"How did Jennifer die?"

Dorothy Speke's loud voice bolted across the dinner table. It was like a gong had been rung. A curious hush descended among Eden Island's elite. Jane and Chief Gabe Kincaid watched the hungry gleam in the eyes of the guests around the table.

"Do tell us," Dorothy persisted.

Gabe watched the eagerness in Mrs. Speke's eyes. "I'm sorry," he said in his most businesslike voice, "Mrs. Madden's death has not been officially—"

"Oh, dear, I knew it! She was murdered! How exciting. Well, frankly, I wouldn't be surprised if it was someone from Eden Island. Money and position don't imbue one with morality, as we all know."

The ensuing silence was deafening. Then Richard Madden rose and faced the empty chair on his right. In a voice that echoed across the room, he raised his glass. "To my wife, Jennifer. Beloved of all who knew her." Glasses up and down the table were raised in silent salute.

All but one. Beside Jane, Philip Lemke's arm barely made it over his bowed head. And if she hadn't been sitting right next to him, she never would have heard the all but muffled sob that escaped his lips.

To Die For

M. J. Rodgers

Harlequin Books

TORONTO • NEW YORK • LONDON
AMSTERDAM • PARIS • SYDNEY • HAMBURG
STOCKHOLM • ATHENS • TOKYO • MILAN
MADRID • WARSAW • BUDAPEST • AUCKLAND

Special thanks go to Jane Jeremy, Chief Deputy Coroner of Kitsap County, Washington, for her graciousness in sharing her expertise and experience

Harlequin Intrigue edition published February 1993

ISBN 0-373-22214-9

TO DIE FOR

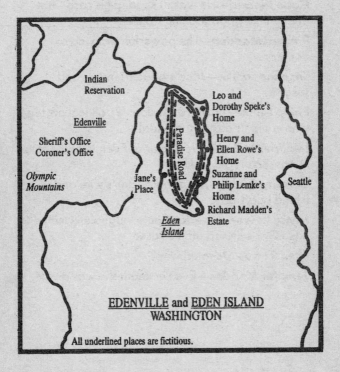

Indian
Reservation

Leo and
Dorothy Speke's
Home

Edenville

Sheriff's Office
Coroner's Office

Henry and
Ellen Rowe's
Home

Olympic
Mountains

Jane's
Place

Suzanne and
Philip Lemke's
Home

Paradise Road

Seattle

Richard Madden's
Estate

Eden
Island

EDENVILLE and EDEN ISLAND
WASHINGTON

All underlined places are fictitious.

CAST OF CHARACTERS

Jane Hardesty—She wanted in on Eden Island's sensational murder investigation.

Gabe Kincaid—He wasn't sharing his case—not even with a good-looking dame.

Richard Madden—The powerful, grieving ex-Senator.

Suzanne Lemke—Jane's good friend . . . and suspect.

Philip Lemke—Richard Madden's political protégé who couldn't afford a scandal.

Leo Speke—Exclusive doctor of Eden Island's elite. What secrets did he know?

Dorothy Speke—The good doctor's wife and Island busybody.

Henry Rowe—Superior Court Judge determined to have Gabe kicked off the case.

Ellen Rowe—Devoted wife?

Jennifer Madden—Even in death she was divine.

Chapter One

Even in death she was divine. A diamond anklet dulled next to the honey sparkle of one slim leg, exposed from toe to thigh. Rich ripples of her thick black hair fanned her face, a glowing summer moon within a swirling dark cloud. Her gently swelling hips plunged into the tender canyons of her waist, then soared to the amber-tipped breasts winking out of her glistening red-satin negligee.

Chief of Detectives Gabe Kincaid raked a paw through his black hair. His throaty growl vibrated through the still air of the dressing room. "What a waste."

Detective Roy Fleming rolled his round frame against the dressing room's thin doorjamb and munched noisily on a bag of peanuts. He didn't comment on his boss's outburst.

Gabe hadn't expected him to. Ever since Gabe had become chief, four years before, Roy had been his right hand. Gabe knew the baby-faced, portly detective could stare death in the face and not flinch—even when it involved a beautiful woman like this one.

At the moment, Gabe envied him. He dragged his eyes away from the vision on the floor. She was the first and only thing he'd noticed since entering the dressing room a moment before. Now he marked the opened bottle of red wine on the dressing table, along with two wineglasses—one used. He read the French label aloud. "Ring any bells, Roy?"

"No, but I'll bet you that's the kind of ridiculously expensive wine the waiters in those fancy Seattle restaurants just pray you'll order."

Gabe dropped to one crisply pressed knee to get a closer, professional look at the corpse. Her facial muscles seemed tense, even in death. Her long, red-tipped fingers lay curled and stiff. A small red streak—probably spilled wine—stained her palm.

He leaned back against his heel, barely resisting an impulse to touch the red, shiny substance and test how it felt between his fingertips. Then he noticed a small crystal decanter that had fallen next to the body. From its size, and the seductive fragrance permeating the room, he knew it had to be perfume.

Gabe looked back at the shiny satin fabric that molded so perfectly to the woman's dark, petite body. He swallowed into a dry throat. "Who was she?"

"Jennifer Madden. Mrs. Richard Madden."

Gabe's head snapped in Roy's direction as memories like newsreels played through his head. "Ex-state senator Richard Madden? But that would mean she's—"

"'Jennifer the Genie.'" Roy's smile barely punctured his chubby cheeks. "Her stage name, of course. Tabloids picked it up to describe her popping up beside the senator when the old wife got the boot. Quite a local gossip item four or so years ago."

Gabe's eyes returned to Jennifer Madden. "The showgirl and the politician," he said, as though reading the headlines in a supermarket checkout line. "Definitely unusual for one of the staunchly conservative residents of Eden Island, who have a knack for washing their dirty laundry in private."

Roy munched on a couple more peanuts. "Yeah. And pretty odd he ended up marrying her, don't you think?"

Gabe's eyes followed the perfection of one amber-tipped breast. "No telling what some crazy fool will do for a ravishing woman."

Roy grunted noncommittally. From the look on his face, Gabe suspected that if he'd substituted the word *food* for the word *woman,* Roy would have been more enthusiastic in his response.

"Where's the husband?"

"Downstairs. Hard to read his reaction. Says he wasn't here last night. Over on the Seattle side, for a business dinner with—" Roy paused to flip the pages of his notebook before continuing "—Jack Carver. Head of the state's party organization. Madden's personal friend. Meeting ran late. They slept there."

"You call this Jack Carver yet?"

"While the crime scene investigators did a walk-through. He says Madden was with him, all right. Had their dinner meeting at the Hilton. Manager says rooms were assigned just after nine."

"Did the husband find her this morning?"

"Nope. Walked in the door right after I did. Took a look at his wife's body, gave me a cursory statement, and then excused himself. Took it all pretty straight-faced. Told me he'd be on the lower east terrace."

"So who found her?"

"Naomi Parisot. Live-in maid. Came in around seven-thirty this morning to clean. She dialed 911."

"Who else lives in the house?"

"Madden's manservant, a Mr. Gnat. Doesn't exactly fit his name. You'll see when you meet him. Slight speech impediment. He says he was in Seattle with Madden last night. Says he doesn't know anything about Mrs. Madden. Kept repeating that *Mr.* Madden was his employer."

Gabe slowly got to his feet, his eyes traveling over the silver carpet to the wallpaper's hand-painted red-and-silver leaves, blowing in an eternal wind. The room was beautiful, as had been its owner. Beauty surrounded by beauty. Damn.

He walked toward the dressing room window and found it locked from the inside. Makeup paraphernalia lay sprawled on the chrome dressing table. An eyebrow pencil was lying next to the perfume bottle on the floor beside her. Had she knocked them down when she fell? Or was pushed?

He turned back into the room and took a quick look through three fully packed walk-in closets behind the mirrored walls. There seemed to be enough clothes here for ten women.

He turned back to Roy. "Any jewelry, valuables missing?"

Roy shoved his skinny glasses back on his pudgy nose and swallowed the peanuts he'd just stuck in his mouth. "Richard Madden hasn't come in to check, but the jewelry box in the bedroom is still full. No sign of forced entry, either."

Gabe stepped through to the adjacent bathroom. Its porcelain fixtures were red, its floor, walls and ceiling mirrored tile. It was even bigger than the dressing room, a gigantic sunken redwood spa sitting at its far end, surrounded by an indoor garden.

Gabe's eyes traveled toward the medicine cabinet. A bottle of aspirin was newly opened, a circular container of birth control pills nearly empty. The crime-scene investigators had labeled the pills for pickup. The contents of the wastebasket were listed simply as expended tissues, and had also been sealed for pickup.

Nothing sinister presented itself, and yet a vague, familiar uneasiness was playing at the back of Gabe's mind. He knew better than to ignore it. "I want you on this case full-time, Roy. Hand off everything else you've got going."

Roy leaned into the bathroom. "You think this one isn't a natural death?"

"We're going to do everything by the book until we find out."

Roy nodded. "Suits me. It will be nice to see how the other half lives for a change. You know, my whole damn apartment could fit in this one dressing area."

Gabe stepped back into the opulent mirrored room, his eyes lured once again to the beautiful, still form on the carpet. He tore them away to see what his new perspective on the dressing area might reveal. It was long, rectangular, and it reminded him of a fun house as his reflection and Roy's bounced back from the floor-to-ceiling mirrors on the walls. Their images resembled geometric figures, Gabe's the tall rectangle, Roy's the short triangle.

Suddenly a new figure emerged in the repeated reflections, an obelisk. Gabe's eyes snapped toward the doorway.

She was lean and willowy, with the kind of height and high cheekbones that fashion magazines preferred. But her bulky black cardigan sweater and long-legged black slacks would never have made their covers. And neither would her hair—a thick blond braid gathered tightly over her right shoulder and reaching down to her breast. She wore the type of shoes women called 'comfortable.'

Not bad, Gabe thought appreciatively. Then he shook the thought aside as the impropriety of this person intruding on his murder scene scraped irritation across his skin. He quickly closed the distance between them.

At six-four and two-forty, Gabe Kincaid knew he looked as intimidating as hell, and he relished it. But he also knew a little charm and a smile were much more effective with the female sex than a flexed muscle. So it was with the former that he greeted this intruder. "You can't come in here."

Her light green eyes swept over him indifferently. She shoved a card into the hand that reached for her as she agilely stepped out of its grasp.

In surprise, Gabe heard a full contralto voice fill the room. "I'm Jane Hardesty, the new deputy coroner. You must be Chief Kincaid." Then, without waiting for a reply, she turned to Roy and held out her hand. "And you are?"

Roy's peanut-greasy hand met hers. "Detective Fleming."

Jane's expression did not change. "Your reputation for thorough reports precedes you, Detective. I'm looking forward to reading those on this case."

Jane quickly and decisively stepped around Gabe to get to the body. She pulled the camera slung across her shoulder into action and snapped several shots of the remains of Jennifer Madden.

Gabe's charming smile withered on his lips. "Now just a minute—"

As she kept shooting, Gabe realized she either hadn't heard him or was ignoring him. His original irritation at her unexpected presence was now rapidly increasing. He took two long steps and held up a hand to block her next shot.

"Look here, Ms.—" He paused to look at the card she had handed him. "Ms. Hardesty. I'm trying to treat you like a lady, but—"

Jane stopped her shooting as Gabe's large, muscular body blocked her view. She looked up at him, her expression retaining its bland look, her voice cool and deep as she interrupted him. "I'm not a lady, Detective Kincaid. I'm the deputy coroner. When was she found?"

Gabe growled as he glowered at her, forgetting all about the charm of his smile. "You'll find out when we send you our report. I've never allowed a deputy coroner at one of *my* death scenes before, and I'm not about to start now."

Up close, Gabe had the impression that the bones of her pale face seemed a bit too strong for the bland expression in her light eyes. Then something seemed to flicker behind them, belying the continued evenness of her tone. "When you find a death that doesn't involve the coroner's office, then you may call it *your* death scene, Kincaid. Until then, all death scenes in this county are under my jurisdiction. And, as you may or may not be aware, an autopsy begins at the scene of a death. Excuse me."

She was angry. But it was a cool, controlled, tough kind of anger that surprised him. She circled around his body block, replaced the lens cap on her camera and knelt beside the remains.

The idea of picking her up bodily and removing her had definite appeal, but for the moment Gabe just twisted in place and watched her scrutinize the body. Her refusal to be intimidated, and that tight control she held on her emotions, had both surprised him. He wondered if she had any more surprises to offer.

After a couple of moments, her deep voice again filled the room. "Looks like it happened sometime last night, and considering rigor mortis is at its peak, I'd say roughly twelve hours ago. Then there are the contributing physical aspects of the room—the lights are on, and she's dressed in that negligee. That, coupled with the wineglasses and the sensuous perfume permeating everywhere, tells us she was waiting for her lover. Doesn't look like he showed. Hmm..."

She was frowning as she continued to study the corpse. "No signs of violence. No noticeable marks on the body. And this is a scene set for seduction, not suicide. I assume everything here is just as you found it? The light was on? There was no empty drug bottle? Kincaid, you didn't tamper with this scene, did you?"

Roy Fleming went into a choking spasm, caused in part by the peanuts that had suddenly gotten stuck in his throat. Gabe's anger at the unmitigated gall of the woman's words flashed hot and sharp. He glowered at Jane in a scalding silence that could have ignited steel.

It didn't even ignite Jane's attention. Her eyes continued to scrutinize the body.

Roy finally cleared his throat sufficiently to speak. "Everything is as we found it, Hardesty."

"Good." Jane's head lifted to Roy as she asked her next question. "She's Jennifer Madden, isn't she?"

Roy nodded, his eyes darting nervously to Gabe's clenched hands. But Gabe had himself under control. His desire to throttle this provoking deputy coroner had once again been overcome by the continuing surprise of her actions. The deepness of her voice and the cavalier way in which she had taken command of his crime scene, spoke of a strong, sure personality. But there was more to her than the professional facade she presented.

His job had taught him how to read people, and particularly people who tried to hide. That bland look in her eyes wasn't quite as detached as she obviously meant it to be. Somewhere beneath that carefully controlled exterior, the real woman was carefully sequestered out of sight. Interesting.

A uniformed deputy called from the door. "The guys would like to bag her now, Gabe."

Jane got to her feet and stood before him. "The transport service is waiting to take her to the Edenville Hospital morgue. I've alerted the radiologist and pathologist, so they'll be expecting her when she arrives. Looks like interviewing the husband is next on the list. You ready?"

Gabe found himself momentarily speechless at the woman's brazenness. He planted his hands on his hips and stepped forward, backing the scratchy roar of his words with a menacing look. "Am I ready? Just who do you think you are?"

The full bluster of Gabe's ire had been known to cower hardened repeat offenders. This woman didn't even flinch.

"I don't *think*, Kincaid. I know. I'm the deputy coroner on this case. We should interview Richard Madden as soon as possible."

Gabe's eyes narrowed into dangerous blue slits. "*We?* No way, Hardesty. You're leaving with the body. That is your only responsibility. Now, I don't know what it was like where you came from, but in this county I'm the one in charge of suspicious deaths. I've put up with a lot from you this morning. Far too much. I'll put up with no more."

Gabe pushed past her and stomped out. He had let his curiosity about her distract him only momentarily. He had no intention of letting a nosy deputy coroner who fancied herself a detective follow him around and undermine his investigation. No woman was that interesting.

JANE HARDESTY WATCHED the arrogant, immaculately clad back of the handsome chief of detectives retreating through the doorway. She'd been warned about Gabe Kincaid. His attempts to intimidate had not surprised her; nor had his assumption that he had the right to order her around.

As a matter of fact, the only thing that had surprised her about Gabe Kincaid was how much calmer and more spacious the room seemed now that he was out of it. The man was like a coarse wool blanket scratching against sensitive skin; she was glad to be rid of him.

Roy leaned away from the doorframe and shoved the almost empty bag of peanuts into his pocket, a thin smile on his thick lips. "You're not much like your predecessor."

Jane looked at him directly. "Is that good or bad?"

Roy's smile expanded into a grin. "I'll have to get back to you on that. Got to go supervise stuff now. See you around."

As soon as Roy left, Jane refocused her attention on the body sprawled on the silver carpet. Jennifer Madden had been alive a scant twelve hours before. Had she been happy? What had been her dreams? And where did they go now that *she* was gone?

Jane gave herself a mental shake. These were the wrong questions to be asking if she hoped to survive in this job. She had to remain aloof, professional, in control. She could do it.

She must do it.

She concentrated her attention on the crime-scene investigators as they collected the tagged evidence from the bathroom. "Don't forget to bag her hands," Jane called to them.

While they prepared the corpse, Jane took a thorough look around the room. Her attention focused on the contents of the woman's closets.

Jennifer had more than a hundred pair of shoes, all spike heels and pointed toes, sequins and satin. Much of her wardrobe was made of see-through materials. Jane's hand passed over scores of low-cut silky daytime dresses. Trimming nearly ten feet of hangers in the next closet were evening gowns even a movie star would have thought suggestive and daring.

A frown gathered on Jane's forehead. Jennifer Madden had certainly been a flamboyant dresser. How had the ex-showgirl's continuing propensity for such outfits sat with her staid Eden Island husband?

As the procession of people with the sheeted corpse of Jennifer Madden slowly filed out the dressing room, Jane followed. She took the wide oak stairs down to the first story of the impressive Madden house.

Only she wasn't impressed. Never had been. As she walked once again through its gigantic entry hall, with its stone floor and its thick, dark wood paneling, she wondered if the impenetrable-looking edifice had dungeons, and if so, who might be buried in them.

Its sixteenth-century-style architecture—half-timbered, with rough brick and bleached stone—had never struck her as particularly warm or welcoming. Now, as she looked up at the banks of brilliant leaded-glass windows cut into its formidable sides like sharp, rough diamonds, and at the gabled slate roof capping its massive, scabrous elegance, she found it no less forbidding. Was its master still the equally forbidding tyrant she remembered?

She escaped down the brick stairs at the entry. She felt a cool, crisp April breeze, and looked up to see the ruffled leaves of fir, spruce, alder, red-barked madrona and centuries-old cedar that ran thick, wild and unchallenged only a few feet from the entrance to the Madden mansion.

They seemed so green, so flexible, so alive, next to the white, stiff, sheeted corpse of Jennifer Madden, which was now being loaded into the transport wagon.

Involuntarily Jane shivered.

Her assistant, a dark, hairy little man who had been with the coroner's office for twenty years and was known to everyone simply as Fast Freddy, was directing the transport driver. She knew Freddy would check Jennifer Madden in at the morgue, maintaining the chain of evidence. Her presence would not be required.

She was glad. She had no intention of going meekly with the body as the overbearing Mr. Kincaid had commanded. Jane had seen things in that dressing room that brought questions to her mind, questions that couldn't be answered down at the morgue.

However, she knew where she might start to get some answers. She turned and headed for her car.

Gabe nodded to the deputy on duty at the rear entrance to the estate as he made his way to the back terrace, and Richard Madden. Twelve years with the sheriff's department, and twenty-six homicide cases, had taught him that wives were generally murdered by husbands. And it was always better to get to them before the attorney was called and the story changed. If he did have a murder on his hands, Richard Madden was his prime suspect.

Gabe picked up his pace in anticipation. He liked this part of his job, and he knew he was good at it. Hell, he wouldn't have shared it with Roy, much less that pushy deputy coroner.

Richard Madden was on the last finger of what looked like a full hand of straight Scotch by the time Gabe found the ex-senator slumped in a deck chair on the covered back terrace. The man's unseeing stare was locked on a wet Seattle sitting across the pewter waters of Puget Sound.

Gabe remembered State Senator Richard Madden well from locally televised congressional sessions. "The six-foot, square-jawed, silver-haired, silver-tongued bulldog," they called him. And when Madden had called Bob Scabre, the president of Washington State's biggest logging firm, an environmental scalper five years before, the state senator had made national news.

Even his supporters acknowledged that he was a hard man to cross. Madden had gotten his bulldog reputation by never budging once committed. He didn't move a muscle when Gabe addressed him by name and introduced himself.

"Sit down. Mr. Gnat will get you something to drink."

Gabe started when, from out of a wall of purple rhododendrons, a dusky, bald man emerged. Gabe had given the terrace a long, hard look a moment before, and he would have sworn Richard Madden was alone on it.

Mr. Gnat was two inches shorter than Gabe's six-four height, but his shoulders expanded like a wrestler's beneath his thick neck. The appendages dropping out of his tight suit jacket looked more like clubs than hands. His puffy-cheeked, expressionless face stared straight ahead. He reminded Gabe of a powerful, precision assembly-line robot in the off mode. Gabe had not the least inclination to flip the switch.

A rainswept gust of cold air rushed Gabe's face as he lowered himself into a deck chair next to Madden. He turned toward the man who looked like a robot and asked for coffee. Mr. Gnat faded once again into the purple rhododendrons.

Gabe gave himself a moment to study Madden's square frame as he slumped back in his chair. Without television's makeup magic, Madden looked his sixty years, and maybe a few more. His left hand hung limp, as did the prominent bags underneath his eyes and at the corners of his black-mustached mouth, the most prominent feature of his face. Unlike his totally silver head, its dense ebony forest showed not one strand of gray.

Gabe leaned forward, positioning his elbows on his knees. "I want to assure you, Mr. Madden, that the questions I'm about to ask, despite how they might sound, are routine."

Gabe paused. Madden continued to look straight ahead. Only the white knuckles on the man's right hand, gripping his nearly empty glass of Scotch, betrayed the tension of his body.

"I understand you were away from your home last evening?"

Madden's tone was that of master to servant. "I already told your people I was at the Seattle Hilton with Jack Carver."

Gabe ignored Madden's attempt to put him in his place. Even a resident of Eden Island couldn't dismiss the law. He took a pen and small pad out of the inside pocket of his suit jacket. "Coming here this morning, I was first interrogated by the security guard at the bridge entrance to Eden Island,

and then by your maid over the intercom before the private electronic gate to your property was lifted. Are these security precautions always in effect?''

''Yes.''

''Are there any others?''

Madden waved at the watery landscape before him. ''Private security guards with dogs patrol the island's beaches for all the residences.''

''So admittance to the island is scrutinized. Does the maid normally screen a visitor and release the electronic gate?''

''Anyone in the house could. Members of the household also have their own remote key to open the gate.''

''How does that work?''

''Just like your garage-door opener, Kincaid.''

Madden's tone continued in its lordly cadence. Gabe was beginning to wonder if the man was so used to dealing with servants and subordinates that the tone had become automatic.

''So you're saying household members have remote-control devices in their vehicles?''

''Yes.''

''Would Mr. Gnat have such a device?''

''He doesn't drive.''

''Mr. Gnat's your butler?''

''He performs that function, and others.''

''He was with you last night?''

''Yes.''

''I understand the maid had the night off?''

''Yes.''

''What other servants do you retain?''

''A part-time cook.''

''The cook has a remote key to the gate?''

''Yes.''

''Was the cook here last night?''

''No.''

Gabe deliberately clicked the top of his pen. ''Are you saying your wife was the only one home?''

The blue veins in Madden's Scotch hand bulged. ''Yes.''

Gabe found it interesting that the silver-tongued bulldog orator had been reduced to one-syllable responses. He gave his pen another click. "Did that happen often, Mr. Madden?"

"Occasionally."

"So if anyone came into the house last night, it's likely your wife let them in?"

"Yes."

Gabe clicked his pen again, watching a corresponding flicker of Madden's eyelash. "Did you see your wife yesterday?"

"In the morning. We had coffee together."

"When was that?"

"Around ten. I left for appointments right afterward."

"Did Mrs. Madden work outside the home?"

"No."

"Do you know what she planned to do yesterday?"

"No."

"Do you have any idea how she died?"

"No."

"Did she take drugs?"

A pause. A tightening along the shoulders. "What do you mean?"

"Sleeping pills, that sort of thing?"

A perceptible relaxing of the shoulders. "No."

Gabe watched the continuing clawlike grip on the Scotch glass. Sorrow? Guilt? Difficult to tell from just Madden's profile.

"Had your wife been despondent, upset, lately?"

Quick answer. Maybe too quick. "No."

"Had she been ill?"

Unequivocal now. "No."

"Who was her doctor?"

"Leo Speke."

"And her medical and life insurance carriers?"

Very quick and unqualified. "She had neither."

Gabe thought it must be nice to be *that* rich. "Do you know where she got the bottle of wine sitting on her dressing table?"

The silver head nodded. Not an obedient follicle moved out of place. "The wine came out of our cellars."

"You bought the wine?"

A nerve flexed and unflexed in Madden's jaw. "I already answered that question."

"What about the bottle of perfume that was lying beside her body?"

"What about it?"

"Did you ever see it before?"

"Probably."

"Did it smell familiar?"

Madden's tense right hand raised the glass to his lips for a quick swallow. His eyes still stared straight ahead. "Her tastes changed frequently. She was always trying something new."

Gabe shifted in his seat. He watched Madden's eyes flick at his movement. Just as he'd thought. The man was wound very tight.

"Did your wife have a social engagement last evening?"

Madden suddenly shifted his grip on the glass of Scotch, setting the ice cubes to pinging against the sides. He gulped a mouthful of the Scotch, leaving only the ice cubes, rattling around in the bottom of the glass. "I called her around eight. She said she had a slight headache and was going to take an aspirin and go to bed."

Gabe's fingers clicked his pen rhythmically now.

"So she wasn't expecting anyone to come by?"

Madden's mouth moved into a tight little twist. Before he had a chance to respond, Mr. Gnat interrupted with a fresh drink for him. Gabe turned to see that a cup of coffee had been set next to his chair. He was disconcerted to realize that he hadn't even heard the servant's approach. He had no time to dwell on it, however, as the voice of a newcomer at the terrace door drew all heads back toward the house.

"Richard, I came as soon as I heard."

The newcomer was a short man, slightly stooped, curly-haired, in his middle fifties, with enormous, soulful, dark eyes, carrying a black medical bag and a heavy look.

Gabe thought he looked more like an undertaker at the moment than a doctor. Even his voice dragged. "Where is her, uh...where is she?"

Madden turned toward the newcomer, giving Gabe a look at his full face for the first time. "Dr. Leo Speke, this is Chief of Detectives Kincaid."

Dr. Leo Speke didn't take Gabe's offered hand. He approached Madden, his voice rising perceptibly. "You called the sheriff?"

"Not now, Leo. I've answered all the questions I'm going to for the present, Kincaid. Gentlemen, I'd like to be alone. You know where the door is."

And with that curt dismissal, Madden turned away from them both, toward the serenely cool Seattle landscape, but not before Gabe had caught the fiery blaze in his black eyes.

JANE HARDESTY BARRELED along Paradise Road, on the southern end of Eden Island, in her two-tone blue 1951 Talbot-Lago. She hadn't been on this end of the high, narrow, mountainous road in years, but she still remembered every inch of it. She knew she'd have to downshift to take the next curve, and she placed the small lever on the steering-column quadrant in second. As she rounded the treacherous corner, with a sheer four-hundred-foot drop below, she stamped on the clutch pedal, and the Wilson preselector gearbox jammed her into second, instantly, flawlessly.

She hummed along. It was a great old car. Throaty. Responsive. Could corner on a dime. It reminded her of her mother, of a time when her world had still been full of possibilities.

Those memories seemed far away.

Suzanne Lemke's estate, which Suzanne had inherited from her family and which doubled as her exclusive lingerie shop, was just a couple of turns away. Jane had known the moment she saw Jennifer Madden's negligee that it had been designed by Suzanne. In a world of off-the-rack clothing, the exquisite beauty of that negligee was a signature clearer than any label.

She also knew it would take the overbearing Gabe Kincaid a while before he figured it out. He was a man of Edenville County—not of the exclusive community of Eden Island. Few outside its borders understood its society, or were invited into it.

Actually, she was glad Kincaid had lived up to his uncooperative reputation. Now she didn't feel obligated to share her knowledge of Eden Island with him. She could carry on her investigation uninhibited. And that was precisely what she intended to do.

Jane's mind was replaying the scene of Jennifer Madden's death as she shifted down to take the next turn. She had no premonition—no warning at all. The other car came out of nowhere, a mere flash in her sideview mirror. And then, suddenly, it jammed alongside her, pounding into the side of the Talbot, locking into its fender, pushing her toward the edge. In the space of a terrified heartbeat, the Talbot was skidding out of control as Jane's strangled scream exploded in her ears.

Chapter Two

Jane yanked the wheel, gritted her teeth and held on as her world spun into a dizzying, blurring funnel. Screeching tires and roaring engines reverberated in her ears. At some point she felt a freeing lurch as the fenders of the two cars were jarred loose. She was too terrified even to consider whether it was a good sign.

Finally, after what seemed an eternity, the Talbot skidded to a stop.

Jane opened her eyes, until then unaware she had even closed them. Her head felt like the inside of a hive, full of angry bees. When it finally cleared enough for her to see straight, she gasped as she found herself at the very edge of the shoulder, looking off into empty space. She twisted her head around as she tried to locate the car that had hit her, peering through the settling dust. At first she saw nothing. Then she heard it—the distant sound of her assailant's whining engine, echoing up the canyon like some demonic cackle.

Jane released a trapped breath, her trembling hands still gripping the steering wheel and her feet still jamming the brake pedal to the floor. Slowly she tried to unwind, drawing her right hand from the wheel to the key in the ignition, switching off the engine. The Talbot seemed to heave a sigh of relief.

Jane put on the hand brake and uncoiled her cramped feet from the brake pedal. Although still shaky, she felt an overwhelming need to get out of the car and uncramp her too-tight muscles.

She opened the driver's door, sucking in a quick breath as she saw the cliff edge mere inches away, and, directly below, waves boiling against jagged rocks.

Jane tore her eyes away from the sheer drop and resolutely refocused on the Talbot's fender. Amazingly, the only evidence of her encounter with the reckless creep who'd hit her was some chipped paint and a small dent.

She realized now that the fool probably hadn't even seen her until the last minute, as he sped around that turn. He must have panicked after he realized he hit her. Still, it burned her that he hadn't stopped to be sure she was okay. She'd like to get her hands on him. Eden Island had always been a safe place to drive. Seemed like there had been a few changes since she'd been away.

Well, she'd take care of reporting the incident later. Not that it would do any good. She hadn't even gotten a look at the car, much less the idiot behind the wheel.

Jane got into the Talbot and backed it off the shoulder, onto the road. Her initial fright had turned into irritation, and some healthy righteous indignation. She gunned the Talbot's engine, determined to resume her interrupted journey to see Suzanne. By the time she pulled into the circular drive that led to Suzanne Lemke's home and business, she'd all but forgotten her close call, her thoughts once again consumed by Jennifer Madden's death.

She parked the car and made her way to the sprawling, elegant French-style château with its central cluster of white mansard roofs extensively dotted with blue-gilded dormer windows. This morning it seemed to perch like some gliding sea gull fifty feet above the rocky beach of Eden Island's eastern shore. Suzanne was already sprinting down the two dozen pyramid-shaped entry stairs before Jane had a chance to reach them.

"Jane, what a nice surprise! I knew it had to be you as soon as I saw the Talbot."

Suzanne flung her arms around Jane and gave her a tight squeeze. Jane felt the wind leave her lungs and marveled at the strength of Suzanne's slim five-foot-six frame.

Suzanne released her and assessed her at arm's length, a frown deepening her brow. "Damn it, Jane, you're hardly more than a skeleton. Hell, I can't keep telling people you were the only woman who could compete with me for those Harvard upperclassmen with you looking like this."

Jane could smell the henna rinse that left Suzanne's chestnut hair full and glowing. Her nut-brown eyes sparkled with health and humor. "Well, you're looking great," she said.

Suzanne dropped an arm around Jane's waist and headed them both up the stairs toward the door. "Stop trying to butter me up. I've got spies, you know. You've been on the island several days and haven't come to see me. Rotten way to treat a friend."

Jane shrugged. "I've been trying to get settled."

Suzanne closed the door behind them as soon as they were inside the ornately appointed entry hall. Jane felt her long, hard look and heard the change in her tone. "I'm beginning to think Philip and I should have stayed with you after the funeral."

Jane shook her head dully. "When someone you love dies, the last thing you need is a bunch of people, however well-meaning, gathered around feeling sorry for you. Just makes the whole process worse. As it was, I had a house full of grieving in-laws for weeks. Not a pretty picture, I assure you."

Suzanne gave her another squeeze, gentler this time. "A year and still it hasn't been enough time, has it? Well, at least you've come back to Eden Island. Your mother would have been glad."

"Yes. She always thought of the Island as some kind of sanctuary—a sort of protection from the evils of the real world. I think the way Dad died left her with a fear of journeying too far. Remember how she even fought my going out of state to school?"

Suzanne tugged her toward the sitting room. "Yeah, she was even worse than my parents, and God knows they were unrelenting. If they weren't happily settled in their Hawaiian abode today, I bet they'd still be trying to live my life. Come on. Philip is at the office, so we have the place to ourselves."

Jane followed Suzanne, sitting down carefully on a French provincial love seat across from her friend. It was a fragile and expensive antique, like everything else in this large, lavish home. Such fine appointments lent just the right background to Suzanne's delicate beauty, but Jane had always felt more comfortable around sturdier stuff. She sat on the edge of her seat. "Do you know I've taken the position of deputy coroner for the county?"

Suzanne's eyes opened wide, and when she spoke her tone was incredulous. "You've given up your medical practice for Karl Daly's job?"

"Not for Karl's job. The coroner's job is an elected position. I'm his deputy coroner, the grunt who does all the work."

Suzanne shook her head as she leaned forward. "But I don't understand. How could you give up medicine?"

Jane rose and circled the couch to look out a nearby window, rubbing her hands together as though to warm them. For a moment she stared fixedly at the fat gray clouds sitting like a blanket above the city of Seattle, in the distance. "What good was my medical training? Gregory still got sick, and there was nothing I could do for him. Except watch him die."

She turned to face Suzanne. "Karl offered me the position when he heard I was closing up my practice in Boston. Sam had retired after twenty-five years. Karl was looking for someone to replace him. Seemed like an answer for us both."

Suzanne's eyes were wide with unspoken sympathy. Jane blessed her for keeping it unspoken. Such sensitivity reminded Jane of why she had befriended this woman in the first place, when they were both in the second grade, and why they had remained friends through time and separation.

"You've moved into your mother's house?"

Jane nodded. "I could never bring myself to sell it after her death. I'm glad I didn't now. It needs a lot of paint and elbow grease, of course. And the gardens are in shameful condition. But I need the activity to keep me busy."

"Then why work? Why don't you just stay at the house and get it into order? Then maybe, in another year or so, you might feel more like—"

Jane interrupted her. "I'm broke, Suzanne."

Suzanne came out of her delicate antique chair, a deep frown puckering her brow. She repeated the word in the kind of whisper a refined lady reserves for an obscenity. "Broke?"

Jane shrugged and looked out the window again. "Gregory's long illness wiped us out."

"You didn't have insurance?"

"It didn't begin to cover all the new experimental and expensive treatments he had to have. And when they didn't work, we'd hear about a new drug somewhere and we'd fly to South America. Or to Europe. I couldn't keep up my practice. Gregory needed me beside him. We grasped at any and every straw. And even if those straws didn't help, I think the grasping did. At least Gregory lived six months longer than any of his doctors predicted."

Suzanne's tone was still verging on the unbelieving. "Even your mother's money is gone?"

Jane turned back into the room. "What's left will just about pay the taxes on the house this year. So you see, I have to work. Will you refuse to be seen with me now?"

Suzanne exhaled her good-natured irritation. "What an idiot you are, Jane. Nearly everybody on Eden Island works these days, including yours truly."

"Yes, but I doubt any of you need to."

Suzanne waved a bejeweled hand, social decorum or friendship, or maybe both, dictating that she deliberately misinterpret Jane's comment. "Of course we need to. I'd be stark raving mad without my lingerie business. And Philip would wither without his politics. Stop trying to press my shock buttons and sit down. I've got Scotch, vodka, rum, brandy, and just about any kind of liqueur you care to name. What'll it be?"

"At this time of the morning, orange juice."

Suzanne looked a little disappointed, but she came back from the portable bar in the corner of the room with two glasses of juice in Waterford crystal. After she handed Jane her glass, she sat, comfortably curling a foot beneath her. "So why do I have the feeling that it's your job that's brought you to see me?"

Jane circled the love seat and sat down again. She took a quick sip of her orange juice, enjoying its tangy bite, knowing that the only way to deliver the news she carried was quickly and quietly. "Jennifer Madden was found dead in her dressing room this morning."

Suzanne gave a little start, uttering some inarticulate sound. "Jennifer Madden? But it can't be! I saw her only yesterday!"

"Business or personal?"

"Business. I had designed some lingerie for her. Jane, this is incredible! How did she die?"

"In your negligee. An absolutely dynamite red satin number. Ring a bell?"

Suzanne's dark eyes clouded as she sank back into the couch, taking a big swig of her drink. Jane began to suspect that her friend's glass had more than orange juice in it.

"I'm not sure of the cause of death yet, Suzanne. The autopsy will be this afternoon, and it should tell us more."

Suzanne's voice sounded far away. "She'd just turned thirty."

Jane saw the look on Suzanne's face and knew what her friend was thinking. She and Suzanne were both thirty-one. All those solid feelings of immortality got a jolt when someone younger died.

"How well did Richard and Jennifer get along?"

Suzanne shook her chestnut curls. "They seemed...
content."

"Did she have any enemies?"

Suzanne's eyes widened. "Jane, why are you asking such
a thing? You can't think—"

"Suzanne, I'm trying to keep an open mind. That's what
my job requires. Are you still videotaping your interviews
with your clients?"

Suzanne nodded dumbly.

"Can I see the one on Jennifer?"

Suzanne got up as though still in a daze and disappeared
into the back room. She reemerged carrying a VHS tape and
scooted it into the machine in the corner, flipping on the
television as she passed by. She handed the VCR's remote
control to Jane.

"I normally erase a taped session with a client as soon as
she's picked up her lingerie. A women's moods and desires
often change dramatically from one session to the next. Retaining old impressions proves a useless waste of record-
keeping, since it's the current moods and desires that have
to be sensually pleased. I was just overly busy yesterday."

"Was Jennifer a regular customer?"

"No. First time she came to me was three weeks ago yesterday. Before that, I had only seen her socially. We never
really talked."

"Will it bother you to watch this again?"

Suzanne shook her head mutely as she reached for her
drink and Jane hit the play button on the video machine.

Jennifer's animated face beamed at them—alive and eager as she sat forward on the edge of Suzanne's sitting room
sofa. Remembering her still corpse so clearly and now seeing her glowing image on the tape gave Jane a skittish sense
of altered reality.

"I've never had lingerie designed just for me and my
personality," Jennifer's excited voice said. "It's a perfect
present to myself for my thirtieth birthday."

Suzanne's taped voice spoke. Jane knew she was sitting behind the video camera, focusing it solely on Jennifer. "You sound comfortable with your age, Mrs. Madden."

Jennifer's smile was broad. "Hell, why not? We women are at our sexual peak, and every other peak, in our thirties. It's a great age! And for God's sake, Suzanne, call me Jennifer."

"Okay, Jennifer. Now, first, I'd—"

"Hey, can I have the videotape, too?" Jennifer interrupted.

"Certainly. I use one tape for several customers, so I'll have to make a copy of your session separately. I can have it ready for you when you pick up your lingerie."

Jennifer smiled as she sat back. "Great. I love videos of me. Have a whole collection of them. You have all my measurements. Now, what do you want to know? I'll tell you anything."

Once again Jane heard Suzanne's disembodied taped voice. "I'd like to start out with your favorite color or colors."

"Crimson and silver."

"Give me a one-word description of how you feel when surrounded by crimson?

"Sexy."

"And silver?"

Jennifer's dark eyes gleamed. "Powerful."

"So you are this sexy, powerful woman. If you had been someone in history, who would it have been?"

Jennifer's head sat tall on her well-shaped shoulders. "Cleopatra."

"Because?"

"She was all woman, and proud of it. I heard that as she set sail to meet Antony one day, she even had the sails of her ships perfumed."

Suzanne's voice grew animated. "Yes, I read about that. And legend has it that even the winds fell in love with the beautiful queen of Egypt, bringing her safely and quickly to the lovers' rendezvous."

A small frown dug itself in Jennifer's smooth forehead. "Love? Those legends were obviously written by men. I think it much more likely that Cleopatra sailed to conquer, employing all her mental and physical strengths."

"I see. So with Cleopatra as a standard, I assume you don't consider yourself a conventional woman, whatever that means today."

Jennifer's laugh was a challenge. "Whatever that means is right! I make it a point never to fit into anybody's definition."

"What gives you the most enjoyment?"

"Living my impulses."

"What type of furniture fits you?"

"Ultraexpensive."

"And your choice in music?"

"Hot. A fast beat. Something that can keep up with me."

Jane listened distractedly through the next fifteen minutes as Suzanne tried to understand her client's flamboyant personality. But then Jane's ears perked up as Suzanne asked a new set of questions.

"The ensemble I will create for you will include a bra, panties, a slip and a negligee. Are any of these to be worn for a special occasion?"

Jennifer's dark eyes sparkled. "My life is a special occasion. But you can forget about the bra, panties and slip. I never wear any of those. I just want the negligee. And I want it so hot he won't be able to resist me."

"I...see. What fabrics do you prefer against your skin?"

"Something tight and tactile—arousing for me and my partner, a sleek, sexy war paint for my body."

"War paint?" Suzanne's voice repeated, sounding stunned.

Jennifer threw her head back, her laugh throaty and raucous. "Of course, war paint. The battle of the sexes *is* sex! And with the right war paint, I make them all my prisoners."

"And a negligee is war paint?"

Jennifer looked delighted at Suzanne's shocked tone. "Of course! A woman's greatest weapon is her ability to fire the dark passions within men."

"Men?"

"Well, naturally I want to attract all men. What fun is it if you can only seduce one? Besides, I like powerful men with silver hair."

"Powerful men?" Suzanne had begun to sound like a parrot.

Jennifer's long red nails dug into her soft palms. "I heat them until they melt, dripping their power into my hands, taking them to the brink."

"When you say the brink, what—"

The confident, dark woman sat forward again in eagerness as her voice descended, low and breathy, interrupting Suzanne. "Death. I want a negligee so enticing a man will not be able to contain his desire for me—even if it means he must die."

An icy chill shot up Jane's spine, despite the fact that she knew Jennifer was only describing a fantasy. Suzanne's taped voice sounded a bit disquieted itself. "He could die?"

Jennifer straightened and smiled warmly. "Yes. But happily. Very happily. You see, I want a man to know that sex with me is worth even death."

Suzanne's taped voice paused for some time before asking her next question. Jane understood. She needed a few seconds to recover, too. "Will you eat before making love?"

Jennifer's dark eyes squinted. "It's important?"

"Yes. If I'm to make this negligee fit you perfectly, I need to know whether you'll be wearing it on a full or empty stomach."

"I see. Well, I really like to eat oysters beforehand. They're an aphrodisiac, you know. But just a few. I want my stomach to feel hard and flat. A pouch takes the sexual edge off, and I want it heightened, not reduced."

"Do you have any alcohol beforehand?"

"A small glass of red wine. Expensive, of course."

"Of course. Well, Jennifer, I have a clear picture now of the type of negligee that would most become you. Crimson crushed velvet and satin will be the fabrics. And the design will be bold, powerful, dangerous—perfectly suited to a sexy woman of bold, powerful and dangerous desires. The creation will be called To Die For."

The petite dark woman beamed on the tape as she came to the edge of her seat. "Yes! That's perfect! When can I have it?"

Suzanne's voice explained to Jennifer that it would take three weeks to select the proper fabrics and fashion them into the fabulous To Die For negligee that would do justice to the woman who would wear it. For the first time in the taped session, Jane could see the disappointment on Jennifer Madden's face. Patience had not been among her character traits.

The screen filled with static as the taped session came to an abrupt end. Jane pressed the off button on the remote and turned to Suzanne. "I'll need that tape."

Suzanne got up to retrieve it from the VCR. She held it out almost reluctantly. "I know I can depend on you not to show this around. My other customers wouldn't feel too secure if they heard about this circulating."

"Yes, being one of your customers, I can safely say I wouldn't have wanted my tape up for public scrutiny."

Suzanne waved her hand dismissively. "It was erased long ago. And even so, as I recall, your session got a G rating compared to most I get. Well, you heard Jennifer, so that gives you an idea. I feel like a psychologist sometimes, delving into the psyches of my clients. I sometimes wished I'd never started the taped sessions."

Jane looked full at her friend. "Why did you?"

"Oh, it was just a fluke. Early on in the business, one of my clients insisted on my taking notes about her preferences. Well, I hate taking notes, as you probably remember from our college days, so I just picked up the video camera and taped her instructions, asking a few pertinent questions along the way. She was thrilled. Told all her friends about my 'psychological evaluation of her sexual psyche.' They came in droves after that, and demanded the taping and questioning, too. Still, you realize I never would have shown even you that tape if Jennifer wasn't dead?''

"I know, Suzanne. And I feel I should warn you. Chief of Detectives Gabe Kincaid might want to talk to you about Jennifer. He's leading the sheriff's investigation into her death."

Suzanne's forehead developed an instant frown. "Why would he want to talk to me?''

Jane got to her feet. "For one, Jennifer's death may not have been a natural one. Two, a record of our conversation will be going into my report, which he gets. Three, remember, it was your lingerie she was found in."

Suzanne threw a chestnut curl behind her shoulder. "That's hardly a strong connection between us."

Jane rested a hand on her friend's arm. "No, but since Jennifer was married to your uncle, your relationship to her was not really all business, was it?"

Suzanne looked very uncomfortable. "I . . . hardly knew her."

Jane watched her friend closely. When she spoke again, her voice was soft and even. "You loved your Aunt Margaret. You nearly came apart at her funeral. She suffered because of your uncle's liaison with Jennifer. And then Jennifer took her place with your uncle. Did you really have no animosity toward the new Mrs. Madden?"

Jane felt a muscle twitch within Suzanne's arm. "It's been four years, Jane. I . . . She was what Richard wanted. He always gets what he wants. He's backing Philip for senator, you know."

"No, I didn't know." The words surprised Jane, although Suzanne's obvious loyalty to her uncle didn't. It had been a lifelong pattern.

Suzanne's forehead twisted into an even tighter frown. "He's less than a five-minute drive away. I suppose the right thing to do would be to pay a condolence call."

Jane heard duty in Suzanne's words, not affection. Seemed some things hadn't changed in her time away. Before she could dwell on that, her attention was suddenly drawn to the slamming of the front door and a male voice calling out, "Suzanne?"

"In the sitting room," Suzanne answered.

Philip Lemke turned the corner a moment later. He seemed to have been expecting Jane's presence, no doubt having seen her distinctive car parked outside. He extended a welcoming hand.

"It's been a while," he said in greeting.

Jane took Philip's hand. He was aging very well. He was forty-two, and his full hair was well into gray now, giving him a dignified look his younger years had never supported. His muscle tone reflected his hour each day on the rowing machine. And although his nose was small, a square jaw added the frame of strength needed for one of his otherwise weak-looking smiles.

Except his current expression was far from strong or a smile. He turned back to his wife after giving Jane's hand an uninspired, perfunctory shake. "Jennifer's dead."

Suzanne had been shaken but composed when Jane had broken the news. But at Philip's words, Jane could see a new jolt go through her friend, almost as though Suzanne were hearing the news for the first time. Before Jane had time to dwell on the surprising second reaction, she was distracted when Suzanne took both of Philip's hands in hers in almost a motherly fashion. "Jane just told me. I'm on my way to see Richard now."

Philip's voice sounded pained. "I should go with you, of course. But, do you mind if I… Will you tell him I couldn't get away?"

Suzanne didn't answer Philip. Instead, she looked anxiously over at Jane, and Jane took her cue. Husband and wife needed to be alone. "Well, I've got to be going. Good to see you again, Philip. I'll stay in touch, Suzanne."

Suzanne flashed Jane a grateful smile as she headed for the door. But for some reason, as she closed it behind her, the lingering image of Philip's strained expression and Suzanne's hands about his kept playing through Jane's mind like some bothersome, flickering silent movie.

She shook the images aside. Thanks to Suzanne's tape, she knew a lot more about Jennifer Madden. Now was the time to get to the morgue and find out exactly how the woman had died.

"HOW DID SHE DIE?" Leo Speke asked Gabe over his shoulder as he began to walk away. It had only taken a few moments for Gabe to confer with Roy Fleming and the crime-scene investigators and agree that their focus should be on the second story of the immense Madden mansion. A parade of forensic specialists marched up the stairs like an invading army.

Now Gabe turned to watch the tight black curls at the nape of the doctor's retreating neck and followed their color change to the woolly white cap they formed at the top of the man's head. Speke's head resembled a two-tone sheep.

"We don't know how she died yet," Gabe said as he lengthened his stride to move alongside the much shorter doctor.

Speke headed directly for a study of ponderous walls and heavy furniture. As far as Gabe could see, nothing in this house but Jennifer's dressing area reflected any femininity. Speke put down his physician's bag just inside the room and reached for the brandy decanter sitting on a table. His direct line to it convinced Gabe of the man's familiarity with the Madden residence.

"I understand you were Jennifer Madden's physician?"

Gabe detected a slight quiver in Speke's hands as the man poured two fingers of brandy into a snifter. He gulped down its contents, his large eyes watering as he choked out his reply. "I've been the Madden family physician for three decades."

"And that included Jennifer?"

"Since she married Richard, three years ago."

"Do you have any reason to think her death might not be from natural causes?"

Speke turned toward Gabe. "Isn't that why you're here?"

Gabe's eyes remained steady. "Doctor, surely I don't have to remind you that our involvement is routine now in all cases of death?"

Speke stared at Gabe blankly for a moment before he gave a short, assertive nod. "Oh, yes. That ordinance that got passed last year about all deaths being investigated. I guess I've been fortunate not to have lost a patient until..."

Gabe watched the troubled stare return to Speke's large, dark eyes. The perpetual hunch in his shoulders deepened.

"When did you last see Mrs. Madden?"

"Yesterday afternoon. She stopped by briefly."

"And where were you last evening and night?"

Speke looked back at the brandy decanter, but he made no move to refill his glass. "I practice out of my home. After my last patient, I worked in my study until seven. Then I joined my wife for dinner and we went to bed early."

"Neither of you left the house?"

"That's right."

Gabe clicked his pen. "Did you know Jennifer Madden well?"

Speke circled the empty snifter in his hand as though it were full. "I told you I was her doctor."

"Did she seem depressed lately?"

The nonexistent brandy got another swirl. "No."

Gabe watched Speke's eyes; they were so large they looked like the exaggerated work of a caricaturist. "Was she physically healthy?"

"Yes."

"What was her emotional state?"

"I'm not a psychologist."

"I understand that, Doctor, but sometimes patients do confide in their family physician."

It was a question, but Gabe could tell by the purposeful straightening of Leo Speke's normally curved neck that he had no intention of answering. Within a minute, the man had gone from being sad to being shaken to being unshakable. Gabe didn't feel comfortable with such quick emotional switches.

Gabe schooled his voice to its most authoritative tone. "Doctor, your cooperation in clearing up this matter would be most appreciated. Naturally, I will need her medical records forwarded to my office immediately."

Speke gave a slow nod.

"Did Jennifer Madden say anything to you that reflected her emotional state?"

Speke swirled his empty brandy glass one more time before answering. "Patients don't always tell their doctors something that just concerns themselves. Their confidences often reveal—"

A noise brought Speke up short. On the far end of the study, double doors suddenly swung open, bathing the dark, ponderous wood with light from an adjacent hall. Gabe blinked through the blinding light as a feminine voice drifted in his direction.

"Leo, thank God you're here. I drove over as soon as I heard. Where's Richard?"

Gabe's eyes adjusted, and he made out the figures of two women—one round and sixtyish, in a large white uniform, the other slim and thirtyish, in a stylishly cut light suit. It was the younger woman who had spoken, and who'd now claimed most of his attention. She had curly chestnut hair, with an erect carriage and a flair for the right makeup and clothes.

"He's on the lower east terrace, Suzanne," Leo said. "But he's asked to be alone for a while. This is Detective Kincaid from the sheriff's office. He's looking into Jennifer's death."

Gabe watched Suzanne's expression and limbs stiffen.

"Suzanne—?" Gabe left the word hanging as he tilted his head encouragingly in her direction.

The pretty, dark eyes squinted at him very unprettily. "Mrs. Philip Lemke."

Gabe turned to the woman in uniform. "And you are?"

Her light eyes stared at him like tiny, bright flashlights beaming out of the fleshy folds of her face. "Naomi Parisot."

"You were Mrs. Madden's maid?"

The woman nodded in a tight affirmation.

Gabe turned back to Suzanne. "And how are you related to the deceased, Mrs. Lemke?"

"Jennifer was married to my uncle."

"You're Richard Madden's niece?"

"That's what I just said."

"Perhaps you wouldn't mind answering—"

"Yes, I would. I'm here this morning to comfort my uncle. I know nothing about Jennifer's death. My husband is a lawyer, and he would insist I have him present before I speak with the authorities. Leo, please, I must talk with you. Naomi, would you see Detective Kincaid out?"

And with that last, parting shot, Mrs. Lemke pivoted on her expensive high heels and headed toward the door, with Leo Speke padding obediently in her wake.

Gabe didn't see any point in making an issue of Suzanne Lemke's curt and suspicious dismissal, but when Naomi Parisot began to follow, he stepped forward.

"Ms. Parisot? A few questions."

She turned back to Gabe, the smug look on her face telling him it hadn't taken her long to learn. "I'm not answering any questions without my lawyer, either."

Gabe nodded. "Yes, I would recommend it if you have something to hide. It's just that you struck me as an honest, hardworking woman. I didn't think you had either the time or the money to waste with hours of questioning down at the station while an expensive lawyer planned his next vacation with your life savings."

A dark shade rolled over Naomi Parisot's smug look. When it unrolled, all traces of smugness were gone, and she was blinking as though the room's light had become too strong. Then she turned from the doorway and found the nearest chair, locking her orthopedic shoes around its straight legs. "What do you want to know?"

Gabe remained standing as he opened his notebook and fiddled with his ballpoint. "How long have you worked for the Maddens?"

"Three years."

"You're a live-in?"

"My apartment is over the garages."

"Did Mrs. Madden hire you personally?"

"She selected me from several agencies' applicants."

"You had superior qualifications?"

"Of course."

"Your duties?"

"I take…took care of her personal needs. Made sure her rooms were tidy. Arranged for her washing and dry cleaning. Did general cleaning around the house. Kept track of her appointments. Got her snacks from the kitchen."

"I thought the Maddens had a cook."

"The Mr. and Mrs. generally just have—had—coffee in the morning. They dine out for lunch. Cook is used to coming in around three and preparing the evening meal. Before she goes home each night, she leaves food in the refrigerator for snacks and such the next day. Just in case the Mr. or Mrs. comes home."

"Did the cook come in yesterday?"

"No. She had the day off."

Gabe studied her face for a moment before stepping away. "You do all the housecleaning?"

The flashlight eyes blinked. "You must be joking. This place is more than twelve thousand square feet. No one person could keep it in order."

"So who does it?"

"A cleaning crew comes in once a week. I direct their work."

"Were they here yesterday?"

"No. They're not due back for several days."

"Were the Maddens home yesterday?"

"They had coffee together in the morning."

"You saw him leave?"

"Yes. Sometime before noon."

"Did Mrs. Madden stay at home?"

"No. She left around three for an appointment. I didn't see her the rest of the day."

"What was Mrs. Madden's appointment?"

"She was picking up some lingerie she'd ordered."

Gabe clicked his pen. "Do you know where?"

"No. Week before, she told me to remind her to leave at three yesterday to pick up her lingerie. That's all she told me."

"So Mrs. Madden left at three, and you don't know when she returned?"

"She gave me the night off. I left the house around six."

"You asked for the night off?"

"No. She told me she wouldn't need me, and suggested I go into town and catch the ferry to Seattle for dinner and a show."

"And you returned?"

"After midnight. Probably closer to one."

"You didn't see Mrs. Madden then?"

"No. I went directly to my room."

"Did you notice if her light was on?"

"I didn't look."

"Were there any cars in the drive?"

"I didn't see any."

"So you found her this morning?"

"When I went up to clean. Her bed was still made. The lights were on. I walked into her dressing room and saw her lying on the carpet. I leaned down to check her pulse. Her body was cold."

Naomi Parisot spoke about finding her employer of three years dead with the same inflection she might have used in discussing spot removal. Gabe took a couple of steps closer.

"What kind of a woman was Mrs. Madden?"

Naomi shifted in her chair. "She was my employer."

"You didn't like her, did you?"

Naomi sat up a little straighter, the small light in her eyes telling Gabe she relished this opportunity to speak. "Jennifer Madden was a woman who went after what she wanted. And got it.''

"What did she want?"

"Everything."

"Can you be specific?"

Naomi Parisot's lips tightened. "You must have heard the stories. She was just a showgirl. Came from nothing. Ended up with Madden—with everything.''

"Everything?"

"Are you blind? Look around."

Gabe clicked his pen again. "Did she have any enemies?"

"How would I know? I was only her maid." Naomi Parisot crossed her arms over her chest. "It's not like we were friends."

And you never wanted to be, Gabe thought. As he watched the angry, triumphant glint in Naomi Parisot's light eyes, he also thought that Jennifer Madden had made a very large error in her selection of a maid. Maybe even a fatal error?

Chapter Three

Jane had been waiting nearly thirty minutes when Gabe walked into the Radiology department at Edenville Hospital. She was irritated at the delay and she felt ill at ease when his blue-eyed scrutiny flashed her way. The previous quiet of the room seemed to shatter.

As he crossed over to where she stood, in front of a wall of illuminated X rays, Jane deliberately turned to her new acquaintances, Sam and Mick, the technicians. They were both standing beneath a scribbled sign over the X ray machine, which happily proclaimed Welcome to the S & M Room. You Slay 'Em—We Ray 'Em.

Her back was to Gabe as he approached. He seemed to close in on her, as though his physical presence were somehow surrounding her. She shook off the ridiculous sensation, tensing at his question, spoken more like a demand: "So what's the word?"

Mick turned his eyes away from the X rays. "Oh, hi, Gabe. We were just telling Jane here that the film shows she's got no broken bones or bullets inside her."

Jane sensed rather than saw Gabe looking back at the empty table. "So where is she?"

Jane turned. His manner seemed to show that he expected a deference she was intent on not supplying. "I had her taken to the autopsy room. Tom Thornton advises me he's ready to get started whenever you are. Detective Fleming persuaded him to wait until you arrived."

Jane had managed to keep the edge out of her voice, but she could tell from Gabe's expression that he understood that, if it had been up to her, they would have started the autopsy without him.

Instead of rising to the bait of her disapproval, Gabe shrugged with irritating nonchalance. "Well, I'm here. Let's get started."

The indignant hair on the back of Jane's neck bristled as she led the way down the hall to the autopsy room. She could feel Gabe behind her, and although he didn't touch her, she had the curious sensation that his body brushed up against her all the way. There was just something about the man that crowded her.

The overpowering smell of formaldehyde immediately burned into Jane's nostrils when she opened the door to the autopsy room. She remembered it well from medical school, when she worked on cadavers to learn the intricacies of the human body. It wasn't a smell that could be forgotten. Jane reminded herself that it was still better than the smell of sickness and death. Anything was better than that smell.

Jane donned a blue hospital gown, an apron and gloves that reached up to her elbow. She kept her mask ready in her pocket so that it would be handy when the bone sawing was done. That was another smell Jane wasn't looking forward to. It always reminded her of her sixth birthday party, when she'd leaned too close to the candles on her cake and her hair had been singed.

One by one they gathered around the stainless-steel table where the body of Jennifer Madden lay, still clothed in the red negligee. Before it could be removed, it, too, had to be carefully examined.

Detective Roy Fleming fidgeted impatiently with the process. "Tom, will you hurry up with those damn shears and get this thing off her? I drew the three-hour discovery-time spot in the detectives' betting pool. Hell, you've already wasted thirty minutes, and you haven't even examined her skin yet."

Forensic pathologist Tom Thornton took a moment to raise some thin, gloved fingers to scratch at his receding hair line before stepping forward and taking the scissors in his hands. "Forget it, Roy. In the four years I've known you, you've never won one of those pools. And if you did, you'd probably fall dead from the shock, and you'd be the next one up on my table."

"You're going to be the next one up on your table if you don't get off my foot, Tom!" Gabe said as he gave the pathologist a shove.

Thornton did a quick little dance forward, only to land on one of Roy's swollen toes. "Get the hell off me, klutz! It's no wonder they don't trust you with live patients anymore!"

Thornton chuckled and then leaned over the remains of Jennifer Madden. "Actually, I switched from the live ones to the dead ones when I found that none of the live women could keep their hands off me. Of course, I still have trouble with the dead ones."

As if it had been a prophecy, one of Jennifer Madden's dead hands sprang up to land on Tom Thornton's arm.

Roy gave a yelp, Jane's hands reached for her throat, and Gabe bounded toward the table.

It wasn't until Thornton's enormous smile turned into uncontrollable laughter that Jane realized they'd been had.

Thornton proudly raised the dead woman's arm to reveal the spring-action catapult hidden beneath. Then his finger pointed to the trail of connecting wire attached to the activating pad he had just pressed with his foot. "Great, isn't it? Got it at the pathologist's convention last month. I think they stole the idea from the morticians' convention the month before."

"To drum up more business, no doubt," Gabe said, his mouth white-lined. Jane noticed he wore a reluctant smirk.

"My brother-in-law is a night call man at Patter Brothers Mortuary in town," Roy contributed, fully recovered and ready to enter into the swing of things. "He told me about this one time when they hid a cordless microphone in the mouth of a dead victim they'd just picked up from the hospital and nearly gave the mortician a heart attack when he—"

Jane interrupted him, not attempting to take the edge out of her voice. "Okay, folks. Can we get on with this?"

Three pairs of eyes turned to stare at her. She returned their stares without blinking. Tom Thornton was the first to look away. He shrugged and reached over to turn on the recorder as a signal that they were back to business. "Deceased female, mature, white, thirty. X rays reveal no broken bones or abnormalities. Skin clear. No marks, cuts, abrasions..."

Gabe's attention drifted as Thornton's voice droned on. Normally he would have joined in more fully with the relaxing foreplay that always seemed to lubricate the tightness surrounding an autopsy. After seeing that beat-up look in Jane Hardesty's eyes, he was glad he hadn't today.

She'd gone ten rounds with someone—or something—that hadn't pulled any punches. He began to wonder who or what it was, and why she had taken the position of deputy coroner for the relatively small county of Edenville.

Edenville certainly wasn't a booming community—probably no more than about fifty thousand residents, not counting the Indian reservation at its northernmost point. It had very little industry apart from logging. Most everyone worked in the sawmills, or for the county government, or in the fading fishing industry, or for one of the few services in town. The community's only real wealth was concentrated on Eden Island, and it was going to stay there. No, this was not a place that attracted outsiders.

Why had she come?

Gabe's thoughts became distracted as he looked at the body on the table. Even his many autopsies, which should have inured him to the procedure, didn't help when that beautiful body was opened up. He felt the lurch in his stomach and looked away.

The minutes dragged by. "Healthy heart," Tom Thornton's crisp voice said from across the table.

On his left, Gabe watched Roy engaged in copious note-taking. On his right, Jane Hardesty readied containers and labels. Gabe concentrated on their activities over the next twenty minutes, on the scrubbed white walls of the small room, on the ventilator fan in the corner, on the shiny aluminum refrigerator door that sat flush with the wall—on anything but the remains of Jennifer Madden.

Tom Thornton leaned over the body. "Damn. Lungs clear and normal, too. This isn't going to be an easy one, folks."

"I'll need sufficient samples of each tissue group," Jane interjected. "If we're looking for something obscure, toxicology will need adequate quantities to last through all the tests."

Tom nodded. "How's that?"

"Good," Jane responded as she tightened the lid on the container of her most recently collected specimen.

"Okay, let's take a look at her tiny tummy. Hmm... Just a few oysters and wine here. Poor thing didn't even go out with a decent meal in her. This enough for you, Jane? A little more from the other side? Okay. Here you go. Now where's that liver? Come on, baby, don't be shy."

Gabe turned and yanked open the autopsy room door. Once outside, he tore off his protective mask and gloves. When he heard Tom turn on the bone saw, he headed for the coffee machine. After three scalding cups, his mouth was still dry. He became aware he was still holding his mask and rubber gloves only when Tom Thornton started removing his as he came through the autopsy room door, nearly three hours later.

"You okay, Gabe?"

Gabe scrunched the empty paper cup and threw it into the trash, along with the gloves and mask. Then he began to fight with the ties on the back of the blue smock. "Just marvelous. What did you find?"

"Nothing that points to death from natural causes or traumatic injury. You know that just leaves one thing."

Gabe tore his arms out of the blue smock and pitched it into the laundry bin. "Poisoning?"

Tom stopped scratching his balding scalp to point his index finger at Gabe like a gun. "Bull's-eye. Jane's messengered the blood samples and tissues from all major organs to the toxicology lab in Seattle. It's up to them now. You didn't find a suicide note?"

"No. What makes you think of suicide?"

"Most poisonings are. Any drugs around?"

Gabe shook his head. "Just some aspirin and birth control pills. We'll have them tested of course. Could something have been in the wine?"

Thornton shrugged his bony shoulders. "Search me. Like I said before, you're in the toxicologist's bailiwick now. But I will tell you this—if she didn't suicide, then you've probably got a very clever murderer, Gabe."

"Because you couldn't find any evidence?"

Jane walked up at that moment, removing her gloves. "I think what Tom means is that poisoners are either very stupid or very clever. The stupid ones use arsenic, strychnine or cyanide. Easy to see in an autopsy. Normally easy to trace to the buyer. But there are an awful lot of subtler poisons out there that are damn difficult to find because they dissipate so quickly. If one of them was used, we may never be able to identify it."

Gabe looked over at Jane. "What kind of poisons are you talking about?"

"Only ones I can speak to are those that leave obvious traces. Whatever was used here didn't."

Tom had begun to walk away. "Look, I'd like to stay and chat some more, but I'm late for a biopsy. Call me when you schedule the probable-cause hearing on this one, if you get that far. Clever poisoners are seldom caught."

As Tom walked away, his words seemed to hang in the chemically tainted atmosphere like some bad-smelling prophecy. Jane sought a nearby exit and some fresh air. Gabe followed.

The afternoon was like the morning, overcast and cool. Jane cupped each elbow with the opposite hand, leaned back against the hospital's rough stucco wall, and stared out at the rain-tinged gloom. "Tom Thornton tells me this isn't the first time you've walked out on an autopsy when the body has been that of a beautiful woman."

Gabe shoved his hands in his pockets, reminding himself to have a talk with Tom about his indiscriminate tongue. "I needed a cup of coffee."

Jane gave him a sideways glance, knowing nobody drank coffee for three hours. Still, it was hard for her to think of him as the sensitive type. He probably just got bored. "Since it looks like she was poisoned, and there's no evidence to suggest suicide, I'd say we've got a murder on our hands."

"Correction, Hardesty. *I* have a murder on *my* hands. You have a death."

Jane took a deep breath as she concentrated on keeping her rising anger controlled. "Look, Kincaid. I happen to be the deputy coroner in this county. Jennifer Madden's death certificate will be drawn up by my office, not yours. I'm the one who will decide if she's been murdered."

"Based on what, Hardesty? Your vast experience? That was your first autopsy."

She looked at him more fully, feeling forced to retain eye contact by his accusing blue stare. He had made a statement, not voiced a question. Her curiosity got the best of her. "How did you know?"

"Oh, you did everything by the book. If you hadn't, Tom would have had no compunction about correcting you."

"Then what—"

"You stopped the joking, Hardesty. A pro doesn't stop the joking, no matter how black it gets. Levity is the way we cope with touching death day after day. A pro joins in and hopes to hell it will help him or someone else from losing his lunch from what has to follow."

He watched her bite her lip and look away. "I see. It was a mistake."

Gabe hadn't expected her to admit it. He looked at her more closely, at the strong bones of her face, seemingly honed, by illness or pain, at her light eyes, their blandness betrayed by the bruises within them. "You've obviously read up on the procedures, and you know your anatomy. Where did Karl Daly find you?"

Jane leaned away from the wall and started back inside. "I wasn't lost."

Gabe followed her. "What were you doing?"

"It's not important."

"A mortician? No, they don't teach that much anatomy to a mortician. A medical student?"

Jane reached the doorknob. "I said it's not important."

"A nurse?"

"Kincaid—"

"Hell, that only leaves a doctor. You must have had a pretty mean malpractice suit to have been pushed out of medicine."

A crusty edge of controlled fury crept into her voice. "I wasn't pushed out."

His lips circled into a small smile. "So you *were* a doctor."

Her lips tightened as she leaned toward him. For a split second, Gabe had the fleeting impression of a flashing spark deep in those bland, light eyes. Then he felt a plastic bag being dumped into his palm. "This is the label out of Jennifer's negligee. It belongs in your evidence room."

Gabe raised the see-through bag with the enclosed silver label, its letters in elegantly scrolled crushed velvet. He read it aloud. "To Die For. Rather prophetic, under the circumstances. Perhaps the lab should take a closer look at the fabric of that negligee."

"Fleming bagged it and is sending it to the lab, along with the wine, perfume and cosmetics. But I seriously doubt that something in the fabric could be lethal."

Gabe fingered the label. "I'm not ruling anything out, Hardesty. Any ideas where Jennifer Madden could have gotten that negligee?"

Jane was quiet for a moment as her hand rested on the back door to the Edenville Hospital, almost as though she were having a silent debate with herself. Gabe didn't expect an answer. When it came, it surprised him. "From an exclusive lingerie establishment on the southern end of Eden Island. I'll have my written report to you this afternoon."

Jane opened the door and disappeared back into the hospital before Gabe had a chance to comment.

Gabe looked down at the beautiful silver label, trying to figure out how Jane Hardesty knew Jennifer's garment came from a specific lingerie shop. Maybe it was just one of those female things. Wasn't Della Street always able to tell Perry Mason about perfumes and pocketbooks he came across in his investigations?

Gabe slipped the label into his pocket. A quick glance at his watch told him it was time to get back to the office and get Roy going on background checks. He was beginning to think a background check on the new deputy coroner was also in order.

"Ms. HARDESTY, WAIT UP! One question, please!"

Startled by the yelling voice, Jane halted in her tracks just outside the door to Edenville's small coroner's office. She turned to see a thin, young male reporter sprinting across the street from the direction of the sheriff's building. Dark locks of stringy, greasy-looking hair flopped on his shoulders as his microphone pointed at her like the nose of a sniffing bloodhound. Behind him loomed a broad, bearded cameraman. Before Jane had time for another thought, they were on her.

"I'm Kenney from channel thirteen. You've just come from Jennifer Madden's autopsy, isn't that right, Ms. Hardesty?"

"Yes, but how did you—"

"What was in the suicide note?"

"What suicide note?"

"So you're saying the sheriff's office didn't find a suicide note?"

"Look, I'm not—"

"But it wasn't natural causes, was it, Ms. Hardesty?"

"Again, it would be inappropriate for me to—"

"Rumor is she was found with liquor and drugs."

Jane's lips drew tight. "Where did you hear that?"

"So there weren't any liquor or drugs at the death scene?"

"I didn't say that."

"So the coroner's office is covering up the facts?"

Jane took a deep breath, fighting to keep her temper and an even tone as she turned to grab the doorknob. "The chief of detectives is in charge of the case. Ask him your questions."

"But isn't it your job to determine the cause of death?"

"Of course."

"Well, you've finished the autopsy. What killed Jennifer Madden?"

Jane fiddled with the doorknob. "Our findings are inconclusive. More tests need to be done."

"More tests? What kind of tests?"

Jane's lips tightened. "Laboratory tests. Now, if you'll excuse me, I have work to do."

But as Jane turned away and twisted the knob, she heard the reporter's last question hit her like a load of buckshot. "Was Jennifer the Genie murdered, Ms. Hardesty? Is that why you won't give the people of Edenville straight answers?"

Jane didn't turn around to face the reporter. She knew any answer she could give to that last question would be wrong. Damn little twerp. How had she gotten suckered into responding to him at all? She was going to have to start rehearsing "No comment" for when reporters approached her from now on. This was one aspect of the deputy coroner's job that she hadn't been prepared for.

She slammed the door shut behind her and turned the corner to her office, dropping her briefcase with a resounding *splat* in the middle of the clean metal desk in the small, square room.

A totally bald-headed man with thick glasses and a thin face shot his head around the doorjamb. "So how did your first autopsy go?"

Jane turned fully toward her boss, Karl Daly, seeing the anxious expectation in his eyes.

The official wording came easily to her tongue. "Inconclusive pending toxicology report."

She knew she hadn't directly answered the real question Karl had asked, but he grunted in acknowledgment. "Do you think it will prove to be natural causes?"

"No, I don't, Karl. I think the woman was poisoned."

Karl stepped fully into the room. "Jennifer Madden poisoned? Well, well... I look forward to reading your reports on this. Anything else?"

"Yes. You were right about Chief of Detectives Kincaid."

Karl nervously shoved his heavy glasses to the back of his long, beaklike nose. "Shame you had to meet up with him the first time out. After Kincaid got through with your predecessor, old Sam just refused to go out to any more possible crime scenes."

Jane fiddled with the few paper reports in her in basket. "How can he get away with it, Karl? Clearly our job requires us to be there in order to examine the evidence."

Karl shrugged. "Jobs get redefined depending on who fills them. I might be able to talk to the sheriff, although I don't know if I'm going to have much luck. Kincaid is overbearing, but he's the best chief of detectives to come along in five decades, and Andy Peck knows it."

Jane watched Karl's face. It looked like he was preparing himself resolutely for a firing squad. He was not the kind of man she visualized as a knight in shining armor riding to her rescue.

"Thanks, Karl, but I'll handle Kincaid." She dug her hand into her briefcase, brought out her camera and began to rewind the film in preparation to removing it.

A whiff of his mint mouthwash wafted toward her from across the room as a look of relief entered Karl's dark eyes.

It switched to one of surprise when he saw the camera and film. "You got pictures of the death scene?"

"A few."

"Kincaid *let* you?"

Jane felt almost amused at the continuing shock in Karl's voice. She was obviously exceeding his wildest expectations. She removed the film and closed the camera's back. "What can you tell me about Jennifer Madden?"

Karl leaned his posterior against the end of the desk. "All I know is what I read about the scandal concerning her and Senator Madden. Once his wife was dead and he married Jennifer, very little news leaked out. Hell, Jane, you know that Eden Island group is a closemouthed bunch."

Jane did know, being one of them.

She stooped to pick up her shoulder bag. "I've got to get on to my reports. Where can I get the film developed? And this tape copied?"

Karl took the roll of film and the videotape of Jennifer Madden from her. "I'll see to it. There's a place a couple of blocks away. Anything else?"

"The body's being released to the family this afternoon. Funeral services will be tomorrow morning."

"So soon?"

"Richard Madden's directions. He called the Edenville Hospital morgue just before I left to make the arrangements for the body to be taken to the mortuary. I think he wants to get the funeral over with before the media has a chance to descend. Judging from the guy who just accosted me outside, looks like he's not moving too fast. I'll be attending the services, by the way."

"You, Jane?"

"Yes, me. I'm doing a thorough investigation, no matter what Kincaid says. This is our case as much as his."

Karl Daly smiled and gave her shoulder a humoring pat. "Of course it is."

AT THE END of his long day, Gabe stopped off at Shenanigan's, a favorite eating and watering hole, just up the street from his two-bedroom condo in the heart of Edenville. He nodded at the regulars he'd shared ball games and a few beers with and slid onto the bar stool. What with the Jennifer Madden death crowding into an already full caseload, and making sure his staff allowed no leaks to the press, he'd missed lunch, and he was both hungry and thirsty.

Harry Pool, Shenanigan's portly owner and bartender, slipped a cold draft beer and a bowl of steaming Irish stew under Gabe's nose as though he'd been expecting him, which, considering Gabe's frequency at the establishment lately, maybe he had.

Gabe didn't like to dwell on how many nights he'd come here in a row, or on the fact that that was indicative of yet another period of growing boredom with the dating scene. He just concentrated on getting the hot, filling stew into his cold, empty belly. Harry left him alone until the bowl got pushed aside and Gabe grasped the beer glass.

"So, Gabe, I hear you're the one who's gonna find out who did in Jennifer the Genie?"

Gabe's eyes shot to Harry's heavy-jowled smirk in unwelcome surprise. "What are you talking about, Harry?"

Harry's beefy shoulders gave an indifferent shrug in response to Gabe's demanding and displeased tone. "Hell, Gabe, no reason to get ticked at me. Ain't no secret what you're working on. Local TV station ran the news brief five minutes ago. And it looks to me like it's about to run again. Here, I'll turn up the tube."

Gabe followed Harry's shuffle to the TV mounted over the back of the bar. He recognized the greasy black locks of Edenville's most obnoxious reporter and was gripped with an irritating foreboding.

"This is Clive Kenney for channel thirteen news with an exclusive interview with Edenville's new deputy coroner, Jane Hardesty, just outside her office." He turned to Jane. "You've just come from Jennifer Madden's autopsy, isn't that right, Ms. Hardesty?"

"Yes."

"What did Jennifer die from?"

"Our findings are inconclusive. More tests need to be done."

"Is suicide or murder a possibility?"

"The chief of detectives is in charge of the case."

"Gabe Kincaid? So what you're saying is that since the sheriff has assigned his ace, Kincaid, the circumstances surrounding Jennifer Madden's death must be suspicious?"

"Yes."

"Well, ladies and gentlemen, you've heard it here first. Once again, that was new deputy coroner Jane Hardesty looking into the suspicious death of Jennifer Madden, the wife of ex-senator Richard Madden, found dead this morning in her home on exclusive Eden Island. Ms. Hardesty refused to comment on whether the former stripper was found with liquor and drugs, but with Chief of Detectives Kincaid assigned to the case, natural causes must be ruled out. We'll keep you informed as further developments come our way."

Harry Pool stretched up to turn down the volume on the TV again. "So you see, Gabe, it ain't no secret that—"

Gabe never heard the end of Harry's sentence. He was already out the door.

JANE HAD BEEN HOME about an hour, trying to find a place for her books on her mother's filled shelves, when the call came in. She expected her caller to be Karl, since she hadn't given her unlisted number to anyone else. But the female voice that responded to her hello was definitely not her boss's.

"Jane, dear, why haven't you called?"

Jane recognized the accusatory but kindly tones of Dorothy Speke immediately. She plopped down on her overstuffed couch. "Dot, it's good to hear from you. Really good. But how on earth did you get this number?"

Dorothy Speke chuckled. "You're asking *me* that, Jane?"

Jane shook her head. It was a silly question. Dorothy Speke's Eden Island information-gathering network was as thorough and extensive as any FBI operation—and, she suspected, ran just as efficiently.

"When did you find out I was back?" Jane asked, out of curiosity.

"Three days ago when you stopped in at the mechanic's to get the Talbot-Lago out of storage. But don't try to distract me with these extraneous issues, Jane Hardesty. You know perfectly well I'm calling to find out about the suspicious circumstances around Jennifer's death."

Jane sat bolt upright. "Dot, who told you there were suspicious circumstances surrounding Jennifer Madden's death?"

Dorothy's voice ascended into incredulity. "Who told me? Jane, dear, you told me, right on the evening news, although I must say I think, as a friend, you could have called Leo and me personally first, before you spread it to the rest of the world."

Jane's stomach did a queasy turn. "The evening news? That's impossible."

"Dear, it's no use denying it. I saw you in that interview with that local news reporter."

Jane tried to steady her swirling thoughts. "It's true I talked with some reporter for a minute or two, but I only told him Jennifer's autopsy was inconclusive."

"Well, that's not how it sounded to me, dear. And, anyway, it's not such a surprise. Leo told me when he got to Madden's place that the sheriff's office was already there, questioning everyone."

"That's normal procedure, Dot."

"Is it? Well, it's not normal procedure for Leo to be worried about *how* Jennifer died."

Jane chewed on her lip. She knew Dot relished the triumphs and tragedies of others' lives, and particularly the lives of those living on Eden Island. Her penchant for gossip always made Jane feel uncomfortable. Still, Dorothy was a source, and at this moment a very good one. And she had a job that involved information-gathering, too.

"Did Leo see anything strange?"

Jane could almost see Dorothy's smile as her voice lowered conspiratorially. "Leo told me he didn't want to talk about it. And he canceled all his appointments this morning and locked himself in his study."

Jane could understand Leo being sensitive to the death of a patient. She couldn't help but marvel at Dorothy's spongelike ability to soak up every ounce of intrigue. Still, a few more questions seemed to be in order. "Was Leo treating Jennifer for anything special?"

"I doubt it, Jane. She looked fine when she stopped by yesterday afternoon. Still, Leo won't confide a thing to me. He can be so very stingy sometimes."

Jane detected the pique hidden in Dorothy's words. In fairness, and in his absence, she felt the need to come to Leo's defense.

"Dot, Leo's always been generous to me. He did a million kind and thoughtful things for me after Mother's death."

Dorothy's tone softened, even became sad. "Yes, dear. I haven't forgotten the loss of your mother or your husband. So young, and you've already known such terrible tragedies!"

Jane was eager to change the subject. Dorothy's weepy condolences at both her mother's and Gregory's funerals had only made things worse. She didn't feel ready for another round of them.

"What did you think of Jennifer, Dot?"

"Oh, she was a man-made woman, dear. You know the type. All come-on. The flesh-and-blood embodiment of those playthings that men drool over in those magazines. There were lots of rumors about her having affairs."

"With whom?"

"The entire male population of Eden Island, if one can believe all the talk."

"Tell me why you think Leo is worried about Jennifer's death?"

Excitement once again skipped through Dorothy's words. "Well, don't you see, Jane? He has to be worried. Jennifer was young, and Leo was her doctor. If it comes out that Leo didn't notice something important that cost Jennifer her life...well, we both know Richard Madden isn't exactly the forgiving type, don't we?''

Jane frowned. "Does Leo think that's what happened?"

"Why else would he have been so upset? I know there's something funny about her death. I just know it!"

Jane squeezed the telephone instrument tight. Dorothy's words bothered her, because Dorothy said what she did strictly out of excitement, and not the least little bit out of fear or worry. And then Jane knew.

Dr. Leo Speke's wife was rather hoping Jennifer Madden had died of something quite dreadful. And if she hadn't, Dorothy was going to be most disappointed.

"Jane! Your interview is coming on again. Quick. Turn on your television! Channel thirteen!"

Chapter Four

When Gabe arrived at Eden Land Chapel the next morning, he could see that the Madden family had barred both the public and reporters from Jennifer's funeral. It couldn't have been an easy task, not after Jane Hardesty's television debut the night before.

As he had anticipated, right after its airing the sheriff's office had been deluged with calls clamoring for information from previously low-key and well-behaved reporters. "No comment" wasn't going to hack it for much longer, not now that Jane Hardesty had revealed his involvement and that damn reporter had speculated about murder.

Murder. Even a whisper of the word around an Eden Island resident caught the interest of both the local news and the national wire services. What should have been a quiet investigation had suddenly turned quite noisy. And he had that damn deputy coroner to thank. Gabe promised himself he was going to wring Jane Hardesty's neck at the first opportunity.

At least whoever was in charge of security here at the chapel and the cemetery had done a good job of situating a circle of guards around the entire perimeter to keep out the curious and the uninvited. That at least made Gabe's identification of the small group in attendance much easier.

He recognized Richard Madden and Suzanne Lemke right away. His question went to Detective Fleming at his side.

"What do you have on the Lemke woman?"

Roy leafed through his collection of faxed photos. "She's the owner of Suzanne's, an exclusive lingerie shop on Eden Island. Caters only to the rich. It's where that negligee came from that Jennifer was wearing."

Gabe looked at Roy. "She made the negligee?"

"She designs them. Picks out the materials. Her employees actually hand-sew the stuff. This was in Hardesty's report. Didn't you read it?"

Gabe scratched his chin irritably. "Not yet. Is the tall guy on Suzanne Lemke's other arm Philip Lemke, the husband?"

"Yep. He's an Eden Island lawyer who's obviously friendly with Madden. They're all sticking close to their lawyers, now that the media has gotten the story. I've gotten lots of cold shoulders when I've tried to make your appointments."

Gabe nodded. "Figures."

"You want to start pressing the issue and pull some of these people in for a face-to-face?"

Gabe's hand straightened his already straight tie. "Meaningless now that their defenses are up. Let's see what we can find out about them first."

Roy pointed a finger. "See the short one with the gray crew cut and chunky frame keeping pace on the other side of Madden?"

Gabe looked down the sight line of Roy's finger and nodded.

"He's Jack Carver, the state's political party chairman and Madden's alibi."

Gabe began checking off names in his notebook. "No wife?"

"Fourth one just divorced him. Carver likes to play around, and apparently keeps getting caught at it."

"Where's our Mr. Gnat?"

"He's waiting next to Madden's silver limo over there. Computer drew a blank on him. No driver's license. No military record. No bank accounts. No nothing."

Gabe's eyes rested on the dusky man. "Keep checking. He didn't just materialize on the planet full-grown." Gabe turned back to the chapel. "Walking up the stairs now is Dr. Leo Speke, and I presume the hefty lady on his arm is his wife?"

"Right. Dorothy Speke. She's an Eden Island blue blood. They've been married twenty-eight years. Kids are grown and gone."

Gabe nodded. "And that's Naomi Parisot, the maid who found Jennifer's body, right behind them. Have you gotten any further on checking out her story?"

Roy shook his head. "The employment agency that placed her with the Maddens promised to have their president call back. I'll let you know. Hey, hey, look who's also trotting up, Gabe."

Gabe's black eyebrows rose as he watched the familiar straight-backed carriage. "Well, if it isn't the honorable 'Hang 'Em High' Henry Rowe. So our infamous superior court judge is also a friend of Richard Madden's. Guess it figures. The magnet of money attracts, and he's the only one of our fearless lawgivers whose chauffeur drives him to work."

"Do you suppose the smartly dressed redhead on his arm is the missus?"

"Probably. Check it out."

Roy closed his folder of computer printouts, and his voice took on a new tone. "And trailing the field is our own infamous deputy coroner, Jane Hardesty."

Gabe clipped his pen to his notepad, frowning. "What in the hell is she doing here?"

Roy's sideways glance shot a dart at Gabe's temple. "You obviously haven't read my reports, either. You told me to check up on her, remember?"

"So what did you find out?"

"She's one of them, Gabe. Born on Eden Island. Her mother's blood is even bluer than Dorothy Speke's. Her father came from humbler origins. He was killed in the Vietnam conflict. She graduated medical school, went into practice, and then got married six years ago. She and the husband settled in Boston. Mother died of a stroke about five years ago. She returned to the island just this week.''

Gabe let the information sink through his initial surprise. ''Without the husband?''

''Yeah.''

''Divorced?''

''Widowed. Year ago.''

''Who was he?''

''Gregory Hardesty. Some lobbyist for a Boston environmental league.''

''How did he die?''

''Give me a break, Gabe. I had no idea you wanted that kind of detail. You know she's called me again asking about our reports on the Madden death. I don't think I can stall her much longer.''

Gabe gave Roy a sideways glance. ''Can't stall her? Roy, I've known you to stonewall all five county commissioners for months without working up a sweat. You letting Hardesty get to you?''

Roy looked away from Gabe as a slight flush erupted beneath his full cheeks. ''Hell, you know it's not that. It's just . . . well, her thorough documentation puts old Sam's scribbles to shame. That autopsy paperwork she forwarded reads like a textbook dream. Feels kind of stingy not to reciprocate with at least something.''

Gabe gave Roy a comforting clap on the shoulder. ''Get the guilt off your shoulders, Roy. I'll take care of Hardesty. Concentrate on getting me thorough background checks on all these people who've showed for Jennifer's funeral. You can get started right away, since there's no reason for you to stay for these festivities. I'll catch up with you back at the office.''

Gabe took the chapel steps two at a time.

''JANE, YOU GROW more and more like your beautiful mother every day. Let's see, the last time I saw you was at Margaret Madden's funeral, nearly four years ago, and before that it was your mother's funeral, what—five years ago?"

Jane took Jack Carver's large square hand; every finger sported the armor of a thick gold ring. "Shame someone has to die before we seem to have a reason to get together, Jack."

Jack's straight, prominent teeth gleamed back at Jane. "Yes. I've shirked my duty, and I'm ashamed."

Jack Carver looked anything but ashamed. "Your duty?" Jane asked, a bit perplexed.

Carver patted Jane's hand in his. "Jane, dear, you know I've always wanted you to look to me as the father figure you were so cruelly denied."

Jane had felt uncomfortable with Jack's clumsy efforts along these lines when she was ten. Now that she was thirty-one, she found them intolerable. The only thing she liked less than child-women were the men who encouraged them to remain that way. She removed her hand from his clutches. "I'll send you my Christmas list."

Jack sailed his rejected hand over the sharp ends of his crew cut, smiling as though he were enjoying the tactile sensation of the short hairs scraping across his palm.

"Don't be too quick to refuse a helping hand, Jane. After your televised betrayal of your Eden Island neighbors, I have a feeling you're going to need all the support you can get to mend fences."

Jane felt a direct jolt at Jack's reprimand. Seeing herself on TV the night before, answering questions she'd never been asked and saying things she had never meant, had both shocked and angered her. Now she realized that to Jack and the other residents of Eden Island that interview must have been positively inflammatory, what with its insinuations about alcohol, drugs, and murder.

Jane's voice rose in frustration. "I was misquoted, Jack."

Jack took a hold of Jane's arm again and gave it a desultory pat that felt more scolding than affectionate. "And that's what you want me to tell Richard?"

Jane wasn't fooled by the evenness in Jack's tone, or by the smile that descended on his lips. She knew her explanation had struck him as far from satisfactory. She extricated her arm from his grip. "I don't want you to tell Richard anything. I can speak for myself."

Jack's smile remained in place as he looked purposefully over her shoulder. "Well, here's your chance."

Jane turned to find herself face-to-face with Richard Madden's black eyes. She flinched; it was a knee-jerk reaction that sprung from youthful impressions of this man, who always seemed larger than life and twice as menacing.

The years had significantly lessened their height difference, but not nearly enough. Madden possessed an authority in his bearing that went way beyond mere size. She paused to take a deep steadying breath. "My deepest sympathy on the death of your wife, Richard."

His mustache curled at the edges, but the shrewd black eyes did not smile. "Thank you, Jane."

He waited, knowing there was more she would say, accepting her automatic homage. She felt his control and power directing her as they always had, and it made her angry. She wanted to turn and walk away. But somehow she couldn't, and it made her all the more angry that he knew she couldn't. "I apologize, Richard, for any distress that television interview might have caused. My answers were twisted to leave an impression that was never meant."

Richard stepped closer, and his strong, powerful fingers suddenly circled about her wrists. "Jane, do not distress yourself. These things happen. I understand perfectly. I think it's time for the services now. Shall we all have a seat?"

His words by themselves were innocent. But the way he timed them, and the inflection he used, gave Jane a definite suggestion of the anger beneath their polished surface. And then there was the tightening grip on her wrists. She waited until he released that grip before she moved away. Far away.

She sat at the back of the mortuary chapel, not feeling at all eager to be within Richard Madden's immediate sphere.

She could remember from her childhood the palpable tension in the air whenever he had entered a room. She had cringed to see how even her mother's carefree, easy disposition sobered at his presence.

Fortunately, she knew, he wouldn't expect her to take a place near him. None of them seemed to this morning. Suzanne and Philip nodded with formal politeness as they passed. Dot and Leo Speke sent a stiff smile in her direction. Henry and Ellen Rowe stared straight ahead without so much as a glance. God, even the maid looked unfriendly!

Jane watched their backs, feeling a separateness that was almost like a wall. Her earliest memories were of these people, and of her mother's smiling insistence that they all be good friends. But not all the friendships had felt comfortable. And except for Suzanne, Leo and Dot, she'd barely thought about them in the last few years. She doubted they'd thought of her at all.

She was a stranger in their midst, supernumerary, and she was wondering if she always had been—and just hadn't known it.

Jane released a sigh and sat back, feeling suddenly weary. Her eyes strayed to the white marble casket, outlined in delicate gold filigree, sitting in state on the ornate altar. Thousands of freshly cut white roses sat in crystal vases, so thick that even the minister couldn't walk through. Only two candles had been lit. Their glow lent a gentle, virginal purity to the scene. Jane shifted uneasily in her seat.

The minister took the white marble pulpit and began to speak in soft, dulcet tones, his words barely reaching Jane in the back row. "...join in his sorrow...such a sad occasion...mourned by all who knew her..." A perplexed frown dug into Jane's forehead.

A morose eulogy. How could these people have arranged such a service? Jane thought of the flamboyant and outrageous Jennifer Madden she had seen on Suzanne's tape. She could almost hear the woman's raucous laugh. Jennifer

Madden would have hated this uninspired, depressing send-off.

Jane didn't like it much, either. Or maybe it was just the fact that it was a funeral, and Jane had already sat through far too many of them. She got to her feet and groped her way down the narrow pew and out the chapel's cold, coffinlike doors into the warm sunshine. She plopped onto the steps at the chapel's entrance and stared at the yellow dandelions twirled by the April breeze.

But what she saw was Gregory's slim, pale form, his brown curls all gone, trophies of the cancer's victories.

Forcefully she shoved the images and pain aside, willing her mind to go blank. She used every ounce of her strength and concentration to focus on the lack of feeling that had become her shield and savior over the past year. As she clasped it tight around her, she began to empty into a cool, accustomed calm.

Then, suddenly, the calm fled, and he was there. She felt his presence even before the slight movement caught the corner of her eye. Jane gave a start as her head swung toward Gabe Kincaid, standing not five feet away.

Her eyes still carried the bland look, but today Gabe could have sworn the bruises behind them were fresh. Confusion in the face of her obvious distress clashed with his initial intent to give her a good tongue-lashing for talking to that reporter. It was an even match, and he found himself stymied into an unaccustomed silence.

Jane looked away from Gabe's uncertain expression and back down to the bright yellow dandelions, furious with him for disrupting her calm, wishing he would go away, knowing he would not. When he finally spoke, his voice had that insistent, demanding quality that incensed her so.

"How did your husband die?"

Jane got up from the stairs, brushing the back of her slim black skirt with an impatient hand. "I'd rather not talk about it."

"Why?"

"Because it's personal."

"Someone dying is personal?"

Exasperation coated her words. "What is it with you?"

Yes, he was sure now. Despite the bruises, there was a spark deep in the very hard fine-grained quartz of her green eyes. It was the flint that could be sparked with the right words, igniting that suppressed emotion. He'd found a few of those right words. He wondered how many others there might be.

"What is it with me? What is it with you? All I asked was how your husband died. Should be simple enough to answer. How bad can it be? Shot by a jealous husband? Jumped off a cliff? Gunned down while he was trying to rob a bank?"

Jane decided that she'd never met anyone more insensitive than this man. She started for her car, in the parking lot, only to find him right beside her.

"So which one was it?" he persisted.

She let out an oppressed sigh. "All right, Kincaid. He died of cancer. Now will you let it drop?"

Gabe had the nerve to smirk. "Cancer? All this fuss over something as legitimate as cancer?"

She paused long enough in her stride for an angry retort. "You're . . . you're . . . !"

His smile was smug. "Yes, I am. So what bothered you about the funeral service just now, a hard seat?"

Jane ground her teeth. She was beginning to feel like a frog that kept getting poked so it would jump. It was an infuriating image. Everything about this man was infuriating. She fired out her question. "Why should something have bothered me?"

"Because you're leaving early. Come on, Hardesty, you must see you can't keep secrets from me. Now what was it?"

Damn, he was a monumental pain in the neck. Maybe if she just told him, he'd go away and leave her in peace. About now she was willing to try anything. She started walking again.

"All right, Kincaid. It wasn't the kind of service Jennifer Madden would have wanted. I can't imagine the people who loved her arranging it."

"You knew Jennifer Madden?"

"No. But the mourners back in that chapel should have."

Gabe shook his head. "I'm not following you."

Jane took another step, with him doggedly staying alongside. She looked meaningly at his feet. "Looks to me like that's precisely what you're doing."

Gabe marshaled another smirk. "Stop trying to change the subject. What's the point you're trying to make about the service?"

"You haven't read my report yet, have you?"

"I was at the autopsy. What's there to read?"

Her chin came up defiantly. "I guess you won't know unless you read it. You can read, can't you?"

Gabe's eyes grew tight. "I can read, Hardesty. Not only did your impromptu interview with the yellow press rate repeating all night long on the TV news, it's also generated a front-page story on Jennifer and her death in the local newspaper. Maybe you've seen it? It's the one picturing Jennifer in her skimpy stage outfit and carrying the headline 'Deputy coroner calls Jennifer Madden's death suspicious.'"

Jane felt her ire rise at his pointed criticism, knowing she was being condemned unfairly. Her fists balled as she fought to keep her temper. "You can't think I'd be so intemperate as to say such a thing. The little twerp maliciously misquoted me."

Knowing the reporter in question, Gabe could easily believe it. But he wasn't about to let Jane Hardesty off the hook. He stepped directly in front of her, looming. He liked looming, and he knew he was sensational at it.

"That reporter didn't misquote you when you identified me as being assigned to the case, and that is why the subject of murder is being bounced around. Now hear me, Hardesty, and hear me good. Your job is done on the Jennifer Madden death, and you are going to fade into the woodwork. I'm warning you—from now on, you'd better keep out of my way. Are we communicating?''

Jane's eyes flashed, as all her careful control crumbled in the press of his physical and emotional pertinacity. Her hands balled; blood rushed into her cheeks. Her voice rose to a roar. "Are we communicating? No, but we're about to, Kincaid. I'm not some timid little fellow who will jump when you order him around, like my predecessor. I've faced hell, and next to it, buster, you're nothing but a puff of smoke. Jennifer Madden's death is as much my case as it is yours, and I will investigate it with every resource at my disposal. So you'd better keep out of *my* way!''

Jane stepped around Gabe and stomped off in the direction of her car.

Gabe shook his head at her retreating figure. Well, he'd struck past that placid facade, all right, and what a conflagration he'd found!

A reluctant smile spread his lips. Once again she had flaunted his authority, ignored his orders, and yelled at him. Why were these far-from-endearing traits beginning to grow on him?

Maybe it was because her face had changed with every ounce of mounting indignation—had become fierce, fiery, alive. *So that's what her anger looks like,* he thought fleetingly. *I wonder how her laughter would sound?*

"Kincaid?"

Gabe instantly turned toward the perpetually hoarse voice that had dominated many a court case in his career. He found himself nearly eye-to-eye with Henry Rowe, a tall, bony man who always stood so erect he looked as if he were hanging from some hook at the back of his suit.

"Yes, Your Honor," Gabe said, forcing the smile to stay on his lips.

Henry Rowe, never exactly a burst of Technicolor, stood before him today like an old black-and-white set whose picture tube was fading. His eyes, his hair, his clothes, even his complexion, looked gray. Gabe couldn't remember seeing anyone who had struck him as so colorless before.

"I hear nothing conclusive came out of the autopsy?" Rowe's hoarse tone said.

"No. Nothing conclusive."

"However, you suspect foul play?"

Gabe's hands had begun to clench. Rowe had no business pumping him. They both knew it. They also both knew the judge could pay Gabe back in court on future cases if he didn't cooperate.

Gabe tried to keep his tone noncommittal. "Naturally, we must pursue all options."

Rowe gave an unsatisfied grunt. "Madden's a close friend and neighbor of mine, Kincaid. His wife's tragic death must be handled discreetly. I won't tolerate unsupported accusations or unwarranted invasions of his privacy, or the privacy of anyone in his circle. You understand me?"

Gabe's short nails pierced his palms. He took a moment to remind himself that he had long ago outgrown foolish macho gestures. Still, it took every ounce of the control he'd learned from years of practice to bite down the blunt words thrashing within his throat.

Henry Rowe nodded curtly. Gabe knew he was taking his stoic silence for agreement. The stiff, washed-out man turned away to join the rest of the funeral attendees, who were now shoving heads and feet into cars for the short drive to the gravesite.

As Gabe watched the man join his wife and Richard Madden, who were getting into the latter's long silver limousine, he made a solemn pledge to himself that Jennifer Madden, Richard Madden and Henry Rowe were all going to get one of the most thorough background checks he had ever run.

"Jane! Wait up!"

Jane swung around in surprise to see Dr. Leo Speke coming up behind her. She stopped at the top of the path leading from the main buildings of the Indian reservation to the parking lot and waited until he caught up.

"You barely said hello at Jennifer's funeral this morning. Why haven't you been around to see Dorothy and me?"

Jane gave Leo's arm a companionable squeeze, noting that he still smelled of baby lotion, even after all these years. "I've been getting settled into my mother's place. I haven't been around to see anyone socially. Are you still spending a day every week here at the reservation?"

"Yes. I think of it as my day of real medicine, away from Eden Island's pampered. How's the new job?"

"It's the reason I'm here. A high-school-age Indian boy was killed in a traffic accident about an hour ago. I had to notify his family."

Leo silently nodded his curly white top. "That's always going to be the hardest part of our jobs."

Jane turned back toward the parking lot and began to resume her interrupted pace. "Not really, Leo."

Speke's large eyes rolled over to Jane as he fell into step beside her. "What could be worse than having to tell waiting family members that someone they love has just died?"

Jane's answer was swift and sharp. "Standing by and watching them die and knowing you can't do a thing to prevent it."

Leo's hand came out to circle her arm. He tugged her to his side. He didn't say anything about Gregory, or about anything else. Jane silently blessed him for it.

"You could help me out here at the reservation if you ever decide to practice again."

Jane shook her head. "I'm better off where I am. You've come here a lot of years, haven't you?"

"Since my internship."

"I've always admired you for that, Leo. Everyone says your grades were so good you could have gone to any of the hospitals in the state. For you to have chosen the Indian reservation—"

Leo held up one hand to halt her. "Purely selfish. My family wasn't born on Eden Island. Didn't have two nickels to rub together. I got most of my medical training through grants and scholarships. The one that went with an internship among the tribe was the most generous.''

"Surely there were others equally generous?''

He smiled. "Okay, I'll confess. Coming to the reservation lets me study native herbs and medications firsthand. And one day, who knows? I may discover an important new drug and become famous.''

Jane circled her arm through his. "Such selfishness. Performing your medical services then and every year since for free. Although I do seem to remember Mother mentioned she had a copy of a book you wrote on the Indian medicines. Did it provide much in the way of royalties?''

Leo looked down at the rocky path they were traveling. Jane got the feeling she was embarrassing him. He gave a small, strained laugh. "Probably sold all of fifty copies. Writing can be a very ego-deflating process. Only recommend it to my worst enemies. Oh, I see you're driving the Talbot-Lago. Amazing, but she still looks as good as new.''

Jane patted the bumper of the car as they approached. "A sweet lady. Remember? That's what Mom used to call her.''

Leo nodded distractedly. "They were both sweet ladies. Newer models just can't compare—with the exception of present company, of course.''

Jane cocked her head at him. "Thank you, Leo, but do I detect something troubling you?''

Speke studied his feet, and the perpetual hump in his shoulders seemed to increase. "I'm concerned for you, Jane. You didn't die with your husband. Don't beat yourself for it.''

Jane started at the unexpectedness of his words.

Leo looked up at her. "Yes, Jane. I know what this new tight control means. I've been your physician and friend a long time.''

Jane released a whisper of a sigh.

Leo gave her arm a gentle shake. "Time to put away the black and start mingling again. Look, Richard Madden is announcing Philip's candidacy Friday night. You know these political dinners attract everyone. Why don't you come join us?"

Jane turned surprised eyes in Leo's direction. "Richard Madden is entertaining so soon after his wife's death?"

Leo shrugged. "My dear Jane, there are only two things I've found that cannot be circumvented in this world, and those are death and political campaigns. Of course, I realize you and Richard Madden were never exactly close, but considering your friendship with his niece, I'm sure he would welcome your presence."

Jane leaned against her car door, her gaze drifting to a patch of ground fog circling like a halo over the straight-limbed Douglas firs surrounding the parking lot. "He's still playing at lord and master, the controlling force of everyone in his circle."

Leo nodded solemnly. "Some men crave power over others. That's why they gravitate toward politics."

"Yes, I suppose that's what drives Richard. I remember going to hear his campaign speeches. Seemed bigger than life to me at the time. Margaret, his first wife, was with him, so supportive and quiet in the face of his excesses. A lot's happened since then. Now he's no longer a senator, Margaret's dead, and his second wife's death is up for scrutiny."

"Scrutiny?" Leo repeated. "Are you now saying there was some truth to that reporter's story after all?"

Jane shrugged. "That reporter misquoted me, Leo, but, amazingly, he got the basic facts correct. She might have been murdered, although admittedly it's kind of hard to think anyone could do such a thing."

"You didn't know her, did you?"

"No, but I did see Suzanne's tape of her. She seemed so—"

The pitch of Leo's voice rose; he was clearly surprised. "You *liked* her?"

Jane struggled through her muddled emotions. "Oh, I realize she was no Mother Theresa. But she seemed so happy and so alive. You know what she told Suzanne? 'My life is a special occasion.' She found such pleasure in it, Leo. And she was so...young."

Leo's voice became gentle. "I think I understand. Your empathy for Jennifer comes from your own recent loss. Gregory was only thirty-three, wasn't he?"

Jane silently opened the driver's door and slipped behind the wheel. "At least he had some time to prepare. Leo, do you think Jennifer would have lived her life any differently if she knew she would die at thirty?"

Leo stooped down until his eyes were even with Jane's. His were a very soft brown, large and soothing. "I think Jennifer lived for today, without thought or care for the future, or for anyone but herself. Now drive safely. I must hurry to make my next appointment."

GABE HEARD THE characteristic *clop-clop* of Sheriff Andy Peck's cowboy boots coming down the hall a full half minute before his ginger-whiskered face turned the corner to frame itself in Gabe's doorway. "Got a minute?"

Gabe put down the final pages of Jane Hardesty's report. "I thought you took the day off, Andy. Something come up?"

Andy Peck's answer came through loud and clear as he closed the door behind him and then plopped his heavy frame down in Gabe's side chair. Nobody in the entire detective unit ever closed his door unless something really big had hit the fan.

A multilegged expectation began to crawl up Gabe's back as he watched Andy nervously finger one of the long cigars in the pocket of his soiled yellow sweatshirt, which proclaimed in black letters across his ample belly Get a Cop to Come—Dial 911.

"No use beating about the sagebrush, Gabe. We've got to go real careful-like on this Jennifer Madden business. Real careful."

Gabe leaned forward, watching the sweat bead on his boss's brow. "Who called?"

Andy made a rude grunting sound as his jelly belly shook. "Who didn't? Damn phone's been ringing off the hook. Madden and friends have got burrs up their behinds because you've been riding roughshod into their private stock to check their brands."

The more nervous Andy got, Gabe knew, the thicker his cowboy metaphors became. He pushed his chair back and landed on his feet. "Look, Andy, I've been proceeding according to the book. Madden's wife is dead. We're taking a close look at him and the other people she knew, and that includes finances, and anything else there is to know."

Andy studied the blank white wall behind Gabe. "Get out of the hot sun, boy. Despite what that damn news reporter said, it's not yet officially a bushwhacking. Death certificate reads 'Undetermined pending toxicology.' Time to rein in. Seattle's got a heap of gang-shooting trouble, and they ain't gonna get those toxicology reports back to us real soon."

"You're telling me I've got to wait? But the trail's bound to get cold every day we—"

Gabe didn't bother finishing his protest. The deepening squint around Andy's eyes, and his own sudden lapse into Western metaphor, signaled its futility. He exhaled a heavy breath as he gave himself a mental dialect shake.

"Andy, what's going on? You've never asked me to back off before."

Andy scratched his head. A piece of hay fell from his scraggly ginger locks onto his yellow sweatshirt as he leaned forward.

"Okay, time for some real plain talk, partner. This is an election year. Now, you know I let you have your head and rope any ol' wayward steer that even looks like he's heading out of the ol' law-abiding herd. Hell, I'm as mellow as a dead pig in the sunshine. Except this ol' ginger porker is gonna be barbecued come November by these filthy-rich Eden Island dudes unless you stop moseyin' onto their private pastureland."

"Andy, you really going to let them ride roughshod over us?" *Damn. He'd slipped into another Western metaphor.*

Andy's complexion deepened to match the ginger of his profuse facial hair.

"Don't go kicking dirt in this old cowpoke's face, Gabe. All I'm saying is, we've got to be careful we don't go roping on the night range and find out in the morning we've corralled nothing but a mighty mean and ornery bull, with horns long enough to reach us on both sides of the fence. Now, you get my drift?"

Gabe exhaled and sank back in his chair. He could feel a brick wall when he was being rammed into it. "If you mean do I understand you're telling me to officially back off Madden, yes. If you mean do I understand that roping-bull analogy coming out of your city-born-and-bred Seattle mouth, you'll have to give me a written explanation. In English, preferably."

Andy Peck gave Gabe a crooked grin as he got to his feet and began his *clop-clop* toward the door. "You keep my humble origins to yourself, boy. Damn. Afraid I got this crud all over your floor."

"Yuck. What is it?"

"What you think? I was mucking out the horse stalls when all those damn calls started coming in."

Chapter Five

Jane was flabbergasted when she answered her doorbell at seven that night and found Gabe Kincaid on her doorstep. He was in the same suit he'd worn to the funeral that morning. Somehow the slacks still had their razor-sharp crease, and his hair was still neat and well-kept. Only the stubble on his chin gave his long day away.

Jane rubbed her dust-coated hands on the pants of her old gray sweats, irritation and a curious expectancy rendering her uncustomarily at a loss for words.

"I've read your report," he said, waving the pages in front of her like a flag of truce.

Jane's nose scrunched up. "Congratulations. Dear God, is that smell coming from you?"

"Uh, probably. The sheriff raises horses as a hobby."

"That doesn't explain why you smell like one."

Gabe grinned as he began to unlace his shoes. "I think I stepped in some, uh, residue from his impromptu visit to my office this afternoon. Perhaps it would be better if I left my shoes at the door?"

"How about outside the door?"

Gabe nodded. "How far?"

"How do you feel about Idaho?"

Gabe dropped his shoes and stepped into the house, his quick and easy grin expanding.

Jane closed the door behind him, feeling unsettled and fidgety. Here he was again, invading her peace and quiet.

The fact that he was wearing a smile this time only seemed to heighten her unease. What was the man up to? "Okay, Kincaid, you read my report. That doesn't explain what you're doing here."

Gabe pulled a videotape out of the breast pocket of his jacket. "I wanted to watch this tape you sent on Jennifer Madden. Where's your VCR?"

"It's in the study, but—"

Gabe gave her shoulder a firm but gentle shove. "Well, come on, move it. We don't have all night."

Jane planted her bare feet right where she stood and stretched to her full five-foot-eleven-inch height. Not that it did a whole lot of good next to a man who towered at six-four, but she was ready to stand her ground. "Now, wait just a minute. What makes you think—"

"Look, I assume you wouldn't have included this tape in your report unless you thought it was important. I don't have a VCR, and the one at the office is broken. Why are we wasting time?"

His words were more of a challenge than a question. Jane couldn't believe that the man had intruded on her privacy and now had the gall to try to make her feel as though she were impeding his progress!

Still, he was willing to view the tape. She supposed she ought to give him points for that, at least. "You could've called first. How did you even know I'd be home or have a machine?"

He grinned. "What can I say? It's a gift. Lead the way."

Jane grimaced at his nonchalance. Damn that easy smile. There was a definite aura emanating from the man, strong and disturbing and positively irritating. She tried to shrug it aside as she led him down a narrow hallway to the back of the house, trying to ignore the way his presence already seemed to be taking over her house.

Gabe glanced around. Although nestled in a lovely alcove where the woods gave way to the sea, Jane's home wasn't exactly one of the Eden Island mansions he had viewed at every turn off Paradise Road. But it was a trim, two-story, ivy-covered affair with overgrown gardens and the graceful feel of the English countryside. A luscious view of the Olympic Mountains spread westward into the setting sun. The walls, by contrast, were covered in dingy beige wallpaper, badly in need of repapering. The natural hardwood flooring needed a good shine, too. Every room was crowded with partially unpacked boxes.

Jane's voice interrupted his scrutiny. "You'll find the VCR in the box sitting on top of the television."

Gabe checked it out. He gave her a look of wonder, his voice a caricature of insincerity. "Your TV isn't even hooked up to the cable. Hardesty, how are you surviving on local channels alone?"

Jane looked away from his easy smile, which was definitely far too charming. The man was up to something. She lifted a box off the study's couch, placed it on the floor, and sat down. "You could have rented a VCR to view the tape."

Gabe had leaned behind the TV to connect the VCR. "I would have had to rent a TV, too."

Jane's voice rose. "No TV? Kincaid, how are you surviving?"

He chuckled at her very good imitation of his earlier tone. She wasn't giving an inch. He liked that.

Gabe shoved the tape in and then tried the TV. All that appeared on the screen was snow. "You'll have to call a cable company to get hooked up to the national TV stations, but the VCR should be working okay. We're going to need some popcorn."

Jane blinked. "Popcorn?"

Gabe's smile was back. "Well, I don't know about you, but I always have popcorn with my movies."

Jane folded her arms across her chest, unamused. "This isn't a movie theater."

"I should hope not. The lighting's terrible. So what about the popcorn? None made, I suppose?"

Damn, but that smile of his could be infectious. She'd have to watch herself. She'd have to watch him.

Gabe dropped the remote control on the couch and lifted her to her feet. "Well, let's get to it. Do you have a hot-air popper, or do you buy the microwaveable stuff?"

His hands rose from her arms to her shoulders as he propelled her toward the kitchen. There was nothing remotely personal about the gesture, but, of its own accord, her body kindled, her blood stirring most annoyingly. She slipped out from under his touch, imbuing her voice with a brusqueness that she was far from feeling. "The popper's still in a box somewhere, but I did pick up a few of the microwaveable bags last time I was at the store."

"Ah, there's hope for you, Hardesty."

She was acutely aware of him standing right beside her as she dug into the grocery bag for the microwaveable popcorn. There was a spiciness to his after-shave that smelled warm and exciting from contact with his skin. His presence seemed to close about her. She had the curious feeling that, however she moved, she would bump into him. She tried not to move at all.

It seemed to take a very long time before she located the popcorn bags. He became immediately impatient as she pulled them out of the grocery bag and began to read the directions.

"Directions are what you go to when everything else fails," he said, snatching the bags out of her hands. "Seven minutes for two should be just right."

She didn't know how he knew, but seven minutes later they were heading for the couch, opening hot, steaming bags of perfectly microwaved buttered popcorn. Gabe settled back and hit the play button on the remote control. "Here we go."

Jane moved to the arm of the overstuffed couch opposite Gabe, trying to sit as far away from him as possible. It didn't seem to help much. She could still feel him there.

As the taped session progressed, Jane stole covert glances in his direction. Her eyes drifted over the aggressive strength of his profile, to the well-cut straight black hair, to the confident jaw. And all the while he seemed to be radiating against her skin like a far-too-hot sun.

Then, toward the end of the tape, Gabe quit eating his popcorn as the corners of his mouth arrowed down in distaste. As soon as the tape stopped, he just sat and stared at the blank TV screen.

When he hadn't moved or spoken for nearly a minute, Jane felt compelled to break the almost palpable tension in the air. "Do you understand now why I considered that chapel service so inappropriate?"

He nodded as he got up to pace, shoving his large hands into the pockets of his suit slacks. "Hell, yes. Woman like that would have demanded nothing less than a circus act to send her off."

The strong emotional undercurrent in his words brought a frown to Jane's brow. "Why does that bother you?"

Gabe only half turned in her direction. "You've seen the tape, and you're asking me? Jennifer Madden got off on playing the grim reaper when she bedded a man."

Despite the covering harshness of his words, Jane detected the disappointment that underlay. That he should be disappointed surprised and confused her. "You know that was only Jennifer's fantasy."

"Do I?"

His tone was upset, challenging. Jane sat forward. "What's really bothering you? Is it that Jennifer Madden was a beautiful woman whose emotional makeup didn't end up meeting your personal expectations?"

He spoke through slightly clenched teeth. "It's my case. If she's been murdered, I'll find out who did it, and they'll pay to the letter of the law. I don't have to like the victim."

"But you did, and it was helping. It helps you to care."

It was a direct hit, bouncing off the back wall of insight and plunging into the open basket of Gabe's suddenly exposed ego. Jane could see by the narrowing of his eyes that he wasn't going to be applauding her accuracy.

He grabbed at his bag of half-eaten popcorn. "So maybe caring for a victim does give more meaning to the job. Didn't it help when you got close to your patients?"

"Not really."

He looked at her then; it was a very deep look. "Not when you lost them, huh? And the husband? Is that why you try to deny your emotions?"

Jane got to her feet, more than uncomfortable to be the focus of such comments, determined to direct the attention away from herself. An edge crept into her voice. "Well, you seem to deny your emotions pretty well by walking away from an autopsy."

Gabe's hands found his pockets again. "Maybe I walk away because I can't deny them."

Jane pushed ahead boldly, resentfully, unsure of why she should be either. "When it's a beautiful woman, you mean. What's the matter? Are there too few of them in the world for you, that you have to personally mourn each one when she dies?"

Gabe's look cut at her so deeply, that Jane quickly took her seat again, wondering whether it had been wise to goad him. She was totally unprepared for the deep, biting laugh that finally broke through. "Too few of them? Hell, in my thirty-five years on this earth, I've barely had enough time for all the lovely ladies who've wanted to take me for a ride. On the contrary, Hardesty. There are too many of them for this man to handle."

Looking at the confident face before her, Jane didn't doubt it. She vacillated between annoyance and some purely female curiosity. As always, her curiosity won out. "Were you ever married?"

His long-legged stride had him back at the couch in less than an instant. He didn't just sit. He claimed. A new gleam entered his eyes. "No. I don't intend to be taken for that big of a ride, so don't get your hopes up."

Jane sputtered, nearly choking on a kernel of popcorn that went sailing up her windpipe at the galling implication in his words. "Why, you—"

Gabe leaned toward her across the couch and gave her back a sharp pat, cutting off the rest of her words. He let out a throaty laugh as she sputtered some more. "This has been fun, Hardesty, but we need to get back to business. And to start off with, I suppose I owe you some thanks. Jennifer's tape has told us several important things."

Jane readjusted her position on the couch, trying to regain her composure and her breath. She was more than relieved to drop his personal life and return to discussing the case. She inhaled deeply, trying to imbue her tone with a calm she was far from feeling. "A glimpse into her personality, certainly."

Gabe leaned back against the opposite end of the couch, hooking one long, muscular leg across its arm. "More than that. Apart from her penchant for the macabre, she was obviously cheating on Madden, probably with more than one man."

Jane sat forward. "You could tell that from the tape?"

"And you could have, too, if you'd been listening carefully. She said it on several occasions. She was out to attract men—not just one man."

Jane wasn't convinced. She leaned back again, grabbed hold of her thick braid and began to twirl it through her fingers. "I know she talked about attracting men in the plural. But just because a woman might want to feel attractive to all men, that doesn't mean she's promiscuous. Remember, that interview reflected Jennifer's sexual *fantasies.*"

"Well, it wasn't just fantasy that Jennifer was found dead in an extremely revealing red negligee, wearing perfume, with two wine glasses on her dressing table, on a night when her husband had told her he was going to be out of town."

Jane nodded. "I see. So the lover she was waiting for wasn't her husband. Does Richard Madden know?"

"Oh, he knows, all right."

Jane looked over at Gabe. "How can you be sure?"

"He saw her body, what she was wearing. And I saw his face afterward. He was furious. I bet he had just found out."

Jane was thinking over Gabe's words and finding herself somewhat surprised, both at their content and at the fact that the man was discussing the case with her. She couldn't help but feel pleased. Was this Kincaid's way of trying to apologize for the rotten way he'd treated her?

Gabe watched her changing expression as her braid got another twirl. "What is it, Hardesty?"

Jane scratched her forehead. "Richard Madden is going through with a scheduled political dinner this week. I thought it was strange that he was carrying on so... unaffected after his wife's death. But if he knew she had taken a lover—"

"He could have gotten mad enough to kill her. Yes, I've already thought of that."

"You suspect him, then?"

Gabe got to his feet again, obviously restless. "Yes and no."

Jane's eyebrows raised. "Well, that covers all the bases."

Gabe flashed her a quick smile. It seemed to brush warmly against her cheeks, and for the moment she felt the beginnings of an answering smile. She squelched it, trying to caution herself not to get too carried away just because the man appeared to be sharing the case. That was his job, after all.

Gabe paced a moment. "Okay, follow me on this. Yes, Madden's a natural suspect, because his wife was cheating on him. No, it doesn't seem reasonable he killed her, because the look on his face told me he had just found out about her betrayal, so if he didn't know before she was dead, why would he kill her?"

"If you don't suspect him, who do you suspect?"

"But I do suspect him. And anyone else who knew her. At this point, I'd be a fool not to. I normally go into a case with a known time of death and a definite cause. I've got neither as of now."

"But we know she died somewhere between six and ten that night."

"That's a four-hour span, Hardesty—a long time. And if she was poisoned, we don't know how it was administered, or when."

"So what you're saying is we can't pinpoint means or opportunity until we get the toxicology results back?"

"That's right. So all we've got to go on is motive. And I'm not one to rely too heavily on motive. People kill for strange, even totally off-the-wall reasons. Sometimes they're not even sure why they've done it. No, I don't like tracking a killer through a motive trail."

"But you're going to try?"

Gabe watched the brightening of her eyes. A pink blush had descended on her face. She positively glowed. He held his breath. It took him a moment before he realized the glow had not been generated internally, but was a reflection of the sunset streaming through the west-facing windows. He looked away, concentrating on the lingering light that was turning the snowy tops of the Olympics into crimson caps, as he struggled to collect his thoughts. "If motive is all I can look for, then it's what I look for."

"What other motives are there?"

"I'd rather not indulge in conjecture. A lot of pieces are still missing. There were some fingerprints lifted from Jennifer's bedroom that weren't hers, the maid's or Richard Madden's. They've been sent to the AFIS."

"AFIS?"

"Automated Fingerprint Identification System, in Tacoma. The crime-scene crew only went through the second story of the Madden estate. Even so, it took them all day. That place is like a damn hotel. Has Madden owned it long?"

Jane watched Gabe run his hand over the growing stubble dotting his strong jaw. It looked like flecks of pepper in the dimming light. Then she realized that she was staring, and that she had yet to answer his question. She repositioned herself on the couch, annoyed at her wandering attention. "He had the original Victorian house pulled down and built that monstrosity in its place about twenty years ago."

"Whatever for?"

"I think he likes the idea of living in a place that looks like a fortress. He uses it for large political parties. As a matter of fact, there'll be a political gathering there tomorrow night."

Gabe grunted. "Who's the candidate?"

"Philip Lemke. He's—"

"I know who he is," Gabe said, interrupting. "You're invited?"

"Well, yes."

"What's Lemke running for?"

"The district's senate seat. Tomorrow night the party leaders will meet to announce his candidacy."

Gabe's fingers continued to play with the stubble on his chin. "Does he have a chance?"

"He's a shoo-in. Only time the district ever lost to the opposition party was four years ago, when Richard was voted out because of the scandal with Jennifer. Even then, he didn't lose by much. Normally, when the money of Eden Island is in back of a candidate, nothing can stop him."

"And Eden Island money is in back of Lemke?"

Jane nodded. "Philip has become Madden's protégé, and when it comes to politics, Richard Madden is Eden Island's king."

Gabe stared silently into space for a moment before he turned back to her. "Can you get me an invitation?"

Jane sat forward. "What?"

"Hardesty, you're neither dumb nor hard of hearing. You understood me."

"Maybe the words, but not the reason. Why would you want to go to one of Madden's political get-togethers?"

"It'll give me a chance to catch my suspects off guard by rubbing social shoulders with them. See the wild animals in their natural habitat, so to speak."

"Can't you just show up officially?"

Gabe turned away and paced the length of the room. He hadn't planned on sharing the truth with her, but at the moment it didn't look like he had any choice. He pivoted and faced her. "The Seattle lab is backed up, Hardesty. We're not going to be getting the toxicological results from Jennifer's autopsy until who knows when. Until we do, it's not officially murder. Pressure has been exerted on me directly and through my boss to pull back from even routine inquiries into the background of Madden and friends. I've got to be invited into their midst."

"Can't you just put your investigation on hold until after the toxicology results have come in?"

"What for? I know what they're going to say, and you do, too."

Jane nodded. "That Jennifer Madden was poisoned."

"And every day's delay in my questioning the guilty party puts me just that much farther away from being able to find him or her."

Jane's hand fiddled with her braid again. Gabe watched its multicolored strands catch the light. They ranged from the palest yellow to a tawny gold. She looked up at him questioningly. "You definitely suspect someone from Eden Island?"

Gabe looked away. "Jennifer obviously was waiting for a lover. According to the security guard on duty that night at the Eden Island entry gate, he let in only five cars. All five were driven by the staff or residents of Eden Island."

Jane leaned forward. "He remembers who they were?"

"No. Only that no strangers came through. That pretty well narrows the field, wouldn't you say?"

Jane leaned back again. "I see your point."

"So all I need from you is the invitation."

Jane's braid brushed her chin again. "I'm sorry, but I have no authority to be issuing invitations to Richard's gatherings."

"But I could go as your escort?"

Jane frowned as she had a silent conversation with herself. She had planned to attend the political dinner at the Madden estate so that she could do some subtle questioning of her own. With Gabe at her side, the Eden Island residents would be sure to avoid her. And him, too. "No, that's a bad idea."

"Why? You afraid of me, Hardesty?"

"Afraid? Not for a second!"

Gabe cocked an eyebrow. "Well, then, you've got nothing to worry about. I'm not afraid of you, either. And I'm warning you that if you try to have your way with me, I'll resist."

Jane felt Gabe's words stab through her control. "If I try— Why, you—"

Gabe's quick laugh cut her off. "Yes, me. Don't get your nightie in a knot, Hardesty. Look, all we need to do is present the appearance of a couple. I assume that even on Eden Island, despite what they believe, social decorum will prevent them from tossing us out?"

Jane's hands found her hips. "So that's what this evening has been all about. Your investigation has been shut down, so you brought that tape over here, pretending to deal with me as a colleague, just so you could worm your way into my Eden Island contacts. Well, it's not going to work, Kincaid. You've done everything you could to keep me out of this investigation. Now we'll see how you like it!"

A lazy little smile played about his lips. "You're wrong, Hardesty. I haven't done *everything* I could to keep you out of the Madden investigation, or any of the other cases that have come across my desk. Not yet."

Jane's eyes flashed at him. "You've tried to bar me from the death scene, the suspects and the media. What's left?"

"Just my department's investigative paperwork."

Jane got a sudden sinking feeling. Her protest sounded far more certain than she felt. "You can't block those reports."

"You think not?"

Jane licked her suddenly dry lips. "Damn it, Kincaid. I'll go to the county commissioners."

Gabe had the gall not to look the least bit worried. "Good luck. Those good ol' boys are my drinking buddies."

Jane didn't doubt the boast for a second. She took a deep breath and counted to ten.

"Come on, Hardesty. It's about time you learned the rules. You scratch my back, I'll scratch yours."

Jane's eyes flashed. "I'd rather scratch a skunk. Listen, Kincaid, and listen good. You'll go as my escort tomorrow night only if I have your solemn word that you'll share with me whatever your sources have revealed about the Madden case and that you will never again deny my office your investigative reports on any case."

Gabe kept the smile off his lips. "That the deal?"

"Yes," Jane said through clenched teeth. "Those are my terms, and they are not negotiable." Jane dug in, expecting a siege, ready to do appropriate battle no matter what form it took.

But, to her immense surprise, it didn't take form. Gabe suddenly held his hand out for a shake, a big smile on his lips. "All right. Deal."

Jane took his hand tentatively, almost as though she expected him to pull it back at the last minute. In reality, it held hers in a firm clasp far longer than necessary, shooting tendrils of warmth up her arm.

She retreated, a bit disoriented by the prolonged contact, feeling as though she'd somehow agreed to something she had not intended, although what that might be she had no idea. Her nerves tingled with an anticipation that was annoying. She put several feet between them before she spoke again. "You'd best not expect too much, Kincaid. Getting these people to open up won't be an easy task. They are politicians, you know."

"I've spent a lot of years getting people to open up. Don't worry, Hardesty. I can read politicians like Richard Madden. I already have, remember?"

Jane shook her head. "Perhaps not. Madden knew you had seen Jennifer's compromising attire. He's not such a fool as to think you wouldn't find out it wasn't meant for him. Maybe he deliberately decided to project the fury of a betrayed husband. Maybe he was only pretending to have just found out his wife was playing around."

Gabe shook his head. "No. Emotion was eating at the man. He couldn't have faked it."

"I won't disagree he was probably emotional. But Eden Island politicians like Richard are very good sellers of human meat—particularly their own. They've got years of experience in putting all their chuck steak in filet mignon packaging. He could have sized you up and put a sale price on the cut he wanted you to buy."

"Why are you so sure Madden wasn't furious?"

"I'm not saying he wasn't. All I'm saying is that you should be cautious about accepting his portrayed emotions. And particularly leery about assigning motivations behind them."

"Hardesty, men find release in anger the way women do in tears."

Jane shrugged, looking anything but convinced.

Gabe watched her reaction with renewed interest. "You don't like Richard Madden, do you?"

"I don't think Richard Madden is the kind of man someone likes—you respect him, you fear him, or you just try to stay out of his way."

"And which of those three reactions describe you?"

"Any and all, depending on the occasion. But he's the uncle of a good friend, so I try to make allowances."

"Suzanne Lemke?"

"Yes."

Gabe watched her closely. "She's a suspect, you know. Everyone who knew Jennifer is."

A frown appeared on Jane's brow. "Yes, I know."

Gabe picked up the tape of Jennifer's session and headed for the front door.

Jane followed, calling after him, "Madden's dinners are black-tie, of course."

Gabe stepped outside, onto the circle of old brick steps that fanned out from the entrance to Jane's home, and leaned down to collect his shoes. He was on one knee, lacing them, before he answered. "Of course. What time shall I pick you up?"

"I'll be ready at eight."

Gabe looked up at her from his kneeling position, then brushed off the knee of his trousers and rose. "What time does Madden's get-together officially start?"

"They'll begin serving cocktails at seven-thirty."

"Then I'll pick you up at seven-fifteen. I like to be one of the first to arrive."

Jane swatted the air in front of her nose with the end of her braid. "All right. I'll agree to about anything right now, if you'll just walk those shoes somewhere else."

Gabe grinned at the expression on her face, at the crinkling of her nose. Suddenly he found himself leaning over to kiss the edge of that nose, and then her mouth, so soft, so full. After only a few seconds, he came to his senses, turned and walked away.

Jane stood at the door, staring at his retreating figure. His mouth had been hard, experienced. Her cheeks were turning scarlet from the sudden rush of blood pounding through her body, forcibly reminding her of many things she had been so careful to forget. Then she began to tremble.

Her fists balled at her side as she fought for control. Damn the man! He'd done that on purpose! He'd bullied and threatened her into taking him to that political get-together and then he'd had the effrontery to kiss her goodnight!

Well, it wasn't going to do him any good. There was no truce between them. She wouldn't allow it. She spun around and stormed into the house, slamming the door shut behind her.

GABE JAMMED THE GEARSHIFT into second and let the engine compression slow his pickup toward the advancing intersection with the red light. He pushed a dark wave of hair off his forehead as he tried to settle his thoughts and emotions.

That they needed settling at all was a bit of a surprise. Damn, there was just something about that woman that made her awfully hard to ignore. Still, she'd hit it on the mark earlier when she'd accused him of just using her to get to Eden Island's elite to look for Jennifer Madden's killer. That had certainly been his intent.

And now? Oh, hell, she was a challenge. He could admit that. It was fun getting her to release all that bottled-up emotion. She was so determined not to, it gave him a kick.

Gabe stomped on the brakes, having almost run through the red light. No doubt about it, even thoughts of the lady were dangerous.

And tonight he'd found the impulse to kiss the pink tip of Jane Hardesty's obstinate nose, and then those invitingly soft lips, entirely too strong to ignore.

He wondered now, if he had stayed, would she have pushed him away or pulled him to her? Hmm... Would have been interesting either way. Next time, he'd have to stick around to find out.

JANE WAS DEAD ASLEEP when the insistent ringing finally broke through. By the time she'd dragged the phone to her ear, one eye had read the time on the clock on the dressing table. It was 2:00 a.m. "Yes?"

The words were low and breathy. She hardly recognized Karl's voice. "Get right over and pick up the body. Here are the directions."

Jane obediently grabbed for a pad and pencil and scribbled down the directions as fast as she could. "And who is the deceased—" she began to ask after the directions ceased, but it was too late. The other end of the line was a dial tone.

Damn. Karl could be cryptic on occasion, but this was a little much. Oh, well, she'd find out soon enough, she supposed. Jane scrambled out of bed and hurriedly put on some slacks and some shoes and pulled a sweater over her teddy. She grabbed her shoulder bag and ran out the door, straight into a freezing rain. She hurriedly went back for her raincoat before resuming her path to the car.

She'd had a couple of late-night calls this week, so she'd learned to keep the Talbot parked in the circular drive at the front of the house. She yawned, operating at an automatic, half-conscious level that took her back to her earlier days, when she'd been called in the middle of the night to go to the hospital for an emergency.

By the time she arrived at the dark, dingy-looking apartment complex on the edge of Edenville, it was nearly two-thirty. It wasn't a part of town she was familiar with, and before getting out of the car she tried to get her bearings by peering out the windshield through the steady sheets of gray rain.

Upstairs, Karl had said. The downpour was so thick she could barely make out the open wooden staircase. Still, people who had just had a loved one die couldn't always be expected to think of switching on a light. It struck Jane as a little surprising that Fast Freddy wasn't here yet with the coroner's van, though. Generally he beat her by several minutes.

As long as she was here first, she thought she might as well go up. She opened the driver's door.

The wind immediately caught the hood of her raincoat and flipped it back, as though some invisible hand were determined to soak her. She grabbed the ends of her hood tightly and tugged it back over her head. The rain and wind continued to bluster noisily around her as she headed for the stairs.

The banister felt wet and splintery beneath her hand. Jane ascended the stairs carefully, feeling their shaky movement beneath her feet, battling with the wind that buffeted her from behind. It seemed a long walk, but she finally made it to the top landing.

The wind pushed and shoved at her as she approached the darkened door. She pulled her raincoat more tightly around her as the rain whizzed by her sheltered face. She felt for a doorbell or buzzer, but could find neither.

She was just raising her arm to knock when suddenly she felt her hood being forced down over her face. Stunned, disoriented, she staggered backward. Strong, rough hands grabbed her from behind, pinning her arms to her sides, digging into her flesh. Terror shot through her. She struggled within the cruel grasp, tried to twist, to plant her feet so that she could resist, but she was blinded by the cloth, and already off balance.

She fell back against her assailant, adrenaline pumping through her without release. She screamed as the heels of her shoes scraped over the floorboards, but her captor only tightened his hold, crushing out the small amount of air still remaining in her lungs. Then the rough arms spun her around and shoved her forward.

The floorboards were no longer beneath her feet. She was falling! It was her last thought before a kaleidoscope of flashing lights exploded in her head, immediately replaced by a dense, immense darkness.

Chapter Six

"How is she, Doctor?"

Gabe felt his first reassurance in over an hour as he watched the smiling expression on the face of the young woman in white as she approached him in the waiting room. "The concussion appears to be slight. Her speech is lucid, and all her reflexes are intact. She's got a humdinger of a headache, of course, but I've given her a shot for the pain and written her a prescription for when the shot wears off. I told her it would be a good idea if she spent today and tonight in the hospital."

New relief washed over Gabe, and a knot in his stomach he hadn't even been aware of began to untie. "What room has she been checked into?"

"She hasn't been checked in, Detective. She ignored my advice. She's getting dressed at this very minute so that she can leave."

Irritation immediately replaced Gabe's relief. "Where is she?"

The doctor twisted so that she could point. "Back there. Two doors on the right. But I wouldn't—"

It was too late. Gabe was already moving, and obviously he would.

JANE HAD JUST GOTTEN her sweater over her head when the door flew open and Gabe Kincaid stomped in. He didn't look at all like himself. His normally impeccable hair was messed up, and he was wearing a pair of old blue jeans and a bulky blue sweater. But his voice had that damn insistent quality that she was all too familiar with. "You're supposed to remain here for observation!"

Jane flashed her back at Gabe, grabbed the ends of her sweater and pulled them down over her breasts. Her cheeks had begun to burn by the time she twisted back to face him.

"I don't need observation, Kincaid. And the next time you come sailing into a room I'm in without knocking, I swear I'll kick you!"

Gabe kept the relieved smile off his face with difficulty. Jane Hardesty was more than all right. She was back to her fighting, feisty self. And the flash of tempting flesh through the lacy black teddy he'd just glimpsed was a bit of all right, too. He leaned against a nearby examining table. "So what in the hell were you doing out in the middle of the night, falling down the stairs of some condemned building?"

Exasperation coated Jane's tongue. It was just like the man to make it sound like her fault. "Look, I didn't fall down. It's like I told the deputy who found me when he stopped to check out my car. Someone pushed me down those stairs."

Gabe came away from the table he'd been leaning against, taking out his pad and pen. "Why don't you go over it again with me?"

Jane tucked her sweater into her still slightly damp slacks. She didn't like repeating herself, but she conceded that at least this part of his harassing her could be viewed as part of his job. She took a steadying breath. "My boss, Karl Daly, called me for a pickup at 2:00 a.m. When I arrived at the address and walked up the stairs to the top of the landing, suddenly someone grabbed me and threw me down. I must have hit my head on the banister when I fell. The next thing I knew, a deputy was shaking me awake. He called the paramedics. They brought me here."

Gabe clicked his pen. "You say someone threw you down. Who was it?"

"I didn't see him. He pulled the hood to my raincoat over my eyes before he grabbed me."

Gabe clicked his pen again. "You said 'he.' You're sure it was a man?"

"No, I guess I can't say for sure. I suppose a woman could have dragged me. I was already knocked off my feet. Maybe Karl can tell you the gender of the voice that called him."

Gabe watched Jane for a moment before speaking. "I've already talked to Karl Daly. He didn't get a call, Hardesty, and he didn't call you."

Jane felt a cold shiver run through her body. She swallowed into a thickening throat. "It wasn't Karl on the phone?"

Gabe's eyes seemed to be piercing deeper through her with every new click of his pen. "Who has your telephone number?"

"Just Karl Daly. And Dorothy Speke."

"I assume you'd recognize their voices?"

"Yes. Of course. Except this voice was . . . well, I guess it was a bit muffled and slurred. I could have sworn it was Karl's. The voice said to get right over."

Gabe watched confusion tumble through her eyes. He'd seen the same expression on many a witness's face. She wasn't sure of the facts anymore. Believing anything she said now could be a mistake. "So somebody with slurring words calls you up in the middle of the night and asks you to get right over. And being half-asleep, you naturally assume it's your boss?"

"Yes."

"I see. You realize, Hardesty, there are lots of bars in that run-down part of town. That call could have been from some drunk who tried to get a ride home and dialed your number by mistake."

Gabe was clicking his pen again, in a steady, irritating rhythm. Jane could feel the vibration along her taut nerves. "I distinctly heard the voice say, 'Pick up the body.'"

"Maybe. Or maybe it said, 'Pick up *my* body,' meaning the guy was too drunk to make it on his own steam."

Was that really possible? Jane discarded the thought almost immediately. "No, somebody was waiting for me out there! Somebody grabbed me and threw me down those stairs!"

"Are you sure? The deputy who found you saw no one. Your purse was with you, and its contents were untouched."

Jane's hands clenched into fists. "Kincaid, I'm sure someone threw me down those stairs, and I'm also sure that if you don't stop clicking that stupid pen I'm going to come over there and shove it down your throat!"

Gabe put away the pen. It had served its purpose. Someone who reacted so vehemently to its clicking was obviously wound far too tight with guilt or fright. Not that he blamed her for being frightened. She'd had an appalling experience. But it wouldn't do to let her descend into paranoia.

He tried to make his tone as even and understanding as possible. "The wind is pretty strong out there. It could have blown your hood over your face. A sudden gust might even have felt like arms pulling you back. Maybe you just slipped on those unsteady, wet stairs, and your imagination did the rest. After all, it wouldn't be the first time that a concussion has left someone confused."

Jane pushed her feet into her shoes and shoved her arms into the sleeves of her raincoat. She fought through her anger for enough breath to speak. "Confused?" She grabbed her shoulder bag and headed for the door. "How dare you presume to render a medical opinion without a credential to your name!"

"What is it you want me to believe, Hardesty? That someone just tried to murder you and bungled it?"

His blunt words stopped Jane in her tracks. Dear God, that was exactly what she was saying! The impact of the knowledge hit her hard and fast. A dizziness drilled through her. She tried to steady herself against the doorframe.

He was by her side in an instant, two strong arms wrapped around her wobbly body. His touch was like an electrifying shock to her limp muscles, startling them back into service. She knew she could push away from him now that she had the strength, but instead she relaxed against the hard flesh that surrounded her. His warm breath stroked her cheek as his temple nestled against hers. "I'll admit you're one damn provoking package, Hardesty, but even I can't imagine your having incited someone to murder in less than a week. Of course, if it had been two..."

His words were as absurd as usual and she giggled in spite of herself. Gabe felt the vibration clear through his bones. His arms tightened, and his voice lowered suggestively. "Time to take you home and make sure you get a good night's sleep. I know a great relaxing technique."

Jane let herself continue to lean against this warm, muscular, amusingly arrogant man for the briefest of moments before determinedly slipping out of his embrace. "Thanks, Kincaid, but I didn't get hit that hard on the head."

Gabe let her go with obvious reluctance. "It may not always be this easy to get rid of me, you know."

Jane heard a husky undertone in his voice that sent a little thrill up her spine. She paused in the doorway just long enough to throw him a last pledge. "It will never be easy to get rid of me, Kincaid, no matter how many stairs I get thrown down, so don't get your hopes up. I'm taking this Jennifer Madden case to the end. Seven-fifteen tonight. Sharp."

Gabe stared after the closed door, the corners of his mouth lifting in amusement. No matter what she had just been through, that old fighting spirit was still intact. And what a surprising and disturbing contrast it had been to feel the feisty Jane Hardesty soft and yielding in his arms.

KARL DALY WAS ON HAND to meet Jane the minute she walked into her office at eight. "Jane, are you all right?"

Jane eased herself slowly into her chair. She felt better after a shower and change of clothes, but she didn't want to take any chance of resurrecting the pain in her head. "Fine. Why?"

"Gabe Kincaid just called to say you'd been hurt. He also said you refused to remain at the hospital for observation. What's going on?"

Jane hadn't counted on Kincaid blabbing about her condition. "I had an...accident, Karl. Nothing serious, really. Just some bruises."

"Bruises? Kincaid said you suffered a concussion."

"That's what a concussion is, Karl. A bruise on the brain. Don't worry. I'm a doctor, and I know the signs to look for in the event of complications. I'll be fine. Now answer a question for me. Did you give my home telephone number to anyone?"

Karl's eyebrows rose in some indignation. "Of course not."

Jane gave him a contrite smile. "Sorry." She should have known that, if anyone had given out her number, it had to be Dorothy.

"Jane, what's all this about?"

Jane looked up at Karl's thin, anxious face and knew she couldn't confide in him. He was a good man, but there was a worried quality about him that seemed to pour out of some deep inner pool of dread. She didn't feel like contributing any more drops to what she imagined to be its murky depths.

"Nothing important, Karl. Really. By the way, I understand Seattle toxicology is pretty backed up. Are there any cases other than Jennifer Madden that we have in a pending status waiting for their analysis?"

"No. She's the only autopsy that's been inconclusive lately. But we did get some preliminary results from Seattle before they got inundated. They checked out the wine, the pills and the contents of the perfume bottle from the death scene."

Jane sat up straight. "And?"

Karl rubbed his beaky bottle nose as if it contained his information genie. "Nothing. If Jennifer Madden was poisoned, as you suspect, it had to have come from something else."

Jane felt a sharp quiver of unease in her stomach. There was only one other item found at the death scene. Suzanne's negligee.

"Jane? What is it?"

She was saved from answering her boss when the telephone rang. Karl shuffled back toward his office as Jane picked up the receiver and announced the coroner's office.

"Jane, it's Ellen Rowe. Have I called you at a bad time?"

Jane leaned back in her chair, somewhat surprised to be hearing from Eden Island's most celebrated entrepreneur. Ellen Rowe was not one to squander her time on someone who could not do her a service. Jane couldn't squelch her curiosity. "No, Ellen, it's not a bad time. I just got in. What can I do for you?"

"You know I'm a blunt woman, so I'll get right to the point. The publicity you've generated about Jennifer's death has not helped you with your Eden Island neighbors. You're either one of us or an outsider, Jane. Straddling the fence will simply not do."

Jane could hear the scold in the woman's deep tone, and she didn't like it. In a carefully controlled voice, she asked, "What fence am I supposed to be straddling?"

"Don't be obtuse, Jane. And how could you stoop so low as to take that deputy coroner's job? You're a Harvard Medical School graduate, for pity's sake! Your mother must be turning in her grave!"

Jane would have been amused if she hadn't been so angry. She kept both emotions out of her tone. "I doubt it, Ellen. She was cremated, remember?"

"I see you've still got a mouth on you, Jane. I had hoped you'd outgrown it. Seems I'm destined to be disappointed by you. Take some friendly advice. If you're going to ridicule your Eden Island friends and roots, go back to Boston. You won't be happy here."

Jane wasn't sure how much longer she could politely put up with this conversation. She thought it best she interrupt while she was still holding her temper. "Ellen, I appreciate your concern for my welfare. Thank you so much for your call."

She hung up without waiting for a reply, then stared at the telephone with a forehead creased in frowns. It had been an infuriating conversation.

Out of all her Eden Island neighbors, Ellen Rowe had always been the most distant to her and her mother. Even as a child, Jane had felt the woman's critical, assessing eyes on her. She didn't believe for a moment that Ellen Rowe really cared if Jane's job meant she was sinking in indignities. It had to be for another reason that the woman was uncomfortable with Jane holding the deputy coroner's position. Did that reason involve Jennifer Madden's death? And if so, how did Ellen Rowe fit in?

GABE WAS JUST GETTING ready to leave for home and a shower and a change of clothes before going to pick up Jane when Roy came bounding into his office. "Gabe, you were right. Checking out Jennifer Madden has paid off."

Gabe returned to his seat. "What did you find?"

"Well, it seems the owner of the nightclub where Jennifer Madden was employed before her marriage claims she only came to him for a job the week before she met Madden."

"Where was she from?"

"Guy says he doesn't know. Jennifer just walked in off the street. Told him she was new in town."

"What was her maiden name?"

"Jones was what she entered on his employment forms. No middle name. Place of birth is shown as this county."

Gabe straightened his already straight tie as though he were trying to straighten out his thoughts. "Jones is the kind of name you adopt as an alias. I wonder if it could be bogus?"

"I wondered that, too. I matched the set of fingerprints from her driver's-license application to the ones taken off her body. They were the same, all right. I also ran them through the AFIS and the FBI's data base. If she ever used another name, I haven't been able to find it."

"Did you find her birth record?"

"Yeah. She was American Indian. Father's name was Saul Jones. Mother's name was Kay. They both lived on the reservation."

"Any other county records?"

"She took out her first driver's license three years ago, after she and Madden were married."

"School records?"

"I'm going to have to check with the tribal council for an address to see where she might have attended."

"What does the marriage record between her and Madden say?"

"No previous marriages for her. Nothing else that wasn't on the birth certificate."

Gabe steepled his fingers beneath his chin. "Did she make any friends at the nightclub?"

"According to the manager, she kept to herself. One interesting thing, though. When she applied for the job, she asked the manager if his place was the one Senator Richard Madden was known to frequent."

Gabe eyes shot to Roy's. "She asked that? Sounds like the lady deliberately set out to meet Madden. We'll have to pursue that angle further. Good job, Roy."

Fleming shrugged as though it were no big deal, but Gabe could tell he was pleased. "You want me to send a copy of my report to the coroner's office?"

"No, not yet. Let's keep trickling the information to our dauntless deputy coroner."

"You did promise her we'd send her the reports."

Gabe smiled. "Yeah. But I didn't promise how soon."

JANE LISTENED to the grandfather clock in the hall chime eight times and felt the annoyance climbing up her spine. Kincaid was late. Again. It would serve him right if she left without him. She promised herself that in another five minutes she would.

She glanced at herself in the full-length hallway mirror and wasn't dissatisfied. She'd taken care in dressing, not only because Richard Madden's gatherings were always first-class, but also because she had several developing bruises to hide.

As her reflection gazed back at her, she knew she'd been successful in covering them. All she had to remind herself of her terrifying early morning experience was the dull headache in her left temple and her recurring dissatisfaction with how Gabe Kincaid had so summarily dismissed her report of the attack. They were more than enough.

All right, she might have been a little disoriented after the blow to her head. But that 'disorientation had quickly cleared. Her memory was intact. He'd had no right to dispute her word as though only his mental processes regarding the experience could be relied on. What consummate arrogance!

Still, she couldn't deny his chilling assertion that her interpretation of the events described a murder attempt. That did sound rather farfetched—didn't it?

Jane came to attention as she heard the tires on the pavement. Well, finally, His Majesty approaches! For reasons she had no intention of acknowledging, she took one last look in the mirror and fluffed her hair before heading for the door.

Gabe did a double take when Jane opened the door. Her dress was a deep jade, an old-fashioned, high-collared, long-sleeved, ankle-length affair that hugged her long, lean frame, revealing curves far more seductively than any bikini could have. Her hair had been released from its traditional braid to cascade over her shoulders in long, thick, glistening blond waves. Her complexion had taken on a luscious flush. She was almost his height now, thanks to three-inch heels.

"You look—" He stopped, barely catching himself in time.

Her lips parted in a Mona Lisa smile as she finished his sentence, much too sweetly: "Confused?"

Gabe laughed, thankful for an excuse to release some of the tension that had begun tightening his stomach muscles in a rather interesting way. "You've got a mean, vengeful streak in you, Hardesty. I like that."

She drifted to the hall closet and came back with something white and soft thrown over her shoulders and a purse clutched in her hand. "What kept you?"

The question was innocent enough, but Gabe saw anything but innocence in her eyes, which had turned mysteriously green and seductive, as they looked up into his. He struggled for an answer. "Some stuff came in on the case."

"Good. I look forward to hearing all about it on our way."

Gabe gave himself a mental kick. He'd said precisely what he had promised himself he wouldn't. The damn woman was far too distracting tonight. Well, he'd just get himself back in hand. No woman was going to upset his control. "My truck's over here."

She halted in her tracks. "We'd better go in my car."

Gabe turned back to her. "You too good to arrive at this shindig in a truck, Hardesty?"

Jane laughed. The laugh was alluring, just like everything about her at the moment, and it grated along Gabe's nerves. "Don't be so dense, Kincaid. You could drive up in a Ferrari tonight and be denied entry. My car is known to Madden's staff. It's only logical we take it."

As Gabe followed in her enticingly perfumed wake, he knew that the thing most irritating about Jane Hardesty at that moment was that she was right.

Jane slipped her hand into her purse for her keys, smiling at Gabe's expression. So far she had appreciated all his expressions tonight—and particularly the one when she'd first opened the door.

Now, as they approached her car, she had an opportunity to notice how perfectly the black tux fit his muscular frame, and how well the blue of his dress shirt brought out the midnight in his eyes.

She shifted her eyes back to her keys and found her palms had become moist. "I'll drive."

He stopped beside the driver's door. "I'd rather."

Jane shook her head. "I don't let anyone drive this car. The special Wilson gearbox is a delicate mechanism and could end up in disaster in inexperienced hands. If you forget what gear you're in, it's all over. Besides, the intercom at the Madden estate is on the driver's side, and I'm not climbing over you to announce our arrival."

The flashing image of a sleek and supple Jane Hardesty climbing over him made Gabe's stomach clench tightly at the intriguing possibilities. He put them aside for the present and concentrated on holding the door open for her. Then he walked around to the passenger's side and got in.

The Talbot's engine erupted into a throaty purr. Jane didn't wait to get right down to business. She felt a pressing need to distract her mind from the large, muscular man in the passenger seat, whose presence felt almost like an embrace in the small sports car. "What was the information that came in on the case?"

Gabe was silent as Jane maneuvered the Talbot out of her driveway. After a short conversation with himself, he decided it probably wouldn't do any harm to tell her, might even make her more cooperative through the evening, thinking she was a real partner in this investigation. "It's about Jennifer's background."

Gabe filled Jane in on what Roy had found out. He was surprised at what appeared to interest Jane most.

"She was an American Indian? With no family?"

"Yes. That bother you?"

"No, I'm just surprised."

Gabe found his right foot stomping on the floorboards as she took a sharp turn along a particularly nasty cliff without slowing down. To his surprise, the old sports car hugged the curve. She handled it well. "You trying to say Madden's prejudiced? After all his publicity about fighting for Indian rights?"

"No, it's not a question of being prejudiced. I just don't think Richard Madden would marry anyone who couldn't offer him additional money or the power of prestige. His first wife, Margaret, came with a fortune and a family on the social register."

Gabe rubbed his hands over the butter-soft leather of the car's seats, enjoying the smooth coolness. "Still, Madden's got money and power to burn now. I doubt he needs any more."

Jane stared at the road intently. Gabe was somewhat surprised at the touch of bitterness in her tone. "Need doesn't factor into it, Kincaid. A man like Madden never thinks of himself as having enough money or power. I think you'll find that on Eden Island those are the addictive substances for which people are willing to sell their very souls."

"But not you?"

No, not her. Maybe that was partly why she had been immediately attracted to Gregory—he'd been idealistic enough not to be impressed by the trappings of Eden Island's wealth and power.

Gabe rolled down the passenger window. Jane's perfume, just like the rest of her, seemed to have an uncanny ability to get under his skin tonight and haze over his thoughts. He inhaled a lungful of the rain-tinged breeze before his mind cleared enough for another question. "Did Madden divorce his first wife after he met Jennifer?"

"No. Margaret died about six months after the affair became public. Madden married Jennifer three months after Margaret's death."

"Didn't do much mourning, did he?"

"I never got the impression Margaret and he were a love match. Like I said before, he married her because of her money and her Eden Island heritage. He didn't even seem disappointed when it turned out she couldn't have children. He'd had affairs before Jennifer, of course. The press just hadn't gotten wind of them."

"How did Margaret die?"

"It was stomach cancer. Although I think what she really had eating at her was Richard's faithlessness."

Gabe rubbed his newly shaved chin. "With his penchant for playing around, you'd think Madden would be content to remain a bachelor after his first wife's death."

"Or at least marry a woman of equal wealth and position. Appearances always seemed to be important to him. After all, a man like Richard could always arrange to have a Jennifer on the side. Unless . . ."

Gabe heard the speculation in Jane's voice and turned to watch her profile. "Unless what?"

"Unless he just simply fell in love with her."

Chapter Seven

Gabe licked his lips as though he had discovered a bad taste. "I'd sooner believe she got something on him and blackmailed him into marrying her."

Jane shook her head. "I guess you would."

Gabe turned partially toward her. "Isn't it possible? She'd gotten close to Madden, apparently far closer than the women in his other affairs. Maybe she found out something sensitive and she used it to convince him to marry her."

"That's a big maybe, and it presupposes there are things about Richard that he'd like kept quiet. You know of any?"

Gabe glanced back at the road. "No. But candidates he's run against have accused him of shady business dealings."

Jane shrugged. "It's certainly possible. Can you trace Richard's financial holdings to see if there's anything to their accusations?"

"That's what I was doing until my boss started getting the pressure put on him. Madden and his buddies took pointed exception to our interest. But I assure you I'll be back at it the second we get the toxicology results back and prove it's murder. Now I'll just have to bide my time and be content with getting to know Madden and friends a bit better on a more social level, like rubbing shoulders with them this evening."

Jane shifted down as she made the final turn. "Well, get your shoulders ready. We're here."

Minutes later, the heavy wooden doors to the Madden estate whooshed open, revealing Mr. Gnat's robotic stance. Gabe could have sworn he heard the squeaks of the heavy man's metal joints as he took Jane's cape without a word and disappeared behind a sturdy closet door.

"What do you know about him?" Gabe asked.

"Not much, really. He's been with Richard for as long as I can remember. He speaks haltingly and only infrequently. No one but Richard knows where he came from, and Richard squelches all inquiries on the subject."

Gabe opened his mouth to ask another question, but halted as a smiling Suzanne Lemke swept toward them in a low-cut, high-hemmed gown of glistening amber chiffon. "Jane, I couldn't believe my ears when Mr. Gnat told me he was buzzing your car through the gate! Yet here you are! And you look great!"

Gabe looked from Suzanne to Jane. Both women were undeniably beautiful, but it was Jane who kept his attention. He didn't know precisely why but he suspected it had something to do with the way she held herself. Or was it just that determined chin she kept shoving out that gave her such a strong and lasting definition?

Gabe refocused on Suzanne reluctantly. "Perhaps you remember me, Mrs. Lemke. Gabe Kincaid?" He offered his hand and a smile.

The chestnut eyes turned frosty, and her handshake was stiff, but he found that Suzanne's tone still reflected the warmth of the polished hostess. "Yes, of course. A surprise to see you, Chief Kincaid."

"Please call me Gabe. After all, I'm not here in a professional capacity tonight."

Her look thawed a bit and darted inquiringly toward Jane. "How... nice to hear."

Gabe laced his arm through Jane's as he smiled back at his hostess. "Yes, isn't it?"

Jane felt Gabe's warm claim on her arm like a jolt of electricity. She hadn't expected Gabe to take his role as escort so much to heart.

"So where's Philip?" she asked, fighting a sudden, disturbing breathlessness and hoping she was changing the subject gracefully.

Suzanne circled to Jane's other side, a speculative smile settling on her face, and began heading them both into the huge gathering room just to the left of the massive entry hall. "He's in the study with Richard and Jack. War talk. They should be out soon. I'm playing hostess for Richard tonight, so I'll need to run. Get a drink and show your escort around. See you later."

When Suzanne was out of sight, Jane's voice lowered to a thick whisper. "Public displays of affection are not required, Kincaid. This is Eden Island society. Understatement is the rule."

Gabe wore a satisfied male smile. He'd sensed Jane's stiffening against him. Whatever she felt, she was determined to hold it in. He was just as determined she let it out. "That was my understatement."

Jane tried to gracefully extricate her arm from his. He held on quite ungracefully, taking a look around the gigantic room they had just walked into. The last time he'd been to the Madden estate, he'd concentrated on the upstairs. Now he stared in awe at this downstairs gathering room, the walls of which were nothing but floor-to-ceiling salt-water tanks containing hundreds of colorful and exotic-looking fish.

It was a room full of light and movement, so much of both that it was difficult to get one's bearings. He felt as though he'd been transported to the Nautilus and Captain Nemo had taken them into a dive. For the moment he ignored the elegantly dressed people.

Gabe moved to the nearest tank, unsuccessfully trying to locate the invisible source of the light that glowed off the bright green algae. Pulsating sedately between the thick sea fronds was a multifinned white and brownish-red striped sea creature, delicate and beautiful. He read aloud the label on the tank's glass. " 'Lionfish—Poisonous.' "

Gabe walked the room's periphery, continuing to read the labels of each tank in turn as he studied its inhabitants. "'Tigerfish—Predatory. Damselfish—Territorial. Crab—Treacherous. Portuguese Man-of-War—Deadly.' Interesting selection."

Jane followed beside Gabe, not really paying attention to any more of the names he called out. She'd been in this room many times, and was familiar with its aquarium specimens. She concentrated on the prosperous human din and the cornucopia of scents.

Jane stopped suddenly when Gabe's arm signaled a halt in front of the last tank, which had been covered with a black cloth.

"I wonder what's behind this one?"

"Why? Haven't seen enough fish?"

Gabe turned toward the room. "Well, you know how it is. Always curious to see the one you can't. Do you know what's in this tank?"

"I don't recall offhand. The aquariums are under Mr. Gnat's care, so he should know. Just a minute. Let me try to catch his eye."

Jane lifted her hand and gestured. A moment later, the servant stood before her. "Why is this tank veiled, Mr. Gnat?"

The big man's face remained expressionless. "Water brown."

Mr. Gnat turned and walked quietly away.

"Does that blank expression ever change?" Gabe asked.

Jane was watching Mr. Gnat's retreating figure thoughtfully. "Actually, I thought he looked worried. These aquariums mean a lot to him. He must be upset over—"

A strong voice coming from behind her stopped Jane in midsentence. "Jane! So you are here!"

Gabe turned to see Ellen Rowe glide their way, her red hair rather startling against her white skin and an off-the-shoulder gold dress that didn't leave a whole lot to the imagination. She was as tall as Jane, and broader, with shoulders like a fullback's. A ruby pendant the size of a boulder flashed at her throat.

Jane took the woman's bejeweled hand, for a small squeeze, rather than a shake. "I hope your presence here means you've taken my advice to heart?"

Gabe watched a still, formal politeness descend over Jane's face. "Do you know my escort, Gabe Kincaid?"

Ellen's shrewd eyes flew to Gabe. He felt her sharp assessment as she offered her hand. "It's chief of detectives, isn't it?"

He smiled. "Just Gabe tonight, Mrs. Rowe."

A finely penciled eyebrow arched. "Off duty? Don't all detectives claim that to get their suspects to lower their guard?"

Gabe's smile broadened. "Absolutely. Did it work?"

Ellen Rowe didn't smile as she turned back to Jane. "I'm disappointed in you, Jane. Very disappointed." And with that curt dismissal, Ellen Rowe pivoted and left them.

"Is bringing me what has disappointed the lady?" Gabe asked as he enjoyed watching Ellen Rowe slink away.

"It's going to disappoint them all," Jane answered as she placed a glass of champagne in his hand. "But then, you knew that."

Gabe was surprised to see the sober look she gave him. "Actually, I hadn't thought about my company ruining your social standing, Hardesty."

"But even if you had, it wouldn't have stopped you."

True enough, but Gabe didn't think admitting it was going to help his case. He took a sip of champagne instead.

Gabe then spied a quiet but quick-eyed Naomi Parisot moving away with a half-empty tray of champagne glasses. She flashed Gabe a furtive look, distracting his thoughts.

"Now there's a lady I wouldn't want washing my windows."

Jane looked up. "Why do you say that?"

"Something about her. Can't seem to get any cooperation out of the employment agency that placed her in the Madden household, either. They've been more than reticent in returning Roy's calls. Maybe they're one of these outfits that have green-card problems with their staff."

Jane sipped her champagne. "Hardly. Ellen's Domestics is not the normal type of domestic employment service filled with foreign immigrants."

Gabe turned startled eyes toward her. "You know about the firm?"

Jane sipped her champagne. "Of course. The owner of Ellen's Domestics is none other than Ellen Rowe, the wife of Judge Henry Rowe and the same lady who was just over here checking you out."

Gabe wasn't taken in by the nonchalance of her manner. He could see the small gleam that had centered in her eyes. "All right, Hardesty. I know you're just bursting at the seams to get it all said. Tell me about Ellen's Domestics."

Jane's smile was smug. "About fifteen years ago, Ellen got the bright idea of starting an employment service made up of women who were divorced, widowed or deserted each year. She insisted her applicants had to be women who had performed as housewives for most of their lives and now found themselves alone and financially destitute. She got them jobs in the homes of the wealthy, most including live-in quarters and full health insurance."

"And now?"

"And now nearly every domestic employee on Eden Island comes from her firm. Ellen's women command a premium wage."

Gabe nodded. "I see. So Ellen Rowe placed Naomi Parisot in the Madden household."

"Actually, Naomi came to work for my mother about ten years ago. She became a part of Ellen's Domestics after her husband skipped out with their bank account and a younger woman. I didn't know where she'd gone after Mother's death until I saw her here at the estate the morning Jennifer was found."

"So her husband skipped out with a younger woman? Maybe that's why Naomi never warmed up to Jennifer. After Madden's scandal with the stripper, I doubt a marriage license would have legitimized their liaison in Naomi's eyes."

Gabe watched the Parisot woman flash another furtive look in their direction. "How well did you and Naomi get on?"

"Actually, I wasn't at the house much in the time she was with my mother. There was school, my internship, then my marriage."

"Gregory wasn't from Eden Island?"

She was surprised that Gabe knew her dead husband's name. She sipped her champagne, more to cover her reaction than to quench a thirst. "No. I met Gregory when I was doing my residency back East. His family was from Boston."

"And you married him after completing your residency five years ago. That was when you officially moved away from Eden Island to live in Boston."

Jane looked over at him quizzically. "No wonder Roy hasn't been able to find out about Ellen's Domestics. He's obviously been too busy checking up on me."

Gabe shrugged, unwilling to rise to the bait. "What can you tell me about Henry Rowe?"

"Henry was born on Eden Island, into an established family of money. Married Ellen just before he left for a private law school back east, when he was nineteen. Everyone considered him a competent contracts attorney until he won his judgeship couple of years back. Pretty unexciting."

"Was Ellen's family from Eden Island?"

"Yes, but not nearly as well-to-do as Rowe's. Still, unlike hubby, she's polished the old tarnished spoon she was born with until it shines. Her domestic employment agency, just like a dozen other projects she's nurtured, has blossomed into a very healthy monetary endeavor. I imagine she could buy and sell her husband four times over now and still come up with change."

"She looks to be in her late forties."

"She's fifty-five, a year older than Henry, although she looks ten years younger. She takes care of herself. They've got longevity. Married in their teens, and still together. One son, Rick. He's thirty."

"Is he around?"

"No, Richard's got him employed in one of his firms in South America. Seems he's convinced Henry and Ellen that Rick needs some hard muscle work to make a man out of him."

"How well did Ellen know Jennifer?"

"I would guess pretty well, since she and Richard have always been tight. Ellen and Margaret, Richard's first wife, got on. Ellen let Margaret help raise Rick, and that gave her pleasure. Henry didn't seem to care about his son. Between the two women, they spoiled Rick rotten. I'm not surprised he's grown up to be a disappointment. None of us other kids could stand to be around him long."

Gabe slugged down some champagne. "Damn. Maybe what I should have done to find out about these people is just send Roy to interview you."

Jane laughed. Her laugh was hearty, deep, just like her voice. The bland mask was gone for once, and her face was flushed and full of soft curves. Her eyes sparkled with a hint of mockery, and he knew she was enjoying knowing more than he did and making him ask for the information. He moved closer.

Jane stepped back in a tactical retreat.

Gabe shrugged. The evening was young yet. "Madden was obviously behind dear old Henry becoming a judge. I wonder who else owes Richard Madden a political favor?"

"Probably most of the people in this room tonight. And speaking of, we might as well start to mingle."

Gabe turned to look around the room, taking a small sip of his champagne. "I'm only really interested in talking with the people at Jennifer's funeral. Who are the rest of these folks?"

"Most are the wealthy property owners of Eden Island. They come to these functions and back candidates for state and local offices who will have a say in local issues. They're all interested in keeping Eden Island as a haven for the elite." Jane waved her glass of champagne in acknowledgment of a few signs of recognition around the room.

"Who were those you just waved to?"

"Just residents of the island."

"They're not coming over to say hello."

"I'm not politically important enough to warrant anything but a nodding recognition at this gathering. They don't want to waste their time."

"You say that rather blandly. You don't think it's rude?"

"They're not being rude. They're being politically astute. I've never involved myself in politics. About all I have in common with most of these people is a residence here on the island."

"Jane?" a male voice called from behind them. She turned toward the newcomer and leaned down to give Leo Speke a brief hug.

"Now this color I approve of on you, Jane. Does Dot know you're here yet?"

"Haven't seen her. Leo Speke, this is Gabe Kincaid."

Leo ignored Gabe's offered hand. As a matter of fact, he seemed to be purposely avoiding even looking in his direction. "We've met. Can I get you some champagne, Jane?"

"No, I've had my limit. From the swaying bodies, I'd say I'm not the only one."

Leo leaned over as though he were imparting a confidence. "Richard's been plying them with it for well over an hour. You arrived late."

"Gabe was . . . unavoidably delayed."

Leo's bushy gray-brown eyebrows met as his dark, soulful eyes rolled toward Gabe's face briefly and then returned to Jane's.

"You came together?"

"Yes, Leo."

A frown erupted on Leo Speke's brow. "I . . . see. . . . Well, I must be on my way. Catch you later," he called as he once again disappeared into the crowd.

"What? Doesn't he think I'm good enough for you?"

Jane ignored Gabe's flip tone. "He's worried about Jennifer's death, is all. He was her doctor."

"And maybe he slipped her something. As a doctor he would know about untraceable poisons, wouldn't he?"

Jane scowled at Gabe.

Gabe nodded as though things were becoming clearer to him. "I take it Speke is your doctor, as well as Madden's?"

"Leo is Eden Island's doctor. Nearly everyone uses him."

"And I bet he knows their secrets. I wonder if one of those secrets is what's making him so nervous around me?"

Although Jane didn't want to admit it, the truth was, Leo did seem nervous. At that moment, the ringing of a loud bell quieted the room's background noise almost instantly. Jane was happy to relinquish her disturbing thoughts to focus attention to the raised voice.

"Ladies and gentlemen! May I have your attention, please?"

Gabe turned in the direction of the voice. Sometime in the last few moments, a small platform had been rolled into the room, and on it now stood the stocky state party chairman, Jack Carver. The chunky face surrounding his thin crew cut beamed with goodwill. Gabe didn't catch all his mumbled words amid the gold glint of his waving ringed fingers, but the final two came through crystal-clear: "Richard Madden." Then Jack Carver stumbled down the platform's one step.

Richard Madden's large, sturdy frame ascended amid enthusiastic clapping. There was no evidence of mumbling in his booming voice. His dark eyes sparkled as his upper lip waved his hefty mustache like a black flag.

"Our last legislative session has seen the passage of an important, history-making clean water and land recovery bill. But we must not lessen our vigil to protect the beautiful waters that surround our lovely island from contamination and our forests from wanton decimation.

"There's only one way to ensure our survival, and that is by electing the man who will be our voice against these greedy conglomerates who prey on all our natural resources. Ladies and gentlemen, friends and neighbors, join me in welcoming Philip Lemke, the next state senator from Eden Island's district!''

Gabe put his hands together a couple of times as the room vibrated with applause. Since Eden Island was only a small part of the total geographical district, Madden's disenfranchisement of the less wealthy residents of Edenville irritated him.

Following the silver bulldog's powerful delivery, Philip Lemke looked and sounded like an undernourished greyhound. Throughout his letter-perfect speech, accompanied by letter-perfect smiles, Gabe found his eyes kept darting to Richard Madden standing behind the platform, as if he expected to see him pushing the remote control buttons.

Lemke finished to a round of enthusiastic applause and urged everyone to join him in the dining room for a long-awaited supper.

Nearly fifty people poured into the next room, the doors of which had magically opened at the end of Lemke's speech. Gabe couldn't believe the length of the room or the length of the massive table, set with starch-white linen, gleaming platinum-edged china and sparkling silver. The flashing jewelry and elegantly dressed shifting bodies around the massive dining table reminded him of exotic flamingos circling a water hole.

He leaned toward Jane's ear. "Where do we alight?"

"Since you want to talk to the movers and shakers at this little soiree, the head of the table. Follow me and sit directly across from where I do."

The head of the table was at the far end of the tunnellike dining room. As he stepped farther into the room, Gabe could see that its dark walls were backgrounds for an extensive display of early weaponry. There were samurai swords, knightly battle-axes, war hammers, flanged Gothic battle maces, courtiers' daggers, Indo-Persian fighting helmets, Viking spears, even a Norman warrior's Bayeux shield and a Scottish targe. It wasn't a room he thought he'd want to get angry at anybody in.

"Nice and homey," he commented in Jane's ear as they finally approached the far end of the table. Gabe could see that Richard Madden had claimed the position of prominence. To his right was an empty seat with a single red rose wrapped to its back with a silver ribbon. Gabe recognized the gesture to Jennifer's memory, but found his reaction mixed as he gazed back at the walls full of weaponry.

To Madden's left sat Jack Carver. Philip Lemke took the place next to the chair with the rose, and Suzanne Lemke eased in next to Jack Carver. Then Gabe watched Jane sit next to Philip Lemke, and he slipped into the chair across from her, next to Suzanne.

Leo Speke sat next to Jane, and Gabe turned to see his wife, Dorothy, taking the seat next to him. On the other side of Dorothy, Henry Rowe sat stiffly. A smiling Ellen Rowe glided into the chair across from her husband.

Jane took a moment to officially introduce Gabe to the people sitting around him whom he had not met. He received a curt nod from Jack Carver, a practiced smile from Philip Lemke.

The room reverberated with the flashes and sounds of tinkling crystal as stiff, correct waiters filled the waiting goblets with more sparkling champagne. Abundance and opulence surrounded Gabe in glittering, shimmering luxury. He frowned, unable to keep from wondering at the impact of such wealth on the psyche of the man who commanded it.

JANE WATCHED Philip Lemke stab two penny-sized raw carrots with his salad fork and then carefully raise the fork to his mouth, shove the carrots in and then drop his fork to pick through the lettuce to stab two more carrots in his salad. For the past few minutes she had found herself watching, fascinated, as he determinedly stabbed that precise number of little orange orbs.

Jane had always thought that the methodical attorney was a poor match for the creative Suzanne. As he concentrated on counting and positioning those silly carrots, Jane had the strong impression that his mind was a million miles away. When Gabe's voice drifted across the table to him, Philip seemed to jolt out of his meanderings.

"Congratulations on your candidacy, Mr. Lemke."

Philip was frowning at the remaining carrot circle in his salad. He seemed in a quandary as to how to eat this uneven orphan. He opened his mouth to respond to Gabe, but he never got a chance, as Dorothy Speke's very loud voice sounded from across the table.

"Detective Kincaid, do tell us—how did Jennifer die?"

It was as if a gong had been rung. A curious hush descended on everyone within hearing range.

Jane noted the appreciative gleam that had come into Gabe's eyes. "Please call me Gabe, Mrs. Speke. I'm not here officially."

"Yes, yes, but do tell us," Dot persisted. "After all, we're her family and friends."

Leo Speke spoke up from beside Jane. "Now, Dot, I'm sure you don't mean to pester Detective Kincaid. He's told you he's off duty and surely your questions—"

Dorothy Speke turned away from her husband's admonition. "I'm not pestering you, am I, Detective?"

Gabe smiled. "Of course not. But please call me Gabe. I—"

"Was it one of those obscure diseases? Surely you know, don't you?"

Gabe wondered at the eagerness in Dorothy Speke's eyes. "Why would you think she died from some obscure disease?"

"Please, we're not fools. We know if it had been something obvious, everyone would have been told by now, Detective."

"It's Gabe, remember? And Mrs. Madden's death has not been officially—"

"Do you suspect she was murdered?"

Gabe was beginning to think Dorothy Speke would have made a good prosecuting attorney. He'd certainly hate to be on the witness stand facing her grilling. "I'd be far more interested in hearing your thoughts, Mrs. Speke. After all, you knew her, whereas I—"

"Oh, dear, it is murder! No wonder you're here looking us over. Well, frankly, I wouldn't be surprised if it was someone from Eden Island. Money and position don't imbue one with morality. Why, Mabel—that's Leo's receptionist—has told me stories that—"

"Dorothy!" Leo Speke's voice boomed out as the doctor sprung to his feet, clutching his napkin. "That's enough. Mabel has no right to be discussing anything with you. I've told you both before that if you don't curb your tongues, I'll have to let her go."

"But, Leo, I—"

"Dot, are you willing to be the cause of her dismissal?"

Dorothy Speke jammed her lips together. She closed her arms across her chest. Her rising purple color gave Jane the impression of expanding gas imprisoned in a fragile test tube.

The ensuing quiet was deafening. Then Richard Madden rose and faced the empty chair on his right. In a voice that cut across the table like a sharp, clever knife, he raised his glass in a toast. "To my wife, Jennifer. Beloved of all who knew her."

Glasses up and down the table raised high in silent salute.

All but one. Philip Lemke's arm barely made it over his bowed head. And if she hadn't been sitting right next to him, Jane never would have heard the all-but-muffled sob that escaped his lips.

Chapter Eight

Jane excused herself and headed for the ladies' room, knowing from the scared look on Suzanne's face when their eyes had met across the table that she'd be followed. When Suzanne's familiar form appeared less than a minute later, Jane locked the door behind her.

She turned to her friend, fighting to keep her tone even. "Philip and Jennifer were having an affair, weren't they?"

Suzanne grasped the counter and lowered herself, stiff and straight, into the room's sole chair. "Oh, God..."

Jane dropped to her knee and put her arm around Suzanne's shoulders. "I'm sorry, Suzanne. I didn't mean to be so blunt. It's just that the revelation threw me. How long have you known?"

Suzanne's face drained white beneath her makeup. Quiet tears strode down her cheeks. "At least six weeks. It's not like Philip told me, of course. He probably still doesn't think I know. But wives get this sixth sense.... But I never imagined it was Jennifer. Not until that morning after her death, when he came home and I saw in his eyes...heard in his voice..."

Jane knew why Suzanne was having trouble completing her sentences. She held her friend's face tight against her shoulder as anger tumbled dry inside her own chest.

Gradually Suzanne's sobs stopped. She raised her head and reached for some tissue to dry her eyes. "This is so stupid. I have no reason to cry. Jennifer's dead. It's all over."

Jane frowned. "Over? Philip just sobbed out there when her memory was toasted."

Suzanne turned away from Jane's searching look and began to powder her face, smoothing away her smudged eyeliner. Jane knew her tone sounded far surer than it had any right to be. "He'll forget. His healing will come in time."

Jane clasped Suzanne's shoulders. "I'm not concerned about *his* healing. I'm concerned about yours."

Suzanne continued with her brave words, her eyes far too bright. "Marriage is a package deal, Jane. Sometimes not all the product is particularly palatable..."

Jane winced at the naked pain in Suzanne's eyes. She brought her in closer for a hug. "And sometimes products aren't up to standard and need to be recalled."

Suzanne shook her head as she moved away from Jane's embrace and got to her feet. "You don't understand. It's over. He needs me now, particularly through this upcoming campaign. We have a chance to get close again." She paused to glance nervously at her wristwatch. "We've got to go back to the table. They'll be wondering what happened to us."

Jane rose to her feet and faced her friend. "I can't just go back in there and sit next to that...that husband of yours, like nothing's happened."

Suzanne grabbed hold of Jane's arm as she took a step toward her. "Yes, you can. Jane, I've always thought of you as the sister I never had—the one who'd come to my defense and stand by me, no matter what. And you always have. Do you remember at my eighth birthday party when that big obnoxious bully Ricky Rowe chased me, trying to dump his ice cream down my back? You were terrific when you grabbed him and smashed that Neapolitan-hot-fudge-and-nuts mess all over him instead."

Jane smirked at the memory. "If you've brought this past episode up to show me the similarity between Rick Rowe and Philip Lemke, you needn't have bothered. I could have seen it for myself."

Suzanne's eyes pleaded. "Jane, you know that's not the reason. Remember, Philip's my husband. I love him. No matter what you think or feel, please keep this Jennifer business to yourself. Please."

Jane gave a little sigh of retreat. "You're a loyal and solid supporter, kid. The rat doesn't deserve you."

Suzanne's smile surprised Jane with the suddenness of its sparkle and pride. "I know."

GABE CHECKED HIS WATCH when Jane and Suzanne returned to the table. Fifteen minutes for a call of nature? Something was up. Jane's mouth seemed tight, and even Suzanne's smiling, freshly powdered face looked a little sallow around the edges. He got up to hold her chair for her. "Your soup is cold."

Her smile didn't quite reach her eyes. "It's vichyssoise, Detective Kincaid. It's supposed to be cold. Oh, I see. You're making a joke. Yes. Funny."

He resumed his seat. "Please. Call me Gabe. Remember my unofficial status tonight."

Suzanne's voice sounded even more distracted. "What does it stand for?"

"Gabriel. My mother was hoping for an angel."

Suzanne's laugh was practiced, hollow.

"All us mothers do," Dorothy Speke said from Gabe's other side. "Don't we, Ellen?"

Ellen's cramped smile was like a continuing reprimand.

Dorothy's comment to Gabe had been the first thing the doctor's wife had contributed to the conversation since her husband's strong admonition to drop the subject of Jennifer Madden. She looked over at Leo now—a quick visual check. Then she put her head down and studied her soup as though she were an astronomer getting her first glimpse of the Milky Way.

Gabe knew Dorothy Speke was just bursting with information, and it wouldn't take much to get her lid open.

But Gabe was aware that ever since Dorothy's earlier comments concerning Jennifer everyone at his end of the table had been listening to their conversation very carefully. Particularly Richard Madden. Gabe was beginning to feel like a well-chaperoned teenager on his first date. Getting Dorothy Speke alone was going to be a bit of a trick.

"What drew you to a career in law enforcement, Detective Kincaid?" Jack Carver suddenly asked him from across the table, waving a hand that glistened with gold rings.

Gabe flashed a good-neighbor smile. "Please, Mr. Carver, my name is Gabe."

"And you must call me Jack. So, how about a life story?"

Gabe leaned back as a steaming, freshly boiled lobster the size of Maine was set before him. "Not much to tell. Born and raised here. Only been out of state once, and that was for college."

Jack Carver leaned forward in his seat, ignoring the waiter who was trying to serve him his lobster, as an inauspicious glint entered his eyes. "I seem to remember a Sheriff Neal Kincaid from about twenty years back. Any relation?"

Gabe stiffened as he cracked the lobster's shell. "My father."

Carver eyed Gabe like a cat ready to play with a cornered mouse. He twisted his pinkie ring between eager fingers. "Very popular with the people, until... What was it? Oh, yes, accidentally shot himself."

The table had gotten quiet again. Everyone seemed to be waiting for Gabe to respond. Gabe's face was blank as he concentrated on pulling lobster meat out of the shell.

Jack Carver's smile turned hard. "Had to resign after that. Lost his popularity, it seemed. County commissioners appointed someone else to fill the job until the next general election. Neal didn't run again."

Gabe kept himself focused on the lobster on his plate as he fought down the very strong desire to punch Jack Carver in the mouth. The man was doing this to goad him. But if he lost his temper, he'd only be playing into Carver's hands. He gritted his teeth.

But Carver wasn't going to let it go. He raised his voice so that all within range could hear. "Whatever happened to him, Kincaid? I've always been curious."

Gabe lifted his head, flashing a tight smile that took all his control. "He retired, just as we all will do some day, Jack. Those of us who know when to quit." After that very pointed and warning remark, Gabe glanced over at Philip Lemke, noting his empty glass and his growing alcoholic flush. "I'd be much more interested in hearing from our district's senatorial candidate, wouldn't you?"

Gabe thought he was changing the subject smoothly. Certainly, at the moment, any subject was preferable to the one at hand. Too late, he realized that he'd said the wrong thing. All of Philip Lemke's gleaming white teeth flashed out at him like a carefully laid porcelain trap. By the time they clamped together again, nearly twenty minutes later, the man had related an obviously well-practiced political biography, devoid of any real information or substance. It had taken all of Gabe's control even to respond with a semblance of interest. Despite the drinks in him, Philip Lemke was a well-rehearsed man.

As Gabe finally and thankfully looked away, he caught the benevolent smile on Richard Madden's face and had the curious impression his host both understood Gabe's conversational blunder and was finding it quite funny.

Things were not going well.

Gabe wished the topic he really needed to discuss, Jennifer Madden, hadn't been so effectively squashed. By the time the dessert came, he had finally admitted to himself that for the most part Jane Hardesty had been right. Coming to this dinner hadn't accomplished much.

Then he just happened to look up to see Jane deliberately knock Philip Lemke's ice-cream dessert into his lap.

"Oh, my. How awkward of me," Jane said serenely as Philip leapt up with a surprised exclamation and displayed a very wet and very gooey crotch.

Ellen Rowe's voice rose censoriously. "Jane! How can you *still* be so clumsy!"

Out of the corner of his eye, Gabe saw Suzanne raise her
dinner napkin to cover her face while her shoulders shook
lightly.

"It's all right, Jane," Philip muttered, in a voice that
didn't sound all right at all. "These things happen. I'll just
go wash up. If everyone will excuse me?"

"WHAT WAS THAT ALL ABOUT?" Gabe asked Jane as soon
as dinner was over and most of the guests were retiring into
the aquarium-lined gathering room for coffee and after-
dinner drinks.

Jane shrugged, an ambiguous smile lifting her lips. "A
private matter. Did I miss anything when I left the table?"

"No. Leo Speke and Madden put an effective lid on
Dorothy. It's a shame. She obviously knows something. I'd
like to get her alone."

Jane looked over at Leo, who was hovering over his wife.
"I don't think you've got a prayer. Who's next on your
list?"

"List? What list would that be, Kincaid?" Henry Rowe's
perpetually hoarse voice asked from behind them.

Jane pivoted around to face the judge, feeling uneasy at
the hefty determination and uneasy suspicion lighting his
gray eyes.

Gabe's voice was even, controlled. "This is an interesting room, don't you think, Judge? All these predatory fish
swimming side by side, where they can see one another and
yet are prevented from getting at one another. Has to be
pretty frustrating."

Henry Rowe's tone gave vent to his own frustration.
"You're out of line, Kincaid."

"And what line would that be, Judge?"

Jane watched the color rising up Rowe's neck. "Don't
play dumb with me. I told you to back off Richard Madden
and those in his circle. You ignored my direction and deliberately harassed the financial institutions that serve Richard and his friends. Well, we've put a stop to that, and we'll
put a stop to you if you persist."

Gabe's eyes narrowed to blue slits, and when he spoke again a new, deadly calm strode through his voice. "What is that supposed to mean?"

Dots of redness swelled beneath Rowe's cheeks. "Whatever I choose it to mean. How dare you show up here! For the sake of Richard and his guests, I said nothing through dinner, but my patience is at its limit."

Jane took a step back. Gabe took a step toward the judge. A vein in his forehead stood out like a blue canal, belying the continued evenness in his tone. "I'm here in a social capacity, Rowe."

Jane caught the increased movement of the fish in the tank alongside them, as though they, too, had sensed the turmoil.

The judge's voice rose into thunderous proportions. "You dare call me Rowe? You presumptuous ass. They said you were better than your father, but I don't see it. Two of a kind, as far as I'm concerned. Neither of you worth a dime! You will address me properly, as Your Honor!"

Neither full stomachs nor emptied champagne bottles could dull the stiffening shock his outburst brought. The room grew immediately quiet. Every head turned their way with juicy interest.

The sparks from Gabe's eyes were like emotional claws of anger edging ever closer to Rowe's throat. "This is not a courtroom."

"It won't take but a call to get you into one!"

The fish behind them darted in agitation. Jane shivered at the deadly quiet of Gabe's voice. "I beg your pardon?"

Jane could see that Henry Rowe had no idea how close he was to being throttled. The man's foolish ego egged him on, bloating his next words, causing him to take a step forward. "You have reason to beg it, Kincaid. And you'll be doing more than begging me before—"

And then, suddenly, Rowe was falling, grasping at air. For one horrible instant, Jane thought he was going to land on Gabe, but in a movement so fast she hardly saw it, Gabe stepped aside, and Judge Henry Rowe collided with a small occasional table, which promptly overturned and followed him to the floor.

Jane was so shocked that she just stood there, looking down at the prone man, who grunted as he tried to get his breath back. She wasn't the only one who had become immobilized. The room suddenly looked as if it were filled with statues.

Then Richard Madden pushed through the silent crowd and planted his feet in front of them. "What's going on?"

The ghost of a smile played about Gabe lips. "Judge Rowe, ah, tripped."

Madden stared at Gabe with his black eyes and flipped his hand to summon Mr. Gnat. The large man was instantly at his side. At another gesture from Madden, Mr. Gnat bent down to assist Henry Rowe to his feet.

Only when Rowe was standing again did Madden tear his eyes away from Gabe to look at the judge's face. It was already draining to its natural gray color. "I hear you tripped."

Henry Rowe blinked uncertainly under Richard's hard gaze. Jane realized with some small surprise that Henry Rowe was afraid of Madden. She watched his eyes drop as his pale lips parted with a mumbled response. "Lost my balance. Most disconcerting."

Richard Madden continued to look at Rowe's bowed head for a moment more before he turned to Jane. His eyes were like burning, angry coals singeing her flesh.

Richard took her hand in his iron fingers. Jane tried not to flinch when he blew a false kiss across her knuckles. "So nice of you to have graced us with your presence this evening. Regrettable that you must leave so early."

Mr. Gnat materialized beside Jane with her wrap.

Jane let Gabe help her into it without comment, all the while feeling impaled upon the anger in Richard Madden's eyes.

It was with profound relief that she stepped outside and heard the door close behind them. She said nothing as she stomped to the car. Once there, she snapped into the driver's seat and gripped the steering wheel.

Gabe slipped into the passenger's seat beside her. "Why do I have the feeling you're about ready to slug someone, Hardesty?"

Jane took a deep breath and glanced his way, her eyes green sparks in the subdued light of the car. "Guess who."

Gabe looked over at Jane, genuinely surprised and amused by her barely controlled anger. "You can't mean me? I didn't start that shouting match with Rowe."

"No, but you kept it going. And you deliberately tripped that pompous ass, didn't you?"

Gabe smirked. "It was either that or get arrested for his murder."

"Damn it, you should have acted with more decorum. You got us kicked out!"

Gabe swiveled in his seat, amused to see who was throwing stones. "I should have acted with more decorum? I wasn't the one who dumped ice cream in the guest of honor's lap!"

Jane glared at him a moment more before memories of the evening's comic elements took hold and her pique turned into a giggle that soon erupted into full-fledged laughter.

Gabe enjoyed her full-bodied laughter; it bubbled through him like a vintage champagne. He joined in wholeheartedly.

"I don't really blame you for tripping him," Jane said a few moments later, when she'd gotten her breath back and was wiping the tears from her eyes. "That insufferable Rowe had it coming. Still, I was surprised you let him get to you. Was it that crack he made about you and your father?"

Jane could feel Gabe stiffen beside her as all traces of his relaxing laughter fled. So there was something there to pursue. How interesting. She started the car and pulled out of the circular drive. "Did he really shoot himself?"

Gabe rolled the passenger window down. "It's a long, boring story. Ancient history."

"History was always my favorite subject."

"I'm telling you that you don't want to know."

Jane's voice rose until it dripped with sweet sarcasm. "I hope this is an earth-shattering secret, considering how hard you're making me work to get it."

Gabe grinned over at his driver as he tore his tie loose and unbuttoned his collar. "That nasty vengeful streak is showing again, Hardesty."

Her eyes flashed over at him, green and mocking. "I thought that was the one trait of mine you appreciated, Kincaid. Come on. Stop stalling."

Gabe exhaled heavily. "All right. My father was a man who fell in love with a beautiful woman who over the years managed to strip him of every ounce of his manhood. All she ever thought about was what other people would think."

Gabe's face looked both hard and sad as he stared out the windshield. "He gave in to her at every turn. She wanted him to make money, so he did. When she wanted him to run for sheriff, he sold his business and ran. But when a sticky political crisis came up during his term of office and he was being forced into making a very unpopular stand, she went into hysterics about how she was going to lose all her friends. So he went out and shot himself in the leg. Claimed it was an accident. Got himself relieved of duty. Someone else made the unpopular decision. Nobody was fooled."

"And you're still trying to live it down."

Gabe turned in his seat to face her. "I grew up in Edenville. I was fifteen when my friend's fathers began snickering about mine, and my friends joined in. When you're shamed by your own actions, you can rectify them. But when you're shamed by your father's, you've got no place to hide."

"Yet you chose the same profession. Doesn't that lay you open more frequently to comments like those made tonight?"

"Undoubtedly. But that's the only way I know how to face a problem—head on. Besides, the people who take a swing at this chin soon learn they're not dealing with my father."

Jane was quiet for a few moments before she spoke again. She was thinking about that adolescent boy being taunted for his parent's fears. How did the boy and the man he'd grown into handle such harassment? Quite well, judging by the uncompromising strength she saw in the profile beside her.

He must have felt her scrutiny, because his deep blue gaze swept her way. Jane quickly refocused her eyes on the road. "The evening didn't quite go the way you planned, did it?"

Gabe shoved his black tie into an inside pocket of his tux. "Oh, I don't know. I found out a few things."

"Like what?"

"Like despite all his unconcerned display, Madden is worried about my investigation. That's why he really kicked us out. Do you think Madden put Henry Rowe up to trying to warn me away tonight?"

Jane shifted down to take a sharp curve. "Richard's not shy. I very much doubt he'd send someone else to do something he'd take pleasure in."

"Hmm... That's what I thought. I'm beginning to think Judge Henry Rowe might have been acting on his own behalf."

Jane looked over at Gabe. "How do you mean?"

"Well, remember when Madden came up and demanded to know what was going on? Rowe said he tripped, but he didn't mention anything about my tripping him."

Jane nodded as the implication sunk in. "That's right! Why didn't he? Unless he didn't want Madden to know he'd been trying to warn you off?"

Gabe smiled at her. "My thoughts exactly."

Jane's head cocked to one side. "You're excited about that for some reason. Why?"

"Well, don't you see? That probably means Rowe isn't as interested in keeping me from investigating Madden as he is interested in keeping me from investigating him. He's got something to hide, and ten to one it has something to do with Jennifer. I wonder."

"You're wondering if Rowe was the man Jennifer expected the night she died?"

Gabe was pleased at Jane's quick understanding. "He fits the description Jennifer left on that tape. He's older, silver-haired, and holds a position of power. Why not?"

Jane was frowning as she pulled into her driveway and shut off the Talbot's engine. "Maybe. Still, that description fits most of the men on Eden Island. And if Rowe was having an affair with Jennifer, why would he kill her?"

"Why, indeed?" Gabe answered, trying not to be distracted by her appealing scent or the way the entry light from her home highlighted the wet glow on her lips. He reached behind him for the door handle. "Invite me in for some coffee. We've got things to discuss."

JANE'S LONG LEGS curled around one of the bar stools in the corner of her cool, crisp kitchen as she cuddled a cup of freshly brewed coffee in her hands. Gabe removed his tuxedo jacket and sat on another bar stool, just a few feet away.

Her nose positioned itself above the china cup as she took a deep sniff. Gabe watched the look of pleasure light her face.

He fingered the glossy ceramic coating of his coffee cup, wondering if her finely modeled cheekbones and the hollows beneath were as smooth as they seemed.

She looked up. "I have to admit Rowe acted very strangely tonight."

"Yes. Guilty. Even fearful. If Jennifer was having an affair with him, it could have gotten out of hand. If Jennifer threatened to expose him, Rowe might have killed her."

"No. Assuming that this affair did take place, if Jennifer exposed Rowe, she'd be exposing herself."

"All right. Maybe she fell for Rowe. Wanted to leave Richard for him. Maybe she didn't care if Richard knew."

Jane shook her head. "I very much doubt a woman who got turned on by the kind of power a Richard Madden wields could be satisfied by leaving him for a flunky like Henry Rowe."

Gabe circled both hands around the warmth of his coffee cup. "You consider Henry Rowe Richard's flunky?"

"You saw him tonight, Kincaid. He looked like a whipped puppy in front of Richard's questioning. I've got no doubt now that Richard controls him."

"Have they known each other long?"

"Henry was Richard's lawyer for many years before Richard decided to back him for a judgeship. Frankly, as afraid as he seems to be of Richard, I rather doubt he would risk the chance of being caught with Jennifer."

"Well, I still think Rowe was involved with her. It's the only thing that explains his wanting to warn me off while not letting Madden know. God, I'd love to catch him with his pants down on this one."

Jane gave a noncommittal shrug.

Gabe drank his coffee. It was rich and smooth. He took another gulp. "Since you're skeptical about Henry Rowe being her lover, who do you think was coming to see Jennifer the night she died?"

Jane eyes darted to her coffee cup, but not soon enough.

Gabe gave a low whistle. "Oh, I see. So that explains the little tête-a-tête with Suzanne in the ladies' room. And the ice-cream decoration on Philip Lemke's pants. He had the hots for Jennifer, didn't he?"

Jane's head jerked up at his words. Her expression brought a smile to Gabe's lips.

"You shouldn't be holding out on me, Hardesty. We're supposed to be working together on this case, remember?"

Jane downed the last of her coffee. It was just like him to throw logic in her face. She just wished she had a suitable rejoinder. About all she could do was stall for time. "You want some more?"

He looked down to see that he was holding an empty cup. He handed it to her and then followed her to the coffee maker.

"Does Suzanne know?"

Jane poured more coffee into both their cups. There didn't seem to be any use in denying it. "Yes."

Gabe shook his head. "So his wife knows, and she's standing by him. Well, good for Suzanne."

Jane's eyes went to Gabe's face. "Is it good?"

Gabe had an interesting expression on his face—his features steady as stone, but the look in his eyes flickering, as though from an unpleasant inner vision. "A man needs his wife to stand by him, especially if he's facing trouble."

Jane suddenly realized they weren't talking about Suzanne and Philip anymore. Her voice tempered as she took a step toward Gabe. "When your father shot himself, your mother left, didn't she?"

Gabe's eyes contemplated the coffee in his cup. His voice was toneless. He could have been talking about the weather, but of course he wasn't. "She said she wouldn't stay around to become a laughingstock. Told me I should go with her. When I wouldn't, she walked out and never looked back."

Gabe drained the rest of his coffee, then raised his eyes to Jane's with a steely composure that stunned her—and made her indefinably sad.

"So what's the story on Philip? Was the affair serious?" His renewed questions signaled their return to business and wiped away the previous moment as though it had never happened.

Jane trotted through her thoughts silently. Suzanne had asked her to say nothing, and she had already said too much.

Gabe read her silence correctly. "Look, I'm only after one person, and that's Jennifer Madden's killer. If your friend's husband is innocent of that, he's got nothing to fear from me. Just tell me the facts and trust me."

Jane turned to study his face, looking for the trustworthiness he advertised. The face of a basset hound looked trustworthy. The face of Gabe Kincaid was once again overflowing with his special brand of well-groomed but rakish charm. His deep blue eyes returned her appraisal with an all-too-appealing confidence.

She looked away, inhaling deeply, disconcerted to learn of this man's ability to tap into so many different emotions inside her. "Yes, I think the affair was serious. He sobbed when she was toasted tonight."

"Okay. That gives us several different motives."

"Which are?"

"Well, Jennifer might have been having affairs with them both. If Rowe found out about Philip or vice versa, either of them might have gotten jealous enough to kill her."

Jane frowned. "Neither Rowe nor Philip strike me as the jealous-lover type."

"There isn't a type, Hardesty. Most men are susceptible under the right circumstances to play the fool over a woman. Then there's Richard Madden. Maybe what you said was correct. Maybe Madden was giving me a show when he played the angry, bruised spouse. Maybe he found out about Jennifer's sleeping around and killed her."

"And Ellen Rowe was very nervous about your presence there tonight. She could be involved in Jennifer's death."

Gabe shrugged. "It's worth considering. The jealous-wife motive is a strong one. Henry Rowe's warning to me could have been an attempt to protect his wife if he knows she killed Jennifer because of him. Any other thoughts as to possible suspects?"

"I set Jennifer's death at between six and ten that night. Do you know where all these people were then?"

"I know where they say they were. Madden claims he was in Seattle with Carver and that manservant. The maid was seeing a show, also in Seattle. Leo Speke was at home with his wife. The attorneys for the Rowes and the Lemkes advised me that both couples were home alone together. Why are you frowning?"

"As a rule, Eden Island couples don't spend their evenings at home. I guess it seems a bit strange to me that all these couples just happened to be home on that night."

"You saying it couldn't happen?"

"Oh, it could. It's just a bit unusual, considering all the normal social engagements they attend."

Gabe ran a hand along the countertop. "You realize that from the viewpoint of motivation, Suzanne Lemke has to be way up there on my suspect list. She might have decided to do away with Jennifer in order to protect her marriage and ensure that her husband wasn't involved in a scandal that could cost him an election.''

Jane shook her head. ''No, Suzanne didn't even know Philip's lover was Jennifer until the morning after her death.''

''So she told you. She could have been lying. After all, poison is often a woman's choice of weapon.''

Jane stiffened, and her tone turned vehement. ''Never. Suzanne's no killer.''

''You're prejudiced, Hardesty. It's my job to be open to all the possibilities and pursue them. It's supposed to be your job, too, remember?''

Jane licked her lips as Gabe's hard, leatherlike accusation threatened to strip them dry. She was happy for the diversion of the ringing telephone. She leaned across the kitchen counter to grab the receiver and said hello.

''Jane, it's me. I'm sorry I'm whispering, but I don't want Leo to know I'm calling you. Can you hear me okay?''

Jane straightened in her seat. ''Yes, Dot, fine. But why don't you want Leo to know?''

''Not now, Jane. I'll come by your place tomorrow morning at eight. Since it's Saturday, I assume you're not working?''

''Well, no, I'm not, but—''

''Oh, here he comes! I can't talk anymore. Tomorrow, Jane. Bye!''

After a quick blast of dial tone, Jane replaced the receiver.

''What was that all about?''

Jane answered Gabe distractedly, her mind still swirling with confusion. ''It was Dorothy Speke. She wants to see me.''

''When?''

The eagerness in Gabe's voice drew Jane's attention. ''Tomorrow morning.''

A speculative gleam entered his eyes. "And she didn't want her husband to know? This sounds very promising. What time is she coming?"

"Eight, but—"

"No time for buts, Hardesty," he said as he grabbed his tux coat off the back of a bar stool and headed for the door. "I'll be here at 7:45."

Jane followed. "No. I refuse to alienate the few friends I still have here on the island by forcing them into confrontations with you when they come to see me."

"Confrontation? What harsh language, Hardesty. All I want to do is talk to her."

"I believe that like I believe I'm going to win the lottery. Besides, there is no way I can explain your just happening to drop by so early on a Saturday morning."

Gabe looked down at the thick, glossy waves of blond hair framing her obstinate, upturned chin. He inhaled her perfume, hot and sweet from her skin. There was a challenge in her green eyes, but it wasn't the one his body had been pressing him all night to answer. He took a step closer. "If she found us having breakfast together in a couple of towels, there would be no explanations necessary."

He watched her eyes widen, then darken. He heard the small intake of her breath as his chest lightly brushed hers. She looked shocked, but he could see the pulse beating wildly in her long, luscious neck, and he knew shock was not all she was feeling. He was disturbing her, getting past her careful control. The knowledge sent a heady percussion through his already thumping arteries.

Jane's thoughts raced around in circles. She could feel his warmth closing dangerously about her as his eyes looked deeply into hers. She had the strange feeling of being unable to catch her breath, as though his lungs were drawing in all the air.

He reached for her, pulling her closer, searching the deepening green in her eyes, feeling the jolt in her muscles as their bodies met. An ache of desire drove through him like a stake, impaling his will.

Then her lips were beneath his, and he was murmuring her name against them, and the desire was spreading like a flash fire through them both.

His touch melted Jane's rigid muscles into a feverish offensive. Her need rose up to meet Gabe's, hot and heady in its sudden intensity. She gripped his shoulders, squeezing herself harder and tighter against him, tasting the fervid flavors of his mouth and pressing greedily for more.

His hands branded her shoulders, her back, her hips, as they hungrily went exploring, caressing. A deep moan escaped from her throat as his lips sank to devour the sensitive skin of her neck. His hands molded themselves to her bottom, pressing her to him. She gasped in pleasure until on some level of consciousness she felt the control that had been so much a part of her for so long fading so quickly away.

A primitive, panicky fear jerked her to attention, stiffened her limbs, had her pushing out of his arms.

Gabe felt the change in her instantly. He leaned back to see her face, fighting to fill his lungs with shallow breaths. "Jane? What is it?"

She was equally breathless, flushed, disheveled, beautiful, passion setting her skin aglow and wetting her lips. But the bruises were back in her eyes, and the word that escaped those lips was the one he hadn't wanted to hear: "No."

"Jane—"

Her fingers dug into his arms, holding him back. "No!" She yelled it like a slap. Then she turned and fled. Gabe watched her plunge down the hall, her long hair like liquid gold melting down her back. He wanted her. Oh, how he wanted her! And he knew she wanted him. But, damn it, he wasn't running after her! He ran after no woman!

He snatched at his jacket, yanked open the door and slammed it behind him.

JANE PLUNGED into the study, not bothering to turn on the light, and sank into the first chair she found. She heard the front door slam, and it sent a cold shiver through her. She kicked off her shoes and curled her feet under her as she sat there in the dark, hugging herself, trembling, confused.

How could she lose all her carefully maintained control so thoroughly? Why had she been so eager to resurrect those rampant emotions that had only caused her so much pain? What was it about Gabe Kincaid that got to her?

Deep at her core she knew, had probably known from the moment she'd walked into Jennifer Madden's dressing room and felt his very presence pressing against her skin. Gabe represented what she had tried so hard to dismiss and yet still couldn't help but desire. He was so irritatingly, aggravatingly, wonderfully alive!

She also knew she'd been spending so much time lately being irritated at Gabe that she hadn't been spending any time at all being sad about Gregory.

Jane got up from her chair and went over to the desk. She turned on the lamp beside Gregory's picture, looking directly into the steady brown eyes. It was no use. Even now she couldn't feel sad, and she wasn't even trying not to. She was trying not to feel so damn excited about Gabe Kincaid.

She switched off the lamp and sank into the high-backed desk chair. She would never forget Gregory. He filled a chapter in her life. But it was a chapter that was over.

A new chapter had started—one full of a big, handsome jerk who described men who cared about women as fools and whose personal relations with women consisted of their taking him for a ride.

No, she knew that wasn't all there was to him. Despite his abhorrence of his father's acquiescent love for his mother, Gabe still wanted the beautiful women whose deaths he avenged to be worthy of the effort. He wanted to care. Caring gave meaning to his work, to his life. She was sure of it.

What she wasn't sure of was whether he could care for her the way she was learning to care for him.

She didn't know how long she had been sitting there, lost in her thoughts, before the light, crunching sounds started to register. But the second they registered on her consciousness, she sat bolt upright in her chair, instantly alert, her ears straining to hear over the sudden, inexplicable pounding of her heart.

Muffled steps outside on the pebble-strewn garden walkway. Cautious. Tentative. Pausing to listen for discovery. Then moving on. Coming closer. Toward the back door to the study.

It was locked, wasn't it?

Jane's anxious mind played back her afternoon. Coming home early from the office to take a pain pill and relax before the evening. Feeling restless, not being able to stay down. Getting up and going out back for a walk in the garden. Coming back through the study door after pulling weeds. Her hands had been filthy. Had she leaned back and locked the door behind her?

Damn! She couldn't remember!

Fear hammered the blood through her arteries. A panicky voice inside her yelled for her to jump up and race for the door to check the lock before it was too late. But that same panic riveted her to her seat. Icy perspiration trickled down her back as her sweaty palms clung to the chair's arms.

Then, suddenly, a shadow was thrown into the room. He wasn't by the door at all! Jane's head jerked toward the far window in time to see a black shape emerge outside it. There was just enough light to see his outline as he tried to open the locked window. He was staring inside. If she had moved that second before, he would have seen her!

There was no question in Jane's mind as to what to do now. She glued herself to the leather of the high-backed desk chair, stiff and immobile. She was barely breathing.

He seemed to stare into the dark room forever. Jane's muscles ached with the pent-up adrenalin in them. Then slowly the prowler leaned back from the window and turned to move away.

A trapped breath escaped Jane's lungs. She reached across the desk for the telephone. She had just picked up the receiver when she heard the doorknob being jiggled.

He was trying to get in!

New fear pounced through her as she grasped the receiver in her hand, the dial tone seeming to blare through the room like a siren. If she'd left the door unlocked . . .

The twisting suddenly stopped. The door remained closed. She had locked it. She was safe! She could hear his footsteps crunching the gravel outside again. He was going away!

Jane sighed in relief. With a shaky hand, she replaced the telephone receiver to better hear the fading footsteps.

But wait—were they fading? No! Suddenly his shadow fell into the room again. He was back at the window! Jane heard the sound of breaking glass in the same instant that new terror gripped her. He wasn't going away at all. He was coming in that window to get her!

Chapter Nine

Jane wrenched open the middle desk drawer as the breaking glass sprayed onto the carpet. The terror that ripped through her drove her like a powerful, clanging engine. She grabbed the revolver that lay at the back, thumbed back the cocking lever, jerked it toward the broken window and fired at the shape coming through.

She knew she'd missed even before the bullet had left the gun.

But the sound of the gun discharging halted her intruder in his tracks. Jane recocked the revolver and lifted her arm to fire again. Her intruder jerked around and jumped headfirst through the window's frame of broken glass. Jane heard him land with a muffled oath on the gravel outside. Within seconds, his shoes were spewing gravel as he ran away.

Jane's arm was still extended, and her hand still grasped the gun. Slowly she willed her arm down and released the gun. It fell with a clatter to the desktop. She sank into the chair, stiff and still. She laid her suddenly throbbing head down on the cool walnut surface before her. There were things she should be doing, but they would have to wait. At the moment, all she could manage was a deep bone-jarring shudder.

GABE HADN'T BEEN HOME ten minutes when he got the call.

"It's Curtis on the night desk. Complaint about an intruder out on Eden Island just came in. You left word that any activity concerning the island should be reported to you.''

Gabe checked his watch. It was after midnight, and he was tired. He didn't relish the idea of driving all the way back to Eden Island again tonight. He hoped it was something inconsequential. He reached for a pen and paper.

''What's the address?''

''Four ninety-five Paradise Cove. Name of Hardesty.''

The pen froze in Gabe's hand. He dropped the phone and started for the door, an unfocused dread suffocating his thoughts.

''WELL, I'VE FOUND your discharged bullet, Hardesty,'' Gabe said as he held up a book Jane recognized as Agatha Christie's *The Murder of Roger Ackroyd,* a rare signed copy her mother had savored for years.

Jane winced as his pocketknife dug into the binding, dislodging a slug. Gabe brought it up to the light for scrutiny. ''Yes, has the weight of a .38. Looks like it hit the metal banding on the corner of the bookcase here and then ricocheted at an angle through the wood shelving into this book.''

Gabe flipped the expended slug as if he were tossing a coin. ''You're not much of a shot. After he came through the glass, the guy couldn't have been more than fifteen feet away. I'll take you out to the range next week.''

It wasn't an offer, or even an invitation. It was an arrogant prediction. So like the man! It annoyed Jane thoroughly, as did the casual way he was treating her and this violent intrusion into her home.

Once she had gotten over her excitement and surprise at finding him so unexpectedly on her doorstep, answering her call about the break-in, she had been deflated to hear him call her by her last name again, to see him able to look so calm and unaffected by what had passed between them scarcely more than an hour before.

It was all the more irritating because she could feel his presence taking over the room again, nudging her however she moved, reminding her of his branding touch, not letting her remain unaffected, no matter how hard she tried. She stepped to the broken window, letting a gust of night air chill her warm cheeks. "Is Fleming outside checking for footprints?"

"Among other things. You sure it was a man?"

"I think so, but I didn't get a clear look. Whoever it was had on a black ski mask and a black sweat outfit. The light wasn't on in the room."

"What were you doing sitting in this room in the dark?"

It was that same demanding tone that she knew so well, the one that reminded her how foolish her churning emotions for this man were. "Thinking, Kincaid. Some people do it, you know."

Gabe almost smiled at her baiting tone. He'd been elated to find her unharmed, but alarmed by her close call. He'd had an insane desire to grab and hold her then, but he could tell just how insane that desire was when he got a glance at the cool control that was back in her eyes.

She'd changed her slinky green dress, too—put on a sweater and slacks of powder blue, both fitting her lean, luscious frame far too well. Her hair was still free and full, the curled ends bouncing across her breasts with every movement. Those movements proved quite distracting.

Gabe's eyes took in the broken glass on the carpet and angled toward the desk. He saw the .38 sitting on top, the engraved nameplate that read Dr. Jane Hardesty, the picture of the smiling man with curly brown hair in the silver frame. It was the latter that brought a frown to his forehead.

He turned back toward the room. "The revolver yours, Hardesty?"

"My mother's. Somebody gave it to her during the Vietnam conflict. The island wasn't as well secured during those times, and some of the more violent protesters had made threats against its inhabitants, as bastions of the establishment."

"Your mother was living alone then?"

"Yes. My father's family was from D.C. They married back there, and then Mother returned here to wait for him when he was drafted. He was a surgeon. He didn't make it back."

Gabe followed Jane's eyes to the mantel in the corner. He walked over to the picture of the smiling man in uniform, sitting behind a desk. He had a round, eager face that seemed far too youthful for the captain's insignia on his collar. His name tag read John Paul Cabot. In the next picture he stood proudly by a tall, slim woman with blond hair and guileless green eyes. Gabe could see that Jane resembled her closely, except that the woman's face was heart-shaped and lacked the definable strength of Jane's square jaw.

Gabe's scrutiny of Jane's parents was interrupted by Roy's tap on the back door. The round detective let himself in, brandishing a large flashlight. "It's mostly gravel back there, Gabe, but I think I found a footprint along the softer edge of the dirt near the shrubs. I'll have the forensic guys come by first thing tomorrow morning to see if they can get an impression."

"Male or female?"

"Hard to tell in the dark."

"All right, Roy," Gabe said. "You might as well go home."

Roy nodded, gave Jane a small smile, and went out the way he'd come in, closing the door behind him.

"Now are you willing to listen to me about what happened last night?"

Jane could feel Gabe watching her closely. "Are you saying you think the two incidents are related?"

"I'm not a strong believer in this many coincidences. I've been back in Edenville less than a week, and I've been thrown down a flight of stairs and my house has been broken into. The odds are heavy against two such violent episodes occurring so closely together. And if I also count the day when that car ran me off the road—"

Gabe stiffened so visibly that Jane stopped in midsentence. "What car?"

Jane related the incident that had happened to her as she'd left the Madden estate and headed for Suzanne Lemke's on the morning Jennifer's body was discovered.

Gabe's voice had an unusual sound to it. "Hardesty, why didn't you tell me about this car running you off the road until now?"

"I meant to report it at the time. I guess I just forgot, what with everything else going on." Jane dropped into the nearest chair. She suddenly felt tired, her spirit sapped and drained. "Besides, what good would it have done? I didn't see the car or driver, and even if I had, you're determined not to believe me."

Gabe came over to her chair and knelt down beside it. He took her cold hand in his warm one. "Who said I didn't believe you?"

Her head came up warily at the sudden gentleness in his touch and his voice. "Do you?"

His eyes were calm on her face, cool and soothing, as was the way he stroked the back of her hand with his fingers. "If I wasn't inclined to rely on your perceptions about someone throwing you down those stairs before, I am now. Do you have any idea who could be doing this?"

Jane felt heartened by his belief. "None."

"Has it occurred to you that these assaults against you could have something to do with Jennifer's death?"

Jane straightened, intrigued by his implication. "Are you saying the person who killed Jennifer is after me? But why?"

His tone had picked up a soft, kneading quality. "You know these people on Eden Island. Maybe something you know, something you're not even aware you know, is providing the impetus for these attacks. Think about it. Someone you've talked to since you've been back. Some little slip of the tongue they made?"

His pulse beat into her hand. He felt suddenly like a warm cocoon she snuggled into. Her mind drifted over the contacts she'd made since her return to the Island. Suzanne, Philip, Dorothy, Leo, Jack, Richard, Ellen. Their conversations hovered over her like slow-moving mists. She could almost make out each individual word. But there seemed to be nothing alarming.

Suddenly the clock in the hallway chimed loudly twice, bringing her abruptly out of her trance. She sat up straight, looking around her as though she'd just awakened. Tardily she began to understand what he'd been doing to get information out of her. The damn man was mesmerizing! She pulled her hand away from his, mortified at how he controlled her. Bitterness coated her words. "It's so easy for you, isn't it?"

Easy? Gabe knew that if he continued to remain so close to this maddeningly uncooperative, ravishing woman he was going to either strangle her or make love to her. Feeling his hands aching to circle her neck, he jumped to his feet and stepped quickly to the other side of the room, turning his back.

It was a moment before he faced her again and spoke. "Look, you ninny, I was only trying to get you to search your memory for the answer to who might be after you. Damn it, I'm on your side."

Jane clenched her teeth. "I don't remember anyone saying anything even remotely unusual."

Gabe exhaled a frustrated breath. What she really meant was that she wasn't even trying to remember anymore. He let his tone become demanding again. "Where will you sleep tonight?"

"Upstairs, in my bed."

Gabe jerked a thumb over to the broken window. "Anyone could come through there now. How safe do you think you'd be?"

"I have a lock on my bedroom door. I intend to use it."

"And tomorrow morning, when you unlock it?"

"There's still Mother's gun. I'll sleep with it under my pillow."

"Who were you planning on getting to fix the window?"

"I know a carpenter. I'll call him tomorrow, early. Now that's all the questions I'm going to answer. You responded to the call. You've gathered the information. You've done your duty. Now you can go home."

Gabe looked at her silently for a moment. She was a stubborn, exasperating woman. He ached to grab her and shake some sense into her, but he knew that if he put his hands on her again, shaking her wasn't what he would end up doing. A retreat was definitely in order. "Well, then, there's nothing more to say, Hardesty. Good night."

And with that he walked out of the room and was gone.

Jane felt curiously abandoned at the sound of the front door closing. All her brave talk about spending the night alone upstairs behind locked doors withered away now that the house was empty again and the darkness from the broken window rushed at her. She went over to the desk, picked up her mother's gun and switched off the lamp. On her way out of the study, she shut the door behind her, as though she could shut out the memory of that broken window and the black figure that had come through it. She ascended the stairs quickly, as though pursued, switching off the hall light as soon as she was ready to enter her bedroom. She locked the door securely behind her.

None of it helped. She kicked off her shoes as she lay on the bed, propped up against the headboard, with no thoughts of getting undressed. She grasped the gun in her hand and listened to the night noises that inhabited her house. She'd never realized how many there were of them or how loud they could be.

She heard other sounds, too. The roar of Gabe's anger, his easy laugh, the insistent demand of his questions, the soothing gentleness in his tone as he'd knelt next to her, caressing her hand. The room was cool, but Jane was suddenly perspiring beneath her sweater. It was going to be a long wait for dawn.

WHEN SHE FIRST OPENED her eyes she couldn't imagine why she was sprawled so uncomfortably across her bed, fully dressed. And then the fuzzy steel object misting before her eyes shot into a clear, hard focus, and she recognized the revolver. With it, memory returned, splashing her soberly awake. She shot up in bed.

So she'd slept after all. Light shone brightly through the eastern windows, casting white columns across her mauve carpet. Her eyes darted to the clock radio on the nightstand, and she groaned when she saw that the time was already 7:50. Dorothy Speke was due at eight. She'd overslept.

She jumped off the bed and headed for the bathroom, knowing she didn't have time for a shower, but determined at least to get her face washed and her teeth and hair brushed. She also needed to change. She'd slept in her clothes, and they looked it. She peeled them off and wrapped a robe about her. She'd think about clothes in a minute, but first she needed a cup of coffee. Badly. She unlocked the door to her bedroom and headed downstairs to the kitchen.

She was at the bottom of the stairs, pointed in the direction of the kitchen, when she got her first suspicion that something was wrong. It might have been a sound, a smell. She wasn't sure.

She stopped as her senses stretched before her, looking, listening, waiting. Then, suddenly, it was too late. Strong arms had grabbed her from behind.

Jane's heart stopped, and her muscles froze in fear. It was yesterday morning's nightmare all over again! She tried to scream, but the terror stuck in her throat like a suffocating sponge. He'd come back to kill her! She must fight back. She must not go meekly to her death. She was just planning a vicious kick to her attacker's shins when a surprisingly familiar voice penetrated in her ear.

"It's okay, Hardesty! It's me!"

As proof, Gabe spun her around to face him, still holding on to her shoulders.

Relief washed through Jane, a relief so deep that it left her legs weak. "I was just about to kick you!"

Gabe's strong arms caught her as her knees buckled. He grinned. "I'm glad to see you, too."

Jane tried to rally the strength to push away from him and his absurd sense of humor. "Glad to see me? Damn it, I should kick you anyway for scaring me like that."

"Sorry, Hardesty, but after your telling me you'd be emerging from your room this morning with that .38 in your hands, I thought it would be safer to approach you from behind. After all, even a poor shot like you could get lucky."

Jane wanted to be mad at him, but the look in his eyes was making it very difficult. His arm still circled her shoulders, and his warmth was pulsing through her with every beat of his heart.

She looked wild and windblown this morning, her hair tangled honey, her white cotton robe slightly apart, revealing the luscious curve of her breasts. Her face was free of the last evening's makeup—clear, translucent. And her eyes! Not bland, not cool, but seductive and shadowed. His heartbeat increased, as though to hasten the emptying of the thoughts from his head.

Jane felt life pulsating from him—so much life. He was such a positive force that he left no room for anything else. She saw his look deepen, and she knew he was going to kiss her.

Slowly, tantalizingly, he leaned toward her, his right arm circling her waist, drawing her into him. She knew he was giving her the chance to pull away first, and if she didn't, his look told her, there would be no second chances. There was more than a kiss in his eyes now. Much more.

Her heart was pounding with a new kind of excitement as his face stopped just an inch from hers, their breath mingling, stirring, becoming quicker. Of course she was going to stop him. Soon. But at the moment all she could concentrate on were the silky waves of pure pleasure radiating from where his fingers traced a line from her cheek to her neck and then headed toward the slit in her robe.

The loud blast seemed to come out of nowhere, bouncing off the walls. Within an instant, Jane and Gabe were several feet apart, both having jumped back in alarm. Except Jane now realized it was only the sound of the doorbell they'd heard, and it was only loud because they were standing directly underneath its chime.

"Dorothy Speke," she breathed in tardy remembrance.

Gabe nodded as he replaced the gun he'd drawn back into the side holster beneath his shirt. The visible tension in his body disintegrated into a smile. "Shall I get it, or will you?"

Jane's palms went to the warmth in her cheeks. "Oh, hell! No matter which of us gets it, you know what she's going to think?" Jane could see from Gabe's smile that her protest was a waste of time. The impression they were about to leave on the biggest gossip on Eden Island was obviously one he had intended all along.

Well, there was nothing for it but to answer the door. She tucked her robe around her as primly as possible and charged resolutely forward.

Dorothy Speke raised an eyebrow when she saw Jane answer the door in her bathrobe. Her entire forehead soared for the ceiling when she got a look at Gabe standing behind her.

"Detective Kincaid! My, my, Jane... What a delightful surprise! I told Ellen and Richard that they shouldn't go jumping to conclusions. Why, I knew all the time that you really brought Detective Kincaid to Richard's party because of mutual attraction. I could tell the moment I saw you two looking at each other."

Gabe stepped around Jane and took Dorothy's pudgy hand, amused by the look of dismay that flashed over Jane. "I'm sure few people can fool you, Dorothy. May I call you Dorothy?"

Dorothy beamed as Gabe took her hand. "But of course, Detective!"

"Now, Dorothy... you must call me Gabe, remember?"

Jane was cringing at every word. She could see now that Gabe was even wearing the same tux pants he'd worn the night before, and the same shirt, with the sleeves rolled up and the collar loosened. He hadn't even shaved. Everything about him gave the impression that he'd spent the night.

If there was any way to salvage the situation, she knew she'd best try to take events in hand. She laced her arm through Dorothy's. "Come into the kitchen, Dot. I was just about to have a cup of coffee. Gabe will be happy to wait in the living room, if what you want to discuss with me is private."

Gabe flashed her an irritated look. Jane smiled back sweetly as she led Dorothy toward the kitchen.

"Well, I really hadn't intended on discussing this with anyone but you, Jane. But I suppose since you and Detective Kincaid are so...well...I guess it would be all in the family, so to speak."

Gabe found his smile again. It was Jane's turn to glare. But the glare melted into surprise as she turned the corner into the kitchen and found the coffee already made, the pancake batter mixed, the griddle warmed, and the kitchen counter set for two.

Gabe stepped briskly forward. "Ladies, you sit right here on these bar stools next to the kitchen island, and I'll pour your coffee. Pancakes will be ready in no time." He actually had the nerve to wrap a towel around his lean middle as an apron and then blow Jane a kiss.

Dorothy looked from Gabe to Jane, inhaling every detail for later broadcast. Jane shook her head, knowing there was nothing she could do about it now. After this cozy little domestic scene Gabe had manufactured, it would be impossible for her to convince Dot that Gabe had arrived this morning and not spent the night.

"What was it you wanted to talk to me about?" she prompted, feeling uncomfortable, with things slipping out of her control.

Dorothy leaned toward Jane eagerly as Gabe poured hot coffee into their cups, obviously ready to hang on to every word. "Well, now, I know you couldn't say much last night about Jennifer being murdered, considering Richard was sitting right there and all, but someone did kill her, didn't they?''

Gabe smiled. "You're very observant, Dorothy. How did you suspect?''

"Well, because Jennifer was having an affair, of course.''

Gabe leaned forward, his face a mask of surprised innocence. "She was having an affair?''

Dot's quivering lips were beginning to blow excited little bubbles. "First you've got to promise you won't tell my husband I've talked to you.''

"Are you afraid of what your husband might do?''

"Well, of course! Why else do you think I don't want you to tell him?''

Gabe shook his head. "I mean, are you afraid of what your husband might do to you?''

Dorothy fell back against her bar stool, as though Gabe had struck her. "What he might do to me? Don't be silly. Leo wouldn't do anything to me. But he'd fire Mabel. Jane knows. He's threatened to do it before.''

"And Mabel is?''

"His medical receptionist. For more than twenty years. She's his right hand. But he'd fire her, Detective. Because he gave his word he would. And Leo always keeps his word.''

"Why would he fire Mabel?''

Dorothy moved a little closer to Gabe and lowered her voice just a smidgen. "Well, she talks to me, you see. She shows me things. How can you blame her? Leo practices out of our home, so poor Mabel is cooped up there all day. Day after day. It's only natural, with my being there and all, that we should talk. Leo gets so wrapped up with patients he barely says boo to either of us.''

"And what is it you and Mabel have talked about?'' Gabe asked.

As this was becoming just a two-way conversation and none of it was coming her way, Jane sat back, drank her coffee, and simply listened.

Dorothy lowered her voice even more, as though she were afraid of being overheard. "Well, we tumbled to it just this week. In the early mornings, Leo goes to the hospital to check on patients. It's just Mabel and me at the house then, and that's when we found Jennifer's record on his desk."

"Her patient record?" Gabe asked.

Dorothy blinked. "Well, yes. What other record did you think I was talking about?"

"I just wanted to be sure."

Dorothy waved aside the interruption. "Well, anyway, we noticed Jennifer's record, and it was just too good an opportunity to pass up. Leo generally keeps all his patient records locked up, but he must have been making some notation in Jennifer's file and left it out by mistake. So we took a peek, and what do you think we found?"

"I can't wait to hear," Gabe said honestly.

"Why, her chart clearly indicated that Leo had prescribed birth control pills for her."

"You knew Jennifer Madden was having an affair because your husband prescribed birth control pills for her?"

"Of course. Richard Madden had a vasectomy more than five years ago."

"And you know this because . . ."

"Well, Mabel showed me his record, of course."

"How did Mabel get his record, if, as you say, they are generally locked up?"

"Well, Leo left his file cabinet keys in his desk at the same time he left Jennifer's file out. He was most forgetful that morning."

"I see. Do you have any idea who Jennifer was having this affair with?"

Dorothy licked her lips. "There's been lots of gossip over the last couple of years. Naturally, we tried to find out which one."

Gabe nodded gravely. "Naturally."

If Dorothy caught the underlying sarcasm in Gabe's words, she gave no sign of it. She offered her explanation with the innocent zest of an amateur detective. "Mabel and

I checked the records of all the men on Eden Island to see which ones hadn't had vasectomies. We were only able to narrow it down to about fifteen.''

Gabe tried to keep any emotion out of his voice. "Are you saying there are only fifteen fertile men left on Eden Island?"

"No, of course not. Naturally, I didn't see any of the servants' records. Leo doesn't treat them. And many of the men were traveling in Europe or other parts of the world at the time. So Mabel and I eliminated them."

"Can you give me the names of the fifteen?"

"Well, as a matter of fact . . ."

Jane listened to Dot give the memorized list to Gabe without hesitation. He halted her after the second one to rummage in his pants pockets for a pen and something to write on. He settled for the back of an envelope.

The names came out in alphabetical order. Jack Carver, Philip Lemke and Henry Rowe were among them.

"You know, Dot," Gabe said as he folded his envelope and tucked it back into his pocket, "sometimes I'm told women are given birth control pills to regulate their periods."

Dorothy shook her head. "Not Jennifer. She was as regular as clockwork. It's all in her chart. No. She needed those birth control pills so she wouldn't get caught like she had been last Christmas."

"Caught?"

Dorothy was beginning to look irritated at Gabe's denseness. "You know. Pregnant. I guess she didn't want to go through another abortion."

It took Gabe a moment to compose himself enough to ask Dorothy his next question. "Are you telling me your husband performed an abortion on Jennifer Madden last Christmas?"

Dorothy's eyebrows did a little jig. "December twentieth. Seventy-thirty. Termination at five weeks. No complications."

JANE CLOSED THE DOOR behind Dorothy Speke thirty-five minutes later, after Gabe had insisted she have two helpings of pancakes, complete with syrup and whipped cream. He gave every impression that he was delighted with his duties as chef, and with Dorothy, despite the fact that she continued to call him "Detective."

Jane shook her head when she rejoined Gabe in the kitchen. "Leo knows better than to let Mabel or Dorothy near his patient files. Why did he suddenly leave out both Jennifer's file and the key to the other medical records? What other matter could have been so pressing as to have drawn his attention? I don't understand."

Gabe poured himself another cup of coffee. "And I don't understand why nothing Dorothy Speke just told us checks out."

Jane turned to stare at him. "What?"

Gabe smoothed a wayward lock on his forehead into place as he took the bar stool next to Jane. "I have a copy of Leo Speke's medical records on Jennifer Madden. I reviewed them thoroughly. There's nothing in them to indicate that he prescribed birth control pills for her, or that he performed an abortion on her last year."

Jane frowned. "But how can that be?"

Gabe took a sip of his fresh coffee. "Well, one of the sources is wrong. You tell me which."

Jane's finger circled the edges of her empty plate, capturing a missed golden trail of syrup. She licked it off her finger as she gave his question some thought. "I've never known Dot to lie. She had to have been telling you the truth."

Gabe was momentarily distracted by the way Jane was licking the syrup off her finger. With her, it seemed, the smallest things were beginning to develop erotic overtones. He tried to get a grip on his straying thoughts. "In her malicious busybodying, could she have looked at the wrong woman's file?"

Jane bristled as she sat up straight. "Look, I know Dot's inordinate interest in other people's business isn't laudable, but there's nothing malicious in her intent. Her sons are grown and gone and are always too busy to return her calls. Leo is tied up in his practice and doesn't see her need. She's a life crying out for a reason to continue living. She finds diversion in following her neighbors' activities."

Gabe watched Jane's face. "She could be doing worthwhile volunteer work in the less fortunate community of Edenville."

"She does volunteer work twice a week. And she runs a charity ball each year to raise money for the homeless."

"She obviously still has too much free time on her hands. She could be doing more."

"Yes, and you could be donating your entire salary to the poor. I don't know any saints, Kincaid. Do you?"

She was a staunch defender of a friend—even one with social warts. He liked that in her. He was liking altogether too much in her. "Let's get back to the original question. Could Dot have looked at the wrong woman's file?"

"You heard her rattle off the names of Jennifer's possible partners, alphabetically, with the correct spellings. Did she strike you as a woman who would mistake one file for another?"

"Then Jennifer Madden's medical file has been altered. And, since we can be pretty sure it wasn't Mabel who did it, that just leaves Dr. Leo Speke."

Jane frowned. "Why would Leo alter the file?"

"Good question. At least Dorothy's information has cleared up one puzzle. When I didn't find a prescription on Speke's medical records for the birth control pills in Jennifer's medicine chest, I just assumed she'd gone to another doctor. Looks like I was wrong. I'm going to be very interested to hear what Speke has to say about all this."

Jane shook her head. "It's so hard for me to believe Leo would falsify records. You realize, if you tell him you know about the abortion and the birth control pills, he'll figure out it was Dorothy who told you?"

"Don't worry. I won't get your busybodying friend into trouble. There are other ways to get her husband to spill his guts, and I'm conversant with them all."

Jane saw the look of hard determination that had suddenly descended on his face. Gabe Kincaid would be a formidable opponent. She felt uneasy that he was about to take on Leo. "Look, Kincaid, if Leo changed anything, I know he had a good reason. Please don't—"

Gabe frowned at her. "Running in to champion his cause, too, I see. First Suzanne, then Dorothy, and now Leo. Has it occurred to you, Hardesty, that your opinion might not be too objective on this case? That perhaps your ethics need a bit of addressing?"

His admonition hit a little too close to home for comfort. It put her immediately on the offensive. "My ethics? Who was it who broke into my home this morning?"

"I didn't break in."

"Oh, yes, you did. Entering through a broken window, even if you didn't break it, is still entering without permission."

"I'm aware of that, Hardesty, which is why I didn't come through the window."

That gave her pause. Kincaid might be arrogant and pigheaded, but she couldn't believe he'd lie to her. "If you didn't come in by the window, how did you get in?"

"Simple. I never left. When I walked out of the study last night, I just opened and closed the front door. I didn't exit through it. I went into the living room. I spent the night on the couch." He paused to rub his back. "It's not very comfortable."

"But why?"

"Not long enough. My head and feet hung over the edges."

Jane was irritated by his obvious equivocation. "I wasn't asking about the comfort of the couch, Kincaid. I want to know why you stayed here last night."

He looked at her a long moment before answering. "From the living room couch I could see the door to the study. If anyone had come through the broken window, I was ready for him.''

Jane was stunned by his admission, but even more so by her reaction to it. She felt thrilled, and profoundly feminine. Her voice suddenly seemed to belong to someone else. ''You were protecting me?''

Gabe could hear her surprising vulnerability, could see it shining in her eyes, moistening her lips. He could barely believe the incredible, mind-boggling, defenseless core that had just opened up to him so unexpectedly.

Her face positively glowed with warmth. Her eyes were jade jewels that turned his mind to mush. She was incredibly beautiful, and he wanted her more at that moment than he had ever wanted anything in his life. And he also knew that she was defenseless, his for the taking.

It was crazy, but it was that latter knowledge that halted him in his tracks. With an insight that hit him hard and fast and mostly below the belt, he realized he couldn't take this defenseless Jane Hardesty.

While he still could, he got up from the bar stool and headed for the living room to collect his tuxedo jacket and leave.

She followed. ''Where are you going?''

Gabe's response came out hoarse. He was glad to be able to respond at all. ''To interview Speke, of course.''

''I'm going, too.''

He stopped in the process of putting an arm in a sleeve to look at her. It was a mistake. He counted to ten as he tried to control his desire and his frustration. ''No!''

''Look, it's my case, too, and—''

''And nothing, Hardesty,'' he said as he looked determinedly away and finished putting on his jacket. ''Our deal says you get the reports my department generates. It doesn't give you a right to be in on my interviews.''

''But I included you in Dorothy's visit.''

''You included me? Ha! I had to force the issue, and you know it. Now call that carpenter and get your window fixed. I don't intend to spend another night on that stupid couch, even if a dozen maniacs with hatchets are trying to get to you. Got it?''

And after that bit of warmth and charm, Chief of Detectives Gabe Kincaid stomped out of Jane's house, slamming the door after him.

JANE'S FISTS BALLED as anger drilled up her spine. What a fool she had been to be swayed into thinking his staying over the night before had had anything to do with genuine care or concern for her. The man was a self-centered, arrogant, pigheaded jerk!

Yet there had been that one moment when he'd looked into her eyes and when she'd thought she saw— No! Impossible! She'd only been deluding herself into seeing what she wanted to see.

Wanted to see?

Jane sank into the living room couch, remembering that this was where he had slept the night before. She leaned down to sniff it, and felt disappointed when she couldn't detect even the faintest impression of his lingering scent. She spread a hand over the soft fabric, then lay on top of it. Her head and feet hung uncomfortably over the armrests. Gabe had an additional five inches on her. It must have been hell for him.

Perversely, the thought made her both sad and glad.

"I APPRECIATE your coming in, Dr. Speke. Since you saw Naomi Parisot in the waiting room, perhaps you know why I asked you down?"

Leo Speke's large, dark eyes stared at Gabe. They were like two endless tunnels. "I don't follow you, Kincaid."

"Well, then, perhaps I should explain. You see, a woman like Jennifer Madden, coming from a very different lifestyle than that led on Eden Island, not always feeling like she fit in, sometimes probably needed to talk to someone who could understand what it's like to have different roots. So, although they were employer and employee...Jennifer Madden and Naomi Parisot exchanging confidences—well,

I think you can appreciate how natural that would have been.''

Leo Speke scraped his palms across his pants.

Gabe leaned back in his chair. "So, Doctor, considering what Mrs. Parisot has told us about some of the more private concerns of Jennifer Madden, I thought it only fair that I give you an opportunity to tell us your side."

Speke's eyes rushed around Gabe's blank white office walls as though he were hoping to find some answers written on them.

"Doctor?"

"If Mrs. Parisot has said something that concerns— You are aware doctor-patient confidences are protected?"

"Doctor, Jennifer Madden is dead. Surely you're aware the doctor-patient confidence does not apply to the deceased?"

Speke shook his head. "It's not that simple. No one lives in isolation."

Gabe got up and circled his desk to sit on the edge in front of Speke. "Are you saying you're hesitant to discuss matters concerning Jennifer Madden because those matters involve others?"

"Not just some vague 'others.' Jennifer's life revolved around the inhabitants of Eden Island, my patients. To relate the more... intimate details of her life would be to expose details in the lives of others. I do not have that right."

Speke's mouth drew tight. Gabe watched it for a moment before he moved off the edge of his desk and began to pace. "Naturally, I can appreciate your reluctance, Doctor, but it's not like you're going to be telling us something we don't already know, is it?"

Speke swallowed. "You know?"

"About Jennifer's lovers, yes."

The moisture seemed to dry in Speke's large eyes. "You can't expect me to—"

"You performed an abortion on Jennifer last Christmas. Was that the first one?"

Speke's Adam's apple began to resemble an up-and-down elevator. "It was a perfectly safe and legal procedure."

"I'm not doubting it, Doctor. I repeat—was it the first one?"

"Yes."

"A bit unusual, wasn't it?"

"I don't know what that's supposed to mean."

Gabe put on one of his nicest smiles. "Well, there is the fact that Jennifer's abortion was nowhere in the medical records you submitted to my office. And Richard Madden obviously couldn't have been the father, since he shoots blanks. Now, Doctor, I don't have to tell you that making false statements and supplying false records to the sheriff's office is illegal, do I?"

Sweat leaked onto Speke's brow. Gabe moved a box of tissues toward the man. He waited as Speke wiped his face and hands.

"Richard Madden is my neighbor and friend. We've known each other more than thirty years. But all those considerations had to be put aside when a patient's trust and confidence were at stake. I've taken an oath. I didn't really have a choice. You see that, don't you?"

"Doctor, are you saying that you performed the abortion on Jennifer without her husband's knowledge?"

Speke took some more tissue. "Jennifer came to me in confidence. As her doctor, I could not betray that confidence."

"Not even after she died?"

Speke wiped his brow again. "All right. I erased that information from the copy of her file I sent to you. Did I do such a terrible thing? Richard had just lost his wife. Did he need to lose his happy memories of her, too?"

"And the information about the birth control pills you prescribed for her?"

"Again, a simple erasure from her chart. These things had nothing to do with her death. Why should they be allowed to infect the lives of those left behind?"

"Doctor, identifying what relates to Jennifer Madden's death is not your decision to make."

Speke folded his arms across his chest. "All right, prosecute me for these acts if you must. If saving a friend from pain and humiliation is a crime, then I'm guilty."

"Is that all you were saving Richard Madden from, Doctor?"

Speke sat up straight and tall for once. "What does that question mean?"

"Did Richard Madden love his wife?"

"Of course he loved her."

"Was he jealous of her?"

A cloud descended over Speke's countenance. "Well, naturally, a man Richard's age with a much younger wife—"

"Is Richard Madden a jealous man?"

Speke's lips drew into a tight line. Gabe slipped back onto the edge of the desk in front of the man's chair and leaned into his face, his voice barely above a whisper.

"Doctor, what you say now could keep you out of jail. Choose your words very carefully."

Speke unfolded his arms as he exhaled his answer. "Yes."

Gabe leaned back and crossed his arms. "Tell me about it."

Speke fidgeted in his chair as he wiped his brow again. "It was last July. Richard had invited us over for a luncheon meeting."

"Us?"

"Jack Carver, Henry Rowe, Philip Lemke and myself."

"Why you four?"

"We're all involved in arranging support and financial backing for candidates to public office. We were going over some names Richard had proposed, when suddenly Jennifer came breezing in to say hello, and Richard blew up."

"Why?"

"It was a hot day. She'd been swimming nude in the outdoor pool. She hadn't bothered to put anything on when she came back into the house."

"So she was naked when she walked in on this meeting?"

"Not a stitch."

"And Richard was upset?"

Speke paused to wipe his brow again. "He got up from the table and dragged her into the next room. They got into a screaming fight. The door was open, so we couldn't help but hear."

"What was said?"

"Naturally, after all this time, I can't remember every word that was—"

"Give me the gist of it, Doctor."

Speke squirmed some more in his chair. "Richard demanded an explanation for Jennifer's behavior and she screamed that she owed him none. There was some back-and-forth where he insisted she act more circumspect and she told him she'd act any way she pleased. Then Richard issued his threat."

"And that was?"

"He told her if he ever caught her fooling around with another man he'd kill her. And then the other man."

"What did Jennifer say?"

"I don't think she said anything. At least if she did, she didn't say it loud enough for us to hear. The next thing we knew, another door had slammed, and Richard came walking through the one that had been left ajar and sat down to resume where we had left off."

"He didn't refer to the argument? Seem upset?"

"Richard can . . . hide his feelings quite well at times."

"And six months later you performed an abortion on Jennifer. Doesn't look like she took her husband's threat very seriously. Maybe her lover did."

Speke's large eyes saucered. "You don't think that he—"

"Who was Jennifer's lover, Doctor?"

Speke gulped. "I never asked. It was none of my business."

"But it was your business to later falsify Jennifer Madden's medical records. Were you afraid of what Richard

Madden might do if he had the evidence of his wife's betrayal?''

"I—"

"Well, Doctor, did you think he might carry out his threat and go after Jennifer's lover?"

Speke clamped his mouth shut. As far as Gabe was concerned, that was as big a yes as he'd ever gotten.

Chapter Ten

"Trying to save money by pumping your own gas?" Philip Lemke's voice asked from behind Jane. She turned, realizing that the noise from the gasoline pump must have drowned out his approach.

"I've always pumped my own, Philip. Don't tell me you've given the chauffeur the day off and come here to fill up the limo?"

Philip stared at her face a moment, a strange, jumping anxiety lighting his eyes. "I saw you as we were driving by and asked him to stop. I wanted to talk to you."

Jane turned away, toward her car, suddenly sure she didn't want to have this conversation.

Philip didn't take the hint. "You know, don't you?"

Jane felt the gas hose bounce in her palm, signaling that her gas tank was full. She extracted the nozzle from the tank.

Lemke persisted. "You dropped that ice cream on my lap last night because of Jennifer, didn't you?"

Jane didn't like being shoved into a conversational corner. But she was determined that whoever did the shoving would find she was capable of coming out swinging. She glanced over at the impeccably dressed man beside her as she replaced the gas hose in the station pump. "What do you think, Philip?"

Lemke wiped his mouth with a nervous hand. "It's not what you imagine, Jane. Actually, it all began quite innocently. She had just dropped by my office to—"

Jane deliberately interrupted. "Suzanne's the one you should be having this conversation with, Philip. Not me."

Philip suddenly grabbed her arm. "I love Suzanne. You've got to believe me. I wouldn't do anything to hurt her. I'm trying to protect her."

Jane tore her arm from Philip's grasp. She hated being manhandled, and particularly by this man. "Your assurances come right off the old philandering husband's cue cards, Philip."

Lemke took a step back as though he'd been struck. His tone turned indignant. "You can't condemn me just because I cared for Jennifer. My feelings for Suzanne haven't changed."

"Look, Philip, Suzanne is my friend. You're not going to get absolution from me for your sins against her, so why are we even having this conversation? No doubt it's as distasteful to you as it is to me. I repeat—if you must talk with someone, talk with Suzanne. This is none of my business."

Something like relief sifted into Philip's eyes. "Then you won't say anything to Suzanne or Kincaid?"

Jane's brow furrowed. "Is that what this is all about? You had your chauffeur stop your car and you came over here just so you could try to talk me into being silent about your affair with Jennifer?"

Philip's face shoved backward into a double-chin square. "I'm not a man who has affairs. My feelings for Jennifer . . . well, they went beyond the superficiality of an affair. Still, I know my duty to my wife. That's why I fully intended to break it off when I went to see her that night—"

Philip stopped in midsentence, his rapidly reddening visage telling Jane he'd clearly said more than he meant to.

"You went to see Jennifer Madden on the night of her death?"

Philip stepped back quickly. "I didn't say that. You didn't hear me say that. I must go. You'll keep this to yourself. If you don't, Suzanne will get hurt, and I know you won't do that to her. We have to think of her now. I must hurry."

And hurry he did. He literally ran back to his waiting limousine.

"You may go now, Mrs. Parisot," Gabe said, bending next to her seated figure.

Naomi Parisot rose on her sturdy orthopedic shoes, her fleshy elbow impaling her purse to her side as the beam from her flashlight eyes focused in on Gabe. "What nonsense is this? First you tell me to come down here. Then you keep me waiting for forty minutes, and now you just tell me to go home without even talking to me?"

"I am sorry for the inconvenience, Mrs. Parisot. But you have been most helpful, believe me. Do you need transportation back?"

"I have my own car," Mrs. Parisot informed him curtly as she turned to go.

Gabe was just about to head back to his office when the desk clerk beckoned him to the phone.

"Kincaid here."

"It's me—Hardesty. I just spoke to Philip Lemke. He went to see Jennifer on the night of her death."

New possibilities flew in elliptical orbits through Gabe's charged cells. "He told you this?"

"Not intentionally."

"You think he killed her?"

"No, I don't. But since he went to see her that night, he might have seen something."

Gabe's free hand scratched the back of his neck. "It appears it's time that Philip Lemke and I had a little talk."

"Our relationship has just hit an all-time low, but if you really want some straight answers out of him, you'd best include me. It would be hard for him to lie his way out of what he admitted to me face-to-face."

Gabe realized she was probably right. Without her in the room to confront Lemke, he doubted he'd get anything out of the politically rehearsed man at all.

"All right, Hardesty. Where would he be about this time?"

"His limo was heading for his offices in Edenville."

"Meet me there in thirty minutes."

JANE WAS JUST OPENING the door to leave when she started as she found Ellen Rowe on her doorstep, staring her in the face.

"Sorry, Jane. Didn't mean to startle you. I see you're going out, but can you spare me a minute?"

Jane decided she'd rather be late than give up this opportunity. She stepped aside to let Ellen Rowe pass.

"May I get you something to drink?" she asked, as Ellen swept onto her living room couch in a graceful wave.

"No. I'm fine. Good of you to see me on such short notice. I just happened to be driving by."

Ellen Rowe had never struck Jane as anything but confident. But today, despite the characteristic ease of her movements and smile, there was a popping-corn nervousness in the movement of her eyes.

Jane chose her words carefully. "The last time we saw each other, I didn't have the impression you'd be seeking out my company again so soon."

Ellen waved a gloved hand dismissively. "I interpreted your bringing Kincaid to Richard's party wrongly, Jane. It never occurred to me— Well, it should have, I suppose. He's quite a handsome hunk. I've had a few like him, uh, cloud my judgment from time to time."

It was obvious from Ellen's comments that Dorothy's grapevine had been squeezing the juice out of her knowledge of Gabe's stay at Jane's place the evening before. Confirmation of their relationship had no doubt reached every ear on Eden Island by now.

"One of his deputies is outside watching your house, you know. I saw him when I drove up."

Jane felt surprise at Ellen's news, and a few other emotions. She tried to ignore them all for the present and respond in what she hoped was a reasonable tone. "I had a

prowler last night. Detective Kincaid's men were here earlier making a cast from a shoe print he left.''

There was no denying the shocked surprise that news
brought to the woman's face. But Jane could have sworn it
was a delighted surprise that laced Ellen's words. ''A
prowler! How extraordinary!''

Jane glanced at her watch. ''I don't mean to be rude,
Ellen, but I do have to leave shortly. What was it you came
to discuss?''

''I haven't come to discuss anything, Jane. I told you. I
was just driving by. I thought we might get together for
lunch next week. A lot has been going on with your island
neighbors during the time you've been away. You should be
brought up to date.''

Jane watched her guest closely. ''What day would you be
free?''

''What day?'' Ellen searched unconvincingly through her
handbag. ''Oh, I seem to have left my appointment calen-
dar back at the office. I'll have to check it and let you
know.''

Jane knew Ellen Rowe hadn't ''dropped by'' to invite her
out to lunch. Despite the dry, contrite lift to her lips, the
underlying tones of oily subterfuge rolled through.

''My throat does seem to be getting a bit dry, Jane. Join
me in a drink?''

''I'm not thirsty. What can I get you?''

''Maybe a glass of water, if it's not too much trouble?''

Jane got up to get Ellen Rowe some water for her perfectly moist throat. Ellen took a perfunctory sip. ''It was a
regrettable incident between Henry and Kincaid last night.''

''Is that what Henry called it?'' Jane asked.

Ellen took another quick gulp of water. Jane was sure that
if the glass had been filled with milk the woman's anxiety
would have curdled it. ''Did Kincaid say anything about it
after you left?''

''Like what, Ellen?''

The tiny lines around Ellen Rowe's cloudy gray eyes and
expertly outlined coral lips deepened. ''Henry told me he'd

taken Kincaid to task regarding some badly prepared court evidence for a past case that resulted in a guilty man going free. Is it true that's what their conversation was about?''

Ellen's anxiety was like a hungry vacuum, sucking up the room's air. Jane had never liked Ellen all that much, but at the moment she felt sorry for her. Was this the real reason the woman had come to see her?

"Jane? Did you hear me?''

"You didn't believe your husband's explanation?''

Ellen's smile was tight. "We've been married a lot of years. I always can tell when Henry's lying. So what were they really discussing?''

Jane took a breath. "Your husband became very angry when Gabe did not address him in what he thought was a respectful manner. He demanded Gabe leave.''

Ellen's tongue darted out to lick her rapidly caking lipstick. "That's all it was?''

"Well, sometimes when people have been drinking, you know, they can take normally harmless remarks and escalate them out of proportion.''

Ellen's sharp eyes dissected Jane's face so well that Jane felt her skin tingle. The woman didn't believe her. Not for an instant.

Ellen stood. "Well, I guess I'd best be on my way. I'll call you to schedule next week's lunch.''

But Jane knew as Ellen Rowe exited her front door that the bogus appointment for the next week would never be made.

"YOU'RE LATE,'' Gabe said as he opened the door to Philip Lemke's law offices for Jane.

"I had a surprise visitor.''

Gabe nodded. "Ellen Rowe.''

Jane sought his eyes. "So you are having me watched?''

Gabe looked away. "After three attempts on your life, Hardesty, what did you expect? Come on, let's get on with this.''

They had approached the secretary's desk. Gabe refocused his attention as he gave the secretary his name and produced his badge. When Philip Lemke's secretary gave them the nod to go in five minutes later, Philip's face fell when he saw Jane by Gabe's side.

He stood nervously behind his desk. "I agreed to see you, Kincaid. Not her. She's the only reason you're here, isn't she?"

Gabe settled in his chair. "No, Mr. Lemke. Your involvement with the dead woman and your false statement to my office concerning your whereabouts on the night of Mrs. Madden's death are the reasons I'm here. Would it surprise you to hear we found your prints in her bedroom?"

Lemke stood very straight and still for a moment before his shoulders slumped and he slowly sank into his chair.

Gabe motioned for Jane to be seated. As soon as she was he leaned forward. "Let's get to it, then. Did you see Jennifer Madden on the night of her death?"

Lemke's eyes rushed around the room, as if he were looking for a place to hide. Gabe saw the red creeping up the man's neck as his glance alighted on Jane. He looked like a trapped animal, and no doubt he considered Jane the trapper.

"Understand, Mr. Lemke. I'm willing to keep this interview off the record, providing you're candid with me. But only if you're honest with me."

The watery eyes blinked and then refocused on Gabe's face. "All right. But this conversation mustn't go beyond this room. Do I have your word?"

"My profession is law enforcement, not journalism. If you haven't committed a crime, you've nothing to worry about."

Lemke squinted at Gabe as he chewed his lip for a minute. Then he exhaled in partial defeat, as though he realized the offer wasn't going to get any better.

"Jennifer asked me to come by at nine. Richard was at a meeting in Seattle. She knew he'd be gone all night."

"So you went to her place around nine for a romantic rendezvous?"

"I couldn't get there that early. I had to have dinner first at the house and then make a detour here to the office to leave my briefcase and make sure my line would be busy if anyone called. I'd told Suzanne I had a late, confidential meeting with a client and I didn't want to be disturbed, but wives can be unpredictable. Suzanne had called me late at the office before. I couldn't risk her doing it again."

Gabe ignored Lemke's attempt at a male-bonding smile. "So what time did you reach Jennifer's?"

The smile withered on Lemke's face. "It was just after ten."

"She let you in?"

"No. She'd told me she would open the security gate at nine."

"Was it open?"

"No. And no one answered when I buzzed on the intercom."

"So what did you do?"

"I was late. I thought she might have gotten mad and closed the gate. I parked my car in front of it and walked the quarter mile up to the house. The front door was unlocked, as she'd promised. I could hear noises from upstairs and see the light on in her bedroom. I went up."

Lemke's voice had dropped, become almost leaden. Jane found herself nervously clasping the arms of her chair as he continued.

"The stereo by the bed was blasting out this loud rock noise. I called out for her. She didn't answer. I couldn't think with all that racket going on, so I walked over to the stereo and switched it off. That was when I became aware of her perfume."

Lemke's eyes dropped to his clasped hands on the desk. "Suddenly it was everywhere, and it was wonderful. It was then I knew she wanted me, late or not. I hurried into her dressing room."

Lemke's voice began to tremble. "She was lying on the carpet. I called out her name. I knelt before her and put my head to her chest, but she had no heartbeat. I knew then she was dead."

Lemke raised his eyes to Gabe's, tears squishing at their corners. His voice broke. "She was so beautiful. I told myself that after I'd had her, I'd be able to forget her. But I had to have her again and again. I couldn't help myself."

Then the dignified candidate for the state senate threw his arms onto his desk and buried his head, sobbing like a baby.

After several uncomfortable minutes, Lemke finally slumped back in his chair, a woebegone expression on his face.

Jane leaned forward. "Philip, you told me earlier today that you were going to see Jennifer on the night of her death to put an end to the relationship. What you've just described as your actions and feelings on the evening in question don't sound like you were ready to call anything off."

"But I was!" Lemke almost shouted as his body shot forward. "I had told Jennifer for the entire six weeks of our affair that it must end. And when she called to invite me over that night, I told her it had to be the last time I'd see her. We couldn't risk it again. Not with the election coming up and the possibility that Richard might discover us at any time."

"Are you saying that it was Jennifer who kept insisting the affair go on?"

"Yes, yes! She was insatiable! Just couldn't get enough! You can't imagine what it was like!"

Jane leaned back. She'd heard enough. Philip might be fooling himself about his desire to end that affair, but he wasn't fooling her.

Gabe was the next to address Lemke. "What did you do after finding Jennifer dead?"

"I left."

"You found your lover dead and you just left?"

The man straightened. "I couldn't be found there! I had no idea her death was anything other than natural. I couldn't be involved. I had to think of my wife! She had to be protected!''

Jane had no doubts about who Philip was really trying to protect.

Gabe leaned back in his chair. "Where did you go then?"

"Back to the office. I telephoned Suzanne, telling her I was too bushed to drive home after my meeting, so I was just going to sleep on the office couch. I was too upset to face her then. Most of the night I just paced up and down. Finally I fell asleep on the couch, and the next thing I knew it was the following morning and my secretary was waking me.''

Gabe clicked his pen. "All right. So we have the night of Jennifer's death cleared up. Now, Mr. Lemke, I want to take you back to last July. You were at Richard Madden's home, along with Leo Speke, Jack Carver and Henry Rowe. Do you remember?''

Lemke looked at Gabe blankly, despite the warming glow of perspiration that played along his skin. "The four of us have been at Richard's home many times.''

Jane didn't know what this was leading to, but she sensed Philip's attempt at subterfuge. So, apparently, did Gabe. "You know the precise incident I'm referring to, Mr. Lemke. I don't see much point in your pretending not to, do you?''

Philip's eyes flashed resentfully. He shoved his words out with a frank vehemence. "All right. Jennifer came in wet and nude from the pool. She was glistening all over. She was the most beautiful woman I'd ever seen. Is that what you wanted to hear?''

Philip couldn't keep up his vengeful frankness. A moment later his face was decaying into a look of self-pitying longing.

"What happened after she came in that way?" Gabe asked.

Lemke leaned back as his shoulders slumped again. "Richard grabbed her arm and herded her into the next room.''

"Then what?"

"He yelled at her. She yelled back. It wasn't like any of us were trying to eavesdrop."

"What did they yell?"

"What you might expect. He made it obvious he didn't like her behavior. She in turn made it obvious she didn't care."

"And then?"

"It got a little rawer. He told her if she was unfaithful, he'd kill her and her lover. She slammed a door in his face, and he came back into the room with us."

Gabe stared directly into Lemke's eyes. "He said if she was unfaithful he'd kill her and then the man?"

"Yes. He said it just before she slammed the door. 'I'll kill you and any bastard who touches you.' Those were his words. Then he walked back into our room and sat down to discuss a fund-raiser, just as cool as you please."

"You resent that in him," Jane said quietly.

Philip turned wide eyes to her. "All right, yes, when it came to Jennifer, I did. She deserved a younger, more physically able man, not one whose juices were all dried up."

"You mean she deserved you," Jane said.

Philip waved his hand as though he were batting a buzzing insect. "I knew it couldn't last. But she was mine for a little while, at least."

Gabe was quiet a moment, leaning back in his chair. "Didn't you take Richard Madden's threat seriously, Mr. Lemke?"

Philip looked down at his hands again. Jane could tell the self-pity was on the rise again. "I told you, I couldn't help myself. I was hooked. If you had met Jennifer—"

"That wasn't the question I asked, Mr. Lemke. I repeat, didn't you take Richard Madden's threat seriously?"

Lemke looked up at Gabe, flecks of fright darting in his eyes. "Only a fool wouldn't take Richard Madden seriously. But Jennifer and I were careful. He didn't find out. He doesn't have to now, does he? Please?"

JANE WALKED alongside Gabe as they headed for their cars in the law firm's parking lot. "Nothing in Roy's reports mentioned anything about Lemke's fingerprints being found in Jennifer's dressing room."

"That's because the prints we lifted were too smudged for an ID."

"But you told Philip—"

"I didn't say we'd found his prints there. I asked him what he would say if I told him we'd found his prints there. His guilty conscience did the rest."

Jane nodded appreciatively. "How did you know about that July incident where Richard and Jennifer argued?"

"A little doctor told me."

Jane couldn't help portray her surprise. "Leo?"

"Only little doctor I know. What is your relationship with Jack Carver?"

"He was after my mother the entire time I was growing up—not that it did him any good. Why do you ask?"

"Would he see you if you called?"

"Probably. It seems my Eden Island neighbors feel a bit more neighborly toward me today, since Dorothy has spread the word that you and I spent the night together. They take that to mean that my bringing you to Richard's last night was only a faulty judgment call due to my attraction for you."

Gabe smiled at the edge of mockery in her voice.

"Glad I could be of assistance. I suppose their attitude toward me hasn't changed?"

"I wouldn't think so. No doubt they think you're just using me to spy on them, which of course, happens to be true. Why do you want me to see Carver?"

"I want to come along and talk to him."

Jane stole a glance at Gabe's profile. "You want to question him next about Jennifer and Richard's argument last year?"

"Good guess. There's a telephone over there. Let's see if he's home."

Jack Carver was indeed home, and he took her call straightaway.

"Jack, I have some questions about Jennifer Madden I'd really appreciate your help with. Can I come by now?"

There was a slight hesitation on the other end of the line. Jane felt the tension in her hand as she squeezed the telephone receiver. "All right, Jane. I have a meeting in about an hour, but I can spare you a few moments before then. I'll alert the servants."

Jane thanked Carver and hung up the phone. She turned to Gabe. "He'll see me, although your presence will no doubt be an unwelcome surprise. I'm beginning to feel guilty about using my friendships this way."

Gabe draped a companionable arm across her shoulder as they headed back toward the cars. Jane could feel her whole body warming to him until she put a tight, conscious halt on her runaway emotions. "All part of the job, Hardesty. When you're after a killer, you use everything you've got and everybody you know. Since he's expecting you, we'll take your car."

Jane nodded as they walked toward her car in the parking lot, his words echoing in her ears: *You use everybody you know.* That's all he was doing with her—using her. She had to keep reminding herself of that.

While on their way to the Carver estate, Gabe filled her in on his interview with Leo Speke.

She shook a disbelieving head. "Amazing the lengths he went to to protect Richard. I'm also amazed that Leo told you so much. He's normally very discreet."

"Well, we detectives have our ways. Still, there were two other people at that meeting, and I'd like to know how they react to the subject matter."

"Judge Henry Rowe and Jack Carver. Did you try to get an appointment to see Rowe?"

"Yes, and I was turned down flat. I didn't even get past Carver's maid to make my request. Catching him off guard this way is the only thing that will work. You're definitely coming in handy, Hardesty."

Jane sighed, absurdly flattered.

THE CARVER ESTATE was a modern, triangular-shaped affair with rising columns of black slate and glass. Although it was not even half as large as the Madden mansion, its bold architecture lent it an unique distinction. Jane had always been impressed by its clean lines and the beautiful blooms of the cultivated crimson rhododendrons that showed the way to the door like a red carpet laid out for royalty.

A neat middle-aged woman guided their way to where Jack Carver waited, in a bold, high-ceiling room of red, white and black with brass accent pieces. Carver was standing next to a slate fireplace that absorbed the room's light and glowed in its own rich, shadow shade.

Carver came forward to take her hand, and Jane noted a quick dart of irritation in his eyes when he saw Gabe. "Well, Jane, I didn't expect you to be accompanied by Detective Kincaid. You should have told me."

Jane held her chin up high and poised as she clasped Jack's hand in a firm shake. "But then you wouldn't have seen me, Jack, and this is very important. I need your help."

Gabe had to admit that Jane was handling the difficult situation well. Her voice held just the right blend of forthright professionalism and personal entreaty. It would have taken a man with far less polish and ego than Jack Carver to refuse her. Carver shrugged as he released her hand and beckoned her to a chair.

Gabe took a second deep black-leather chair, a twin to the one Carver offered Jane. Carver settled on an adjacent zebra-patterned couch.

"So what can I help you with, Jane?"

Jane's voice was relaxed, conversational and yet still had that confident edge of a woman with a focus. "Jack, as you know, I never met Jennifer Madden. Yet part of my job as deputy coroner is to learn as much as I can about the victim of a suspicious death. I need you to tell me what you know about her."

Despite the mild look on Jack Carver's face, Jane could see his hands beginning to make nervous little traces over the black stripe of the couch. "Why don't you ask Richard?"

"I would, Jack, except that I didn't want to dwell on the subject with him so soon after her death. You understand?"

It was a question that had only one answer. Jack shifted his position uncomfortably as he began to finger the pinkie ring on his right finger. "I didn't know her well."

"Did you meet her before she married Richard?"

"Yes. A couple of months before. We had dinner together. My ex-wife and myself, Richard and Jennifer."

"What did you think of her?"

Jack smirked. "She proved a little too much for my ex-wife."

Jane sat forward. "How do you mean?"

"She was wearing this see-through, sequined thing. And all these diamonds and rubies about her throat and arms. I have an eye for a good gem, and these were the best. All from Richard, of course. And on that fabulous body, well, no man in the place could keep his eyes off her. Made my ex, and all the other women there, seem to fade away into nonexistence. Jennifer knew it, too. And she sort of reveled in it."

"Reveled in it?"

"Flaunted herself. The way she'd look at you. Her gestures. Her laugh. She was like a siren calling men to her."

"Did she call you, Jack?"

Jack's practiced smile spread across his lips. "Of course. But my wife was next to me, and Richard was sitting across from me. In those kinds of shark-infested waters, only a fool would have swum ahead."

"So you never had an affair with Jennifer?"

Carver's gray eyebrows rose. "Jane, I'm surprised at your asking such a thing."

Jane didn't think Jack Carver looked surprised at all, but she let it pass. Getting an honest answer to that question wasn't likely. "Didn't Richard resent Jennifer flaunting herself?"

"He saw all the men drooling over her and knew he was the only one who could have her. Men get turned on knowing they possess such a beautiful woman that other men desire."

"But later he didn't like it, did he?"

Carver's index finger began to tap. "Later? What do you mean?"

"I was referring to the argument between Richard and Jennifer last July. The one where he threatened to kill her and any lover she might take."

A careful mask descended over Carver's face. "Last July?"

Jane wasn't fooled by Jack's apparent loss of memory. But she knew it couldn't last after her next pointed description. "Jennifer came in nude from swimming. Walked right into the room where you, Henry Rowe, Philip Lemke, Leo Speke and Richard were meeting to discuss political candidates."

Carver's fingers began to drum a disturbed beat against the couch cushions. His face remained an impenetrable mask. Jane leaned forward. "I respect your desire to protect Richard. But surely you realize we already know she provoked him?"

"He grabbed her, twisted her arm!"

The words had come out rushed, angry, before they could be censored. For the first time in the interview, a flash of discomfort shot through Jack's eyes. Then the practiced smile claimed his features once again. "She was an exhibitionist. It was in her blood and every bone of her body. She never pretended to be anything else. Everyone understood that."

"But Richard didn't seem too tolerant of her exhibitionism that day. He threatened to kill her."

"He didn't mean what he said."

"So you didn't take his threat seriously?"

Jack waved a ring-encrusted hand. "What threat? That business about Jennifer taking a lover? That was all nonsense. Jennifer was a tease. Richard knew she got a kick out of being scolded. Hell, he knew she wasn't an Eden Island blue blood. He got her out of a strip joint, for Pete's sake."

"Yes, he did, didn't he? Why would Senator Richard Madden of staunch Eden Island lineage marry a striptease dancer, Jack?"

Jack's hand had begun to beat out a rumba on the fabric of the couch. "Richard isn't nearly the stuffed shirt you make him out to be, Jane. Oh, he was careful with his first marriage, but that was because he had political aspirations and being in front of the public eye required a circumspect family life. But once the affair with Jennifer became known, and he lost the election and then Margaret died, well, his political career was over."

"So it was safe to marry a poor Indian?" Gabe asked.

Jack's biting brown eyes darted toward Gabe, just a trifle too fast. "Where did you—"

Gabe smiled. "Her birth record."

"Why are you bringing up her Indian heritage? It has nothing to do with anything."

Jane noted Jack's suddenly antagonistic tone with surprise. Despite his denial, Jennifer's Indian heritage apparently did have something to do with something. "What is it, Jack? What's wrong?"

Jack looked at Jane as though she'd just cussed in church. Slowly, with infinite care, his features relaxed. "Nothing's wrong, Jane. What is so unusual about Richard marrying a beautiful Indian? He's always been for Indian rights. Why, he was the chief proponent for the restoration of lands to the Indians that were deeded to the tribes centuries ago."

Jane could see Jack's political mask settle firmly back in place on his chunky face. "Yes, I remember it was in a passionate plea to restore those lands that I first saw Richard display emotion. Jack, he hides his emotions quite well sometimes. Do you suppose he's really in pain over Jennifer's death?"

"He has to be. She was—" Jack stopped himself. "She was his wife, after all," he finished with far less emotion than Jane sensed lay beneath his controlled countenance.

Carver got to his feet. "You'd best leave now. I must make my meeting."

JANE ONLY WAITED until they got into her car in the driveway of the Carver estate before asking the question that was foremost in her mind. "You think he was having an affair with Jennifer, too?"

"I'd bet on it," Gabe said. "Did you catch the anger when he talked about Richard grabbing Jennifer? It was positively seething."

"Yes. Jennifer Madden seems to have left quite an impression on the men in her life." Jane started the Talbot's engine, heading them down Carver's private lane toward Paradise Road.

Gabe raised his hand as he counted off his fingers. "Well, that makes two confirmed: future senator Philip Lemke, and now state party chairman Jack Carver. And probably Judge Henry Rowe, and for all we know, these other two digits have names, too. The lady certainly got around, although I can't say much for her taste."

Jane shook her head. "Frankly, I'm amazed any of these men would take the chance of sleeping with Jennifer. They all heard Richard's threat, and no matter how much Jack tried to mitigate the intent, they must all know Richard well enough to realize he doesn't make idle threats."

Gabe considered Jane's words for a moment before responding. "There are a lot of men who believe a dangerous liaison adds spice to an affair. And you've got to admit, Jennifer spelled danger."

"Still, since Jennifer's death, those three men must be walking on eggshells around Richard. I wonder which one Richard suspects?"

Gabe flashed Jane a meaningful look. "Of sleeping with her or of killing her?"

"You think one of her lovers could have killed her?"

"Well, as you mentioned, sleeping with Madden's wife wasn't exactly a bright thing to do. Jealousy, lust, desperation, frustration, fear—there are a lot of emotions that can come into play under such an arrangement. It wouldn't have been too unusual for one of them to get out of hand. What can you tell me about Carver?"

"In terms of background, not much. He was born into a wealthy Eden Island family. He graduated from Harvard Law. His father was party leader and groomed Jack for the role. When his father retired, Jack took over."

"How does one get prepared to become a party leader?"

"Learn where the money is and befriend it."

"And, naturally, that means befriend Madden."

"Naturally. Where do we go from here?"

"I wish to hell I could get to Henry Rowe about now."

"That reminds me," Jane said. "I think Ellen Rowe's reason for dropping by was to pump me about your disagreement with her husband last night."

"So what did you tell her?"

"Only that Henry Rowe got angry because of the way you addressed him. She didn't believe me. Rowe had told her the argument was over some mismanaged evidence in a trial. She didn't believe him, either."

Gabe's eyebrows rose. "So Henry lied to Ellen about our fight? That makes me more convinced than ever that Henry and Jennifer had something going. Forget about taking me back to Lemke's. Drive me directly to the station."

"You've decided something, haven't you?"

"Yes. I've decided to talk to the sheriff and get the official investigative shackles off. If Andy wants me to stay on this job, he's going to have to let me do it. Step on it, Hardesty."

THEY WERE ENTERING the sheriff's station when Karl Daly waved at them from across the street, in front of the coroner's office. They halted and watched the thin, bald man sprint across the intersection between cars. He quickly caught his breath, shoving his glasses back on his beaky nose as he approached them.

"Jane, I've been looking for you. The toxicology results just came in, and you're not going to believe what killed Jennifer Madden."

Jane could feel the excited tension in the coroner's every gesture. She motioned him inside the hallway entrance and followed. "What is it, Karl?"

"Bad oysters, Jane. She died from eating bad oysters."

Gabe leaned back against the hallway wall and stared at Karl Daly's moon-shaped head as though he were waiting for it to go through phases.

"Jane? Gabe? You heard me? Jennifer Madden ate bad oysters. Can you believe it? The woman wasn't murdered after all."

Chapter Eleven

"It's toxin ingested by an oyster, Jane," Karl continued. "We got lucky. One of the lab guys in Seattle has seen this stuff before. Related to some weird sea creature."

Jane turned as a new figure approached. She saw a short, stocky, ginger-whiskered man in old acid-washed jeans and a new, straight-out-of-the-cellophane shirt. A straight pin still stuck out of its collar.

"Some weird sea creature?" Andy Peck's voice repeated from behind Gabe. Gabe pivoted to face his boss and introduced Jane. As the curious glances increased from passersby, Gabe gestured them all into an empty interview room and closed the door behind them.

Karl turned to Andy. "Yeah, the sea creature produces the toxin that was in the oysters that killed Jennifer Madden. I called Seattle as soon as the messenger delivered the report and asked the technician for a more complete explanation. Here. Just a moment. I wrote his comments beneath the official lab results."

Karl paused to open his notebook and read from a yellow sheet. " 'The toxicity in the oysters was caused by minute planktonic organisms on which a lot of invertebrates, like oysters, feed. Botanists call them dinoflagellates and classify them among the algae, although zoologists consider them flagellated protozoa. The toxin they produce is called gonyaulax. It's quite deadly.' "

"Here, let me see that," Jane said as she lifted the report from Karl's hands and began to read.

Gabe rubbed his chin. "I seem to remember something from Biology 101 about dinoflagellates. Aren't they what cause the red tide?"

Jane nodded. "A species of them. The toxic blooms of the creatures turn sea water brownish or reddish. But the red tides that cause fish mortality are not from the same species of dinoflagellate that produced the toxin that killed Jennifer Madden."

Andy shoved his short hands to his hips. "How do you know that?"

Jane lifted one shoulder. "Being from the Pacific Coast, I was fascinated by the phenomenon in biology. When the red tide makes an appearance, most of the time the dead fish, crabs, turtles, oysters, even barnacles wash up on the sand in the thousands. But the report here describes a toxin-producing dinoflagellate from a specific species that doesn't harm fish. The oysters digest the toxic protozoa as food. The more they eat, the more toxin accumulates in the oyster's tissues."

Gabe moved to Jane's side. "So the oyster was infected, and in turn infected Jennifer Madden when she ate it?"

Jane nodded. "Actually, when she ate them. One might not have killed her. But with four, she didn't have a chance. These lab tests on those oysters show they were full of the toxin."

Andy was shaking his head. "But they didn't die. Why did the Madden woman?"

Jane turned back to him. "This gonyaulax toxin is only fatal to warm-blooded animals. It acts like a nerve poison, actually very similar to curare. It interferes directly with myocardial conduction and has an additional, similar effect through central nervous system action at the level of the brain. It results in cardiovascular collapse."

Andy turned to Gabe. "I don't remember the crime-scene investigators' report mentioning any oysters in the Madden refrigerators, or any residue of shells in the trash. Where did these oysters come from?''

Gabe's attention was still focused on the report. He'd taken it out of Jane's hand. Karl shifted on nervous feet, apparently feeling it was up to him to answer Andy's question. "Well, Andy, since they were raw, I'd say she stopped at one of those bars that serve that kind of hors d'oeuvre with their drinks.''

Gabe looked up at Jane. "How long from the time of ingestion to death?''

Jane shrugged. "Varies. Symptoms can appear from within a few minutes to up to three hours after swallowing a toxic dose.''

"What would Jennifer have felt?''

"Oh, initially maybe a slight topical anesthesia about the lips and mouth on contact. Possibly a slight headache. Later, numbness about the face and in the fingertips. Pins-and-needles sensation at the lips. A general paralysis probably would have followed soon after. Then death by respiratory failure.''

Gabe shook his head as he handed the yellow paper back to Jane. "Why didn't Tom Thornton see any of this in the autopsy?''

"If she'd been ingesting the poisonous fish in small doses over a long period of time, there would have been degenerative changes in the large nerve cells of the spinal cord and medulla. But this was a single, acute poisoning. The Seattle lab finding the poison in her blood and other body tissues along with the oysters in her stomach is our only evidence.''

Gabe was silent. After a moment, Jane exhaled a deep breath. "I know how you feel. I thought it was murder, too.''

Gabe glanced at Jane, the look in his eyes a challenge. "What's changed your mind?''

Andy squinted at Gabe. "What do you mean?''

"Hell, Andy, it's been nearly a week since Jennifer Madden's death. No hospital has notified us of even one poisoning. Have you seen or heard of any similar, recent poisonings from seafood?''

"Well, no.''

"You, Hardesty?''

"Nothing's come through the coroner's office.''

Gabe shoved the hair off his forehead. "Then why is it that Jennifer Madden was the only one unlucky enough to end up with four poison-filled oysters in her stomach? If she had really gotten these oysters from some oyster bar in Edenville, we would have seen other cases of the poisoning.''

Jane's head tilted to one side as she studied Gabe. "Are you saying you think someone deliberately fed those oysters to Jennifer, knowing they would kill her?''

"I don't see it makes sense any other way.''

Karl looked more than uncomfortable. "Damn, I wouldn't want to be the one to take that idea to court. You realize you're going to have to prove not only that someone knew those oysters were poisonous—and that would be a trick in itself—but also that he or she deliberately fed them to the Madden woman?''

Andy's forehead furrowed. "Karl's right, Gabe. How's someone gonna know a bad oyster from a good one?''

"There must be ways.''

Karl shoved his glasses to the back of his beaky nose. "Even if there are, how are you going to prove those oysters were in the murderer's possession? Not just any oysters, but those precise oysters?''

Andy began munching feverishly on his lower lip. "If you can't corral a heap more stray—''

Gabe interrupted. "Appreciate the help, Karl, Andy. But I know the difficulties.''

Andy squinted up at Gabe. "This trail you're taking is leading to Madden, ain't it?''

Gabe's eyes met his boss's nervous squint. "Roy is going to resume digging into his background and everyone associated with him. You got a problem with that, Andy?''

Andy Peck rocked back on the heels of his cowboy boots as he stroked his straggly ginger beard. Jane could see from his pronounced scowl that he had lots of problems with Gabe's course of action. He rocked forward. "Damn. You sure about Madden?"

Gabe exhaled. "I'm only sure it's murder, and I need a free hand and sufficient time to find out the rest."

Andy's teeth pierced his bottom lip. "You gonna try for a search warrant?"

Gabe nodded.

"Judge Henry Rowe's on call this week. You know he's not gonna let you hitch his horses to any buckboard of dynamite heading toward Madden's spread."

"I've got Judge Black's home telephone. He's a square dealer. He'll issue whatever paperwork I need."

Andy's stubby hand tugged at his drooping mustache as his eyes darted to Gabe and then down at the pointed tips of his cowboy boots. "Black's retiring this year. I ain't planning to. Maybe I oughta mosey up to Canada with the missus for a little vacation."

Gabe was getting a feeling of déjà vu. Andy's sidestep was precisely the kind of move he'd watched his father make. Still, he knew there was no use confronting or cajoling the man about it.

"Why not, Andy? No reason for both of us to go down."

Andy's bottom lip disappeared between his sharp teeth. He gave Gabe another sideways look. "If I hightail it out on the next flight, that leaves you top hand. You'll be facing Madden's guns alone, Gabe. You interested in that kind of showdown?"

Gabe's lips tightened. "Get out of here, Andy. You, too, Karl."

Andy turned and clopped hurriedly away. Karl Daly took hold of Jane's arm. "Well, our job is over, Jane. No use in us sticking around."

Jane frowned in some surprise. "What are you talking about, Karl?"

"We got the results. We handed them over to the sheriff's office. We're outa here."

"But we can't leave now. Kincaid's right. Logic tells us Jennifer had to have been deliberately fed those oysters."

"That's not our concern, Jane. We don't get involved in running down possible murderers."

Jane frowned at her boss. "Karl, you can't mean that. We have an obligation—"

Karl interrupted her as he renewed his tug on her arm. "We've fulfilled our obligation. Damn it, Jane, I can't afford to alienate Madden. I'm not interested in throwing away my chances in this next election. Gabe understands why the coroner's office can't be associated with this business anymore. Why can't you?"

Jane gently but firmly pried Karl's fingers from around her arm. "I'm not abandoning justice because it isn't politically expedient, Karl. If that's what you expect from a deputy coroner, then I guess you've just accepted my resignation."

Karl took her hand. "Jane, I..." For an instant there, she thought she saw something like courage trying to form in his eyes. But whatever it was just wasn't strong enough, and the nervousness and fear once again took hold. He nodded his head silently and beat a hasty retreat.

Finding she couldn't watch, Jane turned back to Gabe, much more comfortable with the stiff determination drawing at his lips.

"You sure about what you're doing?" he asked.

"Absolutely. What now?"

Gabe felt a peculiar sensation in the vicinity of his diaphragm as he watched the no-regrets set to Jane's jaw and the focused gleam in her eyes. "Now, I'm going to get a court order to search Richard Madden's house."

"Why?"

Gabe's smile was slight. "Come with me and see."

NAOMI PARISOT curtly informed them that Richard Madden was not at home. Gabe had to show her his warrant before she'd let them in.

"Mrs. Parisot, what was in the refrigerator on the day of Mrs. Madden's death?"

Naomi tucked her hands around her ample waist. "Your men searched it. Why don't you tell me?"

"My men searched it the next day. I want to know what was in the refrigerator on the previous day."

Naomi's mouth twisted. "Some chicken. I had a piece for my lunch. And salad fixings. Milk. Orange juice. Cottage cheese."

"Was there any fish?"

"No. Never. Cook won't keep leftover fish in the refrigerator. What isn't eaten gets thrown out."

"Thank you, Mrs. Parisot. You can return to your duties. Ms. Hardesty and I will find our way."

Gabe headed toward the enormous gathering room. It looked different today, somehow not as large without all the people, and not as alive, either. As Gabe stopped in front of the veiled aquarium tank, Jane sent him a querying look. "Here?"

Gabe took out his pocketknife and began to work at the nails keeping the black drape in place. Jane watched the deft movements of his fingers as the veins in his hands tensed.

The nails were tenacious, but Gabe was more so. A few minutes of concentrated effort, and the black drape fell to the floor. They stared at the tank.

Gabe exhaled a frustrated breath. "There's nothing in it."

Jane did a quick scrutiny. "Look at the identification label. It says bivalve mollusks. Mollusks? Aren't those the ones with shells?"

As though on cue, a beautiful orange shell suddenly took off from the thick, black bottom, rapidly opening and closing, taking water in around the scalloped margin and expelling it in little jets on either side of its hinge line.

Gabe smiled. "Yes, mollusks do have shells, and obviously I was wrong about there being nothing in this tank.

That one just demonstrated its very efficient swimming technique. It's a scallop. See the others sitting on the substrate?''

Jane nodded as her nose rested against the glass. "They looked just like lifeless shells a moment ago. Are they what you expected to find?"

"Actually, I was looking for something else. And seeing that deep black bottom makes me think I might still find it." Gabe's hands had begun to probe the edge of the glass. "Do you know how to get into these tanks? They appear to be flush to this wall."

Jane nodded. "There's an access to them through a closetlike room on the other side. Come on. I'll show you."

Gabe thought it looked more like a long, narrow hallway than a closet. There was a great din from the many air compressors that pumped a steady supply of oxygen into the thirsty salt-water tanks.

Gabe and Jane made their way along the narrow corridor to the enormous tank that held the bivalve mollusks. Gabe pulled up a stepladder to climb to its open top. Then he dipped in a long pole with a basket on the end to stir up the black bottom. The first few times he mostly came up with sand, but finally he was successful and scooped up a couple of shells. Then he filled a pail with sand and sea water and dropped the shells in.

When he had gotten down from the ladder and held out the pail for Jane to view, she watched the shells burrowing into the pail's black bottom. Her voice rose in excitement. "I see. They're oysters! You think these are the same kind of oysters Jennifer ate?"

"Yes. Exactly the same. They've been specially prepared. Look at the color of the water and algae in this tank. They're both reddish-brown. Now look at the other tanks and their algae. The water's clear, and the algae is bright green."

Jane nodded in understanding as her eyes took in the row of tanks. "And that means this tank has something the others don't: a special deadly toxin—the same deadly toxin that killed Jennifer.''

Gabe smiled. "Right. These oysters will prove Richard Madden is guilty of premeditated murder.''

"You want to try saying that to my face, Kincaid?''

Gabe and Jane both started at the sudden booming voice coming from behind them. Blocking their only exit from the aquarium access room was the large, stocky bulldog frame of Richard Madden. His sturdy legs stood apart. His hands settled solidly on his hips. His face was a stone mask. Only the ends of his thick black mustache twitched.

Gabe felt Jane stiffen beside him. He cleared his throat. "I have a court order, Mr. Madden.''

"So Naomi told me the moment I walked in the door. And Henry Rowe tells me you didn't get it through him. And the sheriff has conveniently left town. You ready to tell me what the hell you think you're playing at, Kincaid?''

Gabe hadn't planned on confronting Madden until he had the lab report. Solid evidence was hard for a suspect to argue with. However, as long as the opportunity presented itself, he saw no reason not to oblige. "I'm sending this pail and its contents on their way to be analyzed first. I'll need to use your phone.''

Madden's next words were delivered with a piercing, icy calm. "Will you? What insolence! Accuse me of murder behind my back and then ask to use my phone. Not a real man at all, are you, Kincaid? Having known your father, I'm not surprised. I'll be in my study, if you find the guts to face me.''

As Richard Madden stalked away, Gabe felt the unvented heat of the man's fury—a roaring, scorching, full-blown furnace.

Jane exhaled beside him. "I don't know about you but I feel singed.''

Gabe felt anything but. He felt warmed by the excitement of the chase. "Come on, Hardesty, let's get to that phone. I want a unit to come by and get this pail on its way to Seattle. And then I think we should have a word or two with our host, since he was kind enough to extend such a gracious invitation.''

RICHARD MADDEN was sitting behind a huge mahogany desk in his ponderous study when they walked in fifteen minutes later. Ellen and Henry Rowe stood in back of him, like guard dogs behind the master's throne. Madden's eyes and words shot immediately to Jane.

"Daly tells me you've resigned. Too bad. After your presence here today, I'm afraid you're not going to find any more jobs available to you in Edenville, Jane, dear.''

Jane felt the sharp threat in his cold words scrape through her. She knew she should be afraid, but she wasn't. On the contrary. She was finding that Gabe's eagerness to confront the man had suddenly become infectious. For the first time in her life, she felt quite free of fear of Richard Madden. He had just so clearly exposed himself for what he really was—a small, mean, petty tyrant.

She deliberately straightened before him, squaring her shoulders and raising her voice. "I am not your dear anything, Richard.''

Gabe noted Jane's raised chin and challenging words and smiled deep inside.

Richard Madden's mouth raised slightly in surprised amusement. "Well, well, Jane... Maybe you don't resemble your mother so much after all. How... refreshing.''

Jane was so taken back by his unexpected words that she was struck dumb. Madden turned to the Rowes. "Get on it, Henry. You, too, Ellen.''

Henry obediently started for the door, but Ellen stayed to protest. "Richard, I don't like—''

The mere raising of his hand was enough to silence her. With eyes simmering with frustration, she followed her husband out the door, closing it behind them.

Gabe sat in an unoffered chair and beckoned Jane into another.

"Suppose we speak plainly, Mr. Madden. I'm not after a formal statement. Just some straight answers."

Richard's bushy black mustache waved arrogantly. "That you hope will convict me of the supposed murder of my wife."

"I try to keep an open mind, despite my suspicions, Mr. Madden. But I think you should know we've found your wife was poisoned by a marine toxin contained in some raw oysters she ate just prior to her death."

Not an eyelash flickered above Madden's ebony eyes. "And you've decided I poisoned oysters in my own fish tank and fed them to her."

It was a statement, not a question. Gabe was beginning to think that if Madden was a murderer, he was the coolest one Gabe had met. "Last July you and your late wife had a rather loud argument in your home, witnessed by four people. In that argument you told her that if she ever took a lover you would kill her and her lover. Is that true?"

The ends of Madden's mustache curled. "Yes."

Gabe felt an uneasy perspiration collecting on his palms. The admission had been made much too smoothly. He played another of the cards he held. "Did you know your wife was having an affair?"

"Of course."

Gabe blinked. What kind of a hand was Madden holding? "You knew?"

Madden leaned back in his chair. "I knew about all her affairs. She even videotaped a few of the juicier ones for me. We had fun going over them later. It was a turn-on for us both. She was always good to watch in action."

Gabe swallowed the distasteful phlegm collecting in his throat. With an effort, he managed to refocus his thoughts. "Are you telling me you condoned your wife's affairs?"

"I didn't condone them. I encouraged them. Jennifer was not a rock, anchored to some shoreline, to be worn away by waves of restrictions. She was an exotic pearl, to be shown off and admired. I'd had my share of rocks. I was happy with my pearl."

Gabe took a deep breath and sat forward. "If you weren't upset over Jennifer's affairs, why did you threaten her?"

Madden's hands relaxed over the arms of his chair. "Jennifer was after the men I had invited over. But she knew in that unfailingly female heart of hers that some men require challenge and danger in order to really savor the pursuit and capture. So we staged her nude appearance and the resulting fight. It was the preamble to her conquest. She wanted to tantalize them by a glimpse of her body and then taunt them to want her badly enough to face death."

Remembered similar phrases and images from Jennifer's video flashed through Gabe's mind. Damn, he had to admit it could just be true. But he wasn't ready to swallow it whole just yet. "Do you really expect me to believe that your fight was faked?"

Madden's tone was that of a teacher to a backward pupil. "Come now, Kincaid. Think. I took her into the next room and left the door open while we shouted at the top of our lungs. If I had really been serious about the business, don't you think I would have had brains enough to at least shut the door behind me?"

"When I spoke to you on the morning after your wife's death, you seemed upset. Furious, even."

"Of course I was furious. Wouldn't you have been furious if you'd just lost such a beautiful woman?"

Madden spoke about losing his wife just as he might have spoken about losing an expensive possession—with anger, not sorrow. Gabe got a small chill up his spine.

Madden went on. "At the time, of course, I thought Jennifer died from natural causes. Since you say it was from poisoned oysters, it must have been an accident."

Gabe watched the expressionless face before him, knowing there was no way he could see beneath that practiced facade, no matter how hard he tried. He got the sudden, unwelcome feeling that Richard Madden knew it too. With careful control, Gabe sat back in his chair and relaxed his hands, which had unconsciously begun to curl into fists. "Who were the men she was after?"

Madden waved his hand. "That's unimportant."

"Considering what happened to your wife, I hardly think who her lovers were is unimportant."

Madden sat forward. "Kincaid, get this straight. What happened to my wife is that she ate some bad oysters. That someone deliberately fed them to her is your fantasy, not mine."

"Where did she get the oysters?"

Madden's hand waved dismissively as he relaxed back into his chair again. "Some restaurant, I suppose. Can't stand any raw fish myself. But she loved the things. Said they increased her sex drive. Not that it needed any increasing."

Madden's smile was amused, proud. He could have been talking about a prize racehorse's fondness for oats. Gabe was learning to despise the man more by the minute. "Do you know who she was to meet on the night of her death?"

"No one I plan to tell you about."

The arrogant tone of Madden's voice convinced Gabe it wouldn't do any good to ask. This entire interview was nothing like what he'd anticipated. "You told me you called your wife around eight and she said she had a headache and was going to take an aspirin and go to bed early."

"That's what I told you, and that's what she said. I just didn't feel it necessary to mention who she planned to go to bed with."

"Mr. Madden, I'm finding it very hard to believe that you could love a woman and then let her—"

Madden's black eyebrows raised. "Love? Who said I loved her? Love is a deadly infection in an otherwise healthy self-interest. Relationships work because each party gives the other something they want. Jennifer wanted my money and the circles of influence I command. I wanted her youth, beauty and zest for life. Nothing complicated."

"Can you really sit there and tell me that her being with another man never made you jealous?"

Richard shook his head like a man whose patience was being tried. "If I own a beautiful pearl and stick it away in some drawer, it loses its luster. Certainly my enjoyment of it diminishes. Chances are I might even forget I own it. But if I display my pearl, others envy me my possession, and that envy makes it all the dearer to me. And if I let them temporarily wear my pearl, they covet it even more, and I am reminded anew of its worth."

"I find that to be a very...strange way to view one's wife. Why did you marry Jennifer?"

"Mistresses are not included in social invitations in my circle. I wanted her by my side, and she wanted to be there. Marriage was the obvious decision."

"Was it? If all you wanted was a beautiful woman other men would admire, surely you could have found such a woman in your social circle? Jennifer came from a poor Indian background. She'd chosen to make her way as a stripper. Frankly, Mr. Madden, your decision to marry her doesn't seem an obvious one to me at all."

Madden shifted his position in his chair, his eyes squinting at Gabe ever so slightly. For the first time since the interview began, Gabe was beginning to detect an uneasiness in the man. "I don't care what seems obvious to you, Kincaid. The bottom line here is that neither Jennifer's heritage nor her previous profession have anything to do with her death. Now, I have a full schedule this afternoon. I can waste no more time with you."

Madden rose. "You've made a grave error in trying to take me on, Kincaid, but at least you've shown some guts. It's a regrettable necessity that I shall now have to spread them all over the sidewalk. You both know where the door is."

THEY WERE OUT THAT DOOR and on their way to Jane's car before she fought through her anger sufficiently to speak. "That arrogant swine! How dare he threaten you that way!"

Gabe turned to her, surprised at the vehemence in her voice, but not displeased. "Keep it cool, my little lioness. We've got more serious stuff to contend with than the man's stupid threats. We're missing something. I feel it in the very marrow of my bones.''

Jane swung the strap of her bag over her left shoulder, her fury all but derailed at hearing herself referred to as his little lioness. "I'm not little," she protested.

He smirked at her. "No, you're certainly not."

Jane looked away from the amusement in his eyes, not at all sure how she should take it. But she was sure he was right. Getting angry wasn't going to help. She took a deep, cooling breath. "Yes, we are missing something. Something was making Richard uneasy toward the end there. Do you think he was telling the truth about his relationship to Jennifer?"

"Probably. I can't imagine anybody making up anything so sick. He seems sorry she's gone, but I think his analogy to the pearl is precisely how he feels. He lost an object—not a loved one."

Jane shook her head. "So you think Richard and Jennifer really did stage that fight back in July?"

Gabe circled around the Talbot-Lago to open the door for Jane. "Yeah. Seemed like he got as much, if not more, of a kick out of it than she did. What I can't understand is how incredibly open he just was about all this."

Jane waited to respond until he'd gotten in the passenger's seat and she had started the engine. "That's been bothering me, too. A dose of honesty is the last thing I would have expected from Richard. Unless he told us some shocking truths to hide some of the more devious lies?"

Gabe squinted. "I like the way you think, Hardesty."

Jane turned off Madden's private drive onto Paradise Road and headed north, back into the city, toward Lemke's office and Gabe's truck, feeling a warm tingling up her nerves at Gabe's simple compliment. She was his little lioness, and he liked the way she thought. Ah, such was the stuff that could melt a woman's heart. "Is Madden still at the top of your list?"

"I'll hold my answer to that until after I have the lab report on those oysters. If I can prove he had the means, then the next step is proving he could have fed them to her."

"What time did he arrive in Seattle that night?"

"According to Carver, they both spent the afternoon there, arrived around three. If that was the case, Madden couldn't have fed her the oysters, since she was still alive at six."

"And we know she had to have been alive at six, because that's when Naomi Parisot left for her show, and Jennifer hadn't arrived home yet. And Madden says she was alive at eight, when he called. And Philip says she was dead around ten. So it looks like she died somewhere between eight and ten."

"Right. Unless Parisot's lying. Or Carver. Or Madden. Or Lemke."

Jane shifted down to take a turn. "I wouldn't put it past any or all of them, if it was Richard's wish. Except that if Richard killed Jennifer, what could be his motive?"

"Well, even if he didn't lie about encouraging Jennifer's affairs, Hardesty, there could still be some other reason for him to have killed her."

"Like?"

"Like, despite what Madden would like us to believe, I have a feeling he's hiding something about Jennifer's background."

Jane nodded. "Carver, too, seemed nervous when we were asking questions about Jennifer's Indian heritage. Could that also be what caused Richard's unease?"

Gabe took a look at his watch. "Pull into your driveway here. I'd got to use your phone to check in with Roy."

Jane did as requested and, after parking the car in front of her house, led the way through to the kitchen. Gabe immediately reached for the phone on the counter. Jane remained to overhear what she could.

It wasn't good news. Jane only caught a few words, but it was enough. She was ready for the worst when Gabe hung up.

"It's Madden, isn't it? He's trying to block you again?"

Gabe nodded. "While he was talking to us, he had Rowe rushing through a restraining order to prevent my office from contacting any more banks or institutions with records of his financial affairs. He's also calling each one of the county commissioners personally to pressure them into having me fired for running a false investigation."

Jane's tone ascended with incredulity. "A false investigation? How can he say that when his wife's been murdered!"

"But that's just it, Hardesty. Officially, she hasn't. Roy tells me Karl Daly just messengered him a signed death certificate that reads accidental poisoning. Apparently Madden has also leaned on our county coroner."

"But Karl can't sign off that death certificate yet. He hasn't the right! At the very least, a poisoning like Jennifer's has to go to a coroner's jury for a judgment on cause of death. What he's doing is against all the rules. I'm going down there right now and confront him!"

Gabe caught her by the shoulders. "No, you're not, Hardesty. You resigned, remember? You have no official position on this case anymore. And until it's over, you're staying right here, behind locked doors, with a deputy outside on watch."

Jane was stunned by Gabe's words. "But I can help. You can't mean to keep me out of it now."

Gabe took a measured breath. "But I do, and I will. Hardesty, surely it hasn't slipped your mind that on three occasions during this last week someone has tried to kill you?"

Jane could feel her temper rising. "Well, of course it hasn't slipped my mind, but—"

Gabe gave her shoulders a gentle shake. "No buts. For some unknown reason, someone—no doubt Jennifer's killer—sees you as a threat. The thing you should do now is stay safely behind locked doors and focus your mind on figuring out who that can be. You must see that."

How dare he tell her what she should be doing? Jane felt her temperature quickly escalating to the boiling point. Her words came out in an angry stream. "See it? Oh, yeah, I see it, all right. I see this is what I get for putting everything on the line to back your play—a crummy seat in the stands where I can't even see what's going down!"

Gabe's fingers dug into her shoulders as his voice rose to a frustrated roar. "Damn it, this isn't a game. Madden is doing everything in his considerable power to get me out of the way. If I go, so does your protection. Jane, don't you understand? I've got to get out there and find this creep before he tries for you again!"

Such a simple thing—her name on his lips again—yet the vibration of it flowed through her with a force that left her shaken and breathless. Anger, frustration, elation, vied for control over the words she would speak. Slowly, deliberately, her heart pounding with the effort, she gave them voice. "You are not getting rid of me!"

She was angry and so much more. Her cheeks glowed, her eyes flashed, her nostrils flared, her lips parted as though she might be readying her teeth to sink into his flesh. In a deep, raw, primitive part of himself that he had never dreamed existed, Gabe ached to feel them.

His hands released her shoulders to touch her face, his fingertips gliding lightly over her high cheekbones, into the perfect hollows that slid to the corners of her full mouth. She gasped in pleasure at his touch, and the sound seemed to stop his heart. He did not look away from her eyes, could not look away from her eyes, as they widened and deepened and smoldered into his.

Jane felt the power of his touch sweep through her, burning the thoughts from her head, pounding its claim deeper and deeper with every beat of her heart. Her arms wrapped around the iron muscles of his shoulders, eager to draw him near. Gabe's hands slipped to the silk of her neck, down across her shoulders, to the arching of her back, as she melted into him.

His lips found hers, hungrily, then desperately, as the hot taste of her staggered him beyond the edge of reason. He picked her up and carried her to the bedroom.

He undressed her, his blue-hot eyes burning her naked skin. Jane did not recognize this raw, hungry passion that swept through her, as acute as pain. He stared at every inch of her body as he uncovered it, and the way he stared made her feel more beautiful than she had ever dreamed. And still he stared. And Jane trembled with an anticipation that threatened to shake her apart.

She wanted to undress him, but he was too impatient. She watched him greedily as he ripped off his clothes, the smoky afternoon light like a heated incense against the glistening muscles of his powerful body.

She reached for him, but he stilled her hands, grabbing them, imprisoning them behind her back. His mouth caressed her lips, her neck, her breasts, as he voraciously looted her body of its cries of pleasure. Then he picked her up and laid her on the bed and continued his nipping and stroking until she finally gasped with joy.

When she opened her eyes, he was straddling her, still holding her hands immobile above her head, the hard glitter in his eyes lustful and triumphant. Jane read the message clearly. He was the conqueror, and she the conquered. A small smile circled her lips. So he saw himself as a conqueror? Well, two could play at that game.

Slowly, deliberately, she arched her body, seductively, invitingly, raising one long, silky leg to rub against him, and then the other. She watched his eyes following her movements as the hunger grew in them, and then an overwhelming desperation. He moaned as his hands released their hold on hers and sought a new grip on her hips.

But she had no intention of sheathing him and bringing him to culmination quickly. She dodged his grasping hands and rolled out from under him. As he turned to catch her, she quickly pounced on top of him, pitching him on his back. Before he knew it, she had him in her hands, stroking and exploring him as he had explored her.

His eyes sparkled at this switching of their roles, and she saw the pleasure mount in his face. But she wanted more. She licked and teased until his groans sounded as though they were being torn from his throat and he grabbed her hips in a thrust of desperation. Jane took him inside her with a fierce jubilation as they tumbled together, her legs locked around him, moving with a rhythm that pounded the blood in her ears and at long last erupted, leaving her breathlessly spent and smiling.

"My lioness" was all she'd left him with the breath to say. It was enough. His words circled sweet and hot around her panting heart.

Chapter Twelve

Gabe lay beside Jane, not letting himself think. Thinking was the last thing he wanted to do, when he was this close to that beautiful body. Her head rested against his shoulder, silken strands of her hair trailing across his chest. They were as light as a feather, and yet they seemed to hold him in place more effectively than the strongest chains.

Not knowing why he needed to, he spread his hand across the gentle swell of her tummy to feel the rhythmic rise and fall of her breathing. She was more woman than he could ever have imagined, ripe and lustful as any sexual fantasy, and yet so much more lasting. Perhaps it was the need to understand that better that kept his hand enjoying the wonder of the almost magical ebb and flow of her life's breath.

Just when he thought she might be asleep, her hand covered his. "Gabe?"

He had never heard his name spoken that way before. A feeling of tenderness washed over him, catching him totally unawares. It was so strong, so unexpected, that Gabe pushed away from her and got to his feet, grabbing for his clothes.

He fought for control and an even tone. "Not that this hasn't been a sensational idea, Hardesty, but there are definite flaws in our timing. I've got a murderer to catch."

Jane felt a small, sharp pain in her heart. His words were those of withdrawal. She didn't want that. She wanted long, lingering hours of lovemaking, and words from him that matched the volumes of feelings stirring inside her heart.

Except maybe there weren't any such volumes in him? She had to face it. He'd never represented himself as the kind of man who looked for love and commitment. Quite the contrary. Still, some thoroughly female part of her knew that he couldn't take what had just passed between them lightly, however much he might want to.

That knowledge enabled Jane to accept his current practicality far more gracefully that she might have otherwise. She swung her long legs over the side of the bed. "What can I do?"

Gabe zipped up his pants shaking his head. Damn it, he was still warm and humming from her touch, and she was ready for danger again, as if they'd never been together. Whoever said woman was the weaker sex? He took a moment to swear under his breath before responding. "We've already had this conversation. What you're going to do is stay here behind locked doors."

Jane sprang to her feet, irritation creeping up her spine and into her voice. "Yes, we have had this conversation before, and you still can't seem to remember what I've repeated time and again. I'm not giving up this case, Kincaid. If you won't let me help you, I'll just investigate on my own."

She stood before him, naked, hands on her hips, chin out, green eyes flashing. She had never looked more magnificent or more invincible or more desirable, and he ached to take her in his arms again.

He struggled to regain his sanity, shoving his hands into his pockets. "Jane . . ."

"Give it up, Kincaid. You can't bully me or sweet-talk me out of this, so don't even try. Now, wouldn't it be better if we were working together, rather than at odds?"

Yes, it would be better. Of course, what would be best would be to keep her locked up in a jail cell, where she'd be safe. He knew he couldn't do it, however. Gabe exhaled into a reluctant smile. "I suppose you could go see Ellen Rowe."

Jane reached for her clothes, keeping her triumphant grin to herself. "What do you have in mind?"

Gabe was momentarily distracted as Jane bent over to pick up her slacks. What he now had in mind was far different.

Jane straightened, hitching her panties and then her slacks over her slim hips. Gabe took a deep breath, praying for strength. "Uh . . . tell her you're willing to discuss the real reason for my disagreement with her husband."

"And what would that be?"

"That I suspect her husband of killing Jennifer Madden after she broke off their affair. See how she reacts."

Jane glanced up at Gabe's face in some surprise. "You really think Henry had an affair with her and then killed Jennifer?"

In defense against Jane's all-too-considerable attractions, Gabe deliberately turned away and finger-combed his hair into place in front of the dresser mirror. "I think he had the affair, but Madden's still my number-one suspect for murder. Still, Rowe's behavior tells us he's fearful of something. And Ellen's afraid of something, too. You said that yourself. If we prod them a bit, maybe we'll find what's generating those fears. Can do?"

She nodded as she slipped her sweater on and scrambled for her shoes. "Where will you be?"

"At the office, running interference with the county commissioners."

"I know you won't let Richard get away with trying to turn them against you."

Her words brought his eyes back to her face. She was fully dressed now; it was her look that seduced him all over again. It was without guile or obsequiousness, but rather full of a belief and a certain trust that held him absolutely breathless. For an instant, everything seemed to empty out of him and then refill, but finer, stronger, sweeter, somehow. All he needed now was a dragon to slay. Fortunately, he had one.

She watched Gabe shoving his arms into his suit coat. He stood tall, erect, like a general ready for battle. "Madden doesn't know what a fight is until he's picked one with me. Call me as soon as you learn something."

He leaned down to kiss her lips, in a brief, firm salute that he followed with a smile that radiated an infectious, pulsating energy. Here he was, his job in jeopardy, pitted against Madden and all his money and power, and he was acting as though he couldn't wait to cross swords. Jane's heart was beating with soft, squishy, intoxicating little throbs as she watched him leave.

"I'M SORRY, Ms. Hardesty, but Ms. Rowe is trying to prepare for a very important meeting. She can't be disturbed now, and her time is fully committed for the rest of the day. If you want to call next week, I might be able to—"

Jane smiled. "Why don't you just tell Mrs. Rowe I'm here to see her about her husband's conversation with Chief of Detectives Kincaid. Let her make the decision to see me or not."

The secretary's thin hands waved like blown twigs toward the phone. "I can't. On top of everything else today, the intercom is broken."

Jane leaned over the desk. "Then perhaps you wouldn't mind delivering the message in person?"

Of course she minded, but Jane had asked with a smile in her voice and on her face. The secretary's brow crinkled as she pushed her chair back from her desk. Her body jerked toward her boss's closed door. The hand she raised quivered as she knocked faintly. When an irritated "What is it?" was yelled from the other side, she glanced back at Jane with the look of the soon-to-be-martyred before quickly opening and disappearing behind the door.

She came back out a moment later, her eyes glassy, looking as if she'd just witnessed a miracle. "Ms. Rowe wants you to go right in."

Jane gave the secretary a thank-you as she moved past her into Ellen Rowe's private office.

The room, of glass and chrome, with persimmon and prune accents, looked like the woman's smile—deceptively

warm and open. Ellen Rowe rose from behind her com-
puter-dominated glass-topped desk—the only other object
on it was a silver-framed picture of Ricky Rowe—looking
stiff and uncomfortable in a three-piece suit. Jane could feel
the heat radiating from a humming laser printer lying on the
matching glass table behind her.

"This is more than a surprise, Jane. Please, sit down."

Her tone was mildly inquisitive, matching precisely the lift
of one finely arched eyebrow, but totally out of sync with
the unease in her eyes.

Jane took the offered seat and waited until Ellen had sat
down. "I'm sorry to disrupt your busy day, but I spoke with
Chief of Detectives Kincaid after our earlier discussion. I
thought what he told me about his conversation with your
husband last evening might interest you."

Ellen's blood-red fingernails—the exact color of her
hair—scraped across the edge of her desk. "Yes?"

"I hope you understand that until I spoke with Detective
Kincaid, I wasn't at liberty to be as frank with you about his
and your husband's conversation last evening."

Ellen Rowe was on the edge of her seat. "Get it said,
Jane."

Jane drew out a long breath. "Kincaid thinks your husband may have killed Jennifer Madden after she broke off
her affair with him."

There was nothing for a moment. Absolutely nothing.
Then Ellen Rowe fell back into her well-padded executive
chair and burst out laughing. "Henry? Murder Jennifer
Madden? Ha! What a hoot!"

It was Jane's turn to sit forward. "Are you saying your
husband didn't have an affair with Jennifer?"

Ellen grabbed a tissue to dry the wet laughter leaking out
of the corners of her eyes. "Never an affair. More like a one-
night stand. Or maybe I should say a one-minute stand.
Ha!"

"I don't understand."

"You would if you knew Henry. His posture is about all
that remains stiff about the man for more than sixty sec-

onds." The woman expended a few more cackles. "I'd have loved to have seen Jennifer's face!"

"So you knew about your husband and Jennifer?"

Ellen propped herself on the right armrest of her chair. "I suspected. Jennifer was the kind of woman who always wanted the man she hadn't yet had. And God knows, Henry jumps at any woman who even appears to be willing. Not that it does him, or the woman, that much good. Where on earth did Kincaid ever get the idea Henry could murder someone?"

Jane took the question seriously, despite the renewed gust of mirth that drifted her way. "I've seen your husband angry, Ms. Rowe. Don't you think that if Jennifer ridiculed your husband's... nonperformance, it might have angered him enough to kill her?"

Ellen waved a dismissive hand. "Jennifer was smarter than that. She used men, she didn't ridicule them. No percentage in it. Besides, if I'm not mistaken, Henry and Jennifer's short-lived fling came and went early last November. He probably found himself more embarrassed than anything else."

Jane leaned forward in her chair. "Then, maybe. But Jennifer had an abortion just about six weeks later, Ellen. If the fetus was Henry's, he might have reacted differently when he learned of her unwillingness to keep it."

Ellen Rowe's laughter gurgled anew in her throat. "Henry's fetus? You don't know how funny you are, Jane!"

Ellen's laughter burst forth in raucous waves that bounced off Jane's confusion. Dot's view of Henry's medical records did not show he'd had a vasectomy. Why did Ellen Rowe feel so confident that the fetus Jennifer carried couldn't have been Henry's?

Jane's eyes darted to the framed picture of Ricky Rowe, with his black hair and eyes, thinking she might be seeing it for the first time. The coloring, the square jaw. Yes, the likeness was there, if one knew what to look for. The words burst out of her. "Ricky is Richard's child. Henry's infertile, isn't he?"

Ellen's eyes beamed at her with more pride than resentment. "So you've figured it out. Clever little Janie."

"But how does your husband—"

"Henry and I were pressed into marriage for our parents' convenience—not ours. Henry knows Ricky is Richard's son."

"Well, then, I don't understand. If you weren't concerned about Gabe thinking your husband guilty of Jennifer's murder, why were you concerned about their conversation last night?"

Ellen came to her feet, her fingers gluing themselves to her heavy glass desktop. "I don't like secrets. Now, you'll understand when I tell you I have an important meeting—"

The sound of the door opening behind her brought Jane to her feet. Without a knock or an announcement of any kind, Henry Rowe marched stiffly into the room. "Did you get those changes printed? We're going to be late if you don't—"

Henry Rowe stopped in midsentence as his eyes flew to Jane's face. An uneasy surprise quickly floated through his face, despite the automatic smile that immediately drew the sides of his colorless lips toward his ears.

"Well, well . . . Three times in two days. We're setting some kind of record, Jane. What brings you here?"

As Jane hesitated, Ellen grabbed a closed briefcase from beneath her desk and flitted to Henry's side, entwining her arm in his. "Jane was just telling me that Chief of Detectives Kincaid suspects you of killing Jennifer Madden because she had an abortion after you impregnated her. Isn't that a howl?"

Jane could see that Henry Rowe did not think it was a howl. Shock cut through his eyes as perspiration beaded on his upper lip. Ellen's smile oozed satisfaction as she looked at her husband's whitening face.

Henry Rowe swallowed his wife's incredibly sweet smile like a bitter pill. "We're going to be late."

She scratched at his arm with her fingernails. "As always, my dear husband is right. We really must be running.

Thank you for coming by, Jane. It's been most . . . entertaining.''

But Ellen Rowe didn't look entertained anymore. She moved with an urgency that matched her husband's. Wherever they were going, it was important. And that was when Jane decided what she must do.

"WELL, ROY, this faxed report from Seattle establishes without a doubt that the toxin in those oysters from Madden's tank matches exactly the toxin in the oysters found in Jennifer's stomach. We've got means.''

Roy took the report from Gabe's hands. "Yeah, at least now we're sure where the lethal oysters came from. It won't be enough to go for an indictment against Madden, but at least it's a start. I still don't know how you got such a short turnaround from the Seattle lab. What did you threaten those guys with, anyway?''

Gabe smiled. "I'll leave you the secret in my memoirs. You're sure this report from the forensic guys is right?''

"On the money, Gabe. That imprint they lifted from Jane's backyard was from a relatively small shoe. A small man's, or a woman's. Hell, Gabe, it might even have been from Jane's shoe.''

Gabe tossed the report onto his desk. He leaned forward in his chair and ran his fingers through his hair. Madden had anything but a small foot. "Okay, Roy. By the book. Check her shoes and see if we can eliminate them. Did you follow up on that other possible lead I asked you to?''

"I've gathered every piece of information we have on Jennifer Madden and compared it to what I've been able to dig up on Jane Hardesty. Frankly, I just don't see any connection between the two women. They're not related in any way, and as far as I can see they never crossed paths even remotely before Jane became involved with the body in her professional capacity.''

"Except they both lived on Eden Island and knew the same people—including Richard Madden.''

"Yes, except for that.''

"Did Madden have any grudge against Jane's father, mother?"

"I've got nothing to prove he even knew her father. But he was a neighbor of her mother's for a lot of years. If some friction developed between them, you'll never get that Eden Island bunch to admit it."

Gabe got up to pace. "Damn it, Roy, if Jane really doesn't have any knowledge that could point to Jennifer's murderer, why in the hell is someone after her?"

Roy shrugged his heavy shoulders. He waited a moment before he spoke again. "You worked a miracle with the commissioners, you know. Before you talked to them, all five were ready to kick you out."

Gabe sank back into his chair, his voice deceptively even. "Two are still ready to. Madden's barrage of threats aren't being taken lightly. But I've shamed the others into holding on to some ethics, at least for a little while. How's your sleuthing into the financial part going?"

"It's not, Gabe. The banks and financial institutions Madden does business with are a hell of a lot more afraid of him than us. They've flatly refused to fax his records on even the most routine of transactions, citing Rowe's restraining order."

"Madden's counting on having me out of here before we can make a legal issue of it, no doubt. Well, he's miscalculated. You've got Judge Black's court order. Take it with several of the biggest armed deputies we've got to these financial places of business. If they refuse again to hand over the information, put the presidents and every other employee who refuses to cooperate in handcuffs and drag them to jail. Then confiscate *all* their records. I'm through playing games with this crowd."

Roy's chubby face drew into a big smile as he got to his feet. "I'm on my way. Anything you need before I go?"

"Yes, hand me those files on Jennifer and Jane. I want to take a closer look at them."

JANE FOLLOWED Ellen and Henry Rowe's car as it left the parking lot of Ms. Rowe's business, giving it a spacious head start. As the streets came and went, she began to develop an appreciation of the very difficult job it was to tail another vehicle while trying to keep out of sight. She almost lost the limousine twice when it suddenly turned corners. After that she moved a little closer and stayed in the same lane.

When the Rowes passed across the bridge to Eden Island, she was three cars behind. Fortunately, the drivers of the two cars before her were known to the guard, and they were passed through quickly, as she was, too, when her turn came.

Her hands gripped the wheel as she accelerated until she caught a glimpse of the Rowes' dark blue limousine on Paradise Road. She stayed far behind, watching until it turned toward the Madden estate. Jane pulled her car to the side of the road in some wild huckleberry, watching the car retreating up the private lane.

So the Rowes had just been going to visit Richard. Well, that wasn't earthshaking. Why had she detected such strong expectation on both the parts of husband and wife?

Jane looked in her rearview mirror, preparing to turn the car around and head home. One glance, however, and she stopped dead as another car barreled around the bend behind her and then whizzed by her to turn up Madden's private lane. Jane immediately recognized the yellow-haired driver. Her eyebrows raised in more than surprise. She gunned the engine, eager to get home to use the phone.

"DO YOU KNOW who Bob Scabre is?" Jane asked Gabe.

Gabe cradled the phone in his ear as he leaned back in his office chair, a knowing smile on his face. "That big logging man. And you're going to tell me he just drove up to Madden's place."

Jane felt the wind leaking out of her conversational sails. "How did you know?"

Gabe smiled at both her excited diligence and her decided disappointment. "I'm psychic. Come on, Hardesty, one of my men is following you, remember? He just called in a few minutes ago on his car phone. Why were you following the Rowes?''

''They looked like they were up to something when they left Ellen's office in Edenville.''

''So, are they?''

''They must be. Madden and his people talking with Bob Scabre is very strange.''

Gabe's tone carried a shrug. ''Maybe it just means the men have buried the hatchet.''

''In whose back?''

Gabe leaned forward in his chair. ''Feel that strongly about it, do you?''

''Richard has made a public stand against Scabre, and trust me, Richard's not a man who knows the meaning of the word *compromise*.''

Gabe didn't doubt that for a minute. ''Where's Scabre's place of business?''

''Somewhere on the Seattle side. Why?''

''Since it looks like Bob Scabre may have a prominent role in this little drama, maybe it'd be worth our while to pay him a visit.''

Jane got off the bar stool in her kitchen and laced the strap of her bag over her shoulder. ''I'll look up his exact address and meet you down by the ferry in fifteen minutes.''

BOB SCABRE'S OFFICE was on the twentieth floor of an older building a few blocks from Seattle's Space Needle. He was staring out the window when they walked in, looking like a man who had considered jumping in the recent past. Gabe extended his hand as he introduced himself and Jane.

Beneath his heavy crop of corn-colored hair, Scabre had the ruddy, pockmarked, broken kind of face that suggested he had probably picked a fight at least once a day. He ignored Gabe's extended hand, his expression making it clear that he was ready for another one.

"Get to your business and get out. You don't have jurisdiction here, Kincaid."

Gabe put on a reserved smile as he motioned for Jane to take a seat. "We're not the enemy, Scabre."

Scabre stood behind his worm-eaten ship-captain's desk, his arms folded. "Oh? Who is?"

Gabe relaxed back into his chair. "Richard Madden, of course."

Scabre's florid face deepened as his arms unfurled and his hands clenched into fists. "That bastard."

"As those are your sentiments, I'm finding it curious that you're choosing to do business with him."

Scabre's raw-boned frame listed over his desk toward Gabe. "Choosing? You trying to be funny?"

Jane was amazed at how cool Gabe remained, faced with the overwhelming heat coming from Scabre. "Tell me what Madden's doing."

Scabre's big-boned hands found the solid protuberances of his hips. "My grandfather, my father and I have built up the Scabre Timberland Company with our blood, sweat and tears. That bastard Madden is making me sell all my land back to the Indians at dirt-cheap prices. I'm losing one hundred thousand acres of prime logging land."

Jane leaned forward in her chair. "Your land once belonged to the Indians?"

Scabre flashed her a resentful glance. "The whole U.S. did at one time, remember?"

Jane tried a different approach. "But your land is being singled out for some reason. Why is that?"

Scabre shrugged, losing some of his antagonism. "Early in the century, the U.S. government divided Washington State reservation land into thousands of eighty-acre tracts and allotted the parcels to tribal members. They had the option to keep or sell their land. My grandfather was an immigrant with a few bucks in his pocket and a dream of owning a logging company. He bought his first acre from a willing Indian seller and logged it. From the proceeds of that first logging, he bought his next acre, and so on."

Jane nodded in understanding. "And the land he continued to buy was previously reservation land?"

Scabre's tone flared up again. "It was logging land. When
my grandfather passed on, my father and I continued to
purchase land. We've replanted the logged areas, cleaned up
our slash, made sure the streams and rivers remained un-
clogged. It's my land, damn it. We didn't steal it. We bought
it. My family has owned and worked it for three genera-
tions."

Gabe drew Scabre's attention. "How can Madden force
you to sell it then?"

"He got legislation passed ordering the original land
granted to the Indians to be returned to Indians at its original purchase price. You understand? My grandfather
bought his first acre in 1910 for twenty-five dollars! Do you
know what that same acre of land is worth today?"

Gabe could understand the man's frustration, but he was
more interested in the particulars of the transaction. "What
Indians have come forward to purchase the land?"

"Just one. Some woman Madden's people are represent-
ing."

"A woman?" Gabe asked. "What's her name, Scabre?"

"Jennifer Jones. Just like the old movie actress. Damn
bastard thinks the whole world is his show."

Gabe and Jane exchanged meaningful glances. It had escaped neither of them that Jennifer Jones was the maiden
name of Richard Madden's dead wife. "So that's why you
met with him today?" Gabe asked. "So he could arrange for
this Indian woman to purchase your land?"

Scabre exhaled heavily. "I met with Madden and his slimy
sidekick Jack Carver on Tuesday night, here in Seattle, to
conclude the deal over dinner. My lawyer went over the papers, and I signed. Madden was supposed to take the contract to the Indian woman early the next day for her
countersignature. I was supposed to get my check at the
bank at eleven on Wednesday."

"Supposed to?"

Scabre shoved his hands in his pockets as he turned toward the window. "Henry Rowe met me at the bank and told me my signature was blurred on Madden's copy and new papers were going to have to be drawn up. Damn bastards. Probably just trying to pocket an extra few days' interest before having to turn over the check."

"Did Rowe show you the blurred signature?" Gabe asked.

Scabre turned back to face into the room. "After I demanded to see it. It was blurred, all right. Except they must've tampered with it. It sure as hell wasn't blurred the night before. Anyway, they set up another meeting for early this afternoon to sign again. I had to travel all that way for two minutes with a pen."

Scabre slumped suddenly, his bluster all blown. "Hell, what's the use? It's all over. The check I got is barely enough to buy five good acres of timberland today."

Jane leaned forward. "I'm sorry, Mr. Scabre."

He looked at her with muddy eyes. "The old work ethic was what I was taught. You get off your tail and you work hard and you do good and nobody can take away the fruits of your labor. Only it don't work that way no more. That man has taken everything from me, and I don't for a minute think he was doing it for any Indians."

Gabe leaned forward. "Why do you say that, Mr. Scabre?"

Scabre waved a raw-boned hand. "Madden's a greedy bastard. I never believed any of those do-gooder speeches he gave five years ago, and I don't believe him now. He doesn't give a damn for anybody but himself. Somewhere there's a profit in this for him. You bet on it. Damn hypocrite publicly ridiculed me when he was in office. Kept saying I was raiding the Indian land. Well I know what will happen to that land now. He'll get his greedy claws in it, you just wait and see."

THEY CHOSE TO STAND at the bow of the ferry on the return trip. For the first half of it, they were both quiet, just staring at the whitecaps as the chilling spray dotted their cheeks. It was Jane whose deep voice finally sank into the heavy air, breaking the silence. "Is Scabre right? Has Madden given lip service to Indian rights all these years just in order to orchestrate a land grab for himself?"

Gabe leaned against the rail, face into the wind. "It's a sweet setup, Jane. He fights for the rights of the underdog, and then disguises himself as the underdog when the payoff comes. With Jennifer as his wife, he could put things in her maiden name and still have control over them. I'll bet we've just discovered the real reason he married her."

"Yes, I feel certain you're right, but the rest of this isn't making much sense. Scabre said that Jennifer hadn't yet signed the contract Tuesday night. But if she didn't sign it before then, she couldn't have signed it at all. She was dead the next morning, when Madden arrived home."

Gabe rubbed the back of his neck. "I've been trying to figure that one out, too. In order to make that contract valid, Madden had to find another legitimate Indian buyer to substitute for Jennifer, somebody he could control like he did her."

Jane turned toward him, her voice rising excitedly. "Maybe that's why they smudged Scabre's signature on the original contract—to give them time to locate a replacement and have new contracts drawn up with the replacement's name. Rowe used to be Richard's contract lawyer, so he probably drew up the papers."

Gabe nodded. "Could be. With the state Scabre was in today, I doubt he'd notice a different name in the signature box on the second set of contracts. By then I'm sure all he was concerned about was signing, getting his check and getting out."

Jane watched the ferry's bow, rubbed furiously by whitecaps of turbulent waters. "Well, Richard certainly has this little conspiracy to grab Indian land well thought out, and we know the Rowes and Carver are in it up to their necks. I can't wait to get the particulars and expose their sordid little plan. If Richard thinks he was embarrassed by my last interview with the press, he hasn't seen anything yet!''

Gabe turned to Jane, saw the wind whipping long strands of blond hair across her face. His other thoughts scattered as he held his breath at the vision of elemental beauty she represented. Her eyes swam like the deepest green of the waters. Rain and ocean misted her pale face until it glistened. She stood tall and strong and mystic, like a goddess of the sea—full of fathoms and mysteries and turbulent emotions.

He gathered her in his arms and kissed her streaming skin, tasting the sea and sky, feeling them pour through him. And suddenly he was drunk with the waters of life and the knowledge that it was through a woman like this that a man might discover what he had always wanted to find within himself.

"Gabe," she whispered beside his cheek.

"Hmm?" What was it about the way she said his name?

"Gabe, I'm not complaining about this slight tangent, mind you, but I just thought of something."

Reluctantly, very reluctantly, he leaned back. "Yes?"

"Well, we know that Madden is guilty as hell over this Indian land grab, but what has any of it to do with Jennifer's murder?"

Gabe frowned as the implication in Jane's words set in. He leaned against the sea-sprayed rail, looking out at the overcast day. "Actually, it tells us that of all the people in this world, Madden was probably the one least likely to want Jennifer dead."

Jane nodded. "Yes, I agree. Her untimely death threatened all his carefully laid plans. Still, just how coincidental could it be for his oysters to be infected with the same toxin that poisoned his wife?"

Gabe's forehead furrowed deeper. "Yes, that is entirely too coincidental."

Jane turned to look at his profile, shining with sea spray and new speculation. "What is it, Gabe?"

"What if arresting Richard Madden is exactly what someone wants me to do?"

Jane licked the salt spray from her lips. "Are you saying the killer of Jennifer is trying to frame Richard for the crime?"

"I'm beginning to think so, Jane. Consider the facts. If Madden killed Jennifer, he's been incredibly stupid about it. He waits for a night when she's having a liaison with another man, knowing that she'll be found in a revealing negligee and her affairs are bound to surface and give him a motive. He poisons her with a toxin in oysters from his own tanks. And he does it right in the middle of a land-grab deal that can ruin him if it's exposed. Does any of that make sense?"

Jane's eyes opened wide. "Gabe, you're right! Richard would be a fool to leave such damning clues. But someone else—"

"Let's get to Madden's place."

"You want to talk with Richard again?"

"No. I want to talk with Mr. Gnat."

THEY FOUND HIM on the east terrace of the Madden estate. The sun was peeking through the windswept clouds gathering overhead. Mr. Gnat knelt at a bench in front of a row of recently polished shoes. He was brushing one that he cradled in his left land. He was shirtless, and the top half of his massive body was beaded with sweat. He looked up at their approach.

Gabe smiled, but Jane noticed that he had tucked his right hand into his belt, just inside his coat, where she caught a flash of his .38.

"Mr. Gnat? I'm Chief of Detectives Gabe Kincaid. Do you remember me?"

Mr. Gnat squinted in a sudden ray of the emerging sun. Gabe halted about eight feet from the massive man, Jane right next to him. Mr. Gnat did not respond to Gabe's question, just fixed his blank eyes on Gabe's face.

"What is your first name?"

"No first name."

"It's just Mr. Gnat?"

The bald headed nodded.

"Where were you born?"

Mr. Gnat looked away as his clublike hands rubbed the perspiration beading on his huge, hairless chest.

"Mr. Gnat, did you hear my question?"

The heavy man concentrated on his sweating body. "Mr. Madden no like me to say. No like me to talk."

"You understand I'm with the sheriff's office? That if you refuse to answer my questions, you may get into trouble? Do you think Mr. Madden would want you to get into trouble?"

Mr. Gnat's hands moved methodically over his body.

"Mr. Gnat, Mr. Madden would not want you to get into trouble. He needs you beside him, not locked up in some jail because you would not cooperate with the sheriff's office. You see that, don't you?"

The man's small, dark eyes drifted to Gabe's face. "Here."

"Here?"

"Born here."

"What do you mean by here?"

"Washington."

"The state. I see. That's curious, Mr. Gnat, because I wasn't able to find any records of your birth."

"Born in forest. Tribe keep record."

"Tribe? You're Indian?"

The big head nodded.

"Is the rest of your family on a reservation?"

"All dead. Mr. Madden find me. Head injured."

Mr. Gnat's hands traced the faint lines of an old, thick scar that began at his left ear and climbed to the top of his bald head. Gabe leaned closer to get a better look and winced at what he saw. The man's whole skull must have been opened. It was a wonder he'd survived. Gabe began to think he understood Mr. Gnat's apparent mental and verbal slowness a little better.

"How did the injury happen?"

"Not know. Don't remember time before. Very young."

"How long ago did Madden find you?"

"Many seasons."

"Do you know how many?"

"Not count."

"You've been with him as long as you can remember?"

"Yes."

"Has he been good to you?"

The small black eyes blinked at Gabe. "He save life. He give home. He give job."

"He pays you a salary?"

"No reason for salary. He give everything."

"Hmm . . . Did he give you an education?"

Mr. Gnat looked down at his tree-trunk legs. "I go to school once. I not learn. I come home. Don't go back."

"Can you read?"

"I can sign name. Mr. Madden teach me. I sign name for Mr. Madden."

"But you can't read?"

"I sign name."

"What else can you do?"

The big shoulders squared. "I am strong. No one bothers Mr. Madden. I make sure."

Gabe gave him a small smile. "Mr. Madden must feel very secure with you around him. Do you stay close?"

"I have room. Over garage. Mr. Madden have bell. He call. I come."

"And on the nights when Mr. Madden is away from home?"

"I go. Always close."

"How does that work, Mr. Gnat?"

"Work?"

"Do you share Mr. Madden's hotel room?"

"Yes."

"Did you share a motel room in Seattle with Mr. Madden this last week, after his meeting with Mr. Carver and Mr. Scabre?"

"Yellow-haired man went home. Not live far."

"And Mr. Madden didn't stay in his room all night."

Mr. Gnat's eyes darted to Gabe's face. "He tell you?"

Gabe smiled. "How else would I have known? Now, why don't you tell me where he said you two went next. You do remember, don't you?"

"We take ferry."

"To Mr. Madden's home?"

"To Ms. Rowe."

"Henry and Ellen Rowe's home?"

"He not there. Only Ms. Rowe home. She call. We go."

"She called Mr. Madden at the Seattle hotel?"

"Yes."

"What time did she call?"

"Late."

"Ten? Midnight?"

Mr. Gnat's dark eyes blinked. "Late."

Gabe gave it up. "Did you share the servants' quarters at Ms. Rowe's home?"

His head shook. "I always sleep in car."

"Always? Mr. Madden goes to see Ms. Rowe frequently?"

"Yes. Friends."

"Is Henry at home when Mr. Madden visits his friend Ellen?"

"No."

"And on this night when Ellen Rowe called, how long did you and Mr. Madden stay at her home?"

"I sleep in car all night. In morning Mr. Madden come. He drive home."

"And Mr. Madden arrived home to find his wife dead?"

The big head bent as steel fingers pulled at a loose nail. He tore it off and threw it to the ground. "Yes."

"When we were here at Mr. Madden's party the other night, you mentioned that the aquarium tank had been covered because the water had turned brown. Do you remember?"

"Yes. Tank brown."

"This is important, Mr. Gnat. Did you see anyone put something in the tank before Mrs. Madden's death?"

Mr. Gnat's dark eyes didn't even blink. "No. Tank clear then."

Gabe licked his lips. "The tank was clear *before* Mrs. Madden's death? You're sure?"

"Yes."

Gabe spoke the next words into the air. "Then it was after Mrs. Madden's death that the water changed to brown."

Jane looked over at Gabe. "What is it?"

He turned to face her. "Jane, if the tank wasn't infected before Jennifer's death, then that means the oysters in it weren't the ones used to kill her. And since they came from elsewhere, it also means that someone deliberately fouled the tank."

Jane nodded. "To implicate Richard in Jennifer's death."

"Right." Gabe turned to the servant again. "Did anyone go into the tank room on the day after Mrs. Madden's death?"

"Lot of people here."

"Yes. Mostly people from my office. Strangers. But did you see anyone near the tank room that you knew?"

The big, bald head nodded. "Suzanne."

Jane jumped back, feeling as if she'd been struck. She could barely find enough voice to say the words: "Suzanne Lemke?"

"Yes. She come out of tank room."

Jane continued to step back until Gabe's hand circled around her arm and brought her to a halt. He turned back to Mr. Gnat. "Was Suzanne Lemke carrying anything?"

"She have purse."

"When did you see her coming out of the tank room?"

"Morning you come."

"No." Jane's protest was adamant.

Gabe gave her arm a silent shake. "Mr. Gnat, did you see anybody else in or around that tank room?"

"No."

Gabe thanked Mr. Gnat and began propelling Jane back through the Madden house to reach the front exit. "Gabe, Suzanne didn't do it."

"You said it yourself, Jane. Jennifer might have walked around with that deadly toxin in her for three hours before it killed her. Suzanne could have fed those oysters to her when she stopped by for her lingerie."

Jane bit her lip. "She's not a murderer. I know it."

Gabe picked up his pace. "I'll understand if you want me to question her alone."

Jane's lips tightened. "No. I'm coming. She's my friend and she's innocent. I won't let you scare her."

Gabe stopped and turned to Jane just as they reached the front door. "Is that what you think I'm going to do?"

Jane took a deep breath, hearing the disappointment in his voice and wishing she hadn't spoken without thinking. "I'm sorry, Gabe. I just want to be there."

Gabe laid his hands on her shoulders. "Then you will be."

His warmth charged through her like an invading army. She surrendered without raising even token resistance.

Chapter Thirteen

Suzanne was noticeably upset at Jane's unannounced appearance at her door with Gabe in tow. Jane took hold of Suzanne's hands and tugged her to a seat on the living room sofa. "It's time for some plain talk, Suzanne."

Suzanne clasped Jane's hands tightly for a moment before releasing them. "I guess I knew all along it would come to this." She turned to Gabe. "What do you want to know?"

Gabe took a seat opposite, resting his elbows on his knees. "Mrs. Lemke, we now know Jennifer Madden died from poisoned oysters."

Suzanne blinked several times as she sat very straight. "Oysters? But then it was an accident!"

"No, Mrs. Lemke. Someone deliberately fed poisoned oysters to Jennifer Madden. In your lawyer-transmitted statement to my office, you said you were home with your husband on the night of Jennifer Madden's death. Was that statement true?"

Jane could see Suzanne's anxiety rising as their eyes met. When she answered after a long pause, her voice was barely a whisper. "No. Philip wasn't here."

"Where was your husband, Mrs. Lemke?"

Suzanne's shoulders slumped as she turned back to Gabe. "I suspect he was with Jennifer Madden. That's where he was every other night over the last couple of months when he phoned me to say he would be working late."

Gabe kept his voice gentle. "Why did you lie and say you were at home with your husband that evening?"

Suzanne's color drained beneath her makeup. "To protect my husband, of course. He called around ten-thirty with this story of being so tired he was going to sleep on the office couch. The next day he told me we should say we were together at home during the night of her death. Said he didn't want to expose the confidential client he'd gone to see. I agreed so that he'd have an alibi."

Jane laid her hand on Suzanne's arm in a comforting gesture. But Gabe's next question was far from comforting.

"You're not telling the whole truth, Mrs. Lemke. This is no time to be keeping things back. What exactly were you doing on the night of Jennifer Madden's death?"

Suzanne exhaled a trapped breath as she pulled away from Jane's touch and stood up. "Okay! I lied for myself, too. I was afraid what people would think if the whole truth came out. I wasn't at home... alone."

Jane sat forward. "Suzanne, are you saying what I think you're saying?"

Suzanne swallowed hard. "It wasn't exactly like that, Jane. Philip had just finished calling to say he was spending the night at the office when Henry Rowe dropped by."

Jane sat still and stunned.

"You didn't expect him?" Gabe asked.

Suzanne paced to the back of her couch. "Of course not!"

Jane exhaled heavily. "But you were glad to see Henry Rowe."

Suzanne came around to the front of the couch again and fell into its cushions beside Jane. "I felt like I needed to talk to someone about then. The strain of pretending to Philip that I didn't know..."

"You told Henry about Philip having an affair?"

Suzanne nodded. "He was a shoulder to cry on. He told me what I wanted to hear—that Philip would be coming back to me, that it was probably just a fling he was having. In the meantime ..."

Jane laid her hand on one of Suzanne's agitated ones. "In the meantime?"

Suzanne sighed. "He said he'd be there to comfort me. At first, I didn't ... you see, he was gentle, and I was feeling so off balance. After enduring Philip's unfaithfulness and rising neglect ... discovering another man found me desirable ... wanted me ..."

Jane almost choked on her words. "So you let him make love to you?"

Suzanne's uneasy eyes darted to Jane's face. "Only briefly. I came to my senses after a minute and shoved him away. He didn't persist. He was helping himself to another drink when I went up to bed. The next morning the servants told me they had found him snoring loudly on the living room sofa. When they awakened him, he left."

"And when your husband came home?" Gabe asked.

"It was right after Jane had come by to tell me about Jennifer. It was when I saw his face, you see, that I ..."

Jane's other hand joined her first in cupping Suzanne's. "It's okay. He didn't do it. He found her dead. That's why he was so shook up."

Suzanne slumped against the back of the couch like a puppet whose strings had just been cut. "I didn't really think so, you understand. I mean, I thought maybe an accident ..."

"He wasn't even there when she died," Jane said.

Suzanne's eyes fluttered closed as she exhaled a deep sigh. "So it's over. It's finally over."

"Not quite," Gabe said. "Your husband left here to go to his office in the city before returning to Eden Island and driving to the Madden residence. That gave you plenty of time to get to Jennifer and feed her the oysters before your husband arrived."

Suzanne's eyes flew open as she shot up on the couch. "What? You can't possibly think—"

Gabe's look was hard, uncompromising. "Why did you go into the salt-water tank room at the Madden residence on the morning after Jennifer's death?"

Suzanne blinked as though she didn't understand the question. "The tank room? I didn't go— Oh, yes. I remember now. I did go in."

Jane frowned. "Why?"

Suzanne seemed puzzled. "What can it matter?"

"Trust me. It does."

Suzanne leaned forward on the couch. "Well, when Leo and I left Detective Kincaid in the study, Leo asked me to wait in the dayroom for him. He'd forgotten about an urgent private call he had to make. I got bored waiting and decided to watch the fish in the gathering room next door. I had just walked in when I heard some noise behind the tanks. I went around the side and opened the door to the tank room and called out. I went in a few steps, but I didn't see anyone, and the lights were off, so I came back out and returned to the gathering room. Leo joined me a couple of minutes later. That's all there was to it."

"Were any of the tanks draped that day, Mrs. Lemke?"

"No."

"Was there a brownish tinge to any of the water?"

"No. They were clear."

Gabe leaned forward. "How long was Dr. Speke gone?"

"Four, maybe five minutes."

"And from what direction did he return?"

"Why, from the direction he left, the door leading into the living room, where he went to make his call."

"Was that door open?"

"No. He closed it after him. He said the call was private."

"So you can't be certain he was in the living room during that four to five minutes?"

Suzanne frowned. "Well, I obviously didn't see him, but where else could he have been?"

Gabe's elbows were on his knees, and his fingertips were rubbing together. "Is there another door to the living room?"

Suzanne thought for a minute then nodded. "On the far side. It leads out to the hallway."

"The same hallway that also feeds into the gathering and tank rooms?"

Suzanne looked from Gabe to Jane, then back to Gabe again. "Yes. But I don't understand what all these questions mean."

"Did you notice anything different about Dr. Speke when he returned to you in the dayroom?"

"Different? What do you mean?"

"Was there a splash of water on his pants? Did he seem nervous? Upset?"

Suzanne looked lost. "Of course he was nervous and upset. We both were. Jennifer was dead."

"So you talked in the dayroom?"

"For a few minutes. Then I wrote a quick note to Richard to call me if he needed anything, and Leo and I left. What is it, Detective Kincaid? What do these questions mean?"

Gabe got to his feet. "They mean I'm trying to be thorough, Mrs. Lemke. I'd like to use your phone."

Suzanne nodded and rose. Gabe hurried to make his call. When he rejoined Jane in the foyer a few minutes later, the frown in his forehead had deepened.

"The doctor is at the hospital doing his rounds. I assume you want to be there when I talk with him?"

Jane nodded distractedly as she opened the front door and started for the car.

Gabe hurried to keep up with her long stride. "Jane, you okay?"

At the pressure of Gabe's hand on her arm, Jane came to a halt, turned and managed a smile. "Yes, I'm fine."

Gabe studied her face. "You're not telling me something, Jane. What is it?"

Jane wet her lips. "Did Dot... did Dorothy Speke mention to you that Jennifer came by to see Leo on the day she died?"

Gabe shook his head as he gently rested his hands on her shoulders. "No. Jane, do you know for a fact that Jennifer visited Speke?"

"Dot said something to me about it," Jane admitted. The first time we talked. I didn't think to mention it before."

Gabe's hands tightened. "If Jennifer came to see Leo that afternoon, Jane, he had an opportunity to feed her the oysters. And from what you just heard from Suzanne, Speke could also have doctored the fish tanks in Madden's aquarium."

Jane spoke quickly. "Others had opportunity, too, Gabe. And they had motive. Leo has no motive."

"Remember what I've always said about motive? Who can ever really know what goes on in another's mind?"

Even the feel of Gabe's warm arms failed to soothe Jane's thoughts. "But, Gabe, if it's Leo, that would mean he's the one who's been after me. I know—I just know in my heart Leo couldn't do such things."

Gabe steered her toward the car. "Go home. Get something to eat. I'll commandeer the unit I've had following you to take me to the hospital. When we've got a hold of Speke, I'll send another unit by to collect you. Then we'll talk face-to-face with your doctor friend. And if what your gut feeling is telling you is right, then Speke will clear himself. Okay?"

Jane nodded distractedly.

Gabe watched her face, suddenly feeling strange, confronted with this new, quiet, sad Jane Hardesty. Before he knew it, he had drawn her into his arms. Tenderness swelled inside him as he stroked her hair, but it did not cause the weakness he'd always feared. Amazingly, as everything else with her, there was power in it, such a glorious, burgeoning feeling. He tightened his arms about her.

And then he let her go and headed toward the parked car with the waiting deputy.

JANE LEANED AGAINST the closed front door of her house.
She felt heavy, weighed down. Gabe's words should have
lightened her worries. They hadn't. Because she hadn't told
Gabe everything.

She headed directly for the study. Once she was there, her
hand traced across the wall of books. Most of them had
been her mother's. She lifted the small black book out of its
place, her thumb rubbing off the layer of dust that obscured the gold lettering: *Indian Herbs and Medicines of
Puget Sound.*

Jane sank into her easy chair, holding on to the book. She
opened it slowly, reluctantly. The index directed her to the
appropriate text. She turned to the section and read silently
for several minutes. When the voice came at her from the
other side of the room, she was startled. She got quickly to
her feet, dropping the book on the floor.

"I'm too late, aren't I?" Dr. Leo Speke asked.

His mellow tone drifted over to her as he slowly approached and leaned down to pick up the book. He smiled
ruefully when he saw the page she'd turned to.

His next words carried a tinge of regret. "Yes, way too
late, I see. I can't tell you how sorry this makes me."

Jane was finding she barely had enough breath for a
whisper. "Leo, how did you get in here?"

"This time by a broken window in the utility room. I had
just let myself in when I heard you drive up. I hoped you'd
go upstairs and I could slip in and out without disturbing
you. Just as I hoped to do the other night. I'm sorry if I
frightened you. I was only here for the book, you understand."

Intellectually, Jane knew she should be afraid. But Leo's
mellow tone held no threat, no hint of violence. He had to
be mad, of course. Here he was telling her he was sorry he'd
frightened her, and he'd tried to kill her on several different
occasions. Her senses fought the battle of conflicting perceptions. Wearily she sank back into her chair. "Leo, I don't
understand."

Leo inched his way onto the seat of the opposite chair, still holding on to the book, his book. "I forgot about your mother having a copy of my book, you see. You gave me quite a shock when you mentioned it the other day. Naturally, I realized then that I must make every effort to retrieve it. I was afraid you might read it and start to wonder."

Jane's mind was reeling at the dichotomy of emotional and mental influx. When she finally spoke again, her voice sounded like someone else's. "You really did kill Jennifer."

Leo's large eyes saddened. "As you've just read, I learned about the plankton toxin. The Indian tribes in the Northwest used to collect the mollusks when the sea estuaries turned the characteristic reddish-brown. Through trial, they learned how much would relax the body's muscles, including those of respiration. Error taught them how much would relax the muscles forever."

"How did it happen, Leo?"

Leo fell against the back of the chair, looking old and tired.

"Yes, Jane. I want you to know it all, so you'll understand. Thirty-one years ago, I was only a young intern at the reservation when an Indian woman brought in her badly injured son, a youngster no more than five or six. His head had been split open. She told me he'd been hit by a white man in a fast-moving car. The white man had sped off.

"The regular doctor had gone home, nearly sixty miles away. I knew the boy needed blood and immediate stitching to close his wound. I had to do it, and somehow I did. He took four pints of blood over the next several hours, and all of my prayers. When he was still alive in the morning, I was sure I'd witnessed a miracle.

"The boy stayed at the reservation clinic the next week, gradually getting stronger. During that time I got to know his Indian mother. She was a widow, several months pregnant, with no money. I wanted to help her and the boy. I was angry at the white man who had struck him down. I was determined to find him and bring him to justice. Still, even with the car's description and a partial license plate number, it took weeks before I got any news."

Leo stopped, and his head suddenly sank into his hands. "How many nights I have lain awake since, wishing I had never done so!"

Jane leaned forward. "Leo, why? Who was it?"

Leo's arms dropped over the arms of his chair. His face looked drawn, exhausted. "Richard Madden."

Jane leaned back against the couch, suddenly cold. She rubbed her arms with her hands, but she found that her chill wasn't one that could be warmed by the friction.

Leo's hands raked through his tight curls. "I wanted to turn him in to the authorities right away, but the Indian woman was adamant that I wasn't to go to the sheriff. Her way, the way of her ancestors for centuries, was to have me approach Richard and set her grievance before him and wait to see how he made amends."

"So that's what you did?"

"Yes. Richard admitted he'd been up to the reservation buying fireworks. He claimed he didn't know he'd hit the boy. He readily agreed to pay for all the boy's medical needs and gave his mother ten thousand dollars in compensation as long as the authorities were not brought in. When I told him how serious the boy's injuries had been, how he would need constant care, he agreed to take the boy into his home to ensure that the care was given.

"I tried to tell the boy's mother about courts of law and how they could sue Richard for his actions, but she wouldn't listen to me. Ten thousand dollars sounded like a fortune to her, and Richard's offer to take the boy impressed her. You see, in Indian culture, that is the highest expression of responsibility. She didn't see it as losing a son. She saw it as Richard becoming his surrogate father."

Jane sat forward. "The boy is Mr. Gnat, isn't he?"

Leo nodded. "That's what Richard called him. The boy's name is really Thomas Jones. I didn't understand the Mr. Gnat nickname until I overheard Ellen, Henry and Richard reminiscing one night about their wild ride through the reservation. They had been with Richard, you see. Ellen had gasped when she felt the car hit the boy. She'd turned to Richard and told him to stop, but he'd said there was no need, that he'd probably just run over a gnat.''

Jane's mouth twisted. "Leo, how could you ever have called that man friend?"

Leo exhaled a deep breath. "It was the money, Jane. I was seduced by the money. Thomas grew physically strong, but mentally he was slow, and his speech was halting. Richard taught him basic, repetitive tasks and strength-building exercises. Considering what a lifetime in an institution would have meant, I suppose the boy hasn't fared badly in Richard's care."

Jane's hands still clutched her arms. "And Richard has all the benefits of a loyal, unpaid servant. What happened to Mr. Gnat's—I mean Thomas Jones's—mother?"

Leo's face grew sad. "She died giving birth to her baby girl."

Jane sucked in a breath as realization dawned. "Jennifer Jones! Jennifer Madden!"

Leo's nod was weary. "Yes. She was adopted by another Indian family. After seeing what he termed my 'negotiation skills' with the boy's mother, Richard befriended me, introduced me to his Eden Island contacts. When my internship on the reservation was completed, I married Dorothy, using her family's prestige and those other contacts to begin a lucrative practice, a secure future."

"And then, twenty-seven years into that secure future, Jennifer appeared?"

"Yes. And she was looking for Richard Madden."

"Why Richard?"

"Her adopted parents had told her the story of the honorable white man who had taken her injured brother under his protection. Jennifer was wise to the ways of the world. She didn't buy the honorable-white-man routine. She knew the only person Richard had protected was himself. At first she set out to ruin him. She seduced him and then leaked the news of their affair to the press.

"Richard lost the senatorial race, but it didn't ruin him. It just caused him to go behind the scenes in politics, which he found even more lucrative. And then Margaret died and Jennifer's plans changed. She came to see me and told me she was tired of being a poor Indian. She said she was going to marry Richard and be rich."

"Why did she tell you this?"

"To give me pain. She blamed me for her family's sell-out to Richard. And from my weekly contact with her adopted Indian family, she'd learned I blamed myself. She knew it would hurt me to see her selling out, too."

"So Richard and Jennifer married?"

"Yes. And every time I met with Jennifer after her marriage, she'd tell me about a new affair she'd had and how Richard had encouraged it. I despaired at what she'd become—what he had emboldened her to be."

"Did Richard know about Jennifer's abortion?"

"There was no abortion, Jane. I planted that information in Jennifer's records."

"You planted it? But why?"

"To throw suspicion on Richard after her death, of course."

Jane swallowed hard. "You were setting him up?"

Leo's hands dropped between his knees. "You've got to understand.... She told me about how Richard was planning to acquire hundreds of thousands of Indian acreage by putting her name on the land deeds."

"And you killed her for that, Leo?"

Leo rubbed his face with his hands. "It wasn't planned. Over the years, in my spare time, I'd gone on experimenting with several of the Indian folk cures—particularly the brown-water algae toxin. I was hoping to isolate the right amount for a mild anesthetic. The infected oysters were waiting for my dissecting knife, sitting on the small lab table, when Jennifer dropped by just before six."

Leo lowered his hands from his face. "All she could talk about was the pittance they were paying for the richest logging land in the state. She told me Richard had already gotten a buyer for the lumber, and he was going to clear-cut the entire hundred thousand acres and make a fortune. When I tried to explain she was ripping off her own people, she just laughed at me. Told me to get wise, that this wasn't a world of cowboys and Indians anymore, but of each individual looking out for himself. She had become so like Richard, free of the constricting strings of duty or love or caring. Two exactly matched halves of a rotten whole.

"Then she saw the oysters, and before I knew it, she'd scooped up one and swallowed it. I was stunned, shocked. I opened my mouth to warn her, but nothing would come out. I watched in a kind of horrified fascination as she gobbled up the remaining three oysters. She even licked her fingers and told me how good they were."

Leo's head drooped, and his hands cupped over his white, curly hair.

"Leo, are you telling me you just let her walk out, knowing the poison would soon take effect?"

He raised his head, his large eyes full of pain. "I hadn't planned it, Jane, but when it happened, I began to look on it as fate. Indians have always believed in the power of fate. I told myself I mustn't interfere with their punishment of one of their daughters who had betrayed them."

Jane fought the small shiver that ran down her back. "What about planting the toxin in Richard's tank?"

"The idea only occurred to me the next morning, after she'd been found. I thought how perfect everything would be if Richard were subsequently charged with her murder. Then both of them would meet with justice."

Jane took a deep breath. "So you implicated him deliberately?"

"I put the infected plankton in my doctor's bag. It didn't take but a minute to dump the toxin in the tank, though I had a close call when I knocked over a stool and Suzanne came walking in unexpectedly. But she didn't see me, and then I went home to alter Jennifer's records and leave them where I knew Mabel would find them and share them with Dot. I knew Dot would blab about it first chance she got. I was sure the discrepancy between the record I gave to the police and the one she would talk about would lead to Richard. It was just a question of time."

Jane clasped her hands together. "Except you began to worry that I would read Mother's copy of your book and find the chapter you wrote about the brown-water algae toxin?"

Leo smiled. It was the same friendly smile she had grown so fond of over the years. And then it vanished as his head fell into his hands. Jane leaned forward and rested her hand lightly on his arm. "If you go to the authorities and confess, you can still stop Richard. You can tell them about what he plans to do with the land he's bought from Scabre, how he's hidden behind his wife's Indian heritage. You can expose him, Leo."

Leo's head came up; his large eyes were dry and bright. "I couldn't do that, Jane. I would be exposing myself at the same time."

Jane removed her hand from Leo's arm and leaned back. "But it's only a matter of time before—"

Leo sat up straight. "Haven't you understood the story I've told you? I'm weak. I sold out right from the first. I'm a man who has always taken the easy way."

And at that moment Jane saw him slip the knife from his pocket. An icy fear seized her insides, solidifying in her veins.

Jane wanted to jump up, to run, but all she could do was sit immobile, eyes fixed on the shiny, sharp blade of the knife in Leo's balled hand. And when Leo Speke raised the knife before her and plunged it down, her vocal cords would not even thaw sufficiently to let her scream.

Chapter Fourteen

Jane grabbed for the knife, but it was too late. Its sharp blade had already pierced Leo Speke's chest. He fell heavily to the floor, bringing her with him, as blood splattered over them both. At some level, Jane realized, she had known all along that Leo meant to kill himself, not her. Now she went into action to save his life, years of medical training automatically taking over.

In mere seconds, she had him on his back and had the knife removed, and was applying direct pressure to the wound to control the bleeding. Her hand had stayed his attempt at a deeper thrust. If she could just get an ambulance here quickly... She reached for the phone, but it was too far away, and the sound of her name being called from the hallway made her twist toward it instead.

"Jane! What's going on?" Ellen asked as she rushed into the room.

Jane gave a sigh of relief as she gestured toward the phone. "Call 911, Ellen. Leo's badly hurt."

Ellen turned toward the phone. "What happened?"

"Leo tried to kill himself, out of fear and remorse. You see, he was responsible for Jennifer's death. He's been trying to frame Richard for the crime."

Ellen grabbed up the phone from the table. "Leo? Framing Richard?"

"Ellen, please. Explanations can wait. Call 911."

A angry frown dug into Ellen's forehead as she yanked the phone cord out of the wall and stooped to pick up Leo Speke's knife where Jane had laid it on the floor. "Why should I? The bastard deserves to bleed to death."

Jane was appalled. "Ellen, you can't do this!"

A sly smile drew Ellen's lips as she slipped a lethal-looking pearl-handled gun out of her purse and pointed it at Jane. "Oh, but I can. Jennifer's death nearly ruined Richard's deal. For the last couple of days, Henry's been having to bribe the world to get adoption papers drawn up on Mr. Gnat so that Richard could legally adopt him before Scabre signed over his land. It's been absolute hell! And all because of this fool. He deserves to die for all the trouble he's caused. And so do you."

Jane battled the rising fear constricting her throat. "Me?"

Ellen's gray eyes narrowed to two thin lines. "You don't know, do you? I guess I shouldn't be surprised that mother of yours never had the guts to tell you."

"Tell me? Tell me what?"

"Richard is your father, you fool!"

The words were ludicrous. Jane's eyes flashed. "That's a lie! My father died in Vietnam. I've seen my parents' marriage certificate. It's dated two years before my birth."

"Yeah, two years before your birth. But your so-called father's death certificate is also dated ten months before your birth, and he was in Vietnam for a solid five months before he died. Do I have to explain biology to you, Ms. Doctor?"

Jane wouldn't believe what she was hearing. "My mother never would have let Richard touch her."

"Not in later years, I agree. But she was grieving after her husband died, and Richard was momentarily drawn to that pale, insipid beauty of hers. Their affair didn't last long— just long enough to produce you."

Jane could not accept this woman's words. Ellen was mad—totally mad. But she'd have to humor her. "Even if this were true, what can any of this have to do with you?"

"It has everything to do with me! Remember, Ricky is his, too! And he's a boy! You should be glad you weren't a boy, Jane. If you had been, I would have seen you never survived childhood."

It was all Jane could do not to wince under the woman's hateful glare. Danger buzzed in her ears, like a nest full of angry bees.

"Richard didn't care for girls. He made a will several years ago leaving everything to our son. Except now Ricky isn't clever enough for Richard. Or macho enough. I can see the disappointment in Richard's eyes. Then you came back to Eden Island, and you know what Richard said to me? He said, 'my daughter the doctor is back.' You understand? He'd never called you his daughter before. I knew I had to get rid of you then. I knew he was starting to see in you the legacy of cleverness and strength he wanted in an offspring. And then today, when you stood up to him, and I saw the pride in his eyes . . ."

Ellen stepped closer, the knife and gun visibly shaking in her hands. "You were very lucky when your car didn't skid over that edge. And when the fall down that flight of stairs didn't break your neck. I had to make it seem like an accident, you see. But now, this is much better."

Jane's heart pounded inside her chest. "Better?"

"Don't you see? Leo Speke killed Jennifer. He broke into your house to kill you. You struggled with the knife. After he stabbed you to death, he finally confronted the horror of his deeds and stabbed himself. They'll find you both, Jane. But it will be too late for you both."

Jane knew she had to do something, and quickly. But all she could think about was that if she removed her hand from Leo's wound he would bleed to death. The doctor in her couldn't do it. The knife was coming closer. "Ellen, please—"

But there was no mercy in the far-too-bright eyes only inches from hers as Ellen raised the knife and stooped toward her. Jane felt the terrified intake of her own breath.

"Stop!"

The shout had come from behind Ellen, startling her upright. The world exploded in flame and thunder as Ellen's gun discharged. Jane felt something hot and fast whiz by her cheek at just about the same time a hefty bulk came charging into the room and knocked the woman to the floor. Ellen fell in a graceless heap, hit her head and went out with a painful grunt. Large, capable hands grabbed up the weapons knocked from her hands and pocketed them.

Jane blinked at her rescuer, barely able to believe her eyes. "Gabe!"

Gabe rushed to her, glancing only briefly at Leo Speke's inert form. He dropped down to a knee beside her, his voice full of that insistent quality she'd come to expect, and adore. "Where are you hurt?"

Jane was surprised at his question until she got a look at her sweater, covered in Leo's blood, and understood he thought it was hers. She gazed deeply into his eyes. He looked worn down by the worry that he was determinedly trying to hide. She raised one blood-spattered hand to touch his cheek. "Gabe, I'm not hurt at all. Honest."

He cradled her hand in his, gently, possessively. "When I found out Speke had slipped out from his hospital rounds—and I knew you were alone here—I started to worry that maybe he . . . And I . . ."

"You came to the rescue," Jane said, her eyes shining.

Gabe looked deeply into her eyes and felt the warmth and strength of her belief. "I love you, Jane."

THEY WALKED TOGETHER out of the hospital into bright sunshine. The air tasted of warm spring, and Jane drank it in greedily. Then Gabe's fingers curled around hers, and she marveled at how much more alive she could feel just from his touch.

"Jane, you know Leo's going to make it?"

She looked over at him. "Yes, Dot just told me. He couldn't have really wanted to kill himself. What kind of a suicidal doctor stabs himself in the chest and misses every vital organ?"

"Yeah, too bad. Would have saved the taxpayers some money."

Jane shook her head. "You're such a fraud. You're as happy as I am that he's going to be all right."

Gabe gave her hand a tighter squeeze. "He should be well enough for arraignment in about a week. He told me he doesn't want a jury trial. Just wants to plead guilty in front of a judge and get it over with. I guess he's decided on a new way to commit suicide."

Jane savored the warmth of the sun on her skin, the warmth of his hand in hers. "Despite what he said, I think you should be ready for a change in plans."

Gabe cocked an eyebrow at her. "You know something I don't?"

Jane smiled. "I just had a long talk with Dot. She's determined Leo will fight. Asked me to take over his patients temporarily until she can get him out."

"Does she know the whole story?"

"Yes, he told her. But as far as she's concerned, no matter what Leo has done, he's still her husband, and he needs her now. You should have seen how happy that fact is making her. I'd hate to be the prosecutor going up against the energy of that woman."

Gabe squinted over at her profile. "You've taken those patients, haven't you?"

Jane smiled. "What the heck—it's time for me to get back into medicine. Frankly, I'm looking forward to it."

Gabe gave her a happy smile as he drew her to his side. "Ellen Rowe is scheduled to be arraigned this morning. Want to come?"

Memories of the woman's hateful look as she had pointed both a knife and gun at Jane gave her a shiver. "No thanks."

Gabe's arm tugged her closer. "Seems Richard Madden has also declined. He's sent her the message he didn't appreciate the lady going after his daughter."

His daughter. The words still seemed so alien to Jane. Ellen's claims about her father's death having occurred ten months before Jane's birth had proven accurate, however. Damn the woman. This was one truth Jane really believed she would have been better off not knowing.

Jane's chin came up. "Well, if he's done it on my account, I'm not impressed. I can't change the biological accident that made him my father, but what I've done with my life has nothing to do with him. Even memories of the dead man I thought was my father gave me more love and guidance than Richard Madden."

Gabe drew her very close, very tight, marveling anew at how well she was handling this mind-boggling revelation. He raised a hand to caress her silky hair. "He called to thank me for uncovering Leo's plot to frame him. Told me he'd be glad to support any run I might like to make for sheriff."

Jane stiffened in Gabe's arms and pulled back, her eyes wide and searching. Richard was at it again. Only this time his target was Gabe. Would Gabe—? No, of course not. He was his own man. Every forthright, determined line in that handsome face said so. This man was not for sale at any price. Jane's heart smiled as she asked nonchalantly, "So how did you tell him to get lost?"

Gabe loved the way this woman's belief in him made him feel. A sensation he couldn't have begun to describe poured through his heart at the amazing fact of her here in his arms. His eyes smiled down at her. "I let some dial tone say it for me."

Then he drew her closer in his arms and kissed her eyes and her cheeks and finally her lips, softly, gently—with all the tenderness that gave his heart such strength. "You know, I think maybe we should make sure Leo Speke has a well-publicized trial."

Jane searched his face. "You want the story of the logging fraud to come out, don't you?"

"Can you think of a better way to stop Madden?"

Gabe saw a familiar gleam in her eyes. "He'll hate you for it. He'll use everything in his power to stop you."

Gabe smiled. "And he'll lose."

Jane's face glowed with pride. "Yes, he will. I love you, Gabe."

He'd known she did, of course. Or at least he'd told himself she must a dozen times. But hearing it, seeing her glowing face, her shining eyes, he lost it. He just lost it. Suddenly he was clutching her tightly in her arms, and an ocean of need had filled him. "Jane?"

Jane felt an anticipatory tingle down her spine at the way he said her name. "Yes?"

It was there in her eyes. He could see his next question, already asked and answered. Damn it, but he wouldn't let her second-guess him. "Ah...you were helpful on this case. Without you, it might have taken me another day or two to get to the bottom of it."

Jane drew back, stunned. This was not what she had expected. "I was helpful on this case?" Her hands found her hips as she sputtered with indignation. "Another day or two? Why, you arrogant, ungrateful, pompous know-it-all! You know perfectly well that without my help you would have been completely dumbfounded. Now, why don't you just have the guts to come out and admit it?"

Gabe took her into his arms again as a laugh erupted in his throat. "Only if you'll admit you can't live without me."

"Can't live without you? Such arrogance! Such—"

But Jane never got to the end of her sentence, because suddenly Gabe was kissing her, deep and hard and desperate, and she was responding just as passionately. When he finally drew away, several warm minutes later, his husky voice was low and breathy in her ear. "Jane, there's no use denying it. We were made for each other. Marry me and I promise we'll fight and make love the rest of our lives."

Jane fought down the excited rush his words brought to her heart. She had no intention of giving in easily to what had taken him far too long to say. Her eyes flashed up at him, and her voice asked, much too sweetly, "But I thought you never planned to let any woman take you for that big of a ride?"

Gabe smiled into those devilish green eyes. "Ah, there's that vengeful streak in you that I love so much. Jane, you're not taking me on this ride. We're taking each other. And I promise it will be one neither of us will ever want to get off. Now come here, my lioness. Your mate is calling."

Jane came, her heart purring happily as she nestled contentedly in his arms.

HARLEQUIN®

I N T R I G U E®

43 Light St.

It looks like a charming old building near the Baltimore waterfront, but inside 43 Light Street lurks danger ... and romance.

Labeled a "true master of intrigue" by *Rave Reviews*, bestselling author Rebecca York continues her exciting series with #213 HOPSCOTCH, coming to you in February.

Paralegal Noel Emery meets an enigmatic man from her past and gets swept away on a thrilling international adventure—where illusion and reality shift like the images in a deadly kaleidoscope....

"Ms. York ruthlessly boggles the brain and then twists our jangled nerves beyond the breaking point in this electrifying foray into hi-tech skullduggery and sizzling romance!"
—Melinda Helfer, *Romantic Times*

Don't miss Harlequin Intrigue #213 HOPSCOTCH!

LS93-1

HARLEQUIN®

INTRIGUE®

They say a cat has nine lives....

Caroline Burnes brings back Familiar, the clever
crime-solving cat, his second Harlequin Intrigue
coming next month:

#215   TOO FAMILIAR
by Caroline Burnes
February 1993

A night stalker was about to bring terror to a small
Tennessee town and Cassandra McBeth feared that her
nightmares would become tomorrow's headlines. Then
Familiar came to town with some uncanny abilities.

And be sure to watch for the third book in this
new "FEAR FAMILIAR Mystery Series"—
THRICE FAMILIAR—coming to you in September,
from Harlequin Intrigue.

"Oh, to hell with it." Reaching up, he touched the tip of his finger to her lower lip.

Her mouth opened on a soft gasp and he dipped his head until only a breath separated them. "The second I saw you, I wondered what you'd taste like. If you'd rather me not find out, can you say something?"

Lena blinked. Wow. Her brain had just gone completely blank. "Umm."

"Is that a back-off?" he asked.

"No. No, I don't think so."

"Good."

His mouth came down on hers, easy and light, keeping it slow at first. She opened for him and shuddered as he traced his tongue along her lower lip. He tasted like coffee and chocolate cheese-cake and man. Delicious. Lifting a hand, she placed it on his cheek. There was the faintest rasp of stubble under her palm, very faint. Curious, she trailed her fingers along his neck, dipped them into his hair, but as curious as she was about how he looked, the curiosity was slowly dying under the heat of hunger.

He could kiss.

Humming under her breath, she moved closer and brought her other hand up, resting it on his hip. Lean hips, she couldn't help but notice that. And the body she pressed against was also lean, long and lean. Heat started to pulse through her, but that was little surprise. It had already been on a slow burn from the time she'd sat down next to him.

He skimmed a hand down her spine, resting it at the small of her back. She shivered under that touch and when he pressed her closer, tucking her lower body more firmly against his, the shivering got worse. She almost came out of her skin. Need tightened her belly and she rocked closer, all but ready to ride the hard ridge pressed against her belly.

And she just might have tried to do that—just might have asked him if maybe he'd come back to her place—just might have lost her ever-loving mind.

But a car horn blared, shattering the calm night air, and Lena pulled away, sucking air in desperately.

Her heart. Shit. It was pounding so hard, she thought it just might explode out of her chest.

Swallowing, she licked her lips and then she could have whimpered, begged for mercy, because she could taste him. Taste him, and it made her want to throw herself against him and kiss him. Again, and again . . . and then stop just long enough to lose all their clothes.

IF YOU
HEAR HER

SHILOH WALKER

BALLANTINE BOOKS • NEW YORK

A Ballantine Books Mass Market Original

Published in the United States by Ballantine Books, an imprint of The Random House Publishing Group, a division of Random House, Inc., New York.

BALLANTINE and colophon are trademarks of Random House, Inc.

This book contains an excerpt from the forthcoming book *If You See Her* by Shiloh Walker. This excerpt has been set for this edition only and may not reflect the final content of the forthcoming edition.

ISBN 978-0-345-51753-1
eBook ISBN 978-0-345-51757-9

Printed in the United States of America

www.ballantinebooks.com

9 8 7 6 5 4 3 2 1

Ballantine mass market edition: November 2011

For Lora Leigh and Jaci Burton—thanks, ladies, for helping me stay grounded back when I was trying to get this story together.

For Lynn Viehl, for reading it through when I was trying to figure out if this was even a story worth telling.

For Irene Goodman, my agent—thanks for taking me on in the middle of a mess, for falling in love with the story, and for giving me other stuff to worry about besides the writing.

For my editor Kate—thanks so much for being so excited about this series and for not letting my insanity drive you insane, too.

For my Twitter friend Shannon and her willingness to help me out while I wrote Lena's story.

And last, but never least . . . always, to my family. I love you all. You're my always and my everything. I thank God for you every day, and it's still not often enough.

IF YOU
HEAR HER

CHAPTER
ONE

HER NAME WAS CARLY WATSON.

The final hours of her life were brutal.

She didn't know where she was. She didn't know how long she'd been there. By that point, she was so wracked with pain, so desperate for escape, she barely remembered who she was.

She was twenty-three. She was going to medical school. She was bright, eager, and before she'd fallen into this hell, she had loved life. Now she just prayed for it to end.

She had been stuck in that hellish darkness for hours, days, possibly weeks.

And she knew she would die there.

She knew he was coming back—the door creaked. It was like a death knell, heralding his arrival. As the door swung open, the ancient hinges protested.

A sob bubbled up in her throat as he laid a hand on her calf and stroked up. She cringed away as much as she could, but the restraints at her wrists, waist, knees, and ankles didn't allow for much movement.

When he cupped his hand over her sex, her scream, long and desperate, split the air.

Her kidnapper, rapist, and soon-to-be killer watched,

amused . . . pleased with her terror. "Go ahead and scream, sweetheart. Nobody can hear you."

"Please . . ." her throat was so dry and raw from how she had cried. How she had begged. How she had pleaded. She almost hated herself, for begging. For giving him that pleasure. Some part of her just wasn't ready to accept the truth, wasn't ready to give up.

Even though, in her heart, she knew it was useless. "Just let me go. Please let me go . . . I won't tell anybody, I swear."

He sighed. It was a sigh of long-suffering patience, the one a parent might give a child. He even patted her shoulder as he murmured, "Yes, I'm sure you won't."

A loud sound rasped through the air and she whimpered as she recognized it. A zipper. He was getting undressed—no, no, no . . .

Hysterical panic tore through her and she started to scream.

He raped her again.

Her voice gave out long before she was able to escape inside herself.

This time, though, her escape was final. She had retreated somewhere deep inside herself—somewhere where pain didn't exist, where terror didn't exist.

When he ended her life, she never even knew—she was already gone.

Her name was Carly Watson.

It was a lovely day, the kind of day you just didn't get too often. The air was warm and mild, with clear sunshine beaming down. A soft breeze drifted by. Under the trees, it was just a bit cooler.

The perfect sort of day for a walk.

At least, Lena Riddle would've thought so. But halfway through, her dog started getting anxious. Puck didn't do anxious. Not in the four years she'd had him. But there he was, pulling against his leash, like he was determined not to let her take their normal route through the woods.

"Come on, Puck. You wanted to go for a walk, remember?"

She tried to take another step, but the big yellow retriever sat down. He wasn't going to move an inch.

Just then, faintly, oh so very faintly, she heard . . . something.

Puck growled. "Hush," she murmured, reaching down and resting a hand on his head. He had his hackles up, his entire body braced and tensed. "Easy, boy. Just take it easy."

Standing in the middle of the trail, with her head cocked, she listened. The faint breeze that had been blowing all day abruptly died and all those faint sounds of life she could always hear in the woods faded down to nothingness. A heartbeat passed, then another.

It was utterly silent.

Then it came again. Something . . . muffled. Faint. An animal? Trapped?

She scowled absently, concentrating. There it was again. Her brow puckered as she focused, trying to lock in on the sound better.

Puck whined in his throat and tugged on his leash, demandingly. Lena turned her head, trying to follow that sound. It was gone, though. The breeze returned and all she could hear now were the leaves rustling in the breeze, the sound of a bird call, and somewhere off in the distance, a car's motor.

Still, the faint memory of that sound, whatever it was, sent a shiver down her spine.

"You know what, Puck?" she murmured. "I think you're right. Let's get the hell out of here."

She only had a few hours left before she had to go to work anyway.

*   *   *

". . . there. . . ."

He stood over her, studied her hair.

The gleaming blond strands were shorn now to chin length, perfectly straight, even as could be.

Her eyes, sightless and fixed, stared overhead.

That blank look on her face irritated him, but he wasn't surprised. He had seen this coming, after all. Something about the way she had reacted, the way she'd screamed.

The life had gone out of his girl and once that fight was gone . . .

Well. That was just how it was.

Carefully gathering up the hair, he selected what he wanted and then bagged up the rest, adding it to the pack he'd carry out of here. Later. Few things still that he had to handle.

He studied her body, the long slim lines of it, her limbs pale and flaccid now, the softly rounded swell of her belly. Nice, full breasts . . . he did like a good pair of tits on a woman. The dull gleam of gold at her throat from the necklace she wore. Strong, sleek shoulders.

Stooping down beside her, he hefted her lifeless body in his arms.

What he needed to do now wasn't going to be pleasant, and he wouldn't do it here.

"So what do you think it was?"

"Hell, I don't know." A sigh slipped past Lena's lips as she turned to face her best friend. Just talking to Roslyn Jennings made her feel better. And slightly silly. It had probably been nothing. Nothing . . . although it had bothered her dog something awful. "It sure as hell had Puck freaked out, though."

"You sound a little freaked out, too."

"Yeah. You could say that."

Although, really, freaked out didn't quite touch it.

Grimacing, Lena forced herself to focus. Should pay more attention to what she was doing or she was going to end up slicing up her fingers as well as the potatoes. It wouldn't do the Inn's reputation any good if word got out that the chef was adding body parts to the dishes, she thought morbidly.

For some reason, that thought sent a shiver down her spine.

"It sure doesn't sound like Puck. I mean, that's not like him. He loves his walks, right?"

"Yep. He does. And you're right . . . this isn't like him." She couldn't recall him ever acting quite like that before. He was a good dog, protective, loving . . . a friend.

"Let's talk about this noise you heard. If we can figure out what it was, maybe we can figure out what had Puck so freaked out. It probably had something to do with the noise, right? I mean, it makes sense."

"I can't place it. Weird grunting. Kind of muffled."

"Don't take this wrong, but do you think maybe you heard somebody going at it?" Roslyn's voice was a mixture of skepticism and interest.

"Going at it?" Lena asked, blankly. "Going at what?"

For about two seconds, Roz was silent. Then she burst into laughter. "Oh, sweetie, it's been way too long since you've gotten laid. Sex, girl. Do you remember what sex is?"

"Yes. Vaguely." Scowling, she went at the potatoes with a little more enthusiasm than necessary. Oh, yes, she remembered sex. It had been close to a year since she'd gotten any, and before that? It had been college.

But, yes, she remembered sex.

"So, you think maybe a couple of people were out there screwing? Although, hell, if some guy is going to talk me into stripping nekkid in the great outdoors, it had better be good sex. Bug bites. Ticks. Poison ivy."

"Sunburn," Lena offered helpfully. Perpetually pale, she had to slather down with SPF 60 just for a jaunt to the mailbox. Well, maybe not that bad. But still.

"Sunburned hoo-haa. Heh. Doesn't sound like fun, does it? Although if the guy is good . . . but you were in the woods, right? So scratch the sunburned hoo-haa. So, what do you think . . . could you have just heard some private moments?"

"You're a pervert, you know that?" Lena grinned at her best friend. Then she shrugged. "And . . . I don't know. I really don't know. The only thing I know for sure is that Puck didn't want to be there—that's just not like him."

The dog at Lena's feet shifted. She rinsed her hands and then crouched down in front of him, stroking his head. "It's okay, pal. I understand."

He licked her chin and she stood up.

As she turned to wash her hands again, she heard the telltale whisper of the cookie jar. Smiling, she said, "If you eat all of those, you're out of luck until next week. I am not whipping up another batch tomorrow. You're stuck with whatever you bought from the store. With that wedding you've got planned, Jake and I are going to be busy enough as it is."

Jake was the other chef here at Running Brook. They split the week, Jake working Monday through Wednesday and Lena working Thursday through Saturday—they traded off on Sundays, but with the wedding they had going on tomorrow, they both needed to be here.

"That wedding," Roz muttered around a mouthful of cookie. "Hell, that wedding is why I need the cookie—and store-bought isn't going to hold me right now, sweetie. I need the real stuff. Good stuff. Shit. If I thought I could get away with it, I would have a White Russian or three to go along with the cookie."

"No drinking on the job. Not even for the owner."

Lena smirked. "Hell, you're the one who had to go and decide to start doing these boutique weddings. You all but have a welcome mat out . . . 'Bridezillas accepted and welcomed.'" Shoving off the counter, she joined Roz at the island. "Gimme one of those before you eat them all."

Roz pushed a cookie into her hand and Lena bit down. Mouth full of macadamias, white chocolate, and cranberries, she made her way to the coffeepot. "Since you can't have a White Russian, you want some coffee?"

"No." Roslyn sighed. "The last thing I need right now is coffee. I'm supposed to be meeting the bride and her mom in a half hour to discuss the floral arrangements."

In the middle of getting a clean mug from the cabinet, Lena frowned. "Discuss the floral arrangements . . . the wedding is tomorrow."

"Exactly. Which is why I need cookies." She huffed out a breath. "Damn. I really do need that White Russian, you know. But I'll have to settle for the cookies."

Lena smiled as her friend went for another one. That emergency stash wasn't going to last the day, much less the weekend. She thought through her schedule and decided she might try to make up another batch. She could probably find the time. It sounded like Roz would probably need it. They were all going to need it, probably.

"Does she want to change the floral arrangements or what?"

Roz groaned. There was a weird thunk, followed by her friend's muffled voice. "I don't know. She just wanted to discuss the flowers. She had some concerns." There were two more thunks.

"Well, banging your head on the counter isn't going to do much good . . . unless you hit it hard enough to knock yourself out. Otherwise, all it's going to do is give you a headache."

"I've already got a headache," Roz muttered.

"Look, if she does have the idea of changing the arrangements around, explain to her that the florist here closes at noon on Fridays. Somebody will have already made sure the orders are covered, but changing the orders would just be too difficult, and it could be too chancy to try someplace outside of town. If you lay it on thick enough, she's not going to want to risk it."

"Hmmm. Good point." The stool scraped against the tile floor as Roz stood up. "I knew there was a reason I hired you."

"You hired me for my cookies," Lena said, her voice dry.

"Another reason, then." She took a deep breath. "Okay, no more cookies. I'm going to check on a few things before I go talk to my . . . client."

"Good luck. But do me a favor . . . if she decides she needs a last-minute menu change? Stonewall her. I don't care how, and I don't care what you say. Stonewall her."

"This woman can't be stonewalled." Roz sighed. "I think she might just *be* Stonewall. His reincarnation or something. You can't stonewall a Stonewall, right?"

"Figure a way out." There was no way she was doing a last-minute menu change.

CHAPTER
TWO

August 2010

THE LATE SUMMER SUN BEAT DOWN ON HIS BACK AS Ezra King hauled a two-by-four up onto the deck. Hot as a bitch outside, miserable hot, edging close to ninety degrees, but he didn't let it slow him down.

Nope, he was going to get this damn deck built before fall. He wanted it done so he could spend the cool—assuming it cooled off—fall nights out on the deck, staring into nothingness while he contemplated the best way to waste the rest of his life.

"Anything other than carpentry," he muttered. "Anything."

Once he got through the damned, do-it-yourself hell that was this house, he was done with hammers. At least that was what he told himself. Part of him enjoyed it, though. It was kind of cool, watching something unfold in front of you, something that started with just a bare wisp of an idea. Hard work, money, and sweat was all it took to make that idea into reality.

Ezra had been raised to appreciate the value of hard work—he'd hated it at the time, but now it served him well. Nothing worth having came for free. A guy wants something, he works for it or pays for it. Otherwise, he doesn't get it—doesn't deserve it. That was life.

Like this deck. Ezra wanted it, he wanted it done his way, and he didn't want to pay somebody else to do it for him—he might have some money tucked away, but if he wanted it to last, he had to be careful. So here he was, doing it himself. But damn, he'd be glad when it was done.

Around lunchtime, he stopped, but only because his stomach was growling so loud he could hear it over the hammer. After a messy BLT and half a pitcher of iced tea, he headed back outside and once more fell into a rhythm, hammering nails into the wood, fetching another, and another.

He lost track of time, his mind blanking out on him.

Stripped down to a pair of low-slung khaki shorts and tennis shoes, he worked. A red bandanna held his sweat-dampened brown hair back from his face and sunglasses hid green eyes.

He had a pretty face, a fact he'd been told more than once in his life. Back in school, he'd gotten into more than a few fights because of it. It was just a face, his dad's face, with his mom's green eyes.

Having that face was both a curse and blessing, as far as he saw it. Girls had been flirting with him for as long as he could remember, even before he was old enough to really understand what flirting was. As he got older and started school, all the pretty little girls who flirted with him ended up catching the attention of the boys in his grade and more than once, that had gotten him into trouble.

Eventually, he got to the point where he enjoyed all the flirting enough to ignore the teasing that was directed his way. At least, most of the time.

In his junior year of high school, he got into a fight with one of the other players on the basketball team. His nose was broken in that fight and he was also forced to quit the team after his folks got the call from school.

It had seemed harsh at the time, but looking back, he was glad he had parents who loved him enough to be strict, who loved him enough to enforce their rules, even when it hurt.

To his mother's dismay and his own delight, his nose hadn't healed perfectly straight. That slight crook to his nose made his face just a little less pretty.

Over the years, Ezra hadn't changed much. The dimples in his cheeks had deepened to slashes. He shaved in the morning, but come late afternoon, that five o'clock shadow made its appearance. He was still long and lean, although he'd finally put some weight on in college, thanks to lifting weights.

Now, those muscles were warm and loose. Even the screwed-up muscles in his right thigh. He'd taken a bullet in that leg six months earlier, which was why he was living out here in Ash, Kentucky. He'd walked away from his job, from his badge, and he didn't think he wanted to go back.

He knew his leg would hurt like a bitch later once the muscles tightened up on him. It would be hell come nightfall. But he'd deal with it then.

The deck was shaping up pretty damn good, he had to admit.

He took another short break around three when he heard the familiar rumble of a jeep. The rural mail carrier had bills for him and a box. As the jeep headed off, Ezra jammed the bills in his back pocket and tore into the box—books . . . and hot damn, one of them was a book he'd spent the past few months trying to track down.

Ezra didn't open it, though. He was tempted, but he made himself tuck the book back into the box. For now. If he started reading now, he wasn't going to finish anything else but the book today and damn it, he wanted to get more done on the deck.

After stowing the mail in the kitchen and refilling his

thermos with iced tea, he headed back outside, going through the side door.

He heard the purr of an engine and glanced up toward the highway in front of his house. The sight of the long, black stretch limo made him pause.

Scowling, he unscrewed his thermos and drinking, watched the limo until the gleaming black car disappeared around a curve.

He knew where it was going—Running Brook Inn. When he had visited Ash as a kid, the big old house had been run-down and just this side of ugly. After the owner had died, one of the heirs had the brilliant idea to turn it into a bed-and-breakfast, and the idea took off.

But now it wasn't just a B&B. It had a small restaurant and they also did "boutique" weddings—whatever in the hell that was.

And it all added up to a fairly steady amount of traffic going by his place on a regular basis. He'd come out here seeking the peace and quiet he'd remembered from his youth, not a steady string of cars and limos and traffic.

"Hell. It's not like they're driving through the front yard," he muttered, brushing his irritation aside. Pushing the limo out of his mind, he got back to work. He didn't stop until he began to lose the light.

By that time, the muscles in his injured thigh were screaming, and his head was pounding along, too.

A hot shower, a sandwich, then he'd crash, and he'd be as good as new.

But after the shower, Ezra realized he wasn't in the mood for a sandwich or a microwave pizza, or any of the other fast, cheap crap that currently filled his freezer or fridge.

Not that he had a lot of choices in Ash, but he wanted real food. Since he couldn't cook worth shit, that meant leaving the house.

Since it was Friday, the café on Main Street would still be open. Plus, there was the Turnkey Bar and Grill.

But instead of heading into town, Ezra found himself turning right, heading toward the bed-and-breakfast.

Of course, it was nearly ten by the time he got there.

And as he settled down at the long, sleek sprawl of mahogany wood, he noticed something.

He was kind of underdressed. His jeans and T-shirt did not fit in with the khakis and Dockers and polo shirts.

He couldn't care less. As long as he had some food.

He could smell something mouthwatering. Garlic. Spice. Lasagna, maybe . . .

"Hey, can I get a menu?"

The bartender gave him a friendly, apologetic smile. "Sorry, but the kitchen closed at nine-thirty. We've got bar food, if you're interested. We serve that until eleven."

"Closed," he repeated. His stomach growled demandingly and he wouldn't have been surprised if he'd been drooling . . . whatever had been on the menu? That was what he wanted. Not bar food.

"Yeah, afraid so. Sorry." He glanced at his watch and grimaced.

Blowing out a sigh, Ezra asked, "So what kind of bar food?"

One good thing—the beer was cold. Five minutes later, he was watching the TV mounted over the bar when he caught a glimpse of somebody from the corner of his eye. He also heard the oddly familiar clack of nails on hardwood. Frowning, he turned his head.

The clacking wasn't coming from her, that was certain.

She was a looker.

For the first fifteen seconds, Ezra didn't notice the dog at her side or anything else, because he was too busy staring at her.

Damn—

She wore a pair of sunglasses, despite the low lights

used in the bar. Her hair, dark red and gleaming under
soft lights, was short. The ends curled under, framing a
narrow, feline face and a wide mobile mouth that just
about screamed S-E-X.

Her skin was pale and creamy, the kind of skin that
either got slathered with sunscreen religiously or just
never saw the sun. Tall—he pegged her at 5'9" and most
of it was probably leg.

Damn. She was definitely something worth looking at,
too. Actually, she was probably the best thing he'd looked
at in quite a while. Did she live here? He didn't remember ever seeing her during his infrequent visits in the years
before Grandma died, but granted, he hadn't left the house
that much except to go fishing or take her to church.

He heard that weird clacking again and glanced down.
That was when he saw the dog. A big, beautiful yellow
retriever—wearing a rather distinctive vest. The dog
walked alongside the woman, keeping pace with her perfectly, and with each step, his nails clacked on the hardwood floor. The redhead walked as she stood—looking
neither left, nor right, shoulders back, chin up.

Blind.

Ezra frowned, watching her every step as she neared
the bar.

"Hi, Paul. How's it going?"

"Going just fine, Lena. You want a drink while you
wait for Carter?"

She reached out a hand, brushed it against the back of
one chair at the bar. "Yeah. Rum and Diet Coke, I
guess." With a slow, easy grace, she settled in the chair.

Ezra found himself staring at her mouth.

Staring . . . and wondering how she'd taste.

Her head turned toward him, cocked to the side.
"Hello?"

"Ahhh . . . hey."

The bartender glanced at him, grinned. "She's got ears like a bloodhound."

The woman made a face at the bartender. "I do not. I just felt somebody looking at me." A faint smile curled her lips. "Apparently he's never seen a blind woman."

"It's not that," Ezra said, scowling, a little disgusted at the way she talked about him like he wasn't there.

She shifted in her seat, turning to face him. She rested an arm against the gleaming wood of the bar and cocked a brow. "Okay, so if it's not me, perhaps it's Puck."

"Puck?"

"Puck." The dog at her feet perked his ears and lifted his head. "My dog. Sometimes people don't like seeing him in restaurants."

"Gotcha. No, it's not your dog. Nice-looking animal, but no. And unless he starts trying to eat my food, I'm not worried about him being here."

He had the sexiest damn voice, Lena thought. *Sexiest voice . . . and he was still staring at her, too.*

She could tell, all but feel the warmth of his gaze. Feel it, almost like a ray of light traveling over her body, leaving seductive warmth in its wake. She fought the urge to squirm in the chair, settled for petting Puck. Normally, she'd have the dog lying at her feet, but right now, she needed the comfort of touching him.

"Well, if you're going to keep staring at me, then maybe you should introduce yourself."

"Ezra King. And you are . . . ?"

She held out her hand. "Lena. Lena Riddle."

A warm, rough palm pressed against hers. Strong. Callused, like he spent a lot of time working with his hands. His skin didn't have the crepey feel of an older person. Damn, better and better. Her libido was going to be hard to control here in a minute, especially if he kept staring at her.

"So, Ezra King, why are you staring at me?"

"Because you're beautiful."

Lena didn't blush often. She rarely felt self-conscious. But in that moment, she could feel the rush of blood to her cheeks and she had to fight the urge to squirm around on her seat and fidget.

"Ahhh. Well, thank you." Behind her, she heard the squeak as the kitchen doors opened and she could have heaved a sigh of relief.

"Here you go, Lena." Mike, the assistant chef, set down her lasagna. Her mouth watered at the smell.

"Thanks, Mike."

"Sir, you had the wings?"

"Yeah."

As Mike retreated into the kitchen, Ezra muttered, "I'd rather have the lasagna, though. How come you could still get it?"

"Because I made it and set it aside until I was done with work." She shot a smile in Ezra's direction. "I'm one of the chefs here at the Inn."

"Really?"

She heard him shift, then his voice murmured from just a few inches away. "I really need to come out here the next time you have lasagna."

Man, that voice . . . "Hey, Paul, can you get me a plate?"

As Paul set a plate on the counter, she pushed hers toward Ezra. "Tell you what, go ahead and try some. I won't eat all of it anyway."

He hesitated and Lena smirked. "Come on, you were sitting there griping about not getting any lasagna, so take some. And if you like it, you'll just have to come back before the kitchen closes next time."

"Well, if you put it that way."

She sipped from her rum and Coke while she waited for him to finish. She almost choked on her drink when he asked, "So, the next time I'm out here, maybe you could have dinner with me."

Is he asking me for a date?

She stalled for time by taking another sip from her drink and then set it down. "You want me to have dinner with you?"

"Well, that's kind of what I just said."

"Why?"

She looked cute when she was confused. But then again, Ezra was pretty sure he'd like how she looked no matter what expression she had on her face. "You always question a guy when he asks you out on a date?"

"You're asking me on a date?"

From the corner of his eye, he could see the bartender listening and not pretending not to. The kid barely looked old enough to be out of college—hell, high school.

Tuning the kid out of his mind, he focused on Lena. "Yeah, I'm asking you on a date. At least, I'm trying to. It's been awhile since I've asked a woman on a date, so maybe I'm doing it wrong."

"Well, it's been awhile since a guy asked me on a date, so maybe I've just forgotten how to recognize the clues." That pretty, wide mouth curled up in a slow smile.

She had to say yes. Because he really, really wanted to kiss that mouth. He wanted to fist his hand in that dark red hair and he wanted to press his face between the slight swell of her breasts and nuzzle the soft skin there.

He was a pretty good judge of people—he knew how to read them. Under most circumstances, at least, and he didn't think he was reading her wrong.

If he was reading her right, then she was feeling that same, subtle tug that he felt. Banking on that, he reached out and skimmed his fingers down her forearm. "Well, now that we've figured out what we're doing here, maybe we should try it again. I'd like to have dinner . . . with you. Would you be interested?"

"You know, I don't think I've ever had a guy ask me out on a date within five minutes of seeing me." The smile on her face took on a bitter slant as she absently touched the dark glasses that shielded her eyes. "Usually, within five minutes of seeing me, they're either on the other side of the room or they're trying to cut my food for me."

Ezra glanced at the lasagna on his plate. "I figure if you can make it, you can cut it just fine on your own. And you haven't answered me."

"No. I haven't. I'm still thinking . . . hell. Screw it. You know what, Ezra? I'd love to have dinner with you."

"When?"

"If a late dinner works well enough for you, we can try tomorrow night. I'm in the kitchen until ten. There's no lasagna on the menu, though. Just be here around this time, and I'll make sure I save you a meal. How does that sound?"

"Like a plan."

On the drive home, Lena could feel the weight of Carter's gaze every so often. Knowing she'd be getting it from him or Roz sooner or later, she finally said, "Out with it, buddy."

He chuckled. "Was just wondering about the guy you were eating with in the bar."

"Hmmm. That would be Ezra King." She smiled to herself. Just saying his name had her heart racing a little bit. It had been a long, long while since a guy had made her react that way. She couldn't even remember the last time it had happened.

"Ezra King." Carter said the name a few times, an annoying habit of his, not that she'd tell him. Roz thought his absentmindedness was endearing. "King . . . wonder if he's related to old June King."

"Wouldn't know."

Carter glanced over at her, saw the smile on her face, and laughed again. "Yeah, that's right. You're still fairly new."

"Am not." She stuck her tongue out at him. "I've lived here for years. Just because I don't have family that lived here back when Noah walked the earth doesn't make me new."

"Hey, now. The Jennings clan hasn't been here that long. Maybe since Moses. But not Noah." Scratching his chin, he tried to think through the names he could remember of June King's surviving kin. He couldn't quite do it. She'd had some children, but they hadn't stuck around. Grandkids, too. But he couldn't remember much about them, either. "Well, if it's her grandson, he's probably the decent sort."

"I'm so glad he meets your approval." Lena rolled her eyes.

"Smart-ass." He hit the signal as he drew close to her drive. "So. Are you going to see him again?"

"Technically, I haven't seen him at all. This wasn't really a date. We just met. He was drooling over my dinner—I liked his voice and I liked him, so I shared it. But yeah. We're meeting for dinner tomorrow at the Inn." She turned her face toward him, a look of mock, hopeful innocence on her pretty face. "Is that okay, Daddy? I mean, he's really nice and all and I'll be good . . ."

"You're such a pest." He stopped in front of the house. "But the Inn's a good place. We can make sure he's treating you right."

"Oh, please. Like Puck or me would let him do anything else."

Ezra was back at the Inn at 9:30, and this time, he wasn't wearing jeans. The khaki pants he could handle and he'd found a somewhat faded, but mostly unwrinkled polo shirt tucked in the back of his closet. It was the best he could do, but he did shave and it wasn't until he was sitting down at the bar and waiting for Lena that he started to get nervous.

And he got nervous because he let himself think about what he was doing.

He was waiting on a date.

A fucking date.

What in the hell was he doing?

He didn't need to be dating right now . . . did he?

Head was too fucked-up, and too often, he spent time lost in some black, black moments.

Bad date material. Very bad.

But even as he tried to convince himself of that, he couldn't get up and leave. It was dinner. A meal, right? A meal with a pretty lady, and obviously going by the lasagna from yesterday, a pretty lady who could cook. They could share a meal, some conversation—should be easy, he figured.

His screwed-up head didn't even have to enter into it, right?

Food. Conversation. At the end of the night, they'd go their separate ways, and maybe, just maybe he could get her phone number. Nice and easy . . . nothing complicated about it.

Easy.

And it was, he realized. Sitting back at the bar with her, sharing a meal and some conversation.

He hadn't been lying when he said it had been awhile since he'd asked anybody on a date—it had been months since he'd been on a date, years since he'd really asked anybody out.

But still, it was easy. Being with Lena? Felt easy. Felt . . . natural.

"You haven't lived here very long," she mentioned as she cut into the roasted chicken.

"That obvious?"

"Small town. I'd have heard the name before if you had been living here long . . . although the last name is familiar. You're June King's grandson?"

"Yeah." Small towns were strange places. A guy could forever be known as somebody's son, grandson. This was his particular identifier here—June King's grandson. Not that he minded. His grandmother had been one hell of a lady and it seemed like just about everybody who had known her had loved her. "Did you know her?"

"Not so much." Lena shrugged and took a sip of her water. "I've only lived here going on nine years and I know her health started to slide the last few years she was alive. I met her a few times, though. She seemed like a wonderful lady."

"She was."

"It makes you sad," she murmured. "I'm sorry."

"Loss always sucks." He scooped up some mashed potatoes and took a bite, swallowing despite the knot in his throat. "She was a hell of a cook, too, but I'll tell you what, I think you could have given her a run for her money. How did you get started doing this—did you always want to?"

"You really want to know?" A smile tugged at her lips. Something about that smile had him curious. "Yeah."

"I did it to piss my mom off."

"Piss your mom off?" he echoed. Baffled, he set his fork down and asked, "Just how in the hell does becoming a chef warrant getting your mom pissed off?"

"Well, being a chef involves things like knives, and hot stoves," Lena drawled. An amused grin curled her lips, amused . . . and just a little devilish. "In her eyes, it was a veritable death trap for somebody who couldn't see. She's the overprotective type."

"And your dad?"

Lena sighed, that smile faded from her face. "He's dead. Died in an accident when I was twelve." Absently she reached up, rubbing at her eyes under her tinted lenses. "Dad was always pushing me to do whatever I wanted, whatever I could. Mom was more hesitant, but Dad encouraged her to let me try. After he died, well . . . she reacted by hovering. Clutching me too close. Those overprotective moms you hear about on TV sometimes? My mom could have given them lessons."

She turned her face toward his and grimaced. "Not exactly the ideal date discussion we're having here."

"Says who?" He bumped his shoulder against hers and said, "I'm enjoying the conversation. Sure as hell beats some of the inane crap I've listened to in my life."

"Inane." The somber expression on her face slowly faded, replaced by a smile. "Points for using 'inane,' Ezra. But let's try to lighten things up a little. What brings you to Ash?"

Not the way to lighten things up, he brooded. Trying to keep the edge from his voice, he said, "I lived in Lexington until a few months ago and took some time away from my job. Since Gran left me the house, I decided to come here. Place is getting run-down, needs some work on it, and it's easier to do if I'm here anyway."

"To stay?"

"That's what I'm here to figure out," he said softly.

There was something in his voice, Lena thought.

She didn't know him well enough to entirely put her finger on it, but she could hear the strain. And sitting next to him, she had felt the way he'd gone rigid even though he'd forced himself to relax almost immediately.

But she wasn't going to pry.

At least, not yet.

Maybe if he asked her out again . . .

A nice, easy date.

Comfortable, even, Ezra thought as he followed Lena

through the doors to the verandah that wrapped around the old house. She was easy to talk to, easy to look at it . . . and when she smiled at him . . . well, he couldn't call that easy. It hit him in the chest, in the weirdest damn way.

Like now, for example. She was leaning at the railing, the breeze blowing the dark, gleaming red strands of her hair around her face, the corners of her mouth curving up ever so slightly. As though she had a secret.

Lots of them. Crossing the verandah, he stopped just a foot away from her, studying that secretive, small smile.

It was a Mona Lisa smile, he decided, and now he understood why that smile had captivated millions for centuries. Trying to understand just what it was that had inspired that smile . . . yeah, he could spend quite some time trying to figure out what Lena's secrets were.

"I enjoyed dinner," he said, tucking his hands in his pockets. He needed to keep them occupied before he reached up and brushed that hair back from her face. If he touched her, even in a simple innocent way, he might get a taste for it—want more—and he already knew that wasn't happening tonight.

He didn't live for the frustrated lifestyle.

"I'm glad."

"Although, I'd kind of figured I'd be buying it," he added.

"You're an old-fashioned man," Lena teased, that smile widening ever so slightly.

"Maybe. Or maybe I'm just terrified my folks might hear about it," he said, shrugging and trying not to blush.

"A grown man, living in fear of his folks."

That smile was now an all-out smirk and he was hard-pressed not to lean in and cover her mouth with his. "Hey, you've never met my mom. She could inspire fear in hardened criminals."

"Really?" She cocked her head.

"Yeah." Shit, that smile . . . her mouth. It was killing him.

"Oh, to hell with it." Reaching up, he touched the tip of his finger to her lower lip.

Her mouth opened on a soft gasp and he dipped his head until only a breath separated them. "The second I saw you, I wondered what you'd taste like. If you'd rather me not find out, can you say something?"

Lena blinked. Wow. Her brain had just gone completely blank.

"Umm."

"Is that a back-off?" he asked.

"No. No, I don't think so."

"Good."

His mouth came down on hers, easy and light, keeping it slow at first. She opened for him and shuddered as he traced his tongue along her lower lip. He tasted like coffee and chocolate cheesecake and man. Delicious. Lifting a hand, she placed it on his cheek. There was the faintest rasp of stubble under her palm, very faint. Curious, she trailed her fingers along his neck, dipped them into his hair, but as curious as she was about how he looked, the curiosity was slowly dying under the heat of hunger.

He could kiss.

Humming under her breath, she moved closer and brought her other hand up, resting it on his hip. Lean hips, she couldn't help but notice that. And the body she pressed against was also lean, long and lean. Heat started to pulse through her, but that was little surprise. It had already been on a slow burn from the time she'd sat down next to him.

He skimmed a hand down her spine, resting it at the small of her back. She shivered under that touch and when he pressed her closer, tucking her lower body more firmly against his, the shivering got worse. She almost came out of her skin. Need tightened her belly and she rocked closer, all but ready to ride the hard ridge pressed against her belly.

And she just might have tried to do that—just might have asked him if maybe he'd come back to her place—just might have lost her ever-loving mind.

But a car horn blared, shattering the calm night air, and Lena pulled away, sucking air in desperately.

Her heart. Shit. It was pounding so hard, she thought it just might explode out of her chest.

Swallowing, she licked her lips and then she could have whimpered, begged for mercy, because she could taste him. Taste him, and it made her want to throw herself against him and kiss him. Again, and again . . . and then stop just long enough to lose all their clothes.

"Looks like he's looking for you," Ezra said, his voice hoarse and low.

"Huh? Who?"

"There's a guy in a white Lexus over there—staring up here—looks like he's giving me the once-over."

"It's Carter," she said. Taking a deep breath, she blanked her expression and half-turned, waved at Carter. "The owner's husband. He drives me home after work."

"Then I guess you need to get going." He stroked a hand down her arm, then pressed his lips to her brow. "Thanks for having dinner with me."

"It was my pleasure." Hesitating, she battled down the self-consciousness and forced herself to smile. "Maybe we can try again."

"Definitely."

She gave him her number and in less than two minutes, she was in the car, driving away. She didn't want to leave, though. Actually, she'd rather have Ezra in the car with her, driving her home.

Maybe next time . . . or the time after, she told herself.

*   *   *

Except he didn't call.

Not the next day, or the day after.

Lena thought maybe she'd imagined that heat between them and after a week passed without hearing from him, she gave up hoping she'd hear from him.

It hurt, though. In a way she hadn't expected.

One lousy date, and he'd wormed his way past thick, near-impenetrable shields.

A year ago, she'd casually dated a guy in town—Remy Jennings. Off and on for a few months. She'd liked him and they'd been compatible in bed, but when they broke it off, it hadn't been a sharp pain in her heart.

In college, she'd met a guy she'd fallen for—hard and fast—and she'd thought maybe she was falling in love with him, although he'd never once told her he loved her. Not even after they'd been together six months.

Two semiserious relationships. That was the sum of her experience with guys, that and a few casual dates . . . and somehow, some guy she'd met exactly two times, some guy she'd had one date with, he'd managed to worm his way under her guard.

Unreal.

CHAPTER
THREE

HER PHONE NUMBER WAS STILL SITTING BY THE PHONE three weeks later. Mocking him.

Ezra didn't even need that little slip of paper there. He had her number memorized.

He had almost called her a dozen times.

Only to stop himself, because he had come out here to get his head straight and figure what he needed to be doing with himself.

An occasional, casual date wouldn't interfere with that, right?

But as Lena had pulled away from him after that one intense, hot kiss, Ezra had almost grabbed her back—close. So close. The memory of her taste haunted him, and he could still hear the echo of her laugh.

All in all, it added up to more than just a casual sort of feeling.

His head was too fucked up for anything more than casual. He couldn't sleep without nightmares. Too many nights, he woke up with a scream trapped in his throat, certain he'd find his hands covered with the hot, slippery feel of blood. He was a mess—the last thing he needed to be doing was getting involved with a woman.

Especially after the last one . . .

So he didn't call.

But he wasn't throwing her number away, either.

Maybe it was more to punish himself.

Maybe it was more to remind himself.

Maybe it was a little bit of both, he didn't know.

Or maybe it was because he just couldn't bring himself to throw it away.

"So what in the hell does it matter if he hasn't called?" Lena muttered to herself after she listened to her messages.

She leaned against the counter in her kitchen, drinking from a bottle of water.

Puck was having a drink of his own, thirstily guzzling down the water she'd poured into his bowl. They'd just gotten back from one of their walks through the field. She'd wanted to take the woods path, but Puck hadn't gone for it.

Lately, he was reluctant, although she could usually talk him into it.

Today, though? He'd sat down and refused to budge.

So instead of walking in the relative shade the trees could offer, they'd been in the field, the September sun beating down on them. She'd returned home hot and cranky and the last thing she needed to do was push the button on her answering machine, hoping to find a message from Ezra.

Nope. Two messages from Roz at the Inn, one from another friend, but none from the man who'd all but kissed her senseless three weeks ago.

Grumbling to herself, she pushed the button again and dutifully listened to Roz's messages—ordering problems with some of the ingredients she'd needed for that evening's menu—she'd have to alter it. Fine. Another wedding—the bride had requested a specific menu and Roz needed to run it by her that night at work.

She erased the messages and then headed out of the kitchen. She needed a shower. She was hot, she was sweaty, and if she wanted to be ready when Carter arrived to pick her up, she couldn't stay in the kitchen brooding about why Ezra King had never called her back.

What in the hell did it matter?

They'd had one date.

One very wonderful kiss.

It didn't add up to much.

So what if she'd dreamed about him quite a few times since then?

In the end, what were a few dreams? A few really, really hot, sexy, poignant dreams?

Dreams.

Fuck, Ezra hated these dreams. They chased him. He could drown them out with liquor. He could lose them in a drugged stupor.

He chose to live with them. He might change his mind, though . . . if he lived through the night. This one was choking him.

In the dream, he was back in the alley. Back in the alley where he discovered that his partner, "Mac" Stover, was dirty.

His partner, his friend . . . his lover.

They had known there was a dirty cop involved somewhere. They had spent the past year trying to bust a statewide theft ring and every time they got close, something went wrong. It was a cop—in his gut, Ezra knew it.

But he hadn't thought it would be her. Hadn't thought it would be Mac . . .

"We can't keep this up. Sooner or later, we're going to screw up."

Ezra stood in the shadows, listening. Dark, it was so dark. He should be able to see—shouldn't he? See

*something. Know something. Like that voice—he knew
that voice.*

Who was it?

Who was she?

*"We got a good thing going here. One more big ship-
ment, Mac. Then we're done. One more go-round."*

*A low, tired sigh, followed by a rough, husky chuckle.
"Yeah, one more, my ass. Hell, you know what? I am
done. One more round and I am so fucking done. One
more. That is it."*

*A storm of memories assaulted him as he stood in the
shadows. Walking down the street, side by side with his
partner.*

"Come on, Mac. One more. We can hit one more."

*"Yeah, one more, my ass, pretty boy. One more, and
then you're buying me dinner."*

Mac. It was Mac.

Get out . . . gotta get out. Shit, fuck that. Got to go
knock some sense into her . . . Mac . . . aw, shit.

No.

Get out. Got to get out.

*Couldn't seem to move his legs, though. Damn it.
Like they were stuck in lead, and his head didn't want to
work. Mac . . . his partner. Best friend. His lover . . .
how many times had he held that woman in his arms?
How many nights had they lain awake talking?*

Mac . . . his partner.

Best friend.

Lover.

Killer.

Rational, man, you gotta be rational . . . gotta get
out . . .

*As the world turned to hell, as voices raged, he kept
thinking that.*

Get out—

Ezra tore himself out of the nightmare, ragged breaths

sawing in and out of his lungs, a half scream twisting inside his throat.

He wanted to rub his hands over his face, but he feared, once more, they'd be covered in blood. Mac's blood.

"Lights," he mumbled to himself. "Need the damn lights." He smacked at the lamp on the bedside table until it came on and then he swung his legs over the side of the bed, staring at his hands.

Scarred. Callused. And clean. There was no blood on them.

So why did he still see it?

His memory of that night was a mess. Indistinct. He knew all the medical jargon—head trauma, blood loss, and a bunch of psychobabble shit he had no use for. It was possible he'd recall more of that night in time. It was equally possible he'd go to his grave not knowing exactly what went down.

He knew what mattered the most—Mac was dead. He had killed her. After she had drawn a gun on him. Her lifeless body had been found on top of his, her gun still in hand.

The doctors had spent hours working to save his leg; one of the bullets had nicked the femoral artery. Another had lodged in his bone.

He could have died. Maybe he should have.

He was alive. She wasn't.

He knew Mac—if she had wanted him dead, he would be dead. She wouldn't have missed, would she? Had she spared him? If she had, then what kind of bastard did that make him? He'd killed her. Leveled his gun at her heart and ended her life, just like that.

"Fuck, you can't sit here thinking about this," he muttered.

Guilt. It could choke a man.

"All that time," he whispered. All that time and he hadn't seen it.

Not until somebody made him look. Made him see. Made him think.

He hadn't wanted it to be true, had insisted it wasn't. That's why he had followed her. To prove them wrong.

He had ended up proving them right . . . he had proved them right and he'd killed Mac, almost died himself. She had been his best friend, his lover . . . and now she was dead.

Certain he would never sleep, Ezra glanced over at the clock. Then he closed his eyes and swore. Not even eleven. Shit. Not even a fucking hour of sleep. He'd been so tired, he'd crashed and burned just a little before nine and now he'd be paying for that, probably sleepless the rest of the night.

Except he doubted he'd really want to sleep anyway. Not after the dream. Maybe in a few hours . . . after he leveled out.

Yawning, he climbed out of bed. The shorts he'd worn the day before were draped over the footboard and he grabbed them. After dragging them on over naked hips, he headed downstairs. The muscles in his right leg knotted in warning. Almost in afterthought, he detoured by the bathroom and grabbed the bottle of Vicodin just in case. That ache could go from mild to holy shit in no time flat.

He crashed on the couch. The plan was to watch some TV, veg out. He might not sleep, but he could shut his brain down. Avoid thinking about Mac.

If he could manage to do that, he'd make it through the night okay.

Fifteen minutes after he made it downstairs, his leg let him know in no uncertain terms that he wouldn't be making it through the night without some pharmaceutical help. When he could, he tried to just deal with the pain. But he'd heaped too much abuse on the healing muscles. He washed the pill down with a Diet Coke and remained on the couch, watching the TV and stubbornly refusing to think.

Life was so much easier when he just didn't think.

It took another thirty minutes before he was floating comfortably in a mind-numbed haze.

He might have even made it to sleep.

If it wasn't for the damned four-wheelers.

He hit the front door just in time to see the back end of the last one before it shot off into the dark night.

"Son of a bitch." He stormed outside, the first edge of anger burning through his sleepy brain.

They'd trashed the flowerbeds. Reckless, idiotic kids. They'd been ripping through the back of his property off and on for the past few weeks, but this was the first time they'd ever gotten this close to his house, and they'd never actually done any damage.

Damn it, damn it, *damn it*.

Squinting in the dim light, he stared down at the flowerbeds his grandmother had lovingly tended. A rainbow of petals littered the ground, muddied and mangled.

For some reason, he found himself oddly mesmerized by the sight of the broken and ruined blooms.

Her name was Jolene Hollister.

She was twenty-nine, engaged to be married.

One week ago, she'd been on top of the world, living her life to the fullest.

Now, she was in the lowest level of hell, and she'd begun to pray for death.

In some part of her mind, she thought she should feel guilty for that but she didn't. She knew she should want to fight for her life, for the life she should have had with her fiancé, but she hurt so badly and she was so tired . . .

Death would be an escape. From him.

But as much as she might pray for death, when Jolene realized how loose her restraints had become, she worked them even looser. When she managed to free herself, she crouched in the corner and hid, her hands gripping a metal bar. It had leather cuffs on it and her mind tried to shut down when she remembered what he'd done with that bar.

It didn't matter now. It didn't matter that it had been stained with her blood. Now that bar was a weapon in her hands and she'd use it against him.

But she was so weak.

When he came inside, she swung it at his head. It connected and he went down, but she knew she hadn't hit him hard enough.

Still, she ran.

She'd get away, or die trying.

She only hoped . . .

That had been her only thought and now that thought mocked her. She wouldn't get away and his mocking laughter infuriated her as she thrashed through the woods, struggling to get away from him.

Laughing—the bastard was laughing at her.

Laughing at her while she ran.

Laughing.

Somewhere in the back of her mind, she was furious.

The sick, perverted fuck was laughing.

The rage tried to take control, but the fear wouldn't let it. She had to run. He was coming after her and she had to get away, get help before he caught her.

He's going to catch me . . . I'm not going to get away from him. Despair whispered in her ear, dark and cloying. She tried to shove it aside. She could get away—she'd gotten outside, right? She could get away.

A sob burned inside her abused throat, threatening to choke her. She could hear him, trailing behind her, chuckling as she ran.

She thought she could even hear the sound of his feet

on the hard-packed, uneven forest floor. Above her own breaths, harsh and ragged, she could hear him as she pushed through the night-dark forest.

Or maybe it was just her heart.

She hurt. She hadn't thought it was possible to hurt like this, hurt so that every breath, every move was sheer agony. All she wanted to do was huddle into a ball and whimper from the pain, but she couldn't—couldn't stop running, couldn't stop.

There were lights ahead. She could just barely make out the faint golden glow.

Lights—lights could mean a house. Could mean help. Safety—

Wide-eyed, Jolene looked back over her shoulder and darted off to the left, desperate to put more distance between them. Desperate to get to those golden lights ahead.

She suspected she was going to die tonight, but that didn't mean she was going to give up. Not without a fight.

Her name was Jolene Hollister.

Unconcerned, the man trailed along behind her, a dark, shadowy presence that moved through the forest with ease. He knew the forest, knew it well, knew all the paths, knew where fallen tree limbs or exposed roots waited to trip up the unwary. He'd been walking these paths for years—some of his fondest memories had taken place in these woods.

She was pretty, this new girl. Pretty, quick, not quite so easily broken. Even after a week, she tried to fight. Tried to struggle. Even tried to run, and she ran well, her nude legs muscled and strong. Very strong—he ran his tongue along the inside of his cheek, feeling the open wound where his teeth had sliced him open when she smashed her head into his mouth just a few days earlier.

He'd seen to it that she drank, that she ate, although he had to force it on her. Letting her get too weak from hunger or dehydration was such a waste. Although now he had to admit, if she hadn't been so strong, she wouldn't have slipped away from him, wouldn't even now be running through the woods, screaming.

He hadn't broken her and that was what gave her the strength to run.

Still, although this was making more work for him, it was fun. A lot of fun. His blood pounded hot in his veins and his dick was so hard, so ready, he ached. He was going to have even more fun with her tonight.

Ahead of him, she screamed.

"Help me!"

He laughed, listening as she struggled through the undergrowth. Most likely she was trying to get to the house ahead. From time to time, he caught a glimpse of the porch lights before a bend in the path once more hid it from view. It was still some distance away. He would catch her before she got much closer. He would have to, after all. He liked his games too much to risk them.

As he passed a tree, something glinted on the ground and he glanced down, frowning when he saw the silvery moonlight reflecting off the necklace there.

He'd seen that delicate gold chain before—it belonged to his girl. It was his girl's.

Scooping it up, he tucked it in his pocket and bit back the angry snarl that tried to rise in his throat. It wouldn't have been good if that had been left here. Not good at all.

He'd have to teach her a lesson for that.

Once their game was over. And speaking of games, it must be time for a new one.

It had gone quiet. Cocking his head, he listened for the sounds of her running through the forest, branches breaking, leaves crunching underfoot.

But there was nothing.

She'd gone completely and utterly silent.

"Are we going to hide now?" he asked, stopping in his tracks and turning in a slow circle. "If I find you, does that mean I win?"

A sound caught his ear. Cocking his head, he listened. It was faint, that low, soft moan. The erratic gasps as she struggled to breathe. Quiet, but not quiet enough.

Laughing, he followed the sound.

"Come out, come out, wherever you are . . ."

He hadn't ever realized how much fun it would be to chase them.

Such possibilities . . .

The voice of reason advised caution, though. Wouldn't be wise to make such a drastic change in his game plan, not now.

Lena was dreaming.

She knew it and she had to admit, it was one damn fine dream.

In the dream, she could see. She had vivid memories from back before she'd gone completely blind and sometimes, those dreams taunted her.

This dream wasn't so bad, though.

She was outside and the sun shone down on her, a brilliant burst of light and warmth raining down on her. Tipping her face to it, she stared into the sun until her eyes watered and burned.

"You shouldn't stare at the sun."

The voice was low, rough . . . sexy. And familiar.

Ezra. Damn him.

Couldn't he leave her in peace, even in her dreams?

Lena was a sucker for a sexy voice and he had such a fine one. Hands came up from behind, rested on her waist, and then slid around her, pulling her back against a hard, strong body.

"I don't want to dream about you," she said, but she didn't pull away from him. No, she rested her head against his chest and continued to stare at the golden-white burn of the sun.

"I told you that you shouldn't look at the sun," he murmured, stroking one hand up and cupping her breast. Something hot and liquid flared to life inside her.

"It doesn't matter if I look at it or not. Not now."

"Why not?"

"Because I'm just dreaming. Those pesky UV rays can't hurt me here." As much as she hated to look away from the sun, she did, turning in his embrace to study his face. She wanted to see him, too. See what subconscious image she had cooked up to go with that sexy voice.

And damn, her subconscious had delivered just fine.

Although sometimes she suspected her sighted memories weren't as clear as they could have been, she wasn't going to complain. He looked just fine to her.

Right now, she could see . . .

Right now, she could touch.

And more . . . she could be touched. Touched by somebody who wasn't moved by curiosity or pity, or even worse, some fucked-up male desire to get a unique score he could tell a bunch of his loser friends about over a beer.

No, she was being touched by somebody who very obviously wanted to touch her right back. So what if it was only in a dream? At least here he couldn't disappoint her by saying he'd call and then not follow through.

As he ran his hands down over her body, stripping away her clothes, Lena lifted her eyes upward and stared at the sun again.

Lost herself in the warm golden glow and the feel of a man's hands on her body.

She could see . . . see his face as he guided her to the ground and knelt between her thighs.

She could touch . . . touch his shoulders and fist her

hands in his hair as he lowered his mouth to her aching core and licked her.

She could feel . . . feel the fiery hot pleasure blistering through her as he levered up over her and pushed inside, one deep, smooth thrust that stretched her in the sweetest damn way.

She could hear—

"Help me!"

Lena came awake with a gasp. Her heart knocked against her ribs and she shivered as cool air danced over her sweat-slicked body. A breeze drifted in through the open window.

It was cool . . . not cold. But she was freezing.

Hearing one low, questioning yip, she held out her hand. Puck pressed his nose against her palm and she heaved out a breath. The dog's body was tense—all over tense and he had his hackles up.

"Sorry, boy. Just had a bad dream," she muttered. She'd gone and freaked her dog out.

As she started to lie back down, she heard it.

A voice.

". . . help me . . ."

Puck growled.

Jerking back up, she turned her head toward the window, tried to breathe past the knot in her chest. "What in the hell . . . ?" She closed her eyes, listened. Concentrated.

Puck growled again, louder this time, his voice rough, full of menace, full of warning. Lena shushed him, her voice sharp, her own fear edging its way in.

Through the window, she could hear . . . something. Thrashing in the forest that bordered the western edge of her property. The western edge . . . the woods. That strip of land where lately, her dog didn't like to go. Not for the past few months.

"Somebody, please help me!"

The sound of the woman's screams, raw and agonized, sent a shudder racing down Lena's spine.

"Oh, God," Lena whispered. Her heart slammed against her rib cage as she reached for the phone by her bed.

There was another scream and she dropped the phone. Swearing, she crawled out of the bed, patting around on the floor. "Damn it, damn it, damn it." Icy, cold sweat dripped along her spine as she listened through the window.

Branches snapping. A ragged moan. Then all was silent.

Where's the fricking phone??

Making a sound halfway between a sob and a growl, she stuck her hand under the bed and heaved out a sigh of relief as her fingers brushed plastic. Scuttling across the floor, she pressed her back to the wall and listened, phone clutched in her hand.

Call 911, damn it! She tried to get her fingers to move but terror made them clumsy.

Outside, she heard nothing. She didn't hear anything . . . wait. Yes, yes, she heard something now, but it was quiet . . . somebody, moving quietly and softly through the trees.

If her room had been any farther away from the woods, if she had lived any closer to town . . . hell, if she'd had the radio playing, she never would have heard it. So, so quiet . . .

There was another short, sharp scream—one that ended all too abruptly. The sound of it was enough to get her frozen fingers to move and she dialed 911.

Puck made a rough sound low in his throat and nosed her leg. She patted the space next to her and as he pressed his big, furry body against her leg, she wrapped an arm around him.

"Nine-one-one. What's your emergency?"

"I . . . I hear a woman screaming. She's screaming for help."

It only took minutes. Maybe ten. Logically, she knew not much time had passed before she heard the sirens, but it seemed like an eternity. Too long. Too much time.

She hadn't heard the woman again . . . what if it was too late?

They could have been there for thirty minutes. They could have been there for three hours.

Lena suspected it was somewhere in between, but she wasn't sure.

She was having a damned hard time concentrating.

Nobody screaming for help.

No woman.

No abandoned cars on the side of the road, no wrecks.

Nothing.

They hadn't seen a soul, hadn't found a damn thing.

But she'd heard somebody.

"Ms. Riddle."

Lena folded her fingers around the cup of coffee. "Sergeant . . . Jennings, is that right?" She gave him a faint smile. "I guess you're related to half the town, then."

"Yes, ma'am. I'm Keith Jennings, if that helps any."

The quiet humor she heard in his voice made her smile. "A bit." She sighed and pushed a hand through her hair. "When half the county is named Jennings, even a bit of help is nice."

"Well, to be honest, I think it's only a quarter . . . and I'm a pretty distant cousin."

He was smiling a little. She could hear it in his voice. "You mean there are people here who aren't distant cousins?" The Jennings family practically owned Ash, it seemed.

"Well, you're not."

"True." She tucked her hair behind her ear and sighed. "Did you . . . um . . . was there anybody . . ."

"I'm sorry, but we couldn't find anything." He was silent for a second and then cleared his throat. "Would it be okay if I sat down?"

"Oh, of course. I'm sorry. I . . ."

"It's okay. It's late and all."

She heard the other rocking chair creak as he sat down.

"That sure is a fine dog you've got there, Ms. Riddle. What was his name again?"

"Puck."

"Nice dog."

She heard him snap his fingers and it made her smile. Keeping her hand on the dog's harness, she said, "He won't come to you while he's on his leash. He's working." She adjusted the dark glasses she wore.

"Oh, I'm sorry."

"It's okay. You didn't know."

He chuckled and said, "I guess people do that a lot."

"Some." Lena shrugged. "Not so much around here, though. At least not now. They're getting to know him." She grimaced. "It does happen a lot when I go into Lexington or Louisville."

"People see a pretty dog, they want to pet it."

Lena smiled. "Yes." Puck was a beautiful dog, twenty-eight inches at the shoulder, well-behaved, and although she couldn't see his golden coat, she knew it was shiny and clean. Jennings spoke the truth—Puck was a pretty dog and people like to pet pretty dogs.

But as pretty as Puck was, he was also a working dog. Plus, he was her dog. He liked people well enough, but he preferred her over other people. He wasn't just her dog—he was a friend. It was more than a pet/owner relationship. With a guide dog, it had to be.

Silence fell, stretching out for nearly a minute before

Sgt. Jennings broke it with a question. "So, can you tell me more about what happened?"

"Screaming," she whispered quietly, turning her head to the wooded area that bordered the western part of her property. A knot settled in her throat and she had to clear her throat twice before she could manage to speak. Fear tore into her, brutal and sharp. "Somebody was in the woods. I could hear her screaming . . . screaming for help."

"You're sure it was a woman?"

Lena licked her lips. "Well, no. I can't be positive, but she sounded female. I only heard her voice a couple of times, but she sounded . . . well, female."

"And she was screaming."

"Yes." Lena's hands were suddenly damp, cold with sweat. Swiping them down the front of her pajama bottoms, she tried to pretend they weren't shaking. "That was what woke me up. I heard her scream. I was sitting there in bed, kind of confused . . . you know how it is when something wakes you up, but you're not sure what it is?"

"Yes, ma'am."

"Well, it was like that. I was sitting there, trying to figure out what had woken me up and then I heard it again. Heard her. She screamed, 'Help me.' A few seconds later, I heard somebody thrashing around in the woods and then she screamed again—'Please, somebody help me!' No, that wasn't it. It was 'Somebody, please help me!' Sounded a little closer, too. I grabbed the phone and called nine-one-one."

"After you made the call, did you hear her again?"

Lena shook her head. "No. Just those few times . . . well, three or four, I guess." Then she paused, cocked her head. "No. Five. I heard her cry out five different times. I think her screaming is what woke me up."

"And you're sure you were awake?"

"Yes." She suppressed a sigh as she shifted in the rocking chair. "I was awake, Sergeant. Very awake."

"Okay." The chair creaked under his weight. Paper rustled. "We took a look around the house, didn't see anything."

"She wasn't around the house." Lena pinched the bridge of her nose. A headache was settling behind her eyes—a monster bitch of a headache. "I heard her in the woods. Did you look there?"

"We took a bit of a look around. But, as you can imagine, it's pretty dark . . . hard to see much of anything." He paused, cleared his throat. "However, I can swing by later, after the sun's up. Take another look around when I can see."

Lena grimaced. The woman had sounded so desperate. Could she wait until the sun rose? "There's nothing else you can do?"

"I'm afraid not. I had another one of the deputies check the roads, make sure nobody had been in an accident or anything like that. Could have been an accident victim."

No. That wasn't it. She didn't know why, but she was convinced it wasn't that. It was . . . worse.

Your imagination is running away with you, she thought. A car wreck could explain it just fine.

Except there weren't any car wrecks around.

Feeling his expectant gaze, she forced a smile. "Well, if you would come back and take a look around in the daytime, I'd appreciate it."

CHAPTER
FOUR

"HOLY SHIT," ROZ BREATHED OUT. "ARE YOU SERIOUS?"

Lena rubbed her gritty eyes and said, "Yeah, I'm serious." She checked the time and then stretched out on the couch, cradling the phone between her ear and shoulder. "I swear, Roz, I feel like I've been run over by a bus or something. Last night was the worst night of my life."

"You hear some woman screaming for help, it's not going to make for sweet dreams," Roz said, her voice wry.

"You ain't kidding."

"So what is the sheriff's department doing?"

Her spine stiffened as she recalled the conversation she'd had with Jennings a few hours earlier. "Right now? Nothing. The guy from the sheriff's department who came by last night came back over this morning, walked the main trail and didn't see anything, hear anything. Beyond that, there's not much they can do."

"That's a fucking load of bullshit," Roz snarled.

"That was my first thought, too." Lena adjusted a pillow under her head. "I was thinking about going to the sheriff's office, talking to somebody else. But seriously, I don't know what they can do."

"Want me to come with you?" Roz offered.

"Nah, that's okay. You've got that shower this after-noon, anyway. I'm going to call Law."

"Perfect . . ."

He stepped back and surveyed his handiwork.

She slept, her face slack, her breathing deep and steady. Just a little chemical inducement was all it had taken. He had to keep her quiet, after all.

She wouldn't get free this time. He didn't like using the shackles—he liked the velvet ropes better, loved how they looked against a woman's soft, smooth skin. But she'd gotten free from the ropes and he couldn't risk that happening again.

Idly, he palmed her breast. Her nipples were hard. It was cool in his little place and he knew it was more a reaction to the cold than anything else. At least right now.

He could make her nipples hard for him, and he'd done so.

Just like he could make her wet for him. Just like he could make her come for him.

It was erotic, drawing that reaction from their bodies even as they fought against it. Almost as erotic as the way they struggled when he shifted gears and focused on sweet pain instead of reluctant arousal.

He loved both.

He loved bringing a woman to climax and he loved bringing a woman to pained screams.

He loved the response . . . and she wasn't giving him one.

She lay still, practically lifeless. Watching her face, he pinched her nipple cruelly, watching as she whimpered in her sleep and tried to twist away. She could only move so far, though.

So perfect and petite, her sleek, shining hair swinging

just below her shoulders, her skin smooth and pale and perfect, a narrow waist, high, small breasts, and long, strong legs.

So beautiful.

So beautiful . . . and such a fucking cunt. Too close. As erotic as it had been, as much as he'd loved hunting her down, it had been dangerous. Risky.

Memories danced through his mind and he shuddered, lost in them. Just thinking about last night was enough to make his dick hard as iron, even as his mind clinically, coolly listed and analyzed all the many, many risks.

Exciting. But too fucking risky.

She wasn't quite so perfect now.

Red scratches and scrapes marred her pretty skin and there were mottled bruises at her wrists and ankles. When he'd managed to catch her, she'd been filthy, covered with dirt, her feet black from her run through the woods. He'd bathed her, then cleaned himself and burned the clothes he'd worn on his run through the woods. No evidence . . . none.

Now he had to figure out what to do.

He had to be careful.

Especially after this latest . . . complication.

He flicked a glance at his watch. Another half-hour, and he'd slip away. He had things to do. Plans to make.

*   *   *

I feel sort of weird about this. I mean, it's not that I don't appreciate how you're trying to help me—

*   *   *

I'm not trying to help you. I'm trying to help me.

He hit Enter and watched as his reply popped in the IM box.

Edward Lawson Reilly wasn't lying. This would help him. He skimmed a hand through his hair, but the light golden-brown strands fell right back into his eyes. Ignoring it, he pulled open a drawer and reached inside, pulled out the faded, tattered picture.

It was a picture of him from high school. Next to him was Hope, her long hair flying around her face. A happy smile curled her lips. Next to her stood the boy she'd married not long after she'd graduated.

They had all looked so young. So happy and hopeful. Innocent.

Hope's innocence, her hopes, her happiness, they'd all been shattered. Hell, Hope was all but shattered.

A grim-faced, unsmiling little yellow emoticon appeared in the IM box, followed by a reply.

I find it hard to believe you can't find anybody more qualified than me to help you out. Qualified, and a hell of a lot closer to where you live.

Law snorted.

I live in Mayberry, Hope. If I ask anybody around here, everybody and their best friend's dog will know. Besides, it's not like I need somebody to write a doctoral thesis or something. I need somebody to help with paperwork, organize shit, and I want somebody I know to do it. Somebody I can trust.

Law . . .

She was trying to talk herself out of it—just like she had done for the past year. He didn't need to see her to know that. He knew Hope too well.

Look, Hope, I really do need some help here. I'm tired of doing all this shit myself. I'm drowning. Are you going to come help me or not?

It wasn't a lie. He needed help around here and there wasn't anybody he trusted as much as he trusted Hope. It was the God's honest truth. So what if he would feel a lot better knowing she was someplace safe, someplace where she would feel safe . . . where she could heal.

The phone rang. For a second, it caught him off guard. It wasn't quite nine in the morning and only a couple of people would think to call him this early on a weekend.

Still, he wouldn't look a gift horse in the mouth. He had a way to get out of the talk with Hope and he planned to take advantage of it.

Hey, phone. Gotta go. You'll be here soon, right? I'm telling you—I am drowning here.

He closed the window before she could answer.

One thing about Hope, she had a hard time telling people "no." Even when she really wanted to do just that.

Glancing at the caller ID, he grinned when he saw the familiar number.

He grabbed the phone and drawled out, "Hello, gorgeous."

Huddling over the desk, Hope Carson stared at the laptop and the inactive IM window. She didn't bother trying to send him another message. She knew Law. Once he got an idea in that hard head of his, he didn't let go of it.

Still, she wasn't sure she wanted to move to that small town.

Weary, she rubbed her eyes and leaned back in the chair. Tilting her head back, she stared at the ceiling. Small towns made her nervous. She knew small towns. She and Law had grown up in one—the sort of place where everybody knew everybody else's business.

She didn't want anybody knowing her business.

But the fact of the matter was, she didn't have a lot of options.

She was running out of money, she had no family, and if she didn't find a job, she was going to end up living out of her car. Job choices weren't exactly huge—she had no experience being much of anything, except a wife.

Closing her eyes, she ran her limited choices through her mind yet again.

Find a minimum-wage job and see if she could get an apartment. With no references, no credit history. Nothing. And she didn't exactly want to leave a paper trail that could be easily followed, either. If possible, she'd rather leave no trail.

She couldn't go back home, even if she wanted to, which she did not. Clinton, Oklahoma, wasn't going to welcome her, not after what she'd done.

"No." She opened her eyes and straightened in the chair, staring at the grim-faced woman in the mirror hanging over the simple utilitarian desk. "I'm not the problem. He is. I didn't do a damn thing. He did."

She couldn't go back home, though, no matter what the reasons.

Not like she even had a place to go, anyway.

Her ex-husband, Detective Joseph Carson, had been found not guilty of spousal abuse and even now was living in the house where they'd spent the past ten years of their life. He had the house, he still even had his fucking job. Hell, while she'd been locked away like a prisoner, he had gotten a promotion.

He had everything.

Hope didn't have jack.

"Stop," she muttered. Rubbing the back of her neck, she forced her thoughts away from Joey. Feeling sorry for herself, feeling angry, none of it would help. She needed to focus on her next move, not think about the wreck of her life.

Shame tightened her belly as she thought about Law's offer.

She could either hope she could find a job and a place to live, or she could turn to a friend.

"You look exhausted."

"Law, I am exhausted." Lena smiled at the concern she heard in her friend's voice. Chances were, she looked like shit, but he was too nice to point it out so bluntly.

She slid her feet into a pair of flats and went to get her purse.

"Maybe you should try to get a nap instead of going into town," he suggested.

Grimly, she shook her head. "No, I need to get this done." She wouldn't sleep until she'd at least talked to somebody. Not that she expected the talk was going to do much good.

After all, what could they do?

Nothing.

Shut up, Lena thought, snarling at the quiet mental voice. "Come on. I want to get this over with."

Off to her side, Law sighed. The floorboards creaked under him as he came to stand beside her. "Somehow, I knew you were going to say that. So why are we going to the county sheriff's office? The Jennings boy and his friends hit your place, too? I heard them out on the road near my place around eleven or so. Looks like they tore up old Mrs. King's front yard some, too. Saw it when I was driving in—the new owner is going to be hot."

New owner—Ezra. *Oh, yeah. He's hot, all right.*

Her belly fluttered at the thought, but fortunately, she was so damn tired, that was about all she was capable of at the moment. Sighing, she shoved her hair back.

"No, it wasn't that." Man, what she wouldn't give for her problem to be anything so mundane. "Look . . . I'd rather not go into detail about it right now. I'm going to have enough of a headache explaining it once."

Excuse me, Sheriff, but I really think you and your deputies need to do something about the woman I heard screaming last night. No, sir, I don't know who she was. No, sir, I don't know where she was. No, sir, I don't know where to find her. No, sir, I have no idea what should be done, but there has to be something.

"Hey." Law brushed his hand down her arm. "What's going on, Lena?"

"Just a lot on my mind," she said, forcing a smile for him. "Come on. Let's get this over with."

He had woken up in a lousy mood.

Ezra figured he was entitled. Little sleep, lots of pain, torn up front yard, all of it on the heels of one of those damn dreams. He wasn't going to be in the mood to make nice.

Especially not with the village idiot.

Although, for the life of him, he could not figure out how in hell that village idiot had wound up wearing a badge.

"Look, Gomer, I don't give a damn if they are just kids or not." He glared at the round, ruddy face of Deputy Earl Prather.

Who gave you this damn job? Is your mama on the town council or something? Ezra couldn't figure it out, no matter how hard he tried. A functioning brain stem was still a requirement for law enforcement, or at least he'd thought it was. "I'm tired of those punks joyriding on my property."

"Mr. King—"

"Detective King," Ezra snarled. He was being an asshole and he knew it, but he didn't really care. He was too tired to care. His leg hurt, his head hurt, and he was still carrying around the weight of that bad dream—like a nasty, clinging hangover. Only worse.

His leg was fucking killing him, knotting and cramping up on him. He had the bad, bad feeling if he kept putting weight on it, he was going to end up on his ass when it gave out under him and wouldn't that just top off his morning nicely?

After those kids had woken him, it was nearly two before he was able to fall back to sleep. It had also required the help of another Vicodin. The quiet country nights didn't help, either. He was used to the city and last night, the quiet had seemed almost oppressive. He'd ended up putting on his headphones and listening to Aerosmith on his iPod as he waited for the narcotics to kick in.

His mood wasn't any better when he awoke and saw just how extensive the damage to his yard was. Half of his grandmother's flowerbeds were trashed. Some of those pretty flowers he could remember watching her plant when he'd been a kid and now they were trampled—completely ruined.

He'd thought he could come here, get this complaint filed and hopefully the guys here could deal with those stupid kids. They'd been ripping through the back of his property with their four-wheelers off and on for weeks, but this time, they'd gone too far. He wanted to get this done with, then go home and grab a nap.

He hadn't counted on running into some dumb-ass county deputy who couldn't seem to understand the simple issue of trespassing.

"It's not Mr. King, it's Detective King and I'd appreciate some simple courtesy here." Hell, he didn't even need any kind of professional courtesy. He just wanted the man to do his job.

Prather cocked a brow. "Detective? With who?"

"Detective with the Commonwealth of Kentucky. I'm

on official leave from the state and I'm pretty damn sure that nobody went and changed the laws on trespassing in the six months since I went on leave."

"On leave for . . . ?"

Ezra narrowed his eyes. "I'm also pretty sure you don't need to know that information to get the damn complaint filed against those kids."

"Look, Detective." Prather sighed and scratched his chin. "I know these kids don't have any right going out on your land with their four-wheelers without your permission. Your grandma didn't much care for it, either." He lifted the paper that Ezra had given him and wiggled it. "It's just that I think the owner of this particular four-wheeler is Brody Jennings." He glanced at Ezra as he said the name.

"I get the feeling that name should mean something to me," he bit off. He paused for a few seconds. "It doesn't."

"He's Hank Jennings's son—Hank is the mayor."

"Then the mayor needs to get his kid under control." Ezra didn't care if the kid was a blood relative to the Queen of England. He could be the president of the United States for all Ezra cared—trespassing was still trespassing. Destruction of property was still destruction of property.

But Prather wasn't paying attention. The deputy gazed off behind Ezra, a frown settling on his round, ruddy face.

Automatically, Ezra glanced over his shoulder, following the deputy's gaze.

He almost swallowed his tongue when he saw her.

Shit.

Lena Riddle.

It wasn't possible, but she looked even better now than she had when he'd first seen her three weeks ago. That deep red hair, gleaming under the harsh fluorescent lights. The pale, pale skin. She wore no makeup, and her unpainted mouth was set in a grim, hard line.

Man, that mouth, so full and lush—he could almost

feel it under his all over again. Looking at her mouth had him all but drooling for another taste, just like looking at her body had him wanting to touch.

No. Forget want. Need. He needed to touch.

Shit.

What was she doing here?

He hissed out a breath between his teeth, seriously glad the deputy's attention was focused elsewhere just then. Ezra was having trouble thinking in coherent terms—much less speaking in them.

One of the deputies approached her. She said something and the deputy absently gestured toward Prather.

Prather mumbled under his breath, his words too low to hear.

But it sounded distinctly irritated.

"Mr. . . . ah . . . Detective King, I think I'm needed, so if you'll . . ."

Ezra dropped into a chair. "Oh, by all means. I can wait a few minutes. We can take care of that report after you're done."

He certainly wasn't in any rush to leave—he wanted to sit there a few more minutes and just stare at her. Drink in his fill. No—not just.

What he really wanted to do was walk over there and tell her, *I'm sorry. Sorry I didn't call. Can you give me a second chance? My head's all screwed up, though, so I can't promise I won't do the same thing again . . .*

"Fine. Fine," Prather muttered. Resigned, the deputy edged around Ezra and started toward Lena. Perfectly content to stare at her, Ezra crossed his arms over his chest and waited.

As Prather drew even with her, Ezra continued to watch. The deputy had a genial smile on his face—the same smile he'd given Ezra. "Hope you're not here about anything important, darlin'," Ezra muttered. Gomer didn't seem too keen on the idea of doing actual work.

What in the hell was she here for? he wondered as concern started to edge in, replacing the surprise.

They were too far away for her to have heard him, but her head turned his way. Something low in his gut started to heat, but he tried to ignore it. She might have good ears, but she couldn't know he was in here, not from that far away.

Whatever she said had Prather shaking his head and then he stopped, glanced back at Ezra. Ezra smiled and saluted the deputy. Slouching down in the chair, he straightened his right leg out in front of him, absently massaging his thigh.

Tired as he was, he wasn't leaving just yet. He had a complaint to file . . . and he figured he really should talk to Lena. Maybe it was just divine intervention that had them both here on the same day.

Prather's shoulders rose and fell in a shrug and then he shifted, reached over to take her arm. But the second his fingers touched her, Lena stepped back.

That was when he noticed the man with her.

About the same age as well, Ezra figured. Light brown hair, tanned. Jeans, a T-shirt.

Ezra watched as the man moved to her side and offered his arm. Ezra scowled as she accepted and through narrowed eyes, watched as the man guided Lena to the conference room. He dipped his head to murmur in her ear. She smiled and said something back.

Ezra clenched his jaw as the bastard reached up to touch her cheek, his fingers lingering on her soft skin before he moved away. He strode away, head bent low.

Ezra remained where he was, battling an irrational bout of jealousy. He didn't like seeing her touching somebody else. Even if it made sense.

"Looker, ain't she?"

Ezra glanced up, realized somebody had noticed his preoccupation. He spun the chair around and met a pair of amused blue eyes. Cocking a brow, he asked, "Excuse me?"

The man gestured toward the woman. "Lena Riddle. She's a real looker, huh?"

Ezra cocked a brow and studied the man in front of him, looked him over from head to toe, taking in the suit and tie. Pretty-boy lawyer—blond, blue eyes, a suit that cost more than some people made in a month.

Pretty-boy lawyer held out a hand and said, "You're June King's grandson, aren't you?"

"Yeah." He glanced at the offered hand before giving it a brief shake. Then he went back to rubbing his aching thigh. "Ezra King."

The blond leaned against a desk. He rubbed his jaw absently and said, "Last I heard, June had two grandsons— one was a carpenter, one was a cop. You're the cop."

"If I hadn't made you for a lawyer the second I saw you, I might be impressed." Ezra looked away, his eyes seeking out Lena one more time.

The blond laughed. "Guilty."

Somebody across the room called out a name and the blond pushed away from the desk. "About time you showed up, Les." He gave Ezra a friendly smile and said, "It's nice to meet you. I'm Remy Jennings, by the way."

Jennings—

But the blond was already striding across the office, entering a different office. In that moment, Ezra was more interested in Miz Lena Riddle than finding out if the lawyer was any relation to Brody Jennings.

Just what had brought Lena in here on Sunday?

He'd get the answer to that question. He knew who to ask, how to ask. He'd just have to bide his time and he could do that.

He was a patient man . . . usually. Generally, he was also one who minded his own business, but five minutes later, both traits were being put to the test as voices rose in the conference room. Prather's ruddy complexion was now a florid shade of red. The deputy stormed to the door, skirting around Lena. The door to the conference room opened and the voices grew louder.

"I told you—I wasn't asleep," Lena said stiffly. "Can't you at least listen to what happened?"

Deputy Prather, his tone condescending as hell, replied, "I've read Sergeant Jennings's report, Ms. Riddle, and I understand what you believe happened. Sometimes we can have dreams. Very realistic dreams. Is it so hard to think you just had a nightmare?"

"Yes."

"What about cats?"

"Cats?" Lena repeated, dumbly. What in the hell did cats have to do with this?

"Yes. There are an awful lot of strays, or farm cats. If there's a female in season and a tom catches her scent, well . . ."

She narrowed her eyes as she realized what he was implying. She clenched her jaw and mentally counted to ten. *He's doing his job. He's exploring all the angles. He's—*

He's being an asshole.

An insulting asshole.

"Deputy Prather, I'm pretty sure a couple of cats aren't going to be able to scream 'Help me,' even if the female is in heat, not even if she's being gang-raped by every fucking tom in the county. I heard screams," she snapped, not bothering to keep the scathing tone out of her voice. "I heard a woman screaming. I heard her. It wasn't cats and I wasn't dreaming."

"Nobody else reported hearing anything."

"I live five miles outside of town," Lena bit off. "My nearest neighbor is a half mile down the road."

"You are pretty isolated. Perhaps . . . well, I realize it could be pretty unnerving, living out there all by yourself. Especially at night. Have you ever considered getting a live-in companion?"

Oh, you son of a bitch.

Lena realized she was clenching her hands, her nails biting into the palms of her hands so hard it hurt.

A live-in companion.

"Why in the hell would I be unnerved to live by myself?" She just barely managed to keep her voice level. Barely.

"It is rather isolated. Big old houses like that, they can be spooky."

"Spooky." Lena spat the word out like it tasted bad. "I lived in that house until I was eight. I moved back into it nine years ago and I know it pretty damn well. Why in the hell would I have moved back to it if I found it spooky? Do I look like a damn middle-school kid?"

"There's no reason to be so upset, Ms. Riddle. I'm just trying to cover plausible scenarios here."

"And you think it's more plausible that I'm imagining things? That's more believable than something really happening? And you think it's plausible that I should be unnerved to live alone, or that I'd need assistance. Because I'm blind." She paused and then asked pointedly, "Am I understanding you correctly?"

"It stands to reason."

"Actually, no. It doesn't. I'm blind, Deputy. I'm not helpless, nor am I an idiot. I've been living on my own for quite some time now and that doesn't have one damn thing to do with what happened last night." She paused and took a deep, slow breath. It didn't do anything to ease the rage inside, the insult. She was so deeply insulted, so furious, she wanted to hit something. Wanted to scream.

But it wouldn't do a bit of good and if she knew a damn thing about Prather's type, he'd just use that as more of an excuse to write her off.

In his mind, he already had plenty of justification to do just that. She'd be damned if she gave him any more.

In a stiff voice, she said, "I'd like to speak with somebody else."

"Ms. Riddle—"

"Somebody else," she snapped.

Lena couldn't fucking believe this. Couldn't believe him.

"Ms. Riddle, you're the one who came wanting to talk to me, remember. I'm sorry if you don't like what I have to say."

"You're sorry?" she demanded. "You stand there and insult me, imply I don't know what in the hell I'm talking about, that I'm some helpless, useless, handicapped female, but you're sorry I don't like what you have to say?"

By her side, Puck shifted, his big body tensing as he reacted to her distress. Forcing herself to relax, she rested a hand on his head.

"Ms. Riddle, I don't know what exactly you want me to do. You say you heard screams, but Sergeant Jennings didn't find anything, didn't see anything out of the ordinary. Nobody else has reported hearing anything unusual. So what exactly do you want me to do?"

Lena smiled sweetly. "I already told you. I want you to find me somebody else to talk to." She had brushed up against a chair when she came into the office and now, she turned, took a couple of small, slow steps forward. When her toe bumped against the chair, she slid a hand down the arm and then settled down. Crossing her legs, she lifted her face to the deputy.

"I'd be more than happy to wait. Right here."

For as long as it takes.

"It's Sunday, Ms. Riddle. We don't have a slew of people around right now."

"Are you telling me there's nobody else to speak with?"

"What I'm telling you is that there's not much else we can do at this point. There is only so much we can do when one woman claims to hear screaming, but nobody reports it, and our searches turn up nothing unusual."

Puck rested his chin on her knee and she reached down, stroked his head. "As I said, I'm more than happy to wait right here, Deputy."

The heels of his shoes thudded dully against the floor and then stopped. "Ms. Riddle, around here, we work. We don't have time to chase down every little imagined problem, spend hours following up just because one person insists she heard something weird—"

"Actually, that kind of is your job."

A new voice. A deep, low rumble of a voice—and very, very familiar. Pretty much the last voice she would have expected to hear. Narrowing her eyes, she turned her head toward the sound of the voice. "Ezra King."

"Hello, Lena."

Don't you "Hello, Lena" me, she almost snapped. She managed to bite it back simply because she didn't want him to know she'd been looking forward to him calling her . . . like he'd said he would.

Bastard.

"You okay, Lena?"

"Oh, I'm just peachy," she drawled, resisting the urge to cross her arms over her chest. Just the sound of that low, sexy drawl had her body doing bad, bad things— her nipples beaded up, her belly went hot and loose, and her heart was racing.

Sexy, so damned sexy, the sort of voice a woman

wants to hear murmuring in her ear during just the right moment—hell, with that kind of voice, any moment would be right.

Like a phone call.

A phone call would have been nice.

But he never called—

Focus! she told herself as Prather said, "Mr. King, if you don't mind, this doesn't concern you, so if you'll just wait for me where you were . . ."

"Actually, I do mind—and I've already pointed out, it's not Mr. King, Prather. It's Detective King. Detective. Got it? It sounds rather obvious to me that you have some sort of problem doing real police work, Prather, but I feel the need to point this out—chasing things down is kind of what us cops do."

Detective? Us? You're a cop? Arching her brows, she interrupted Prather. "Excuse me, Ezra—do you work here?"

Please, please, please say yes, she thought. Forget the fact that he hadn't called her. If he worked here, she could totally forget that, because she already knew he'd do something more than Prather.

Hell, the person who'd greeted her at the desk had been more helpful than Prather.

Footsteps, drawing closer—the steps sounded uneven, like he put more weight on one foot than the other. She'd noticed it before, but it was more obvious this time . . . she thought.

"Sorry, Lena. I'm with the state, and I'm on leave. Of course, I don't think the deputy really works here either. Seems he just pretends to."

Well, hell. But the sense of disappointment faded as a slew of other emotions swarmed up to surprise her.

He was closer, now. Close enough to touch. Close enough to pick up on a few other things, too, like the slow, steady cadence of his breathing and his scent—he smelled good. She remembered that from the two other times she'd been this close.

The sound of his voice, the woodsy, male scent, the warmth of him, the entire package had her heart racing and she had to forcibly throttle down. He'd made it clear he wasn't interested enough to call, so she wasn't going to humiliate herself by letting him see just how . . . interested she still was.

But that heat didn't want to be ignored, and for about five seconds, she couldn't think of a damn thing beyond him.

Her heart skipped a few beats, her breathing hitched, and liquid warmth spread through her, starting in the pit of her belly and spreading outward until it encompassed her whole body.

Cool it, she told her libido.

Said libido didn't want to listen. It had been being ignored for way too long. Lena was too much a control freak to let lust drag her along on a choke chain, though. Inwardly, she wrestled it into submission and outwardly, she just smiled.

"I must admit, I'm inclined to agree with you about the deputy and his lack of interest in working."

"Are you now?" That sexy voice rumbled out, stroking her senses like a velvet glove. "Since he doesn't seem to give a damn about doing his job, I think he probably needs to go get somebody else."

"Look, King—" Prather snapped.

"Somebody else, Deputy. Or I'll find somebody." The authority in that voice demanded obedience.

Prather gave in, stomping away. He grumbled under his breath and not a thing he said was complimentary, but Lena was content to tune him out. She'd much rather talk to Ezra than Prather—even if she was still pissed, even if she was still sulking over the fact that he hadn't called.

"You okay?" he asked as the heavy tread of Prather's feet faded away.

"No, I'm not. I'm fucking pissed," she bit off. "That moron actually had the nerve to imply I should get a live-in companion to stay with me at night."

For about fifteen seconds, Ezra was completely silent. Finally, he said, "He implied what?"

"You heard me."

"Why?"

The obvious dismay in his voice soothed the raw, ragged edges a little. So what if he wasn't interested? At least he didn't view her as some sort of weak, helpless invalid. Forcing herself to smile, she shrugged and said, "I don't know. I guess he views blindness on the same level as Alzheimer's or something. Moron."

"I think moron is being kind when it comes to him," Ezra said. He was quiet for a moment and then, softly, he added, "I've got to say, I wasn't exactly expecting to see you here today—you're pretty much the last person I was expecting to see."

"Am I?"

"Yeah." Ezra resisted the urge to shift on his feet—he wasn't some high-school kid who'd been caught cheating on his girlfriend. It was a phone call. Not a lifelong commitment . . .

But it was one he'd really wanted to make.

"I'm sorry I never called you," he blurted out, feeling the hot, slow crawl of blood as it crept up to stain his cheeks red.

He hadn't even realized he was going to mention it.

Lena's reaction was to laugh. A low, amused chuckle that had him blushing even more—exactly as if he *was* some idiot high-school kid who'd been caught cheating.

"No, you're not," Lena said, shaking her head. "Look, it's no big deal. It was a phone call—you changed your mind. No harm, no foul, right?"

"I didn't change my mind." Swearing, he shoved a hand through his hair and started to pace. The stiff muscles in his leg protested, but he ignored them. There weren't many places to sit and all of them put him too close to her. "I wanted to call. Hell, I've still got the number sitting by my phone, even though I don't need it—I had it memorized before I pulled into my driveway. But . . ."

"But what?"

He blew out a breath and turned to look at her. The sight of her, shit, it still hit him like a punch, straight in the solar plexus. No other woman had ever hit him like that—not even Mac. He'd liked her—in some way, he'd even loved her, although it wasn't the kind of love that would have him down on bended knee, and both of them had known that.

This woman in front of him, though, whom he had seen exactly three times, now? She hit him, knocked the breath out of him, and left him standing on uncertain ground.

"I came back to Ash because I needed to get my head on straight—went through some bad shit not too long ago. And it dawned on me that the last thing I needed was to get involved with anybody."

"I wasn't aware we were anywhere close to getting 'involved,'" Lena said. "We had dinner once. You had my number. That's a far cry from a declaration of marriage. It's not even anything we could call a casual dating relationship—I think we'd need at least two or three dates for that."

"I look at you and feel anything but casual," Ezra muttered. "Shit."

"Ahh . . . what?"

"Nothing. Look, I just wanted to tell you I'm sorry, okay?"

She looked like she wanted to say something, but then she just sighed and averted her face. "Fine. You're sorry. It's over and done with."

"Yeah. Over and done with." He hesitated a second and asked softly, "Friends?"

A deprecating smile curved her lips. "Friends. Sure. Why the hell not?"

Shit, what a fucking mess. Ezra absently rubbed the heel of his hand over his chest. The forlorn, tired expression on her face did bad, bad things to him. He'd backed away from her after one fucking date because she made him feel things he knew he wasn't in any shape to feel— not while his head was still so screwed up over Mac.

Don't think about that right now, he told himself. It was the last thing he needed—the absolute last thing he needed.

"I had some idiot kids out joyriding on my property last night, did some damage. Came in here to file a report on it. What brings you in here?" he asked.

Lena grimaced. "Don't ask."

"Too late. Already did." He'd heard some of it . . . and it hadn't settled that well. Screaming. She'd heard somebody screaming. "Why don't you tell me about it?"

"Why?" Lena asked wearily. What in the hell did he care? Shifting in the chair, she crossed her legs and listened as Ezra moved across the linoleum floor, his footfalls a bare whisper. If it wasn't for the faint unevenness she detected in his gait, and those rubber-soled tennis shoes squeaking on the linoleum, she doubted she would have heard him at all. "What does it matter what I'm doing here?"

"Isn't that kind of what friends do? Ask how the other is doing?"

Friends. Lena curled her hand into a fist and tried not to think about the knot of disappointment that had settled somewhere in the vicinity of her heart. He hadn't called because . . . what was it again?

Irritated all over again, she started to tap her fingers on the arm of the chair. "Look, you know what, Ezra? I don't think friends will work. I've got plenty of friends. If you're here to get your head on straight, fine. You do that. But you don't need some mock 'friendship' with me to do that. So you can shelve the mock concern, too."

Ezra was silent for five seconds, but she could feel the intensity of his stare, all but burning into her. "Did it occur to you for even five seconds that I could have just walked away when I saw you in here? I didn't need to come over here. Didn't need to humiliate myself and admit to anybody—much less a beautiful woman that I'm seriously attracted to—that I'm a total asshole."

"And exactly when did you humiliate yourself?"

"Oh, fuck it," he muttered, shoving upright. He started to pace, but the muscles in his leg decided he wasn't going to pace and the leg tried to buckle under him. Swallowing the groan of pain, he slammed a hand down on the table and managed, just barely, to stay on his feet.

"Ezra?"

Blood roared in his ears and he barely heard her soft voice above it. His heart raced in his chest and a cold sweat broke out all over him. Carefully, he eased his weight back against the table—it was either that or end up on the floor. Breathing shallowly, he waited for the wave of pain to pass and that was when he realized Lena was on her feet and moving closer.

"Are you okay?"

"Fine," he gritted out.

She brushed her hand against his arm. Ezra nudged her away and said, "I'm fine."

"No, you're not. You're sweating. What's wrong with you?"

"Nothing," he bit off. Sourly, he added, in an echo of her earlier question, "What does it matter?"

She scowled. "Are you sick?"

"No." Snagging a chair, he spun it around and used the table and his good leg to maneuver himself into it.

"Look, I messed my leg up a few months ago. Acts up sometimes. Pushed myself too hard yesterday and now I'm paying for it. That's all."

"What . . . what did you do?"

With a dry laugh, he said, "Careful, Lena. You're almost acting like a concerned friend there, you know."

"Jackass." She glared at him and then sighed, returning to her chair. "Let's try this again, okay? I mean, I liked you a few weeks ago. And even right now, when I'm trying to not like you, I find myself still wanting to like you . . . even when I don't want to, and yes, I know that doesn't make sense. So let's just wipe the slate and try this again. Maybe we can try . . . well, being friends."

Studying her from under his lashes, Ezra debated on whether he should tell her or not—there was no way he could look at her and think friends. But he could fake it. After all, how likely were they to be around each other?

"Okay. Friends. So, about my leg . . . I messed it up on the job a few months ago. It's still trying to heal."

"A few months ago? You must have messed it up something awful," Lena said, her brow puckering in a frown.

Yeah. Steel plates. Two surgeries. Safe to say he'd torn it up something awful. But he didn't go into detail. "Okay, so I gave. Now it's your turn. You want to tell me why you're here? What's the deal with this screaming you say you're hearing?"

"I don't say I'm hearing it. I heard it," she bit off.

"Okay. What's the deal?"

Frowning, she said, "Why?"

"Call me curious. Besides . . . isn't this what friends do?"

Was it wishful thinking or did he not sound quite so . . . dismissive? Annoyed with herself, Lena started to swing her foot back and forth. Prather had gotten under her skin with those sly little jabs. And having Ezra here? Man, that was making it worse . . . so much worse. He got under her skin, too. In so many ways . . . oh, so very, many ways.

"Friends or not, Ezra, I'm already freaked out by this, and I don't want to have to go into detail about it any more often than necessary," she murmured.

Besides, she'd just met this guy.

Even if she'd had one rather nice date with him, she didn't really know that much about him, and those screams had her . . . unbalanced.

FIVE

WELL.

Law hadn't been kidding, Hope decided as she slowed to a stop.

Ash, Kentucky, had a roundabout.

A town square.

More stop signs than stoplights and she'd actually had people waving at her as she drove through town. It didn't make her feel welcome, although she imagined the smiling townfolk probably hadn't planned to freak her out.

It wasn't exactly their fault that small towns made her teeth grit and her skin crawl and her hair stand on end.

If there was one thing that Hope Carson had hoped to avoid, it was small towns.

They absolutely freaked her out.

She felt trapped in them.

Hell. She *had* been trapped in one.

A horn honked behind her and she jerked herself back to awareness, realized she'd been sitting there, staring stupidly at nothing for the past minute or so. Waving at the driver behind her, she pulled forward and found a parking spot off to the side of the county building. Although it was Sunday, there weren't many open spaces and she could see people bustling all over the place.

It might be a small town, but it was a lively one.

With curious, curious people.

Feeling the weight of the stares, she debated about whether to just turn around and leave town.

She could get in touch with Law and tell him she'd changed her mind.

Yeah, she knew he was expecting her—he hadn't been at home when she'd gone by his place. She hadn't been able to just sit there and wait.

Hope wasn't too good at sitting and waiting.

She'd spent too much time doing just that.

Don't think about that right now, she told herself. She couldn't think about that and make any sort of logical decision and she needed to be logical right now. Logical, not emotional.

Taking a deep breath, she unclenched her fingers from the steering wheel and made herself climb out of the car. She'd just take a walk around. Judging by the number of little shops and restaurants around, this town probably saw plenty of weekend tourist traffic from Lexington or Louisville. Hope and Law had grown up in a town not too different from this one. If she just wandered around, she'd blend in. But if she sat in her car like a freak, people would stare at her. Pay attention.

She didn't like it when people paid attention—

Stop it.

Her hands were sweating, she realized.

Wiping them off down the sides of her jeans, she tucked her keys in her pocket, checked to make sure she had her cash, the one credit card she had in her name—for emergencies only—and her ID. It was all she ever carried.

Everything she owned was in that car.

She'd left all her belongings in another small town. A

beautiful home, a closet full of lovely clothes, and a life that had been a lie.

People said taking the first step was the hardest, but they were wrong.

She'd taken that first step more than two years ago when she'd finally decided she couldn't keep living that life and she was still walking, putting more and more distance, more and more time between herself and that life—him—and it was still hard.

Because of the memories . . .

Because of locked doors and white rooms and whispering voices . . .

Stepping away from the car, she started toward the sidewalk. For some reason, it felt like she was severing a lifeline.

It hadn't been this hard before.

She knew it hadn't.

She had no trouble leaving that small, cramped hunk of junk when she was crashing in some no-tell motel for a night, or when she was bussing tables, cleaning houses, whatever she could find in exchange for quick and easy cash. There were times when she hated that car.

Because it was so hard to walk away, she made herself do it. Absently, aimlessly, she wandered down the sidewalk, staring blindly into the glass-fronted shops and fighting the urge to turn back to the car—run back to it, dive inside, and drive away.

Get away from this little town.

Why?

Was it just because it was a small town so like the one where she'd been trapped?

Was it because of Law and his determination to get her to stop running?

Logically, she had no reason to keep running. There was no legal reason and if she was honest, probably no tangible reason.

Do you really think I'll let you leave me? You're mine, Hope. I don't let go of what is mine . . .

Working on a Sunday was the last thing on earth Remy wanted to do, but sometimes, a man had to do things he didn't want to do. Since he'd rather get it over with early, he'd attended the early service at Ash Methodist and headed into the office, dealt with his business, and swung by the sheriff's department.

The church service, like the work and the visit to the sheriff's office, was necessary. If he didn't go, his mother would know. And he would then have to answer to her. Nobody could work a guilt trip quite the same way a mother could.

Besides, there was something . . . soothing about it.

He wasn't entirely sure if he believed in any greater power—he believed in justice and he believed in the law, but more than that? He didn't know.

But it was peaceful, and Remy didn't find peace in many places.

Since it was peaceful, and since it only took forty-five minutes or so, and it kept his mother happy, he attended church, and he did so willingly.

He'd needed that bit of peace, too, as he dealt with his business.

Especially today.

There were times when he wished he wasn't a lawyer.

There were times when he wanted to use his fists, instead of his wits and mind.

Especially today.

Moira Hamilton was in the hospital again, this time with a busted jaw and a broken arm.

Her damned husband had beaten the shit out of her. Again.

The kids were now out of the house and if Remy and Social Services had anything to do with it, they would not be going back. The twelve-year-old, poor kid, had seen the whole thing and he knew that girl was going to relive that night in her dreams for years.

Possibly her entire life.

Before, Pete Hamilton had always whaled on his wife when the kids were either asleep, out of the house, or just out of the room. But this time, Bethany had seen it. She had been crouched on the landing with a phone in hand, calling the police.

Poor girl.

Brave girl.

Smart girl.

She'd seen what her mother couldn't. Or wouldn't.

The mom wouldn't get help for herself, or for them, so the girl had taken matters into her own hands.

He'd spent the past hour going over the report at the sheriff's office. As the Hamiltons' big old house was outside the city limits, the sheriff's department had to handle the call—and apparently they'd had another call last night.

Ash was a quiet town. They had their share of crazy nights, but it wasn't unusual for them to go a night or two, even an entire weekend, without much of anything happening.

This weekend had been different.

Very different.

Pete's brutal attack on his quiet, soft-spoken wife, in front of their kids.

Then the very, very strange call from Lena Riddle.

Very strange, from what Remy had been able to put together.

Lena . . . he ran his tongue along his teeth, thinking about her. The thoughts were enough to bring on a wave of nostalgia, and not a little bit of lust. He hadn't had another woman in his life since he'd broken up with her and he missed her—missed the sex definitely, but he missed her, too. Missed that lazy, easy humor of hers, that sexy laugh and her smile.

If he hadn't been so damned tired, he might have joined her when he saw her talking to Prather.

But he had been too tired, Prather grated on his nerves, and he had a few more things to follow up on with the Hamilton case.

By the time he'd finished, Lena had been gone and he figured it was best if he stayed out of it anyway.

All she had was an unusual—very unusual—complaint. It was weird enough that he was glad she had that dog of hers, but he had his hands full. Besides, things between them, while their relationship hadn't ended badly, were strained.

Remy had wanted . . . something more, although he didn't really know what.

Lena had liked the status quo and when he'd pushed—awkwardly, he could admit now—it had changed things between them. The easy friendship they'd shared before they started dating had changed.

Jumping in would probably just stress her out more, he had figured, and he could tell she already had enough stress going on, just by looking at her. He suspected she could have used a shoulder, but Law could handle that.

Remy had seen the other guy on his way into the station. Law had been waiting in the lobby, fiddling around on his iPhone, seemingly oblivious to the world. Remy knew better. He hadn't been too surprised when he'd seen Lena—one thing could make Law wait patiently, and that was Lena.

Weird that Lena hadn't ever realized that. She was so insightful about things, but about that particular thing, she was clueless. It was clear as day—the word "smitten" probably had Law's picture next to it in the dictionary. But Lena didn't seem to have any idea.

He finished up his business in record time and headed

out of the small municipal building shared by the minuscule city police and the county sheriff department. Outside, the sun was blazing down with brutal intensity. It hit him like a fist. Slipping out of the summer-weight jacket, he threw it over his shoulder and started toward his car.

He had half a mind to spend the rest of the afternoon napping out in the hammock on the balcony. The next few days would be busy as hell for him. Whether Moira Hamilton cooperated or not, he planned on busting that bastard husband of hers and come Monday, things would really start rolling.

Maybe he should spend the day in the hammock— likely wouldn't have many chances to do it again anytime soon. If he knew anything about his town, it was that when one weird thing started, it was followed by another, and another.

Hamilton's arrest was probably the start of another flood.

Yeah, he really should enjoy the day while he could . . . maybe pick up a book from Shoffner's, spend the afternoon emptying his mind. He probably needed to do just that.

With his mind set, he turned east instead of heading to the car he had parked just a few yards away. He almost changed his mind when he recognized a familiar form—

Prather.

Remy curled his lip.

Man, he couldn't stand that bastard.

He was a throwback to the days when small-town America consisted of nothing but the good ol' boy network. Anybody who wasn't a white male who fit society's version of normal was placed in the "inferior" category.

He was condescending, he was an idiot, he was oblivious, and very often, he was a pain in the ass for the sheriff, Remy, three-fourths of the town council, and just about everybody else who came in contact with him.

He was also only a few years away from retirement and unfortunately, he'd never done anything to justify getting kicked out, so they just had to deal with him.

Somebody else caught Remy's eye and if he hadn't seen her, he might have headed back to his car.

But once he saw her, he found himself staring, oddly unable to look away.

The breeze kicked up, blowing long, dark hair around a slender, almost waiflike form.

He didn't know her.

Remy had been born in this town—on the stroke of midnight, New Year's Day. He had gone to school here until he left to attend college and after he finished up with college and law school, he'd come back home. He knew everybody here.

But he didn't know her.

She stood staring into the window of Shoffner's, but something about the way she held herself, the way she stood, made him think she wasn't debating her book purchases or trying to decide if she should splurge or not.

She looked like she was lost in another world.

No.

Trapped.

Trapped . . . and utterly alone.

Somebody bumped into her and she jumped.

Even from fifteen feet away, he could see the way the blood drained from her face, could see the way she darted away, plastering herself against the plate-glass window.

There was a plant stand there, one she didn't see, and she bumped into it, sent it toppling over.

Prather was closer than Remy was and for reasons that he couldn't even explain, dread filled him.

All Hope saw was the uniform.

When he touched her, she freaked out.

Jerking away from him, she smacked at the restraining hands, trying not to scream, trying not to cry.

No, no, no . . .

"Miss, you need to calm down—" Hard, big hands with blunt, strong fingers manacled her wrists and she could feel her airway constricting, trying to shut down. Dark pinpoints flooded her vision and she fought the onslaught—

Can't pass out, can't, can't, can't . . .

Passing out was always bad. When she passed out, that was when she woke up and found herself . . . *no, no, no . . .*

She didn't know she was moaning, soft and low, under her breath, and she was barely aware of the fingers tightening on her wrists as she jerked and twisted once more, trying to escape.

Then, abruptly, she was free, resting with her back against the cool, smooth glass window, blood roaring in her ears, trembling all over, shaking like a leaf.

But free.

And very much the center of attention. The deputy was staring at her, as were several other people on the street. Covering her face with her hands, she tried to gather her wits, tried to calm down.

"Damn it, Jennings, what in the hell is your problem?" the deputy demanded.

"You big idiot, are you blind? Can't you see she's terrified?"

The words were delivered in a flat, level voice, one that managed to pierce the shroud of terror enveloping her. Hope lowered her hands, watching from the corner of her eye. Whoever he was, he wasn't looking at her—he was glaring at the deputy.

Good. That made it a little bit easier for her to breathe.

"She bumped into a stupid plant—she ain't got no reason to freak out over that."

"You really are blind." The blond gave him a scathing glance and then shifted his eyes to Hope. The impact of that gaze, for reasons she didn't understand, hit her clear down to her toes. "Are you okay, ma'am?"

Hope swallowed the knot in her throat. *Oh, God . . . Can I even talk?* "I . . . ah, I'm fine." She cleared her throat, or tried to, and then focused her attention on the deputy she'd stumbled into.

All she'd done was knock something over and crash into him, but the sight of his uniform had set her off. She felt like an idiot—a world-class idiot—and worse, she was still scared, still shaking.

That was all sorts of bad, too. She couldn't let them see, couldn't ever let them see the fear. Swallowing the spit pooling in her mouth, she tried to smooth the fear away from her face, but she knew she failed. It would be like trying to calm the ocean . . . impossible.

It didn't help when the deputy's eyes narrowed on her face.

"No reason for her to be afraid." Studying her with suspicion, he said, "Unless, of course, she has a reason."

Hope had every damn reason to be afraid of people wearing a uniform—she knew how many hid behind one. But she'd be damned if he made her feel like she was some kind of criminal. Hoping, praying her voice wouldn't shake, she stiffly said, "You scared me." She glanced at the badge he wore, his uniform. County. "My apologies, Deputy, but you scared me. I don't like being touched and you just startled me. I overreacted."

The other man stood off to the side, watching them. The deputy shot a look at him, a look that was heavy with dislike if Hope could still read people worth a damn. Of course, her faith in her ability to read people was pretty much nonexistent these days. Her faith in herself period was nonexistent.

She'd misread the most important person in her life, and in the worst way imaginable, for the longest time . . .

The deputy looked back at her. He gave her a terse nod and then gestured to the busted pot at her feet. "Well, then, ma'am. I guess I should be sorry if I scared you, but I was just trying to help. You do know you will have to make reparations for that."

"Oh, don't be silly."

Hope cringed inwardly at the new voice. From the corner of her eye, she saw a woman—petite, with hair the color of brick, bright blue eyes, and a face that looked like it had seen the inside of a tanning bed a little too often.

"It's a damn plant, Earl, not a Ming vase," the woman said. "You go inside, help yourself to some coffee, and don't worry about it."

"Too hot for coffee." The deputy straightened his uniform and stalked off.

Somehow, it lacked the authority he was probably reaching for, Hope decided. Licking her lips, she debated on who to look at first.

She decided on the woman. Maybe the guy would just walk away.

The woman wore a shirt almost the same blue as her eyes, with "Shoffner's" embroidered over her left breast. There was also the logo of an open book. From the corner of her eye, Hope could read the lettering on the window. Shoffner's.

"I'm sorry. I'm usually not so clumsy," she said, her voice stilted.

"You weren't," the woman said, shrugging. "I saw it from the counter. Somebody bumped into you and just kept on going. You stumbled into the plant stand. It's not a problem and it's not your fault. Really. I'm Ang Shoffner—my husband and I own the place."

She gave Hope a wide smile and winked. "I'll just take

it out of his pay." That smile, it was so friendly, so warm and welcoming. It did something to ease the knot in Hope's belly.

But it returned as the man shifted around to stand by Ang. "Prather's day is all ruined now, Ang. He couldn't arrest some brute of a felon for vandalizing your ficus."

"It wasn't a ficus." Then she cocked her head and studied the plant. "I don't think." She peered at Hope and asked, "You know plants?"

But Hope couldn't think.

Couldn't speak.

Swallowing, she just shook her head.

The urge to run to her car was back. *Run. Run away.* Very, very far away, and all because this man had shifted his gaze her way.

He was smiling at her, a friendly, easy smile.

Not at all threatening. Not at all predatory.

Just the same friendly, easy smile Ang had given her. His eyes were blue, too, but not that bright blue—no. His eyes were the dark, dark blue of the eastern sky just as the sun sank below the western horizon. Dark, dark blue . . . so dark a blue they were nearly black, ringed by a thin band of even darker blue. Spiky, thick black lashes framed those amazing eyes, and his hair was gilt-blond—he looked like an angel, she decided.

And he had a friendly, easy smile.

His voice was deep, low and smooth, a slow and easy drawl. He could have made millions with that voice, she suspected. The voice, just like the face, was perfect.

Their gazes locked—that dark, dark blue with her green. The smile on his mouth softened, warmed. Those eyes . . . so blue.

Hope felt like she was falling.

Sucking in a deep breath, she tore her gaze from his and stared at the sidewalk, keenly aware of the fact that he was still standing there, still staring at her . . . keenly aware of the fact that her heart was racing, her belly felt hot and tight.

Heaven help her.

Swallowing, she darted one more look at him and just as quick, she looked away.

For reasons she couldn't even begin to understand, he terrified her.

Her hands were sweaty and shaking, and the bones in her legs felt like they were made of rubber. Blood roared in her ears, and her heart felt like it had taken up permanent residence in her throat. Worse, her belly was pitching and rolling. If she didn't get out of here, and soon, she was going to end up puking or passing out.

Or both.

Licking her lips, she whispered, "I have to go." Digging into her pocket, she pulled out her money and with shaking fingers, counted out twenty precious dollars. "Will this cover . . ."

"Honey, I meant it when I said . . . hey, are you okay?"

"Here, take the money."

"No," Ang said, her voice firm. She gripped Hope's wrist and forced Hope to close her fingers around the money. "Girl, it's a stupid plant, one that half dies every time I'm off of work for more than two days at a time. The planter cost five bucks at Walmart and the plant probably cost less than that. Listen, why don't you come in and have some coffee, some water . . ."

"No. I . . . I have to go."

This time, she didn't bother trying to fight the urge.

She ran back to her car, and she locked the door behind her.

She was twenty miles away before she made herself stop.

Before she reminded herself she'd made a promise.

Two promises. One to Law. He was counting on her,

and whether he really needed her around or not, she'd told him she'd come.

But she'd also made herself a promise.

She'd promised herself she wouldn't let herself get trapped again.

And what was this but being trapped?

Trapped by fear.

She ran so fast, that long, luxurious brown hair streamed out behind her like a banner.

Her eyes had connected with his, and for a few endless seconds, he'd felt lost in the soft, dreamy green of her eyes. Before she had looked away. Before she had started to think.

Before some dark, icy fear had settled deep inside her and she had taken off, running like the hounds of hell were at her heels.

Watching after her, half stupefied, Remy didn't say anything for nearly a minute. He had never in his life had a woman run away from him. Not even once.

He didn't like the feeling it gave him. Not at all.

Ang stood next to him, as silent as he was.

As the woman's tires squealed on the pavement, Ang sighed and said, "Dear Lord, I hope she doesn't do that anywhere near Prather. He'd just love to pull her over and write her up—just to be mean."

"Yeah." Frowning, Remy reached up and rubbed the heel of his hand over his chest. "You ever seen her around here?"

"No." Then she pushed her fingers through her wiry red curls and said, "And I doubt we'll see her again, either. That girl, she's running from something."

Yeah. Remy had that same sinking sensation.

Those eyes of hers, something about them, they had gotten to him—right square in the heart.

CHAPTER
SIX

IT WAS ALL OVER TOWN BY NOON.

Law sat at the table across from Lena, watching her pale, strained face and wondering if she was going to talk to him.

Oh, she'd told him what had happened.

Once they'd left the sheriff's office, she'd confessed what was going on and he had been hard-pressed not to go through the roof of his car.

No wonder she'd looked so pale.

No wonder she'd looked so worried.

Shit, why hadn't she called him? That night? Why hadn't she called him when it happened? He would have been there in a few minutes—been there with her.

But hell, of course she wouldn't call him. Lena didn't look at him that way—didn't think of him that way. She might call him for a ride into town, for a ride to the county sheriff, but she sure as hell wouldn't call him when she needed a shoulder, in the middle of the night when she was alone . . . scared.

When she heard some woman screaming.

Screaming . . .

Jennings. Keith Jennings. Law ticked through his mental file until he placed a face to the name and he figured it could have been worse.

Jennings was quiet—sometimes a little too quiet, in Law's opinion—he liked when people talked, did stuff, because that made it easier to figure them out. But Jennings focused on his job and tried to be fair and thorough, from everything Law had seen about him. In a small town like Ash, it was easy to watch, too.

Watching was kind of his thing, anyway.

Jennings did his job.

Yeah, could have been worse . . . could have been Prather. If that idiot had been on the night shift that weekend, Lena's report might still be in the process of being written. Hell, Prather might have tried to figure out a way to not even write the damn report.

That man could fuck things up seven different ways to Sunday and manage to make it look like the other person's fault.

A soft, tired sigh drifted from Lena.

Leaning back in the seat, Law crossed his arms over his chest. "So. You going to tell me about it or what?"

"I already did," she said, her voice weary.

"No, you told me exactly what you told the cops. You haven't told me how you are, what you're worrying about, thinking about. Things you'd normally tell me. You're not. You going to?"

She caught her lower lip between her teeth and then reached up, slipping her fingers under her glasses to rub her eyes. She had a headache. He could see it, tell it by the way she was rotating her neck, rubbing the back of it.

"Come on, Lena. Talk to me."

"I'm scared. I feel sick. I feel helpless. And I'm pissed off."

"Why are you pissed off?" he asked.

She smacked a hand against the table. "Because there's somebody out there—or there was. Maybe it's too late, I don't know. But she needed help—she needed it, Law, and nobody helped her. And nobody can find her. Is anybody even going to look?"

"Jennings did look," he said softly. "You tried to help. You called the cops."

Lena snorted. "Fat lot of good it did." Slowly, she reached up and took off her glasses, revealing the pale, almost crystalline blue of her eyes. She'd been born blind in her left eye. Until she was ten, she'd had vision in her right eye, but she'd gotten injured playing baseball with some friends . . . and not wearing any safety equipment. Apparently it was a big risk for people who already had a vision impairment. She'd been hit in her one good eye and the injury had resulted in vision loss in her right eye as well.

He loved her eyes. He knew she was self-conscious . . . well, maybe that wasn't the right phrase. Lena wasn't always patient with people—she didn't mind people asking her questions, but too many people would rather stare than ask. She knew when people stared—she could feel it. She was too attuned to people, too sensitive.

She wore the dark, tinted lenses because she had some idea that it might keep people from looking at her as much. Law could have told her it was a waste of time— people had a habit of staring at what they didn't quite understand. And then there was the case that with Lena, she was just one of those women that people noticed—she was attractive, yeah—but it went deeper than that. She had that . . . spark.

Logically, he knew he wasn't looking at her from unbiased eyes; he thought she was absolutely beautiful. But she had something special, she had a way about her. People noticed her. The way she moved, the way she held herself, the way she laughed. Her confidence. Everything.

And right now, he couldn't help but notice the strain on her face, and the very unfamiliar look of self-doubt. "It's because of me," she said quietly. "I know Sergeant Jennings at least made the effort to look around, but Prather? He didn't even bother. And it's because of this."

She passed a hand over her eyes and shook her head. "If I could see, he would have paid a little more attention to me."

"Oh, bullshit." He snorted. "Then he would have written you off because you're female. 'You know, a woman really shouldn't live in that big house all by herself . . .' some crap line like that. Don't tell me you can't hear him saying something just like that."

"Oh, I can totally see him saying something like that. He already implied I should have some sort of *companion*." She all but spat it out, fury vibrating in her voice.

Law narrowed his eyes. "Companion?"

"Yes." She sneered, the derision dripping off her words. "It's a big house, too spooky at night. Somebody with me might help."

If he thought it might help, he might have voiced the rage that made him feel. But he knew it wouldn't help her. Still, he had a vision of meeting up with Prather, telling the fool a thing or two, assuming he'd understand. "I suppose you disabused him of that idea?"

"There's no point." She shook her head. "You know, he isn't that old. Why does he act like a dinosaur? I wonder if his folks were dinosaurs."

"Some people just have it in their genes, maybe," Law said, shrugging.

Leaning forward, he covered her hands with his, stilled the nervous twirling of her glasses. "You can't let him get to you, Lena. You know what you heard, and you did what you could. You can't do any more," he said quietly.

"If I could see . . ." She tried to pull away, averting her face. A muscle twitched in her jaw.

"If you could see and you went outside without knowing what was going on, I'd have to wonder about your intelligence, honey. That's one of those TSTL things—too stupid to live. You don't go plunging headlong into something without knowing what kind of environment you're putting yourself into. Not smart, Lena. If it's a dangerous environment and you're not absolutely convinced you can handle it, then your best bet is to do just what you did—call for help."

She made a face.

Law laughed. "It's the truth. When you dive into something, if you can't handle it, then you risk making two victims instead of one—how does that help anybody?"

"You're right." She sighed and rested her head against the padded bench. She closed her eyes, the thick fringe of her lashes lying against her ivory skin. "I know you're right. I just wish . . . I don't know. I just have a bad feeling about this, Law. Really bad."

All over town—damn it. They were talking about it all over town.

How could she have managed to cause this much trouble?

Fuck, it had been two A.M. and miles outside of town. One neighbor—only one. But that one neighbor had heard her.

As he stopped at the counter to pay for a Coke and gum—neither of which he needed—he heard Adrienne Cooper talking about it to Deb. He just barely managed to keep from snarling.

Deb Sparks was more effective at getting news out than any modern media known to man. Tell her and in a matter of hours, people who no longer even lived in Ash, who hadn't lived in Ash in twenty years, would hear about it. Family members who only visited every other year would hear about it.

Hell, maybe the whole world.

Not good.

Not good at all.

Judging by the strange glitter in Deb's eye, she was miffed, too. Probably irritated that she hadn't been the source of all the excitement instead of Lena.

Too bad it wasn't Deb.

Too bad indeed. She might know how to spread the word, but she was also known for spreading . . . less than reliable words.

Somebody called out his name and he only paused a moment in the swinging glass door. "I've got to get back, sorry!"

Yes, he had to get back.

Had to figure out what to do. Had to decide.

The drive back to his place hadn't yielded any miracle answer.

Distracted, he paced the hard-packed dirt floor and studied his territory.

It was dimly lit, the light provided by battery-powered torches or gaslights. Completely self-contained, completely his. He had spent a great deal of time in this place, perfecting it until it was exactly as he wanted it. Some of his tools and his toys he'd crafted with his own two hands.

He took a great deal of pride in this place.

His own little world.

And he'd come close, too close to being discovered. If he was discovered . . . well, it had always been a risk, but he hadn't exactly envisioned it being a risk quite like this. Hadn't imagined it happening quite in this fashion.

She was strapped down to the cot, her face slack, her chest rising and falling in a rhythm of deep, deep sleep.

She'd tried to rouse twice, but he'd just given her more Valium. Right now, he needed her quiet. So he could think.

He'd think easier away from here, but he couldn't seem to pull back just yet.

It was like a drug, he realized—an addictive, dangerous drug that was sure as shit going to fry his brain if he wasn't careful.

As close as he'd come to being caught, it had been such a thrill. And as chancy, as dicey as things were now, what was he doing? Cleaning up his trail? Getting rid of her?

No. He was out here, all but whacking off and remembering it all over again.

The hours he'd spent in town hadn't helped him find answers, and while he'd intended to go home and clear his mind, he hadn't been able to.

What to do?

Yes, somebody had heard her.

But it wasn't like it was the most reliable witness. Nobody had seen anything.

This was new. Unusual for him. To feel so . . . unsure. And on the flip side, so exciting. Part of him raged at what she'd done. Part of him wanted her to do it all over again—so he could feel that rush, all over again.

Mouth dry, he stopped in the middle of the floor and turned back to look at the door. Right there. He'd barely made it inside before the lust got control of him. Once he'd caught her and gotten her back here, all he had been able to think of was taking her—hard, fast, brutal. He hadn't even attempted to bring a response from her this time.

Once he'd gotten her back inside his spot, he'd slammed her against the dirt wall. With his hand over her mouth, he'd fucked her again, relishing every last struggle, every choked, muffled cry. She'd been unconscious when he was done, and as his mind cleared and his blood cooled, he realized he'd need to keep her that way for a while.

Just in case.

It had been a wise call.

Even as he had gone about dumping her on the bed, he'd heard the distant wail of sirens.

He hadn't panicked. Even then, he hadn't panicked. Panicking never served a wise man. Instead, he dealt with his girl, using a syringe to give her a heavy dose of Valium. It would keep her unconscious for the next little while. After taking care of that first, pressing need, he'd checked the door, made sure his place was still secure, still hidden.

Then he'd gathered his belongings and debated . . . did he slip away? Did he wait here?

Too close . . . last night had been far, far too close.

He'd spent the morning in town, listening to the chatter on the gossip grapevine.

After all of these years, after so much care, he'd messed up. He'd almost been caught.

Now he had to decide what to do.

Careful . . . he had to be careful now, even more careful than before. He had to think it through. Had to plan. While part of him insisted he kill her before this place was found, he knew that might not be wise.

The sooner he killed her, the sooner he'd have to dispose of her body—that was always the riskiest time, aside from actually bringing her in. If he killed her now, then he'd have to get rid of the body soon, and people would be too watchful for a few days.

Needed to wait. Yeah. That was best. Yes. Yes. That was it.

That had to be the way.

Besides, he couldn't make his plans until he knew what the sheriff's department planned to do about Lena Riddle's report. Lena Riddle. That was a hot topic in town today. Too many people talking about what she'd heard, whether or not she'd really heard anything, whether or not her sanity was in doubt.

She wasn't crazy, though. And too many people knew that.

That was the entire problem.

Hope woke to the sound of rain, and her cell phone buzzing on the bedside table.

She glanced at the display and grimaced. Huddling under the blankets, she sat up and answered the insistent ring. She could ignore it, but he'd just call back. And keep it up until she answered.

Law was rather insistent that way.

"Hey."

"You're not here."

"No. I'm not there. I'm here."

"And where is here?" he asked, his voice level.

He wasn't mad—she knew that. He was worried, and he'd continue to worry and she could tell him she was a grown woman and could take care of herself, but that was a lie; she absolutely sucked at taking care of herself.

He was just being Law, but she suspected that if she told him she was at a hotel only twelve miles from his place, he might get mad. So she kept that quiet.

"At a hotel. It's in Kentucky," she said. "I was just too tired to finish the drive and now . . . well, I need a day or two."

"For what?"

"I just do," she said, keeping her voice flat.

For a moment he was quiet, and then quietly, he asked, "Are you okay?"

She knew what he was asking. "I'm fine. Really. I just need some time. I'll be there soon. Okay?"

Over the line, she could hear him sigh. "Yeah, you told me that last week. You actually coming?"

"Law, I told you I'd be there," she said. "I already am here . . . I just need to . . . get my head on straight." Not that she was very likely to do that in the next twenty-four hours. She really, really had planned on heading back to his place the day before.

But something about the confrontation with the deputy, and then the strange, tense minutes that followed after he'd left, had set her on edge.

And that guy. The blond. Why had he affected her like that? What was the deal?

She was so jumpy right now—a door had banged in the room next to hers and she'd flinched. She was literally five seconds away from hiding under the sink counter.

She might not get her head on straight, but she could at least pretend that she wasn't just a whisper away from the funny farm.

Funny farm.

Uniforms.

Shaking her head, she thought, *It's almost like old times*.

"Hope?"

"Yeah, I'm here. Sorry, I'm just thinking. Look, I'll be there."

"When?" Law asked. "You've been telling me this for weeks and then another week passes and you never show."

She sighed, rubbing the tense, aching muscles of her neck. She couldn't even explain, exactly, why she wasn't there right now—it wasn't like she was far away. It wasn't like she had a whole hell of a lot of money, either. She was down to her last couple hundred dollars.

But she needed to settle her brain, settle herself, especially after the episode earlier. She couldn't do that in the few minutes it would take to get to his place—she knew she couldn't, but she also couldn't go there until she was a little less on edge.

"Hope?"

She swallowed and closed her eyes. "Yeah?"

"You're not coming, are you?" The flat, grim sound of his voice made her wince.

"I am coming." She closed one hand into a fist, fought the tears that rose in her throat. "I am coming. I'm just . . . I need a couple more days."

Silence hung between them and finally, Law sighed. "Yeah. Whatever."

But she could tell he didn't believe her. "I'll be there, Law." Damn it, she couldn't keep running. She had to stop at some point, at some time, and the time was now. "I'll be there. Three more days, Law. I'll be there in three more days."

"You're sure?"

"Yes, Law. Three days, Law. I promise."

A huge sigh whooshed out of him. "Good. Good."

She could picture him, clear as if he stood there, running his fingers through his hair and smiling that way he did when he got his way. And that's what had happened—he was worried about her and he wanted her someplace where he could take care of her and that meant having her closer to him.

If she wasn't so desperate, if she had anyplace else she could go . . . if she didn't really, really need a friend, there was no way she would do this. She didn't want to lean on anybody and she didn't want to need anybody.

But it was Law.

If she was going to put her life together—hell, she didn't have a life right now. She had to build one, and she needed a friend, she needed a job, she needed a place to live. Law was her best, and only, friend and he was offering the job, and that would help her find a place to live.

If she couldn't let herself lean on her oldest, dearest friend, then she couldn't really lean on anybody.

Maybe she should have more pride, but considering the hell her life had been the past few years, she knew how very little pride actually meant. She had her freedom, and she had a friend willing to help her. That had to mean more than pride.

Quietly, she said again, "I'll be there soon."

Then she hung up the phone and stared at the mirror.

CHAPTER
SEVEN

It was Monday—a rainy, dreary Monday. Lena lay in bed, listening to the rain falling outside and trying to work up the interest to get dressed. After the hell of yesterday, when she'd finally lain down, she'd gone straight to sleep, dropping down like a stone.

But dreams plagued her.

Dreams plagued by a woman's screams.

Dreams where Lena was running through the woods, being chased. Chased by some nameless, faceless monster.

Dreams about Ezra.

She'd had another one of those dreams, full of heat and hunger and lust and laughter. Ezra's humor, that sexy innuendo as he talked to her . . . except, of course, he wanted to be friends.

Because he wasn't ready to get involved. He needed to get his head on straight—and what in the hell did that mean anyway?

And then her dreams circled back around to that night, of the woman and her screams.

"God." Closing her eyes, she clenched her jaw and tried to tell herself she'd done everything she could do. There was nothing left for her to do. She'd called the sheriff's office. She'd gone out there.

A fat lot of good it had done.

Down on the floor, Puck shifted, giving a little doggie yawn, followed by an impatient yip. Lena rolled onto her back and rubbed her hands over her eyes. "Yeah, yeah. I'll be up in a second," she muttered.

He yipped again.

Despite herself, she had to smile.

"Let me guess . . . it's seven-oh-five." Reaching out, she pushed the button on her clock and grinned as the voice recited the time. "Yep. Seven-oh-five."

The dog's internal clock was as reliable as any man-made clock. Come 7:05, it was mealtime. She could feed him a little earlier, but never any later, not without hearing it from him. Blowing out a breath, she sat up and kicked her legs over the side of the bed.

She needed to get up anyway.

It might be a rainy, dreary Monday, but it was Monday.

And on Mondays, she had a standing breakfast date.

"Anything weird happen last night?"

The concern in Law's voice was a balm to her soul. Lena might not have accomplished anything with her visit to the sheriff, but Law believed her.

He was one of her closest friends and she knew she could count on him.

"No. Just a quiet night."

Quiet, but plagued by restless dreams, sex dreams and nightmares.

They were on their way into town for breakfast at the Nook Café. For the past few years, they'd had breakfast there just about every single Monday. Although she was dead tired, she hadn't canceled. She needed to get out of the house and relax, stop brooding.

"You want to go by the sheriff's office again after breakfast?" he asked.

Lena blew out a disgusted sigh. "What would be the point?"

"Because you deserve to have some sort of answer?"

"They don't have one." She grimaced and tried to relax. Tension had her muscles tied into knots. "They didn't see anybody, didn't find anything. I don't think there's much more they can do."

Her hands were damp, she realized. Cold and clammy. "Look, Law, I don't really want to talk about this right now. I need a break from it. It's all I've been able to think about since it happened."

"Sure." He reached over and caught her hand, squeezed it gently. Turning her palm up, she laced her fingers with his. He had strong hands, callused, gentle. Just being around him made her feel safer.

It took twenty minutes to get to town and by the time they got there, the café was already packed. "I'm going to let you and Puck out at the door. I'm going to have to park down the street. I see Roz's car, so she's probably already got us a table."

The car stopped and Lena waited as Law hopped out. Behind him, somebody honked their horn. Rolling her eyes, Lena asked him as he opened her door, "Did you double-park?"

"No . . . I'm not parking. I'm unloading," he said. She could hear the grin in his voice. The other door opened and then shut. Puck was at her side and she gripped his lead. "Forward, Puck."

The rain was cold and the wind gusting down the street didn't help. By the time she made it to the door of the café, her clothes were soaked and her hair was dripping. Puck shook himself and she scowled as he flung more water on her.

The bell over the door chimed as she opened it.

"Hey, Lena."

It was Cassie, the granddaughter of the café's owner. "Hi. Is Roz here?"

"Yep. Front corner, near the windows. I'll walk you over. Nasty day, huh?"

Lena reached out her hand and caught Cassie just above the elbow. "Damn nasty," she agreed as the young woman led her to Roz's table.

"You look like you got a little damp."

She snorted. A little damp. Yeah, that about described it. And now she smelled like wet dog. Shivering, she breathed out a sigh of relief as Roz called out her name and said, "I've already got coffee waiting for you, Lena."

"Gimme." She slid into a chair as Puck settled down under the table at her feet.

Halfway through the first cup, she started feeling almost human. "Nature is screwing with us," she muttered. "Eighty-eight degrees one day and then sixty-two today and pouring down rain. I hate it. And I hate cold rains."

"You and me both," Law said, joining them. He took the chair at her right.

Lena reached for her coffee, but she did it a moment too late. Law had already helped himself. "Damn it, get your own coffee."

"That's the thanks I get for letting you out at the door so you don't get soaked."

Roz snorted. "Oh, that's as much for your benefit as hers."

Tapping her fingers on the tabletop, Lena said, "If you don't give me my damn coffee, Law, I'm going to beat you bloody."

"Violent woman." He pushed the cup into her hands.

She kept it close against her until he got a cup of his own.

"I hear you had a rough weekend." Carter, Roz's husband of four years, spoke up, his voice low and quiet.

He was a soft-spoken man and until he got to know somebody he kept to himself. That he was even asking her about her weekend was, she knew, a sign of his affection for her.

But she still didn't want to talk about it.

"Rough enough," she said, cradling her nearly empty coffee cup.

"Is there anything we can do to help?" Carter asked.

"No." She softened the curt response with a smile, shaking her head. "Not much anybody can do."

Roz reached over, covering Lena's hand with her own. "You know, you're welcome to stay with us for a while. So you wouldn't be alone. You know we've got the room."

Just then, Puck shifted by her feet. With a smile, Lena shook her head. "I'm not alone. I've got Puck with me."

Roz chuckled. "Yes, and if a stranger shows up, your pooch will be more than happy to show him where to find all the silver."

"He would not." Lena pursed her lips. "He's only nice to you because you sneak him treats."

Desperate to get them talking about something—anything—else, she shifted the focus to Carter. "How is work going for you?"

She hadn't been joking when she said she didn't want to talk about it. If she had her way, she'd tuck the night away and forget it ever happened.

Not that she'd have much luck with that.

Brooding, she listened with half an ear while Carter talked about his pottery. Occasionally Law would ask a question, which sent the discussion spiraling in a whole new direction. Lena kept up as much as she could, but she couldn't concentrate on much of anything.

In the back of her mind, she kept hearing that poor woman's voice.

Put it away, she told herself.

But that was so much easier said than done.

"I'd better be going," Carter said. "These projects are nice to talk about and all, but they won't get done if all I do is talk. Lena, you be sure to call us if you need anything."

She forced a smile. "I will. But don't worry. I'm fine."

As Carter left, the three friends fell silent. "You're not fine," Roz said quietly. "You're worried sick. I can see it."

"There's not much I can do about it, though, is there?" Lena asked. Weary, she slid the tips of her fingers under her glasses and rubbed at her eyes.

She had another headache, a bad one. All she'd done was nibble at her food. The French toast she'd ordered—one of her favorites—lay mostly untouched, cold syrup congealing around it.

"The police didn't see anything to worry them. Nothing happened last night, and nobody else reported anything weird, no reports of anybody getting hurt."

She shrugged and lifted her hands. "I just can't really do anything else. Although it would have helped if the damn cops had listened to me."

"They didn't?"

"Shit." Curling her lip, she leaned against the padded bench. "Jennings, the guy who came out that night when I called nine-one-one, he at least listened to what I had to say. But when I went in to see if there was anything else they could try to do, that moron Prather was more interested in convincing me I'd been imagining things."

Lowering her voice, she said mockingly, "It's got to be unnerving for a woman like me to live out in a house all by my lonesome."

"He said that?" Roz demanded.

Lena smiled at the disgusted rage she heard in her friend's voice. It helped, having her friends pissed off for her. "Yeah."

"The sheriff's office was a waste of time." Law's voice was calmer, steadier, but she still heard the undercurrent of irritation there.

It soothed the ragged edges. A lot. Enough that she was able to give them a real smile. "Nah. Not a total waste. I mean, at least I wasn't sitting at home and wondering if maybe I should go in and see if there was anything new. Now I know the answer. That's better than not knowing, right?"

Just then the bell over the door rang. Roz shifted on the seat across from her and in a low voice, she muttered, "Wow."

Faced with nothing but week-old pizza in his refrigerator, Ezra had to face the unavoidable.

He needed to go into town and buy some damned groceries. He couldn't have picked a worse day to run out of just about everything, either. Sheets of water all but obscured the roadway, and when he hit the main strip, traffic was moving at a crawl.

It was about as much of a traffic jam as the small town of Ash probably ever saw, he figured. A neon sign caught his eye and he glanced over, saw the little café. His stomach growled at him, reminded him he'd decided against the pizza. He could either stop to get a bite to eat before hitting the store or he could wait another couple of hours to eat.

His stomach wasn't very impressed with the latter idea.

When a van started to back up just in front of him, he took it as a sign. After he parked, he made a dash through the rain. He was soaked to the bone by the time he hit the door. The scents of bread, bacon, and coffee mingled in the air and he was all but drooling as he stood there, dripping water onto the floor.

Shoving his wet hair back, he glanced around absently. A familiar, dark red head of hair caught his eye.

Every time I turn around, he thought . . . Hell. Maybe this was some sort of sign. He started toward her table, but halfway there, he realized she wasn't alone.

No, she was sitting at a table with two other people. A woman, about her age, Ezra figured. She was a looker, too, blond, blue-eyed and tanned. Her blond hair was worn short and sleek. Her eyes rested on his for a few seconds in female appraisal.

Ezra looked at the guy, recognizing him from the other day. He'd been with Lena at the sheriff's office. Judging by the look in his eye, the man had more than just a casual interest in her.

He glanced at Ezra and then leaned forward, murmured to Lena. Ezra didn't catch a word, but Lena straightened and turned in his direction as he drew even with the table.

"Morning, Lena."

"Ezra."

A slow smile curled that pretty mouth. She cocked her head. She shifted in her seat, crossed one slender, jeans-clad leg over the other. "We're about done, but you're welcome to join us. We're just talking and drinking coffee. Avoiding the rain."

From the corner of his eye, he saw the look in her friend's eye.

"There's plenty of rain to avoid. Are you sure you don't mind?" he asked.

"Of course not. After all, isn't that what friends do?" she asked.

Maybe it was his imagination, but he thought her smile was just a tad bit mocking.

He managed not to wince. Friends—shit, that was the last thing he wanted . . . well, no. Not really. He did want to be friends with her. He just wanted more than that. A lot more.

Wanted, but couldn't. Needed, even. Hell, he couldn't quit thinking about her and he had to.

"I guess so," he murmured, well aware of the daggers the other guy was drilling into him with his eyes. Ignoring him, Ezra settled into one of the empty seats—it hadn't been empty long, though. The remains of somebody else's meal still sat there.

"I'd love to join you for some coffee. Might get a bite to eat, too."

"By all means." She made the introductions easily, either unaware of the undercurrent of tension or just unfazed. Ezra decided she probably wasn't aware of it.

The guy's name was Law Reilly. Law—what the hell kind of name was that?

Ezra wondered how long he'd been mooning over Lena.

He didn't wear his infatuation very well, either, Ezra decided as Law pushed back from the table in under two minutes flat. "Lena, I've got to run down to the post office. I'll be back in about twenty or so."

"It's pouring down rain."

"Just water." Law shrugged as he dug some money out of his pocket and dropped it on the table. "I'll come back inside to get you when I'm done. Maybe it will stop raining by then."

He lingered only long enough to drop a kiss on Roz's cheek and then he was out the door.

"Friendly guy," Ezra said, keeping his voice neutral.

Roz gave him a knowing smile. Lena might not realize her buddy had a thing for her, but this woman did.

"Law only behaves in public when he sees the point," Lena said, shrugging it off. "Small talk isn't something he sees much point in, especially if he doesn't know you. He wasn't trying to be rude."

Ezra wasn't so sure of that, but he didn't much care.

The waitress showed up to clear the area in front of him, take his order, and pour coffee. After she left, Ezra slumped in his seat and stretched his stiff right leg out as much as he could. Absently, he massaged it. Damn rain.

"So you're June King's grandson?"

Ezra looked up, met the woman's curious, vivid blue eyes. Roz. Lena had said her name was Roz—Roslyn Jennings and she owned the bed-and-breakfast close to his place. "Yes."

A warm smile curled her lips. "I knew your grandmother. She used to come out to the gardens a few times a year, back when I was still trying to get things going with the Inn."

"You own the Inn?"

"Yes, I do. Miss June gave me some advice about the gardens and she used to fuss at me about my roses."

"That sounds like her."

"Were you close?"

Ezra looked down at his coffee, staring into the dark brew as though it held the answers to life itself. "We were. Especially when I was a kid. But then I graduated from high school, went to college. Got busy." He sighed. Distracted, he shoved a hand through his wet hair and leaned back in his seat, staring off into the distance. "Time slipped away and before I realized it, it had been a year before I'd seen her. I'd come out and see her at Christmas, stay for a few days, and I'd try to come see her in the summer when I could. I didn't do as good a job of it as I could have."

"You did a lot better than some do, though," Roz said. "I think I saw you at the funeral, with your folks. I didn't stay very long. I don't much care for funerals."

"Who does?" Shifting his gaze to Lena, he asked, "You have any trouble last night?"

"Nice, subtle change of topic there, Ezra," she said, her voice dry.

"Yeah, I'm a smooth operator, all right. And you didn't answer me."

"No. I didn't." She took a sip of her coffee. "And no. There wasn't. Can we talk about something else?"

"Can't give you any points for subtlety—you don't even make an attempt," he said.

Lena lifted a brow. "I don't see the need to pretend. I don't want to talk about it."

"Not talking about it doesn't solve the problem."

"Talking about it doesn't solve it, either," she snapped. Then she sighed, a soft, weary sound.

Ezra watched as she lifted a slender hand, rubbed at her temple. Then she lowered it to the table, curled it into a fist. A tight, white-knuckled fist. "I'm sorry. Look, I just don't want to talk about this. I really, really don't."

"I can understand that." He could—and he did. But his spine was itching. She hadn't wanted to talk to him yesterday at the sheriff's office, but that hadn't kept him from asking around.

He knew how to ask around, and what little he'd picked up was enough to leave his skin crawling. That, combined with the fear he'd glimpsed on her face, the fear and the worry, added up to one thing in his mind: bad news.

Screaming—in the dead of night.

Prather might want to write her off, but Ezra wasn't about to do the same.

Not with this burn in his gut. As much as he'd like to believe it was just indigestion, he knew better. His instincts might have let him down a time or two in the past, but he knew to listen when they were singing like this.

Something was going on.

Leaning forward, he covered her fisted hand with his. "You don't want to talk about it. I get that, I really do. But think about it—is hiding from it the smartest thing to do?"

"So what can I do?" Her mouth twisted in a scowl. "I already called the police and a fat lot of good that did. What more can I do?"

Rubbing his thumb along the back of her clenched fist, he said, "Well, you could start by telling me what you told the county sheriff. Tell me what happened."

"Why?" she asked quietly. "What's the point? You said it yourself, you work for the state."

"Yeah, but I'm still a cop. And unlike that prick, Prather, I don't always have my head up my ass—I know how to listen. Maybe . . . well, maybe I'll think of something they didn't."

"Like what?" she muttered. She tugged her hand away from his.

The loss of contact left him with a weird ache inside, one he couldn't entirely explain. He was prepared for her to tell him to just let it go, tried to find another argument to convince her.

But to his surprise, she just sighed and said, "There's not that much to tell, Ezra. I was sleeping. It was late. Something woke me up and it took me a minute to figure out what it was. But it was screaming. A woman. She was screaming for help. I heard her call out four more times. And then . . . nothing."

"Where did you hear her?"

"In the woods, off to the west of my house. Probably in a hundred feet or so. It couldn't have been too far, or I wouldn't have heard her." A faint smile curled her lips and she said, "I can hear well enough, but not that well."

"Any idea if she sounded young? Old?"

"I . . . don't know. A woman, not a kid. But she could have been in her twenties, her thirties, forties . . . she wasn't old as in needing a walker old, but for all I know she was in her fifties or sixties. I just don't know." She shook her head. "All I can say for sure is that she sounded . . . terrified. Desperate." She averted her face and he watched her throat work as she swallowed. "Completely terrified."

When she faced him again, she had a cocky, somewhat forced smile in place. "So, Sherlock, any brilliant deductions?"

"Not just yet, Watson."

Roz leaned over and wrapped an arm around Lena's shoulders. "Lena, sweetie, are you sure you don't want to come stay at the house for a while? Man, I'm scared just thinking about it."

"I'm sure." Lena reached up and patted Roz's hand. "But thanks."

She reached for her coffee, and closed her hands around it, lifting it slowly to her lips. "Sergeant Jennings came back out, took a look around, but he didn't find anything," she said.

"Jennings?"

"Yes. He's with the sheriff's department," she answered. "He wanted to take a look at the woods when he had some light, but he couldn't find anything."

"Hmmm. Actually . . ." Ezra reached up and scratched his chin. *What in the hell are you doing?* "I was kind of thinking of coming by your place. Having a look around myself."

I'm trying to be a friend. Remember?

Then he grimaced and glanced out the window at the deluge. "Not that I expect I'll find a whole hell of a lot with all this rain. But still. A look around in the daylight, even after a downpour like this, who knows . . . maybe I'll see something they missed."

"Why do you think you'll find something when the deputies didn't?"

"Sometimes people don't see things because they don't expect to see things," he said, shrugging.

For a long, quiet moment, Lena said nothing. Then slowly, she lowered her coffee cup to the table. "You believe me."

"Why wouldn't I?"

She swallowed, shook her head. "I . . ." Licking her lips, she took a deep breath and murmured, "It's just that . . . well, Sergeant Jennings listened, but I'm not all that sure he believes what I'm saying. I think he believes *I* believe but . . . that's not the same thing as *believing* me. And Prather sure as hell didn't believe me. Why do you?"

Reaching out, he caught one of her hands and this time, when she tried to tug it free, he wouldn't let her. "Lena, you just don't strike me as the type to dream up something like this, and you definitely aren't the sort to make up something like this. If you say you heard a woman screaming, then that's exactly what I think happened."

A slow, shaky smile curled her lips. "Really?"

"Yeah."

In fact, he was pretty damn sure of it.

Maybe it was because of the tight, strained look on her face as she'd been talking to Deputy Dickhead Prather.

Maybe it was the grim, worried look on her face.

Or maybe it was because he could all but feel something buzzing inside him.

He didn't know, didn't entirely care just yet.

But something was going on.

He wouldn't be much of a cop if he didn't listen to his gut.

He wouldn't be much of a man, if he could look at Lena's tight, drawn face and not feel . . . something.

Luck was with them. By the time Law was done at the post office, the rain had stopped. He arrived back at the café just as Ezra had finished eating. The two men didn't speak more than three words to each other, but that didn't surprise her, especially not on Law's part.

"What do you think about him?" Lena asked as she walked with Law back to his car.

"Who?"

She frowned. He sounded . . . irritated. "Ezra."

"Beats me. Just met the guy. Didn't hang for the breakfast chat, either."

Sighing, Lena said, "Law, you notice people. You notice things about people that people probably don't even notice about themselves. Geez, you probably know what color socks our waitress had on. Wouldn't surprise me if you'd noticed if she was wearing a thong or regular panties."

A few seconds of silence passed and then Law sighed. "Actually, she wasn't wearing either, I don't think."

"Eww. Okay, that was a little TMI, buddy." She jabbed at his side with her elbow.

He grunted as her elbow bounced off—it was a lot like she'd bumped into a wall.

"He limps when he walks," Law said. "Did something to his right leg. Noticed him rubbing it a few times. Looks like he notices just about every damn thing, too. Wouldn't surprise me if he was a cop."

"Hah. See? You do notice things. He is a cop—he's with the state police. Maybe you should be a cop."

"Hell, no. The pay sucks and the hours aren't any better." Law was quiet for a few seconds and then he added, "He was checking you out. Just you. Watches you, like he doesn't really see anything else, even though you can tell he sees everything."

"What do you mean . . . like he was checking me out?"

"Shit, Lena. What in the hell do you think?" Hot temper edged his words, and under her hand, the muscles of his arm were tense and tight.

"What's wrong?"

"What's wrong?" Law stopped in his tracks and turned to stare at her. There was barely an inch's difference in their height and he was so close, he could see his face reflected in the dark surface of her shaded lenses. She rarely took them off, even around him.

One of her best friends.

Fuck, that hurt.

Five years and she still hid herself from him.

Five years and he'd been half in love with her the entire time. She was clueless about it, too. So fucking clueless, as evidenced by the fact that she was standing there with a mixture of temper, hurt, and concern on her pretty face as she tried to figure out what the hell his problem was.

His problem. What would she do if he showed her just what his problem was? If he tried to kiss her?

Shit, he was too messed up to do this today. Worried about Lena, worried about Hope. Half sick with jealousy at what he was hearing in Lena's voice when she mentioned that guy. Half sick with fear over how long it was taking Hope to get here.

Get it together, he told himself. He had to get it together, or just outright tell Lena what his problem was—or at least part of what his problem was, and wouldn't that go over swimmingly?

You. It's you. I'm shit-faced in love with you, and you can't even see it and you're wanting me to give you details about some other guy who's got a thing for you . . . and you've got a thing for him, too.

He could tell. He'd seen it on her face.

Yeah, he noticed things, all right.

Reaching up, he cupped her cheek in his hand, brushed his thumb over her silken skin. So soft. So strong.

I'm not ever going to have a chance with you, am I? he thought miserably.

She reached up, curled a hand around his wrist. "Law, what's going on? Are you okay?"

"Just dandy," he muttered, his voice hoarse. No. He

wouldn't have a chance with her, even if he could ever work up the courage to try. She wasn't into him, and he wasn't about to ruin a friendship. Wasn't about to strain a friendship. Leaning in, he pressed his lips to her brow. "Come on. Let's get back to the car before the rain starts back up."

They finished the walk to the car in silence. He opened the door for her and waited until Puck had jumped inside. But when Lena would have climbed in, he caught her arm. "I guess I'm just worried about this mess you've got going on. Reckon the last thing I want to think about is you hooking up with some strange guy."

An amused grin on her lips, she said, "He's June King's grandson, Law. It's not like he just dropped down out of nowhere. I don't exactly know him, but people around here do. And he's a cop."

Snorting, Law said, "You know, I realize this 'He's June King's grandson' is kind of like some sort of written seal of approval for some people, but you're forgetting something. I never really got to know June. Besides, even if she was a great lady—and yes, I've heard she was a great lady—but even if she was, that doesn't automatically mean her grandkids are all great by default."

"You're such an optimist," Lena said, grinning. "I really, really admire your upbeat, positive outlook on life and mankind." The humor on her face faded and she leaned back against the car, sighing. "Besides, there's nothing there. We . . . ah, actually had dinner a few weeks ago. He was going to call me, changed his mind. We're friends."

He heard the mocking sarcasm in her voice, thick and heavy, but it didn't quite hide the disappointment.

"Shit, Lena, if that guy wants to be just friends, then I'm a chorus line dancer."

"Really? Do you wax?" A reluctant smile curled her lips. "Look, we're just friends. I'd thought there was something there, but we've talked, and we're just going to be friends."

This was killing him. Seriously. Law figured it might be less painful just to ram his head against a brick wall until he either passed out or drew blood . . . or both. "Hell, maybe he wants to be your friend, but it's not just that."

"You don't like him."

He just barely managed to keep from swearing. Just barely managed to keep from snarling. Just barely managed to keep from punching something—like the nearby metal light post. Instead, he jammed his hands into his pockets and said, "I don't know him one way or the other—can't say if I like him or not."

Her shoulders slumped.

Law's heart squeezed inside his chest and he blew out a breath. Closing his eyes, he muttered to himself, "I'm going to so fucking regret this."

"What?"

"Nothing. Just muttering to myself." Rubbing the back of his neck, he shifted so he could stand next to her, leaning against the car, their shoulders almost touching.

At that moment, a fat drop of rain fell down and plopped right on his nose. It was followed closely by another. The coward in him wanted to beg off—they could get in the car, be nice and dry—have this conversation later. Never sounded good.

"So the fuck what if he's saying he just wants to be friends? You might not be able to see the way he's looking at you, Lena, but I do and trust me, honey, it's not the same look you give your friends." He took a deep breath, blew it out. "If he's pulling back, maybe he just needs some space, maybe he needs his head examined, I don't know. But he's not looking for a fishing buddy, I promise you that."

Her brow creased and she scowled. "So . . . what, you think I should ask him out? Just leave it alone?"

"Hell, I don't know. Look, I don't know him. But he seems like a pretty stand-up guy. If that's what you're wanting to know."

She leaned against his arm. "Stand-up, huh? Like a co-median act?"

"Har-har." He reached over and tugged on a lock of her thick, gleaming hair. "I don't know if this little town is big enough for two stand-up acts."

She was smiling again.

The knot in his chest eased a little and he figured it was probably worth it. Hell, he'd already accepted the fact that she wasn't ever going to be interested in him anyway, right?

"So he seems pretty decent, you think?"

"Yeah." He wrapped an arm around her shoulders and hugged her. "But I think you'd already figured that much out or you wouldn't be interested in him. So why are you giving me the third degree? What does it matter what I think?"

She made a face. "Let's just say that right now, I'm questioning myself. He says he'll call, then he doesn't. He says he wants to be friends, but that's not exactly the vibe I'm getting . . . and hell, friend isn't really what goes through my mind when I talk to him—and that doesn't make much sense, seeing as how today is only the fourth time I've even talked to him. And then there's that little fact that I'm questioning myself . . . a lot."

"Well, stop." The rain was coming down harder now, a light, steady downpour. "If you're that interested in him, and if he's got you that confused, then maybe you should push a little harder, see what the deal is. You've never quit on something, once you've set your mind to it. Why stop now?"

Lena smiled. "Good point."

"Now that we've had this little heart-to-heart, how about we get out of here?"

They were halfway down Main Street when the light, steady downpour became a torrent. Blowing out a sigh, Lena muttered, "At least it waited until we were in the car."

She pushed her hair back from her face and turned toward Law. "Ezra's coming out to my place. Today."

In that moment, Law was damn glad she couldn't see him. He clenched his teeth, just barely managed to keep from swearing. "Yeah? He's moving fast, especially for somebody who just wants to be friends."

From the corner of his eye, he saw the confusion on her face, saw it fade as a slow blush took its place. "Eh, not for that. Don't I wish. He's going to look around in the woods. See if he can see anything."

"The sheriff's deputies already did that."

"Yeah." A somber frown on her face, she used the tip of her finger to trace a circle on the console between them. "But I don't think they thought they'd find anything. Do you think when somebody expects to find nothing, that's exactly what they find?"

"Could be." He ran his tongue along his teeth. "Look, if he's coming by, I'm hanging out at your place. Don't take this wrong, Lena, but with all the weirdness you've got going on right now, I'm not going to trust some guy who just up and appears. I don't care if he's a cop, I don't care if he's June King's grandson. He could be June Cleaver's grandson for all I care."

Lena chuckled. "Gee, Beave. If you insist."

EIGHT

FOR SOME REASON, EZRA WASN'T THE LEAST BIT SUR-
prised to find Law Reilly at Lena's place.

Torn between the resolve to keep things on a friendly
basis and all but drooling over the way her butt filled
out the seat of her jeans, he felt a pair of eyes on him.
Even before he looked up, he knew who it was.

Shrewd hazel eyes bore into him like lasers and if
looks could kill, Ezra would have been bleeding from a
dozen vicious wounds. "Hey . . . ah, Law, right?"

"He wanted to go with us," Lena said. She gestured
toward the living room where Law waited. "Go have a
seat. I forgot to dig out my hiking boots. It's going to be
muddy and I'm not wearing my tennis shoes."

"You're coming?"

She cocked her head. "Yes. That a problem?"

"No." He heard an edge in her voice and he had a
feeling he knew what had caused it. Uncertain how to
proceed, he decided to take the safest course—silence.

"Good."

She disappeared up the stairs. Law waited a few more
seconds and then he snapped, "She's blind, you know.
Not helpless. If she wants to go walking around the
woods, she can."

"Did I say she couldn't?" Ezra asked, tucking his hands into his pockets.

"You might as well have."

Ezra sighed. "Look, I didn't say that and I didn't really think it, either. My mind might have started down that road, but it's pretty damn clear that woman knows how to handle herself." Then he rocked back on his heels and studied the man in front of him. "And that's not what your problem with me is, either."

"I don't have a problem with you. Don't know you." Law crossed his arms over his chest and leaned against the arched doorway that led to the living room. Then he shook his head. "Wait, scratch that. I do have one problem—if you weren't going to call her, why did you say you would?"

Fuck. Blowing out a breath, Ezra said, "Don't you think that's kind of between me and her?"

"Not when it hurts her," Law said softly.

"She's a big girl. I don't think she needs you hovering over her to kiss her bumps and bruises." He turned away, staring out the window. She had flowers planted, vivid bursts of them dotting the landscape here and there. "But I did plan to call her. It just dawned on me afterward that it was probably better for her that I didn't call." Shooting a look at Law over his shoulder, he said, "And that's not your problem with me. Or maybe, that's just part of it. She's interested in me, and whether I'd called her or not, you'd still find a reason to be pissed off at me. You got eyes. You know I'm interested in her. I got eyes, too. I know you're interested in her. Problem is that she doesn't seem aware of your interest . . . and she is aware of mine."

Something hot and angry flashed in Law's eyes. "She's a hell of a woman. She deserves to be treated right. She doesn't deserve to be strung along."

"I agree with you. And that's why I didn't call her."

"You didn't call her because you knew you'd string her along if you did?" Law said, scowling.

Ezra rubbed a hand over his face. Just why had he started this conversation?

"I didn't call her because until I can tell if my head is in the right place, the last thing I need to do is get involved in anything more than a casual relationship. And again, I'm failing to see where this is much of your business. It's not like we were getting married—we had one date, and I had her phone number. For all you know, a second date would have resulted in the two of us hating each other."

Although Ezra knew that wasn't likely.

He'd spent much of the past three weeks thinking about her, and ever since he'd seen her in the sheriff's office, she'd all but dominated his thoughts. Shit. She'd dominated his thoughts since the first second he'd seen her. If he was one to believe in love at first sight, he'd almost swear he was hooked.

"I hope you're doing a better job at convincing yourself than you are at convincing me," Law said, shaking his head. He glanced toward the stairs and then back at Ezra.

"Shit, no," Ezra muttered. He could talk friends all he wanted and it wasn't going to do a damn bit of good. He didn't want to be her friend—or at least just her friend.

A grin twitched the corner of his lips and as he met Law's gaze, he saw a similar smile echoed there.

"So how come you're here? Chauffeur? Making sure I behave? Keep my distance? Make sure she keeps her distance?"

Law snorted. "That one date you had definitely didn't teach you much about her, did it? People don't keep Lena from doing what she wants. Not once she makes her mind up." He shot another look toward the stairs and then sighed. "Just worried about her. Want to keep an eye on her."

Understanding dawned. Reluctant admiration followed. "You're watching me. She hears screams, some new guy suddenly pops onto the scene and seems to believe her when not many others do—made you suspicious." As his grin widened, he studied the other man. "How close am I?"

"Dead on." Law shoved off the wall and retreated into the living room. "Might as well have a seat. Lena will be a few minutes if I know her." He flopped on the couch, focused those shrewd, insightful eyes on Ezra's face once more. "I know a couple of state cops. Based out of Berea."

"Yeah?" Ezra chose the chair closest to the doorway, stretching his legs out as he studied the room.

"Yeah." He had a serious look on his face, and his eyes slid down to Ezra's leg. "I guess I can understand why you need some time to make sure your head is in the right place."

Ezra narrowed his eyes. Something hot and tight worked through his gut, spread through him. Irritation, anger, guilt. All of it, twining tighter and tighter, rising higher and higher. "You checked up on me."

"Damn straight. Sounds like you're lucky you can still walk with that leg—hell, lucky to be alive. Femoral artery—people can die when that one gets nicked." Something that looked like sympathy darkened those hazel eyes. "Heard a friend of yours died, too."

Tension climbed up his back, and he had to consciously work to relax those tense muscles. "You did more than a little asking, if you got that much." Asking, and getting answers—just who in the hell had he talked to, and why the hell had he been told so much? But Ezra already had an idea why . . . whoever he'd talked to trusted the guy.

"I'm nosy. What can I say? Besides, I wanted to make sure you are who you said you are. Lena matters to me—I'll do what I need to, to make sure she stays safe."

Because Ezra could understand that, he told himself to let it go. Taking a deep, slow breath, he eyed Law closely. "Ever been told you're paranoid?"

"Part of my charm." Law shrugged, unperturbed.

"It's not really that charming. But then again, I guess I can't really be surprised. I've always heard that writers can be a nosy, paranoid bunch of bastards . . . aren't they, Ed O'Reilly?" He had the pleasure of watching Law stiffen as he threw the guy's pen name out there. Surprise and aggravation danced across his face.

Satisfied, Ezra smirked. "Come on now. Big shot crime-fiction writer like you, what would one of your cop characters do in this situation? He'd run everybody even remotely connected to the heroine, of course. And you're connected."

"You did a run on me." Law's eyes narrowed.

"Damn straight." Ezra flashed him a grin and added, "You made a real killing with your last few books. Damn good racket you got going there."

Abruptly, the disgruntled anger on Law's face faded, replaced by amusement. "You know, I almost hate to admit this, because I get the feeling Lena's falling for you—and if you hurt her, I'm going to kick your ass in a major way—but I think you might actually be an okay guy."

"So you'd rather her fall for a bastard?"

Law scowled. "No. I'd rather her fall for me." He glanced past Ezra to the stairs. "But I never made a move and I get the feeling it's a little too late now to even bother trying."

When she got downstairs, the two men were talking books.

Law's voice had that animated, excited tone he always

got whenever he was in the presence of another biblio-phile. Smiling, she stood in the door. "Oh, how sweet. You two went and bonded over books."

In a scathing voice, Law said, "Your cop friend here doesn't have the sense God gave a goat. He thinks Dean Koontz is the be-all and end-all of modern fiction."

"Heaven forbid," Lena said, tongue in cheek. "It's got to suck to be that wrong. Everybody with any brain knows that's a toss-up. It's between Linda Howard, Lynn Viehl, and J. D. Robb."

"Lena, you cut me deep," Law said, blowing out a heavy sigh.

She laughed and shook her head. "Somehow, you'll survive. I need to put my dog out before we go."

"You're not taking him?" Law asked.

Lena grimaced. "No. He doesn't like the woods much these days. I'll take my cane—between you and the cane, I'll be fine." She skimmed a hand through her hair and shrugged. "I can probably get him to go with me since I have you along, but I don't want to stress him out."

"You'll just stress me out. Thanks."

"You're welcome." She grinned and called out, "Puck!"

She had a fantastic smile, Ezra decided. It lit her face up—like the sun slipping out from behind the clouds. Em-barrassed by the strangely fanciful turn of his thoughts, he turned away and studied the movies lining her shelves. She had a hell of a lot of movies, too.

"So, cop. If we do find anything in the woods, not that I'm expecting we will after all that rain, but if we do, what exactly do you plan to do?" Law asked as Lena put Puck outside.

"Depends on what we find," Ezra said, glancing over his shoulder.

Lena remained by the door, waiting for Puck to finish up his business. While she waited, she angled her head toward Ezra. "You really think you can find anything?"

"No." Ezra studied the leaden gray sky, wondered if the rest of the rain would hold off or end up drowning them while they were out tramping around under the trees. "But that doesn't mean I won't look."

"Any idea what you're looking for?"

"Ideally? I'm looking for a woman in distress who would have been screaming at approximately two A.M., two days ago." Then he shrugged. "But that's a lot to ask for. I'd settle for anything that just looks . . . out of place."

What he found was wet, wet, and more wet.

The rain held off, but that didn't mean it was anything close to dry under the trees. Rain dripped from the leaves, and water puddled on the ground. Thick columns of mist hung in the air, giving the entire forest a surreal, almost spooky look.

"Any idea how much area the trees cover?"

Lena shook her head. "I don't. I only hike the area that borders my house. Too far back and there are cliffs. I don't do cliffs without having somebody with me, which isn't often around here." A faint grin tugged at her cheek and she murmured, "Law doesn't share my love for the great outdoors."

"I've got no problem with the great outdoors. I just have problems with bug bites. Mosquitoes. Poison ivy. Snakes." Law stopped in his tracks, staring around him, but Ezra had the feeling he wasn't seeing the trees around him. He looked like he was rummaging through some unseen mental file.

Under his breath, he muttered, shook his head, squinted.

Lena paused, one hand lifted. Automatically, Ezra extended his. Their fingers brushed and she slid her hand up, tucked it into the crook of his elbow. "He talk to himself a lot?" Ezra asked, trying to distract himself. It was either that . . . or lean in and press his face against the curve of her neck. She smelled good, something light, almost citrusy, but not quite. Female, and sexy. Completely delicious.

Friends, he reminded himself. They were just going to be friends.

Fuck . . . that smell was killing him. He desperately wanted to find the source of it and just start licking it right off her skin.

"He's thinking," Lena said, tilting her head up and grinning. "He doesn't think in silence well. Give him a minute. If he's heard the figure, he'll remember. Sooner or later."

Law continued to mutter. He paused and shot a glance at Lena. "Who's the guy who owns the property adjacent to yours? On the western side?"

"Ohlman." Once Law went back to his muttering, Lena added a mutter of her own, under her breath. "Mean old bastard."

"Huh?"

"Ohlman. The old man who owns the property along the western border of mine. Technically, I own about thirty percent of the woods. He owns the other seventy percent and he wasn't happy when I moved in, either. Not that he really wanted anybody living here. He—"

"Five hundred acres," Law announced, cutting into their conversation.

"Five hundred."

He nodded. "Yeah. I'd been reading up about land surveys and area history a few years ago. The Ohlman property was one I'd checked out—been in his family since before the Civil War."

"Doesn't sound like standard reading material for a thriller writer."

"Was thinking about doing something a little different. Idea didn't pan out."

"Um, excuse me. Just one minute." Lena's brows winged up. "How did you know about Law's writing? It took me more than a year to get that out of him," she interjected.

"He did a run on me," Law said, scowling.

Ezra snorted. "Hey, don't look so disgusted. You went and checked up on me, too, remember?"

Now her jaw dropped. "A run? What in the hell . . ." Comprehension dawned and she snapped her mouth shut. A muscle twitch and for five seconds, she looked like she couldn't decide if she was going to implode or explode.

Ezra winced as she went with explosion—he couldn't say he was surprised. Why should she suffer the headache when they were the ones responsible? But man, he wished he'd kept his mouth shut. Although it would have slipped out sooner or later, right?

"Why in the hell are you two doing runs on each other?"

"I'm a cop," Ezra said, shrugging. He tucked his hands into his pockets. "It's just kind of what I do, especially when there's something weird going on. You're at the center of it—only makes sense to eliminate those around you. He is around you."

Lena tugged her tinted lenses off and reached up, pinching the bridge of her nose. He caught a glimpse of pale, pale blue eyes. They sparked with temper and irritation. She might not see, but those eyes expressed emotion just fine, he decided. She slipped the glasses back on and then focused her attention on Law.

"What's your damned excuse?"

"What, I need a reason to worry about a friend of mine? You go through something majorly fucked up, the local law enforcement doesn't seem too concerned, but for some reason, some hotshot state cop seems to think there's a problem? That doesn't strike you at all strange? How in the hell was I to know he wasn't the guy who was out there hurting that girl?"

Lena made an exasperated sound. "Oh, for crying out loud." She turned around.

Behind her back, Law and Ezra exchanged glances.

He suspected they both wanted to come out with something equally mature, like . . . "See what you did?"

Instead, they just shrugged. Law crossed his arms over his chest.

Ezra hooked his hands in his back pockets and shifted his weight, trying to work some of the tension out of his right leg. Hiking was one thing he hadn't done much of since his injury and he had a feeling he'd be paying for it later. Paying in a major way. He wondered how many pills were left in that prescription bottle.

Lena turned around. Although her face was smooth and expressionless, he could tell she was still pissed. She didn't burn when she was angry—no, she went straight to ice. Butter wouldn't melt in her mouth.

Why in the hell did he find that so damned appealing?

"I'm trying to decide which I find more insulting . . . that a friend gets it into his head to use his connections to investigate somebody who is doing me a favor, or that a cop is investigating a friend of mine, just for being a friend of mine," she said, her voice flat and level.

Law said nothing.

As Lena's face angled toward his, Ezra scowled. "Hell, like you said, I'm a cop. If there's something weird going on, then you're damn straight, I'm going to nose around, and at this point, I'm curious enough that I'm going to nose around whether you want me to or not."

Lena rubbed her hands together. Her head cocked, her gleaming red hair swept down to brush against her shoulder. "I'm curious, myself. Just why are you so curious, Ezra King? Why in the hell do you care if I heard screams or not? This is a little out of your . . . what's the word . . . jurisdiction. And you're on leave."

"Doesn't matter if I'm on leave or not." Ezra sighed

and rolled his shoulders. It didn't matter. Just like it didn't matter if this was out of his jurisdiction. He saw a puzzle and he was going to get to the root of it. That was just how he worked. "I'm a cop. It's just how I am, Lena. Besides . . ."

He snapped his mouth shut before he could finish that thought. He wasn't quite sure he wanted to go there just yet.

"Besides what?"

She lifted a brow.

Blood rushed up, staining his cheeks red. Shit. Hunching his shoulders, he turned away, even though it didn't do a damn bit of good. She couldn't see him anyway—didn't keep her from sensing how uncomfortable he was, he had a feeling. And Reilly, damn it, he'd already seen it, and would probably have a laugh or two about it later.

"Besides, what?" Lena persisted.

"This is a small town," he said, hedging. He could talk his way around it. He didn't need to get into discussing the fact that he'd already gone and developed a personal concern for her. Even as a friend, he was allowed to have a personal concern, right?

Of course, he knew his personal concern went deeper than friendship and it didn't matter that they'd only been on one date, that they'd only known each other a few weeks, that they'd already decided to just be friends, right?

She already mattered to him. But he didn't need to get into that.

No, no reason at all to go into that. "You know how small towns are. The minute you mentioned this to anybody, then everybody knew about it."

"And your point is . . . ?"

He turned back, watched her face. From the corner of his eye, he also watched Reilly's face. He'd already figured it out, Ezra realized.

Lena hadn't, though.

"If somebody was out there, hurting a woman, Lena, then you heard it. That makes you a witness . . . of sorts. Makes you a liability. And now the whole damn town knows about it. If whoever did it lives here, then he knows about you."

She was naturally pale, the clear ivory complexion of a natural redhead, and it didn't seem possible that she could get any paler.

Obviously, he was wrong.

He'd seen corpses with more color than her, and for about five seconds, he had to wonder if she was going to pass out. Through the tinted lenses of her glasses, he could just barely make out the shape of her eyes, could see the way her lashes fluttered, then lowered as she closed her eyes. She took a deep, steadying breath.

"Shit."

"You hadn't thought quite that far ahead," Ezra said.

With a raw, humorless, laugh, Lena said, "You could say that." Her hand swung out as she swept her skinny, flexible cane across the ground. It brushed against a tree and she made her way over to it, sagged against it as though she couldn't entirely support her weight just another minute.

"No," she said. "I hadn't thought of that. And I don't know why. Sergeant Jennings—the one investigating that night—he had mentioned an accident, but even when he said it, I knew that wasn't it. There was something in her voice, something about the way she was crying for help. It wasn't an accident. Whatever had been done to her—it had been done intentionally."

"Accident victims can get pretty traumatized."

Lena's mouth twisted in a sad smile. "You probably think I'm being overly dramatic." She sighed and pushed her glasses on top of her head, rubbed her fingers against her eyes. "Believe it or not, I'm not prone to drama. I'm just not. I'll leave that to Law. There was just something . . . something in her voice. I can't explain it. But it sounded like hell—hell on earth. And . . . I don't think she was alone."

"What do you mean?"

Lena lifted her cane, absently twisting it in her hands. "I keep thinking it through. Over and over. Hell, I don't know. Maybe I do have some latent drama-streak in me after all. But I think there was a second set of sounds. Her screaming, running through the woods. And a quieter sound. Somebody who walked . . . instead of running."

"You could hear that?"

Lena pressed her fingertips to her eyes, sighed. "Yes. It's quiet where I live, Ezra. Very quiet. I know the sounds. And like I've mentioned before . . . while my ears might not necessarily work better than yours, I listen to them better. I could be wrong. It's entirely possible I am."

"But you don't think you are."

She lifted her face to his. "No. I don't think I am."

"If there was another person in the woods, then maybe she had somebody trailing her," Law suggested.

"Maybe." And that was the conclusion Ezra had already come to—one he didn't like much, at all. Slowly, he straightened and turned around, studying the uneven, ragged terrain around them. "Come on. Let's see how much ground we can cover before the next downpour starts. Lena, try to get us close to the area where you think you heard the screams."

She sighed. "We're already there, the best I can tell. It wouldn't have been much farther away than this." She remained leaning against the tree, her ivory complexion drawn and tight, her sightless eyes staring off into the distance. She tugged on her lower lip with her teeth, an absent, nervous gesture that Ezra doubted she was even aware of. "I can't be exactly sure of the direction, but if I had to guess, it would be around here."

Ezra studied the terrain, searching for something, anything. Catching Law's eyes, he said, "I'm going to take a little bit of a look around. Then we'll shift around, maybe move to the north. Do the same thing."

Law caught his unspoken signal and moved to join Lena.

Lena smirked as a branch broke under his feet. "You here to play babysitter?"

"No, I'm here to sit down. I didn't come on this little jaunt to play Boy Scout. He wants to run through the woods, let him."

"Nice cover. I even believe that's half true," she murmured.

Damn rain.

Anything he might have been able to find was likely gone now. Still, Ezra looked anyway, moving slowly, covering as much ground as he could.

There wasn't much to see. Wet leaves, exposed tree roots. The occasional cigarette butt or beer bottle—people out on Lena's land, hunting or goofing off, probably.

He combed through the woods carefully, but as he'd expected, he found nothing.

Nothing he could see anyway.

Nothing he could find.

But there was something there.

In his gut, he knew it.

He could all but feel it as he slowly made his way back to Lena.

He'd be back.

Maybe he wouldn't find anything the next time, or the next time, but sooner or later . . .

CHAPTER
NINE

"So." Sheriff Dwight Nielson flipped through the pages of the report and then closed the file, tapping his fingers on it. Mondays were always a nuisance, but this one was proving worse than normal.

He had Pete Hamilton in lock-up for beating his wife. The bastard had secured a scum-sucking lawyer from Lexington who was trying to claim it was anything but spousal abuse, even though the daughter's story was just about as solid as they came.

The daughter—if this went to trial, Remy Jennings was going to have to put a twelve-year-old girl on the stand. There wouldn't be any way around it, and it turned Dwight's stomach. He imagined Remy wasn't feeling too hot about it, either.

But they wouldn't have a choice, unless by some miracle Hamilton agreed to a plea.

Putting a child through that . . . shit.

The whole damn thing gave him one massive headache.

And then there was the story with Lena Riddle. A very strange, very curious story, and one Nielson would like to just ignore.

But duty wouldn't let him, and as he skimmed through

the report, he had a weird tingling sensation in his gut. He couldn't ignore that either. Blowing out a sigh, he looked at Jennings. "About Riddle. What's your call?"

"Well, she's not lying." Sergeant Keith Jennings sat in the chair, back straight, feet flat on the floor. He'd been a soldier in the Army—did eight years and then came back home and joined the sheriff's department. He hadn't tried to play off the distant relationship with the mayor, or the DA, either. Nielson appreciated that; he respected it. "But that doesn't mean things happened just as she says they happened, either."

"Shit." He smoothed a hand over his bald scalp. His hair had started to thin in his twenties and rather than fight the inevitable, he'd kept it cut close. For the past few years, he had been shaving it. Easier than messing with haircuts, in his opinion. He had a narrow face, and dark, intelligent eyes, and he had little tolerance for bullshit.

He didn't much like having something muddy the waters in his quiet neck of the woods.

Lena Riddle's report definitely muddied the waters. It didn't fit.

"Why couldn't it have been Deb Sparks?" he mused out loud.

"Because that would have been too easy." Steven Mabry smiled over his cup of coffee. His deputy sheriff's round face was serene and pleasant, and hid a mind that was as sharp as a steel trap.

Deb, their local gossip, busybody, and general pain in the ass, lived just a mile or two away from Lena Riddle. If it had been her . . .

Routinely, she made calls complaining of suspicious activity.

If it wasn't a serial killer's van patrolling the highways at night, then it was a meth lab or a Peeping Tom or white slavery rings. Also included, for variety, she'd accused a local kid of trying to poison her cat, a niece of trying to steal her dog, and three different times, she'd accused her mailman of tampering with her mail.

The complaints ranged from tedious to strange.

She liked attention, and Dwight gave each of her reports the needed attention to make sure there wasn't any real danger, a little extra consideration for Deb, and then it was done. After that, she'd find something else to focus on for a while—something in town, usually, inappropriate books at the library, or a historical building that was going to be renovated in a way that would "harm the historical significance."

It was always something with Deb, and because of that, if she had made the call, he figured he could send Jennings out there one more time just to be sure, then they could move on.

Lena Riddle was a different story altogether. Because Lena Riddle did not make calls.

"How long has she lived here now, do you remember?" he asked, glancing at Jennings.

"She moved here a little before I came back home." Jennings remained sitting, so stiff, so straight, he could have been at attention. "A year or so before, I think. Would be close to nine years."

"Yeah. That sounds about right." It was right about the time Dwight had settled into office here. "Nine years, Keith. She's been here nine years and to my recollection, this is the first time she has ever had us out to her property."

Dwight plucked the report from the folder, studying it. "Go back out there. Talk to her again. Get the story one more time and do another walk through the woods. See if anything changes."

As Jennings left the office, Dwight turned away and stared out the window. Her story wasn't going to change. He knew it.

A nice, quiet little town. He wanted it to stay that way.

Yet he had that itch in his gut.

Something very, very bad was going on.

So he hadn't found much in the woods out by Lena's place. Yet.

But Ezra wasn't one to sit around and wait, either. The day after he'd prowled around through the trees, Ezra found himself waking up early with the sole intention of going into town. Or at least it seemed early to him.

Over the past six months, he had become a little too lazy. Getting out of bed before nine or ten was to be avoided at all costs, if possible—one of the new rules he had established when he decided to waste the rest of his life.

Noon sounded ideal to him.

But today made the second day he'd been up before eight, and he wasn't even grouchy about it.

Right now, he had a mission. Right now, he had something to focus on, besides the damn deck, besides working himself into exhaustion so he'd sleep too deep to dream about the night his life had gone to hell.

He even had a focus that wasn't entirely centered around Lena. Yeah, he knew he needed to keep his distance. That was the wise thing to do. The smart thing.

Although the longer he thought about it, the more he thought about her, the more he wanted to say, *The hell with being smart.*

Maybe you're just so hard up for her, you're imagining things, he tried to tell himself. *Creating some mystery where there really isn't one.*

But that wasn't it.

There was something fucked up in the works—he knew it, as well as he knew his own name.

After hauling his tired ass out of bed, he spent a few minutes stretching his right leg, doing the exercises he knew he needed to do, even though he skipped them half the time. All in all, his leg didn't feel that bad, considering he'd spent a couple of hours tramping through the woods the day before.

He felt almost optimistic, almost useful. Up at a decent hour, had a goal, had something resembling a plan.

It wasn't until he was in the shower that he started to question himself.

So what are you going to do when you get into town, slick? You don't have a badge to flash. Nobody here has to tell you anything. What do you think you're going to accomplish?

The first question was easy—he wanted to know if the sheriff's office had much of anything, although he really doubted it.

And yeah, he knew pretty damn well nobody needed to tell him anything. He could ask all he wanted, but that didn't mean anybody had to answer.

That last bit grated on him, burned him, like salt in a fresh wound. For the first time in six months, he was questioning whether or not he really wanted to walk away from his badge. If he had a fucking badge, he could do something.

Before, he'd always been in a position where he could help and now? He just didn't know.

Maybe that was why he had to try.

He couldn't ignore the feeling in his gut, couldn't ignore what his instincts were telling him. Even if all he could do was watch, even if all he could do was ask questions, at least he was doing something.

The thought of doing something left him with some sense of satisfaction—the kind of satisfaction he hadn't felt in months. Not since he walked away from his job.

Being a cop was more than carrying a badge, more than carrying a gun—and shit, he didn't know if he wanted to carry a gun again. Maybe he missed that sense of purpose, but he didn't miss the responsibility that came with it, and that was part of the reason he was still on leave.

Blood—blood on my hands . . .

Before his mind could travel down that path, he jerked it back in line. He didn't need to be thinking about that. Not at all.

No, what he needed to be doing was making some coffee, getting dressed. Then he needed to get his ass to town. Mind made up, he set about doing just that.

Thirty minutes later, he was in town. What little morning traffic this town had was already cleared. The hot, late summer sun beat down on his head as he climbed out of his truck and started toward the sheriff's office.

It was housed in a plain, squat building of gray brick across from the town hall. Some optimistic soul had planted flowers in cheerful red, white, and blue in the beds in front, hoping to cheer up the look of things.

It didn't do much good.

It looked like exactly what it was.

Nothing could really pretty up a place like this—it might be a little different in small towns, but basically, cop shops were all the same. Full of cops and the occasional lawyer. Hell, they even smelled the same.

It was busier now than it had been the last time he was here. There was a kid sitting slouched on the bench just inside the front door, a sullen look on his face. He had a fat lip, and the swelling just under his eye was going to be one hell of a shiner before much longer.

There was another kid somewhere close by, arguing. Judging by the sound of his voice, these two had gotten into it.

There were also other people, including one woman sitting in front of a desk and staring despondently off into the distance. Unlike the boy by the front door, this woman's bruise wasn't fresh. Somebody had whaled on her and hard. The discoloring had faded to a sickly yellow, and it spread from just over her left brow to more than halfway down her cheek.

Sensing his attention, she glanced up and away.

Afraid of her own shadow. Ezra knew the type, and he imagined he even knew the type who had put the mark on her face. He also suspected she'd be going back to him when she left here, even though part of her already knew she shouldn't.

There were times when this was the most frustrating job in the world.

"May I help you?"

He stopped and met the harried gaze of a woman whose head barely came to his chest. She had a steel-gray helmet of hair covering her scalp, and the glasses she wore were about the same shade of gray. Her eyes were a bright, vivid green and they glared at Ezra with biting impatience.

He flashed her a smile.

She lifted a brow.

Okay, so charm wasn't going to work. "I'm looking for Sheriff Dwight Nielson." No, the charm hadn't worked, but it had given him the two seconds he needed to rack his brain and remember the name of the man he needed to speak with.

Surely by now, there was some sort of report . . . right?

Might as well see if he couldn't sit down with the top dog and find out whatever there was to find out.

The woman turned out to be Nielson's secretary.

Ezra wondered if she'd been a dragon in her former life—the kind who guarded some secret treasure locked away in a cave or something. He wouldn't be surprised, considering how she acted—much more befitting a treasure than the affairs of a small-town sheriff.

Maybe she was buffing up for a job with the Secret Service.

She kept him waiting for close to forty minutes before he was told in a lofty voice that he could have a few minutes—if he could wait another forty minutes.

Seeing as how he'd already wasted half the morning, he figured he might as well do what he came for, and he gave her an easy, completely fake smile. "Sure. Got nothing better going on right now," he said.

She sniffed and dismissed him.

He killed the time reading magazines from the last decade and staring out the window, watching the town go by.

Forty minutes later, on the dot, to the second, he was ushered into the sheriff's private office. She pointed to a chair and Ezra just lifted a brow. "I'm good, thanks."

She opened her mouth and the sheriff cut her off. "Ms. Tuttle, if he wants to stand, let the boy stand."

Boy? Ezra thought with an inner smile.

She gave another one of those disdainful sniffs and left. As the door closed behind then, Ezra studied the other man. He didn't look like a cop—unless you looked in the eyes.

More than anything, he looked like a professor. Maybe a preacher. A skinny face, his eyes dark and watchful, mouth unsmiling.

"So." Nielson leaned back in his seat and said, "I'm going to take a shot in the dark here and guess this isn't about the trespassing out at your place the other night."

Ezra shrugged. Hell, he'd half-forgotten about that, not that he was going to point that out. "Well, as irritated as I am, I wouldn't hang around this place for nearly an hour and a half over trespassing."

"Figured as much." Nielson straightened in his chair and leaned over his desk, rummaging through the files and folders. "Although while you're here, if you intend to file that complaint, you need to go ahead and finish it. You left it unfinished."

"Well, you can thank your deputy Prather for that. I hope you don't mind me pointing this out, Sheriff, but I've seen hall monitors more capable than him," Ezra said. "He spent a good ten minutes trying to talk me out of filing the damn thing."

"Did he now?" Nielson smoothed a hand back over his head and lowered his gaze, studying something on his desk.

The report, Ezra assumed. "Yeah. Something about the kid who owns the four-wheeler is the mayor's son—the deputy seems to think it would be problematic for a citizen to actually expect the mayor to have law-abiding kids." Then he shrugged. "Not that he said it in so many words."

Nielson made a sound in his throat that could have meant a thousand things. He shoved the report toward Ezra and said, "Well, if you want to file the report, just sign it and we'll get things rolling. Or . . ."

Ezra scowled.

Nielson caught the look on his face and smiled. "Hear me out, Detective. Jennings isn't a bad kid. He's just . . . well, his mama died a few years ago. Cancer. She was only thirty-eight. It hit them all pretty hard, as you can imagine. Brody and his dad . . . well, they're going through a rough patch."

"Aw, hell." Ezra turned away and reached up, pinching the bridge of his nose. He didn't give a damn whose kid it was, but hearing something like that . . . well, hell. Yeah, it changed things, some. Plus, it helped that it was coming from somebody who didn't come off as a total asshole.

"Somebody has to talk to that kid and his friends," Ezra said, before he changed his mind. "I won't file the complaint this time, but the next time he's on my property . . ."

He let his voice trail off.

Nielson nodded. "Understood. And it's appreciated." He gave a slow smile and said, "I'm sure his dad will appreciate it, too. Brody, probably not so much, especially at first. But we will talk to him. Now . . . why don't you tell me just why you decided to spend nearly an hour and a half waiting to talk to me?"

"Lena Riddle."

The man would have made one hell of a poker player, Ezra decided. He didn't flicker an eyelash. "And what about Ms. Riddle brings you here? You can't tell me she was out four-wheeling on your property."

Giving in to the ache in his leg, Ezra settled on the one chair in the room that wasn't stacked with files, boxes, or something else. Now that the dragon wasn't on guard, he might as well sit. "No. It's about what happened out at her place the other night. I'm curious as to what you plan on doing about it."

"You're curious."

Ezra shrugged. "You have to admit—kind of odd. Disturbing. Dead of the night. Woman hears screams. Nobody finds anything. No accidents reported nearby. Odd. Not the sort of thing you could just ignore, really."

"That's assuming she really heard anything."

"You think she did," Ezra said, narrowing his eyes.

"I didn't say that."

As Ezra studied him, Nielson returned the favor. The man in front of him looked like exactly what he'd expected to find—a cop. Young, just enough of an edge to him, and still some idealism left in there, too.

He either hadn't been on the job long enough, or he was just one of those who kept that idealism the whole way through.

No, Nielson wasn't surprised by what he saw in Ezra King, nor was he surprised to see the state cop in his office. King had been seen with Lena at the café, and while that wasn't a declaration of marriage, seeing as how

Lena hadn't had a meal with anybody other than Law Reilly and Roz Jennings since she'd broken things off with Remy Jennings a year earlier, well, it said something.

Besides, he had ears.

More than a few of his deputies had commented on Lena's visit to the office Sunday, and the fact that Ezra King had also been around.

The man in front of him might well be a cop—being on leave was irrelevant—but he was also a man. It wasn't just a cop's interest that had Ezra in his office. Nielson knew it as well as he knew his own name, as well as he knew his town.

Made things dicey.

Nielson had no problem sharing some information with a fellow cop.

Had a bit more difficulty sharing it with a man who had a personal interest in somebody the sheriff's office was viewing as . . . a person of interest.

"At this point, I've yet to make any decision," Nielson hedged.

King snorted. "You can try that line on somebody who doesn't know the routine, Sheriff. Look, I just want to know if you plan to pursue this."

"Do you mind if I ask why?" Nielson asked. "Other than your . . . interest in Ms. Riddle? You do have an interest, am I right?"

"That interest, whether I have one or not, doesn't have any bearing on why I'm here." He reached down, rubbed a hand on his thigh, an absent expression on his face.

"On the job?" Nielson asked as King shifted his gaze away, staring out the window.

"Yeah. Six months ago."

"You going back?"

King's gaze, a vivid and clever green, slanted toward Nielson. "Don't know." He hesitated and then, finally, he added, "Not sure if I can."

Those words carried a world of weight to them. Understanding, Nielson nodded. Story there, he suspected. But
he wasn't going to pry. The man's eyes, they held dark,
sad secrets. Nielson would leave them alone.

"Look, I'm not trying to piss you off here or anything." King leaned forward, bracing his elbows on his
knees. His eyes met and held Nielson's easily. "This is
your place, I know that, respect that. But let's just say I
overheard how your deputy was talking to Lena on Sunday and I wasn't impressed with the amount of concern
he was showing her. That dipshit Prather couldn't have
been any more dismissive of her if he'd escorted her to
the door the minute she stepped foot inside. That one?
Major asshole you got there, Sheriff."

Actually, that was putting it mildly. Prather was more
than an asshole, but Nielson had learned to work with
him. He wasn't at all surprised to hear that the man had
been dismissive of Lena Riddle's case—a little irritated,
but not surprised.

He'd have to have a word with Prather about that, too.

A faint smile tugged at the sheriff's mouth. "I'll take
that under advisement. But that still doesn't exactly tell
me why you're so concerned about this."

Ezra figured that question, or a variation of it, would
pop up and he'd already figured out how to answer.
Slouching in the chair, he kept his face carefully blank.
"I've got a friendly interest in Lena Riddle—at this point,
just a friendly interest. I want her safe. That part is personal. Then there's this part—I'm a cop. Whether I'm on
leave or not, I'm still a cop and it pisses me off to no end
to think there could be something majorly fucked up going on just a few miles from where I live and the woman
who is a witness—and that's what she is—is being dismissed on account of the fact that she can't see."

"Lena Riddle's inability to see doesn't mean jackshit
to me," Nielson snapped.

Ezra believed him. Mostly. The guy struck him as the fair, level sort, the kind who'd look at a matter from all angles. "I'm glad to hear that. However, you're letting at least one of your deputies write her off on that basis alone, and there's no way in hell you can deny that. Hell, that fuck implied she ought to have a live-in companion there with her at night—hell, he didn't imply it. He said it. She's not a damned invalid. She can't see. Your deputy obviously can't think, and I don't see him applying for a live-in companion."

Something that might have been humor flashed in Nielson's eyes, but it was there, then gone so quick—Ezra couldn't be sure.

"Look, Detective King, I understand where you're coming from. I really do. And I don't plan on just shelving this complaint." He sighed and leaned back, smoothing a hand over his scalp in what Ezra had decided was a nervous, habitual gesture. "But there's also the plain and simple fact that we can't find a victim. Ms. Riddle heard screams. If we could find a victim, if we could find a body, if we could find some evidence of a crime . . . something . . . then that would make it a lot easier to proceed."

He met Ezra's eyes and spread his hands. "But right now, there's nothing. What would you have me do when there is absolutely nothing to go on?"

"Do you believe her?" Ezra asked.

He didn't want to answer. Ezra could tell by the look in the sheriff's eyes. He didn't want to answer that question, for some weird reason.

Leaning forward, Ezra pressed, "Has she ever done anything like this before? Ever caused any sort of trouble? Ever given you a reason not to believe her?" He studied Nielson's face, but suspected he already knew the answer. Lena wasn't a troublemaker. She wasn't an annoyance, either.

Nielson met Ezra's gaze levelly. "No. Which, I figure,

you'll find out on your own—that's the only reason I'm telling you, Detective."

"Understood." He absently massaged his leg and stared out the window. It was a pretty view of a quiet, peaceful-looking town. He could understand Nielson's urge to protect that.

"She's not the type to imagine it, either," Ezra said, recalling the way she'd moved through the trees with him and Law. Steady and confident—a calm, confident woman. She wasn't going to imagine something like this. "My gut says if she claims she heard screaming, then she heard screaming."

Nielson scratched his chin and said, "And as I've explained, the problem is that we can't find a single soul who could be responsible for the screams she heard."

Then you didn't look hard enough, Ezra thought, but he kept that quiet.

"Besides, it's just the one incident. Until something else turns up, there's just not much more we can do. But . . . I'm not going to shelve this. I'll have my boys come out there every now and then, do a pass through the woods where she says she heard the screaming. Do random drive-bys. If something is going on, sooner or later, we'll see something."

Hell.

It wasn't much, but Ezra had to admit it was better than nothing.

As he left Nielson's office, the green-eyed, steel-haired dragon shot him a glare. "Next time you need some of the sheriff's time, try calling for an appointment," she said.

"Absolutely." Ezra ambled past her, well aware that she was drilling daggers into his back with her eyes.

As he left the sheriff's office, he debated on what to do next.

He didn't want to work on the damn deck.

He couldn't concentrate worth shit and he knew it. He'd end up smashing his thumb or fucking up his plans, which would require fixing the screw-up, and his patience was absolutely shot to hell.

No . . . what he wanted to do was go out and see Lena.

It was an edgy, burning need, one that crawled around under his skin and tore at him, ate at him. It was a hunger, a need, an ache, and one he had to listen to, or it would drive him insane. But he also knew listening to it was a bad, bad idea.

Bad idea, very bad idea, he told himself. *Friends, remember? Just friends.*

"Yeah, and as a friend, I can go out there and see how she's doing, right? I mean, after the weekend she had, what could it hurt?" he muttered to himself.

Trying to talk himself out of that idea, trying to cool the need, the fire in his gut, he decided to stop by the store. His last grocery store run, he'd been distracted—and without a list. Today, he was still distracted, and still without a list, but one thing he'd realized he needed was deodorant, so he made himself stop before leaving town.

He made it halfway through the store, congratulated himself for not thinking about Lena. But as he stopped in the microscopic health and beauty section—crap, why did they put men's deodorant in the beauty section?—he found himself in front of the display of condoms.

Shit. Shit. Shit. Shit.

He did not need condoms for a friendly relationship.

Once more, his focus was right back on her, and this time it had nothing to do with the strange mystery of the screams and everything to do with the shape of her mouth, the round curve of her ass, and the weird way he found his heart skipping when she stood close. The way he smiled when she laughed, and the way his chest ached when he saw that sad look on her face.

It was almost like the way he felt when he'd first

started dating Stacy Traynor back in high school—first major crush—that hot, fiery burn of young love.

But the deal with Lena? It was worse. Way worse.

Shifting his weight away from his stiffening right leg, he grabbed a box of Trojans and threw them in his hand-held basket before stalking out of the aisle. Fine. So what? He'd bought a box of condoms—he was being practical. Nothing else.

Just practical.

Except he was having a hard time thinking about practical when it came to thinking about sex and Lena at the same time. It gave him the weird sensation of burning his brain cells—causing little microscopic implosions—and he could almost hear the neurons blowing up, one by one.

In self-defense, he started thinking about something else—and the best way to distract himself was to focus on the puzzle. The screams.

"Not a car wreck. We pretty much know that," he muttered.

There would have been records at one of the local hospitals, a vehicle, even just the sign of an accident, something.

That was off the list.

Missing person? Somebody had been kidnapped, maybe escaped only to be recaptured by her abductor?

Problem with that line of thinking, in a town the size of Ash, if a person disappeared, people would notice, and he figured the sheriff would have mentioned it if somebody had fit that bill.

"Could be somebody not from around here, though . . ."

"Ezra!"

Stopping in his tracks, he winced. That creaky voice was familiar. Normally, he would have welcomed it, but he really, really wasn't in the mood for the thirty-minute distraction that was Lucy Walbash.

Miss Lucy had been his grandmother's best friend, and

Ezra had known her for as long as he could remember. When he'd come back home for his grandmother's funeral, Miss Lucy had sat in the front row, right next to him, and she'd held his hand, patted it as he tried not to cry.

When he hadn't been able to fight it anymore, she'd whispered, "She was a fine woman, you know. Would be a shame if you couldn't shed a few tears for her, I think."

She was, without a doubt, one of his favorite people in the world, and probably his favorite person in Ash . . . with the possible exception of Lena.

But he really didn't want to talk to her just yet—especially not with the box of Trojans sitting right there in his basket.

You're a grown man. Thirty-six years old. The fact that she used to teach the Sunday school classes when you went to church with Gran doesn't change the fact that you're a grown man, he told himself.

As she drew nearer, he angled the basket so the box of Trojans slid around—score—they fell down and got lodged on their side, no longer quite so prominently on display.

"Hey, Miss Lucy."

She shook a finger at him. "Don't you hey, Miss Lucy me. You've been telling me for the past month you'd be coming by for a visit and you still haven't done it. What is your excuse this time?"

"Ahhhh . . ."

She sniffed. "You went and forgot." She gave a theatrical little sigh. "You young people, always forgetting about us older folks."

"Now, come on, Miss Lucy . . ." Chagrined, he shifted on his feet, feeling the same way he'd felt when she'd discovered him reading a comic book during her Sunday school class instead of paying attention.

"Grandma, leave Ezra alone. He's been busy, that's all."

As her granddaughter came sauntering up behind her, Ezra managed to muffle his sigh of relief. Natalie was pushing along a mountainous cart of groceries—probably helping her grandmother get her monthly shopping done.

She met his eyes and smiled. "Don't pay attention to her nagging. It's just her way of showing affection."

Lucy sniffed. "Affection. Why should I show affection to a boy who can't even keep his word and come by to visit me? All he does is sit out there at his place and brood." The teasing light in her bright eyes faded, replaced by a serious, somber intensity. "I hate to think of you just sitting out there, day after day. You're a young man, Ezra . . . you've still got your whole life ahead of you. Can't let that leg slow you down forever, you know."

Natalie reached up and patted Lucy's narrow, stooped shoulder. "Now, Grandma, you're meddling." She winked at Ezra and then added, "Besides, you're also slipping. Otherwise, you'd know that Ezra was out at the café yesterday—had breakfast with Lena Riddle, too."

"Lena . . ." Lucy peered at him. She pursed her lips and then, a slow, pleased smile curled them. "Lena Riddle. Oh, pretty girl, that one. Been living here nine years now. She's a nice girl, too. Not afraid to work, and my goodness, she can cook . . ."

One good thing about a small town was how easy it was to find out information on a person.

One mention of her name and Ezra had inadvertently ended up hearing a Reader's Digest version of her entire life. Only child, had been born in Ash, but her parents had decided to move to Louisville when she was young. Her father had died in an accident when she was twelve.

Went to school in Louisville, ended up graduating,

and bought the house that used to belong to her parents, before they moved.

She was a chef—of course, that fact he already knew, but now he knew her schedule, her specialties, and if he was smart, he'd ask her to whip him up some white-chocolate, macadamia, and cranberry cookies.

She took a break long enough to skim her list. "Natalie, we're done, right?"

"Yes, Grandma. And you told me once we had every-thing on the list, to make you get in line—you didn't want to do any of that 'evil impulse buying.'" She deliv-ered that last line with a deadpan expression on her face.

Ezra studied the heap of groceries in the cart, then glanced at the minuscule piece of paper Lucy held. "You actually had all of that on the list?"

"Oh, a lot of these are staples."

Ezra craned his head and studied the neat little stack of paperbacks tucked in the front part of the basket. "Books are staples?"

She arched snow-white brows. "Books are one of the most important staples. And you mind your own business about the groceries and I won't mention that personal item I saw in your basket."

Blood rushed up his neck.

He was not blushing. No way in hell had an eighty-year-old woman managed to make him blush over a damn box of condoms.

Natalie gave him a look of sympathy. "She's got eyes like an eagle. They keep saying eyesight is one of the first things to go when you get older, but I swear, her eyesight gets better."

"My hearing is just fine, too," Lucy said smartly, march-ing ahead of them toward the lines. "So. Lena Riddle, Ezra? Is she the reason you haven't come by to visit?"

This could be a land mine, he decided. Lucy wasn't a gossip, exactly, but she heard things. If he let her assume he was dating Lena when he wasn't . . .

Shit. This woman was like super-mom or something. She had the ability to make him feel like a teenager, sneaking outside after curfew. And he'd only done that like twice.

"We're not dating or anything. Just friends," he said, blowing out a sigh.

"A nice girl—you could do a lot worse, you know. I haven't talked to her much, mind you, but she seems to be quite a nice girl. After all, Natalie likes her."

Natalie smiled at her grandmother. "Lena's a sweetheart."

Lucy inspected the contents of Ezra's handheld basket and shooed him in front. "You go first. You've only got a few things there." Then she winked at him. "And it's not like you have to hide your purchases, after all."

Courtesy demanded he decline. But then he looked at Lucy's heaped basket. Forget courtesy. Besides, he really would rather get out of there before she decided to strike up a conversation regarding his "purchases."

"If you don't mind?"

She beamed at him. "If I minded, I wouldn't have offered, now would I? Natalie, didn't Lena date Remy for a while?"

"I think so," Natalie said, her voice distracted. She was scanning the magazines on the rack, nibbling her lower lip.

"If you're talking about Lena Riddle, yeah, she dated Remy. Almost a year, I think." That came from the cashier.

Natalie and Lucy didn't look at all surprised and Ezra stood by, a little bemused as the woman jumped feet-first into the conversation. "A few people were talking like it was kind of serious and then they just stopped going out. Never did hear why."

Ezra frowned as he tried to place the name. Once he did, the frown threatened to turn to a sneer—Remy Jennings. Yeah, he knew that name. The pretty-boy lawyer he'd met in the sheriff's office that day, and he was more than a little disgusted to think of the pretty boy putting his hands on Lena.

Remy Jennings—who might or might not be related to the kid who had been driving all over his property, too—an issue he had agreed to let go, he remembered. Scowling absently, he dumped his stuff on the conveyor belt as the cashier decided to prattle on, at length, sharing all she knew about Lena.

She knew quite a bit. As far as information went, the woman had it nailed. She knew how often Lena had her dog to the vet, to the groomer's, how often she went into Lexington, how often she went to Louisville. Her brother-in-law had done some contract work out at Lena's place, and how it was just plain odd that a blind woman would choose to live so far out in God's country when she could be living back in Louisville.

"Maybe she likes living in God's country," he said when the cashier stopped to take a breath.

"I don't see why. I mean, it's not like she can drive herself into town or anything."

"Yeah, because driving into town is of the utmost importance in everybody's life," Ezra said.

She just blinked at him, looking vaguely confused.

He took advantage of that to push the money for his stuff into her hands and make a break for it. He needed to get the hell out of there before he did something really humiliating—like pry for more details about this so-called relationship between Lena and Remy Jennings.

Man . . . he had it bad.

*   *   *

"Deputy, did I ask you what your thoughts were about that complaint?"

The sheriff kept his voice mild.

Nielson wanted to make absolutely sure that Prather got this message.

He was still pissed off—he'd kept it hidden well, he knew, but Detective Ezra King's visit had not started his day off in a good manner.

He'd made a few calls and discovered pretty much what he'd expected to discover.

King was a good cop. Had a bad case six months earlier and could have died—it was the sort of case that could break a good cop. Could break a person.

King hadn't broken, but only time would tell if he could go back to the job or not.

Having a good cop in here, telling him about one of his own cops—a lousy fucking cop—set his teeth on edge, but it only made it worse because King wasn't wrong.

Prather wasn't dirty, but he sure as hell wasn't a good cop.

He also didn't know how to control his temper worth shit. He glared at Nielson with eyes that all but glowed with all the anger he had trapped inside him. Nielson wished, just once, the man would let some of that anger slip . . . in his direction, of course. If he could put it in writing that he felt Prather might prove a danger, he could boot the bastard out.

But Nielson couldn't do it just because he didn't like the bastard, and the man hadn't crossed the line in any way that could get him fired, either.

"What is the problem, Sheriff?" Prather asked, his voice stiff and level, despite the rage that had his face red and snapped in his eyes.

"My problem is that we had a civilian call with a valid concern and you did everything but shove her out the door when she came in to discuss it."

"A valid concern?" Prather snapped. "She didn't see anybody—she *can't* see anybody. She heard something and nobody else heard it. Nobody fucking believes a word . . ."

"I do," Nielson said, his voice cool, quiet. Yelling at buffoons like Prather might make him feel a little better, but he'd learned a long time ago, those buffoons listened better when he didn't yell . . . and there was something about a cool, quiet voice in the face of temper that just unnerved people. "She's not a quack, she's not a flake, and if she claims she heard a woman screaming, and very explicitly details the screams, the words, and even the direction and general area of the screams for my deputies, then I'm more inclined to believe her. This isn't like the crock-of-shit reports Deb Sparks calls in, just to get one of us out there."

Then he leaned back in the chair and pinned his deputy with a direct stare. "What's more, Jennings feels there's something odd going on. As does the state cop you insulted when he was here. You're making an ass of yourself on this and you didn't just insult a civilian, you also insulted a fellow law-enforcement official. Are you trying to cause me problems, Deputy? Or is it just natural?"

Prather's chin rose a notch. "What does it matter if King believes her or not? It's not like he's out here investigating anything. He's on leave."

You're so damned stupid. Nielson resisted the urge to pinch the bridge of his nose. He'd woken up with a headache—it was a sign, he realized, a sign that today would be a crap day and nothing else. That headache had only gotten worse as the day went on.

When Prather came swaggering in just before two, the

headache had grown to gargantuan proportions. The bastard was an insult to his uniform, and every year that passed, he just got worse.

Taking a slow, calming breath, he focused on Prather's face and said, "No, Detective King isn't out here on an official investigation, but then again, that's not going to keep him from poking around if he decides to poke around, is it?"

"He ain't got no fucking reason to poke around. Nothing happened."

As if Prather hadn't said a word, Nielson continued, "Not that I much care for having some state big-shot messing with my territory, but then again, considering he's gone and developed an . . . interest in Ms. Riddle and you were about as insultingly rude as you could get, how could I expect him to do otherwise?"

Prather's face went pasty white, then back to ruddy red, all in the span of five seconds. "Now listen here, Sheriff, if that woman is claiming I acted improper somehow, she is lying—"

"Did you tell her she should consider getting a live-in companion?"

Prather gave a restless, jerky shrug. "And how is that insulting?"

Gently, using the same tone he used when explaining something to a five-year-old, Nielson said, "She's blind, Prather. She can't see, but she's not mentally challenged, she's not helpless. She has a rather demanding, chaotic career, which she manages to handle without a companion, she's lived on her own here for quite a while, and I do believe I've heard she's a college graduate—that doesn't sound to me like somebody who needs to be on the receiving end of companion services."

Prather just blinked.

He really didn't get it.

Rising from his chair, Nielson leaned over his desk,

hands braced on the surface. "You don't get it. I can't make you get it, even if I paint it on a billboard. Yet you seem to think she's the one who needs assistance," he muttered, disgusted. Why in the hell did he have to continue putting up with this?

CHAPTER
TEN

THE STORY WASN'T MOVING, AND HADN'T BEEN FOR about the past week.

Plain and simple.

Law tried to figure out if the problem was the story, or him. He had too much shit on his mind, there was no doubt about that. Maybe that's all it was, and he certainly hoped that was at least part of it, because he'd spent the past six months working on the current book and if it turned out the book was the damn problem, then he had a major damn problem, because there was no way he could start from scratch and still meet his deadline.

Law didn't miss deadlines.

Period.

Blowing out a breath, he stared up at the ceiling, absently throwing an old baseball up, catching it, and then tossing it up again. Over and over.

He let his mind drift and hoped that it would settle on whatever was blocking him.

And to no surprise, it wasn't the book.

He found his thoughts torn between two women— two women who meant a lot to him. Lena, a woman he adored, and Hope, one of his dearest friends. Worry for the two of them ate at him.

Hope should be here by now and she wasn't—she'd said she'd be here within the week and that was six days ago. She was stalling, he knew that, and he even understood.

She had given him her word and she wasn't here.

Hope didn't break promises.

He'd have to call her if she didn't show by nightfall, because this worry just wasn't going to go away. He knew she was a grown woman and if she'd decided not to come, there wasn't anything he could do about it. But . . . shit, what if that bastard ex of hers had tracked her down?

Hope insisted it wasn't likely, but Law knew all about obsessions, and Joey had one major, hard-on obsession for his ex-wife. She'd walked away from him and Joey hadn't ever been one to handle people walking away well.

And Lena.

Lena. Ezra. Shit. Not that he'd seen anything to say otherwise, but Law knew it was only a matter of time before the cop decided to forget the "just friends" bit. He could tell by the way Ezra looked at her that he didn't think friendly thoughts about Lena.

Jealousy ate at him, but the part of him that wanted, needed to see her happy . . . well, his gut told him the cop might be able to do that for her.

Aside from the jealousy, though, there was worry, and he couldn't deal with worry as easily as he handled jealousy.

Law was, by nature, the suspicious type. Even when he'd been a kid. He'd had conspiracy theories running wild in his head before he even understood the concept.

It was probably why he did so well writing suspenses. He was one of those who always saw the sedan in his mirror as one that might be following him and even when he wasn't speeding, he always watched the cop cars in his rearview mirrors, certain they'd turn around and pull him over for something.

Conspiracy theorists R us. He was a card-carrying member. Or at least, he might have been, but he was a little too normal for most of the conspiracy theorists—they drove him bonkers.

Sometimes, actually, all too often, his imagination got a little carried away.

But something hadn't felt right in the woods by her place when they'd been out there earlier in the week.

He couldn't figure out the right way to describe it, but something hadn't felt . . . right.

Heavy.

Oppressive.

The right kind of atmosphere for a woman, hell, anybody to scream desperately for help.

Not that they'd found anything. At all.

And King had looked . . . and looked. And looked.

Abruptly, Law straightened in his seat and bent over his computer. Pulling up the browser, he went to BING and keyed in Kentucky + Missing Persons + females.

Then his eyes widened as he saw all the names.

Whoa.

Okay, so this was local and fairly recent.

"Let's try giving it a few days."

That cut down on some of the results. But still so many . . .

Absently, he clicked on one. It was a woman, but her disappearance was too far back, he figured. Carly Watson. Missing for six months. Long time. More than likely, if she was still alive, she was just living the good life under a different name.

It happened sometimes, he knew. He'd even written a book about a woman who'd gone and done just that—it hadn't been published yet, but he'd started it after he'd done the research on how Hope might be able to "disappear," if that was what she'd wanted.

Closing out the page on the article on Carly Watson, he went back to the search results. Needed to narrow it down more, he figured. Wondered if he could do it by location . . .

The doorbell rang.

He rose, padding on bare feet across the polished hardwood floors. He had hopes that it would be Hope, but still, he wasn't exactly expecting it to be her.

That made it a double surprise when he opened the door to see her standing there.

A slow, hesitant smile curled her lips and she went to hold out a hand.

"A handshake, Hope?" he asked.

When he held out his arms, she launched herself at him.

Though they had kept in contact, it had been years since they'd seen each other and Hope wasn't sure how she'd feel when she saw Law.

But the moment his hazel eyes met hers, all the fear, all the nerves and anxiety melted away. As his arms closed around her, she settled against his chest and let herself breathe.

She felt . . . safe.

She hadn't felt safe when a man touched her in a good long while, and she hadn't realized it could still happen. But it could.

Pressed against Law's chest, his hand gently cradling the back of her head, she sighed and tension she'd held in check for years slowly began to drain out of her body.

Suddenly, she was no longer questioning why she'd come. She remembered now.

Because it was Law.

Because this was her dearest friend and this was the

one person on God's green earth she knew she could trust. Sniffling, she squeezed her eyes closed against the tears that threatened.

"You took long enough," he said teasingly.

"Yeah . . . yeah, I think maybe I took too long," she said, her voice hoarse and rough.

A couple hours later, they sat down in front of a huge flat-screen TV with *Lord of the Rings* playing. There was a half-eaten pizza in front of them. Law had a beer, she was drinking a Diet Coke and she felt . . . almost normal. With their backs braced against the couch, she tried to focus on the movie, but she couldn't.

Her mind wouldn't settle.

It felt odd, she realized, being in a house, being with another person—a friend. For the past two years, the only people she'd let herself be around had been strangers—safer that way, she had thought.

Easier.

But maybe she hadn't needed to stay away from Law. Maybe she did . . . hell, she didn't know. She'd needed to get away from Joey, and maybe she'd needed the time to stand on her own two feet. If she'd run straight here, straight to Law, he would have taken care of her and was that really what she'd needed?

"You're thinking awful hard about something," he said softly, tugging on her hair.

She rested her head on his arm. "Yeah."

He smelled like books. Books and grass and a guy who liked to spend as much time outside as he did inside. Looking up, she studied his face and found the boy she remembered from high school lingering in the faint smile on his face.

That teasing, gentle smile wasn't much different, although his eyes were. Older. Wiser. More tired. Sadder. *How much of that was because of her?* she wondered with not a little guilt. Grimacing, she reached up and traced the shadows under his eyes. "You're not sleeping well."

"I'm fighting with a book. Never sleep well when I'm doing that."

"You fight with them a lot?" she asked.

"Almost every damn one of them," he said, grinning now. "But that's the job."

"Is it what you expected? The writing?"

"Hell, no." He kissed her forehead. He wrapped a friendly arm around her shoulders and hugged. "It's a hell of a lot harder, and I spend half the day questioning my sanity . . . on the bad days, at least. When we were in school, I had this crazy idea that if I just sold the book— never thought past selling the one book—all I had to do was that and everything would be easy."

"So it's not easy?"

Law laughed. "Hell, no. And it's never just the one book. I never thought past anything other than writing, and they don't tell you about the other shit. You have to figure that out the hard way."

"What other shit?"

He slanted a grin at her. "I'll tell you about that later. Because some of that other shit is why you're here. I don't want to scare you off just yet."

"Like I've got a whole lot of choice." She gave him a wry smile. "I'm just about out of cash, almost out of gas, and not a lot of choices."

"Gee, so you're here now because you're out of options," Law said, giving her a forlorn look. "Thanks."

She poked him in the ribs. "I'm here because it's you. And you know it."

He grinned down at her and she smiled back.

It felt strange.

She'd forgotten, she realized. Forgotten what it felt like

to be with somebody whom she could actually tease, somebody she could actually smile with, laugh with. She'd forgotten what it was like to just . . . be.

Reaching out, she grabbed his hand.

"Law, thank you."

To her surprise, he blushed.

Friends, Ezra reminded himself as he showered that morning.

He was going to Lena's. Was going to ask her out for lunch. Not exactly a date. Just a nice, friendly meal. He owed her that, after she'd cooked dinner for him the other day. They didn't even need to call it a date, right?

It was just a friendly meal.

Ezra had spent the past week being friendly with Lena, and actually, it wasn't hard.

She was easy to talk with, she made him laugh, and she could cook like nothing else.

The hard part came when he had to restrain himself . . . when she smiled at him and he found himself remembering the way her mouth felt against his, the way she tasted. The hard part came when his hands itched to touch her and he knew he couldn't.

"Friends," he muttered. "Stop thinking about touching her, tasting her . . ."

Which was impossible, especially considering that his cock ached like a bad tooth. Groaning, he slumped against the tiled wall and reached down, closed his fist around his length and stroked. Pictured her mouth. His cock jerked. Stroked harder. Remembered her taste, the way she'd moved against him.

The hot water beat down on him as he pumped his fist up and down, picturing Lena's face in his mind, her body moving against his—her long, slender torso, those sleek, subtle curves.

Her mouth, fuck. Her mouth, pressed against his, moving against his. The taste of her, the feel . . .

With a harsh groan, he came.

As the water washed the evidence away, he stared up at the ceiling. "This friends-only shit is not working."

He couldn't get her out of his mind, out of his thoughts. Scowling, he finished up his shower and climbed out, drying off with a towel and slinging it over his shoulders. When he opened the medicine cabinet, the box of Trojans sitting there all but mocked him.

Swearing, he grabbed his razor and slammed the door shut so hard, it was a wonder the glass didn't break.

Friends. "My ass," he muttered.

Twenty minutes later, he was heading out to the car, a weird mix of excitement and dread curling through him. He wanted, needed to see her, but at the same time, he knew it was going to strain his . . . ah . . . patience. Already, his skin was humming, his heart racing at the thought of seeing her.

Abruptly, he climbed out of the car and headed back to the house, jogging up the stairs as quick as his right leg would let him. Opening the medicine cabinet, he stared at the box of Trojans, a muscle twitching in his jaw.

"Shit," he muttered. Then he grabbed the box. "The Boy Scout motto . . . be prepared."

Even if it was just driven by wishful thinking. On his way back out, he opened the box and tore packets off the strip, tucking them into his wallet. The rest, he threw into his glove box.

Her house was only a couple miles out from his and he used those few minutes to try to talk himself down.

It wasn't happening, though.

Every time he saw her, every time he talked to her, he wanted her more, liked her more.

Needed her more.

Stopping in front of the house, he turned off the car and sat there a few minutes, studying it.

The house itself was painted a fresh, gleaming white, the shutters a dark red that matched the front door. There were window boxes with flowers in front of the windows on the porch, and a swing at the far end. He climbed out of his car and pocketed the keys.

Lunch.

They'd do lunch. And if there was an . . . opening, he'd see if maybe she was open to pursuing something beyond friendship. He'd apologize for how he'd screwed things up, and they could see where things went from there.

He mounted the steps and knocked on the door, jamming his hands in his pockets, feeling as nervous as a damned teenager on his first date.

She opened the door, keeping the chain in place. "Yes?"

"Uh . . ." *Oh, wow, slick. Don't you sound all suave?* He swallowed and then tried again. "Hey, Lena. It's—"

The door opened a fraction more. "Ezra," she said, stepping around so he could see her through the narrow opening.

"Yeah." He smiled a little.

Lena's lips curled upward and she murmured, "So . . . what are you doing back out here? I didn't forget about something, did I?"

Mentally, he rehearsed the invitation to lunch. A nice, easy friendly meal.

Mentally, he reminded himself they were supposed to be friends. Just friends, and they could share a meal, right? He owed her a meal, anyway.

Shit, screw that sideways. He had no problem being friends with Lena, but he wanted . . . hell, he needed more than that.

He hadn't had this sort of personal attraction—so hard, so strong, so instantaneous—to a woman in a long time. Shit, what he'd felt for Mac had paled in comparison. Mac had been a friend, yeah. A lover. He'd loved her . . . in a way. He'd been attracted. But nothing like this.

He didn't think he'd ever had a woman hit him over the head quite the way Lena had.

Instead of lying, instead of hedging, he just stared at her. "Ah, well, I'd kind of planned on seeing if you wanted to go out, maybe get a bite to eat," he finally said, even though right then, he wasn't at all hungry.

Not for food, anyway.

"Kind of planned?" she echoed.

"Yeah. Friends do meals, right?"

She laughed. It was a low, quiet sound, sexy as all get-out. "Sure, Ezra. Friends do meals." Then the door closed, briefly. He heard the metal links of the chain clink and then the door opened.

Sucker-punch, right to the solar plexus. She wore a pair of black cotton pants that rode low on her hips and a skinny-strapped tank top that didn't quite reach the waistband of those pants, leaving several inches exposed. He found himself staring at her navel and fantasizing about going to his knees in front of her and tracing it with his tongue and then going lower, lower . . . lower . . .

His cock twitched and he groaned inwardly. Fuck, he wasn't entirely certain he could manage a normal conversation—not considering that the longer he looked at her, the more turned-on he got.

He cleared his throat, reminded himself that he wasn't a pig—not normally, not really. But then he noticed something else. She wasn't wearing a bra. Oh, hell.

"You're staring at me again, aren't you?" Lena asked.

Jerking his gaze upward, he saw a faint blush settle on her cheeks. "Yes, ma'am. I'm definitely staring at you again." Staring, fantasizing, and getting harder by the second.

Trying to distract himself, he studied the door and then looked at her. "You know, not that I really want you to leave me standing on the porch or anything, but you might want to think about being more careful who you open that door for."

"I'm not too worried about opening it for you. It's not like this is the first time you've been here," she said, shrugging. "Besides, Puck likes you."

Ezra glanced at the dog at her side, smiling a little. "He tell you that?"

The small smile on her lips widened. "Sort of. His tail started wagging when you spoke. That's a glowing recommendation from him."

"Still . . . you should be careful."

Lena smirked. "Yeah, I should. Especially since God knows if I try to call nine-one-one, they may just hang up on me. Or worse, my luck, they'd send Prather out here."

"Eh, don't feel bad. I don't think it's a personal thing—the way he acted toward you. I think he's just an ass with everybody," Ezra said, tucking his hands inside his back pockets. "The reason I was out there that day was because I had some kids joyriding on my property—they did some damage and Prather kept telling me I really shouldn't file a complaint against the mayor's son."

Lena made a face. "Brody." Then she skimmed a hand through her hair. "While I couldn't care less whose kid he is, he's had a rough time of it. But I think getting in trouble might do him a world of good. Sometimes that's what people need to get their heads out of their asses—a good hard knock across that head. And he's getting worse."

She paused, cocking her head. "So . . . you didn't file the report, did you?"

"Shit. Are you psychic?" Ezra kicked at the floor.

"No, I didn't file the damn report, but it didn't have a damn thing to do with Prather. That idiot can shove it sideways for all I care. But Nielson asked that I let it go, this one time, and I agreed, on the provision that somebody talk to him."

"Somebody will, if the sheriff said so. He'll probably get Remy to do it."

Remy. He ran his tongue along the inside of his teeth, trying to ignore the burn of jealousy at the sound of the guy's name on her lips. Didn't matter—so she'd dated him. So he'd probably gotten to put his hands all over that nice, long, sleek body . . . oh, fuck, he was so into self-torture.

She gestured him inside. "Why don't you come in? It's too damn hot for me to stand here with the door open. Come on in and we'll talk about lunch."

As he stepped over the threshold, he passed close enough by her that he could feel the heat of her skin. Smell her—she smelled like peaches.

Peaches . . . man, he loved peaches.

You're a fucking goner, he thought, brooding. He came to a stop in the middle of the foyer. The floors were gleaming gold hardwood, devoid of any area rugs.

"So . . ." Lena murmured. "About lunch."

She brushed past him and headed into the living room.

He trailed after her into the room. It was large and airy, almost stark in its simplicity. A couch against one wall, an overstuffed armchair that flanked a fireplace, and an entertainment system along another wall.

Lena settled in the big chair, curling her legs up, loose and easy. Trying not to stare at the way her dark nipples pressed against the cotton of her tank, he moved to study the entertainment system. The TV was a smallish flat screen, but there was an excellent sound system and a pretty extensive collection of DVDs.

Crossing over to them, he studied the movies, curious.

Each of them was marked with a label that had a series of raised dots—Braille?

"You like movies?" he asked, glancing back at her.

"I love movies," she said, that faint smile on her lips. "I can't see the action, but I can hear it. What I can't see, I just let my imagination fill in for me."

"There's something to be said for an imagination." He crossed over to the couch and settled down, watching as she tracked his movements. He stretched his right leg out in front of him and automatically rubbed his thigh.

"Your limp—you mind if I ask what happened?"

Startled, he glanced at his leg and then up at Lena. "You can hear me limp?"

"Your gait is uneven. I can hear that." She shrugged. "If I'm being nosy, feel free to tell me. I've always much preferred people ask me things if they're curious rather than just stare at me and wonder. I tend to do the same thing."

"No. You're not being nosy—well, yeah, you kind of are, but I don't mind." Frowning, he looked at his leg. He didn't mind her being nosy. He didn't mind telling her he'd gotten shot in the leg. But the rest of it was harder—talking about Mac was harder.

Although if he was going apologize, ask for a chance to try things over, yeah, if she did ask, he needed to be able to explain . . . something.

Slowly, he said, "I took a bullet six months ago. That's why I'm on leave."

She was quiet for a minute. "Six months seems an awful long time to be out. Was . . . was it bad?"

He shrugged and then scowled. Shrugs, nods, all the normal body language people used wasn't exactly going to work with somebody who couldn't see it, right? Sighing, he rubbed his hands over his face and said, "Bad enough that I had to take some time off—I've had two surgeries, physical therapy, all that crap. It's not bad enough to keep me from going back."

"I get the feeling you're not sure if you want to go back," she said softly.

Blood . . . blood on his hands . . .

An image of Mac's face flashed before his eyes and he waited for that breath-stealing pain, that slow, insidious wash of guilt.

The pain was there, a quick jab, square in the heart. The onslaught of guilt didn't threaten to cripple him this time, but still, it was enough to leave him tied into hot, greasy knots.

The blood . . . shit, the blood.

Fuck, fuck, fuck. He covered his face with his hands, grinding the heels against his eyes, trying to drive those images from his head. Mac—hearing her laugh, remembering how many hours she'd spent at his side, the nights she'd spent in his bed.

Put it away.

Fuck, he had to put this away—had to. How could he even hope to have a chance with Lena when he was letting the guilt over Mac eat at him like this? *Put it away*, he told himself. *Now*.

If only it was that simple.

Shoving to his feet, he paced over to the window and stared out into the front yard. Bright bursts of flowers grew around the big oak and in a flower bed in the center of her yard.

"I'm not sure," he finally admitted. "All I ever wanted was to be a cop, you know? Even when I was a kid. Didn't really understand why then, although as I got older, I started to. It was just there, inside me. I wanted to make a difference. Help people."

Then he sighed, rubbed at his neck. Tension settled there and the promise of a headache whispered at him. "But sometimes when you try to change things, help people, you learn things you'd rather not know. I'm still trying to come to grips with something I learned. If I can't do that, I can't go back. And I'm still trying to figure out if I want to."

Lena was quiet for a moment and then, softly, she said, "If I'm being too intrusive here, tell me to shut the hell up. Was . . . was there a woman involved in this?"

"A . . . what makes you ask that?" Ezra asked, his voice rusty and tight.

"Something in your voice. Instinct. I don't know. And the fact that you didn't outright say no when I asked just now tells me I'm right." She drew a leg up and rested her knee on her chest. "Ezra, I like you. A lot. And yes, I know we're tossing this 'friends' line back and forth, but I also suspect you know as well as I do there's something more than 'friends' between us, or there could be." She licked her lips and asked, "Am I right?"

"Yeah."

"Okay. Then tell me the truth here. If you're pining over some woman you lost back on your job, I need to know. I'm not interested in playing with some guy who's on the rebound."

He laughed—it hurt, like he was choking on broken glass. "Rebound. Shit. Trust me, what I am is not rebounding. I can tell you that the last thing I had in mind when I came here was falling for somebody. The last thing I wanted was to meet somebody . . . you. You, this, hell, it just sort of happened."

Sighing, he turned around and rested his back against the wall, staring at the floor without really seeing it. "I had a partner. Her name was Mac. MacKenzie. We'd been together for close to three years. We . . ."

Sighing, he reached up and rubbed the back of his neck. "We were lovers. It's not exactly the ideal situation, but we weren't planning on getting married. It was another one of those things. It just happened. We were friends, we understood each other, liked each other. We were compatible."

"Friends with benefits?" Lena offered.

"Yeah, I guess." He smiled halfheartedly. "She was one of my best friends. At least I always thought she was. The last year I was on the job, we'd been working this one job—theft ring. We'd get close, and then boom— nothing. Over and over and over." A muscle throbbed in his jaw. There was only so much he could tell her—only so much. Too much was classified, some, he still didn't remember.

Fumbling for the words, he haltingly continued, "I had suspicions that there was a cop involved. Proving it, though, that was damn near impossible and I . . . well . . ."

"It was Mac."

Tearing his eyes away from the floor, he looked at Lena's face. "Yeah."

"That's . . . hmmm." She paused, pursed her lips. "Well, that's bad."

Reluctantly, he smiled. "You're a master at under-statement, gorgeous, you know that?"

"Well, I was going to say, that's so beyond fucked up, but I was trying to be polite."

" 'Fucked up' describes it pretty well, though," he muttered.

"Is she in jail?"

Jail.

Blood. The blood.

Shit. Images flashed through his mind—the crime scene photos—why in the hell had he looked at those? Mac's lifeless face, her eyes in that death stare, forever imprinted on his memory.

"No."

"No? Why in the hell not?" Lena demanded.

"Because she's dead." Ezra turned away and stared out the window. He couldn't see the colorful bursts of flowers now. Couldn't see the vibrant green of the grass or the cool shade cast by the trees.

He saw an alley, the echo of a memory.

"She's dead, Lena. The reason my leg is all fucked up is because she shot me—I took two bullets in the leg—I don't remember her shooting me, I don't remember shooting her, but I did and when I shot her, I shot her dead in the heart and killed her."

He said it so calmly, so matter-of-factly. He could have been giving her a weather report, Lena thought. Except the weather forecasters often got more excited about their reports.

But there was an underlying tension in his voice, and she suspected there was a world of pain hiding inside him.

All of a sudden, his retreat a few weeks ago made sense.

A lot of sense.

"Damn, Ezra. When you said you'd gone through some rough shit, you weren't kidding, were you?" Lena said softly.

He was silent, but she hadn't exactly been expecting a reaction.

"Can you tell me what happened?"

"No." There was a heavy, tired sigh. "Technically, I shouldn't. But even aside from that, it's not even possible, because I don't remember. The doctors don't know if I'll ever get those memories back. I'd had a tail—a couple of Internal Affairs cops following me—and pretty much everything I know about that night is based on what they saw."

"I'm sorry."

"Hell, you didn't do anything."

"No. But it hurts you. It hurts you a lot." She nibbled on her lower lip and then slipped off the couch, crossing the floor to stand beside him. Lifting a hand, she held it out until her fingers brushed against his back. Moving her hand up, she rested it on his shoulder—and tried not to think about that very nice back. A long, ridged line of muscle. Nice, nice, nice . . .

Comfort, not seduction, Lena.

"For some reason, us humans are prone to feeling guilty when we shouldn't. You ever noticed that?" she said, lowering her hand to her side before she gave in to the urge to let it roam where it would.

"You think I shouldn't feel guilty for killing my partner?" he demanded.

"Oh, I can't comment on that . . . although, if it was me . . . well, I'm fond of life. While I might regret that it was necessary, I think I could kill in defense of my life," she said, shrugging. "But that's not what you're feeling guilty about, or at least that's not the majority of it. If it was a guy, or even a woman you weren't sleeping with, would you have felt so guilty?"

Silence. Just silence.

"I don't think you would," Lena murmured. "Ezra, this weighs on you, I can tell, and I don't want to make it worse. You cared for her, I know. But have you ever wondered if maybe she . . . encouraged a physical relationship just for a reason like this? To make it harder on you if you ever found out what she was doing?"

He blew out a hard breath. "Shit. Yes, I've thought of it."

"Could she have done that?"

"Yes," he said, the word rough, raw, and slow, like she was dragging it out of his chest with a rusty hook.

She turned to him and reached up, rested a hand on his chest. His heart bumped against her hand, a strong, steady beat. "You did your job, Ezra, and you did it despite the fact that it cost you a lot, on a personal level. Don't let her take anything else away from you."

She would have gone back to the couch then, but before she could, he caught her hand.

"You know, for somebody who can't see anything, you sure as hell see a lot."

"You'd be surprised at the things you can learn about people when you don't rely on what you can see." She shrugged. "But there wasn't really anything complicated about this . . . it just sounds like something a woman would do, you know?"

He rubbed his thumb along the inside of her wrist. "Why a woman?"

"It's manipulative." Lena grimaced and shrugged. "That sounds terrible, I know, but it just sounds . . . well, like a female ploy. No great psychology feat there."

He was still stroking her wrist and it was doing mad things to her pulse. Lena disengaged as casually as she could and made her way over to the couch, sitting back down. Even getting away from him didn't help much. Damn it.

He was getting to her, way too fast, way too much.

No wonder he'd pulled back.

"I can't say I don't understand, but you shouldn't let what she did tear you up so much, Ezra. You deserve better than that," Lena said quietly.

"I wouldn't be so sure of that," Ezra muttered.

"Sorry. You've already got me thinking you're a nice guy. You're stuck with it."

"A nice guy." Pushing aside the dark thoughts, or trying to, he turned around and studied her. "I wouldn't be so sure of that, beautiful."

Crossing the floor, he sank down on the ottoman in front of the couch and studied Lena. Nice guy? If he was a nice guy, would he be sitting there and mentally undressing her?

As she shifted on the couch, one of the straps of her tank top drooped down over one shoulder. Through the thin, white cotton, he could see the dark circles of her nipples all too clearly and if he was a nice guy, if he was any kind of gentleman, he'd put some distance between them and stop staring at her.

Screw being a nice guy. Screw being a gentleman.

"Are you so sure I'm a nice guy, Lena?" he asked, hoarsely.

"Ahh . . ." She wiggled around on the seat and then lifted a hand, tugging the strap of her tank top back up.

Under the material of her shirt, her nipples were hard, peaked and pressing against the fabric. His mouth was all but watering.

"You're staring at me again," she said, softly. She blushed and folded her arms over her chest, hiding those small, round breasts from his view.

"How can you tell?"

She scowled and hitched a shoulder up. "I just can. I can feel it—don't tell me you've never had the feeling that somebody was looking at you, even if you couldn't see them."

"I've had that feeling plenty. Does it bother you?"

She licked her lips and he muffled a groan, watching that pink tongue slide over her lips and wishing she'd do that to him. She could lick any damn thing she wanted on him.

"I'm not sure," she said, and her voice was hesitant. She nibbled on her lower lip. "If we were really just friends, it would probably confuse the hell out of me, because I don't have too many friends who stare at me the way you seem to."

"I sure as hell hope not." He wanted to see her eyes. He didn't give a damn that she couldn't see him, he needed to see her. Needed to look into that blue-ice gaze. "I've got to be honest here . . . I really, really planned on giving the 'friends' thing a try, but I don't think it's going to take."

Her breath hitched in her throat. "It doesn't seem to be taking very well, does it?"

"I don't want to be your friend . . . or at least I don't want to be just your friend." Reaching out, he laid a hand on her leg, just above her ankle. She tensed, but didn't pull away. "Does it bother you that I like to stare at you?"

"If I said yes, would you stop?"

He flexed his hand, traced his thumb along the back of her foot. "Yeah. It would take some work, but I'd quit."

"What if I said I didn't want you touching me?"

He tensed. His stomach knotted, something ugly and bitter burning in the back of his throat. Slowly, he pulled his hand away and stood up. Hell, was he really that screwed up in the head that he'd been reading her wrong?

"Then I'd quit." The burn of hunger that had boiled inside him from the first time he'd seen her turned to ash, left him feeling cold inside. Yeah, he wanted her. Thought she'd wanted him back—he'd acted on the belief when touched he her, but now he had to wonder—

Fuck. Just get the hell out, okay? Made a big enough fool of myself already. His leg felt a hell of a lot stiffer than it had a few minutes ago and he scowled, listening to the sound of his own footsteps as he headed out of the living room.

"Ezra."

He paused in the doorway and looked back. She was still sitting on the couch, her face turned toward him. She was blushing, that soft pink glow along her cheeks, down her neck, disappearing under the low neckline of her tank top.

He tore his eyes away, made himself stop looking, even though he couldn't keep himself from wondering just how far down that blush went. "What?" He stared at the door, hands fisted inside his pockets.

"I didn't say I don't want you touching me. I just asked what you'd do."

Slowly, he turned around. Narrowed his eyes.

She straightened on the couch and then slid her legs down, rose to her feet with that slow, easy grace. Ezra watched as she reached for her dog and rested a hand on Puck's head, murmured something too low for Ezra to hear. The dog settled on the floor, resting his head on his paws as he watched his mistress.

Ezra watched her, too. Hell, he couldn't take his eyes off her as she walked toward him. He tensed as she stopped just a breath away—literally just a breath. He could feel the warmth of her skin, see his own reflection in the dark glasses she used to shield her eyes. "If I didn't want you touching me, believe me, you wouldn't have gotten in the front door," she said. "The friends thing was your idea in the first place, not mine. Remember?"

His mouth went dry as she reached up and, with unerring accuracy, laid a hand on his chest. "So does that mean I don't need to stop staring at you?" he asked and his throat was so damned tight he could barely breathe.

"Stare all you want." She slid her hand higher, toyed with the neck of his T-shirt. "I want to know what you look like . . . can I?"

"You can do anything you want."

If anybody had told him that having a woman touch his face could be that damned erotic, Ezra would have laughed.

That was until Lena Riddle put her hands on him, tracing the line of his lips with her fingertips, doing the same with his jawline, along his cheekbones, feathering across his eyes and nose.

She took her time with her tactile exploration of his face, combing her fingers through his hair, even tracing his ears with her fingertips.

Every single touch, every single stroke, seemed to arrow straight down his spine, striking him square in the balls.

Damn it, he hurt. His cock was rigid, painfully hard,

and he was ready to do damn near anything if it would get her to wrap those soft, cool fingers around him. He was all but shuddering with the need to touch her, taste her.

By the time she finished and lowered her hands to his shoulders, Ezra was strung tight and hovering on the edge of his control.

"What color are your eyes?"

"Green." His voice was hoarse, tight. Hell, he was so damned turned on, it was a miracle he could even speak. Reaching up, he caught her glasses and tugged them off, setting them on the small table just inside the doorway. "I want to see your eyes."

She averted her gaze but he reached out, caught her chin in his hand, and tugged until she was once more facing him. "You've got the prettiest damn eyes," he said, staring into the pale blue. He closed the scant inches between them and angled her chin upward. "I want to kiss you . . . if that's a problem, then do me a favor and just tell me no, right now."

A grin flirted with her lips and she swayed closer. "Not a problem. Not at all. Unless of course you plan on deciding in a few hours you're not sure you really want to try this thing out, after all."

Ezra nuzzled her mouth. "Hmmm. Not going to be an issue, although I think it's time I apologized. I'm sorry about that. Seriously. Could we maybe rewind and just start over? Try it again?"

"No . . . no do-overs." She raked his lower lip with her teeth. "I get why you pulled back. It makes sense. Just make sure you really want to go forward before we . . . do whatever."

"I'm sure. Damnation, I can't get you out of my head, Lena. You're everywhere." He cupped her face in his hands, angling her head back. "Can't stop thinking about you, not from the first time I saw you."

"Hmmm. Well, that's pretty much mutual . . . now why don't you stop talking and kiss me already?"

Anything else she might have said was muffled against his mouth. She moaned and he swallowed the sound down, licked her lips, demanding that she open for him. She did and he shuddered as her taste hit his system with supernova force. It was like kissing the damn sun, blistering hot but so damn sweet. Growling against her lips, he hooked a hand over the back of her neck and tugged her closer.

She came willingly, sliding her arms around his shoulders and plastering that long, perfect body against his. He rested his free hand on her hip and just barely managed to keep from rocking his hips against her, cuddling his aching dick against her belly. Before he could give in, he stroked upward, tracing the line of her waist, up, up until the heel of his hand stroked over the outer curve of her breast. She caught his hand, but instead of tugging it away, she pressed him against her.

Tearing his mouth away from hers, Ezra rested his brow against hers. "Damn it, Lena. Are you trying to kill me?"

She smiled and arched against him. "No."

"You should be more careful," he rasped, torn between the need to just keep right on touching her and his muddled thoughts—too quick. Moving too damn quick, but damn if he didn't want to just go with it, ride it out . . . ride her.

She shrugged and stroked a hand down his chest. "I usually am." She laughed softly as she slid a hand under his shirt, resting it just above the waistband of his jeans. "I'm usually a lot more careful than this."

He believed her. "Good." Then he grabbed the waistband of her shirt and shoved it up, baring her breasts. "I'm usually a fucking Boy Scout . . . fuck, Lena. You've got the prettiest damn tits. Hell, everything about you—so damn perfect."

Stooping over, he caught one swollen pink tip and sucked it into his mouth. She cried out and dipped her hands into his hair, holding him tight. "Ezra . . ."

He growled against her, using his tongue to push her nipple against the roof of his mouth, drawing on her flesh and shuddering as her taste flooded his senses. She tasted like peaches, too. Ezra loved peaches. He rested his hand on her hip, easing it lower and lower, under the waistband of her pants to find her naked under them. Swearing, he tore his mouth away and rasped, "You're not wearing any underwear."

"Wasn't exactly expecting company." She tugged on his hair, trying to guide his mouth back to her breasts.

Ezra wanted to do just that, bury his face against those small, plump mounds, fill his hands with the subtle curve of her ass. He wanted to strip her pants away and push her thighs wide, press his mouth against her pussy and see if she tasted as sweet there as he thought she would. But his control was already damned shaky and if he was going to stop, now was the time. Slowly, although it damned near killed him to do it, he stopped touching her and forced his hands down to his sides. "We need to stop now."

"Why?" she asked, leaning against him. "You didn't go and change your mind on the friends thing again, did you?"

"Yes . . . no. Shit. I want us to be friends—yeah. Just want more than that, too, and this is rushing it and if we don't stop now, I don't know if I'll be able to stop later." He pressed his mouth to her neck, raking his teeth along her skin. "You're killing me."

She smiled. He could feel it against his chest, feel the soft kiss of her breath drifting over his flesh. "I don't want to stop," she whispered. "It's just getting fun."

Then she reached between them and tugged on the button of his jeans. "I don't want to stop," she repeated, freeing the button and then catching the tab of his zipper and easing it down.

Ezra swore as she slid her hand inside his jeans, inside his underwear and closed her fingers around his dick. "Damn it, Lena. You've known me for a few weeks. That's it."

She pressed her lips to his chin. "I know enough. I know that my dog likes you. I know you've got one of the sexiest voices I've ever heard. You don't seem to feel the need to hold my hand or cut my food because I can't see and you don't seem to care one way or the other about that, either." Her lips, soft and warm, brushed along his jawline, then down his neck. "I know that you got pissed at yourself because you touched me and you thought I didn't want you touching me . . . and you would have left me alone, as quick as that. And that right there says a lot about you, Ezra King. It says a whole helluva lot."

He shot a hand into her hair and tugged, guiding her face up so that he could stare down at her. He caught her hand, and as much as it damned near killed him, he tugged her away until those clever, cool fingers were no longer tormenting him and threatening him to destroy what little trace of control remained.

"You're too damn trusting, baby. You think some slick bastard couldn't make you think just those very things, play on it until you were willing to do just this?"

Lena laughed and pushed up on her toes, pressed her lips to his. "I'm sure some slick bastard could try to do just that . . . and several slick bastards have tried, tried and failed miserably. I've got good instincts, Ezra . . . and you may be slick, you might even be a bit of a bastard when you want. But you're not one for games." Then she bit his lower lip. "I'm not much for moving quickly, but I am one for listening to my instincts . . . and everything inside me wants you."

Fuck . . .

Ezra's hand tightened in her hair and he slammed his head back against the wall, staring at the ceiling. *Count to ten.* Ten didn't work. *Try twenty—*

Fuck it. He could count to fifteen million and it wasn't going to do a bit of good. He was burning, his cock hard, his balls on fire, and the only thing that would soothe that blistering heat was Lena. "I should know better than this," he muttered, lowering his eyes back to her face and staring down at her. "I really, really should. But screw it."

A smile bloomed on her lips just as he crushed his mouth to hers.

She moaned into his kiss and rose on her toes, arching against him. Her breasts pressed flat against his chest, her belly cradling his cock. Sliding his hands under the waistband of her trousers he shoved them down as far as he could without breaking contact with her mouth. "Naked, Lena. Get naked for me."

She shimmied her hips and the black cotton fell into a puddle at her feet. Then she leaned back, reaching for the hem of her shirt. Ezra beat her to it, stripping the skimpy tank away and staring down at her. His mouth went dry.

Her breasts were perfect, small, firm mounds, pale as cream, topped with hard nipples. Dipping his head, he caught one in his mouth. Wrapping his arms around her waist, he boosted her up and turned, pressing her up against the wall. She tangled her hands in his hair and arched against him, whimpering under her breath.

Ezra worked a hand between them, unwilling to let her go, but he had to touch her, had to touch her more, had to touch her everywhere. At the first touch of the slick wet heat between her thighs, he shuddered and groaned. "Fuck, Lena . . . you're wet."

She arched against his hand and gasped as he plunged two fingers inside her. The walls of her pussy clenched around him, tight and greedy. "Put me down, Ezra."

"Why?" He pressed his mouth to her neck and bit her. "I like you just where you're at."

"The bedroom." She whimpered and rocked against his hand. "The bedroom's upstairs."

Ezra kissed her, keeping the contact light. "No bedroom, baby. Right here . . . I'm going to die if I don't fuck you right here, right now." He pressed his brow to hers and said, "Is that okay? Please, please, please say that's okay."

"Um . . . that's more than okay," she said, her voice breathless.

"Good." He circled the tip of one finger around her clit, smiling as her long, slender body arched and shuddered. "So damn hot and tight. You're already so wet for me."

Her eyes widened, her mouth parted. The heat of her body seemed to skyrocket. Laughing, he leaned in and nipped her lower lip. "You like dirty talk, Lena?"

"Yes." Then she blushed and tangled her fingers in his hair, tugging him close. "I like it when you talk, period."

If he had any semblance of control left, he just might have pressed his lips to her ear and given her all the dirty talk she could handle, told her how he was dying to bury his mouth against her pussy and see what she tasted like, that he loved the way she smelled like peaches and moved like sin, but his brain was shutting down on him. Shutting down, drowning out anything but the need to lose himself in her.

"I'll give you plenty of dirty talk. Later. Right now . . ." He slowly lowered her to the floor and then reached for his wallet. Yeah, just call him a Boy Scout. He grabbed one of the two rubbers he'd shoved inside it and then he dropped the wallet to the floor. He could get it later— he'd need it later, because this first time wasn't going to last, and there was no way he could get his fill of her in a few minutes.

Hell, a few decades . . .

He tore the foil wrapper open, but before he could put it on, Lena reached between them. She took it from him, holding it in one hand while she slid her other hand down his chest, along his belly until she could wrap her fingers around his cock. "Carry rubbers around all the time?" she asked, fumbling a little as she unrolled it down over his length.

"No . . . but hope springs eternal." He adjusted the rubber and then reached for her, pulling her into his arms.

"Your leg."

"Leg's fine," he rasped, slanting his mouth over hers and boosting her up. It wasn't—already the muscles were knotting up on him, but he didn't give a damn. The pain in his thigh was nothing compared to the ache in his cock, in his balls. "Wrap your legs around me, Lena . . . hold on to me."

She did and he shuddered as it opened her folds. Nudging against her with the head of his cock, he leaned into her, sank inside . . . lost himself. He stared into her sightless eyes and felt stripped bare as she curled her hands around his neck. "Fuck, Lena. . . ."

She arched against him and he sank deeper, deeper inside that long pale body, until the russet curls between her thighs tangled with the thick, coarse hair surrounding his cock. Buried inside her, he blew out a harsh breath and tried to suck in more air. "You okay?"

"No . . ." she whimpered, working her hips, trying to ride him.

"No?" He could feel her, through the thin latex barrier; she was slick as satin, wet as rain, and burning—burning him, wrapping hot fiery tendrils around his balls and squeezing tight, tight, leaving him torn between exquisite pleasure and near pain. "Not okay?"

"Hell, no. I won't be until you move."

He gave a pained laugh and then started to move, stroked deep inside her honeyed depths and shuddered. "Then maybe I should move . . . like this?" He pulled out until just the head of his cock remained in her snug heat.

"Hmmm. That's a good start."

"What about this?" He pushed deep, but stopped a few inches shy of complete impalement.

Lena pouted and rolled her hips against him. "Not so good there . . . damn it, Ezra, don't tease me."

He would have, though. If he could breathe. He would have teased, toyed, and played with her until she was the sweating, desperate mess that he was—until he thought she was even half as desperate for him as he was for her.

But he couldn't because he couldn't breathe, couldn't think—couldn't do a damn thing but swivel his hips and bury his length inside her. Again. Again. Her pussy went tight around him, gripping him convulsively, milking him like a hot, tight little fist, and he groaned, desperately.

He was going to lose it—going to come before he'd even had a couple of minutes in heaven, before he gave her even a tenth of the pleasure she was giving him. Working a hand between them, he pressed his thumb against her clit and stroked.

Lena stiffened in his arms and arched up, her head slamming back against the wall. A wild cry escaped her lips and he swore, crushing his mouth down on hers, swallowing her cry, swallowing her moans. "Come for me," he muttered against her lips.

Too soon—he wasn't giving her enough—

But she came—like she was already primed for him and all she'd needed was that teasing, taunting touch.

Hot and wild, she exploded for him, her hands tangled in his hair, her legs tightening around his hips. The ache in his balls expanded and he growled against her lips, but now he fought back his own release with a vengeance. Again—he wanted to see it again, and this time, he wanted to watch her as she came, see it in her eyes.

He held back and shifted, reaching down and hooking first her left thigh, then her right over his elbows, leaning into her. Holding her open, exposed, he slowed his thrusts and eased back, stared, watched as he fed one slow inch after another into her heat. She was so fucking wet, so damned soft. Beads of moisture gleamed in her curls and he groaned. Needed to taste her—had to, but couldn't stop.

"Touch yourself," he rasped and she did. With rapt fascination, he watched as she worked a hand between their bodies and circled one fingertip around her clit. Quick, light circles. Her breathing sped up and he gritted his teeth as she went tight around him. "Don't come again, not yet, fuck it, you're killing me. Give me your hand, give me a taste."

She hesitated.

"I want to lick your fingers, Lena . . . one taste, give me a taste," he ordered, staring down at her pink pussy, so desperate to taste her that he might have pulled away and gone down on her, fuck his bad leg, fuck his aching balls. Worth it to taste her—but then she reached up, seeking out his mouth. He leaned in and caught her fingertips between his lips, sucked on them.

Sin. She tasted like sin. Hot, dark, and ripe—

"Fuck, Lena, we should have gone to your room. I want a better taste of you." He leaned in and kissed her, plunging his tongue inside her mouth and gorging on her. Sweet, she was sweet everywhere.

She arched up against him, moaned into his mouth. Her pussy flexed around him—milked, squeezed . . .

Ezra lost it. Hard and fast, he shafted her. She cried out against his mouth, and he swallowed it down and rode her until she cried out again, and again, and again . . .

as she came apart in his arms. And then it was his turn, his orgasm ripping from him with near-painful intensity.

He let go of her legs and wrapped his arms around her torso, banding her against him and shuddering, shaking like a man caught in the grip of fever. Shaking. Shuddering. All but dying.

ELEVEN

IT WASN'T ENTIRELY UNUSUAL TO SEE A VEHICLE PARKED in front of Lena Riddle's house.

But he knew the cars he expected to see there.

He was careful—after all, this was his territory and he made sure he knew exactly what took place in his territory.

The truck parked in front of Lena's house now wasn't one he wanted to see there.

It belonged to a newcomer.

It belonged to a cop.

One who'd been in the sheriff's office last week.

One who'd been talking to Lena Riddle in town last week.

One who'd been talking to Lena Riddle rather often, as a matter of fact.

Seeing that truck parked in front of the woman's house now had him furious—for so many reasons.

He'd finally made a decision about what to do with his girl, and he'd come to take care of things, and now, he couldn't. Not while there was a cop a few hundred yards away.

"Why?" he muttered to himself as he retreated into the trees.

Why in the hell was the cop there? What did he want with Lena?

He'd done some asking around about Ezra King. Knew the state cop was on leave.

On leave. And out of his jurisdiction. But that didn't mean much to some cops, he knew. Apparently King was one of those, the kind who'd caught a scent of something and he didn't want to let it go.

Or maybe all he had caught scent of was Lena. Still, on leave or not, he was showing too much interest in that woman, an interest that hadn't started until after the phone call reporting the screams.

Damn it.

Damn her.

Right then, he didn't know if he was damning Lena, or damning his girl, or damning them both.

As he got farther from the house, he broke into a run. It was hot out, hot and muggy and sweat dripped down his arms. Under the long-sleeved shirt he wore, sweat stung the scratches on his arms. Scratches from her, from his pursuit of her through the woods.

Fortunately, considering his job, it wasn't unusual for him to be seen wearing long sleeves, and nobody would think twice of it. The scratches would heal, and they weren't deep enough to scar.

New plans. He needed to come up with a new plan, something that might deter the cop. Give the cop something else to focus on.

The cop—damn it.

The anger ate him, but he'd be careful.

He was good at his games and he knew, better than most, just how important it was to be careful.

"I don't know if my legs are gonna work," Ezra mumbled against her neck.

They still leaned against the wall and Lena was pretty sure that if he let go of her, she would just sag to the floor, maybe sleep for an hour or two. Or ten. Then, she just might find the energy to walk.

"You're gonna have to walk, Slick," she said, turning her head and kissing his ear. "If I have to stand here too much longer, I might decide to spend the night here."

"Night's still a long time away. I might be able to move before then."

She laughed and pushed against his chest. "Move." She grinned, lifting her face to his. "Come on, I'll show you my room."

"Hmmm." He dipped his head and rubbed his mouth against hers. "Okay. I'm always up for dessert."

"There's no dessert in my room."

Ezra trailed his fingers down her side, over her hip, dipping them between her thighs and stroking the slick, sensitive folds there. "There will be if you're in there."

She blushed. She could feel the heated flush as it formed on her chest and crept upward until her cheeks flamed with it. "I haven't been called dessert before."

"Hot and sweet, sounds like dessert to me." He took a deep breath—she could feel it against her breasts, hear it whisper along her skin.

"My room. Now." She swallowed and pressed against his chest. "Or better yet, yesterday."

She took a step away, but there was something on the floor. She stumbled, slamming a hand against the wall, but the heel of her palm just glanced off the edge as the wall curved into the arched doorway of the living room.

But she didn't fall. Hard, strong hands caught her, steadied her. "Shit, Lena. I'm sorry . . ."

She turned her head toward him, following the sound of his voice as he knelt down.

"It . . . ah . . . it was my wallet. I dropped it."

Lena reached out, brushed her fingers against his cheek. He caught her hand and pressed it against him as he stood. Under her fingers, she could feel the prickly, rough growth of stubble and his skin—hot—too hot. She heard the strain in his voice, recognized the embarrassment easily enough and it helped ease her own.

"Hey, it's okay. My parents knew better than to name me Grace, you know." She softened the words with a smile and leaned in, pressing her lips to his. "Didn't you say something about dessert?"

The first couple days Hope had been there, Law had kept her busy with movies and inane talk . . . when she wasn't sleeping. Oddly enough, the insomnia that plagued her all too often had eased, and the first night she was there, she slept for fifteen hours. The second night, she slept for twelve hours.

On the third day, though, she decided that if he really wanted her to work, then she was going to work.

She half-expected him to tell her to alphabetize the books on his shelves or something.

But when she walked into his office, the first thing he did was jump up from his desk with a look of relief on his face and grab a huge box from the floor.

"Here. Been saving this for you," he said, pushing it into her hands.

Hope scowled at the ridiculous piles of loose paperwork, a jumbled mess of receipts, printed pages, and handwritten notes and then she looked up at Law. "And I'm supposed to do . . . what?"

Law peered into the box. "Organize it. If it looks like something I'll need for taxes this year, set it aside. If it's a letter from a reader or something like that, put it in a file—I think I read them all, and I only print out a few of them, but I want to make sure I go through them."

"How am I supposed to know what you need for

taxes?" Hope asked, dismayed. The box probably weighed ten pounds.

He crooked a grin at her. "Well, if it's anything related to my office, books, writing, research, promotional crap like bookmarks, pens, postcards, or postal costs like stamps, envelopes, et cetera, et cetera . . . all of that is going to be needed for taxes."

"I thanked you the other day," she mumbled. "I think I'm going to take it back."

"Yeah, probably. In a few days, I'll be kissing your feet and begging you to stay, I bet. I wasn't kidding when I said I needed help, Hope. I really, really wasn't."

Hope studied the mess of his office and sighed. "You've managed without an assistant before this."

"Barely." Law skimmed a hand through his hair and said, "Look, some of this crap I can keep doing, but I can write more, focus on my writing more if I've got some help, and there's a bit of a problem with living here and getting help here. There are exactly three people whom I would trust with telling about this and none of them can help me."

He spread his hands wide and said, "They work full-time, they got stuff going on, and this is going to be a time-consuming job, especially at first."

The master of understatement.

That was Law Reilly, Hope decided hours later as she sat at the second computer station he had set up in his office. At first, she hadn't realized it was a computer station. The computer had been hidden behind the books, boxes, the books, the padded mailers, the books . . . the books. As she stretched her arms, she studied the floor-to-ceiling bookshelves he had along the length of one wall.

He owned more than one copy of eight of the books she had cleared off this desk. Of course, Law had insisted otherwise until she had shown him the duplicates, sitting on his shelves. Then he had shrugged. "I'll send them to Goodwill."

Well, that had cleared out more than a dozen books and she had a feeling she could clear out probably twice that if she could get away from that eagle eye of his. The phone had started ringing a few times and she'd hoped he'd answer it, maybe wander out of the office—he never seemed to sit still unless he was writing—but all he did was ignore the phone.

Each fricking time it rang. And it rang a lot.

He ignored it with aplomb. She'd almost think he wasn't even aware of it. But she knew better. The man seemed to notice everything.

Like the way she eyed his bookshelves. The few times she'd inched closer to study the titles, he had looked at her like she was about to pounce on a fuzzy, helpless little baby bunny, instead of looking for duplicates of books he already owned.

She might have risked it, but if he really expected her to actually work for him—and she was starting to realize he did—then she needed someplace halfway organized to do it.

That meant clearing off that frightening nightmare he had insisted was a desk.

Two and a half hours later, she had taken care of the books, somehow managed to organize most of the receipts, filed about half of the papers into recognizable order—research info, reader letters, letters from his agent—she assumed—a few reviews torn out of magazines, and a rather disturbing pile of postcards.

Blank postcards.

More than a hundred of them. She flipped through them, studying the images on the front before flipping them over. Some of them had been sitting around long enough to have the edges worn and ragged, while others looked brand-new.

"What's with the postcards?" she asked, glancing at him.

"Possible book locations," he replied, his tone absent. He had a glazed look in his eyes, almost hypnotized.

She lifted her brows. "You plan on writing a book in . . . Adair, Iowa? What exactly is in Adair, Iowa?"

"Nothing . . . that I know of." He slanted a grin at her. "That means there's probably something. There's always something, somewhere."

"You're strange, Law. Very strange."

His only response was a grunt.

Looking back at the postcards, she grabbed a pencil and the notepad she'd been using. If he was going to keep a running list of possible locations, he could keep them more organized, she figured. A photo album would hold them all just fine. Add that to the list of fifteen other things she needed.

Along with cleaning supplies. Those bookshelves of his had a fine layer of dust, and Hope didn't want to think about how long it had been since this room had been cleaned.

He had somebody who came out and took care of the house, but she wasn't allowed in his office—he even had that written into a contract. The cleaning lady wasn't allowed to open the door. Period.

He was strange. Strangely paranoid.

But then again, he was Law.

Blowing out a sigh, she looked back at the desk, ready to tackle the next chore only to realize she could actually see the desk.

It was clear.

Mostly.

Which meant she could possibly start on the mess of

paperwork in that box, the one by her desk, all but waiting to attack her. It seemed like that pile loomed higher and higher . . .

And his paranoia is rubbing off on you.

"Hey, can you take care of my e-mail for me?" Law called out.

Spinning around in her seat, she stared at him. "Your e-mail. Geez, Law, exactly how much junk do you plan on dumping on me?"

"As much as I can get you to do?" The smile he gave was the same one he'd given when they were kids and he'd tried to talk her into doing something she knew she shouldn't. But it faded as he rubbed a hand down his face. "You remember how I told you I was drowning? I wasn't lying. The last time I looked at one of my e-mail accounts was four days ago and there were over three hundred messages. It's the one I use for my website—a catch-all e-mail."

Hope narrowed her eyes. "Maybe we should discuss some kind of wage here."

He named a figure that had her jaw dropping.

"You're not serious. For answering e-mail? Filing? Cleaning up this sty you call an office? You could hire somebody for half that."

"I am hiring somebody—you. And it's worth it if it's somebody I know will actually hold up her end of the bargain, not leave me hanging, and is actually going to understand the whole reason I use a pen name." He eyed the box on the floor by her desk with the same level of dislike she had given it and added, "Besides, it's getting rather necessary and it's not just about the filing or the e-mails. There's more, but we'll work up to that. It's about saving my sanity, but you have to agree to not leave me in the lurch—if you up and decide this isn't working out and you have to take off, you can't just disappear. Give me a warning, at least." There was a strange look in his eyes as he said it.

Something inside her rebelled at the thought—a leash. Too much like a leash . . . a cage. Even though she realized he had every right to expect some warning if she decided to bail, that wasn't what this was about. He was doing what he'd been trying to do ever since he'd figured out what was going on.

He was trying to look out for her.

Part of her even wanted to let him, but Hope needed to figure out how to stand on her own two feet.

Still, she had to see this for what it was—a friend's concern. This wasn't a cage, and Law would never try to trap her. There was no door locking her in, no key.

She could walk away when she chose.

She had a choice.

He was manipulating her to some extent; she wasn't so naïve that she didn't see that, but a part of her understood. He was her dearest friend, just as she was his, and if he'd disappeared for weeks, months, years . . .

Don't go there, Hope. Don't let those memories pull you back.

She looked away from him, staring out the window. "I won't be able to stay here."

"Why not?"

Hearing the frustration, and the worry, in his voice, she looked back at him and smiled. "I didn't mean *here* here, as in the town. I meant your place. I can't stay here indefinitely. Sooner or later, I'll need to look for my own place." Then she grimaced. "Not that I'll have an easy time finding a place. No credit history, no references."

"I'll give you a reference. And around here, people don't tend to worry as much about things like credit histories," he said, his voice soft. "Small towns aren't always bad, sweetheart."

Not always a cage. That was what he meant, even if he didn't say it.

"And what do I tell people when they ask me what I do for you?" She tried for levity, waggled her eyebrows. "Am I your mistress? Your housekeeper?"

"How about just my keeper? Half of them think I'm crazy anyway." He grinned as he said it and she saw some of the strain leaving his eyes.

She hated how much he worried about her, hated how guilty he felt. It wasn't his fault. There was nothing he could have done, after all. He hadn't caused it.

You did—

No. You didn't cause it and you're not doing this, she told herself.

Once again, the phone started ringing and she sighed quietly in relief—a distraction, even if it was just from her memories. "Does answering the phone come into play?"

"Nah. I hate talking on the phone and most of the people who need to talk to me know that." He grabbed the phone off his desk and eyed the caller ID. "It's my agent. She can e-mail me."

Hope rolled her eyes. "What if it's important?"

"All the more reason to e-mail me first and let me know it's important, because otherwise, I'll forget the important details."

"You don't forget jack."

"Sure I do." With that charming smile that seemed to get him what he wanted every time, he leaned back in his chair. "I forget . . . and I then remember later, but never when I need to. It's all in a jumble, and e-mail makes it less jumbled."

"You're full of shit."

He winked at her. "Yeah. But I'm not completely lying. My brain works on a priority scale and right now, this story is priority . . . especially now that you're here."

Taking a deep breath, she looked at Law. "Okay, boss. What e-mails and what passwords and exactly what am I supposed to be doing?"

She had a knack for this but Law had already figured that much out. Hope was the organized type, and she always had been. In school, she was the meticulously organized one who had known exactly where all of her assignments were and when they were due . . . and usually his and Joey's, as well.

In the past few years, even though she hadn't lived anywhere close to him, she was the one who helped him manage little details he would have forgotten ages ago, e-mails and names he never would have thought to keep track of.

She didn't seem to realize it, but she had been doing this sort of thing for him unofficially for years, except for . . . no.

Best not to think about that time right now, because if he did, she was going to pick up on it and he'd already seen how hard she was fighting to keep level, to keep straight.

He didn't want to rock her boat.

But he did want to kill Joey Carson in a slow and painful manner. Then he wanted to kick his own ass, but he'd been doing that for the past couple of years. Once upon a time, his gut had whispered something very ugly about Joe . . . very, very ugly, but he hadn't listened.

And look what had—

"Law."

He glanced up, saw the look of pale strain on Hope's face. The past few years hadn't been kind to her, but she still had the sweet, soft beauty that had drawn so many boys to her when they'd been in school. The kind that had Law hovering over her like the protective older brother he'd always felt like.

"Law, focus."

He scowled and narrowed his eyes on her face. "I'm focused. What's wrong?"

"That writer, Cassia Hughes—you knew her?"

Knew . . .

"Yeah, I know Cassia."

"She had a heart attack." Hope's eyes went dark, sad. "She died this morning."

TWELVE

It was past six on Tuesday and Lena felt utterly decadent. Most of the past two days had been spent in bed with Ezra. Well, in bed, in the shower . . . once on her back porch.

Right now she was back in the bed, wrapped around that long, oh so nicely muscled body of his.

"You know, I've spent more time in bed the past week than I usually do in a month," she murmured, smiling a little.

"You complaining?"

"No. Just a comment."

His hand stroked up and down her back. She traced her fingers along his torso, taking quite a bit of pleasure as she learned his body. And damn, what a body. He had a hard, flat belly, long, lean limbs, and his hands . . . whoa. He could do things with his hands that just might be illegal in some countries.

Then there was his mouth—his mouth could almost put his hands to shame and if she wasn't careful, she just might start whimpering in need if she thought about it too much.

He was smiling. She could feel the curve of his mouth

pressed against her temple. "Glad you're not complaining, because if you were, it would be your fault."

"Really? How is that?"

"Well. I didn't see you for three days."

Lena laughed. "I had to work," she reminded him. She hadn't seen him at all Thursday, Friday, or Saturday—he had called shortly before she was supposed to leave on Saturday, but she hadn't had much time to talk.

When he'd shown up at her doorstep Sunday, she'd tried to keep it cool, casual . . . letting him inside, offering to cook dinner.

They'd made it halfway through the foyer, and he'd stroked a hand down her back.

That was all it had taken and she'd just about pounced on him. Since then, the hours had passed in a drugged, sexual blur of pleasure.

Lena's sex life had been . . . limited. The last guy she'd been serious with had been Remy—sex with him had been fun, hot, and easy. They had been compatible in bed, but it hadn't compared to this.

She and Ezra weren't compatible.

They were damned near combustible.

It went deeper than the heat, though.

He made her laugh.

He made her smile.

Hell, he just made her happy.

Sometime around eight or nine last night, they'd realized they'd sort of forgotten about eating for most of the day. Starved, they'd hit the kitchen and she'd been delighted when he had ended up making them breakfast. Bacon, eggs, and toast, which they had eaten in the living room while watching the first in a series of very bad B horror movies.

Then they'd fallen asleep on the couch.

She'd woken to his hands on her hips, his mouth between her legs.

Lena was pretty certain she'd had more orgasms in the past two days than she'd had in the past two years, combined. And that probably included those she'd given herself.

She knew she'd laughed more, smiled more since they'd decided to rethink the "friends only thing."

Sex and laughter, they were good things to have, she decided.

For the most part, she was normally kind of reserved, held herself apart—it was instinctive. She wasn't shy, but she kept her circle of friends small, and close. She kept the walls around herself high and tight.

Ezra had a way of smashing through those walls. Actually, it was kind of like the walls just fell down. They didn't even exist for him.

Smiling, she rubbed her cheek against his chest and sighed.

He combed a hand through her hair, absently toying with the ends. "You've got that smile on your face again," he murmured. "Like Sylvester the cat just got ahold of Tweety Bird, once and for all."

"Do I?" She smirked and sat up, stroking a hand down his chest.

"Yeah. Kind of makes me wonder what you're thinking about."

"Nothing . . . exactly. Just this." She shrugged, absently circling a finger around his navel.

He jumped and caught her hand. "Quit that."

A grin tugged at her lips. "Quit what?" Unable to resist, she wiggled around until she was sitting up and raked the nails of her other hand down his side. When he flinched and caught that wrist as well, she started to chuckle. "You're ticklish."

She wiggled her hand free and poked him in the side again and he swore, catching her.

She tried to roll away and they ended up wrestling

across the bed, laughing and swearing—although most of the swearing came from Ezra every time she managed to get free long enough to poke him in the ribs, under his arms. Even a light touch across his spine was enough.

"Whoever would have thought the big, tough cop would be that ticklish?" she teased as he rolled and pinned her beneath him.

"Brat," he muttered, stretching her arms over her head and holding her wrists in one hand.

Biting the tip of her tongue, she twined a leg around and managed to stroke her big toe down his instep. He swore again and used his knee to press her thighs apart, pinning her hips against the bed. "Would you quit it!"

That last move had the length of his cock pressed snug against her sex. Her breath lodged in her throat and she shivered, moved against him as best as she could. "Ahh . . . you know what? I bet you could distract me, if you really, really tried," she suggested.

"You've been torturing me and you think I should make love to you?" He paused. "Okay."

But when he reached down and touched the tip of his fingers to her swollen folds, even that light touch was even to make her flinch—flinch in pain. Ezra eased back. "You're too sore," he muttered.

"Am not." Well, maybe, but she didn't care.

"Yeah, yeah." He nipped her chin and started to move lower, kissing a line down her body, blazing a trail from her mouth all the way down to her navel, her pubis.

By the time he reached the sensitive folds of her sex, she was all but ready to beg him. Bending her knees, she dug her heels in the mattress and pressed down, arching her hips upward.

He cupped her butt in his hands and blew a cool puff of air against her.

She cried out.

The feel of his tongue against her was like the silken lash of a whip—pained pleasure. Each touch, each stroke against her swollen tissues had her heart racing faster, her blood pumping hotter.

"More," she muttered, rocking against him and reaching down, fisting her hands in his hair. It was thick, soft as silk under her hands.

The hunger was a burning, empty, aching knot inside, growing, spreading. It was going to consume her, drive her insane and still . . . he taunted. Teased.

As she panted and cried out, he lifted his head and traced his tongue around her entrance, teased her clit.

"Damn it, Ezra," she whimpered.

A hard, callused hand closed on her ankle. For some reason, that firm, unyielding touch had the knot of hunger inside her tightening, twisting. "What, baby?" he muttered, his breath hot against her wet flesh. "What do you want?"

"I want . . ." The words were trapped in her throat. Slamming her head back against the mattress, she jerked her leg against his restraining hand. He tightened his grip and dipped his head.

His teeth lightly grazed her clit and she froze. He did it again and then, he bit down and gently tugged.

Lena came with a harsh, nearly breathless scream.

She was blushing.

Wrapping his arms around her middle, Ezra rubbed his chin against the soft curve of her belly and smiled as he watched her squirm.

Damn it all but he loved the look of her. Her eyes were all heavy and sleepy from sex, her cheeks flushed, a faint smile curling her lips even as she squirmed in embarrassment. "You know, I'm really glad I don't have close neighbors," she said, her voice husky and soft. "They would have had the sheriff out here eight or nine times in the past two days."

"Nah. After the first time or two, I would have convinced them everything was okay." He pressed a kiss to her hipbone.

She opened her mouth to say something else, but her belly interrupted with a loud, demanding growl. Amused, he nuzzled the silken skin there and then sat up. "Maybe we should go eat. Fuel up for the next twenty-four hours."

Lena grimaced. "Food sounds good, but we can't do another marathon like this . . . at least not tonight. I've got to do some running around town tomorrow, otherwise I won't be able to until Sunday or Monday. I hate trying to get it all done before I have to work at the end of the week."

"Does that mean I can't stay the night?" Ezra asked, trying to ignore the hollow feeling he had inside when he thought about walking away. *Slow, remember? You were supposed to be friends, and then you were going to take it slow . . .*

And how fucking slow were they taking it? He showed up on Sunday, without calling, again planning on a casual meal, and they hadn't so much as left the house. Unless you counted having sex on the porch as leaving the house . . .

He needed to back off a little, he figured. Back off. Slow down. Give her some space.

But even as he tried to convince himself that was the best thing to do, Lena caught his wrist and turned her face to his hand. "Oh, I'd love if you stayed the night. We just can't have crazy monkey sex all night and I've got to be up early for Puck." Then she grimaced. "Plus, I've been bad—I need to take him out for a walk tonight. I try to walk him every day and I didn't yesterday."

"You're too sore for crazy monkey sex. Plus, I think we're running low on condoms." He ran a hand through his hair and stood up, grimacing as he studied the bed. "Your bed is a mess, beautiful."

She flashed him a grin. "I'll tell you what . . . I'll do dinner. You do the bed. Sheets are in the hallway closet."

Lena was adding a little more seasoning to the steaks when the phone rang. Absently, she answered, her mind more on Ezra than anything else.

"Hey, it's me."

"Hey, Law. What's up?"

"Listen, I know I'm supposed to run you into town tomorrow, but I can't. I'm on my way to the airport in Lexington right now. Heading out of town for a few days."

Lena frowned and closed the cabinet, trying to pinpoint the heavy, somber tone she heard in Law's voice. He sounded nothing like himself. She'd heard him irritated, impatient, charming, and mad, but she hadn't ever heard him sound so . . . sad.

"Is everything okay?" she asked, gripping the phone nervously.

His sigh drifted over the receiver. "No. I just got word that a friend of mine died this morning. I'm flying out for the memorial and funeral. Will you be okay—maybe your cop can run you into town or something?"

"Law, I'm so sorry." She swallowed, at a loss for anything else to say. What could she say? Hearing Ezra coming into the room behind her, she turned toward him and automatically reached for him.

It felt so natural, doing just that. Something she'd never done before, something she'd never had before . . . yet it felt so natural with him.

And he was there, catching her hand with his and offering silent support without even asking. He didn't have to, she knew. He realized something was wrong, and he wanted to be there.

Lacing her fingers with his, she closed her eyes and focused on the phone, and Law.

"Will you be okay for a few days? If your cop isn't free, maybe Roz can run you into town?"

"I'll be fine. I'm the last person you need to be worrying about right now," she told him, her voice thick, her heart aching for her friend.

"Not entirely true. You're a friend—friends don't get relegated to the back burner." He paused, sighed. "I've got to go."

As Law disconnected, Ezra stroked a hand down her back. Absently, without even realizing it, she leaned against him, resting her cheek against his chest.

"Everything okay?"

"A friend of Law's died this morning."

Ezra was quiet for a moment and then murmured, "Cassia Hughes, maybe?"

Lena lifted her face to his. "Cassia? Cassia Hughes. I know that name. Mystery writer. He has a friend—Cassie . . . he talked about Cassie a lot. She was . . . yeah, she was a friend. She's dead?"

"I saw the news feed when I was online earlier, checking my e-mail. She had a heart attack. They were friends?"

"Yeah." She rested her head against his chest and slid her arms around his waist. "I lost my dad and that just about did me in when I was a kid. You never really get over it, but Dad's the only one I've ever lost. Law's lost his parents, and now one of his best friends. Man, I hurt for him. This is awful."

The air around Ezra was tense, tight. A soft, rough sigh shuddered out of him and he said, "Awful doesn't describe it."

Remembering what he'd told her about his partner . . . his lover, she winced. "I'm sorry. I just went and put my foot in my mouth, didn't I?"

"It's okay." He kissed her brow. "A heart attack, fast and peaceful, probably isn't a bad way to go."

Lena made a face. "There's a not-bad way to go?"

"Oh, baby. There are ways so awful, I can't even begin to describe. Fast, peaceful? I don't want to kick it any time soon, but if I had to choose a way, a major heart attack probably wouldn't suck, at least." He nuzzled her cheek and stroked a hand down her back. "Is he okay?"

"As okay as he can be, I guess. Worrying about me." She made a face. "That's Law for you. A friend of his died and he's worrying about how I'll get to town. He usually drives me in on Wednesdays."

Tipping her head back, she pressed a kiss to the corner of his mouth. "You maybe want to take me into town tomorrow?"

"Sure. When?"

"Just sometime in the morning—well, any time works. But Puck never lets me sleep in." Resting her head against Ezra's chest, she traced out a pattern on his chest and said, "So . . . you said something about staying the night?"

Fucking bitch.

By the time the week was over, Prather had worked himself to a fever pitch, so damn furious, he could barely see.

A week. He'd been stuck working the desk all fucking week on Nielson's say-so.

It was all that bitch's fault, too.

Fucking Lena Riddle.

He was tempted, by God, he was tempted. Wanted to go out there and give that high-and-mighty little snot a piece of his mind. Then he wanted to punch that smug state boy right in his mouth. King had gone and had a talk with Nielson, that was another part of the problem, and Nielson, being the ass-kisser he was, he'd gone and caved.

Playing nice, that's what he was doing. Wanted to brown-nose anybody he thought might do him good. Looking good for some smart-ass state cop was more important than standing up for his own people. Fuck Nielson, too.

Hell, they could all go fuck themselves.

They needed to give Lena Riddle a bad guy and that's what Prather was for them—the bad guy, even though all he'd done was try to help that stupid, irritating cunt who couldn't figure out what was good for her.

Stupid whore. His eyes narrowed as he thought back to how she stalked onto his grounds and demanded he do something. Bitch had nerve. Had that fucking puppet of hers with her, too. Law Reilly. Boy was always sniffing around her like she was a bitch in heat.

Hell, he might be in on this, too. Probably was.

They needed to be taught a lesson.

All of them.

That was what they needed.

THIRTEEN

HER NAME WAS JOLENE HOLLISTER AND SHE KNEW SHE was about to die.

Oddly, she found she was ready.

She didn't want to die, but she didn't want to face anything else this bastard had to hand out either.

Ever since she'd tried, and almost managed, to escape, he had . . . changed. If a monster could become more monstrous, then that was what had happened. He hadn't touched her—not since the day he'd dragged her kicking, struggling, and trying to scream, back inside this place, her private, personal hell. After that final, brutal rape, he hadn't touched her, but he still scared the hell out of her.

He hadn't touched her, and he hadn't tried to force her to eat, either. Once or twice a day, he forced water down her throat and that was it. It was as though he wanted to do the bare minimum to keep her alive.

She was weaker now, no longer able to do much more than shove at him as he freed her and pulled her off the small cot where she had lain restrained for the past week.

The thing stank to high heaven because he hadn't let her free, not even once. So she had lain in her own filth. His hands weren't gentle as he hauled her to the small, hand-rigged bathing area she'd used before and as he doused her with cold water, her weakened legs gave out under her.

He didn't say anything, didn't attempt to force her to stand.

It was like he no longer saw her as a living, breathing creature—not even a plaything.

Yes, he had become more monstrous . . . in some ways. She was no longer remotely alive to him, and in some ways that terrified her more than anything else he'd done to her.

But at the same time, it was a relief. If he no longer saw her as alive, it was because he meant to see that she didn't remain that way much longer.

And Jolene—*please God, forgive me*—couldn't live like this much longer.

She wanted, needed, craved death and soon, he'd give it to her.

It was a chore, he was disgusted to discover.

She lay under him like a limp dishrag, boneless, barely breathing, the healing bruises standing out against her pale, pale skin. Her pupils were mere pinpricks, and there was little life left in those hazel eyes.

Of course, when he lifted his hand and started to methodically beat her . . . that changed.

For a moment.

The brilliant, stark light of pain flared in her eyes.

Her screams once more rang in the air.

But even the pain in her eyes faded, and her screams went silent far too soon. Reaching down, he closed a gloved hand around her throat, squeezing, squeezing, until she gasped and groaned and whimpered her way back into consciousness.

And still, she looked at him out of swollen, bruised eyes . . . dull eyes.

Setting his jaw, ignoring the stink that lingered in the air, he went to the small footlocker and withdrew a clear bottle. She was lax and limp—it was like trying to initiate intercourse with a corpse and while he could deviate from the plan, he chose not to.

He didn't like using the lubricant unless he was taking a woman anally, but he wasn't about to fuck a dry stick, either. Sometimes, the violence alone was enough for him, but she had to struggle, had to give him . . . something.

She had nothing for him now. Barely any life left in her.

He didn't let it anger him, though.

As he turned back to face her, he smoothed a hand over his bare scalp and knelt down next to her. "You really were one of the best . . . for a while," he said.

It should have ended better than this. So much better.

Her eyes were dull as she stared straight ahead and when he covered her body, she didn't even flinch.

In her mind, Joely was already drifting away. She knew what he was doing. Pain blistered through her, but she was only vaguely aware.

He would rape her again, she realized. She'd thought he was done with that. But no. He'd do it again and she didn't want to be here for it.

Let him do it.

In her mind, she cried out for Bryson . . . for her fiancé, the man she loved. In her soul, she wept for him.

And in her heart, she mourned the life she could feel slipping away.

In life, she'd been very lovely—that serene, almost peaceful, angelic beauty covering an impish sense of humor and wicked intelligence.

In death, that serene, peaceful beauty was broken, shattered. He'd taken his time with the rape, taken his time before he slowly choked the life out of her, and by the time her life ended, her face was so swollen, not even her own mother would have recognized her.

He didn't care for that, but it had been necessary for his plan, and in the end, it didn't matter to him how she looked now. Even as he carefully trimmed her hair to chin-length, he was more focused on how she had looked before.

That night.

Forever, he would remember how Jolene Hollister had looked that night when he had dragged her back into his place and flung her against the wall—her eyes bright with terror, her heart racing, and her strong, slim body struggling. So alive. So alive, so defiant. Even as she fought him and lost, she'd been strong and defiant . . . and his.

Only his.

He took care to clean up the loose hair, taking only what he needed and tucking it safely away, then gathering the rest to be disposed of. He could do that easily enough in the morning.

Tonight, he had another task to see to, and instead of his normal routine, he had a new plan in mind.

He took little notice of the bruises as he cleaned her carefully, wrapping her body in a sheet of plastic before carrying her out of the trees under the cover of darkness.

This was a risk, but it was a calculated one.

One he felt he needed to take.

He'd made a bad mistake in judgment thinking nobody would pay any attention to Lena Riddle if she reported anything unusual. She'd reported it, and yes, people had paid attention. So it was time to give them something to find.

From his truck, he could see the lights on in the house, could see the shadow of the occupant moving around. The shades were drawn, but he could still see movement, the odd flickering light that told him the TV was on.

A night owl, a fact that had played in his favor.

Lena Riddle was a problem. One he needed to deal with, and over the past few days, he had come up with a solution.

There was one major problem and that was Lena herself, but there were smaller problems that added to the whole.

She was so sure of herself, so cocky and confident.

Too many people seemed to believe her, and part of that was just because she was so cocky and confident.

Shake that confidence, even a little, and like a house built on sand, the entire structure might very well collapse.

And even if it didn't . . . well, they needed a body.

So he would give them a body . . . and a bad guy.

She'd forgotten how damned eerie and empty a big house could be at night.

Especially when you couldn't sleep.

The floorboards squeaked.

Outside, the wind wailed.

A storm was blowing in and although it wasn't cold, she found herself rubbing her arms, chilled to the bone.

She thought about turning on the TV, but this late at night, her best bet was infomercials, lousy horror movies, or worse. Something gross and scary, the last thing she needed when she was already freaked out for reasons she couldn't entirely explain.

As midnight edged past and she still couldn't settle her restless mind, she thought about reading. Absently, she realized the wind was dying down. Maybe the storm would blow over. She sighed and moved over to the window, absently adjusting the blinds.

And that was when she felt it.

The eerie sensation of . . . wrongness.

Her breath lodged in her throat and she peeked through the blinds, staring out into the darkness. Her breath came in hitching gasps as she tried to breathe past the knot that had suddenly lodged itself in her throat. Tried to breathe . . . and couldn't.

Tried to breathe . . . and damn near screamed. Clapping a hand over her mouth, Hope Carson breathed out a prayer against her muffling palm. One step after another, she backed away from the window.

She'd just seen a shadow.

Out there in the darkness, where she shouldn't be seeing anything.

Moving toward Law's workshop.

A man.

Carrying . . . something.

Phone calls at close to one A.M. were bad news.

Really bad news. Nobody called at one A.M. just to chat, so whoever was on the phone must really need to talk . . . but he was still going to commit bloody mayhem.

Grouchy, irritable as hell, Law grabbed the cell phone from the bedside table and snarled, "What?"

"Law . . ."

Hope's shaky, terrified whisper was a splash of icy cold water, and one hell of an effective wake-up call.

"Baby, what's wrong?"

"Huh?"

Lena knuckled her eyes and tried to make sense of the words coming out of the receiver, but so far, they weren't making much sense.

"Where's your cop? Is he there with you?"

"My cop? You mean Ezra?" Lena asked. Coffee. She needed coffee—especially if she was supposed to make sense of a phone conversation with Law at . . . what time was it again?

"Yes, Ezra, unless you're shacking up with Prather now, too. Damn it, Lena, wake up, this is important."

"Law, honey, trust me. Whatever weird story question you got, it needs to wait until—"

"It's not a fucking story!" Law snarled.

If it wasn't for the underlying fear she heard in his voice, that tone alone would have had her back going up and she would have torn into him. As it was, it served to wake her up. Very, very well. Slowly, she sat up. "Okay, then. What's going on?"

"Is he there with you?"

"No." *More's the pity* . . . Part of her wanted to make some snide comment about him being presumptuous—except Ezra had spent four nights with her this past week—and just think, last week, they weren't even really talking. Sighing, she rubbed her neck. "He had a doctor's appointment with a specialist in Lexington and said he wouldn't be fit for human consumption, so he was heading home once he got back in town."

"Is he in town?"

"Yes," she said slowly.

"Call him. He needs to come pick you up." Law blew out a breath. "I need you to go to my place and you need to do it now—have him come pick you up right away. It's got to be him, Lena. Nobody else. Not Roz, not Carter. Ezra. You understand?"

"No. Not in the least. Law, what's the deal?"

In a grim, angry voice, he said, "I've got to call the police."

"The police . . . what in the hell is going on?"

"I . . . I've got a friend staying out there. She thinks she saw somebody out near my workshop—I don't know. But I can't call the sheriff and report it until somebody else is out there. Lena, if she sees a uniform, she's going to freak out. I need you there." He hesitated for a few seconds and then quietly, his voice a raw plea, added, "Please?"

*   *   *

The phone rang.

Ezra came awake instantly, even though he'd been caught in the midst of one weird-ass dream involving a physical therapist, his high-school gym teacher, clown school, and Nascar.

Shaking the weirdness from his head, he grabbed his phone from the bedside table. Seeing Lena's number had his heart skipping a beat, but he forced the fear down, buried it under a layer of ice. "Hey, beautiful. Kind of late . . . are you okay?"

"Yeah, I'm fine," she said, her voice husky, soft and sleepy. "But apparently there's something weird going on at Law's."

"I thought he was out of town."

"He is. But he's got a friend staying there. Look, this is a fricking mess and I need coffee before I can try to explain. Will you pretty please just come over here and pick me up? Drive me over there?"

He looked at the clock. Shit. "You do know what time it is, right? It's just a few minutes past one."

"I know." She muffled a yawn. "Trust me, I know. But . . . hell, Ezra. Law never asks me for anything and he sounded . . . scared."

Shit.

He was pretty sure there was something in a relationship handbook somewhere that required him to help out his woman's friends in times of need.

Even if those friends were like Law—a guy who was dying to get inside her pants. Scraping his nails down the heavy growth of stubble on his face, he sighed and stood up. "I'll be there in about ten minutes. Less."

After he disconnected the phone, he got up and walked over to his closet. There was a fire safe on the top shelf. Even touching it was enough to make him break out in a sweat. But he did it anyway. Before slamming the door, he grabbed his shoulder holster as well and a lightweight denim jacket.

Dressing quickly, he took the fire safe into the kitchen. By then, his hands were shaking so bad, it took two tries before he could get the little silver key on his key ring to go into the damn lock.

Opening it up, he didn't give himself time to think, he just grabbed the matte-black Glock and loaded it.

In another minute, he was heading out the front door.

To keep from thinking about the gun, he focused on Lena. Only on Lena.

FOURTEEN

"I'M GOING TO POUND HIS DAMN ASS INTO THE ground," Ezra snapped.

"He wouldn't have asked if it wasn't important." Lena rested her head against the back of the seat and tried to quell the churning in her gut, but it wasn't happening.

"Shit. That guy gets the basics of law enforcement— you suspect an intruder, you call the cops."

"He's got a friend there," Lena said, her voice quiet. "Law just doesn't have friends out at his place. He doesn't. And he doesn't ask for favors. But he asked me for one. I can't tell him no."

Ezra almost missed the turnoff. Law liked his privacy— guarded it the way a dog guarded a beloved bone, one might say. Paranoid—had Ezra called him a little paranoid? He hadn't been detailed enough.

Exactly what was the deal with this friend, anyway?

"There are lights on," Ezra said softly, as they rounded a bend. "A lot of them. No county cars here yet."

"Law will be giving us time to get here." The car stopped in front of the house and she climbed out, called for Puck. The dog jumped out, but there was a reluctance to his steps. He made a sound low in his throat, tugging against his harness.

For reasons she couldn't explain, it made her heart skip a beat.

"Ezra, you don't see anything, do you?"

"If I did, you really think I would have let you get out of the car?" he asked. His voice was weary. "Puck is staring off toward the woods. Past the house. It's not Law's place that's got him spooked . . . it's something else, out in the woods. Whoever it is, whatever it is, don't think he's still here, though. That bruiser of yours is too calm. He doesn't like being here, but I get the feeling if somebody was still out there, he'd be all but dragging you inside the car."

"Hmm." Lena rested a hand on Puck's head and smiled. "Hear that, boy? He's calling you a bruiser." In that moment, she was feeling very, very appreciative of her dog, too.

An eerie, cold tingle raced down her spine and she gripped Puck's leash tighter. *Hope you've called the sheriff's office by now, Law,* she thought. "Hey, do you . . . ah, do you have a gun?"

There was a brief pause. "Yeah. I've got one." His voice was brusque, hoarse. "Seriously hoping I don't ever need to use it, but I've got one and yes, I brought it."

Blowing out a breath, he said, "What's the deal here, Lena? Why was it so important that we come here before he could call the police?"

"I don't really know. All he told me was that he had a friend here and that if she saw a uniform, she'd freak out."

He started to swear, long and hard.

"Stop," Lena said. "Whoever it is, it's not because she's had trouble with the law. He's not a pushover. If whoever it was had legal trouble, they'd just have to deal with it— Law wouldn't be dragging me out of bed over something like that."

She pushed her hair back from her face and sighed.

"You're right, you know. Law does have a decent understanding of how things in law enforcement work—he really does. He wouldn't have asked this if it wasn't important."

Ezra's only response was an irritated grunt.

Resting her hand on his arm, she said, "Come on. Let's go talk to this friend of his."

Law couldn't have timed his call to the police more perfectly. Lena had just knocked on the door when they heard the first wail of sirens.

She heard footsteps, but they froze, as though the woman inside had heard the sirens, too. "Hope . . . ? Hope, my name's Lena. Law called me, asked me to come over. He figured you'd want somebody else here . . ."

The door cracked open.

Lena stood there waiting, Puck at her side, Ezra at her back.

"Law called the police." A soft, thready voice came from inside the house.

God. There was so much terror in that voice, Lena thought. Four words . . . and there was more fear in those four words than Lena thought she'd ever heard in her entire life, more fear than Lena had ever felt in her entire life.

What had been done to this girl to make her so scared of cops?

"Yeah. He was worried about you . . . said you saw somebody moving around outside. He wants to make sure you're safe."

Hope gave a strained, tight laugh. "Safe."

The door inched open just a tad bit wider. Reaching up a hand, Lena rested it on the door. Then she turned her face to Ezra. "Maybe you could wait out here a little bit . . . give me a minute?"

Ezra sighed. "Yeah." He caught her arm, tugged her close. Dipping his head, he murmured softly into her ear,

"It's not going to help much, though. They'll have to talk to her. And Law wasn't wrong. She's so damned scared, she looks like she's about ready to go through the roof if somebody even looks at her wrong."

The last damn person Ezra wanted to see climb out of that county car was Earl Prather.

As it slowed to a stop, Ezra closed his eyes, muttering under his breath, "Please not him. Please. I'll be good. I'll go to church and sit right next to Miss Lucy. I'll put fifty—no, a hundred bucks in the offering plate next Sunday. I swear."

As Prather climbed out, Ezra shot a dirty look up at the sky. "Not much for deal-making, huh?"

But he wiped the disgust off his face and by the time Prather drew even with him, he had his legs stretched out in front of him and his hands folded on his belly. All he needed was a bottle of beer and he couldn't have looked more relaxed. Sometimes, as much as he hated to admit it, appearances were everything.

"Nice night, huh, Deputy?"

Prather gave him a look of acute dislike. "What are you doing here?"

"Lena got a call, was asked to come over. As she can't exactly drive over, I gave her a lift."

"You just happened to be handy?" Prather asked, narrowing his eyes.

Ezra gave him a slow smile. "Well, I won't go into detail about that. My mama raised me right, you know, and she'd have my hide if I was talking about a lady that way."

"Humph. So why in the hell did Reilly call Lena and nine-one-one in the middle of the night?"

"Hey, I'm not the cop here." He shrugged and played dumb. "On leave, remember? Plus, I'm out of my jurisdiction. I'm just playing chauffeur tonight. I heard somebody was nosing around the back, though." He arched his brows and said, "Hey, maybe he's still back there . . . hiding. You could catch him and bring him in."

As Prather waddled away, Ezra rolled his eyes and stood up. *Idiot.* Then he slipped inside the house. He hated like hell that he was going to have to scare the pretty girl inside the house, but she was going to have to talk to Prather and maybe, just maybe, he could prepare her for that a little bit better.

He hoped.

He had cop eyes.

That was the first thing Hope noticed as he came into the room, limping just a little.

The second thing she noticed was the way he lingered by the pretty redhead and stroked a hand down her hair, rested a hand on her shoulder. Lena reached up and covered his hand with hers.

Something about that simple, sweet gesture made Hope's throat ache.

She remembered that kind of touch from her childhood— her mother and father had shared them, all the time. God, what would they think if they could see how things had turned out for her? If they hadn't died in that car wreck?

Shame, slippery and tight, washed through her and she looked away.

It wasn't just shame, though. Envy curled through her and that left her feeling more than a little dismayed. After Joey, she hadn't thought she'd be able to see those casual little touches between a man and a woman and feel even the slightest bit jealous, but here she was.

Although the thought of a light, gentle touch was enough to make her break out in a light sweat, she found herself wondering what it would be like to have somebody touch her like that . . . just because. That "I'm touching you because I can't not touch you" sort of touch. The way her parents had touched each other.

Joey had liked to touch her in public. A lot. But it had been a possessive thing—as in, she was another one of his possessions. He'd liked to touch her that way. He'd liked to . . .

No. No. No. *No.*

You're not there anymore, she reminded herself.

She focused on her reflection in the mirror and reminded herself where she was . . . and where she wasn't.

Then she turned around and looked at the cop, made herself look at him and that was when she noticed something else about him. As he took a seat a few feet away from her, she saw that while he had cop eyes, there was also kindness in them.

Joey's eyes hadn't ever really been kind. He'd used to hide behind a beguiling veneer of charm and affability, but kindness? No. He didn't have it in him. It had taken her years to realize that, though.

"Hey." The cop smiled at her and it was the same slow, gentle smile one would use with a scared child, a stray dog.

Hope hated that she felt about as likely to bolt as a nervous, scared stray. Although it felt like her face might crack, she gave him a nervous smile in return. "Hi."

"You look like you're having one hell of a night. I'm Ezra . . . Ezra King. A friend of Lena's, a friend of Law's. And you're Hope, right? You okay there, Hope?"

Hope shrugged, a jerky, restless shrug. Her head was pounding, aching, and her shoulders were so tight, so tense, one wrong move felt like it would cause her to shatter.

"Seeing somebody out there where they shouldn't be—that's going to give anybody a bad turn." He took a deep breath and then said, "The county sheriff's office sent a deputy out. He's taking a look out back, but he'll have to talk to you. Just tell him what you saw—it will take a few minutes, then you're done. Lena can stay in here with you, if you want."

Hope swallowed. Her throat was so dry, that simple action hurt.

"Yes. Please. If you don't mind, Lena." She hated having to ask that of a total stranger, but oh, hell, if she had to be alone with a sheriff's deputy—even the thought of it was enough to make her hands start to sweat.

Lena smiled. "Nah, I don't mind. Trust me, you aren't getting me out of this house until you get me some coffee . . ." The dog at her side sat up, his head cocked.

Hope watched as his owner leaned forward, rested a hand on his head. "What is it, pal?" she murmured, stroking his head.

The dog just sat there, watchful. Alert. Listening.

Looking away from the dog, trying not to think about the county deputy wandering around outside, Hope said, "So, um. Coffee. I can make coffee. It's never any good, though. Want me to try anyway?"

The man stood up. Slowly, she noticed. Like he was trying to do his best not to freak her out.

It was nice of him, she knew. But she was so freaked out already, it didn't matter. "How about we all go in the kitchen? You can show me where the coffee is and I can take care of it. I'm an old hand at coffee."

"Oh. Okay. Maybe I can find where Law keeps his doughnuts stashed."

A grin slashed across his face.

And Lena chuckled.

"Cops and doughnuts," she murmured. "Tell me, Detective . . . there any truth to those myths?"

He sighed and patted his flat belly with a lean hand. "Me and doughnuts have this love-hate relationship, just like lots of other cops and lots of other doughnuts. It's a personal thing."

She could smile, Hope realized.

Five feet away from a cop, even though he wasn't wearing a uniform or flashing a badge at her, there was no mistaking it—he was definitely a cop. But he didn't make her want to run screaming. And she could sit there and smile.

It was a start, right?

Less than a minute later, the lighter atmosphere shattered as they heard the wail of other sirens.

Followed by more.

When there was a loud, booming knock on the door just a few seconds later, the pit of her stomach crashed to her knees. Her heart jumped to lodge in her throat, and dread crawled along her spine as Ezra moved to open the door.

Even if she didn't know something about how law enforcement worked, Hope would have realized something was wrong just by the way Ezra's eyes darkened, the way his mouth went tight.

Prather might be a lousy cop, but he was still a cop, and Ezra knew by the look in his eyes there was something seriously wrong, and unless the idiot was even more of a clown than he had thought, then it was bad wrong.

"What's the problem, Prather?" Ezra said, using his body to block the door when Prather might have tried to push his way inside.

Three cars came pulling up behind him and out of one of them came Sheriff Dwight Nielson. He made a bee-line for the porch, but Prather was already in Ezra's face, and judging by the glint of battle in Prather's eyes, the boy was gunning for blood.

"Where in the hell is Reilly?"

"A little unavailable," Ezra said, keeping his voice mild. Until he knew what exactly was going on, there was no need to share more than that.

"Deputy, you need to step back," Nielson said.

Prather all but vibrated, all but shook as he turned to stare at Nielson. "I always told you that man had something wrong with him—something seriously fucked up, and I was right. We need to—"

"Right now," Nielson said, his voice low, cold, and all the more effective for it. "It would seem we have a crime scene that needs to be processed, so instead of getting in this man's face, maybe we should take care of that."

Ezra didn't look away from Prather.

But his question was directed at the sheriff. Nielson was the only one, so far, who'd showed any appreciable amount of common sense.

"Crime scene?"

"You're on leave, city boy, remember?" Prather jeered.

"Prather, you're about to find yourself on leave—unpaid—if you don't shut the flying fuck up," Nielson said. His gaze cut to Ezra's and he said, "You're welcome to come along, but remember . . . you have no authority here."

No authority—Ezra had no problem with that. Hell, he didn't want any authority.

He shut the door behind him and followed the sheriff out behind the house. Hell, knowing Prather, it was nothing more than . . .

Death.

Even from out here, he could smell it.

Remembering the eerie way Puck had been staring off into the woods earlier, he was suddenly damned glad of the solid, heavy weight of his gun.

Law grabbed the phone off the bedside table and punched in Lena's cell phone. Damn it, if she didn't answer this time, he was going to wring her neck.

Halfway through the second ring, she answered.

"You're an impatient bastard, buddy, you know that?" she said in lieu of greeting.

"What in the hell is going on?"

"Don't know yet," Lena said, sighing. "County sheriff has men out here and Ezra is out there with them, but that's all I know right now."

Hope was quiet, hadn't said a word since Prather had all but knocked the door off its hinges. Lena wished there was something she could say to calm her down, but she didn't know what would do it. Hell, she wasn't exactly calm. She'd been doing okay up until Ezra had slipped outside, but now . . .

He'd been too quiet.

Something about that silence . . . Shit. Lena wouldn't have minded being able to see just then—being able to see his face, look into his eyes. Have something else to go on besides that odd tension in the air, the fury she'd heard in Prather's voice.

"Hope's okay, right?"

"Yes. Scared. But she's fine. Nobody has been inside the house," Lena said. "You want to talk to her?"

"Yeah. Put her on."

Lena held the phone out and gave the other woman a smile. "It's Law."

The brief conversation did nothing to soothe Law's edgy tension, and he was up, prowling the room after he'd hung up. He wouldn't sleep, he already knew. He wouldn't sleep and he needed to be on the phone, booking a flight back home. But he didn't want to tie up the phone. Not until he knew what was going on.

Shit, why had he left Hope there alone?

Joey—fuck. Had he tracked her down?

The bastard had said he wasn't going to let her go. Had he tracked her to Law's place?

*   *   *

"What's going on?" Hope asked, her voice shaking, so nervous and small. "Why are there so many cars? What's with the van?"

Lena sighed. She felt utterly useless. Pushing upright, she gripped Puck's harness and followed the sound of Hope's breathing. She was pretty sure Hope was over by the window—she breathed in soft, erratic stops and starts, almost like she had to remind herself to breathe.

"I don't know," Lena said, once she stood next to her. Resting a hand lightly on the other woman's shoulder, she squeezed gently. "But don't worry. I won't be going anywhere. Law and I have a mutual dislike of that idiot, Prather, so as long as he's on Law's property, I'm not leaving."

There was a brief pause, and then quietly, Hope said, "The guy is a jerk."

"Yep. He thinks that badge makes him something special."

"A lot of them do." There was an undercurrent of resentment, of anger in her voice. And fear—so much fear. "Think it makes them untouchable."

"Nobody is untouchable." She squeezed Hope's shoulder once more and let her hand fall away. "I might not be able to see, but I get the feeling Ezra was about to put the guy on his back for a minute there. The vibes in the air? Talk about tension."

Hope shifted.

Nervousness had a sound. A habit of swallowing a lot, the restlessness of constant movement, as if stillness was just too hard. Hope's nervousness somehow conveyed a pain, a misery that managed to leach its way inside Lena's heart, and in such a short time. No wonder Law had been so worried. Lena barely knew more than this girl's name and she wanted to protect her.

"Why don't you tell me what you see? Maybe we can figure it out."

"Something's wrong," Hope said softly. "And it's more than just me seeing somebody running by Law's house." She hesitated and then softly, she added, "I . . . I think he might have been carrying something."

"Who? The guy you saw?"

"Yes."

Lena processed that, going cold inside. She was hearing sirens again, but this time they were all in her mind, wailing a warning. She was utterly freaked out. She hoped it didn't show on her face. "Carrying something . . . like what?"

"I don't know." Hope swallowed and then whispered, her voice hoarse, "Something big. Over his shoulder. Almost like a . . ."

She didn't finish the sentence, though. Almost like she feared doing it.

Like a body? Lena wondered as she found herself remembering a scream. A woman's desperate voice.

Being away from the job for a few months hadn't made it any easier, or any harder, to look at the violence one could do to the human body. She'd probably been pretty once, although under the bruising and swelling, it was hard to tell.

Ezra suspected she'd been raped, and probably more than once, judging by the bruising on her thighs and hips. Some of the bruises were almost healed, others were almost new.

She had scratches and scrapes on her body, especially her outer arms and legs—Ezra found himself frowning at those and wondering.

The sort of scrapes one might get in the woods, he wondered? Running through the woods? Maybe that was the cause of the banged-up condition of her knee, too. Those weren't the sort of injuries to happen in a beating—he wasn't a doctor, but he was pretty damn sure of that.

Standing off to the side, Ezra watched as Nielson directed his men in a calm, competent manner. The man had worked homicides before, there was no question of it.

Prather, though . . . Prather was proving to be one major, major pain-in-the-ass kind of problem.

"Fucking pervert—I always knew he was messed up," Prather muttered as one of the deputies had to leave the scene to go puke his guts up.

Prather looked a little green and his eyes glittered with anger, but unfortunately, he wasn't going to excuse himself from the scene.

Too fucking bad. "Always knew that Reilly was a sick sumbitch," he said. "Always knew it."

Running on too little sleep, his mind whirling with too many angles, Ezra opened his mouth when he shouldn't have. "Reilly didn't do this."

Prather's eyes narrowed. "You sound pretty damn sure of that."

"I am sure of it," Ezra said. Hell, he was allowed to have a personal opinion on that. He wasn't involved in it and this wasn't his jurisdiction. Besides, he also knew for a fact Law couldn't have done it.

"You're sure."

Behind him, Nielson opened his mouth, but Ezra caught his eye and gave a quick shake of his head. Nielson cocked a brow but remained silent.

"Yeah. I'm sure." He shoved away from the wall and moved toward the body, crouching down beside her. She'd been young—too young—and somebody had brutally, painfully cut off that life.

A few short hours ago, she'd been alive.

"Well, Mr. Big City Cop, let me spell something out for you, although you shoulda already figured this out, being so smart and all. This here is what we call a crime scene. We got us a dead body and as this is Reilly's home, he's going to be the prime suspect."

Ignoring Prather, he glanced at Nielson and asked, "You got a pair of gloves?"

Nielson, without comment, passed them over.

A humorless smile curled Ezra's lips as he studied the way the blood had pooled in the lowest points of her body. It was no surprise that when he touched the woman's body, she was still warm. Cooling, but warm.

Pity and anger churned inside him as he saw the bruises that also marred the girl's buttocks.

I hope they find who did this to you, sweetheart, Ezra thought sadly.

He didn't do anything else. This wasn't his case, this wasn't his jurisdiction, and he hadn't ever worked homicide. But he knew the basics. The woman hadn't been dead long. Law wasn't in town, hadn't been for a couple of days. Stripping off the gloves, he balled them in his fist and met Prather's gaze.

"You are an idiot," Ezra said shortly. "The biggest fuck-up excuse of a cop I've seen in a while, and I've seen some fuck-ups."

"You stupid son of a bitch—"

Dismissing Prather, Ezra looked at Nielson. "I imagine you've got all sorts of questions for Law Reilly, and if I were you, I'd have them, too. But you need to start rethinking those questions. Law Reilly has been out of town for three days. Nobody knew this but Lena, me, and the friend he has staying in his house.

"So," he said, shooting a thin smile at Prather. "Being a big city cop and all, let me tell you what you have here . . . it's definitely a murder. But it's a setup. And fifty bucks says she wasn't killed here."

Sometimes, once the shit started rolling, a guy just couldn't get out of the way fast enough.

This was one of those weeks, it seemed.

Law lowered the phone and stared at it stupidly for a

second, convinced this was some sort of prank call. Then he lifted it back to his ear.

"You need me to what?"

Lena sighed. "Hang up and call from wherever you're staying—not your cell phone, either. A land line," she said tiredly. "Call the number I gave you. I can't explain any more than that."

Can't. He heard the fury vibrating under her voice and he knew he needed to hang up and do just what she asked, but first . . . "Lena, just tell me Hope's okay."

"She's fine, Law. She's not hurt, I promise."

When he called the number Lena had given him, it was Sheriff Dwight Nielson who came on the phone, and he was about as informative as Lena had been. But the fact that he had a law-enforcement official on the phone was a bad, bad sign, one that had his blood turning to ice.

"Thanks for your cooperation, Mr. Reilly. I'm going to have to ask you to return home immediately. I realize this might be bad timing . . ."

"Bad timing," Law drawled as he sat down on the edge of the bed and then lay back, staring up at the shadowed ceiling. He was staying at Cassie's place—her husband, also a friend, had insisted. Law knew the poor old guy just didn't want to be alone yet, and he couldn't blame him. "I helped bury a friend today and you realize this might be bad timing."

"I'm sorry for your loss, but this is urgent."

Scowling, Law said, "Well, if it's so urgent, you can tell me what in the hell it's about. Otherwise, I don't see any reason I should cooperate."

Five seconds passed, then ten. Finally, Nielson said, "Evidence of a crime has been discovered on your property, Mr. Reilly. That's about all I can divulge at this time. You need to come home. Immediately."

*   *   *

It was hours later.

Dawn was nothing but a memory, and the need for sleep was weighing on all of them, but none of them could sleep.

Hope had come home with Lena—Lena had insisted, and Hope had been shell-shocked enough to agree.

"A body?" Hope whispered, her voice hoarse, almost broken. There was a look in her eyes, one that said she couldn't quite believe what Ezra had told her.

Lena sat silently on the couch next to Hope. Puck sat between Lena's legs, and she kept hugging the dog, stroking a hand down his back. Shaken . . . scared.

Ezra couldn't say he blamed her.

Especially since she'd already made the possible connection he'd made himself.

"Ezra, what if it's the woman I heard screaming that night?"

"There's no way we can know that," he murmured.

Not unless the killer up and confessed. But Ezra knew. He suspected Lena knew it, too.

Ezra had a feeling things were going to get worse.

This whole thing had been orchestrated to throw attention away from what Lena had heard, to focus it on an actual crime—with an actual victim, with the focus on an innocent man, one chosen with a specific purpose.

It wasn't any secret Lena was close to Law. Ezra suspected that was why he'd been targeted.

It was a pretty damn clear setup in Ezra's mind, although there was no telling if the guy had planned other shit. That thought made his gut tighten in dread. What else? What else might the killer be planning?

And what in the hell would he do once he figured out his little plan had just been blown to hell and back?

Any attempt to make it look like Law was the killer

would now pretty much fall flat—all because the killer hadn't realized Law was out of town.

"Is he always this quiet about stuff?" Ezra asked abruptly. "He takes off and only a couple of people know?"

Lena smiled tiredly. "Ezra, if it wasn't for the fact that he usually runs me into town on Wednesdays, I might not have known. Hope only knows because she was staying at his place, and you only know because you were with me when he called about leaving. Law is kind of . . . private."

"He would have checked, though," Ezra muttered. "He wouldn't have just dumped the body."

Hope paled and under her breath, she made a soft, broken little sound—almost a sob, but she cut it off before it could fully form.

Wincing, Ezra said, "Shit . . . uh, shoot. I'm sorry, Hope."

Her face wan, she said, "I was up late. I . . . I have trouble sleeping a lot and I was moving around. Maybe . . ." she swallowed. When she spoke again her voice trembled at first, and then slowly, it steadied, firmed. "Maybe whoever it was saw me moving and just figured it was Law."

Lena frowned. "They wouldn't have been looking very hard, then. There's no way anybody who can see is going to mistake Hope for Law."

"Well, if they look and expect to see Law . . ." Ezra shrugged. "He's not exactly Mr. Social, right? There weren't any extra cars parked in front of the house, right?"

Hope gave a wan smile. "I've got a car, but I parked in the garage. He's got room for a small fleet of cars in there."

"Law likes his toys," Lena murmured.

"So if nobody has reason to expect to see anybody but Law, then nobody is likely to look for anybody but Law,"

Ezra murmured. He rubbed his jaw and scowled at the stubble. Hell, he needed a shower. Needed to shave. Needed another five hours of sleep, and then, maybe a few dozen cups of coffee. Blowing out a breath, he looked at Hope.

No, there was no way somebody who had actually seen Hope would confuse her with Law. But if she hadn't been seen . . . he closed his eyes and pulled up a mental image of the house.

Lights blazing. Blinds drawn. All of them, from what he could tell, looking at the front of the house.

"When we pulled up in front of the house, the blinds were drawn," he said, flicking a glance at Hope.

She nodded. "Yes. I had a lot of lights on, but kept the blinds closed."

"If the blinds were drawn, how did you see the man moving?" Lena asked softly.

"I looked out." She rubbed her hands down her arms, staring off into the distance. "Law's house, well, I'm just not used to it. It's so big, and quiet. Worse at night. I was wandering around, in the TV room. The blinds on one of the windows . . . the slats weren't even." She grimaced. "I'm weird like that. I went to fix them and I felt . . . I don't know."

She licked her lips and then, her voice hushed, she murmured, "You know that expression, a ghost walked over your grave? Where something just feels really, really wrong? That's what I felt. I looked out the window, just peeked through the blinds and that's when I saw him."

"You're sure it was a man," Ezra said.

"Yes." Hope nodded and looked down at her hands. "He moved like a man. He was already close to the workshop, near the door. The top of his head was pretty close to being even with the top of the door—most women aren't that tall."

Ezra smiled at her. "You've got good eyes, Hope. You notice things."

Hope didn't say anything, just stared solemnly at him, her pale green eyes huge and scared. He gave her a reassuring smile. "It will be okay," he said quietly. "Law wasn't even in the state. He can't get in trouble for this."

She didn't look convinced.

Lena slid a hand along the surface of the couch until her fingers bumped Hope's leg. Gently, she patted the other woman's knee. "Relax. Law's going to be fine, okay?" Then she faced Ezra and gave him a breezy smile. "You know, this is kind of like my own personal version of *Law & Order,* or something." She waggled her eyebrows at him. "It's kinda sexy."

To his surprise, Ezra found himself blushing and it got worse when he saw Hope darting a curious glance between him and Lena. "Yeah, police procedure is sexy, all right," he mumbled, shoving up from the couch.

Behind him, Lena said to Hope, "I think I embarrassed him. Is he blushing?"

"Ah . . . yes. Um. I think he might be."

"Shit." Ezra scrubbed his hands over his face and shot Lena a dirty look. She might not be able to see it, but he'd bet his left nut she sensed it. She had an impish smile on her face, impish and unrepentant.

"So is he cute when he blushes, Hope?"

Now Hope was blushing and staring studiously at her hands, like they fascinated her. Chuckling despite himself, Ezra said, "Lena, now you're embarrassing her, too."

If the smirk on her face was anything to go by, that had probably been her intention—distracting the other woman.

"She's probably more embarrassed with you pointing it out," Lena said, grinning. "Why don't you go make us some coffee or something?"

It sounded like a dismissal, but in that moment, he

didn't mind. Caffeine was probably the last thing they needed on top of tired, addled brains, but he needed a few minutes to clear his head.

A few minutes to think.

And plan.

There was a woman dead now.

If it was the same woman Lena had heard a few days ago, then there was a problem.

Until a body was found, the only thing the sheriff's department really had was speculation, instinct . . . and the word of a woman who wasn't really known for making complaints.

It wasn't a lot, but it wasn't nothing either.

Now, there was a body.

But the body had been planted, and very deliberately planted.

If it had anything to do with what Lena had heard, then there were now a lot of problems for somebody in this small town.

The killer might not yet realize it, but his entire ploy had been shot straight to hell the second he decided to plant the woman on Law's property.

Straight to hell.

And he'd been seen.

Lena had heard the screams.

Hope had seen somebody.

If it was all connected, once word of that got out, those two women were very likely to be in a lot of danger.

CHAPTER
FIFTEEN

"NOBODY, AND I MEAN NOBODY IS TO BREATHE A word of this to anybody," Nielson said, pausing to look each of his men in the eye. "Not your wives, not your priest, not your fishing buddy, nobody. Not even anybody else in the department. If the person wasn't on the scene last night, they are not to be told a damn thing . . . am I clear?"

There was a low murmur of assents. Prather sat at the table, staring stonily outside.

"Prather?"

The sullen eyes that lifted to his had Nielson biting back a snarl. "I heard you well enough."

"Anybody talks about this, I'll find out. Until we figure out just what is going on, we keep this quiet."

"I know what's going on. A woman's dead and she was found on Reilly's land. He had to have something to do with it," Prather snapped.

"And if he did, we'll figure it out. But for now . . . nobody talks. Now all of you go, get some sleep." It was Saturday and most of them weren't even supposed to be on duty today. Nielson wouldn't be sleeping anytime soon. He'd gotten a message from Reilly—the man would be arriving in Lexington in two hours and Nielson would be meeting him.

He wasn't going to have any more fuckups happen on this.

Law had seen dead bodies—in person, not viewed on a computer, pictures, but actually in person. Twice. He'd even been to an autopsy—once. It wasn't an experience he ever wanted to repeat. Ever.

But he'd rather look at those bodies in the flesh than at the digital stills of what had been done to this woman.

Bile churned in his throat, threatened to boil up, choke him, explode out of him as he reached up and touched the tip of one finger to one particular image.

She had a butterfly tattoo on the back of her right shoulder. It was a pretty, flighty little thing . . . so lively, so full of life. For some reason, seeing it on her lifeless body made his throat ache.

"You ever seen her before?"

Swallowing around the knot, Law said gruffly, "I don't think so."

It was hard to be sure, though. Her face was so battered, so bruised and broken. "Shit, what kind of person does it take to do this to another?" he muttered, more to himself than the sheriff.

"That's what I plan to find out." Nielson's voice held no emotion, but when Law glanced up, for just a second, there was a flicker in the other man's eyes. "So, you don't know her?"

"I can't be sure, but I don't think I know her. It's hard to say, though. Whoever did this, he beat the hell out of her."

Looking up, he said quietly, "Do you know who she is?"

"We're looking into that," Nielson said. He placed

another photo before Law. "What about this . . . you recognize it?"

Law scowled and cocked his head. "Yeah. That's my workshop."

"Your workshop?"

"Yeah." He grimaced. "I had this idea I was going to start fiddling around with woodwork or something. I dunno. I had a building off the main house—was mostly just used as a shed type of thing. Kept pool chemicals in there, lawn mower, that sort of junk. Converted half of it to a workshop but never really got around to using it much."

"Why not? It looks like you invested some money in it."

He had. But then he got bored with the idea. Plus, it had aggravated his wrists. Rotating his right wrist absently, he glanced up and said, "I ended up not liking it as much as I thought. Yeah, I invested the money, but I wasn't thrilled with it once I started messing with it. So I stopped. I do that a lot."

He looked back at the picture of his woodshop, a muscle twitching in his jaw. "You found her in there, didn't you?"

Long, long moments passed before Nielson finally admitted, "Yes. Yes, she was found there."

God. Law closed his eyes and leaned forward, resting his head in his hands. Hope. He'd left Hope there. Alone. She was already so battered . . .

"Was she killed there?" he asked gruffly.

"I can't tell you that."

Law's temper snapped. Swiping out with his arm, he sent the pictures flying across the room. "Don't give me that shit," he snarled, surging to his feet and driving his hands down on the table. "I left one of my best friends in that house—alone—and a woman turns up dead a few hundred feet away from her. Did somebody kill that woman on my property?"

"Do you have reason to think Ms. Carson might be in danger?" Nielson asked mildly.

"Oh, fuck yeah, do I have reason. But you didn't answer me. Was she killed in my workshop?"

Nielson opened his mouth and then abruptly he stopped, sighed. "Okay, let's try it this way. I can't give you all the answers you want . . . Ed O'Reilly."

Law blinked. Then he slumped in the chair and rubbed his hands over his eyes.

Nielson chuckled. "Relax. I don't plan on plastering it on the front page of the *Daily*. Although it would make great copy, I imagine. But I've known what you do for a few years and I haven't mentioned it yet. Don't see any point why that needs to change now."

"A few years?" Law repeated, narrowing his eyes.

"I like knowing what's going on around my town," Nielson said, simply. "So here's the deal. You're an imaginative guy, a smart one, and you know a bit more about typical police procedure than the average Joe. You understand I can't tell you everything—you know that. And you also know the more information I have, the quicker I can figure out what's going on. So . . . if you'll tell me what you can, I'll answer what I can."

"I'm not answering jackshit unless you tell me whether she was killed on my property," Law said. He had to know. Had to—hell, he was going to raze that workshop to the ground anyway. But if some psycho had killed a woman in there . . . fuck, how could he tell Hope? He'd brought her here so she could feel safer . . . start to heal.

"Okay." Nielson's eyes held his. "You understand nothing I tell you leaves this room. I know you're good friends with Lena Riddle, and you're probably on a friendly basis with Ezra King. But you tell nobody."

"I need to know . . . for me," Law snapped. "Besides, King was out there. I bet he probably has an idea whether she was killed there or not, and if you don't give me an answer, I'll go ask him, and I just might do it in public where anybody can hear. He's not too fond of at least one of your boys, Sheriff. Chances are, if I play it right, I can ask in front of Prather and I can do it in a way that Ezra will answer me just to piss Prather off . . . and you know it."

"You can be a prick," Nielson said. Then he sighed. "No. I don't think she was killed there. I can't be sure, but my gut says she was killed elsewhere, then placed there."

It made it a little easier to think about going back to the home he loved. A little.

Not a lot.

Hope stroked a hand down Puck's back, taking comfort in the warm, solid feel of him. He didn't seem to mind her touch, but she didn't think he was overly thrilled with it either.

It was weird the way he changed after Lena had put his harness on. He'd scampered and played around the house like any normal dog, although he'd stayed very, very close to his mistress, but the minute that harness went on, the dog was all business.

Something drifted through her mind and she said abruptly, "I'm not supposed to be petting him, am I?"

Lena smiled at Hope over her shoulder. "Normally . . . I'd say no." A stern look crossed her face and she said, "And he knows it, too. When he's got the leash on, he's working. But the three of, hell, the four of us—Puck included—have had a shitty twenty-four hours. Just don't do it outside the car. He likes to test things, especially in new environments, around new people. Just to see how much he can get away with."

Hope pulled her hand back into her lap, and Puck shifted his big, brown eyes in her direction, giving her a sad doggy stare. Maybe he liked the petting more than she'd realized. Still, if she wasn't supposed to be petting him, she wasn't going to. "Don't give me that look," she said, keeping her voice low. "You're on the clock."

In the front seat, Ezra smiled a little. She was more at ease around the dog than anybody else, he'd noticed.

"Think Law's done with Nielson yet?" Lena asked softly.

He shrugged. "Probably. Nielson doesn't think he did it—this is just procedure, but he's got to cover all the bases anyway." He hesitated for a minute and then said, "I want to have something to eat in town."

Lena grimaced and touched a hand to her belly. "Ezra, I can't eat. I can't."

"I'm not hungry," Hope said.

Ezra glanced at her in the rearview mirror and she looked away. "But I don't mind drinking some coffee or something."

He focused on the road and said, "I'm not hungry, either. But I still want us to sit down somewhere with Law. Someplace public."

Something in his voice must have caught Lena's attention.

"Why?" she asked.

She had her shaded lenses on and he couldn't very well study her face while he was driving, but he didn't have to see her face to know she was probably looking at him with suspicion in her eyes. Smiling a little, he shrugged.

"I know small-town semantics. Whoever did this is probably just waiting around to see what happens. And that somebody is probably going to be shocked as hell when Law walks out of that sheriff's station, free and clear."

Lena nibbled on her lower lip.

"Won't it be hard to tell if anybody is paying special attention?" Hope asked, her voice nervous and soft. "I mean, this is Small Town, USA, and Law . . . well, this is going to sound weird, but I get the feeling that the people around here seem to think Law is half off his rocker anyway. And a dead girl was found at his place—everybody is going to be looking at him."

A grim smile curled Ezra's mouth. "I don't think everybody knows a dead girl was found at his place. Matter of fact, I know not everybody knows. Nielson was keeping that very, very quiet until he'd talked to Law. The cat will probably be out of the bag by later today, but for now . . ."

There was silence for a few minutes, nothing but the sound of the car speeding along the winding country road. Then Lena broke the silence. "A lot of the people around here do think Law is a little weird—some people think he's into drugs, and there are a hundred stories to explain how he has the money to afford the place he built, even though he never leaves it for 'work.' He has a solid alibi, right? But still, there are going to be people grumbling." She leaned her head against the back of the seat and sighed. "Poor Law."

"Nobody who knows him could really think he'd kill somebody," Hope said.

For once, that uncertainty wasn't in her voice. There was a thin, unyielding layer of strength there that brought a faint smile to Ezra's lips. He could tell by looking at her she'd been through hell. But she hadn't broken—and if what brought that steel to her voice was the defense of a friend? He had to admire that.

"Plenty of people here don't know Law." Lena grimaced. "He prefers it that way. Hell, some of the rumors amuse him—I bet he probably feeds half of them, even though he denies it when I ask him about it."

"The rumors that come out of this won't amuse him," Ezra said.

"No. You're right." Her scowl darkened, anger bringing a flush to her face. "I'm damn well not amused right now."

He reached out and caught her hand, twining his fingers with hers. As they finished the drive into town, she stroked her thumb along the back of his hand.

They were in one hell of a mess, he knew. And everything in him was on edge, alert. It was somehow connected to Lena.

Nothing would happen to her.

Nothing could.

Amazing how somebody he'd known such a short time could already be so necessary to his life.

Friends . . .

He smiled a little.

Hell, what had he been thinking?

SIXTEEN

LAW REILLY WASN'T UNDER ARREST.

How in the fuck had this happened?

Not under arrest.

A woman's body found on his property. Turning away from the municipal building, he started to walk. Couldn't linger. Couldn't have anybody notice him acting weird.

Well, weirder than normal.

He took a few minutes to duck inside the bookstore, picking up a cup of coffee, a few books he'd ordered in. On the inside, he twitched with nerves, but on the outside, he was calm, collected, carrying on a conversation with Ang as he perused the shelves.

She was a fount of information. Not a gossip like some, but she knew things. Heard things.

As he picked up a paperback, she glanced across the street and said, "Something weird is going on."

"Huh?" Giving her a vaguely confused look, he glanced up.

"I'm not sure what, but Nielson doesn't go in on Saturdays unless there's something major and there are more deputies hanging around than normal." She pursed her lips and shook her head. "Something weird."

"Hmmm."

Weird was right. So far, he hadn't heard a damn thing about his girl or Reilly. Somebody should be talking. People talked in a small town and they talked a lot. This sort of thing should have people talking up a virtual storm.

But nobody was. It was like nothing had happened—like nobody knew a damn thing.

Almost like she hadn't been discovered.

He wasn't stupid enough to have lingered—he knew better than that. But they did know—the police had discovered the body. For some reason, they were just keeping it quiet.

Keeping a lot of things quiet.

Disgusted, he thought about all the trouble he'd gone to, all the plans he'd made.

All for nothing.

Law Reilly was walking around a free man.

Pretending to read, he watched as Law headed across the street. An unfamiliar dove-gray car, fancy as hell, pulled into a parking spot just a little down from the bookstore and he watched as the doors opened. He didn't recognize the car, but he recognized the gleaming, dark red of Lena's hair just fine.

And the cop.

There was a woman with them—unknown . . . no. He did know her. Or at least he'd seen her.

The little mouse from the other day, her long hair pulled into a ponytail. She wore a T-shirt that swallowed her skinny body and worn, faded jeans. She was the last one out of the car, but the first one to reach Law Reilly, running toward him and as she drew near, the man's arms opened to enfold her.

So. The little mouse wasn't just passing through town?

Law pressed his lips to Hope's forehead and then raised his head and stared into her pale green eyes. She opened her mouth and he snapped, "If you say you're sorry one more time, I'm going to get mad."

"I'm so . . . um. Okay."

"Hope, it's not your fault, none of this. So quit apologizing." He tugged on her ponytail, like he had done a thousand times in their youth.

"I feel like I'm just supposed to say something," she mumbled.

He sighed. "Yeah. But there's not much to say." He glanced up, looked from Lena to Ezra. "Thank you."

"Under normal circumstances, I'd tell you I'd deck you if you ever drag me out of bed at one A.M. again, but these are pretty abnormal circumstances," Ezra said, his smile humorless. Then he glanced at Hope. Although nothing showed in his eyes, Law could tell—the cop got it. He understood. "Besides, you had good reason."

Lena reached out a hand and out of habit, Law caught it. She squeezed his fingers and said, "Was he able to tell you anything?"

"Yeah, just a little bit more than nothing." He wanted to go home. Shower. He felt dirty, inside and out. "Can we get out of here?"

"Well . . ." Lena licked her lips and turned her face to Ezra's.

"I want to hang around town awhile."

Seeing the way Law's face tightened, Ezra lifted a hand. Then he dipped his head and murmured in Lena's ear, "Can you give me a minute? I need to talk to Law without Hope. I don't want to freak her out any more than she already is."

"Hmm." She turned her face to his, touched her lips to his. "I'll buy that. But you better not be doing this out of some weird desire to coddle me."

Ezra chuckled. "If I tried to coddle you, I think you might decide to shave me bald while I slept."

"Oh, now there's an idea." She smoothed a hand up his neck and then pushed her fingers through his hair. "I don't think I'd do a tidy job, either.

"Hope, why don't we head down to the Grapevine? It's a little coffee and dessert café on the other side of the square. I don't want much in the way of food, but I could use an iced latte or something."

As they walked off, Ezra jerked his head toward Law and they started to walk as well, following the same path as the women, but slower. "Nobody knows what happened at your place yet," he said, keeping his voice low. He slid a pair of sunglasses down over his eyes, even though the day was overcast. "Nielson didn't want anybody knowing until he'd spoken with you—especially since it looked like it was done to frame you—and a shitty frame, I've gotta say. So nobody but the sheriff, his boys, and us know."

"And the man who killed her," Law said, his voice harsh.

"Yes. And chances are, that guy is expecting to hear that you're in jail. He's probably expecting to hear all sorts of wailing, gnashing of teeth, wringing of hands."

"You can't hear people wringing their hands." Law kicked at a pebble on the ground, watched as it skipped along the surface.

"You get the point. He's expecting certain reactions . . . and I bet anything he's here waiting. Just waiting and watching."

Law slid Ezra a sidelong glance. "And you want to parade me around like a monkey in a tuxedo, see if you can see who's watching?"

"You're a quick study." He went to say something else, but a kid crashed into him—a surly kid with angry eyes, a cigarette jutting out of his mouth, and all sorts of attitude hanging from him.

Without bothering to apologize, the kid shoved off Ezra and turned to glare over his shoulder. "I said no fucking way."

Ezra glanced up and found the object of the kid's ire.

It was the lawyer from the sheriff's office.

Jennings. Remy Jennings—Lena's ex-boyfriend.

"And I said, yes, fucking way, Brody, and as luck would have it . . ." Remy gave Ezra a narrow glance. "Ezra King, correct?"

"Yeah, but I'm a little busy."

"This won't take much time." A thin smile curled his lips. "This boy is Brody—I believe he did some damage to your property a couple weeks ago. I meant to drag his sorry butt over there to help with the cleanup, but I've had my hands full with a case. It's probably a little bit late, but have you already finished cleaning up the mess he made?"

"Actually, no. Haven't even started." Ezra crossed his hands over his chest, studying the sullen boy's face, although he made sure he could still see Lena and Hope. Law was doing the same thing, he noticed. Watching the women.

Glancing back at Brody, he asked, "How old are you, kid?"

"Fourteen."

"Huh." Shooting out a hand, he plucked the cigarette from Brody's mouth and dropped it on the ground, grinding it under his foot before the boy had even processed what he'd done. "You're underage."

"You fucking asshole!"

"Yeah." Looking back at Remy, he waited.

"Brody's going to come help with the cleanup—"

"No, I ain't."

"Because if he doesn't, I'm going to make sure that complaint gets drawn up, I'll make sure it gets signed, and I'll personally deliver it to my brother," Remy said, continuing on as if Brody hadn't spoken.

Aggravated and only listening with half an ear, Ezra tracked Lena and Hope's progress around the square. Behind the shield of his sunglasses, he was able to watch, without looking like he was watching—a skill picked up during years on the force.

"Will that work?"

Ezra glanced at the skinny kid, let his brain catch up with the conversation. "Right now, my hands are a little too full to worry about dealing with the damage he did."

"I understand that easy enough. However, he either needs to pay for the damage or fix it himself." Remy cocked a brow. "Personally, I think it would do him a world of good to fix it himself."

Personally speaking, Ezra agreed with the lawyer. But he didn't have time to deal with a pissed-off teenager— even if the kid was going through a bad spot.

The skin along the back of his spine started to crawl and he shifted his glance, focused his eyes once more on Lena and Hope.

They'd stopped dead on the sidewalk. Puck was standing stiff-legged next to Lena, and although it was too far away to be sure, it looked like the dog's hackles were up.

A chill went down Ezra's spine.

The dog was protective, but well-behaved. Protective as hell, but he was an easygoing companion. He had to be.

He watched as Lena tugged on the dog's leash, but Puck wouldn't budge.

"Law."

"Yeah. I see it."

"You ever see him do that?"

"No."

Remy glanced behind, his eyes following the direction of their gaze, curious. The lawyer was sharp, pinpointed what they were looking at too damn quickly. But Ezra didn't wait long enough for him to ask any questions. Glancing at the kid, then at Remy, he said, "Once I'm ready to get to work on the yard, I'll try to remember to call. But he'll work and when I say work, I mean he'll work his sorry butt into the ground."

Then he and Law started forward.

Puck's body was all but vibrating under her hand. He was growling, too, a low, warning growl that would have terrified her if she had been on the receiving end of that growl.

"We need to head back to the guys," Lena said softly, trying not to let her unease show in her voice. Squeezing Hope's arm, she started to turn around, even though she had a bad, bad feeling about giving her back to anybody. She wasn't going to keep standing there, either.

A target—

Shit. That's what she felt like.

A damn target.

Lena didn't do vulnerable. She'd worked too damned hard to build a life—on her own—and she was proud of the fact that she'd done just that. Vulnerable implied a weakness.

But just then? She felt vulnerable, like a rabbit out in an exposed field, just waiting for a hawk to swoop down.

Eyes . . . she could almost feel them crawling all over her.

"What's wrong?" Hope asked, her voice quiet, just the slightest bit shaky.

"Puck." Now that they were moving away, the dog was willing to move. But for a few minutes there, he hadn't been willing to go forward, and he hadn't let her move, either. His body had stiffened and he had stood there, growling in his throat, a low, threatening growl.

It wasn't directed at her—she knew that.

He'd seen something . . . someone.

"Come on, boy," she said, guiding him around as they started down the street. He came along easily, his big body a solid weight at her side, pressing close as though to remind her he wasn't about to let her change her mind—or her direction.

"What's wrong with him?"

Lena turned her face toward Hope, unsure what to say. She licked her lips and finally just murmured, "I'm not really sure."

She could still feel it, the weight of somebody's gaze drilling into her back.

"Something, or somebody, back there bothers him. He doesn't want me near whatever, whoever it was." She felt Hope's intention and she tightened her grip. "Don't look back. Whoever it is. Don't look back. There's a good chance they won't pay much attention to me," *liar*, "or Puck, but don't let anybody see you looking for them."

She lied. She knew she lied. Whoever had been watching her was paying way too much attention to her.

But that person wouldn't see her as a threat. It wasn't like Lena could pick somebody out of a lineup. No, he might be watching Lena with burning interest, but he also would have seen Hope and if he thought Hope might have seen him . . .

"Shit," she whispered. Her stomach was jumping, knotting with fear.

What in the hell was going on?

She heard Hope swallow, heard the unsteadiness in the other woman's voice as she said, "I see Law and Ezra. They are heading our way—fast. Law looks pissed. Ezra . . . he, uh . . . he's got his cop face on."

"Then he's pissed, too." Lena didn't even have to see him to know that.

Odd, how she could so easily peg him, how well she already knew him.

The men were in front of them twenty seconds later. She all but felt the force of Ezra's personality beating at her, the heat of him, his concern . . . everything that made him who he was. His hands cupped her face, arched it up to meet his.

To all the world, it might have looked like a lover's kiss . . . and it was.

But nobody other than Hope or Law could have heard his softly whispered, "What's wrong?"

Lena rubbed her lips against his. "I don't know. Puck . . . he just all of a sudden stopped. He was growling. I reached down to touch him and his hackles were all up. He doesn't act like that, Ezra. Ever."

"Actually, he sort of did." He stroked his thumb over her cheek and then slid his hands down to her shoulders, rubbing at them restlessly. "That night at Law's. Remember how he acted? He didn't want to get out of the car. He kept staring into the trees."

"Like somebody was there . . . or had been," she murmured. She swallowed, her stomach crashing to her feet. And somebody had been there . . . long enough to leave a woman's lifeless body behind.

"This was worse, though," Ezra said.

"Yeah." Crouching down by Puck, she stroked a hand down his head, scratched him behind his ears. He whined low in his throat. "Shhh. It's okay, boy. It's okay. Maybe he saw him, or smelled him."

Law's voice was a low, threatening snarl. "Who?"

"The same guy he smelled that night." She rose. Her hands were shaking, she realized. Sweaty and shaking. She was afraid. It fucking pissed her off.

Law brushed past her. Reaching out, she caught his hand. "Where you going?"

"Just want to take a look around."

"And look for what? And how will you manage to do it without looking conspicuous?" Lowering his voice, Ezra said, "If there's a chance he's here, and you go looking around, you're doing it with a big fat warning sign on your forehead. Be smart. Okay?"

The last thing Law wanted was to be smart. Lena knew him too well. But in the end, he relented. She had to wonder how much of that had to do with her and Hope, though. If it was just him, she suspected he might prowl the town until he found something; no. Someone.

Resting a hand on her belly, Lena said, "Ezra, I know you want to sit around town for a while. And I'm sorry. But I really, really want to get out of here."

Hell. What she wanted was to go home, climb in her bed with Ezra next to her, cuddle up and just stay there.

But somehow, she knew that wasn't an option.

"You can't be serious, Uncle Remy," Brody snapped.

Remy wondered if the kid had realized that he had actually called him "uncle." It had been months, maybe even a year . . . longer since he had done that. Reaching up, he grabbed the pack of cigarettes from Brody's hand before the kid could shake one loose.

He shoved them in his pocket, crumpling the flimsy pack in his fist. "Yes, Brody, I am serious. Dead serious. And by the way, if you don't quit smoking, I'm getting serious about a couple of other things, too."

"Hell. You used to smoke when you were a kid. What the fuck is the problem?"

"Part of the problem? I'll tell you." Stepping closer to the teenaged boy—already so close to being a man, yet still just a kid—he reached up and caught the gold chain that peeked out from under the ragged neckline of the boy's black T-shirt.

It held a gold cross. It had belonged to Brody's mother. "Your mom just died of cancer, Brody. Her dad died of cancer. And here you are smoking. What are you trying to do, break your dad's heart?"

For about two seconds, the sweet kid Remy remembered seemed to stare back at him—sad, angry, young, and so vulnerable, but then he was gone. "Not like he gives a fuck anyway."

As the teen stalked off, Remy pulled the mangled pack of cigarettes out of his pocket and studied them. He'd quit smoking ten years ago. But there were times when he really craved it. Right now? One of those times.

Tossing the cigarettes into a nearby waste receptacle, Remy was about to head back to his car. He had plenty of work he had to get done. Plenty.

A familiar, dark red head of hair caught his eye and he found himself studying Lena's averted profile. Law Reilly and Ezra King were with her. So was another woman. She looked vaguely familiar. A breeze kicked up, whipping her long brown hair around her shoulders. That was all it took to trigger the memory.

The square. Prather. The bookstore.

Standing next to Lena's long, leggy form, she looked delicate. Delicate had never really done much of anything for Remy. So why was his mouth going dry?

She reached up and caught her hair in her hand, trapping it in a loose tail. Reilly edged closer, angling his head down to talk to the woman. There was something intimate between them—a connection, Remy realized.

Okay. Now his mouth was dry, and he was feeling oddly . . . jealous.

Scowling, he shoved his hands in his pockets and turned away. He didn't have time for this shit.

He had to be in court on Monday and there was way too much work to be done still.

Halfway to his car, he damn near collided with Dwight Nielson. The sheriff looked tired, distracted. Worried.

He looked like he had aged ten years overnight.

With a sinking sensation in his gut, Remy plastered a fake smile on his face. This better not be about Hamilton. Even as he thought it, logic tried to step in. *Can't be. You would have been called.*

Remy just couldn't think of too many things that would put that look on the sheriff's face, though. The man was pissed off, running on fumes and emotion. But if anything major had happened, Remy would have heard about it through the gossip grapevine. Hamilton was the only big thing going on right now.

"You look like you had a rough night."

Nielson glanced at him. The faint twitch of his lips didn't even pass for a smile. "Rough doesn't even describe it."

A car rumbled past and out of habit, when Nielson glanced at it, Remy did the same. He saw Lena and caught a glimpse of the dark hair of the mystery lady in the backseat.

Who was she?

Hooked up with Reilly somehow? *In for disappointment there, sweetheart. He's stuck on a woman who doesn't realize he's got a dick.*

Law Reilly wasn't ever going to stop mooning over Lena.

Shoving those thoughts aside, he looked back at Nielson, only to find the sheriff tracking the car's path with his eyes until it disappeared around the bend of the road. The dark look in the man's eyes suddenly had Remy's instincts swinging into full alert.

"So . . . what's going on?"

Nielson's gaze slanted his way. "Meaning . . . ?"

"Well, you look like shit. You're looking at Lena Riddle like she's a key witness." Remy angled his head and counted the patrol cars in front of the municipal building. "And I'd say you've called in every part-time deputy you can get your hands on."

Blowing out a sigh, Nielson slicked a hand back over his bald scalp.

"Shit. This is going to hit the fan in the next little while or so anyway."

SEVENTEEN

"WE CAN'T KEEP THIS UP. SOONER OR LATER, WE'RE *going to screw up.*"

The voices—*he should know those voices.*

"We got a good thing going here. One more big shipment, Mac. Then we're done. One more go-round."

A low, tired sigh, followed by a rough, husky chuckle. "Yeah, one more, my ass."

A storm of memories assaulted him as he stood in the shadows. Walking down the street, side by side with his partner.

"Come on, Mac. One more. We can hit one more."

"Yeah, one more, my ass, pretty boy. You're buying me dinner."

Mac. It was Mac.

The gun . . . where had his gun come from?

Ezra found himself staring at it, appalled.

What in the hell was he supposed to do with it?

But he knew. Looking up, he found himself face-to-face with Mac. Found himself watching—like it was a live feed or something—watching as he pulled the trigger.

There was a scream.

Blood—explosions of it. It painted the entire world

red as he watched, and screams, hers, his, echoed through the air. Ezra rushed to Mac's side, but then everything changed on him and it wasn't a city alley any longer.

It was the woods—night dark and thick with underbrush that grabbed at him, tripped him up. When he fell, he landed in a puddle of blood.

Her blood.

Lena's blood.

Lena's face shifted, re-formed . . . and it was the woman. The woman found at Law's, her battered, ruined face staring lifelessly up at the sky.

He dreamed, knew he dreamed, but he couldn't make himself wake up.

Even as the woman morphed from the dead woman to his lover to his partner, over and over in an unending circle, he was helpless, trapped, unable to stop it, unable to change it—

"Damn it, wake up!"

Breath ripping out of him in sobs, Ezra tore out of the dream and sat up, staring at the pale oval of Lena's face.

"Shit. Fuck."

A cold, nasty sweat drenched him, and he fought his way out of the blankets, stumbled over to the doorway, hit the light switch. Lena sat in the bed, staring in his direction, her sightless eyes huge and frightened. She had the sheet clutched between her bare breasts, her hand balled up into a fist.

"Are you okay?"

"Bad dream," he said, his voice rusty. He leaned against the wall, rubbing at the knotted muscles in his leg.

"Bad dream?" she echoed. She gave him a faint smile. "Ezra, when I dream about waking up naked in front of my high school English class while giving a report on women's rights, that is a bad dream. What you were having . . . I don't think bad dream describes it."

She held out a hand. "Come back to bed?"

He didn't want to. He was shaking, like a leaf, he realized, and half sick. But at the sight of her slender hand, reaching out to him . . . well, walking away was one thing he just couldn't do.

Swallowing against the tightness in his throat, he walked stiffly over to the bed and sank down on it. Lena shifted around and when he lay down, she guided his head to her lap. "Your leg is bothering you," she said quietly.

Ezra didn't answer. Mind over matter. Psychobabble shit. If he ignored the leg, didn't think about the dreams . . .

"Tell me what you were dreaming about," she said softly, combing a hand through his hair.

No.

That was the last thing he wanted to do.

No. No.

"Was it your partner? Mac?"

"Yeah," he whispered, his voice hoarse.

She stroked a hand down his arm. "I know you probably can't tell me. But if you ever need to . . . I'll listen," she murmured.

"I shouldn't tell you," he said. He really, really shouldn't.

But five seconds later, it started to rip out of him, a nasty, vile spew of poison. Like a river breaking free of a dam, he couldn't keep the words trapped inside him, not for another five seconds.

Lena was silent the entire time, doing nothing but listening and stroking those long, slender fingers through his hair. When he finally fell silent, her hand stilled and he caught hold of it, brought it to his lips.

"It's really no wonder you don't know if you want to go back," she mused. "Must be hell when you don't know if you can trust that the good guys really are the good guys, huh?"

"There's always going to be dirty cops," Ezra said roughly. "Always. But I . . . I never thought I'd be so easily suckered in. Shit. And if she . . ." A dull, hot flush crept up to stain his cheeks red as he said, "If it turns out the reason she was sleeping with me wasn't because of me, but because of what she was doing . . ."

"Then it has nothing to do with you, and everything to do with her," Lena said. "Ezra, she's the one who screwed up. She was dirty, and maybe she was using you, maybe she wasn't. But that doesn't change who you are."

"Maybe it does—shouldn't I have been able to see it? Shouldn't I have seen her?"

"I didn't know you then, but I'd say you were probably a pretty good cop. She was just a better actress. She was the one who messed things up, baby. You can't bear her sins."

"Can't I?" Rolling to his back, he stared up at the ceiling. "Maybe if I'd seen it sooner, maybe if I'd looked, we could have taken her down a better way, she'd still be alive."

"And if she hadn't pulled her gun on you, would you have shot her?"

"Hell, no."

"Okay, then." Lena bent down, curling her body in until she could press her lips to his. "Her sins, her flaws, her mistakes. Not yours, Ezra. Not yours."

She waited until some of the tension eased before she straightened up. Then she went back to combing her hand through the tumbled, shaggy strands of his hair. "You have these nightmares a lot?"

"Off and on." He shifted in the bed, pulling away, but before she could be disappointed, he settled down next to her, sitting side by side, echoing her position with his back braced against the headboard. "They usually don't get this bad anymore, though."

"I'm glad." She grabbed one of the blankets and drew it up, snuggling into his body, hoping the heat of her body might warm his. He felt so cold. His nightmare . . . she wasn't going to tell him, but it had just about broken her heart. He'd sounded . . . broken.

Ezra wrapped an arm around her shoulders. Tucking her head under his chin, she sighed.

"The girl at Law's . . . seeing her body, I think it screwed some things in my head up. Hell, even touching the gun. It's a problem for me—part of why I can't go back right now. I can't even think about picking up my gun without having . . . well . . . issues." He laughed, but there was no humor in the sound. It was dry, dark, and ugly. "Issues. Fuck."

"Ezra, everybody has issues from time to time." She caught his hand, lifted it to her lips. "Tell me about the dream."

"It's always been pretty much the same, but it was changing around on me this time. Kept changing from Mac to that girl . . . to you."

"Me?"

"Yeah." He wiped his hand over his mouth, wished he could do something about the knot of nausea that still gripped his gut.

Two seconds later, Lena was on her knees, straddling his lap. She had her fingers wrapped around his wrists, guiding them to her breasts. "Well, you can stop thinking about the dream, then. Think about me. I'm here and I'm fine," she said. "See?"

Resting his head on the headboard, he murmured, "You trying to distract me, Lena?"

"Yes."

"Hmm. I think it could work." Lowering his gaze to her chest, he stared at the way her flesh gleamed pale as ivory against his darker, rough hands. Her nipples were pink, stabbing into his fingers when he pinched them lightly.

As he slid a hand down her torso, she arched her back, a graceful bow.

Ezra's mouth went dry.

Pressing his lips to her torso, he rolled forward, pushing her to her back and sprawling between her thighs. "I want you," he whispered, kissing a hot, burning line down the length of her body. "Fuck, do I want you."

The dark red curls shielding her sex were already damp, already gleaming.

He parted her with his tongue and groaned against her. The taste of her exploded through him and he shifted, grabbing one of her knees and pushing it up, opening her folds wider. Then he pressed his mouth more firmly against her and thrust his tongue inside her.

Her strangled cry bounced off the walls.

She tangled her fingers in his hair, rocking against him, greedy and desperate, driving him on.

Whatever remnants of the dream might have lingered faded away as she came apart for him, crying out his name. When she reached for him and he moved up her body into her open arms, he could think of nothing but Lena, could see nothing but her.

With hands that shook, he grabbed a condom from the bedside table and put it on. Tucking the head of his cock against her swollen entrance, he slanted his mouth over hers. As he sank inside her slick, wet heat, he claimed her mouth as well.

Lena caught his tongue between her teeth, nipping him, sucking on him, driving him to the edge of sanity. Her short, neat nails raked down his back, leaving little trails of fire.

The satin-slicked walls of her sheath clenched him, gripped him rhythmically, milking him . . . pulling him in.

Losing myself, he thought. He could lose himself in her. In the sweetness of her body, in the warmth of her smile . . . in her arms. All of her. He could lose himself in her, happily, leave the nightmares behind, forget about the world outside the house.

Forget about everything but her . . .

Cupping one breast in his hand, he pushed it up and closed his teeth around the tip of one swollen pink nipple. She whimpered and arched closer, pressing herself more firmly against him.

"Ezra," she whispered.

Fuck, he loved the way she said his name.

Swearing, he released her breast and lifted his head, slanted his mouth over hers. "Say it again," he muttered against her lips. "Say my name again."

She smiled. "Ezra . . ."

Stroking her fingers through his hair, she fisted her hand in the strands and tugged his head. With that feline, female smile on her lips, she twisted her hips against his and said, "Make love to me, Ezra."

He cupped her hip in his hand, tucked her close. "I could die happy doing just that."

Doing just this . . .

He rode her, keeping the pace lazy, slow, though the need building inside was dark, bordering on dangerous. He wanted to watch that lazy smile turn into slow and easy pleasure, wanted to see it bloom on her face, lift her slowly.

It was sweet, somehow, Lena realized. Sweet, gentle . . . and healing, maybe.

When he shuddered against her, she wrapped her arms around him. When the need burned too bright and too strong to be ignored, she locked her legs around his hips and rose to meet each thrust. With one hand resting on his heart, the other gripping at the ridge of muscle atop his shoulder, she clung to him.

As the orgasm broke over them, she cried out his name.

Her name was a sigh on his lips as he eased back down.

With his head resting on her breasts, she wrapped her arms around him and held him close.

He didn't rest for a long time.

Until she felt the tension ease from his body, she didn't let herself seek sleep, either.

No more nightmares, she thought. Not tonight.

He could hear them in there, through the crack in her window.

Grunting. Fucking like animals.

He wished her room wasn't on the second floor.

He thought he'd like to watch her. Wondered what she'd look like naked.

Maybe he'd find out one day. Soon.

But for now, he needed to back away.

It was nearly four A.M. and that meant one of the cruisers would be coming around on one of their routine drive-bys. Routine for the past few weeks, ever since the week after Lena Riddle had reported the screams.

"You're not serious."

He could have misheard her. After all, it had been a rough few days.

The nightmare might as well have been a harbinger. The past few days had been full of tension and dark, ugly memories. Ezra had too much emotional upheaval . . . *shit, listen to me. Did I trade in my dick or what?*

Get it together, he told himself. He'd been off balance for the past few days and it wasn't getting any easier, either.

Partly because of the dreams, partly because of everything that was going on, partly because of Lena, and partly because of the mess inside him.

He couldn't think about that now. He needed to focus on Lena.

Raking his fingers through his hair, Ezra peered at her, tried to see if maybe she was joking. But she looked pretty serious.

"What did you just say?"

"You heard me well enough."

"No. Because what I heard you say was that you're going in to work. And that just doesn't seem right."

With an easy shrug, Lena said, "I don't see why not. After all, I do have a job. It is Thursday. That's my normal workday."

How could she sound so fucking normal? How could she be serious?

She couldn't be serious. Going to work? How in the hell could he keep an eye on her if she was at work?

What if the bastard was somebody she worked with?

In his gut, Ezra knew it was somebody who was at least familiar with the town. Had to be. The screaming Lena heard, the dead woman, it was all related. He *knew* it.

Dumping the body on Law's property—hell, it had just been dumb luck that Law hadn't been in town when it had happened. Sheer, dumb luck.

Whoever had killed that woman knew this town, probably even knew Lena, probably knew Law. Might even know Ezra, although he didn't know all that many people yet.

And Lena wanted to go to work?

What if . . .

Scrap that thought, he warned himself. He was already walking a hair trigger right now, on too little sleep and stress. Plus, seeing the woman's lifeless body had stirred up all those bad memories Ezra was still fighting.

He was on edge and he knew it. Certain images in his head? He did not need them at the moment.

"You seriously want to go to work," he said slowly.

"It's Thursday," Lena repeated. "I work on Thursdays. Unless I'm sick or the Inn isn't open. I'm not sick and the Inn is open. That means . . . I'm working."

"Have you forgotten what happened?"

Her smooth, ivory complexion seemed to pale a shade

or two, but if he thought that might change her mind, he thought wrong.

"No. I haven't forgotten. As much as I might wish to. It's not something I'm ever going to forget." She skimmed her fingers through her hair, a tired sigh escaping her. "But I'm not going to let one tragic accident stop me from living my life. Ezra, I can't. I've worked too hard to build a life. I'm not letting some psycho take it away."

"And what if he tries to do just that?" Ezra asked. "What if he decides to try to come after you, Lena? Answer me that. What if he decides you're next?"

Lena's lips narrowed into a thin, tight line. Without saying anything else, she turned and moved into the living room. "You know, I've already thought of all that shit, hotshot," she said as he followed her. "Besides, we don't even know if any of this is related, for crying out loud."

"Oh, don't give me that bullshit," Ezra snarled. "You know damn well it's related."

"No. I think it probably is. That doesn't mean it is."

Bracing a shoulder against the door, he jammed his fists into the front pockets of his jeans. "Then why are you so willing to take the risk?"

She swore under her breath and took off her glasses. Pinching the bridge of her nose, she said, "What kind of person does that to a woman, Ezra? What does it bring them? Why does he do it?"

"I'm not a profiler, babe. You're asking the wrong person."

A humorless smirk curled her lips and she leaned back against the couch. "Just humor me, babe. You might not be a profiler, but you're a cop and you're a smart guy. And don't tell me you haven't been doing some reading . . . you've been on my computer, remember?"

Ezra sighed. "Ego. God complex. All sorts of crazy shit can drive a person to kill. The need to control another—make them feel fear. It's not like taking a Pola-roid picture, Lena. Profiling is pretty damn complicated, and it's a little out of my league."

"The need to control another," she said. She lifted her face toward his. Her crystal-blue eyes stared just past his shoulder. There was knowledge in those eyes, the kind of knowledge he'd rather she never have. "To make them feel fear."

Clenching his jaw, he watched as she slipped her glasses back on. Her armor. Her mask. In a lot of fuck-ing ways.

"Do you think that's why he did it? To scare her? Hurt her?"

"Didn't I just say that I'm not exactly profiler mate-rial? I handled theft rings, Lena. This is out of my circle of expertise."

"Humor me."

"Fine," he bit off. "Yeah, I imagine that is why he does it—or at least that's part of it." *A big part,* he admitted to himself. "He needed, wanted to control her—it wasn't about revenge, or violence, it was about control."

"By staying here, inside this nice, supposedly safe house, I let him win," Lena said, pushing to her feet. She called for Puck and walked past Ezra into the anteroom. She felt on the hook on the wall for the dog's harness and leash. "I'll be damned if I let some sick pervert scare me out of my independence, Ezra. You don't have any idea how fucking hard I had to work to get it. I'm not staying cooped up in this house—I've got a job. I've got a life."

"You think I want to see you cooped up?" he snapped, turning to glare at her slender back as she got the dog ready.

"It doesn't matter what you want. I'm not staying home. I've got a job, and I'm going to work." She stood and turned to face him. Lifting one slender brow, she asked, "Are you going to take me, or should I call Carter?"

Clenching his hands into fists, Ezra closed his eyes. Took a deep breath. Counting to ten didn't do a damn bit of good.

When he looked back at her face, she had an amused smile on her face. "Praying for patience, baby?"

"Trying. It's not working. Damn it, Lena."

"You can't expect me to stay home because some woman I don't even know was found dead a few miles from here," she said, her voice flat.

"Yeah . . . on private property—your best friend's property. Not too long after you reported hearing some woman screaming. And now a woman is dead—probably the woman you heard screaming. You can't tell me you're not a little freaked out by the weird shit that's going on."

"No. I can't. I'm plenty freaked out, but that doesn't mean I'm going to quit my job!" she half-shouted. "Shit, Ezra. You've known me a few weeks and we're sleeping together. Fucking me doesn't give you the right to tell me whether or not I'm allowed to go to work."

"I'm not trying to allow or disallow jackshit," he bellowed. "And it's got nothing to do with whether or not I'm fucking you. I think I'm half in love with you and I'm terrified that something's going to happen to you if I'm . . . not . . . shit."

Blood rushed up his neck and he turned away, scrubbed his hands over his face.

Shit.

Shit.

Shit.

Had he really just . . .

Shit.

He had.

Muttering to himself, he crossed the foyer and dropped onto the first step. Sitting there, he dropped his head into his hands.

"What . . . ah . . . what was that again?"

"Haven't you told me, more than once, that your ears work just fine?" Ezra snapped. Then he sighed. "Ah, hell. I'm sorry. Look, I'm being a bastard and I know it. I'm sorry. I'm just . . ."

Hearing the soft, quiet sound of her footsteps, he glanced up, watched as she moved toward him. "Maybe my ears don't work as well as I thought," she said, her face unreadable.

"Lena . . ."

She knelt in front him.

He could see the vague blur of his reflection, distorted by the glasses she hid behind. Reaching up, he pulled them off and set them aside. "I hate these things, you know," he said quietly.

"I get tired of people looking at me."

"The glasses don't make them not look," he whispered. Catching her face in his hands, he pressed his lips to one eye, then the other. "People are either fucked up, stupid, cruel, or curious . . . wearing the glasses doesn't change that. It just gives you something to hide behind."

She wrapped her fingers around his wrists. "Nice, subtle way to distract me. But I asked you a question. What did you say?"

The words were trapped in his throat. They didn't want to come out. It had been easier, he realized, bellowing it out in a fit of temper and worry. But now, with her so close, and that soft, almost wondering look in her eyes . . . his heart did a strange little skipping thing in his chest and he leaned in, pressed his lips to hers. "I think I'm falling in love with you. I didn't want this, I sure as hell didn't plan this, but it's there anyway and damn it, Lena, it would kill me if something happened to you."

She sighed against his mouth and he caught her lower lip between his teeth, nipped on it gently. As she opened for him, he wrapped an arm around her waist and pulled her into his lap.

She hadn't pulled away.

Hadn't shoved his ass out the door.

That counted for something. Clumsy delivery aside, it counted . . . right?

"You've known me for five weeks, Ezra. Five weeks. And you admitted it yourself not that long ago . . . you just came through a really, really bad experience," she said quietly, cupping his face in her hands. "How can you think you love me?"

He laid a hand on her heart. "I think I started to fall in love with you that first night. You blushed when I called you beautiful . . . and then you shared your food with me. You got so nervous when I asked you for a date and I was scared as hell you would say no." Smoothing his hand up, he rested it on her neck, used his thumb to angle her chin up. "I started to fall for you that night, Lena. I guess it's why I backed away . . . maybe I didn't think I could handle it."

"And what makes you think you can handle it now?"

"Oh, I'm pretty sure I can't. But then again if I wait until I can handle things, then I never would do anything," he murmured, rubbing his lips against hers. "Things happen when they happen, not when you're ready for them."

She sighed against his mouth, a smile curling her lips. "That sounds kind of . . . well, romantic, Ezra. Never would have thought it of you."

"Hmmm." Lifting his head, he smiled at her. "Oh, I can get plenty romantic."

Slipping his hands under her tunic, he caught her breasts in his hands, stroking her through the silk and lace. She made a purring sound low in her throat—a sound that had the blood draining out of his head, straight to his cock. "I want you naked," he muttered.

"Lover, that's not romance. Is this your way of distracting me?"

Ezra scowled, lifting his head. "Hell, no. I pretty much always want you naked. And why should I try to distract you?" Then he trailed a hand down her torso, cupped his hand over the heat of her sex. Through the cotton of her trousers and her panties, he could feel her. He stroked her through the material, smiling as her body shuddered. A glassy, dazed look entered her eyes and he shifted her around so that she sat on his lap, her back against his chest.

He touched her again, this time pushing his hand inside her trousers, inside the flimsy barrier of her panties. She was slick, swollen, and when he pushed a finger inside her, she bucked against him. "I want you," he whispered, raking his teeth down her neck. "I don't see a day going by when I won't want you."

"Ezra . . ."

He used his free hand to guide her face around, catching her mouth with his.

He had wicked hands, Lena decided. Wicked . . .

And his mouth was just as bad. They'd been arguing—just minutes ago, she thought.

And now he had two fingers moving in and out of her pussy, one thumb rotating against her clit, and he was kissing her, like he was dying for her, starving for her.

Need knotted her middle and she braced her hands against his legs, her nails biting into the sturdy material of his jeans. As the orgasm bowed her back and tore through her body, she whimpered his name.

She was still shuddering, still shaking when she drifted back to earth a few seconds later. And still sitting on Ezra's lap, her legs spread as much as her trousers would allow, with his hand between her thighs, still cupped over her sex. A firm, possessive touch.

He had his free arm wrapped around her waist, holding her close.

The length of his cock was pressed against her butt, throbbing and insistent, but he made no other move.

All he did was hold her close.

Head spinning, Lena whispered, "I think we've both gone crazy."

"It's possible."

"Hmmm." She shifted and squirmed until he let her go. Rising, she straightened her pants and then returned to him, curling up on his lap, taking care not to put too much weight on his right leg. Carefully, she rested a hand on it, wincing as she felt the muscles knot under her touch. "I hurt your leg."

"I'll live."

Pressing her face against his neck, she sighed and breathed him in. Man, she loved how he smelled. Warm, strong . . . male. Like sun, wood, grass, and heat. Like Ezra, she guessed. It was something that was uniquely him.

"Did you mean it?" she asked, tracing the tip of her finger in a pattern on his chest.

"I'm not much in the habit of saying something unless I mean it, babe," he said, sighing.

"This is crazy, you know. How can you know me well enough to love me?"

"Lena." He pressed a kiss to her temple. "I know what I need to know. I know that your laugh makes me want to smile, and I know that when you're sad, it bothers me. I know I love to watch you, I know you blush when you realize I've been staring at you, even though it makes you smile, too."

He combed a hand through her hair, angled her head, and bussed her mouth with his. "I may not know everything there is to know about you, Lena, but I do know I'd like to spend my life learning the things I don't know."

Her heart was racing, she realized. Racing, dancing,

skipping, and doing all sorts of other things the heart just wasn't supposed to do. Taking a deep, slow breath, she said, "Okay, so maybe you do know me. Somewhat. And maybe I know you. Somewhat. But we've only known each other a few weeks."

"Doesn't matter. I don't know if I believe in fate and all that crap, but I do know the only time I've ever felt this complete in my life is when I'm with you." He hooked his hand around her neck and pressed his brow to hers. "I'm not going to rush things—it's not like there isn't enough insanity going on around us, anyway."

Insanity.

Yes. Things were mildly insane right now. Mildly insane. Majorly insane.

Screams.

Dead women.

Somebody trying to frame Law.

A sexy state cop thought he might be in love with her.

Lena wasn't entirely certain, but she was starting to think she might be in love with the sexy state cop, too.

Rubbing her cheek against his shoulder, she said, "I kind of like having you around, Ezra. I think I like it a lot."

His laugh was dry, self-deprecating. "You know how to stroke a guy's ego, gorgeous, you know that? I tell you I think I might be falling in love with you and you tell me you like having me hang around."

"Your ego doesn't need stroking." Slipping her arms around his neck, she said, "Slow. We need to go slow with this, because it's majorly unfamiliar territory for me. But . . . well, even with the mind-blowing sex, if I didn't have feelings for you, what you're telling me would have me so freaked out, I'd be all but shoving you out the door. But you're still here. Does that count for anything?"

He nipped her chin. "For now. Yeah." Then he sighed. "You still insist on going to work?"

"Yes."

"Shit." Nudging her off his lap, he said, "Fine. I'm driving you. I'm picking you up. If anybody says one wrong thing to you, tell Puck to eat him."

A smile tugged at her mouth. "You bet."

"And stop humoring me."

She wiped the smile off her face. "You bet."

Sighing, he brushed her hair back from her face. "You're a smart-ass, Lena Riddle."

"You bet." Leaning in, she pressed a kiss to the corner of his mouth. "Relax. The Inn's always got plenty of people around. And I'll have Puck with me. It's not likely anybody would mess with me with him around."

CHAPTER
EIGHTEEN

Scuffing his shoes along the sidewalk, Brody tried not to think about the argument with his dad and Uncle Remy.

He wanted a cigarette. Needed it.

But he couldn't get his hands on any cigarettes and none of the guys who would usually buy them for him would do it now. Curling his lip, he wondered if his uncle had gotten ahold of them.

He might have thought it was his dad, but he knew better.

The only time his dad cared about him was when Brody was causing trouble.

Hunching his shoulders, he tried to block out the memory of their voices. His dad's raised, Remy's soft, and low, as though he realized it was all the more effective for not yelling.

The worst of it, though, was that look in his dad's eyes. The look that made him wonder if maybe his dad did still care. That sad, heavy weight.

The disappointment.

Probably wished Brody had been the one to die instead of Mom.

Brody wished it, too.

Ever since she'd died, things had been different. Real different. His dad, man, he was hardly ever home. Gone all day, sometimes half the night. It was as though there were two strangers living in their house, not father and son. There were days when his dad couldn't even look at him.

A familiar engine caught his ears and he looked, watched as an old white Ford work truck rumbled down Main Street.

Ezra King.

That ugly, dark rage took root inside him. Uncle Remy was good and pissed at him—all over a bunch of fucking flowers.

Bastard.

Paranoia was bad anywhere.

A drive into town proved that, actually, Ezra wasn't as paranoid as he'd thought he was. He was actually doing just fine. These people? They were paranoid.

It was ugly. It was bad.

Bad for business . . . unless you owned a hardware store or sold guns.

It was bad for customer relations, as evidenced by the constant sniping that led to a catfight breaking out between two ladies at the Community Bank on Main Street. It might have been amusing, except the ladies were in their sixties and one of them had possibly broken her hip when she fell.

Paranoia, in under a week, had turned the small, tidy little town of Ash into a fricking nightmare.

Ezra climbed out of his truck and watched as eyes slid his way, danced off to the side the minute he made eye contact, only to lock on his back as he headed into the café.

It was Thursday afternoon and he was hungrier than hell. The café was his best bet, unless he wanted to trek out to the Inn, and even though he and Lena had made up after their argument, he figured it would be better if she didn't feel he was hanging around her every step.

He was tempted, though.

". . . in jail already. Just don't understand."

"No proof. Everything has to have proof these days. A shame, that's what it is."

Ezra was careful not to turn his head and look, although he didn't need to. He wasn't hearing anything he hadn't heard before over the past week.

Half the town was ready to lynch Law.

Even though he hadn't been there.

Shit, what would they have done if Law had been around?

No fucking telling.

His appetite faded and a lead weight settled in his gut, but Ezra didn't get up. Law wasn't coming into town much and neither was Lena. Ezra wasn't quite settled into town life just yet, so if he wanted to hear gossip, he had to do it the old-fashioned way.

Eavesdrop.

"What more proof does he need? They found the . . . the . . . body."

"I heard she was violated."

Ezra curled his lip. Violated. That was such a civilized word for what had been done to that girl. Prettied it up—sounded so much nicer than raped. Assaulted. Sodomized. Beaten.

"What can I get you?"

Lifting his head, he met the curious gaze of the teen-aged waitress.

She paled, and backed up a step.

Taking a deep breath, he blanked his expression and gave her a weak, lopsided smile. "Sorry. I was distracted there. Just give me whatever is up for the lunch special."

Not like it mattered. Whatever they served him, it

would taste like sawdust, it would go down like sawdust, and it would sit in his stomach like sawdust mixed with lead for the next few hours.

As she walked off, he tugged the phone off his belt and studied the time.

It was just after four.

He had a good four hours before he could head out to the Inn, and another six hours before he could hustle Lena out of there, take her back to her house and get her naked, get her into bed, and make love to her.

Wrapped in her arms, he could maybe get some sleep, forget about the ache in his head, the weight on his shoulders, and the unsolved mystery of a dead girl's body.

A dead girl who still had no name.

"We have a name," Nielson said quietly, addressing the few men he'd selected to help work this team. "There was some sort of computer error, otherwise we would have had a name before now—this woman's been listed as a missing person for the past three weeks."

He was keeping it close and tight—one screwup, that was all it would take for somebody to try to get this away from him. But the memory of that girl's face . . .

Focus, man. Focus. The job.

"We have a name," he said again. "Jolene Hollister, aged twenty-nine. Engaged to be married. She disappeared twenty-one days ago from Cherokee Park in Louisville, Kentucky. She'd gone there to go running—her car, her purse, her keys were all found there by her fiancé, who reported her missing. I'm still trying to contact her next of kin. Her only family is a cousin—out of the country."

He took a picture of Jolene from the folder he held and studied it.

Young. Pretty.

She looked like she had her whole life ahead of her.

She'd only had months.

Setting his jaw, he pinned the image of her smiling face up on the board, next to one of the images taken at the scene.

It was almost obscene, the difference between the two. Obscene.

There was something else about her that bothered him, but he wasn't quite ready to discuss that with anybody yet. Wasn't sure if anybody besides him had noticed.

Turning back, he studied the faces of his men.

Sadly, one of those faces was Prather. He hadn't had much choice—if he didn't let Prather in, considering Prather had found her, it was going to cause problems.

Nielson just hoped letting the fool in didn't prove to be more of a problem.

"So. Let's see what we can do to help find some justice for Miss Jolene," he said, turning away from the image of her smiling hazel eyes.

"Shit, business had better pick up," Roz muttered.

Lena rotated her neck, wincing a little at the stiffness there. "It will. Give it a few more days." She grimaced. "This is . . . unusual . . . for Ash. Only type of violence people see around here is the occasional barfight or a drunk-driving accident every now and then."

"Don't forget about Pete Hamilton."

Lena scowled. "Shit. Why not? I say we throw that bastard in a dark hole filled with rats and forget completely about him. Until he's nothing but bone."

"Oh . . . gory image. Nice."

"Sorry." She finished wiping down the counter and said, "Bastards who knock their wives around set me off." She washed her hands and turned back to face Roz. "I heard the daughter saw it all."

"That's what I heard, too. Word is Remy Jennings is

planning on putting that bastard behind bars for a good long while."

A smile tugged at Lena's lips. "If anybody can, Remy can do it."

He was sharp, determined, and focused. She'd admired that about him, respected it.

"So . . . think he might have any idea on who else he might be putting behind bars?"

Roz's attempt at subtlety fell flat. Shoving off the counter, Lena tucked her hands into her pockets and balled them into fists. "Meaning . . . who?"

Long, awkward, awful minutes of silence passed. "Lena, you know who."

"You actually think Law could have killed somebody?"

"Well, no. But, Lena . . . the body was found at his house," Roz said.

"Yeah, and he wasn't there."

"You're sure about that?"

Lena opened her mouth, closed it because she wasn't sure she could say anything coherent—except a long, nasty stream of swear words. Finally, she managed to say, "What do you mean, am I sure about that? Hell, yes I'm sure. He wasn't even in town, and besides, it's Law. He wouldn't ever do that to a woman."

"I don't want to think he would, either," Roz murmured.

But Lena heard the doubt. And it twisted her stomach and made her see red. "Then you don't think it, Roz. If you believe in him, if he is your friend, it shouldn't be that fucking hard."

"Lena, he is, but . . ." Roz's voice trailed off.

An awkward silence fell between them. As the knot in her gut twisted tighter and tighter, Lena finally shoved away from the counter. Under her breath, she muttered, "Fuck it."

"Lena, I want to believe in him, too, you know. And if you're sure he was out of town . . ."

"Roz? Do me a favor and be quiet," Lena said. She made her way around the kitchen until she reached one of her cabinets. The rum she kept in there was generally just used for baking, but right then, she didn't care. She pulled the bottle down and got herself a Diet Coke and some ice.

"Yes, Roz. I'm sure he was out of town, attending the funeral of a friend. He wasn't anywhere in the state, so yes, I am sure."

"Lena, don't be mad. He's my friend, too—"

"Don't," Lena said quietly, her voice trembling just a little with rage. She set the glass down. Carefully. Very carefully. Because she was tempted to slam it down, just to hear the glass shatter. Curling her fingers around the edge of the cool marble countertop, she said again, "Don't, Roz. Don't stand there and tell me that he's your friend right after you ask me if I'm sure he didn't brutally rape and murder some woman. You don't have the right to call him a friend."

Abruptly, she yanked her tunic off and grabbed her phone from her pocket. "I'm going home." She dialed Ezra's number, ignoring Roz's stammering voice as he came on the line. "Hey, I'm done here. How soon can you be here?"

"Five minutes, actually. I was already on my way. I had planned to get a bite to eat."

"I'll make you something at my place," Lena said. She had to get out of there before she exploded. All night, she thought, steaming. All night, she had felt some of the weird looks coming from people. Most of the people who worked at the Inn knew Law well enough to realize he wasn't a psycho, even if they did think he was a little weird.

But Roz . . . hell, Law considered her a friend. And this was what she thought of him?

"Lena, it's only eight-thirty. You can't leave."

"Want to bet?" she asked, baring her teeth in a sharp smile.

"Lena, honey, I'm sorry. I didn't mean to upset you . . ."

"Upset me?" Lena's jaw dropped. Snapping it shut, she took a slow deep breath, tried to get her temper under control. "You think I'm upset? Roz, what I am is fucking *pissed*. Law's being treated like a pariah in this town because some psychotic pervert decided to fuck around with him. You should know him better. You're supposed to be his friend, but you actually think he could do that to a woman. You think he's capable of that."

"Lena, of course I don't. I don't really think he could kill somebody . . ."

Lena laughed. Even to her ears, the sound was cold, harsh, and brittle—as though it might break in her throat, shatter, cut, and choke her. "Shit, Roz. Almost anybody could kill under the right circumstances. Self-defense, to protect somebody you love? I'd certainly try. But what happened to that girl? That wasn't killing."

Ezra knew the details. He hadn't shared them all, but she'd pried a few of them loose. Besides, the grief, the rage she heard in his voice? That spoke more than any words possibly could.

"What happened to that girl is something only a monster is capable of," Lena said softly. "And you stand there and make implications that Law, one of my best friends, could be that monster. One of your friends. But you're sorry."

"Damn it, Lena. What else do you want me to say?" Roz shouted.

A warm, furry weight pressed against Lena's legs and she reached down, rested a hand on Puck's head. His big body was tense, and she could feel his unease. He growled softly and she whispered to him, "It's okay, boy. Calm down. We're just pissed off." She couldn't do this around him—he was too sensitive to her moods and she didn't need him developing a dislike for one of her best friends. Although damn it, right now, *she* had a dislike for her best friend.

"Nothing," she said, focusing her attention back on Roz. "You don't need to say anything."

"Damn it, Lena," Roz said.

Spine rigid, Lena ignored the other woman as she heard the door to the kitchen open. Thank God, she thought. Grabbing Puck's leash from the hook, she crouched down by the door.

It wasn't Ezra, though.

It was Carter.

"Ahh . . . is everything okay in here?"

"Just peachy," Lena snapped. Gripping the dog's leash, she rose and headed to the kitchen's north entrance. She'd wait for Ezra out in the lobby. "Come on, boy."

"Are you okay, Lena?" Carter asked.

"No. I've got a headache, I'm pissed, and I'm leaving," she said, biting off each word.

"It's not closing time yet."

"And we're dead in here. If somebody comes in, give them bar food, tell them I started puking all over the floor—I don't care—but I'm leaving," she said.

"Lena, I can see you're upset . . ."

Upset—damn it, if one more person called her upset, she was going to start gouging out eyes.

Unaware of how close she was to screaming, Carter continued. "I know we're friends, but you are an employee. Now if you're ill, I understand, but if not . . ."

"If not, what?" she demanded scathingly.

"Lena, we need to talk about this," Roz said.

"The hell we do!" she shouted. "I'm not talking about this right now."

Puck's growling grew louder. Shit. She was freaking her dog out.

"Lena, I don't know what the problem is, but you don't speak to my wife that way and you can't just walk out in the middle of your shift, either."

"And what if I do, damn it?" Reaching down, she laid a hand on Puck's head. "If I walk out that door, you'll what? Fire me? If that's what you need to do, then you do it, because I can't stay here another minute—if I do, I'll say something I'll regret."

She didn't wait long enough for him to come up with an answer.

"What just happened?"

Gaping, Roz turned and looked at her husband. The misery on her face twisted at something inside him. Sighing, Carter crossed the room and wrapped an arm around her shoulders, tucking her against him.

"Baby, what just happened?" she said again. "I . . . damn it, I don't get it. We've never had a fight like that. She's never acted like that."

"What started it?"

Roz sniffled. "Me." Then she started to cry. "I just can't help it. I'm scared. I'm worried. And . . . well, all this crazy talk about Law, I don't really think it's him, but what if it is? She's so close to him and she . . ." She sobbed against his shirt.

Carter rubbed his cheek against her short, soft curls. "It's okay, darling. I understand. We all love him. Nobody wants to think he could do this. I don't think he did. But we worry."

Roz continued to cry.

He simply stood there and held her, stroking her back. There wasn't much else he could do.

His nice, quiet little town had gone crazy, Remy realized with more than a little dismay.

It was early Friday morning. He needed to be in his

office, and instead, he was trapped in the doorway of the café. In his left hand, he held his laptop bag. In his right hand, he held a cup of coffee that had already started to cool.

Keeping his frustration hidden, he stared into Deb Sparks's eyes and tried to figure out just what in the hell she expected of him.

"Well?" she demanded, her voice shrill, strident.

Her eyes, a pale, almost colorless shade of blue, peered at him and he could tell by the stubborn set of her shoulders, the lift of her chin that she expected an answer.

She wasn't the only one, either.

She had four other people with her.

Earl Prather was standing there, just a few feet away and he was watching the whole damn thing with just a little too much amusement for Remy's liking. "Ms. Sparks, I can't issue a warrant when there is no proof," Remy said. He'd already mentioned that little fact three times.

"You have proof," she snapped.

Remy barely resisted the urge to wince. Her voice could break glass, he'd swear to it.

"No, we don't. What we have is a body that appears to have been placed there. Law Reilly wasn't on the premises when she was put there. He wasn't in the state when she was killed."

Her eyes widened. In a dramatic voice, she said, "They can fool coroners, you know. Putting the body on ice, all sorts of things. I've seen it on *Court TV, CSI, Law & Order*. And just because he claims he wasn't in the state doesn't mean he wasn't. Did you look for ice? Did you?"

Ice. What in the hell? Shit. *Put knowledge in the hands of stupid people, and it just made them more stupid*, he thought.

"No, I didn't look for ice. However, I'm sure the deputies did. And deputies from the sheriff's office spoke with a number of people who can testify to Law Reilly's whereabouts," Remy said, looking at Deb's face and then at Prather, then to each of her loyal little crowd of followers.

Slowly, as though he was speaking to a child, he said, "Law Reilly was not in the state. And, while I'm sure you're just trying to help, this really isn't anything I can discuss with you—any of you."

"Why not?" Deb stomped her foot. "I am a taxpayer. I pay your salary, Remy Jennings, and don't you forget it. That means you answer to me."

Oh, now that did it. "No. It does not mean I answer to you. I answer to my superiors, and if you have a problem with how I do my job, take it up with them." He made a display of taking a look at his watch. "Now, if you don't mind, I do have other cases, other taxpayers who are depending on me."

"Your mama should be ashamed of you, letting a sick pervert like that walk around when you've got the power to stop him!" Deb proclaimed.

Remy couldn't decide what was more annoying—her strident tones or her habit of making everything sound like a matter of life or death. Turning to look at her, he said, "Ms. Sparks, believe it or not, if I thought Law Reilly was guilty, I'd be out there combing through every square inch of the county on my hands and knees myself, looking for proof. But he's not a murderer."

He pushed through the small crowd only to come to a dead stop as he started to swing left.

Law Reilly was standing there, his face an unreadable mask. The woman was with him, her long brown hair swept back and braided, falling over her shoulder in a tail that damn near touched her waist.

Law might have been wearing a mask, but the woman . . . she wasn't.

Her face was pale, but her sea-green eyes snapped with fire. She wasn't looking at him, though. She was staring past him with disgust at the people gathered at the foot of the steps.

"Bunch of hyenas," she muttered, her voice a low, soft drawl.

Then her eyes cut to his. Their gazes locked for a few seconds and she looked away, staring at the concrete as though it held something uniquely fascinating.

Hell, Remy found *her* fascinating.

She crashes into a plant stand and gets terrified, but somebody insults her lover and she looked ready to rip throats open?

Tearing his eyes away from her pretty, heart-shaped face, he looked at Law. "Reilly."

Law cocked a brow. "Good morning, Counselor."

At the sound of Law's voice, the small crowd at the café door went strangely silent. One by one, they eased down the steps, glanced at Law, and then started to slink away.

Law would have let them do just that.

The woman, though?

"Such a nice town, here, Law. So nice of you to invite me for a visit . . . they stand around talking about you behind your back, but they don't have the courage to look you in the eye when they realize you heard every damn word," she said. "They think you're the sort of sick, murdering coward who could beat and murder a woman, but they don't have the guts to say it to your face. I love a hypocrite, don't you?"

That soft, low voice of hers could carry, Remy realized.

Amused, he shifted so he could see the reaction from the corner of his eye.

Two of them kept walking. One paused and looked back at Law, then at the woman, shamefaced, before hurrying on down the sidewalk.

But Deb, damn her—was she stupid or was she just that fond of causing trouble?

Lifting her chin, she came closer. Giving Law a nasty look, she then focused her eyes on the woman—Remy still didn't know her name, shit.

"You're making a mistake with this one, young lady." Deb sniffed. "I should know. He's lived here for years and after you've lived near a person for that long, you get to know them. He's trouble, mark my words."

A cool smile spread over the woman's face. "After you've lived near a person for years, huh?" She smirked. "Then I should know. He may be trouble, but he's no murderer. I've known him since I was in diapers. He wouldn't hurt a woman. He doesn't have it in him. And that is something I have on good authority—you can mark my words."

A strange, faraway look entered her eyes, one that left Remy with a bad, bad taste in the back of his mouth.

Then she blinked and the moment shattered. Looking back at Deb, she said, "Whatever you think you know, you're wrong. You'll figure that out soon enough."

She looked away from Deb then, effectively dismissing her. "Come on, Law. Let's get out of here. We can grab some coffee at the bookstore or something. Suddenly, I'm not hungry."

As they headed down the sidewalk, Remy fell in step with them. He could have given them several reasons—if he didn't get away from Deb, he might do himself bodily harm, jab himself in the chest with his pen, beat himself in the head with his iPhone until he broke the skin—just to have a reason to escape. But he also needed the woman's name.

Even if she belonged to Law, and it looked like she did. Whether Law was still hung up on Lena or not, the woman was loyal to him.

But Remy wanted her name—the slim brunette who

had cowered in front of Prather but stood up to the worst gossips and bitches this town had to offer. Who was she to him?

"It will get better," he said to Law.

"Shit."

"It will. Right now, it's just . . . news." He grimaced as he said it. It was morbid, it was awful, and it was, plain and simple, true. "But sooner or later, people will find something else to talk about."

"Maybe if we could find who really did kill her, that might help," Law said, his voice sharp.

"Yes." Remy narrowed his eyes. He'd like that. A lot. He wanted that fucker caught, locked away. He wanted a part in it.

"Thinking how nice and shiny that might look on your résumé or whatever in the hell you lawyer types call it?" Law asked cynically.

"No. I'm thinking how nice it will be for people around here to be able to stop worrying every time their daughters, their wives, their sisters leave the house for work, school, groceries," Remy snapped. He stopped in his tracks and glared at Law. "I don't need my ego stroked and I don't need big cases to feel important—if that was what I wanted, I'd be practicing someplace other than here. I just want this town to go back to what it was. Safe."

Law's lids drooped, shielding his eyes. A sigh escaped him and he looked away. "It's not ever going to be the same town again, Jennings. Not after this. Even if we find him. What he did, it ripped something here and even after it's mended, the fabric of the place? It's torn."

The woman reached out and caught Law's hand, squeezed it. "But finding him will make it better. At least it will mend things, instead of leaving a big hole, right?"

Her eyes darted toward Remy, bounced away before really making contact.

Law reached out and caught a strand of her hair, tugging on it. It looked like a familiar habit, one he'd done a thousand times. "Yeah, I guess." Then he frowned and glanced at Remy. "Guess I should introduce you. Remy, this is my friend, Hope. Hope, this is Remy Jennings. If somebody had decided I needed to be arrested, most likely he would have been the one getting the warrants and all that official stuff."

Her pale green eyes cooled—from spring green to arctic ice in the span of seconds, Remy realized. He wanted to glare at Law, but managed not to. Barely. "Nobody is going to arrest you without some sort of proof and there isn't any," he said.

"Law isn't a murderer," she said, her voice flat.

"I agree with you," Remy said. He held out his hand, wondered if she'd accept.

He was mildly surprised when she did. The hand she put in his was small, and slim, as delicate as the rest of her. She gave his hand a quick shake and then pulled back, as if that small touch was all she could stand, or all she wanted. "You're a lawyer?"

"Yes." He gave her the same charming smile he'd used to coax his mother into letting him stay up late, the same charming smile he'd used to coax Sandy Reynolds into going to the prom with him . . . and into losing her virginity with him later that night. It was the same charming smile he'd used on women most of his life and it worked on a pretty regular basis.

But she just stared at him, her gaze unreadable, her mouth a flat, unsmiling line. She didn't look charmed at all. Matter of fact, she actually looked a little irritated and she looked like she'd like to get as far away from him as she could.

Then she pointedly turned away and focused on Law. "Are you still hungry?"

Sixty seconds later, he was standing on the sidewalk and watching her walk away with Law.

She never spared him so much as one backward glance.

Well, Remy thought, at least he had a name.

It was better than nothing.

Although why in the hell it mattered, he didn't know.

Hope was clearly not interested.

And she was clearly all about Law Reilly.

NINETEEN

"EVERYBODY IN TOWN WANTS TO KNOW WHY IN THE hell we haven't arrested him," Prather snapped, jutting his chin up as he faced Nielson.

Everybody? Nielson barely managed to avoid rolling his eyes. "Just who the hell is everybody?"

"Everybody in town." Prather glared at him.

"Really." Shooting a look at Keith Jennings, he lifted a brow. "Sergeant, you live in town, right?"

"I do, Sheriff."

"Okay. Are you wondering why I haven't arrested Reilly?"

"Not for a second." Jennings just smiled. "We don't have the sort of proof we need to arrest anybody. Not even Reilly, as much as some people might like to think otherwise."

"Okay." He looked back at Prather. "You can relax now. It's not everybody wondering it."

"Damn it, Sher . . ." He snapped his mouth shut, sucked in a slow breath. "I apologize. But I have to wonder why you're so dead set on not arresting him."

"Because, Deputy Prather . . . I don't see enough proof, and because I know the man has a solid alibi." He looked away, focused on the reports he'd been dis-

cussing with Keith before his current pain in the ass had
stormed into the office.

He didn't need Prather's help to see that more than a
few people were of a mind that Law Reilly should be
arrested. It didn't matter to them that there wasn't really
any hard-core evidence pointing toward Law, other than
the body that had been found on his property.

"Next time you talk to everybody, please make sure
you let them know we only arrest people when there's
real, serious evidence," Nielson said as he skimmed the
report. He still needed the deceased's next of kin. Apparently she was a reporter or something, working out of
the country on an assignment—tracking her down wasn't
proving to be easy. If he didn't get in touch with her
soon, he'd have to notify the fiancé. They always notified
the next of kin first, but when the next of kin wasn't
reachable. . . . It looked like he'd have to call the fiancé.

Fuck, he hated this part of the job. Hated when he had
to shatter a life like this. Although he'd never had anything like this. Never. Violent deaths, yes. But to this
degree . . . no. Never anything so brutal, so violent . . .
and they had no suspect. No suspect, no possible suspects. No fibers. No prints. No fluids.

It was like a ghost had left that body at Reilly's place.

A ghost.

Or a cop . . .

Somebody who knew an awful lot about cleaning up
a body, that was for sure. But then again, anybody with
access to cable or the Internet could learn all sorts of shit
about forensics these days.

". . . so?"

Scowling, Nielson looked up at Prather. "Look, there
is no way in hell I could possibly make an arrest on
Reilly stick, assuming I even thought he was guilty, which
I don't. Now if you have something other than this to
talk about, please do. If not?"

"Maybe it's a team thing," Prather suggested, narrowing his eyes.

"A team thing?" Jennings echoed, lifting a brow, a smile quivering at the corners of his mouth.

Yeah. Jennings might find this all amusing. Nielson didn't. "For fuck's sake," he snarled, hurling his pen down on his desk and rising. Glaring at Prather across the desk, he leaned forward. "Have you seen the woman he's got staying at his house? Let's assume, just for the hell of it, that he is some sort of psycho killer. Do you really think he's stupid enough to orchestrate some murder when he's got a woman staying at his place? He'd want privacy, Prather. Get that? Privacy."

"He's an arrogant bastard. Could do that to avert suspicion."

"Get out of my office, Prather. Now."

Dropping back behind his desk, he kept his attention focused on it as he waited for the sound of the slamming door. Fifteen seconds later, it came. He looked up and met Keith's gaze.

"That man causes more trouble every damn day."

Keith opened his mouth, then closed it.

Nielson lifted a brow. "Yes?"

"You stating a fact or asking my opinion?"

"Technically, I shouldn't do either." Sighing, he rubbed his hands over his face. "This whole mess has my head so screwed up."

"It should. This isn't supposed to be easy on us, is it?" Keith mused.

"No. No, it's not." He pinched the bridge of his nose and then focused on Keith once more. "You think there's any merit to what Prather was rambling about?"

Just how honest could he be here? Keith wondered. Rising, he absently linked his hands behind his back. Years out of the military and still, those habits were ingrained. "May I be completely honest, Sheriff?"

"If I didn't want your honest opinion, I wouldn't have asked for it," Nielson pointed out.

"It's my honest opinion that Prather wouldn't have an idea with merit unless somebody picked it out for him, wrapped it up, and presented it to him with a big, shiny bow."

For a moment, Nielson stared at him. Then he started to chuckle. "You're probably right about that. Shit." He looked back at the reports on his desk and sighed. "This is such a damn mess."

"That it is." Keith shifted his gaze to the board standing in the corner, his attention focused on the victim's face. She'd been pretty. Happy. She'd had her whole life spread out before her. All that bright hope . . . ended.

"Such a damn tragedy," Nielson muttered.

Keith looked over and saw that Nielson was studying the victim's face as well. "Yes," Keith said softly. "A waste."

Abruptly, Nielson sighed and looked back down at the reports on his desk. "I need to go over these again. There's got to be something I'm missing."

"If you'll let me see the coroner's report, I'll go through it again."

Silence fell, finally broken by a grunt from Nielson. "Yeah. You do that. I need to shoot off an e-mail."

Nielson reckoned something in his tone alerted Jennings.

"An e-mail."

"Yeah." He swallowed and glanced at the board, at Jolene's pretty, smiling face . . . and the ruin next to it. "It's her next of kin. The lady is out of the country. I finally got a way to contact her."

Jennings grimaced. "Hell."

Made sense, in Prather's mind. But what he needed was proof.

Clean. Too clean.

Almost like a cop was in on it . . . A cop.

As he stomped down the street, he tossed that idea around in his mind.

Yeah. Maybe. Maybe that was it. They alibied each other. Stupid city fucker knew how to clean things up, after all.

Proof. Needed to get proof.

Only one way to do that, though, since Nielson wasn't listening to reason.

"The hell you are."

Hope glared at Law over the box packed with envelopes and books. "You told me you were hiring me to do a job. That's what I'm trying to do. Some of these packages have been sitting around so long, they've got dust on them."

"So what?"

Hope tried to ignore the itchy, crawling sensation dancing along her spine. "I'm just driving into Lexington. I'll be gone long enough to find a UPS store and a Target. I need some clothes."

"Fine." He gave his desk a disgusted look and started rummaging around for his keys. "I'll come."

"No." Pivoting away, Hope hooked her hands behind her neck and said, "Law, you know I love you, right? You know I wouldn't say anything to hurt you . . . intentionally. Right?"

He remained silent. Shooting him a narrow look over her shoulder, she said, "I'm suffocating and if I don't get a little bit of breathing room, I'm going to have a breakdown." She wasn't exaggerating, either. Earlier, she'd tried to turn the doorknob to get out of the bathroom, and she couldn't get it open—she'd forgotten she'd locked it. She'd started to panic—*locked in, locked in, locked in*—

Even the memory of it was enough to have panic trying to creep in and she had to throttle it into submission,
beat it down before she turned to look at him. "I'm fine,"
she said. "I am. But I need to get out of this house . . .
for just a while."

"It's not safe."

"Law, nobody is after me."

"We don't know that!" he shouted.

She flinched and when the self-disgust glared in his
eyes, she could have kicked herself. "Don't we?" Slicking
her hands down the front of her worn jeans, she said,
"Don't tell me you haven't already had somebody check
up on Joey. I won't believe it."

He said nothing. Neither did he look away. The truth
was there, in those uncompromising hazel eyes. With a
faint smile, she said, "It's not him. If Joey wanted to get
to me, he'd come after me. Not some woman I didn't
know. And other than you, nobody here knows me."

"Psychotics don't always target people they know,"
Law pointed out.

"And do you really think he's going to come after me
in broad daylight? I'll be gone two or three hours, Law."
Her hands were starting to shake, she realized. Shaking,
sweating . . . closing them into fists, she sank her nails
into her skin, hoping that mild, minor pain might clear
her head.

"Part of the reason why I left him was because I
was tired of being afraid all the time. Tired of feeling
trapped—" tired of being trapped. "If I let something like
this cage me again, then it was all for nothing, Law."

She swallowed the knot in her throat. "I can't live like
that. I can't go back to that . . . that thing he made me
into. I can't."

"And just letting me tag along, what does that hurt?"

"You've always made it so easy to lean on you, Law."
Blowing out a sigh, she looked up at him. "And right

now, I want that. I want it too much, which means I can't let myself do it. I spent the past two years standing on my own. I've come too far and I won't let some monster take this away from me. Not now."

"Hope . . ." Something sad, dark moved through his eyes.

"Don't." Shaking her head, she held his gaze. If he kept pushing, she'd give in, and she'd hate herself. She had to do this, had to make herself be strong. It was getting too easy to lean on him, too hard to fight the need to do it. If she couldn't make herself stay strong around him, then she wasn't going to be able to stay here.

She studied the box in front of her and then looked at him. "Come on, use that brain of yours. Is it really very likely somebody's going to try to hurt me? Nobody knows me. I don't know anybody."

Law reached up and pressed the heels of his hands to his eyes. "Shit. This is insane. I am not doing this, not thinking this."

"Three hours. I just need three hours."

He snorted. "You expect me to believe you'll be there and back in three hours? You did mention a Target, right? The word shopping?"

"I'm not the clotheshorse some people are." She shrugged. "I just need a few things."

He rested a fist on the box sitting on his desk. "Anything happens to you, I'm going to be really pissed off."

"Me, too." Eyeing the box on his desk, she said, "How much money is that going to cost?"

Law shrugged and unearthed a wallet from somewhere. The man had already made his desk a disaster zone again. Hell, he was a disaster zone. He pushed a few twenties into her hand and said, "That ought to cover it."

The box was addressed to his agent. Sealed inside were padded mailers, smaller boxes, and envelopes. When asked about that peculiarity, he'd shrugged and said, "People can look at postmarks. My luck, somebody from here would win a book and put two and two together. This way, she mails them out—they're postmarked from New York and I'm happy with my little paranoias."

As long as he was happy with his paranoias . . .

"You're sure you can find your way around okay?" he asked.

"I'm fine." She had to get out of here, and as much as she loved him, even as much as she was tempted to lean on him, take comfort in how solid and steady he'd always been, she needed a breather from Law. She adored the man, but ever since . . . that night, she couldn't go fifteen feet without him poking his head out of his office to check on her. He wouldn't leave the house without her, and the few times they'd left the house together, it hadn't been pleasant.

Half the town had painted him a murderer in their minds.

Many of the others were all eaten up with curiosity for gory details.

People, Hope had realized, were sick.

Despite her best intentions, she found herself drawn to the window, staring out at the workshop where the woman's body had been discovered.

It was still off-limits, but it didn't matter. Hope didn't ever want to go in there. Ever.

She should be terrified, she realized.

And she was uneasy. Her gut churned and twisted and every second she stood staring at the workshop, it got worse.

But the thought of leaving Law's, where she felt safe, didn't turn her into a tangle of nerves and terror. It should. Once she found a safety zone, she didn't leave it easily and even finding some place where she felt safe didn't mean she wasn't cringing in fear inside.

It was because she was away from Clinton, she figured. Away from Joey.

And she had done that. After all the times he'd told her . . .

"Earth to Hope."

Blinking, she looked at Law and smiled. "Sorry, I was just thinking." Then she forced a smile when she saw the concern in his eyes.

"You know, the longer I think about this, the less I like the idea." He had a grim look in his eyes, his mouth a straight, solid line.

He wasn't sleeping. Even if she didn't hear him pacing the floor at night, she would have recognized the signs of it on his face, in the dark shadows under his eyes, the tense set of his shoulders.

"I'm fine," she said, trying to put a little bit of force in her voice.

Circling around the desk, she leaned her hips against it and crossed her arms over her chest. "Law, you've got to quit beating yourself up over me."

"Can't." He caught a lock of her hair and tucked it behind her ear. "If I hadn't waited so long . . ."

He wasn't talking about what had happened here recently, she knew. Sighing, she caught his hand and squeezed it. "Don't. Okay? Just don't. The ifs here belong to me. Only me. If I had listened to my gut the first year, and left then, things would be different. If I had told you there were problems when you first started getting worried, things would be different. There are a lot of ifs, but I was the only one who could make something change. Me, Law. Not you."

He reached out and hooked an arm over her shoulders, tugging her close in a hug. "It's not good enough, sweetheart. It's just not. I swear, I want to kill him. I want him dead so bad, I can taste it."

"Don't." Hope eased back, shaking her head. "Don't. Don't think it. Don't try for it, don't plan it. Don't do it."

He could. She knew that. He was more than capable of killing, and that mind of his? It could probably come up with a very clever way—one that might never be traced back to him.

She caught his face in her hands, staring into hard hazel eyes. So often, those eyes were distracted, distant, focused on worlds that existed only in his head. But now they were cold, brittle as glass.

"He deserves to die for the shit he did to you."

"I won't lie and say I disagree," Hope said. "But if he dies, it would come back on one of us. He's already destroyed half of my life and I have to start over. If you do anything to him, he's going to do the same to your life. He isn't worth it."

"But my friend is."

Her heart broke a little. Rising on her toes, she pressed her lips to his cheek. "Why in the world couldn't I have fallen for you?" she asked, her voice cracking.

Law blushed. But he stroked a hand down her hair and gave her a sheepish smile. "You're like a sister to me, Hope."

"I know. And you're like a brother to me." She reached down and caught his hands, twined their fingers together. "You are a brother—in my heart, even if we're not related by blood. You're the only real family I have left. And because of that, I'm asking you . . . let it go. If anything happened to you because of him, Law, it would tear me apart."

His eyes narrowed. "That's playing dirty." Then he squeezed her hands. "Fortunately for you, I'd already come to that conclusion." Letting go of her hands, he tugged on her hair once more and said, "But that doesn't mean I'm not going to spend a lot of time thinking about painful, slow ways I could make him die."

"Okay." As long as he didn't try to put that twisted imagination of his to use, she was good.

She didn't want her ex dead. Well, she did. But she didn't need him dead. She didn't. She just needed peace. Closure.

And clothes. Glancing down at her worn, thin T-shirt, she stepped back and circled around the desk. "Okay, boss. Time's a wasting. I've got money to burn and clothes to buy."

Law lifted the box before she had a chance. "I'll carry it." On the way out, he said, "Have I mentioned that I don't like this?"

"Yes. You were pretty clear about that." She shot him a narrow glance. "Law, I can't stay inside all the time. I can't. I'll only be gone a few hours. Promise. And I've got your phone, I've got the GPS."

He rubbed the back of his neck. "Doesn't matter. I still feel really wrong about you being out by yourself right now."

"Well, maybe Lena might come . . . ?"

CHAPTER
TWENTY

"Shopping," Ezra repeated.

Law swore and muttered, "Shit, don't give me a hard time. I kept trying to talk her out of it, but she won't listen."

"I didn't realize I was giving you a hard time." Heaving out a sigh, Ezra pinched the bridge of his nose. "Law, you can't really expect her to stay trapped inside your house for the next six weeks . . . six months. Six years."

There was silence on the other end of the phone. "So, you don't think it's a problem. I'm being an idiot to worry."

"Lena went to work on Thursday—we ended up getting into an argument over it." Ezra stared out the window at her front yard, brooding. Things were still a little too unsettled between them, and he had no idea how to handle it. None. Unsettled. But not just because of the fight.

He'd told her he was falling in love with her.

"I fucking hated every second . . . but I can't make her quit her job, man. And you can't expect Hope to spend the rest of her life hiding in your house."

"It's not the rest of her life. It's just until this is taken care of."

"And what if he isn't caught?"

"Shit."

"That about sums it up," Ezra agreed. He shot a glance toward the ceiling. Lena was still sleeping. The nights she'd worked, she'd come home in a dark, bitter mood—while they were still getting used to each other, he was pretty sure this wasn't routine for her.

Something was going on at work, but she wouldn't talk about it.

Whatever it was, she was pissed off about it, though.

She'd been burning hot with fury when he'd picked her up late Saturday night, and that fury had remained just as hot, just as bright throughout the drive back to her house and once they'd gotten there . . . well, he wasn't going to complain about that.

Hot, edgy sex had finally let her sleep, but it hadn't eased her misery.

Sunday, they'd gone to his place and she'd sat outside with a book while he worked on the deck. At the rate he was going, he wasn't going to be done by fall—hell, he'd be lucky to be done by next fall.

Lately, he was at Lena's more often than he was home, anyway.

She wouldn't talk to him—tell him what was bothering her. He didn't like that. Part of him worried it had something to do with the bomb he'd dropped on her, but his instincts said otherwise.

He'd almost called out to the Inn and asked Roz, but decided against it. If they were seriously going to try the relationship thing here, he needed to be getting the information from Lena . . . not her friends.

Besides, he had a feeling Roz was part of the problem. He didn't know the woman, at all. But he knew Lena and Roz were friends, and nobody could piss a person off as well as a friend . . . or a lover.

Jerking his attention back to the phone, he listened as Law finished up a rather long, disjointed monologue.

"So you really don't think there's any reason she can't drive to Lexington?"

Ezra rolled his eyes. "She's got a license, right?"

"Yeah, she's got a license, but that's not why I'm asking," Law snapped. "What if . . ."

"Shit." Pinching the bridge of his nose, he leaned back in the chair and focused on the ceiling. "There's no reason to think Hope's in any danger, Law."

"Good. Because she's heading your way. She wants Lena to go with her."

Ezra managed to bite back the automatic "Hell no" that sprang to his lips. But just barely. Hearing the soft pad of Lena's footsteps on the stairs and the rhythmic click of Puck's claws, he spun around in her office chair, waited for her to appear in the door. She had an unerring radar, it seemed, able to figure out almost exactly where he was with very little effort.

"Morning, sleepyhead."

She gave him a tired smile. "Did I hear you talking?"

"Yeah. Law's on the phone. Apparently, Hope's got a wild hair to do some shopping in Lexington and she wants you to go with her."

Lena yawned and leaned against the wall. Puck came up, nosing at her legs. "Shopping?" She wrinkled her nose. "I'm not usually much for shopping."

"I think it's more because she needs to get out of the house than anything," Ezra said. She stretched her arms over her head and he tried not to stare at the pale strip of flesh exposed as her shirt lifted.

Under the fabric, he could see the darker circle of her nipples, stabbing into the cotton. Now his mouth was starting to water.

On a sigh, Lena said, "Getting out of the house doesn't sound like a bad idea." Then she grimaced. "As long as it doesn't involve going into town. Sure. I'll go shower."

Irritated, aggravated, and now sexually frustrated, he

stared at her ass until she disappeared around the corner. "She'll go," he said, his voice rough.

Law laughed. "You sound about as thrilled about it as I am."

"If we try to follow, think Hope would notice?"

"Probably."

A few seconds later the shower came on and Ezra said, "Besides, while they're out of town, maybe you and me can poke around a little."

"Poke around. Where exactly?"

Ezra slanted a look out the window. "Lena's woods. That's where the weirdness started, right?"

"We already tried that."

"So we try again. They'll be out of town, and together—plus, they'll have Puck. Whoever it is, Puck's got a nose for him, and he doesn't like him. If he starts getting that Cujo growl going on, Lena's going to haul tail . . . but, I don't think anybody would mess with the two of them together. And nobody's going to risk getting around that dog. He'd take a bite out of a crocodile if it got too close to his lady."

"Puck's not bulletproof."

Images of blood flashed behind Ezra's eyes.

Blood . . . blood on my hands . . .

Fuck. Lena's blood. Nightmare—that was nightmare material, there. And something he didn't need to be thinking about.

His throat constricted. For five seconds, he didn't think his heart beat at all. "Neither is Lena. Neither is Hope. We want them out of this mess, we need to start looking around, because frankly, I don't think Nielson has a clue."

"You're a cop. Aren't you supposed to be saying the police will handle this?"

Absently, Ezra massaged his thigh. "I'm on leave."

Besides, from where he was sitting, this wasn't exactly being handled.

* * *

"I'm not much help when it comes to trying on clothes," Lena said dryly, sitting in the corner of the dressing room. Puck had his head on her lap and she didn't have to see him to know he was giving her puppy-dog eyes and sending her subliminal messages along the lines of, *Can we leave, please please please . . . ?*

Stores were not his favorite place. At all.

Hope grumbled under her breath.

"What?"

"I hate trying clothes on. Stupid jeans. They barely cover my butt," she snapped.

"That's the style." Lena shrugged.

"Stylish—for people to see my butt hanging out when I bend over? That's not style—that's trashy."

She grumbled a little more under her breath and then sighed. "I'll just order some longer shirts online or something."

Lena listened to clothes rustling as Hope methodically went through and tried on more jeans, shirts, and a few sweaters. "Can I ask you a nosy question?"

The wariness coming from the other woman was almost palpable. "Ah . . . it depends," Hope said, her voice slow, reluctant.

"It's about Law. Just wondering what the story is between you two."

"Story?" She sounded puzzled. "What do you mean?"

"Well, you two seem pretty close."

Hope sighed. "We are close. I've known him my whole life. We were best friends in elementary school, middle school, right up through high school."

"So it's a friend thing?"

"What does it matter?" Hope hesitated for a second and then said, "I'm not trying to be rude, but you're pretty involved with Ezra. Even a blind . . . oh, shit, I am so sorry. I can't believe I just said that."

Lena laughed. "Hope, I am blind. And yes, even I can see that I'm pretty involved with Ezra. But that's not exactly why I'm asking. Law is a friend of mine. He has been since he moved here . . . he's one of my best friends. Mostly, I'm just being nosy. Law doesn't talk about himself a whole lot. I've never seen him have company, he's never mentioned his family, doesn't talk about them. As far as I know, he doesn't even date and if he had, I would have heard something, even if he didn't tell me. Then you show up. There doesn't seem to be any romantic interest going on there, but . . . well, like I said, I'm nosy."

"There is nothing romantic between us. Law is kind of private. That's just him. We're friends, best friends, but just friends."

There was sadness in her voice, Lena noticed. A lot of it. Sadness, pain, a reluctance to talk.

"So, if there's not much of a story between you and Law, maybe you can tell me your story." Rising, Lena took one step forward and reached out a hand. Her fingers grazed Hope's arm and she moved her hand up, rested it on the other woman's shoulder. "Now this isn't me being nosy. Really. Although you might have a hard time telling the difference. But I get the feeling you haven't ever really talked about it, whatever it might be. Maybe you need to."

"Thanks for the offer," Hope said, her voice faint, unsteady. "But this is one of those things you just can't talk about. I think if I tried, the words might choke me."

"Sometimes keeping them trapped inside will do the same thing."

"So what's the story with you and Hope?" Ezra asked as they followed the winding trail into the woods.

Law smacked at a bug. "There isn't a story with me and Hope. She's a friend. She needed a job. And I had a job that needed to be done. It would've worked really well, if some psychotic hadn't gone and dumped the body in my workshop."

"Known each other long?"

"You sure as hell are nosy," Law muttered. "Yeah. We've known each other pretty much our whole lives. My dad and I lived next door to her folks when we were kids. Lived in a small town, went to the same schools, graduated together."

Ezra was quiet for a minute—the better to enjoy Law's grumbling as they cut through the underbrush. "She looks like she's been put through hell."

"She has been through hell. Fuck, she's pretty much lived in hell ever since we got out of high school." His voice had a bite to it, heavy, hard with self-disgust.

Pausing, Ezra looked back at the other man. He had stopped on the trail, staring off into the distance.

But Ezra suspected he wasn't seeing the trees, or much of anything. "You okay?"

Law slanted him a look. "You ever suspected in your gut that somebody you loved was in trouble?"

Ezra thought of Mac. Yeah, he had loved her. She had been in trouble, all right, but he hadn't suspected. Not once.

But Law didn't seem to need an answer. "Big trouble. So you ask, but you're told everything is fine. Just fine. And because she's never lied to you before, you believe her. Couple years go by, and it turns out she *was* in trouble. And now it's worse—a lot worse. It's the kind of trouble that you may not be able to help her with. And if you had just pushed, before, back when you first suspected things were wrong, then this wouldn't have happened."

"And if you had pushed, maybe you would've made things worse." Off to the side of the trail, there was a fallen tree, covered with moss. Ezra made his way over to it and sat down, stretching his leg out in front of him.

"I'm not going to ask you for any information. I don't need to. I've already got a rough idea of some of the shit she had to deal with. She was married. And he beat her." He cocked a brow at Law and waited.

"That's the short and sweet version. It gets worse—a lot worse."

"Was he a cop?"

Scowling, Law demanded, "How the hell did you know that?"

"It wasn't that hard to figure out if you know what to look for. I knew she'd been married—I can still see where she wore a ring, even though it's been awhile since she's worn it. Plus, you can tell just by the way she acts that she's been mistreated more than once in her life. That girl's never been in any kind of trouble, so it's not that. Only thing that makes sense is that she was knocked around by a cop. So I just put two and two together." Even the thought of that was enough to have Ezra seeing red. "Did she try to get help?"

"Yeah. And a lot of good it did her. His dad was the chief of police. His mom? She was one of the two doctors in our town. He had been the football captain, was on the student council. Our town's golden boy. He never got in trouble, one of those kids who could do no wrong. He and Hope started dating when we were sophomores. They got married the summer he graduated from college, although I think the mental abuse started well before that. Everybody thought they had one of those sweet little fairy-tale romances." Law turned away and started to pace, scuffing his booted feet through dead, dry leaves. "Hope told me everything was fine for the first couple years—but I don't think it was. Maybe she just needed to believe that."

"She got away from him. You're kicking yourself and I probably would be, too, if I was in your shoes. But she got away from him. That's something you need to remember."

"Yeah." Coming to a halt, Law shoved his hands into the pockets of his jeans. In a flat, emotionless voice, he asked, "You ever fantasize about killing somebody?"

The wash of blood . . . the scent of it, the feel of it. Ezra could remember that, even when he could find no other memory of that night. He'd rather remember nothing than to have the one clear memory be that of Mac's blood covering him.

"You really want to know what it's like to kill somebody, do you, Law?" Ezra asked, forcing the words out of his tight throat. "You want to walk around with that weight on you?"

"That's not what I asked." Law turned and met his eyes. Head cocked, hazel eyes shrewd. "Different thing—killing somebody and fantasizing about it. And it's a different story, probably, thinking about killing somebody who really does need to die, and being the one who had to pull the trigger for . . . whatever your reasons were."

With a fist gripping his throat, Ezra looked away. Whatever his reasons were.

His reasons? He hadn't been worrying about reasons. He had seconds—less—to decide. Did he pull the trigger or did he risk dying himself?

"What was his name? The bastard who whaled on Hope?"

Law's mouth twisted in a bitter snarl. "Joe. Joey. There was a time when I'd called him a friend, too. And that's a punch in the stomach, I'll tell you."

"I reckon it would be." Ezra shoved off the trunk and studied the woods. It was darker here under the canopy of leaves and relatively cooler—relatively. But it was hot as a bitch outside and relatively cooler wasn't really that much cooler. His shirt clung to him and sweat trickled down his neck and back. "So this guy, Joe. He was a cop. And it sounds like he's a bastard and a half, beating on his wife. He's got half the town where you lived eating out of his hand. He still got his badge?"

The look on Law's face was enough of an answer.

Ezra's gut clenched, turned hot inside him and twisted. Dirty cop—dirty cop. Maybe not on the level that Mac had been dirty. But a cop who could beat his wife, and get away with it . . . what else could he call it? That was about as dirty as they came, really.

That hot, greasy knot in his gut started to claw and climb up his throat. Blood roared in his ears.

Put it away. Put it away, he told himself.

"So he's still got his badge." Ezra blew out a breath. "So here's the problem for you . . . aside from the fact that he shouldn't still have his badge. The fact is, he does. And if you keep thinking about doing things, sooner or later, you might decide to act . . . you ever thought about taking it beyond the fantasy?"

"My problem is that I know it would cause hell for Hope if I tried," Law said bitterly.

"And she's been through enough hell."

"Yeah."

"Okay. So maybe you should stop fantasizing . . . and put her ex out of your mind. Besides," Ezra said, studying the trees, "we've got enough to deal with around here now, just trying to figure out what's going on."

"And exactly how are we supposed to do that?"

"Beats the hell out of me," Ezra muttered. "But for now? We keep prowling around these woods until we see something, find something. Or somebody."

"Shit. You know we could be here for a while." Glum, Law stared into the trees.

"Nah. We won't be here any more than another hour or so." Ezra shot a glance at his watch. "Lena and Hope will be heading back by then and we're not leaving them alone."

*   *   *

Slowly, Nia Hollister read the e-mail again.
What is this? she wondered.

Please call me the moment you receive this e-mail . . .
Extremely urgent . . .
. . . regarding your cousin Jolene Hollister . . .

Jolene.
She rubbed her eyes.
Why would a sheriff in Ash, Kentucky, be e-mailing
her over Joely? The words tripped around, ran together
in her mind, not making much sense. It was getting late,
she'd had a long day, she was tired—but not that tired.
Go to sleep . . . call in the morning. After you've rested,
she told herself. She swallowed, wanting to do just that.

Extremely urgent . . .
. . . your cousin Jolene Hollister . . .

She stared at the contact numbers he'd left. One matched
the number included in the little signature line at the
bottom. The other he'd told her was his cell. He'd included all the necessary information for her to make the
international call as well—thoughtful of him.
Why . . . ?
Tears were blurring her eyes. Somehow . . . she knew.
Nia surged to her feet and started to pace the small,
tight confines of her hotel room. No. A sob built up in
her chest.
Joely . . .
Pressing one shaking hand to her lips, she tried to hold
back the scream, tried to keep from sobbing.
This wasn't real.
Taking a deep breath, Nia grabbed her phone. She'd
call them. They'd be wrong. Yes. Wrong.

As she waited to connect, she sat at her computer and pulled up a map of Kentucky.

Just where in the hell was Ash, anyway?

Nielson glanced at his computer, checked the e-mail.

Checked his cell phone. Although he hadn't expected an immediate response, part of him still wanted one. He needed to speak with Nia Hollister. Get this over with.

The silence in his office was interrupted by a brisk knock and he looked up, saw his administrative assistant standing there, her bright green eyes locked on his face.

Something in those eyes warned him. He tensed.

"Yes?"

"There's a Ms. Hollister on the phone," she said. The stern mask she wore cracked and for a moment, he saw the pity there as she shifted her gaze past him to stare at his murder board. "It's the victim's next of kin."

"Shit."

He'd seen them enter the trees.

The two men. Law and King.

Law. Fucking Law Reilly—bastard. Fury all but turned his vision red, choked him.

After all this time, why were things going wrong now?

What were they doing in his woods?

Too close.

Even if they were moving off in the wrong direction.

Too close . . .

None of this had gone as planned. Setting his jaw, he backed away.

None of it.

But then again, it had been awhile since things had gone as planned.

Stupid fucking bunch of flowers, Brody thought, kicking at the dead and dying blooms. The driveway was empty, the house quiet. He'd come out here to talk to King and see if he couldn't get his uncle to back down, change his mind on this lame-ass unofficial "community service" bit—Brody sure as hell wouldn't be bringing his four-wheeler around here again, so it wasn't like King wouldn't get what he wanted.

Right?

But the man wasn't here.

Probably over at Lena's.

"Dumb-ass flowers," he mumbled. He kicked at a tumbled bunch of brightly colored golden blooms. Their fragile blossoms trembled and fell and he ground them down under his heel. Flowers.

The first time his dad had really looked at him in weeks, and it was with disappointment in his eyes. Over a bunch of damn flowers.

Swallowing past the knot in his throat, he shoved a hand in his pocket and pulled out the battered pack of cigarettes. He'd stolen them—Marlboro Lights, but it was the best he could do right now. He lit one and then crouched down, the match still burning and he held it to one of the petals, watching with narrowed eyes.

It burned down to his fingers and he dropped it.

But staring at the singed petal, even with his fingers burning, he felt a little better.

Thunder rumbled warningly through the air. Hope grimaced and shot the darkening sky a nervous glance. "It's looking ugly up there," she said softly, trying not to let the damned fear edge in on her voice.

She was so tired of being afraid. So tired of letting fear dictate everything.

"Why don't we just head to my place for now?" Lena said as the rain started to come down.

"Law will have my head if I'm not home soon," Hope murmured, trying to smile. She didn't want to worry him any more than she already had. He'd spent too much time worrying over her, for her, about her.

"Then we'll call him." Lena pulled a phone out of the backpack she had stashed at her feet. Two minutes later, she tucked the phone away and shot Hope a smile. "That's lucky. He was with Ezra and they're heading to my place now as we speak."

The downpour got harder and the next few minutes passed by slowly, the miles inching along at a crawl. "Man, I'm glad we didn't hang around Lexington any longer," Hope muttered.

"Chances are this will be over within five minutes after we get inside." Lena sighed. "I'd almost lay money on it."

Hope's head was pounding by the time she finally found Lena's driveway. A huge breath whooshed out of her in relief as she parked in the drive, right behind Ezra's big white pickup. "Ezra's here, too," she said.

"Yeah. Maybe he and Law decided to do some sort of male-bonding thing since we went shopping." Lena smiled a little as she said it. The rain came beating down on the car and she grimly reached for the door handle. "It's going to stop raining. The second I hit the porch. Bet me on it?"

Hope shot a look at the sky. She didn't know. It looked pretty ugly to her, and the rain looked like it wanted to hang around for a while. She was just glad they'd been almost home before it started. Driving from Lexington to here in this would have given her a nervous breakdown.

She'd had enough of those, thanks.

Peering through the rain, she said, "They're waiting for us."

"Then by all means," Lena muttered. "Come on, Puck . . ."

TWENTY-ONE

THE HOUSE WAS DARK AND QUIET—TOO DARK. LAW tried the light switch by the back door with no luck.

"You think you lost power?" Hope said softly, trying not to cling to his back, even though that's exactly what she wanted to do.

Law shrugged. "I don't know. I'll check down in the basement, make sure I didn't trip a circuit or something."

Swallowing, Hope studied the dancing, flickering shadows cast on the floor as the lightning flashed. Another storm was rolling in. The thunder crashed and she had to bite her lip to keep from shrieking.

"You okay?" he asked softly, stroking a hand down her arm.

"Just jumpy," she said, trying to smile. Trying, failing miserably.

"I'll light a couple of candles before I go downstairs," he said. "That will help."

Normally, the soft golden glow of candlelight would have helped, but some reason, tonight that soft, golden glow didn't seem so warm and welcoming—it was sinister, secretive, hiding something in its shadows.

Hope huddled by the counter, arms wrapped around

her midsection as she watched Law grab a flashlight from some junk drawer on the island.

As he left the room, that taunting, numbing fear wrapped a fist around her throat and tried to choke her.

She squeezed her eyes closed. *I can do this. I don't have to be afraid . . . I don't have to live like this, I don't, I don't . . . I don't and I haven't.*

As the lights came on, flooding the house, she sucked in a deep breath and sighed. "Oh, shit." Light-headed with relief, she pushed off the counter and staggered a little with her first step.

Light. Sweet, bright light. Moving toward the arched entryway, she started for the stairs. "I'm going to get out of these wet clothes," she called toward the basement.

From the corner of her eye, she noticed the door to Law's office was open.

Frowning, she stopped.

He never left that door open.

Never.

Not when he was working.

Not when he was sleeping.

He didn't leave it open.

Her heart bumped against her ribs and she backed up a step. As she did, she saw . . . something. Something spreading across the gleaming, golden wooden floors of his office. Red.

An ugly, red stain.

No.

Hearing the footsteps behind her, she spun around and saw Law.

He caught sight of her face and concern flashed through his eyes.

For a few seconds, just the sight of him made her feel better. But then his eyes flicked past her shoulder, landing on something behind her.

That dark, ugly red stain, perhaps. She didn't know

and she couldn't turn to look, because there was a shadow coming up behind him, huge and dark and looming.

Screaming out his name, she tried to knock him out of the way.

But she was too far away, and far too slow.

As his long, lean body went sprawling on the floor, Hope stumbled to a stop. With her heart knocking against her ribs, and her throat trying to close down on her, she stared at the dark, faceless shadow.

She was keenly aware of the fact that Law lay still, motionless at her feet. Too still, with a slow spread of red seeping out of his head to spill across the floor.

Law.

Law . . .

No.

As the shadow lifted a hand toward her, she backed away, one shaking step at a time.

The wind whipped her hair back from her face. Standing on the porch, Lena lifted her face to it. The rain was cold, cold enough to send a chill down her back despite the muggy heat still lingering in the air.

"What are you doing?" Ezra asked from behind her.

Smiling over her shoulder, she said, "Just standing here. I love storms." She breathed in the air. She smelled the rain, the scent of grass. Faintly, she could smell Ezra. And . . . something else.

There was an acrid scent.

She took in another deep breath.

Acrid. Sharp.

Smoke.

"Something's burning," she murmured. "Wonder if lightning hit something."

Warm, solid arms slid around her middle and she smiled, leaning back against him. "You and Hope shouldn't have been driving around in this," he murmured, skimming his lips along her shoulder.

"Hmmm. Well, the rain didn't blow in until we were a few miles away. They didn't say much of anything about storms this morning, just a chance of rain." She arched her head to the side and shivered as he shifted his focus to her neck. "By the time the rain decided to be a thunderstorm, we were almost here. Spending a thunderstorm on the side of a little Kentucky country highway? Not supersmart, in my opinion."

The scent of smoke was getting heavier in the air. Thicker—thick enough to penetrate the fog that had begun to wrap around her. Easing away from Ezra's arms, she asked, "Can you smell the smoke?"

Stroking a hand down her back, he said, "Nah."

But then she heard him inhale. "Well, I dunno. Maybe."

Ezra skimmed the skyline. Hard to see much of anything with the low, thick cover of clouds and the rain, and he couldn't see anything a foot or two beyond the tree line—it was just too dark. Shifting his gaze to the west, he followed the road. It was darker there— smoke . . . maybe?

He squinted and then swore. Dread, low and ugly, curled inside his gut. It was smoke, he was almost sure of it. Hard to tell at first, the clouds were so dark, so thick.

But the longer he stared at them, the more certain he was—those black plumes curling against the sky weren't clouds. It was smoke.

His voice gritty, Ezra said quietly, "Lena, I think that might be my house."

The drive didn't take more than eight minutes. He knew that. But the seconds dragged on forever and by the time he and Lena pulled to a halt in front of his house, he felt like he'd aged two decades.

Halfway there, they'd heard the wail of sirens, but he already knew it was pointless.

By the time the fire department arrived, the only thing they'd be able to do was extinguish the blaze.

"Ezra?" Lena murmured.

Sitting behind the steering wheel, his hands gripping the plastic, he said, "Yeah?"

"I . . . I don't know."

She felt like there was something she should say. Something she should do. But what? Reaching over, she sought out his hand, found it resting in a fist on his thigh. It was rigid under hers, bunched and hard. For a long moment, he did nothing and then, he opened his hand, gripped hers so tightly, it almost hurt.

A few seconds later, they pulled up in front of the house.

"I want to make sure there's nobody here," he said softly. "Will you stay in the truck?"

"I'd like to come with you."

"No." He took a deep, slow breath. "Please don't. It looks like the fire's contained to just the house, but the fire department's going to be scrambling around. It will be easier for them to do their job if they aren't worrying about anybody else. I can stay out of their way, get back here quicker if it's just me."

She bit her lip, told herself not to take it personally. She could feel the pain in his voice, the anger. "Okay." She forced a smile and said, "Just hurry back."

"I will."

The door to the truck closed quietly and she suspected he had to restrain himself to keep from slamming it.

He stayed out of the way.

Even when a couple of sheriff's cruisers arrived, he kept out of the way, circling around the perimeter of his property, staring at the blazing remains of his grandmother's house.

Her house—not exactly his. At least not yet. He'd been

working on making it that way, but he hadn't exactly put his mark on it yet. Other things . . . like Lena . . . had kept getting in the way.

Not that he minded having Lena in the way.

A muscle pulsed in his jaw and he barely resisted the urge to hit something—anything. Not that he had a lot of targets just then. Kicking at the muddy ground, he stared at the flames. Rain dripped down his face, into his eyes, but he ignored it, the same way he ignored his sodden clothes, the same way he ignored the few glances that drifted his way.

Who in the hell had done this?

Lena had said lightning, but that didn't settle quite right in Ezra's gut. Too neat. Too easy. Caught in the middle of a fucking mess, there wasn't going to be a neat, easy answer.

"Shit," he muttered. He glanced toward his truck. Through the rain, he could barely make out Lena's silhouette behind the glass. He needed to get back to her— needed to be there, but he had to cool this hot, burning anger first.

Was this connected to the body? To the screams? Why? What was the point? Shit, burning his house down wasn't going to get him away from Lena, if that had been the intention.

Spinning around, he scrubbed his hands over his face, then hooked them behind his neck. Lowering his head, he stared at the muddy ground.

Something caught his eye.

It was muddied, almost buried.

If he hadn't been standing exactly where he was, he wouldn't have seen it.

As disgust curled through him, he crouched down on the ground.

He could have left it. He probably should have. The cop inside him knew that.

But for reasons he couldn't explain, he reached down and scooped it out of the mud and tucked it inside his pocket.

When he rose, he looked back at the house, and then at Lena.

The anger continued to bubble and burn in his gut, but it eased enough to let him start his way back to the truck. Back to Lena.

Halfway there, the sheriff intercepted him.

"You know, before you showed up, Ash used to be a pretty quiet town." Nielson scowled at Ezra.

Frowning at the blazing ruin of his house, Ezra said, "You figuring I'm to blame for this?"

"Shit, no. But it sure as hell looks like you're a magnet for disaster, sometimes." He jerked his head toward Lena. "What is she doing out here?"

"Wasn't about to leave her alone, not until I knew what was going on." Ezra shifted from one foot to the other and shoved a hand through his dripping hair. "Do we really need to stand here in the pouring rain and chat right now?"

"Actually, no. What we need to do is swing by and check on Law Reilly and his visitor."

Cocking a brow, Ezra said, "Hope? Why?"

"Because of that," Nielson said, gesturing to the fire. "Right now, I'm operating on the basis that when one weird thing happens with one of you, it affects all four of you. So we're going to drive out there and talk to those two."

Ezra knew the fire had nothing to do with Lena, Hope, or Law.

But there wasn't any way he could point that out. Not unless he wanted to share with the sheriff what he'd found just a few minutes ago.

Shit.

"Fine. Let's get it done. I want out of the rain."

*   *   *

The tension coming from Ezra was thick enough to choke her. Resting a hand on his thigh, she rubbed it, wished she could think of something to say that would make it better. Make him feel better.

But what could she say?

"The sheriff doesn't think they're in trouble, does he?" she asked, cutting into the silence as it started to weigh too heavily on her.

"I don't know," Ezra said, his voice quiet. Distracted.

Lena bent down and felt around the floor for her bag. The cell phone was tucked into a pouch on the strap and she pulled it free, punched in Law's home number. He wouldn't answer, but if he or Hope was in the kitchen, maybe they'd hear the answering machine come on.

After the fourth ring, the machine came on.

"Hey, it's Lena. We're on our way over . . . ah, the sheriff is going to get there before we do. He's just a few seconds ahead of us. But, well, I wanted to give Hope a heads-up. I know how she is with cops and stuff." She paused, wondering if either of them would answer, but no such luck. Sighing, she disconnected and tucked the phone away again.

"Let's hope Nielson is just erring on the side of caution," she said, forcing herself to smile.

Ezra remained quiet.

Hope's eyes jumped to the phone as Lena's low, smooth voice rolled out of the answering machine.

Sheriff.

Lena . . . and Ezra.

Her heart raced and part of her wanted to hope.

But she knew better.

He stood behind her, big, hard hands on her shoulders. What was he going to do . . . ?

But even as that question rolled through her mind, he was already doing it.

The last thing she remembered was a hot, bright flash of pain.

Then darkness.

TWENTY-TWO

MAYBE IT WAS JUST EZRA'S QUIET, TENSE MOOD. Maybe it was just the culmination of her own tension. After all, the past few weeks had been sheer chaos. The most terrifying night of her life, Ezra's appearance in her life, the discovery of the body at Law's place—it was enough to make anybody paranoid.

Then there was Ezra himself, and all the . . . personal changes he'd brought to her life, and even though the changes were all for the better, it seemed, they were still drastic changes.

Too much going on, that's all it was. That was why she was so on edge. At least that was what she wanted to think, what she tried to make herself believe.

That was why she had the hot, restless feeling crawling around under her skin all of a sudden.

As they pulled up in front of Law's house, she wanted to believe it was something not real—just her imagination. Just stress. Just . . . something.

Because she couldn't think about how to handle it if by some slim chance Nielson was right. It was a thought that had crept in only seconds ago and it wouldn't let go. With its claws sinking deep inside, the worry and doubt twisted and turned inside her, tearing and gnawing.

The car slowed to a stop and she took a deep breath. *Everything is fine,* she told herself. *Everything is fine.*

They'd get up there and they'd knock on the door and Law would open it and everything would be fine.

Gripping Puck's leash tightly, she opened the door and climbed out. Her heart was racing. The skin on the back of her neck stood on end. Everything inside her was on red alert. She was strung so tight when Ezra moved up to stand beside her, she jumped, even though she heard him coming.

"Are you okay?" he asked.

"Just a little edgy," she murmured. "Is the sheriff already here?"

"On the porch, waiting for us."

Reaching for his arm, she took a deep breath. "Then we shouldn't keep him waiting."

Mentally, she told herself, *Let's get this over with. We'll see Law, see Hope, and everything will be fine.* But the closer she got to that house, the more wrong everything felt. And it didn't help when Puck whined, tugging on his leash.

Not fighting her, though. Pulling her, toward the house. When he got to the door, he started nosing at it, and to Lena's surprise, he scratched at it, a soft, low whine coming from his throat.

Lena crouched down by Puck, curling a hand around his neck and scratching his ears. "What's wrong, boy?" she murmured.

Nielson didn't seem to notice as he knocked on the door.

There was no answer and after another thirty seconds passed, Puck scratched at the door again.

"Think they might have gone somewhere?" Nielson asked as he knocked again.

Puck was getting more anxious by the second.

Trying not to let her voice shake, Lena said, "We need

to get inside." Sliding her backpack off, she unzipped it and started digging around inside for her keys. Ages ago, Law had given her a spare set. He was notorious for locking himself out of the house, or losing his keys, so she kept a spare set for him.

As she pulled the keys out, Nielson said, "Ms. Riddle, I can't just enter a private residence."

"Fine. You don't enter. I will."

"Give me the keys, Lena," Ezra said quietly. He reached over and tugged them gently from her hands, and just as easily, he nudged her side. "Let me go in first."

"Ezra . . ."

He dipped his head and brushed his lips over hers. "Just stay with Puck, Lena. It's going to be fine."

She was so pale, he thought. They had left in such a hurry, she'd left her sunglasses at home and right now, her crystalline blue eyes were almost glassy with worry, fear. Tearing his gaze from her face, he looked at Nielson. "Something has her dog freaked out. If it comes down to it, I'll take the heat on this. I'm here as a private citizen anyway, and Lena's got keys to the place, so she has a lawful right to enter."

He eased the door open and slid inside. It didn't take any time to realize there wasn't going to be any heat coming down—extreme circumstances covered all sorts of bases.

Lena lifted a hand and covered her nose. "Holy shit, what is that smell?" she asked.

"Lena, you need to wait in the car," Ezra said quietly.

"What?"

"Take Puck and go wait in the car."

Lena balked. But Puck was tugging at the lead, whining low in his throat. He gave a low bark and tried once more to tug Lena inside the house. "I'm not going to the car," she said softly.

Ezra went to grab her arm and Puck whirled, hackles rising. The dog bared his teeth, snarling in warning.

Instinctively, he backed away and it gave the dog the few seconds he needed to guide his mistress inside. "Damn it, Lena. There might be somebody in here," Ezra snapped.

"Don't you think Puck would know if there was?" she said, her voice oddly calm considering how pale she was.

"You want me to trust a dog."

She tossed him a grimace over her shoulder as she let Puck lead her deeper into the house. "Why not? I do every day of my life."

Shit, shit, shit—

Nielson followed and the look in his eyes was one of disgust and resignation. He knew the stink in the air, knew it as well as Ezra did. "She needs to get the hell out," Nielson said as they moved to catch up with her. "We can't be certain the house is secure."

"Actually, I think we can," Ezra said, although he definitely wasn't too big on just trusting a dog's instincts. "If there was anybody here who was a danger to Lena, her dog wouldn't be walking her inside—I guarantee that."

Apparently both dog and woman were on a mission and it took less than thirty seconds to find out why.

The metallic, coppery scent of blood was stronger than the stink of death, now. "At least let me check things out," Ezra snapped, easing past her in the hallway. Slowly, he opened the door, scanning the brightly lit kitchen. The smell of blood was getting stronger and stronger.

The source of it lay on the floor, completely and utterly still.

"Oh, fuck," he snarled.

"What?" Lena demanded, her voice trembling. "Law?"

"No. It's Hope. She slit her damned wrists, looks like."

There was a scream in his head—warning, warning, warning—something wrong. Way wrong.

There was a gun lying discarded by the kitchen island, dropped there almost like an afterthought.

A baseball bat.

One sharp-ass knife.

Kneeling in the growing pool of Hope's blood, he grabbed her wrists. Thank God—her skin was still warm. She was pale, but her skin was warm. "Lena, call nine-one-one."

Nielson said, "I'm already on it." He stood in the doorway, his face grim, his eyes dark. "Think that's what the dog was going on about?"

Silence fell, stretched out forever. "Where's Law?" Lena whispered.

Ezra looked up and met Nielson's stare. "Can you search the house?"

The sheriff nodded and as he quietly slipped out of the room, Ezra concentrated on Hope. Concentrated on making the blood stop. Concentrated on anything but the wooden baseball bat that lay just a few feet away from him. On one end, it had bloody handprints on it.

Prints too small to belong to a man. On the other end, there was more blood . . . and something else he didn't want to think about.

"Ezra, is she okay? Is . . . is she going to be okay?" Lena asked quietly.

Gruffly, he said, "I don't know, baby. She's not conscious, but this didn't happen long ago. The blood . . . I think it's clotting up."

"Why would she . . . ?"

Tearing his eyes away from Hope, he looked at Lena. "I don't know. I just don't know." It didn't make sense, none of it.

Like she'd read his mind, Lena shook her head. "Something's not right, Ezra. She was fine when she left my place—fine. Why in the hell would she have done this?"

Ezra didn't know what to say to that.

More often than not, Lena was content with her lot in life—she couldn't see, so what? She had her own life, had a job she loved, had friends . . . and for the past few weeks, she even had a lover, a man in her life who liked her just fine, the way she was.

But right then, she wanted to be able to use her eyes.

All but trapped in the corner of the kitchen, she couldn't do anything but listen as the paramedics barked at each other—it sounded like a foreign language, clipped phrases, numbers rattled off in seemingly random order.

The air in her lungs shrank down to next to nothing. All she could smell was the blood—like it lined the inside of her nose. She desperately wanted to leave the kitchen, even if it was just to go out to the porch, but she was afraid to move, afraid she might get in their way just then. Hope—had she really . . .

No.

Lena shook her head. Closing her eyes, she said quietly, "No."

Even though she said it just to herself, it helped. It wasn't right—the pieces didn't fit.

The paramedics had arrived in a loud, fast rush, and in a loud, fast rush, they were gone. The silence was so sudden, it left her head spinning. Reaching down, she touched her hand to Puck's head. "Find Ezra," she murmured.

Her head was spinning. Blood roared in her ears.

Shock, she told herself.

That was why she was still hearing the echo of paramedics talking.

She crashed right into Ezra. He'd disappeared only seconds after the paramedics showed on the scene—she had no idea where he'd gone. Burying her hands in his T-shirt, she curled her fingers into the damp, worn material.

"Damn it, where have you been?" she demanded and she hated the pitiful whine she heard in her voice.

"Lena . . ." He lifted his hands. They rested on her shoulders.

When he leaned in and pressed his lips to her brow, she sighed and relaxed against him. "I'm sorry. I think I'm freaking out a little bit here. Where in the hell is Law?"

A loud, booming voice drifted from somewhere . . . somewhere close.

"BP is stable . . ."

Swallowing, Lena pulled back.

Okay, she had heard that. And that was not one of the paramedics who had been working on Hope, either. So it was another paramedic. And if there was another paramedic here, that meant there was somebody else hurt.

No. Oh, no.

Tension mounted inside her, turning her muscles rigid. "Ezra. Where is Law?" she asked, her voice soft, all but soundless.

He stroked his hands down her arms. "We found him in his office, Lena. He . . . ah . . . somebody worked him over pretty bad. The paramedics are with him, getting him ready to take to the hospital."

"Wuh . . ." She licked her lips. "What do you mean, somebody worked him over?"

"He's been beaten. Bad."

"No." Lena shook her head. "That's just bullshit. He was just over at my place. A couple of hours ago. He was fine. Hope was fine. She went shopping. She had fun. Law is fine. Nobody would . . . no. Nobody would hurt him," she said, her voice breaking. "I need to see him. I have to talk to him."

"You can't, baby. Not right now." Ezra caught her in his arms and pulled her close. "The paramedics are taking him in, Lena. They have to get him to the hospital. He's been hurt really bad and they have to get him to the hospital."

Hospital . . .

Law.

"Oh, God," she whispered. Burying her face against the front of Ezra's shirt, she started to cry.

Rocking her, Ezra stroked a hand down her slender back. The sobs wracked her entire body, nearly choked her. Helpless in the face of her grief, he murmured to her, kissed her temple, and held her. There was nothing more he could do.

When the paramedics rolled Law by, he lifted his head and stared at the battered face of Lena's best friend.

No.

There was one other thing he could do.

He was going to find out who had done this.

He didn't carry his badge anymore, but this shit? It was going to stop.

There was a third body left in the house.

There was no need for an ambulance, though.

Crouching down by Prather's lifeless body, Nielson sighed and tried to figure out just what in the hell was going on.

"What in the world were you doing here, son?" he muttered.

His team was outside, waiting for him to clear them in, although there wasn't much point in keeping them out. This scene had already been blown to hell and back. Hope Carson's suicide attempt, Law Reilly's brutal assault, and Earl Prather's murder.

It was one big tangle and somehow he knew getting

the snags out of this wasn't going to be easy, fast, or pretty.

"What was he doing out here?"

Glancing up, he saw Ezra King standing in the doorway, his arms crossed over his chest, a grim light glinting in his eyes. "Your guess is as good as mine," Nielson murmured.

"He's not in uniform."

"No." Not that Nielson had needed that pointed out. Prather had on jeans and a T-shirt, now liberally splattered with blood and body fluids. Whoever had shot him had planted that bullet in his gut. A slow, painful way to die. If Prather had gotten help, he might have lived.

His killer had likely known that—which would explain the smashed cell phone lying a few feet away, and the equally destroyed cordless landline on the other side of the desk.

"Today was his day off," Nielson said softly. "He worked the weekend so he had today and tomorrow off."

"Law didn't do this," Ezra said, his voice sharp as a whip. He came into the room, stopping a few feet away. Crouching down, he peered at the body. "He's been dead more than a few hours and Law was with me, hiking through the woods over at Lena's place until just over two hours ago—been there since early this morning. Hope was shopping in Lexington with Lena."

"You'll give a statement to that effect, of course," Nielson said, nodding. No, he didn't think Law had done this. Law Reilly could kill. Hell, most people probably could kill, under the right circumstances. But Reilly would do it straight and quick.

Prather had suffered for some time before he'd died. Had crawled around trying to get out of the room, to a phone to call for help—that much was evident in the blood smears all over the place.

His killer had tormented him with the pain of his impending death, Nielson suspected.

If nothing else, he suspected Reilly lacked the patience for that.

TWENTY-THREE

THERE WERE CERTAIN SOUNDS THAT NEVER CHANGED, no matter where you were.

Like the beeping sounds you heard in a hospital.

The squeaking sound a nurse's tennis shoes made on linoleum.

The smells weren't much different.

The smell of hospital-grade disinfectant, used to eliminate the stink of death, decay, and disease. Flowers. The bland foods.

Hope knew, before she even opened her eyes, that she was in a hospital.

Trying not to panic, she lifted her lashes and stared around the room, tried to remember what she was doing there.

But she couldn't. Couldn't remember, couldn't think. She remembered Law—they'd been at Lena's house. She thought. Driving back to Law's place. The rain.

And then . . . nothing. Just a blank. The harder she tried to remember, the more scared she became. The fear wrapped around her, suffocating her, a fist around her throat.

It hazed her vision, clouded her head. Dazed, barely aware of what she was doing, she started to clamber out of the bed. Law. She needed to find Law. He was in trouble. Where . . .

Something dark . . . it tried to creep in on her vision. A shadow. Death. Danger. Shit. Shit. Shit. She needed to find Law. As panic tried to settle in, she fought to push it back.

A cheerful, chirping voice rang through the air. "There you are now, all wide awake."

Startled, Hope looked up. The nurse wore a set of pale blue scrubs and she had that professional, blank smile on her pretty young face. Hope had never seen the woman before, but she recognized that smile all too well. "Where's Law?" she asked, her voice cracking. Her throat. Dry—so dry.

"Why don't you just lie back down . . ." The nurse went to ease her back on the bed.

But at the first touch, Hope's nerves shattered.

She swung out. For a split second, the sight of the bandage on her wrist startled her, but only for a second. She was back in a hospital, damn it. Not again—

Remy Jennings stood at the nurse's station, his arms folded over his chest, dread burning and twisting inside him.

He'd caught one glimpse of her face before the curtain had been drawn.

Hair tangled, hanging in her face, clad in one of those ugly hospital gowns, half-falling off one skinny shoulder.

Listening as she screamed and swore, he looked back at Nielson and then studied the reports.

"It's not very likely she did it," Nielson said, glancing toward the room as a particularly vicious curse rang through the air.

Remy looked up. "Why? Because she sounds so meek and mild?"

"She's got a bit of an alibi," Nielson said. "She was with Lena Riddle for more than half the day, shopping in Lexington."

Remy grunted. Yeah, pretty decent alibi. But still . . . there was something really strange going on with that woman. "Were there fingerprints on the gun? The bat?"

"Yes. We're running them." He scowled and reached up, rubbing the back of his neck. "And my gut says they'll be hers. But my gut also says she didn't do it."

Remy frowned. "Then find me proof. We've got a dead deputy on our hands. We need something more than your gut instinct." He glanced toward the other end of the small emergency department. In the large room there, he could see Law Reilly.

He hadn't woken up.

There was swelling on the brain, and according to the doctor Remy had spoken with, it was entirely possible Reilly could die in the next twenty-four hours. Bringing the murder count up to two.

Could that shy, nervous woman have killed both of them?

If he went with his gut, he had to agree with Nielson.

"What in the hell is going on here lately?" he muttered.

But the sheriff didn't have an answer for him.

Lena held Law's hand in hers.

They'd moved him to ICU sometime the previous night. She had lost track of time—hell, she wasn't entirely sure what day it was. Sometime early Tuesday morning, she thought. She was pretty sure only a little more than a day had passed since she had gone shopping with Hope in Lexington.

A day.

Shit.

Tears leaked out from under her closed lids and she squeezed Law's hand. "Come on, Law, wake up," she whispered.

She wouldn't let herself think he might not wake up. She couldn't think that way. Couldn't. He was strong, he was stubborn—so what if he had some bruising and swelling on the brain? He had a hard head—he could handle it. The rest of it, broken ribs, a busted radius, those would heal. Bruising and swelling on the brain shouldn't even slow him down.

A sob slipped out of her.

"Damn it, wake up," she snapped.

But he made no sound. Made no move.

Sighing, she sat up and wiped the tears from her face. Time was slipping away from them, she knew. She didn't know much about medical shit, but she vaguely remembered hearing something about the fact that the more time passed without him waking up, the worse it got. In her mind, that meant he'd already been out of it too long.

Way too long.

A door opened and she heard the heavy tread of shoes, a familiar gait. The feet paused at the foot of the bed and she shifted to face the visitor.

"Any change?" Sheriff Nielson asked, his voice quiet.

"No."

"I didn't think so." He sighed. "Ezra's dozing out in the waiting area. Your dog looks kind of pissed about being out there instead of in here with you."

"At least this way, Ezra can take him outside every little while," Lena murmured.

An awkward silence fell and finally, the sheriff cleared his throat. "Ah, Ezra said you were in Lexington most of the afternoon shopping with Hope."

"Yes."

"You're sure you were in Lexington?"

Lena rolled her eyes. "We don't have a Target anywhere around here, do we?"

"No. Did you buy anything?"

Lena shrugged. "Hope did most of the buying. I think I bought a CD." She bent down and grabbed her backpack, only to stop. "Yeah. I did, but I left it at home."

"The receipt as well?"

"Yes." Tapping her fingers on her knee, she asked, "Why do you want to know? What's going on?"

Come on, man. Wake up, now. You had me dragging my butt out of bed to go help your friend, now it's your turn. She needs some help, Law, and she needs it in a bad, bad way.

It was Lena's voice. Law would know her voice anywhere.

But he couldn't figure out what she was talking about.

What friend?

And why did he have to wake up now?

He was so fucking tired . . .

Drifting away, he tuned her voice back out.

A hand caught his. Squeezed. Hard.

She's in trouble, Law. They are saying she put you here. Come on, Law. You can't let them do this. Wake up. They are going to put her away—they are saying she's crazy. Hope isn't crazy, Law. You need to wake up and tell them that.

Hope. Crazy—fuck, not this shit again.

Something stirred in the back of his mind.

Memory.

Hope . . . standing in his hallway.

A look of fear flashing across her face.

Shit.

Pain exploded through his head as he tried to think.

Groaning, he went to lift his hands to cradle his head, but he couldn't even move.

Weak, weak as a kitten.

The low, pitiful sound would have been more suited to a baby animal instead of a grown man. But it was angel's music, as far as Lena was concerned.

Resting a hand on his chest, she trailed her fingers up, touched his cheek. "Hey . . . you awake in there?" she asked, trying to sound teasing, joking.

She was just a breath away from tears.

He grunted. Then sighed and shifted. And his hand, the one she still held, squeezed hers.

Twenty-four hours later, Law Reilly sat up in his bed—with the aid of the adjustable head of the bed and a few pillows. Staring at the sheriff, he said quietly, "You want to run that by me again?"

"I might have to arrest her. They also want a psychiatric evaluation, and she's being held in the psych ward for the time being," Nielson said.

He looked completely disgusted as he said it, but it didn't help Law's state of mind at all.

"Stop it. All of it," Law snarled. "And get her out of the damned psych ward."

"I can't," Nielson said. "I tried to keep this from happening, but her prints were all over the gun that shot Prather, and all over the baseball bat that was used to clobber you."

"I saw Prather lying dead in my office before somebody hit me, and she was gone all fucking day, so she didn't kill him," Law said, trying not to lose his temper. He'd get her out. He would. She'd be fine. "She didn't do this to me—I was looking at her when somebody hit me from behind. Hope didn't do this."

Nielson sighed. "Look, Reilly, I believe you. And once

we get your report done up, I'll take it to Jennings my-self. Maybe that will change things. But . . ."

A muscle throbbed in Nielson's jaw and Ezra had a bad feeling he knew what the sheriff was going to say.

"But what?" Ezra asked softly when Nielson remained quiet.

"It appears she's got a history of mental imbalance."

"What she has is a history of being abused," Law said shortly. "Her fucking husband created the 'mental imbalance' picture to make it easier for people to ignore her and his fucking . . ."

He cut himself off before he could finish. That was Hope's private business—she probably wouldn't thank him for sharing it. Shaking his head, he said, "She is not crazy."

She wasn't.

But if he didn't get her out . . .

Don't think like that, he told himself. *Just don't.*

She'd gotten out before. She'd do it again. And this time, she wouldn't have to handle it alone.

This time, that crazy, cruel bastard ex of hers wasn't around.

This time was different.

Flexing his left hand, he stared at it and tried to remember something else. Anything else. But there was nothing. He was nothing but one big bruise all over, and he didn't remember much—he remembered seeing Prather's body sprawled on the floor of his office, and he remembered a look of fear, horror racing across Hope's face in that last moment, just before something hit him in the back of the head.

Hearing footsteps, he glanced up. Nielson was leaving.

"I look like I went a round with a Mack truck, don't I?" Law said quietly. He knew—he'd seen his reflection for the first time that morning. He hadn't been able to make it to the bathroom to piss without holding on to the damned IV pole.

"You look . . . rough." Nielson stopped in the door, waiting.

"Yeah. Rough." He looked down at his right forearm, broken. The doctors thought he'd probably blocked a blow to his head with it. This was one way to get him to use that stupid voice software he hated so much. "Takes a lot of strength to beat somebody black and blue, even if they are using a baseball bat."

Looking at the sheriff, he said softly, "Hope look like she's got the physical strength for this?"

"I already told you I don't think she did it," Nielson said. "What else do you want me to say?"

"Convince Jennings it wasn't her. Don't let him have her arrested, Nielson. If he tries to issue a warrant, talk him out of it. I'm telling you—she can't handle it. She's already been through hell, and this will only fuck her up even worse."

Nielson sighed. "I'll do my best, but people around here are gunning for blood. Half of them are convinced your friend is the one who killed that woman. Hell, Hope might even be safer if she was in jail for a few days—let everybody cool off. I don't really think Remy suspects her anyway, but we have to go by the evidence, Reilly. Not by our gut, but by the evidence."

"Then find the real evidence . . . not the bread crumbs some sick fuck spread out for you."

Then he closed his eyes. He wasn't tired, but he needed to rest. Needed to heal. He couldn't walk out of here today—he'd barely made it to the bathroom. But one day soon—hopefully tomorrow, he would walk out of here.

As soon as he could, he was going to track down Remy Jennings and plant his fist in the bastard's face.

Good thing he was almost as good with his left hand as he was with his right.

Trapped.

The door wasn't locked, but she wasn't fooled by that. She was trapped here.

Hope curled up on the bed, staring at the plain white walls and trying not to think.

As long as she didn't think, Hope was mostly okay.

Lena had come by earlier, told her what the nurses wouldn't.

Law was okay. He'd woken up and he was talking.

That was all that mattered, really.

Law was okay.

Two different shrinks had tried to talk to her, but Hope was tired of talking to shrinks.

She wasn't crazy, was so tired of them trying to tell her she was. She'd lived through that already, and she was almost certain she'd rather die than do it again.

Almost.

But then she'd look at the healing, neatly stitched wounds on her wrists and fury would take over.

A lie. Those wounds were a lie.

She hadn't done that. No matter what the doctors told her, no matter what anybody said, she hadn't done it. Somebody had done that to her.

Law.

No. Can't think about him . . .

But she couldn't stop herself.

She needed to think about him. Needed to talk to him, needed to tell him. There was something important. But it was so hard to think . . . all that crap they kept giving her. Every time she thought she'd be able to think again, they showed up again . . . and oh, shit . . .

The door opened.

Deep inside, something wild started to shudder. Shake.

It was the nurse again. And she had two of the male nursing assistants with her.

Drugs.

They were going to drug her again.

Hope drew her legs close to her chest, told herself not to fight. The more she fought, the crazier they thought she was, and the more they'd do this.

But instinct took over when she saw that needle and she couldn't stop it. Swearing, she lashed out with a foot and hot satisfaction rolled through her when she managed to kick one of the nursing assistants right between the legs.

Remy stood in the door. For a few seconds, he couldn't think. Then, finally, fury had his leaden muscles moving and he strode forward.

"What in the hell are you doing?" he snarled, glaring at the nurse.

"Sir, you'll have to wait in the hallway."

"I don't think so. What are you doing?"

Two men, wearing stark white scrubs, stood on either side of the bed, holding Hope Carson pinned. One held her arms just above the healing wounds at her wrists. The other held her knees.

"We need to administer her medication," the nurse said. "Unfortunately, she's resistant."

"She's allowed to resist," Remy snapped. "Unless somebody has power of attorney and insists she's to be medicated whether she wants it or not. You can't make her take the drugs if she doesn't want them."

He waited a beat and then coolly asked, "Does somebody have power of attorney?"

"It's for her own good. Without the medication, she becomes agitated, irrational . . . dangerous."

Remy smiled. "Dangerous. I've been outside at the

nurse's station for the past thirty minutes on a call and I haven't heard a sound from this room. How dangerous can she be?" He looked at the nursing assistants and then at the nurse. "She was perfectly fine until the three of you stepped in here."

Moving around, he stopped at the foot of the bed. "Let her go," he said, his voice flat and hard.

"She's a violent criminal," the nurse snapped.

Hell. Were these people blind? he wondered. The woman lying handcuffed in the bed was terrified, and she'd fight when she was cornered, but a violent criminal? Shit. Again, he said, "Let. Her. Go."

The assistants slowly removed their hands and Remy studied Hope's face. She blinked. Those pale green eyes were clouded. Hell. How much crap had they pumped into her system? "Do you know where you are?" he asked softly.

The nurse snapped, "She won't talk. She hasn't talked to anybody since they brought her to the unit."

Hope curled her lip and gave the nurse a look of such withering disgust that Remy had to hide a smile. Then she looked at him and swallowed. "Yes," she said, her voice raspy and rough. "I know where I am."

"Do you know why?"

Her lashes drooped low over her eyes and she sighed, her narrow shoulders rising and falling. "I don't want to talk to you." She glanced at his face and then lay down, drawing the blanket over her shoulders. "I don't want to talk to anybody."

"Fair enough. But I do want you to answer this question, and it's important. Do you want any more medication? To keep you calm? For your own good?"

Hope sat up and this time, though her eyes were still clouded, they snapped with fury. "I don't need medicine. If they wouldn't keep sticking me with needles, they wouldn't need to worry about calming me down, either.

No, to answer your question, I don't want any more medication."

Then she shot the nurse a look of pure, undiluted disgust. "Irrational. I wonder how fucking rational you would be if you were put in a psych ward for no fucking reason and had some nurse pumping you full of drugs you didn't need. How fucking rational you would be if people were calling you a violent criminal. What in the hell ever happened to innocent until proven guilty?"

"You haven't been proven guilty of any crimes," Remy said, although he knew that wasn't going to make any difference to her.

In the eyes of some people in this town, she was guilty.

Her pale green eyes went cold as ice. "So this is how you treat everybody who gets assaulted in this town," she said, her voice thick with sarcasm. "Lovely."

She reached up and rubbed absently at one of her arms. Remy scowled when he saw the multiple, mottled bruises there. Bruises in the shape of hands. Fuck, how often had they been drugging her? Why had they been drugging her?

Because of what had happened to Law? Or was it something else? He didn't know and just then, he didn't care.

He only knew two things—none of this fit and she had bruises on her.

Those bruises really pissed him off.

Focus—he needed to focus.

He shoved all of that out of his mind and looked up, staring at the nurse, who was still there, holding that damned syringe in her hand. "Why don't we step outside?" he suggested softly.

Reaction settled in and left Hope shaking. Grabbing the blankets, she hauled them up and huddled under them like a rabbit. Staring out the narrow window, she wished she could just fade away, fade away and disappear. Forever.

But she knew she couldn't.

She might have escaped another forced dose of some sedative, but this wasn't done.

That was the lawyer.

Remy Jennings.

She remembered him.

He was probably here to get her to say something, make it easier for them to arrest her.

CHAPTER
TWENTY-FOUR

"Is there anything left?"

A cool breeze kicked up, blowing her hair back from her face. She could smell the scent of wet, charred wood, grass, and the coming promise of fall.

Next to her, Ezra sighed. "The frame of the house, walls. That sort of thing. Sure as hell doesn't look like much of anything can be saved."

She caught his hand and squeezed. "I'm sorry."

"Thanks." He laced his fingers with hers.

"It was a waste of time, wasn't it?"

"What?"

She lifted a shoulder, shrugging. "Well, if whoever did this had anything to do with that woman, if they burned this place down, thinking that would make you leave, it was a waste of time. You're not going to leave as easy as that, right?"

Ezra chuckled. It was a hoarse, rusty sound. "Hell, no, I'm not leaving. Guess I'm going to have to look for a place to rent, though."

"You got the money for that?"

After a brief pause, he said, "Yeah. I'm good on that front. My grandmother . . . well, let's just say she hid it well, but she knew how to play with money."

She wasn't even aware the fear had been there until it loosened inside her heart. Wasn't aware she'd had the fear until it seeped away. He wasn't leaving. Closing her eyes, she leaned against his arm. It felt good, she realized. Leaning on somebody. Leaning on him.

Maybe it wasn't such a bad thing, to lean on somebody. Maybe he'd even lean on her every now and then.

Tired, Lena whispered, "Sometimes I wonder what would have happened if I hadn't woken up that night. Would any of this have happened?"

Ezra pulled her in front of him, cupped her face. When he stroked one thumb over her lower lip, she sighed and shivered. "Well, I know one thing that might not have happened," he said quietly. He dipped his head and brushed his mouth against hers.

"This." He nibbled on her lower lip and then lifted his head a little. With his brow pressed to hers, he said, "Seeing you at the sheriff's office made me open my eyes. Maybe I would have done it sooner or later anyway, maybe not. But I'm not sorry I saw you there and I wouldn't have seen you there if you had slept the night through."

Then he straightened. With strong, steady strokes, he moved his hands down, rubbing them down her arms, then back up. "Besides, if you waking up that night is what is bringing all this on, then it's a good thing. Sooner or later, he's going to screw up—that's how he'll be caught. And stopped. Keep that in mind when you start getting mad, frustrated, or scared."

"Mad. Frustrated. Scared." She slid her arms around his waist and pressed close. "That pretty much describes my state of mind at any given time anymore."

In a low, heated voice, she added, "I fucking hate it. All this shit, it's in my head almost all the time and I can't turn it off, can't stop it, and it's driving me nuts."

Her voice cracked as she whispered, "Damn it, Ezra.

What is this? What else is going to happen? Your house. Prather—hell, he was an ass but I didn't want him dead. Law almost gets beaten to death. Hope's locked up like some lunatic on the crazy floor at the county hospital and they're talking like Remy might have to arrest her. I just don't get it. I don't understand any of it."

"Lena." He closed his eyes. Shit. Blowing out a breath, he eased back and cupped her face in his hands. Stroking his thumb over the full curve of her lower lip, he murmured, "I don't know what's going on with Law or Hope, but . . . well, what happened here, it's not related to anything else, I don't think. I can't prove it, but I'm almost positive."

Her brow puckered. "What do you mean?"

"Just call it instinct. I can't say anything else about it until I know, but I don't think the fire is related to what happened at Law's house. None of it."

"But . . ."

Dipping his head, he bussed her mouth. "Stop," he whispered against her lips. "You've got enough on your mind right now. Just stop worrying about the house. It's just a house, anyway."

She rested her hands on his chest, stroked upward. Resting one hand on his cheek, she shook her head. "It wasn't just a house to you, Ezra. It was your grandma's house. Don't tell me that didn't mean something to you. You might not talk about this place much, but I hear your voice when you talk about her. She meant a lot to you."

"Yeah. She did. And she'd be glad that nobody was hurt, before anything else," Ezra said, turning his face to her palm and kissing it. He couldn't deny the ache in his chest, though. Looking up, he studied the rubble and what little remained of the house his grandma had been so proud of. The important stuff, like his grandma's quilts, her wedding picture, those things had been given to his mother or aunts. Thank God.

The house itself, yeah, it had meant something and he was madder than hell over the destruction of the pretty old house.

But as he stood there with Lena in his arms, he found himself thinking about Hope and Law.

Hell, what if Nielson hadn't had that weird instinct to check on Hope and Law? Either of them, both of them might be dead.

What if he'd left Lena at the house when he went to investigate the fire?

What if the bastard had gone to Lena's house instead of over to Law's?

It might have been Lena lying in a pool of blood.

Involuntarily, he tightened his arms. Raggedly, he whispered, "Shit, Lena. I don't think I ever want to do without you in my life, you know that?"

It just wasn't thinkable.

Not anymore.

How had this happened?

So quick.

So strong.

So certain.

Lifting his head, he cupped her chin and guided her face up. "Ever," he muttered.

She sighed against his mouth as he kissed her and when she twined her arms around his neck, aligned her body to his, his heart stuttered, skipped a few beats.

She already mattered so much.

Meant so much.

Everything.

Distantly, he heard a car motor and he swore, lifting his head to watch as a truck rolled past, driving at about half the speed limit. Even from here, he could see the driver and the passenger gawking.

"Let's go back to your place," he mumbled against her lips. "This is a regular tourist attraction out here."

* * *

He cruised along down the narrow little country high-way, easily navigating the sharp, winding curves in his big, white van. He could see the back of King's pickup truck up ahead of him. Part of him wanted to get closer. And when he saw King turn off onto Lena's driveway, he was tempted to drive just far enough down the road and do a U-turn, come back, watch them.

For now . . . they had their hands full. Things were a mess, although one thing was certain—they weren't thinking so much about screams, and he doubted they were so curious about the woods or what secrets they might find there.

Things hadn't exactly gone according to plan, but re-gardless, these thorns in his side were now focused on other issues.

And that gave him the time he needed to make sure he had dealt with his issues.

Caution.

It was all about caution, after all.

If he had been more cautious in the beginning, none of this would have happened.

True, he'd had some fun and he didn't regret it, but in the future, he'd be much, much more careful.

So instead of turning around, going back to Lena's house, he kept driving. And because it amused him, when he neared Deb Sparks's house, he slowed down to a near crawl until he saw her shadow in the window. The curtains parted. Fluttered. She disappeared and then he chuckled to himself, slid a hand back over his smooth scalp.

Yes, he had to be cautious, but he could still have fun. And it was a lot of fun to toy with Deb, always had been.

Part of him wanted to toy with Lena, the same way he often toyed with Deb.

But again . . . caution.

The police radio started to crackle.

He'd be long gone before the first cruiser even got here.

As Ezra came to a stop in front of her place, Lena asked softly, "So how much are you wishing you hadn't ever decided to move here?"

"Not even a little." He pulled the keys out of the ignition and opened the door. She was already climbing out by the time he got around the truck. Caging her in, he leaned in and rubbed his lips against hers. "Fucked up as everything is, I'm where I want to be, Lena. That's all there is to it."

Her sigh caressed his mouth. "You're a strange man, Ezra."

"No. Just one who's willing to deal with the bad shit. You got to take the good with the bad, darlin'. That's how life plays out."

She laughed, but it was a sad, lost sound. "The good with the bad. There's a dead woman, a dead cop, my best friend is in the hospital, and one of his best friends is being held in the psych unit. Your house gets burned to a crisp. That's an awful lot of bad shit. Where's the good to balance it out?"

"Right here." He hooked a hand around the nape of her neck and touched his brow to hers. "I've got all the good I need right here."

"Ezra, honey, I've got to tell you, I'm flattered, but I don't think I'm good enough to balance out that much bad shit."

"Yeah. You are." He caught her mouth in a soft, slow kiss, ending it with a series of lighter, teasing kisses that he brushed over her cheek in a trail up to her ear. "Here's the thing—this bad shit? It's going to pass. It will. Always does. But I plan on sticking with you, so you're always going to be here."

Reluctantly, she smiled. "You sound so sure of this. How can you be so sure of this? Of us?"

"Because it just feels too right. Nothing's ever felt quite as right as you do, baby," Ezra murmured, nuzzling her neck. "You'll figure it out, too. But until you do, I don't mind waiting."

I'll figure it out? Hell, the guy already had her heart melting in his hands. But Lena, as much as part of her wanted to make that jump, had caution bred into her. Bringing one hand to his face, she said, "You're doing a pretty good job of convincing me, Slick."

Rising on her toes, she pressed her mouth to his. "Now . . . maybe I could convince you to come inside . . . and take me to bed."

No convincing was needed, but Ezra doubted he needed to tell her that. Trailing after her, he waited while she took Puck off his leash and although his hands itched to touch her, although he ached to hold her, he waited by the door while she played with the dog for a few minutes.

The moment the retriever came off the leash, he was like a puppy, bouncing around and wagging his tail like crazy. Lena chuckled and said, "Yeah, I know. It's been a crazy few days, hasn't it, boy? Maybe we'll take a walk later."

When she straightened and turned to face him, he crossed the floor and reached up, drawing the dark glasses from her face and putting them on the table. Then he dipped his head, pressed his mouth to her brow. Her lashes fluttered low, shielding her eyes. He pressed a kiss to each closed eye and then skimmed his lips along one cheekbone down to her mouth.

"Wasn't that long ago I didn't even know you," he muttered against her lips. "Now I can't think about going through even one day without seeing you."

He cupped her breasts in his hands. "Touching you."

He caught her lower lip between his teeth and tugged on it gently. "Kissing you. Tasting you."

"Ezra." She whispered his name, her voice shaking, husky with hunger. Sliding her hands up his chest, she linked them behind his neck. Need had her shaking. The tenderness in his voice, the gentleness in his hands made her heart clench and ache in the most beautiful way.

Tears burned her eyes as he cradled her face in his hands and took her mouth with his. "Nothing happens to you," he said against her lips and the words were like a promise and a plea, all at once. "You understand?"

"I understand." She slid her fingers into his hair. "Same goes, though, Slick. Nothing happens to you."

They started toward the steps, and a walk that normally took just seconds took five minutes and they left a trail of clothing behind them. Her shirt was off before they hit the staircase. His followed shortly after. When they hit the landing, he stopped her to remove her shoes and jeans, and when she would have climbed a few stairs, he stopped her with his hands on her hips, pressing a kiss to her spine, and then another, inching lower and lower.

Each light kiss left her quivering. When he reached the small of her back, her knees melted.

As she grabbed onto the handrail, Lena's head fell back and she swayed, certain she was going to collapse, fall into a puddle at his feet if he didn't stop.

His lips brushed against her left buttock, his teeth raking over her skin lightly. She opened her mouth, to beg, to plead . . . something.

But he turned her around and whatever words she'd been about to say died in her throat as he nuzzled her between her thighs. Through the cotton of her panties, she could feel his tongue.

She went to push them down and he caught her wrists. "Not yet," he murmured, kissing the inside of her left wrist, then her right. "Not yet . . ."

She would have groaned in frustration but he was

already on his feet, covering her mouth with his, and any sound she might have made faded away under his kiss. Oh, could he kiss. She loved his kisses, could get lost in them. Sighing into his mouth, she leaned against him and curled an arm around his neck.

He stroked his tongue against hers and she nipped him lightly, then sucked on him. He growled and the sound had her shivering all the way down to her toes. He tore his mouth away from hers, resting his brow against hers. "Bed," he muttered. "Right now."

"Bed," she agreed.

Ezra took her mouth again, tangling his hand in her hair, the other hand curving over the sleek curve of her hip, holding her steady as he rocked against her. His cock ached and his balls drew tight, heavy against his body in warning.

Shit, she totally shattered his control, made him feel like a teenager. Made him forget everyone, everything. But her. She was all that existed for him.

Tearing his mouth away, he let her go and said again, "Bed."

She laughed, a slow, female smile curling her lips and then she turned, one hand resting on the banister. He waited where he was until she was five feet away, but that in itself was its own sweet torture.

He stared at the narrow, delicate curve of her hips and ass, his mouth watering. The simple black cotton of her panties rode low on her hips and he wanted to peel that barrier away—maybe with his teeth—and spread her out on the bed, stare at her, at each and every curve, learn them all over again, with his eyes, his hands, his mouth.

His cock jerked and he pressed his hand against it, swearing.

Starting up the stairs, he followed her into her bedroom. He paused in the doorway only long enough to strip out of his jeans and boxer briefs, tossing them into the corner so she wouldn't trip over them if she got up before he remembered to move them.

As she neared the bed, he came up behind her and slid his hands up, cupping her breasts. She arched into his hands, a soft, shaky sigh escaping her lips.

Pressing his mouth to her nape, he murmured, "I love you."

A soft flush turned her cheeks pink. A nervous smile curled her lips. "Ah . . . yeah. I'm starting to believe that. And I'm starting to think maybe I love you, too."

It hit him, like a sucker punch straight to the heart.

Shaken, he hauled her against him and sank down on the edge of the bed. Burying his face against her hair, he rocked her. "Serious?"

Her hands stroked his arms. "Yeah. I'm not much for saying things I don't mean either, Ezra. I'm serious. I don't entirely understand it . . . none of this makes sense and it's happening so fast, but yeah, I mean it."

She shifted and squirmed around in his lap until they faced each other. Lifting her hands, she stroked them over his face, over the straight slashes of his eyebrows, his cheekbones, the hard, firm curve of his mouth. Dipping her head, she pressed her lips to that mouth. "As crazy as my life has been the past couple of weeks, it feels . . . complete. And it's because you're in it."

"Lena . . ." His mouth moved against hers, but other than her name, he said nothing.

But Ezra couldn't figure out what he wanted to say. There were words—a hundred of them, a thousand. But he couldn't figure out what they were.

Her hands came up, pushing on his shoulders, easing him back on the bed. He fell back, staring up at her. Two seconds later, his breath lodged in his lungs as she reached down and closed cool, slender fingers around his cock. She tucked the head against her entrance and his eyes damn near crossed as she started to sink down on him.

Skin on skin . . . nothing between them. Shit, shit . . .

"Lena, condom."

She stilled.

Staring up at her, he gripped her hips. Hell, she felt so good. Silky and sleek and soft.

"Do we need it?" she asked quietly. "I'm not going to get pregnant—not right now. And other than that, there's nothing else I need to worry about."

Bad idea—

It was the capital of bad ideas. Involuntarily, his hips jerked and he sank another inch inside her satiny depths. "No. I'm clean, but . . . fuck."

She clenched around him.

"We should know better," he muttered. Then he arched up. At the same time, he started to rock her against him. "But screw it."

She smiled and leaned forward, bracing her hands on the mattress just above his shoulders. It brought her breasts just in line with his mouth.

Ezra lifted his head and closed his lips around one pink nipple, catching it between his teeth, biting gently.

Lena whimpered and clenched around him. Milking him, a silken fist. When she sobbed out his name and shuddered, when her nails bit into the skin of his shoulders, it felt like glory, like heaven . . . completion. Skimming his hands up over her sides, he cupped her shoulders in his hands, rolling them over.

He needed to see her, needed to watch her face. He caught her hands, lacing his fingers with hers and rested his brow on hers. "Lena," he whispered.

The thick, dark fringe of her lashes lifted and she raised her head, pressed her mouth to his. Her legs wrapped around his waist and she rose to meet him, strong, steady and sure.

Their bodies strained, breath mingled. Hearts raced as one. Her cries rose in the air, underscored by Ezra's low, rough groan. Her name was on his lips as he came and when it ended, he collapsed with his head resting between her breasts, weak as a kitten, barely able to breathe, and his head, his heart, and his soul completely full of her.

She was all he could think of.

All he could feel.

Reaching up, he caught her hand, held it in his. "Lena . . ."

"Hmmm?"

He shook his head, surprised he had the strength to even do that. "Nothing."

Shifting in the bed, he moved up next to her, tucking her body against his. She curled against him and he wrapped his arm around her waist, resting his chin on her head.

He held her in his arms as she drifted off to sleep, his eyes on the trees just beyond her window.

TWENTY-FIVE

She woke in bed alone. But she wasn't alone in the room.

Her skin prickled and for the span of two heartbeats her body was tense and her fingers curled into the sheet while her mind raced.

But then her sleepy mind caught up and she remembered falling asleep . . . in Ezra's arms. She'd slept next to him, and now she was awake and he was here. It gave her the weirdest sense of satisfaction. Completion—somehow.

"Hey," she said softly.

"Hey, yourself," he said from over by her window.

She listened as he crossed the hardwood floors and joined her on the bed.

"What are you doing?" she asked as he stretched out next to her.

"Just thinking." He sighed, and she could hear the frustration, the anger lingering in his voice. His house, she knew. He was thinking about his house. "I'm going to have to see if I can't find a place to rent in or around town. Call my insurance agent."

She stroked a hand up his tense back. Sitting up, she laid her hands on the knotted muscles there and started to knead them. He groaned and his head fell forward.

"It could be worse," she said quietly. "I'm just glad you weren't in the house."

Her gut twisted even thinking about it. She'd just found him . . . what if he had been in the house? What if she'd lost him just when she'd finally found him? Just when she was ready to admit what he meant to her? It made her heart hurt to even think about it.

"Hey."

He reached up and pulled her down in front of him. Staring at her again—she could feel it. Blushing, she buried her face against his chest and wrapped her arms around his waist. "Sorry. I just . . . I don't know. Just kind of blindsided me all of a sudden. What if you'd been asleep? What if you'd gotten caught inside?"

"Don't." He tilted her face up to his and pressed his lips to hers. "Those are the kind of games that can drive you out of your mind. Trust me, I know. I wasn't in the house, and I didn't get caught. I'm fine." He took her hand and pressed it to his chest. "See? I'm fine."

"I know . . . it's just . . ." To her horror, Lena realized the burning in her eyes was tears—she was getting ready to cry. "Oh, shit. What is wrong with me?"

"Reaction." He kissed one eye, then the other, and when a tear broke free, he wiped it away. Wrapping his arms around her, he rocked her.

Pressed close against him, listening to his heart beat, she ran her hands up and down his sides, reassuring herself that he was fine. He was here. Right here . . . with her.

Right where I want him to be, she realized.

Right where she needed him to be.

That thought lingered in her mind even after the tears passed.

Dashing them away with the back of her hand, she murmured, "I feel like an idiot."

"You shouldn't."

Sighing, she rested her head on his shoulder.

There was a breeze drifting in through the window cool, damp with the promise of more rain. Fall was moving in on them, hard and fast, it seemed . . . she could smell it on the air.

She found herself thinking about the woods bordering her house.

And her.

The woman.

That night . . . the screams.

"It's not over, is it?" Lena asked softly.

Ezra stroked a hand down her back and rested his chin on the top of her head. "My gut says no."

"The woman found at Law's . . . you think it was her?"

"I don't know. But whether it was or not, it's not over." His arms tightened around her waist and he pressed his face against her neck. "Shit, I don't like to think about you being alone out here, Lena. There's just too much crazy shit going on."

She didn't answer.

She wasn't about to give up her independence over crazy shit.

But . . .

As they sat down to eat, sandwiches and soup, Lena tried to calm the butterflies in her stomach.

It was a logical decision.

Based on not just her heart, and not just her head.

But both.

There was definitely crazy shit going on lately, and too much of it seemed somehow related to her.

And she was crazy . . . crazy about Ezra. She hadn't ever rushed headlong into a relationship in her life, and she knew she shouldn't do it now—but this didn't feel like a rush.

It just felt . . . right.

He felt right.

The same way it had felt right to major in culinary arts.

The same way it had felt right to take the money that had been left to her by her father and use it to buy the house that had once belonged to her parents when she'd lived here with them as a child.

The same way it had felt right to take the job working at Running Brook.

Even the way it had felt right to make that damned phone call that might have started all this trouble.

Whether they'd known each other a long time or not, if it felt right, what did it matter?

It doesn't, she told herself.

And once she realized that was the truth of it, it was that much easier to think about it . . . and smile.

"What's got that cat-and-canary grin on your face?"

Glancing up, she shot a smile in Ezra's direction. "I dunno . . . I guess I just figured something out." She took a bite of her sandwich and then set it down. Licking her lips, she wiped her hands on a napkin and then took a deep breath. While she had the courage, she needed to get this done.

"I was thinking . . ." Holy shit. *I really am going to do this, aren't I?*

She thought about how it had felt, falling asleep with him. Waking with him there.

"Don't go looking for a place to rent. Stay here."

The only response was the sound of silverware clattering to the table, and then to the floor.

Ten seconds of silence stretched into twenty, and her heart raced as he said nothing. Absolutely nothing.

After another twenty seconds of absolutely nothing, she forced a smile. "I guess I wasn't exactly expecting you to be stunned into silence."

"Maybe I'm just a little confused about why you're suggesting that," he said, his voice hoarse.

Lena licked her lips. Her throat was dry. Painfully. She reached for her water and took a sip, then a larger one. After she'd drained the glass, she set it down. Still thirsty, still trying to find the words. "Well, it makes sense. You need a place. I've got room."

"So this is a rational, neighborly type of arrangement?"

"No." She reached for the water glass again, more to have something to do this time. Pushing back from the table, she walked over to the kitchen counter. Why did it suddenly seem like that walk took a lot longer than normal? She could feel his eyes, all but boring a hole into her spine. Willing her to turn around so he could see her face. She didn't have her sunglasses, and she realized she was nervous about facing him without them.

Coward.

Filling her glass, she turned around and faced him.

She'd been so distracted, so caught up in her thoughts, she hadn't realized he'd gotten up until one of the floorboards squeaked under his weight. Catching her breath, she held still as he reached out, stroked a hand down her face.

"Is it because you're freaked out by all the crazy?" Ezra said softly. "I can't say I blame you there."

She scowled. "All the crazy, as you call it, would be enough to freak anybody out, but no. That's not it . . . or not all of it. It's . . ." She stopped and closed her eyes. "I liked falling asleep with you. I liked knowing you were there when I woke up. I like knowing you're here right now."

Licking her lips, she reached out and hooked a hand in the front of his jeans, tugged him close. "I just kind of like having you around, Ezra King. What can I say?"

He caught her face in his hands and tipped her head back. "You kind of like having me around?" he echoed, reluctant amusement underlining his voice.

"Yeah. Like you said earlier, it feels right." She hooked

her hands around his neck and pressed her mouth to his. "I'm big on doing what feels right. And you . . . Ezra, you feel right to me. You feel all kinds of right."

"Do I?"

"Yeah." She nibbled on his lower lip. He opened his mouth and she hummed in satisfaction, sliding her tongue into his mouth. Man, she loved his taste. Loved the way he let her kiss him without trying to control it the way some guys did.

He boosted her up on the edge of the counter and moved between her thighs, resting his hands just below her hips.

But when he reached for the hem of her shirt, she pulled her mouth away and batted at his hands. "Stop it. You're going to distract me. We were talking about something."

"Hey, I can multitask. I can talk and undress you at the same time," he said, slipping his hands under the shirt and cupping her breasts.

Lena swallowed a groan and just barely managed to keep from shivering as he pinched her nipples. "You can undress me when we're done talking. What do you think? Good idea? Lousy idea?"

"Oh, it's definitely a good idea." He paused long enough to nip her chin. "I'd say I'd move in as soon as I could pack, except . . . well, there's not much to pack."

The heavy irony in his voice had the smile fading from her face, and she reached up, rested a hand on his face. "I still can't believe you lost it all—everything."

"I didn't. I've got everything that matters," he said quietly. "Right here."

He kissed her softly. "And if you're sure, if you're serious, hell, yes, I'd love to move in. But are you sure?"

"Yeah." She gave him a nervous smile. "I'm not exactly ready to talk wedding rings and all, but we've already kind of established we're serious here." She caught his hand and pressed a kiss to it. "You need a place to stay, and I think we'd both feel better if I had somebody here with me right now anyway. And I'm pretty certain I don't want anybody else in my personal space other than you. It's logical. It makes sense."

He chuckled. "You're such a romantic, Lena. You're making me blush here."

"Oh, I can make you blush," she said, giving him a sly smile. Then she shrugged. "It's not just the logic, though. It's because it's you . . . and it's me. And it's right. That's enough for now, isn't it?"

His response was to press his mouth to hers.

They made love right there, on the kitchen counter.

When it was over, he murmured, his breathing still ragged, "Yeah. It's right."

It was enough.

For them. For now.

Author's Note

Some creative license was taken with this trilogy. Carrington County is a fictional county set in Kentucky, roughly an hour away from Lexington.

While I spoke with several lawyers and law-enforcement professionals while writing the stories, I realize certain aspects are still not going to be completely true to life. I hope it doesn't take away from your enjoyment of them.

Acknowledgments

There are an awful lot of people who helped me with this book, but some were an unbelievable help, and I want to offer my thanks. Without your help, this book might not have gotten written.

Thank God for letting me live my dream, allowing me to use it in a way that lets me provide for the family You've given me.

Another mention to Shannon, whom I met in the blog world . . . for answering a bunch of my weird and random questions.

Terrie and Kristeen—I met Terrie at the American Printing House for the Blind and she was wonderful with answering questions, offering insight when I was first putting this book together. She introduced me to her friend Kristeen, who helped with all questions I had related to guide dogs . . . and there were many . . .

Detective Todd H, who didn't close the door late one night when a weird writer showed up asking yet more weird and random questions . . .

Other people who answered weird and random questions . . . Karin Tabke, Nicole P, and an odd fruit by the name of Lime . . .

Read on for an exciting preview
of Shiloh Walker's next thrilling romantic
suspense novel

IF YOU SEE HER

"SHE'S A DISTURBED WOMAN, I'M AFRAID TO SAY."
Remington Jennings pinched the bridge of his nose and tried not to think about the sad green eyes and silken brown hair of one Hope Carson. "Disturbed, how? Can you help me out any here, Detective Carson?"

On the other end of the line, the man sighed. "I . . . well, I'm reluctant to do that. You see, I wouldn't have a DA on the phone, asking about my wife, if there wasn't trouble. And I don't want to cause her trouble."

"She's your *ex*-wife . . . and she's already got trouble. Do you want her to get the help she needs or not?" Remy asked, his voice taking on a sharp edge. Hell, anybody with half a brain could see that woman wouldn't hurt a fly unless she was just pushed . . .

"You want to help her, is that it, Jennings?" The detective laughed, but it wasn't a happy sound. It was sad and bitter.

"If I didn't, I wouldn't have called. I'm not trying to lock her up and throw away the key here. Help me out, Detective." *Damn it, Carson, gimme a break.*

"Help you out. You mean help you help Hope." Once more, Joseph Carson sighed. He was Hope's ex and a cop from out west. He was also proving to be one hell of a pain in the ass.

Faintly, Remy heard a heavy creak. "Mr. Jennings, pardon my French, but you can't help Hope, because she doesn't fucking *want* help. She's a very troubled young woman. She . . . shit, this is hard, but we hadn't been married very long when she was diagnosed with borderline personality disorder. She's manipulative, a chameleon—she can make a person believe whatever they need to believe. You might *think* you're seeing a woman you can help—if she'll just *let* you. But that's not the case. You're seeing what she *wants* you to see."

Remy clenched his jaw, closed his hand around the pen so tightly it snapped.

Shit—that . . . no. Not right. Everything inside screeched just how *wrong* that was. It couldn't be right—it just couldn't.

But his voice was cool, collected, as he said, "Borderline personality disorder, you said? Does she have a history of violence?"

Long, tense moments of silence passed and finally, Carson said, "Yeah. There's a history of violence. Only against herself . . . and me. I kept it very well hidden. I didn't want people thinking bad things about her, and on my part . . . well, I was ashamed. For her, for myself, for both of us. It wasn't until things got really bad that I couldn't hide it anymore."

"You're telling me she was violent with you?" Remy knew he needed to be making notes, processing this.

But he couldn't—couldn't process, couldn't even wrap his mind around it. That woman lifting her hand against somebody?

No. The picture just wasn't coming together for him.

"Yes." Carson sighed once more.

"So you're telling me she *does* have a history of violence?"

"Shit, didn't I just go through that?" Carson snarled.

Remy clutched the phone so tight, it was amazing the plastic didn't crack. This was wrong—so fucking wrong, and he knew it, knew it in his bones.

She's manipulative, a chameleon—she can make a person believe whatever they need to believe. You might think you're seeing a woman you can help—if she'll just let you. But that's not the case. You're seeing what she wants you to see.

Damn it, was he just letting her lead him around, he wondered?

Right then, he wasn't sure.

He took a deep, slow breath, focused on the phone. "Can you give me some examples? Tell me what happened?"

"Examples . . . shit." Carson swore and then demanded, "Why should I tell you this? Just answer me that."

"Because if she's got a mental disorder, then she *does* need help and if she needs help, I'd rather her get help than get locked up. You should know her better than anybody. So if you do care about her, help me help her. Come on, Detective. You're a cop. You're sworn to uphold the law, to protect people. If your wife could prove dangerous . . ."

"You fucking lawyers, you always know what to say," Carson muttered. But there was no anger, no malice in his voice. Just exhaustion. "Yeah, you could say she has violent tendencies. You could say she has a history of violence. She's very manipulative and all those violent tendencies get worse when she doesn't get her way. She becomes unstable, unpredictable. There is no telling what she might do to somebody she perceived as being in her way."

Abruptly, his voice lost that calm, detached tone and

he snarled, "There. I gave you all the dirt you needed
and don't tell me you can't use that. God help me, I hate
myself even though I know she needs help. Now tell me
what the fuck is going on!"

Remy blew out a slow breath and said, "She's in the
hospital at the moment—attempted suicide. Plus, there
was an attack on a friend of hers. It looks like she might
be responsible."

"Fuck." The word was harsh, heavy with fury and
grief. "She's tried to commit suicide before, so as much as
I hate to hear it, that's not a big surprise. But the friend . . .
you said there was an attack on a friend?"

"Yes." Remy scowled absently at nothing. "Maybe
you've heard of him—it seems like the two of them go
back quite a while. The name's Law Reilly?"

"Reilly." Carson grunted. "Yeah. I know Law. I wish
I could say I was surprised to hear that she'd turned on
him, but Hope's always had a way of turning on those
who've tried to help her. Those who care about her."

Remy closed his eyes.

Damn it, was there anything this guy could say that
would make it a little bit easier for him to figure out
how to handle Hope?

Of course if he *wanted* her put away, this guy would
be making his whole damn night.

But right now, he could almost hear the cell door swinging shut on her and it was just turning Remy's stomach.
"So you think she could have hurt Mr. Reilly?"

"With Hope, I just don't know. The one thing I *do*
know? She's capable of just about anything. I also know
that I wish I could help her. Hell, I'd like to believe *you*
can. But I know I can't, and I can't believe you can either. She doesn't want help, won't admit she needs it.
I . . . look, if there's anything I can do to make sure she
gets that help, just ask. I don't want her in trouble, but I
do want her to get help. Before it's too late."

Remy barely remembered the rest of the conversation. He was too busy finally processing the fact that he'd more or less gotten the supporting evidence he needed.

Hope Carson's fingerprints had been found all over the weapon used to beat Law Reilly.

She had slit her wrists.

She had a history of violence.

A history of turning on people who cared about her.

According to her ex-husband—who seemed to care about her—she was manipulative, prone to doing whatever it took to get her way.

Fuck and double fuck.

Instead of feeling satisfied with what he needed to do, what he *could* do, he found himself thinking about those sad, sad green eyes . . .

Fuck . . .

By the time she landed at Blue Grass Airport, Nia Hollister was so damned tired, she could barely see straight, so sick at heart, she ached with it, and she longed to curl up in a dark, quiet room and just . . . sob.

Giving in to tears had never been her way, but this time, the temptation was strong, so overpowering, there were times when she felt the tears swelling in her throat like a knot. And a scream—just beyond the tears, there was a scream begging to break free.

She kept it held inside through sheer will alone.

Now wasn't the time to scream, or to cry.

Somewhere inside her heart, she still wanted to believe they were wrong.

All of them.

Joely wasn't dead. She couldn't be. They were like sisters—almost closer than sisters.

They rarely fought. They were best friends, in their hearts, their souls. Even when Nia was on the other side of the country for half the year—or *out* of the country . . .

They could be wrong. All of them—Bryson, Joely's fiancé, who wouldn't even go with her to identify the boy, the cops who insisted it was Joely . . . everybody. They could all be wrong.

It might not be Joely.

But if it wasn't her cousin lying dead in a morgue in Ash, Kentucky, then where was she?

Her fiancé hadn't seen her in more than a month.

She wasn't answering her cell phone or e-mail.

It was like she'd dropped off the face of the earth.

No . . . she hasn't dropped off the face of the earth. She's been lying dead in the deep freeze in the morgue, you selfish bitch, while you're off on assignment.

Abandoned—because law enforcement always turned to family, although Bryson might have been able to do it if he'd pushed, especially since Nia hadn't been reachable. Out of contact—*fuck.*

She hadn't been around, while her cousin was kidnapped, hadn't been around while she was killed, hadn't been around at all and because of that, Joely was treated like some worthless piece of garbage.

Nia hadn't been around. *Oh, God . . .* Tears pricked her eyes. She'd been out of contact for almost three weeks. Joely could have reached her, but would she have shared that information with her fiancé? Probably not.

With weariness and grief dragging at her steps, she lugged her carry-on through the airport. Years of living out of a suitcase had taught her to pack light and the bag was all she carried. The rest of her stuff was being shipped back to her house in Williamsburg.

Soon, she'd have to find a Laundromat and wash her clothes, but that was a problem for another day.

Now, she needed to get a rental car. Rental car. Then she needed to . . .

She stopped in front of an ad—it was brightly colored, displaying a chestnut horse racing across a field of green grass. Numb, she just stared at it for a minute and then once more started to walk.

Rental car. Ash, Kentucky. She needed to get there. Needed to . . .

"Miss?"

Nia started, then found herself staring dumbly at one of the airport security guards. Blinking, she glanced around. She wasn't sure where she was, or how she'd gotten there.

He eyed her with a strange mix of concern and caution. "Are you okay?"

Nia swallowed. That knot in her throat swelled to epic proportions and she realized those tears were even closer than she'd thought. "I . . . rough few days."

"It looks like it." He gestured with his head off to the side. "You've been standing in the middle of the hall for the past five minutes. Can I help you find where you're going?"

Nia pressed the heel of her hand against her temple. Shit.

The ache in her chest spread.

Ash—she needed to get to Ash, wherever in the hell that was.

But if she was standing around like a zombie in the middle of an airport, the last thing she needed to do was get behind the wheel of a car. Reality breathed its icy cold breath down her spine and she sighed. "I guess I'm heading outside to catch a cab to a hotel," she finally said.

Getting to Ash would have to wait until morning.

She loathed the idea, but her pragmatic side was strong, even in grief. As exhausted as she was, it would be suicide to get behind the wheel of a car and she knew it. As desperate as she was to get to Ash, she had some damn strong inner demons.

Besides, maybe she'd luck out . . . she'd go to sleep

and wake up, realize this was nothing but one awful, horrid nightmare.

The conversation with Detective Joseph Carson was still ringing through Remy's mind hours later as he tossed and turned on his bed, trying to sleep.

Settling down wasn't happening, though. It was past midnight when he finally slept.

There were nights when he hit the mattress and sleep fell on him like a stone. As one of the two district attorneys in the small county of Carrington, Kentucky, he had helped put away meth dealers, a couple of child molesters and rapists, more than a few drunk drivers, several wife beaters, and he routinely dealt with petty theft.

Even in his small, mostly rural county, crime wasn't nonexistent.

He enjoyed what he did.

But tonight, sleep didn't come easy. Hell, screw *easy*—it didn't want to come at *all*.

Every time he closed his eyes, he thought of a green-eyed brunette and he thought about what he had to do in the morning.

It wasn't a job he wanted to do.

It was a job he'd give just about anything to *not* do.

But he hadn't taken this job just so he could walk away from the hard ones.

All the facts pointed to one thing: Hope Carson was a violent, disturbed woman.

His gut screamed *Screw the facts*. But he couldn't ignore what he saw, couldn't ignore the evidence, couldn't ignore what he'd been told and what he'd learned.

His job was clear.

And his job, sometimes, sucked.

It was well past midnight when he finally fell into a restless sleep, and into even more restless dreams.

Nightmares.

Dreams where he saw her as he'd seen her that night in the emergency room. Covered in blood.

Pale.

A disembodied voice whispering, You did this . . .

"No, I didn't. No, I didn't," *Hope said, her voice shaking, but sure.*

Remy stood there, horrified. All he wanted to do was pull her into his arms, take her away from this, away from all of it. But then Nielson, the sheriff, was there, pushing a pair of handcuffs into his hand.

"You want us to arrest her? Fine. You do it."

But that wasn't Remy's job—he wasn't a fucking cop. He didn't arrest people. He got warrants. He prosecuted.

"Yeah, you make us get our hands dirty. But you want her arrested, you do it yourself."

And that was what he did. Remy put cuffs on wrists that seemed too slender, too fragile for such a burden.

Remy was the one who led her to a cell.

And when he opened the door, she walked silently inside. But he saw it in her eyes.

I didn't do this . . .

As he turned away, the screams started. Endless, agonized screams. But he didn't know if they were hers . . . or his own.

That was how he came awake.

With the sound of screams echoing in his ears.

"*Shit,*" he muttered, jerking upright in bed, fighting the sheets and blankets that had become ropes around his waist.

With his breath sawing raggedly in and out of his lungs, he sat on the edge of the bed and stared off into nothingness. His gut was a raw, ragged pit and his head throbbed like it hadn't since his college days. Back then, he had thought he could get by on naps and caffeine.

In a few hours, he was supposed to meet the sheriff at the hospital.

Hope Carson was being arrested today, and there wasn't a damn thing Remy could do about it. That woman had the ability to turn him into knots just by looking at him. No other woman had ever done that to him. Not a one. Shit. This was a mess.

Not that she knew.

Nobody knew, thank God.

At least he'd managed to keep that much hidden.

But shit, he had to get it together.

Had to get his head together, his act together, had to do . . . something.

Shoving to his feet, Remy shambled naked toward the bathroom. Maybe if he blasted himself with enough hot water, and then flooded his body with enough caffeine . . . maybe.

Maybe, maybe . . .

He hit the lights, but they hit his tired eyes with the force of a sledgehammer and, groaning, he turned them off again.

No light. Not yet.

Shower. Caffeine.

Then light.

Maybe.

Not that he really needed light anyway. Not like he needed light to shower . . . or even to get dressed. If he didn't have any light on, he wouldn't have to worry about seeing his reflection, right?

And the last thing he wanted to do just then was look himself square in the eye.

No matter what the evidence said, no matter what the logic pointed to, it just didn't feel right.

It just didn't feel right . . . at all.

There were days when Hope Carson wished she'd just driven right through Ash. Instead of stopping in the small

Kentucky town to see her friend, like she'd promised, she should have just kept on driving.

No matter how much she loved Law, no matter how much she'd missed him, missed having a friend, there were days when she wished she had broken that promise and never stopped.

Maybe she should have driven straight to the ocean.

Hope had never seen the ocean.

She'd wanted to go to the ocean for her honeymoon, but Joey . . . her not-so-beloved ex-husband hadn't liked the idea.

Everybody goes to the beach. Let's do something different.

They'd gone to the mountains.

Skiing in Aspen.

But Hope hadn't been very good at skiing. And she hated the cold . . . it was like it cut right through her bones. She'd fallen down so many times, and had so many bruises.

"Should have just kept on driving," she muttered as she listened to the voices just outside her door.

Would have been wiser, that much was sure.

Desolate, she stared out the window and wondered if she'd have a room wherever they were taking her next.

Would it be another hospital?

A jail?

She just didn't know.

Another hospital, probably. One with real *security.*

Dark, ugly dots swirled in on her vision.

Fear locked a fist around her throat. *Locked . . . trapped . . .*

She barely managed to keep the moan behind her teeth.

When the door opened, she stifled her wince.

Barely.

It was just one of the nursing assistants—this time.

But soon . . . soon, it would be uniformed deputies. She knew it.

Hearing the quiet, muffled sound of shoes on the linoleum, she stared out the window and tried not to think about what was coming.

No matter what, she had to be grateful for one thing.

No matter what, she wasn't trapped back in that house in Oklahoma with her husband, and she wasn't trapped in that hospital where he had complete, total control over her.

She'd almost willingly be held for a crime she didn't commit rather than go back to that particular hell.

At least she wasn't anywhere close to Joey.

At least she wasn't under his control, in any way, shape, or form.

That counted, for a hell of a lot.

But it wasn't enough and the longer she stared at the plain, white walls of the small hospital room, the more they resembled a cell. So instead, she stared out the window—a reinforced window, one she couldn't open. Not that she'd tried.

But the nurse had been a little too free with that information, right after she'd come in to check her blood pressure and *offer* her the medications—just an offer this time.

Nobody had tried to force it on her again.

Not since Remy . . .

She swallowed and tried not to think about that. It really, really wouldn't do her any good to think about that, about him. As humiliating as it had been, for anybody to see her like that, it had been nothing short of a miracle in the end. Whether he'd said something to one of the doctors after he'd left or just scared the hell out of the nurses . . . well, nobody had tried to force any more drugs on her.

No antipsychotics, no tranquilizers, nothing. That

fancy law degree of his, Hope imagined. She didn't know, and honestly, didn't care.

As long as nobody was forcing drugs on her she didn't need.

Her head was completely clear. She should be grateful.

And she would try to be.

But her gut told her she hadn't seen the last of Remy Jennings, and the next time she saw him, it wasn't going to be over the drugs the hospital staff had been forcing on her.

No, the next time it would be over the night she'd been found unconscious, just a few days ago, her wrists slashed open, her prints on the bat that had been used to beat a man damn near to death.

Her best friend—the people here thought she was capable of that.

They wanted her in jail for it.

Closing her eyes, she rested her head against her pillow and sighed. It wouldn't be long now, either. She'd seen it in the doctor's eyes when he'd been in to see her yesterday.

Sympathy, knowledge . . . and a grim acceptance. She was no longer in need of the medical services a hospital could provide. And they weren't about to let her traipse away where they couldn't keep her *secured*.

In their eyes, she'd done something awful, and it was time she paid for it.

But I didn't do anything . . .

The sad, forlorn whine wanted to work its way free but she swallowed it, shoved it down inside. She sure as hell wasn't going to go meekly along with whatever they had in mind, but she was done with wringing her hands and moaning, too.

She just needed to figure out what she *was* going to do . . .